Spirit of Fire

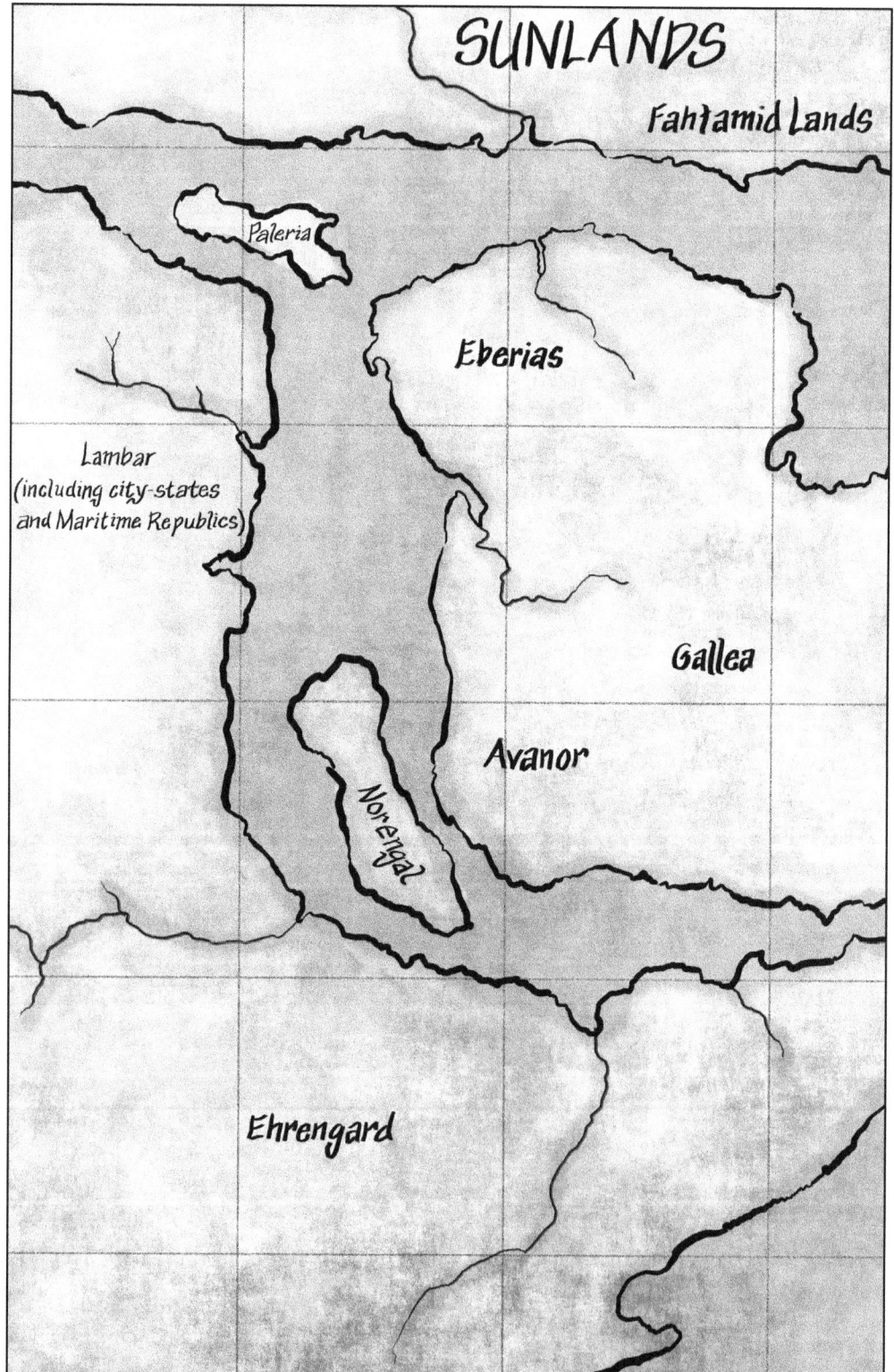

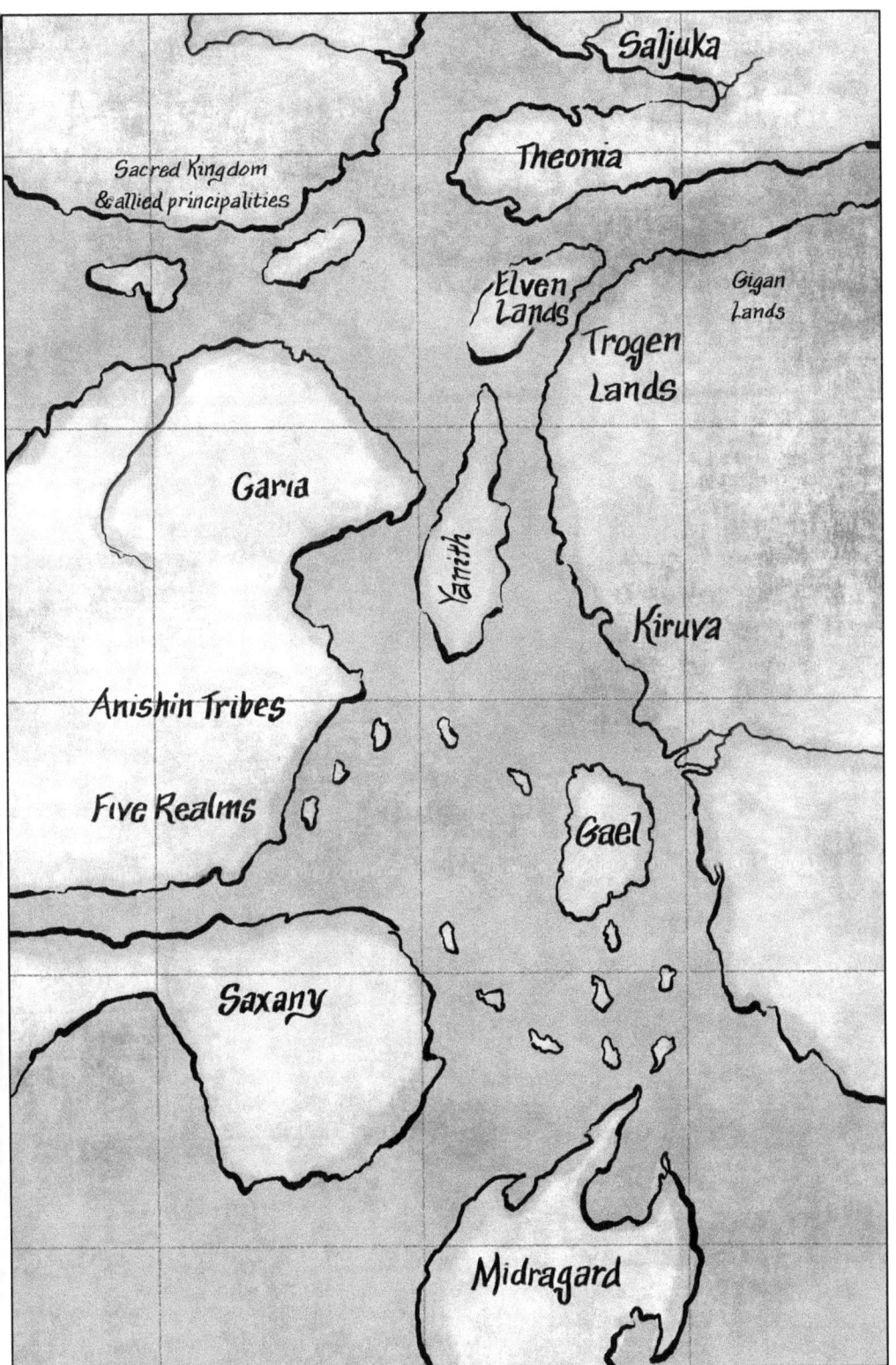

Spirit of Fire

STEPHEN ZIMMER

SEVENTH STAR PRESS

Cover art and illustrations: Matthew Perry
Cover art and illustrations in this book Copyright © 2012 Matthew Perry
& Seventh Star Press, LLC.

Editor: Karen M. Leet

Published by Seventh Star Press, LLC.

ISBN Number 9781937929855

Library of Congress Control Number: 2012908918

Seventh Star Press
www.seventhstarpress.com
info@seventhstarpress.com

Publisher's Note:
Spirit of Fire is a work of fiction. All names, characters, and places are
the product of the author's imagination, used in fictitious manner. Any
resemblances to actual persons, places, locales, events, etc.
is purely coincidental.

Printed in the United States of America

First Edition

DEDICATION

To the original Author, whose grand story unfolds
across all time and space.

To my mother, who continues to show a spirit of fire
in the face of great adversity.

To all others who reach down inside and choose to embrace the
person they are. You will find that your potential is without bounds
when you are the truest manifestation of yourself.

ACKNOWLEDGEMENTS

To Karen Leet: I can't say enough about my wonderful, meticulous, and sagacious editor on Spirit of Fire. Another great experience, and I am so glad that the "Literary Commando" was on board for this next step of the journey. You were thorough as always, and your suggestions and insights were of great value in crafting this installment of the series. I am very fortunate to have you as my editor, and I will always give you every last ounce of effort to bring you the best work that I can.

To Matthew Perry: Artist extraordinaire, and friend extraordinaire, thank you for the perseverance and dedication on this journey. I cannot say it often enough, I am really blessed to have your artwork in these novels. I hope that Ave has been a fun and interesting place for you to play in as you explore it artistically. I know that it has been very hard work, and the road has not been an easy one, but a wonderful body of artwork has been growing that will stand the test of time. Onward and upward!

To Mom: You have a true spirit of fire! Your courage in the face of so many hardships continues to inspire and teach me, and I hope that my novels, in some small way, bring you a little comfort and help make the road still worthwhile to travel. I am so incredibly lucky and honored to have such a great mom. I love you!

To my wonderful Reader-friends: There are so many things that an author has to worry about in today's publishing world. It is an around the clock challenge for someone like myself that puts everything I have into what I do. This is much more than a career or a pursuit for me; it is a big part of who I am. Fatigue, frustrations, and all manner of challenges lie in the road, and it is all of you that help me navigate this difficult path. Your encouragement and support lift me up on the tough days, and take me soaring higher on the good ones. As always, I give you my utmost commitment, and if you stick with me, I will work as hard as I can to bring you ever greater adventures and worlds to explore in the future.

"There is nothing impossible to him who will try."
- Alexander the Great

"Humans are amphibians – half spirit and half animal. As spirits they belong to the eternal world, but as animals they inhabit time."
- C. S. Lewis

"Faithless is he that says farewell when the road darkens."
- J. R. R. Tolkien

"Dig within. Within is the wellspring of Good; and it is always ready to bubble up, if you just dig."
- Marcus Aurelius

"We must expect reverses, even defeats. They are sent to teach us wisdom and prudence, to call forth greater energies, and to prevent our falling into greater disasters."
- Robert E. Lee

"He is a man of courage who does not run away, but remains at his post and fights against the enemy."
- Socrates

"Be faithful in small things because it is in them that your strength lies."
- Mother Teresa

section 1

SAXANY

To the northeast of the Plains of Athelney, a motley assemblage sprawled across an expanse of open ground. Located adjacent to a lake, upon the outskirts of an extensive range of forested hills, the gathering was not too far removed from the place where one tendril of the invasion force had already run into stout Saxan resistance.

The surface of the water was choppy, buffeted frequently with brisk surges of wind. A considerable tension clung to the steadily cooling, evening air, empowered by what had taken place, and what was to come.

The earlier thrust of the Avanoran invaders had endured an unexpected, thorough destruction. Battered survivors trickling back spoke with shaky voices, and wide, frightened eyes, telling of brawny, non-human warriors with gray hides. A horde of the creatures had emerged seemingly out of nowhere, without warning, to shatter the Avanoran encampment and slaughter all but a remnant of the force.

The Saxans that had been arrayed in the hills presented no threat anymore, having been broken and scattered just prior to the deadly ambush. But the brutish interlopers that had decimated the Avanoran force were still an obstacle to be wary of, and reckoned with. They were about to be countered with a most chilling solution.

The deepening unease gripping the assemblage was enough to rattle the nerves of even the most seasoned, hardened of veterans, whether Trogen or human. The disquiet had a single, dreadful source, one that was living, or at least animated to a mockery of life. It was hard to discern which, as the normal vibrancy of life was not present within the hooded being standing tall among the throng of warriors.

The grave apprehension was deepened even further by two huge objects borne into the midst of the warriors, at the dark figure's command. The winged monstrosities that had carried the pair of elongated shapes to the lakeside now rested on the ground, their vast wings tucked in.

The two Darroks were intimidating sights to behold on any occasion, but they were not the cause of the elevated alarm and distress pervading the scene. Between the Arcamon and the hellish cargo of the Darroks, the gathered warriors were truly caught between a hammer and anvil of cold fear.

Mounted upon the Darroks' backs were immense cages, fashioned of timber and iron. The interior of the cages was hidden from view, with long horizontal planks of wood affixed to their frames, the timber lengths fully covering the sides.

The cages themselves were of a respectable height, enough that the tallest amongst the Trogens could walk into them with ample headroom to spare. But the great length of each cage was what made them most unusual.

The ongoing work involved with the pair of enclosures was conducted with extreme diligence and focus. The assiduousness was bolstered by the fact that most of those laboring with the cages wished to keep their attentions diverted from the foreboding entity silently watching over their progress.

With the ends of its long, dark cape undulating in the winds, the Arcamon sat astride its infernal steed. Exposed so prominently atop a small rise in the middle of the host, the entity conveyed an image of authority. The Arcamon's raised hood was a mercy to the surrounding warriors, shrouding the entity's nightmarish face within caliginous shadows.

The glowing embers of the Arcamon's gaze were fixed upon the mass of individuals handling the makeshift network of ropes and pulley-driven cranes, the latter similar to those used on ships at quays, to lower the giant cages.

The Arcamon's grotesque winged steed, scaly, sinuous, and serpentine, followed its master's every directive with rigid discipline. It was now brooding and silent, patiently awaiting its master's next command.

Though the shrouded figure appeared impassive to all eyes, a mounting impatience was welling up within the Arcamon. Of the four of its kind loosed at a tremendous expenditure of energy from the fiery depths of Jebaalos' realm, two were now aiding the assaults upon the Saxan kingdom.

That alone reflected the tremendous importance the Unifier placed upon subjugation of the Saxan lands. The invasion was a pivotal element of the final series of conquests, which would bring all of Ave under one authority; outwardly that of the Unifier, though truly, through the Unifier, Jebaalos.

The Arcamon's fury had soared throughout the report informing of the sudden Unguhur attack, which had blunted the Avanoran efforts to break through to the northeast of the Plains of Athelney. The force should have been able to hook around through the mountains, to pour down and ambush the main Saxan forces on their exposed right flank, out on the Plains of Athelney.

The worst aspect of it was that the Saxan ranks arrayed to oppose the Avarnoran maneuver had been dislodged and broken, leaving the way clear for all aims to be achieved. All had been thwarted by a horde from a brutish race that now held the Arcamon's malefic ire.

At the moment, the battle at the Plains of Athelney should have been over, and the interior of the Saxan lands left wide open. The Kingdom of Saxany had likely exhausted itself in the musters for the Plains of Athelney, and for the smaller force deployed to face the woodland incursion.

Unlike the Trogens, humans, and others around it, the Arcamon knew much about the Unguhur. The primitive creatures had emerged from the depths of their underworld dominion, having been well-hidden from the extensive scouting from the skies and on the land.

The human and Trogen leaders had been confounded. To the few that had even heard of the underground race, the Unguhur existed only within legends, or as wisps of tales. Things of legend and myth were certainly not foremost on the minds of the invasion force's command. In a practical sense, the existence of an underground population of Unguhur, right under Saxan lands, was something entirely unknown; and altogether unaccounted for.

Nevertheless, the Arcamon had confronted many of the Avanoran lords after the terrible debacle. Its dark presence had driven each one of the fierce, haughty commanders to become sniveling, groveling fools in mere moments. Mortals confronted by an immortal from the afterworld itself, its very existence boggling to their minds, several had broken out in cold sweats. Others had openly trembled, unable to stifle the terror wracking their spirits

Failure for any reason was never to be lightly taken, whether in the infernal realms or in Ave. The Arcamon had faced the Avanoran lords as if they were going to be made to answer fully for the considerable losses.

Using mystical arts from the abyssal depths, the Arcamon had implanted stark images directly into the minds of the Avanoran lords, one by one. Shadows of madness, visions of monstrosities in chasms of sentient blackness, and searing vistas of blood-drenched infernos filled the thoughts of the Avanoran lords, as they were given the briefest of glimpses into the nether kingdom of Jebaalos.

They were unable to avoid the terrifying spectacles by shutting their eyes, forced to endure the waking nightmares for what threatened to be an interminable ordeal. A couple openly wept, others shook as the cold sweats streaked down their faces, and still others collapsed to the ground in quivering, sobbing heaps. The Arcamon knew their minds were not equipped to handle such sights for very long.

After their humiliating, terrifying experience had reached the very edge of a place from where it could not return, on the brink of madness, the Arcamon finally, and suddenly, withdrew its hellish grip. The entity consigned the horrific visions to the subconscious regions of their minds.

The Arcamon knew every thought going through their minds as they were loosed. The seeds of many future sleepless, nightmare-flooded nights had been sown, but the Avanorans had blinked and gasped in surprise, and relief, as they were released. They quickly regained their focus, but found to their great agitation they had absolutely no recollections of the previous several moments.

For them it was as if time itself had skipped forward. Greatly disconcerted, their hearts still beat rapidly as an icy fear danced on the edges of their awareness.

The Arcamon had then turned immediately to the issue set before all of them, breaking the defenses of the Saxans, and those that aided them. Whether the main invasion force had broken through or not out on the Plains of Athelney, it was advantageous for the Avanorans to secure an open passage into the northern lands of the Saxan kingdom.

The Unguhur were the only real threat standing in the way. To confront them, and root them out from their underground domain, the Arcamon quickly settled upon a strategy that would exact a terrible vengeance in the process of achieving their aims.

A summons had been sent by way of another of the Arcamon's dark, mysterious arts back to Avalos itself. Two young Darroks were being harnessed shortly thereafter, on open grounds just outside of the great city. Though not fully trained, the pair of Darroks were the only ones out of the Unifier's brood not currently committed elsewhere.

A small crew of fiercely loyal, carefully selected Avanoran warriors had then guided the giant winged beasts to a faraway, hidden place. It was a location known to very few, and all of those were beholden to the Unifier and Jebaalos.

To assault something of the underworld, the Arcamon had chosen to send something from the darkest depths of the underworld. The creatures granted to the bidding of the Arcamon were not entirely unknown to the surface world.

Their subterranean kind had risen up before, making their presence known many times over the long ages of the world of Ave. They had reached the surface through deep lakes and rivers, ascending from the gaping depths of the underworld itself, becoming creatures of great myths and legends themselves.

Two of the creatures had been obtained to serve the Arcamon's bidding, each one of them a veritable juggernaut. Their bodies were akin to enormous serpents, covered with hardened scales that were collectively as good as a solid sheath comprised of the finest crafted armor.

Of massive girth, their bodies were as thick as the trunks of the oldest, largest trees in all of the Saxan forests. Neither of the fully-grown monstrosities was less than seventy feet in length.

Their appearance was also as beautiful as it was terrifying. The scales forming their natural armor were themselves comprised of a variety of vibrant colors, amid others that seemed to blaze like tongues of fire when caught by the light.

The deadly beauty reached its pinnacle atop their great heads. As if kings and queens among the ancient race of snakes, they were crowned with natural diadems. Great, sharply pointed horns sprouted up from each side of their massive heads. In the center of their broad craniums, at the forward end of a fiery red crest, was what looked to be a radiant, sparkling, crystal, bisected by a prominent, blood-red streak.

Their enormous heads contained a gaping maw lined with an arsenal of spiky, rear-curving teeth, forming an inescapable prison for anything caught within the creatures' awesome bite. Two massive fangs, like gleaming, deadly sabers being pulled from scabbards, extended downward whenever the creature opened its mouth with the intent to strike.

Just a few tiny drops of venom from one of the creatures' fangs were more than enough to kill the strongest of humans. One full injection from the dual fangs imparted a comparative torrent of lethal poison, which no creature living on the surface of Ave could withstand.

In the abysmal reaches of the underworld, the beasts could pass through great depths of water, navigate the most powerful of currents, and weather the greatest turbulence. Their bodies could handle great extremes of temperature, and withstand exceptional pressures. On solid ground, they moved with tremendous bursts of speed, dizzying to behold.

There were very few creatures in all of Ave that had the kind of size and power to even have a chance to contend with the colossal serpents; and most of those were now regarded in a mythical state themselves.

Yet they were not invincible, having one major place of vulnerability on their bodies. Located seven spots from the base of their heads was a susceptible point where a solid, penetrating strike could instantly incapacitate the giant beasts. The knowledge of the location was largely delegated to obscure lore, known currently only to a few handfuls of people whose ancestors had encountered the horror of the deadly creatures in past times.

The Uktena were virtually without rival, exactly the kind of formidable creature the Arcamon could use to beset their underground adversaries.

In a shrouding darkness secure from the reach of the sun, the Unifier was keeping a number of the fearsome creatures. Tended closely by the Unifier's Sorcerers, the Uktena were controllable. Using their secret arts, the Sorcerers had lulled the creatures into a deep, trance-like slumber, before a cadre of highly-unnerved Gigans had laboriously gotten them into the lengthy cages.

The creatures had not stirred in the least, as the cages were then mounted up onto the young Darroks' backs, but the huge flying beasts instantly sensed the nature of their deadly passengers. It took a highly concerted effort from their flyers and Sorcerers alike just to calm the surge of agitation in the Darroks. The titanic steeds rumbled and snorted, loosing short, sporadic bursts of fire, even after they had been brought under an outward semblance of control.

Two of the exalted Sorcerers of Avalos accompanied the beasts on the ensuing journey, keeping the Uktena in an unconscious state throughout the entire flight. At the moment, a Sorcerer attended each cage, as they were tediously lowered and angled off of the backs of the Darroks.

Under the increasing weight of the Arcamon's spectral gaze, the small host of men and Trogens, augmented by horses, and a pair of the powerful Gigans, continued to strain with ropes secured to the cages. The wood of their assembled cranes creaked and groaned with an unnerving tenor, the ropes taut as the tremendous weight of their burden drew the hempen cording to the limits.

Just alongside each team, the stoic form of a Sorcerer kept a wary eye out for even the slightest sign that the Uktena might be awakening from their deep slumber. The Arcamon paid no heed to the nerve-wracked state of those handling the cages, who feared that the serpentine monsters could be roused at any moment by the jostles, shakes, heaves, and lurches that the enclosures endured. The noise generated by the effort was considerable as well, as both man and animal grunted in their exertion, and those in authority shouted out orders, whenever sudden adjustments were needed.

When the cages were completely free from the Darroks, and were finally resting upon the ground, the handlers mounted the huge sky beasts and guided them away from the lakeside. The two creatures were given a wide berth as they lumbered forward, many scrambling in haste to avoid being caught in the titanic beasts' path.

The agitation in the Darroks, which had emanated ever since they had taken to the skies with their fearsome burden, finally ebbed as they gained distance between themselves and the cages' occupants. Yet the Darroks' gazes returned to lock upon the extended contraptions, when their handlers drew them to a halt and allowed them to lie upon the ground again.

Like a shadowy wraith, the dark figure on the rise then spurred its scaly steed to flight, and glided down to land close to one of the cages. A number of men and Trogens shuddered reflexively, as if an icy chill had abruptly fallen upon them.

With the Darroks in their place, the Arcamon signaled for the cages to be fully disassembled. Only the Arcamon could have elicited the assiduous response of the apprehensive laborers, transcending the grave dread that permeated the vicinity of the cages.

Trogens and humans opened the locks that secured iron chain links running between the long, modular segments of the great cages. Slowly, the sides of the cage sections were lowered on their hinges, the latter affixed at the bottom.

The dropping of the sides bared the lengthy, gigantic forms within to the eyes of all gathered, exposing the bodies of the Uktena to a host of individuals seeing the creatures in their entirety for the very first time. Expressions of fear and awe filled the faces of the hushed observers. Only the terrified whinnies and stamps of the frightened horses broke the silence, as their handlers labored to keep the wide-eyed equines under control.

The Arcamon felt no pity for what the Unguhur were about to be subjected to. In his view, the Unguhur should have stayed huddled below the surface, and let the matters of the surface world take their own course. The Unifier would probably have even tolerated the existence of the foolish creatures, if they had chosen to remain sequestered away from the upper world.

Their fateful decision to take the side of the Saxans in the war was now going to bring a terrible wrath down upon them. The Unguhur would reap the lethal harvest of what they had sown.

The two immense, serpentine forms, now still, would soon be brought back to full awareness. It would not be much longer before the Unguhur were introduced to the two creatures of legend, and experienced what they were capable of. The Arcamon savored the thoughts of the Unguhur's impending doom, with malice-drenched pleasure.

AETHELSTAN

"I humbly give you thanks, Khan Treas ... Khanum Vuriant," Aethelstan stated solemnly, bowing deeply from the waist.

The Saxan thane was grateful for the strange pendant he had borrowed from the outlander Lee. The object allowed the foreigners to speak to the Unguhur without need for any translation. A gift of the Wanderer, the amulet's power still astonished him.

Aethelstan raised back upright, slowly. A saddened mien permeated his face, his heart growing increasingly leaden with the dread he felt gathering within.

The icy tendril of fear he harbored gained potency with every passing moment, for he knew the colossal power of the enemy they all faced. The Unifier would never forgive the Unguhur's interference in His dark designs. He knew his anxieties would only get worse the longer he remained underground, in light of the thickly veiled mystery surrounding the inevitable enemy response.

Aethelstan was among the last group of Saxans still remaining within the underworld realm. Over two hundred and fifty warriors had already departed for the surface, eager to be under open skies in the world above.

Unaccustomed to living underground himself, Aethelstan could not deny he was looking forward to the simple joys of sunlight, fresh breezes, and the sight of clouds drifting overhead. So many things he had taken for granted had been transformed into treasures during the brief period of exile spent within the shadowy, sunless underworld.

"You are welcome, Aethelstan. All of what you say may be true. You may be far wiser than any of us. Your warning is taken. We may regret that we did not join you," Khan Treas addressed the Saxan, in a somber tone. "We must all make our choices ... and then live with them."

"May good fortune come to the Unguhur," Aethelstan replied, with as much of a tone of hopefulness as he could muster. Inwardly, he felt increasingly grim, knowing in his heart the Unguhur Khan did not fully realize the vast strength, and ruthlessness, of the enemy facing them. "May the light of the Creator shine upon your path, and that of all the Unguhur."

It was difficult to look upon the Unguhur rulers. A part of him felt he had personally failed in his effort to warn them and convey an appreciation of the genuine, existential threat facing the underworld race.

Undeniably, the Unguhur could display ferocious countenances when angered, augmented by their elongated teeth, and wide, powerful jaws. They had strikingly large canines, the sight of which still unsettled Aethelstan.

Yet the concave shape of their faces lent them naturally saddened expressions, especially when they held a softer look within their eyes. The Khan's eyes now held a genuine sense of compassion and kindness, and it tore Aethelstan up inside to take in the words of the Unguhur leader.

Turning, with the burden of an increasingly heavy heart, Aethelstan kept his eyes lowered as he strode slowly across the elongated chamber. He steeled his resolve, as he departed under the watchful eyes of Unguhur elders, situated to either side of him.

Two Unguhur warriors stepped aside at the chamber's entrance, allowing Aethelstan to pass without impediment. A familiar human figure awaited him just outside.

"And?" Gunther queried, using the Saxan tongue requiring no art of the pendant Aethelstan wore.

A single glance from Aethelstan conveyed the answer.

"I thought as much," Gunther said evenly.

"The only thing that remains is to leave, and join the others above," Aethelstan replied stonily.

"Fate is such a weaver of irony," Gunther said, shaking his head slowly. "Once I sought refuge within your forests, to avoid the affairs of the world of kings and emperors. Now, it may be that some of the most important of individuals … at a crucial time … need my help in that world, in a way that cannot be justly denied. I will be going with you, Aethelstan."

Aethelstan smiled, as a couple of worries within the tumult of his mind eased. A part of him was relieved that the eccentric, forest-dwelling, warrior-hermit, forced by harsh circumstances back into the greater world, had come to agreement with Aethelstan's assessment of the looming threats to the Unguhur realm.

"Your words encourage me, Gunther. It is likely we shall shoulder some desperate trials together," Aethelstan responded. "But if we are to face trials, I know it is indeed good fortune to have you with us. Are those in your charge prepared to leave?"

"Of the four-legged ones, I have no worries. Of the two legged ones, it remains to be seen," Gunther responded gruffly.

The woodsman turned, and curtly gestured towards the four outlanders, who were milling about close to the blocky corner of one of the stout Unguhur dwelling structures. Two of the foreigners, the younger boy, and one of the females, exhibited brooding, sullen countenances. They stood together, set markedly apart from their comrades.

The others had looks of trepidation splayed upon their faces, though a little indignation flashed up whenever they glanced towards the sulking pair. It was quite clear to the thane there was a sharp division within the quartet.

"Guilt, I presume?" Aethelstan remarked, looking at the tense postures of the glowering pair.

He knew full well of the story regarding the two outlanders' foolish foray to the surface. Their blundering sojourn had nearly ended in grisly deaths, at the jaws of ferocious Hyaeds.

The thought of their recklessness made his spirit cringe, knowing what kinds of mortal dangers lurked in the depths of the uninhabited stretches of Saxan woodland. The Saxan wilderness was certainly no place for foreigners to rove blindly.

The two outlanders had needlessly courted absolute disaster, and Aethelstan could only imagine how furious their two comrades had been with the whole debacle. The looks in their eyes spoke loudly enough.

"Stupidity, born of stubborness, as it is for most of our kind," Gunther grumbled, casting his own sharp glare towards the heedless duo.

Aethelstan understood the woodsman's frustration. Instead of standing tall, accepting admonishment, and growing in character, the moping pair appeared to be exhibiting nothing more than defiance and immaturity.

"They will have to remain with us from now on, Gunther," Aethelstand stated calmly. "If they wander again, after being given a second chance, I am of the mind to leave them to their own fates … no matter who they are. I do not wish to ask any more risks of my warriors. Enough has been asked of them already. And I certainly will not risk them for acts of sheer folly.

"Nor do I wish to risk any of my Jaghuns, who do not merit the harvest gathered from seeds sown by fools," Gunther replied, his face darkening. "Yet I am still torn, Aethelstan. I have always known the voice of my heart to be true, and it speaks louder to me than it ever has. There is something of great importance with these four. There had better be, as much has been suffered for lending help to those four … far too much, if you ask me."

Aethelstan thought of the latest loss among Gunther's family of Jaghuns, in the fighting to save the foolhardy outlanders from the Hyaeds. Aethelstan understood the Jaghuns were not mere beasts in Gunther's eyes.

The thane sorrowed for the woodsman. The loss had been wholly unnecessary, if the two outlanders had possessed even a modicum of discipline and maturity. It sparked his ire just thinking about it.

Gunther looked over to Aethelstan, iron conviction permeating his timbre, "Be assured, Aethelstan, those two sulkers will be under my watch … right under it … and they will be of no trouble to your men."

"Then we are resolved to our course," Aethelstan responded intently. He felt his mood lightening, as he took his mind off the offending pair of foreigners. "Then let us tarry no further. It is long past time for us to depart these caverns. We court great peril with every moment spent down here."

"Truly spoken," Gunther replied. He turned back towards the foreigners, speaking loudly, in a tone that brooked no argument. "We are going to be leaving, now. All of us. We have a long journey ahead, once we are out of these caverns and back on the surface. Now let us head down to the shoreline, where the rafts are."

"Just a moment," Aethelstan said, remembering one more detail needing attending to. He slipped the mystical pendant off his neck, eyeing the deep blue of the lustrous jewel set within the metal framing. "I almost forgot. I must return this to Lee."

Aethelstan waved for Lee to come over to where he and Gunther stood, calling out his name. The outlander hesitated for a moment, before breaking into a trot, quickly crossing the distance between them.

As Lee approached, Aethelstan extended the borrowed pendant towards him. "I thank you for letting me have the use of your gift."

Lee had a puzzled expression as he reached forth, accepting the pendant. He immediately slipped it around his neck, and the inset blue gem settled down to rest against his chest.

"I am sorry, I could not understand your words for a moment, Aethelstan," Lee said, his own words sounding in perfectly rendered Saxan.

"Of course, and I should have thought of that," Aethelstan responded, marveling at the pendant.

Of the four outlanders, he had a growing affinity for Lee. He sensed that Lee was one reason why the foreigners had not already incurred absolute disaster.

"It is easy to forget that one has this on. It makes things very easy," Lee remarked, with a grin.

"That it does, and since you now understand me, I must repeat my gratitude for your kindness … in letting me wear the pendant for my audience with the rulers of the Unguhur. I was able to speak my mind and heart clearly, in a way I never could have, without it."

"I will do anything I can for you," Lee replied. He shot a sideways glance towards the two sullen-looking ones in his group. His next words were melancholic in tone. "We've already given you all more than enough trouble, and I am so sorry about that."

"Do not be hard on yourself, Lee. Theirs was not your choice,"

Aethelstan replied evenly. "Each must answer for their own decisions."

Lee nodded wordlessly, staring down at the ground and looking uncomfortable. Aethelstan knew the man had more than enough on his mind to have to bear feelings of responsibility for the wayward pair.

Yet Aethelstan could deeply sympathize with the otherworlder. He knew what kind of burdens a leader took upon himself; especially leaders with heartfelt concern towards those they were responsible for.

"We should move on, without further delay," interjected Gunther curtly, a suggestion Aethelstan did not disagree with in the least.

Aethelstan accompanied Gunther, as the woodsman led the four outlanders down the long set of broad stone steps, running from the level with the Khan and Khanum's audience chamber to the ground. After they reached the bottom, they continued onward to the water's edge.

The thane took note of the hard glances cast towards Gunther from the impetuous male youth, the one named Ryan, and the morose young lady named Erin. Yet despite the sour attitudes, they cooperated with Gunther readily enough.

The Saxan thane's long, hastened strides kept pace with the woodsman. They continued to the shoreline together, accompanied by the sounds of their leather shoes scuffling against the gritty surface.

Gunther's remaining Jaghuns were already gathered together, awaiting the others with a skittish energy. The adult Jaghuns circled and whined, wagging their tails furiously as the woodsman moved into their midst. The younger ones jumped about excitedly, tumbling around Gunther's legs, their small paws scrabbling for purchase upon the pebble-ridden shoreline.

A couple of bare-chested Unguhur, and one of the warriors, wearing the distinctive hide-tunic, assisted the humans as they boarded the bobbing rafts tethered there. Within a few moments, both humans and Jaghuns were securely on the rafts.

The Unguhur raft pilots lifted the tethers from their rock moorings, and shoved off from the shore, starting across the dark surface of the lake. Oranim, the great underground city of the Unguhur, soon began to fall away behind them.

All the rafts' occupants, save for the pilots, were turned towards the sight of the sprawling city carved from the rock of the immense cavern. A mix of feelings churned within Aethelstan as he silently beheld the city.

An uneasy calm permeated the expanse of stone-carved constructs. The many Unguhur moving about the terraced structures appeared to be subdued in manner.

There were no sounds of Unguhur youth playing vigorously, a common enough presence before the Saxans began their departure. Nor were there any signs of spirited exchanges between brash young males testing each other's strength and skills, coming into their own as they continued along their passage into full adulthood.

Aethelstan had no doubts that news of the Saxans' departure had been dispersed all throughout the cavern-city. With what he understood of the underground dwellers, and their superstitions, Aethelstan surmised that most Unguhur viewed the hasty exodus of the humans as a foreboding sign with the storms of war sweeping across the lands above them.

A few fishing rafts were out on the lake. Aethelstan noticed the operators seemed to be making every effort to avoid making eye contact with members of the departing group. Their backs squared towards the rafts bypassing them, they attentively focused upon the glimmering lake surface, with spears poised and in hand.

Even the Unguhur piloting the raft carrying Aethelstan was largely unresponsive. The Saxan had no illusions that the creature was doing anything more than fulfilling an ordered task. No shred of conversation emerged voluntarily from the Unguhur, whose dusky gaze was set firmly towards the direction they were traveling in.

Aethelstan could sense the extreme unease of the Unguhur reflected in the pronounced tautness of the creature's jutting, lower jaw, and the tight movements of its back and shoulder muscles. The strained atmosphere was unsettling, but Aethelstan knew he could not take the standoffish gestures personally.

The woodsman had helped him know the reasons, explaining that the Unguhur had a highly pronounced fear of the unknown. They lived in a world that remained relatively constant, and had little interaction with others.

So much upheaval had befallen them, in such a short amount of time. All of the Unguhur knew by now that a war was raging in the lands just above them, and that their kind had taken an active part in the fighting. Seeing Aethelstan's contingent leaving the cavern-city with urgency could only serve to empower fears swirling within the atmosphere of uncertainty.

Passing close by three large gallidils floating lazily along the lake surface, the rafts finally exited the cavern. The pilots carefully maneuvered the rafts as they glided through the narrow river-tunnel.

In a few moments, as the passageway arced around a long, curving bend, they finally lost all sight of the incredible Unguhur city, Oranim. A feeling of regret touched Aethelstan, as well as a stark sense of finality.

Shadows flickered, playing about the ceiling and sides of the damp rock passage, as they wended their way through several twists and turns. Their only illumination came from the strange light emitting from the glowing fungus cultivated, and utilized so effectively, by the Unguhur.

A specter of peril flared when the raft collided with an especially oversized gallidil, which was also navigating the tighter confines of the tunnel. The bulky creature had come upon them without warning, and while it did not intend to strike the raft, its side grazed the edge. Fortunately, although the raft rocked violently at the initial impact, tilting dangerously, everyone aboard managed to keep from falling off.

Aethelstan's heartbeat was spurred considerably by the incident. He was far from alone in his rattled demeanor, noticing Jaghuns and humans alike huddling more closely towards the raft's center. He inwardly offered a prayer of thanks to the All-Father, grateful that he was not splashing about in the cold waters with such a monstrosity.

The river finally emerged from the tunnel, into the spacious cavern housing the mushroom forest. A few Unguhur were idly standing about the edge of the rock platform serving as a quay for the rafts. Their scant attire identified them as laborers.

It was clear they had just been engaged in conversation, but they hushed quickly upon sight of the raft and its occupants. Faces as stony as the shade of their hides, they slowly walked away from the docking area, heading quietly towards the mushroom forest.

The raft jostled as it bumped into the edge of the rock platform. The Unguhur guide on Aethelstan's craft quickly looped a couple of rope tethers over the large boulders on the landing, anchoring the boat firmly into place.

Aethelstan, Gunther, and the others stepped off the rafts and passed by the Unguhur pilots. The Jaghuns bounded to the solid ground, and padded around the humans. Gunther thanked the Unguhur for helping them, and Aethelstan paused to utter his own gratitude, using some of the Unguhur language he had learned during his stay.

The large figures nodded quietly in response, remaining fixedly by the large rafts, their task now finished. It was clear they intended to go no further.

Aethelstan and the others strode briskly forth from the riverside and continued into the sprawling growths, taking the pathway navigating through the midst of the thick, unusual forest. The four otherworld guests gazed about the area with widened eyes, occasionally craning their necks back, as they filled their eyes with the sights of the towering stalks and broad, fungal umbrellas overhead.

Aethelstan could not fault them for their wonderment, as the cavern-forest was likely just as strange to his own eyes as it was to theirs. His studious gaze greedily drank in the sights of the Unguhur-cultivated forest, as they walked onward.

All of them were bathed in phosphorescent light, the copious fungal glow from the large patches positioned on the cavern walls. The looming growths of the mushroom forest appeared to be holding the same, distanced observance of their departure as were the Unguhur themselves. The feeling of being watched fell heavily upon the thane, and he stared towards the tops of the stalks, even searching for signs of eyes on the mushrooms themselves.

He caught himself as he sensed his rising paranoia, and took a slow breath, knowing his mind was getting a little too imaginative. Conferring sentience upon giant fungal stalks was a good indicator that he was drawing excessive conclusions from the strange environment.

Presently, they came to the fissure at the far side of the mushroom forest, and the sharply inclined passageway leading upwards, to the back entrance of Gunther's residence. Aethelstan strode through the deeper darkness filling the rock tunnel, using his right hand to keep appraised of the tunnel's rough-hewn wall. Without any significant light, as the passageway was entirely devoid of the illuminating fungus used in the cavern and tunnels below, his sense of touch was his only reliable means of guidance.

When they were finally through the rear entrance to Gunther's abode, and back up on the surface, Aethelstan almost bumped into the woodsman, who had come to an abrupt halt. Gunther lingered for a few moments in the broad front room, and it looked to Aethelstan's eyes as if a very sentimental moment was occurring with the woodsman.

Some manner of unseen thoughts or memories tugged at the

woodsman, and Aethelstan was careful not to disturb him. He certainly could not fault Gunther when it came to the emotions attached to an individual's home.

The woodsman's eyes were gazing upon the place where he had attained freedom and tranquility for so many years, leaving behind a tumultuous world that had given him no peace. Regrets were undoubtedly gripping the woodsman, finding himself thrust from his temporary haven back into the throes of a world he had so diligently strived to avoid.

Aethelstan was perfectly willing to wait in the shadowy gloom, as they could all afford to spare a little time for the woodsman who had given up so much for everyone. Even the Jaghuns did not bother their master, the young ones and adults clustered to one side of the room.

As if the necessities of the moment regained priority within his mind, pulling him out of transfixing ruminations, Gunther suddenly straightened back up. Without a word to anyone, he walked forward, passing through the front entrance with purposeful strides. The others followed behind him, moving into the fresh outside air and the sight of the surrounding forestland.

After being underground for an extended period, Aethelstan took in a long, slow draught of the woodland air, thoroughly cherishing the feel of it entering him and swelling his lungs. It felt so good just to feel the sun's rays touching his face once again, even if the sudden encompassment of brighter light was momentarily glaring, to his ill-adjusted sight.

A number of Saxan warriors lounging among the trees rose to their feet at the group's appearance. They were readied for departure, with rations and supplies tucked away in small leather pouches, attached to their belts, and in the bulging haversacks they carried over their shoulders. All looked relieved to see Aethelstan, and he did not miss the fact that every last one of them had weapons close at hand.

The recognition that threat and danger now reigned in the Saxan lands brought a sharp pang of sorrow to Aethelstan. Yet he knew they could not relax in their vigilance, not when enemies could manifest at any moment.

Gunther's Jaghuns bounded about the area, clearly ecstatic to be back in the upper world, and oblivious to thoughts of possible encounters with the invaders. Aethelstan envied the creatures in their simplicity, as they were not plagued with nagging trepidations.

"A hard march lies ahead," Aethelstan said aloud, stepping forward into the midst of the gathering Saxans. "We should not linger a moment longer."

The warriors were not about to grumble, plainly harboring a sense of great urgency. Aethelstan did not think any of them wanted to loiter about the very channel into the lower world that the enemy forces had so recently probed.

With the enemy withdrawn, and likely readying themselves to deal with both the Saxans and the Unguhur, there was not a warrior in Aethelstan's force that would want to personally witness the result of those preparations. There would be no new suprises awaiting the enemy, who were by now well aware of the Unguhur, and the existence of the underground passage. The knowledge the Avanorans had gained at the price of their own blood would be put to use. When the countering blows arrived, they would be heavy and overwhelming.

With a chorus of clinks, shuffles, and rustlings, the Saxan force assembled into a loose column, and then began moving out from Gunther's hillside dwelling. The Jaghuns fanned out, trotting among the trees as Gunther moved to the forward tip of the column. Aethelstan was glad to have the capable animals serving in a role similar to that of advance scouts, providing keen eyes and sensitive ears for the nearly three hundred-strong contingent.

A full day's march lay ahead of them, towards the safer havens of the northeastern highlands of Saxany. Aethelstan blocked thoughts of the considerable length of the journey out of his mind, numbing the anxieties inherent with the pressing travel and foreboding circumstances.

The thane instead turned his mind's focus towards the condition of his warriors. For the most part, the legs of the healthier Saxans were fresh and well-rested. In general, an uplifted attitude pervaded the group, their hearts strengthened and emboldened now that they were back within the familiar atmosphere of forest surroundings.

Aethesltan was simply glad there were enough men of recouped strength who could assist those yet struggling with grevious wounds, or rendered lame by battlefield injuries. Overall, enabled by the cooperation of the hale Saxans, a steady pace could be maintained. That was a very welcome boon to Aethelstan, who knew that each and every moment was of the essence.

His worries eased a little further, as he walked among the men of the column, taking closer account of their demeanor. Not altogether surprising, only the outlanders Ryan and Erin seemed unaffected by the return into the upper world.

Shaking his head in consternation at their stubborn, sullen stupor, he paid them little further heed. As far as the two morose outlanders were concerned, Aethelstan could only deem they were people who never knew when to be simply grateful.

The Saxans were free of the underground world that could have become a lethal trap. They were still alive, and acting of their own accord. For his part, Aethelstan was eminently thankful for those two graces alone.

There was much to occupy his thoughts regarding the needs of his men, and what lay immediately ahead of them. His distress about the fate of the Unguhur still pulled at the edges of his conscience. But despite the weightier issues, his step was undeniably livelier with every passing hour. So much had been lost, but the Saxans he led still possessed a fighting chance. That was all he could really ask for, living in the midst of the dark storms breaking over all of Saxany.

JANUS

Janus pounded his fist in sheer frustration against the hard oak of the ship's hull. He was rewarded with scraped skin, and a jolting sting that ran down the length of his arm. But it still felt better than the uncertainty that was becoming maddening.

His three companions were sitting idly in the shadowy murk, as they had been since being ushered from the presence of Fulk and thrust below deck. Kept in an almost-barren space, apparently used otherwise for foodstuffs and supplies, there was nothing to occupy their attentions.

Shortly after they were consigned to the gloomy, musty hold, the movements of the vessel, generated by the sea, became more sharply pronounced. Janus knew the ship had taken in its great anchor, and set its sails.

There were only a couple ways out of the lower hold, and they were both firmly shut. Standing outside, just above them on the upper deck, were a pair of humorless guards.

The immediate surroundings were beyond meager. One rickety wooden chest and a pair of hard cots on the timber decking comprised most of their accommodations, with the exception of a circular metal bowl sitting on the floorboard in the corner, to Janus's right. It did not take much imagination to realize the bowl was intended for bodily waste. In the dimness of the hold, Janus felt it would be quite an achievement to even utilize it.

Janus flinched slightly, feeling a hand settle down gently upon his tensed shoulder. Looking about in the scant ambience afforded by the light trickling through the edges of the opening to the main deck, he could tell that Erika was sitting beside him. She gave him a reassuring smile, with no hint of fear or worry present in her face.

"You stay strong," Erika said in a low voice. "You need to follow your own advice … the advice you gave to Antonio. I couldn't offer you anything better than that …so listen to yourself."

"It is sometimes easier to see from without, than from within," Janus muttered, staring at the wooden planks underneath. "I'm not feeling very strong right now. And I still don't know what to make of all this."

He listened to the creaking of the wood, feeling an unsettling lightness within his belly as the ship was lifted, and then brought down heavily, by the ocean's rolling surface. The first tickles of a clammy chill brushed his skin, and he could only hope that motion sickness did not envelop him.

"Who knows what to make of anything, right now?" Erika responded, after a few moments. "You've seen what's happened. They're keeping us for an important reason. They aren't going to kill us, not a chance. That I'm sure of."

"At least not right away," Janus replied disparagingly. "How long until they figure out we're not that valuable?"

Erika grinned, shaking her head slightly. "Well, I consider myself valuable, by any standard. And there's the fact we did come from another world. No denying that … and let's make sure they don't forget that, either. We may truly be valuable to them, even if they don't know exactly how. Use your head … this thing, here, on your shoulders…"

Playfully, she laughed, lifting her right arm and rapping lightly on Janus' head with her knuckles, as if knocking softly upon a door. The gesture pulled a grin through Janus' morose countenance.

The sounds of bolts being retracted filled the room. The movements sounded loudly within the still hold, jarring the occupants from their subdued states.

The farther trap door to the upper deck swung slowly upward, allowing copious amounts of light to flood the lower hold. The light revealed the massive form of an armored, helmeted knight. The big warrior momentarily blocked the incoming sunlight, stepping slowly down the short flight of steps to the lower decking.

Janus could not read the man's expression, encased within the full helm, but he doubted it held anything friendly. The silhouetted knight worked his way methodically towards the captives.

Hunched over within the cramped conditions, the enormous guard finally entered their area of the long hold. Two others like him followed, after descending the short staircase. When the three had drawn near to the captives, they occupied most of the available space.

Without a word, the guards trailing the giant strode forth, and set about binding the wrists of the four prisoners. Unceremoniously, they assisted the captives to their feet.

"Come along now, and give me no trouble!" the large warrior grunted, when the four prisoners were on their feet. With his large hands, he grabbed Logan roughly at the shoulder, and yanked him forward.

"Lay off him!" Antonio said angrily. "You must feel pretty tough with all that armor on!"

Janus froze in disbelief at Antonio's sheer recklessness. In the next moment, he could see that Antonio's brain was quickly catching up with his impulses, but his mind had not been fast enough. The damange could not be undone, and the young man's eyes were widening in fear and panic.

The knight stopped, and whirled toward Antonio. Janus could feel the hot wave of indignant ire pouring from within the darkness of the helmet's eye slits. The knight tromped over and threw a heavy, unforgiving punch with his mail-covered fists, straight into Antonio's unobstructed gut.

Antonio buckled over, falling to the floor timbers like a dead weight, gagging and coughing. A wave of nausea overcame him, causing him to vomit, as he continued moaning in pain.

"All is just in war. Enemies, above all, deserve no honor," the knight hissed at Antonio, before planting a solid kick to Antonio's exposed side.

Antonio howled in agony, and Janus, Logan, and Erika reflexively rushed the knight. Despite the fact of his restricted hands, Janus was desperate to halt the beating of their friend. All caution and thoughts of what he might incur fled in the surge of righteous fury.

Janus and Erika were forcibly restrained, as the other guards wrapped their arms tightly around the struggling pair. The knight grabbed Logan with both hands, gripping the collar of his woolen tunic. He lifted Logan upward with ease, such that only the tips of Logan's shoes brushed the planking.

"Do you want what he got? Are you that stupid? Perhaps I can share the wealth your friend gained," the knight shouted, almost nose to nose, the iron of his helm pressing against Logan's bare flesh.

"Proud talk, coming from a man wearing armor to a bound man without it," Logan growled defiantly.

"Fulk wants them up here, now!" called an aggravated, impatient voice through the open trap door.

"Luck is with you today, cur!" the burly knight snarled, the words sounding as if they came through clenched teeth.

He jerked Logan down with a heavy thud, turned him about, and shoved him gruffly towards the steps leading upward. Twisting, the knight reached down to where Antonio was still clutching his stomach. With one arm, he wrenched him violently to his feet.

An icy wave passed through Janus, witnessing the power and dexterity of the knight, whose thuggish rancor the captives had barely avoided. If it were not for the voice intervening from above, he and his companions would have soon joined Antonio on the flooring, with heaving stomachs.

Antonio swayed and vomited again, as the knight unmercifully jostled him forward. The four prisoners were herded towards the square of light beckoning to the open deck of the ship. To Janus, the light was a great boon, after having endured the dark, cramped conditions of the hold.

Upon his emergence onto the upper deck, Janus saw that the ship was moving along at a brisk pace. The huge lateen sails were unfurled and filled generously with the winds.

A multitude of rigging and tackle had been set to position the enormous yards, so the great sails could most efficiently catch the gusting winds. The passage of the ship was rhythmic, rising and falling as it glided over the undulating waves.

Sailors labored with the substantial array of ropes and rigging, as orders for adjustments were called out. It was an impressive operation, and the sheer scale of the yard arms amazed Janus.

The four were led across the deck, towards another staircase ascending to the level with Fulk's quarters at the stern. On the way, they passed a number of Harraks being attended by several crewmen. The latter were busy adjusting saddles and harnessing.

Fulk was on the platform just above the one with his living quarters, reached by a few steps located to either side of the stern cabin. Seeing the approach of the prisoners, he dismissed a couple of warriors he had been in conference with.

"You will be in Avalos soon enough," Fulk proclaimed to the prisoners, stepping down to the level where the prisoners were gathered.

Janus kept his visage serene, and his mind focused. During every moment he was with the Avanorans, he knew something could be gleaned of their captor's attitudes and values, if he stayed alert.

Fulk walked up to Erika, and slowly ran his finger just underneath her chin. The left corner of his lip turned up in a smirk, and Janus did not fail to catch the desire sparkling in the man's eyes. Anger whipped through him at the recognition, though he kept his composure.

"Do not fear Avalos, or Avanor. Under the guidance of the Unifier, it is free from strife among barons and dukes. You will find much to your liking there. Perhaps there will be a man of nobility who might find interest in you, within the great city," Fulk stated, keeping his eyes upon Erika. Letting the insinuation sink in, he smiled at the other three. "Perhaps there will be a noble woman attracted to one of you … gaining service in one of Avalos' great households would be a boon to you, if you are of no use to the Unifier.

"You will see that Avalos has every pleasure known to the world. All manner of food, drink, spices, and herbs, acquired by trade with the realms of the world. There are those who do not enjoy the benefits of the Unifier's vision and generosity to the fullest, but their influence fades."

"Generosity, like my friend getting beaten to the floor by an armored man?" Logan interjected, glancing towards Antonio, who was hunched over and cradling his stomach, and still looked queasy.

Fulk stared at Antonio for a moment, before looking back to Logan and the others. "I apologize for the precautions we must take.

Many of my men must remain garbed for war. We do not know you, and the times are uncertain. We must remain prepared for anything," Fulk stated, in a cool tone.

"We all understand," Erika said, with a sweet smile, before Logan could reply. Janus could see she wanted to placate the Avanoran ship commander.

"So what do you hold in esteem, in Avalos? As a foreigner, I know little of your ways," Janus queried. While he wanted to help Erika distract the Avanoran from Logan, he was curious about the sort of standards the more dedicated followers of the Unifier openly adhered to.

"Order ... security ... freedom," Fulk replied, with a charming smile replacing the icier one of moments before. "The Unifier is bringing the entire world together, in trade and mutual respect. The wars being fought now are the wars to end all wars. Once all of Ave is under the Unifier's guidance, you will see a golden age come into being."

Janus kept his face calm, as he took careful note of the Avanoran's words and tone. The reverence in Fulk for the Unifier bordered on more than a mere respect for authority. It was as if the Unifier was something more than any king or human leader. Fulk was clearly a powerful man, but there was no mistaking the awe in his voice as he spoke of the Unifier.

"Truly, we are freeing the world," Fulk then added.

"So, how far away is your lovely city of Avalos?" Logan questioned Fulk, with obvious sarcasm in his tone. Janus grimaced, as Fulk's mouth grew taut. "And if you value freedom so much, and are forcing this freedom on other lands, then how is it we were treated to a feast in the Five Realms, and allowed to go about unfettered? And we are bound up, intimidated, and given nothing in our first interactions with people from your blessed realm?"

"We are not far from the port in Thessalas, from which our ships departed, but you will be sent west upon Harraks," Fulk said, turning to indicate the group of winged steeds on the deck below. "As to your treatment, as I said before, there are precautions in times of war. Once you are in Avanor, you will experience freedom."

"I'm so sure you are right," Logan retorted laconically.

Janus feared that Logan was treading close to an invisible line, or that he had crossed it. But Fulk did not show any signs of anger. He merely swept his gaze beyond the prisoners, towards the steeds, and nodded, as if in response to someone.

Janus followed the Avanoran's gaze, and saw a pair of Trogen warriors standing by the steeds. The Trogens were looking back towards Fulk, with attentive expressions on their dog-like faces.

"Get them onto their mounts," Fulk commanded the trio of guards escorting the prisoners.

Janus felt his arm grabbed firmly, as his group was taken to the lower deck and led towards the Harraks. With their wrists bound, the mounting of the steeds was an awkward process. The hulking knight and the other two guards pushed and shoved the prisoners into place on the saddles.

The Trogens trudged over, and inspected the captives as the human guards stepped back. The tall beings tied extra leather straps around the hips and legs of the prisoners, securing them further to the saddles.

Janus found himself marveling at the Trogen working on his own saddle. Engrossed as it was in its task, it did not take notice of his attention.

He studied the canine-like visage, with its high forehead, framed by a mass of dark hair, the latter much like a mane in how it framed the Trogen's face. He noted the stout, sharp fingernails at the ends of its strong hands, like claws of a moderate size.

'He flinched, seeing the creature's golden eyes peering up into his. It had taken notice of Janus' close scrutiny, and for the slightest moment, the lips of the creature pulled back in an expression that was either a scowl or snarl, revealing its long, sharp fangs. Though the Trogen was probably just irritated at the obvious gawking of the prisoner, the raw, feral look unsettled Janus nonetheless.

Fulk stepped into view, in front of the sky steeds. He addressed the group in a formal tone, "You will now go to Avalos, where you will see the ways of the Unifier. You will realize the wisdom and guidance that the Unifier is bringing to the world."

Looking to the Trogens, who had now mounted their own steeds, he made a curt hand gesture. The Trogens nodded, and took up the reins of their Harraks.

After a couple of shouted commands from the Trogens, the winged beasts launched into motion, bounding down the open deck and leaping upward. Their powerful wings beat up and down as they clung to the air and began ascending. The steeds of the prisoners followed suit, responding to the vocal commands. Once airborne, the group gained altitude rapidly, on a sharp incline.

Looking downward, Janus watched as the huge warship became smaller and smaller, just one of several in the fleet streaming back towards the port city of Thessalas. He felt a great anxiousness at the fact that his hands were tied together in front of him. Even though the Trogens had taken additional precautions to tie him into the saddle, his nerves remained frayed, even though he knew if he fell from the height they were flying at, the result would be the same whether or not his wrists were tied. Nevertheless, he would have felt much better were he not constricted.

The skies above were thickly clouded, and the darker tinge to the vaporous formations evidenced a gathering storm. Passing through a swathe of low-hanging clouds, he felt cool moisture dampening his face.

The Trogens leveled out their flight pattern, about a hundred feet above the low cloud layer. Though resigned to the situation, Janus felt frustration welling up inside. Thrust into a vast unknown, Janus and the others could not begin to get their bearings with chaotic events overtaking them at every turn.

Turning his head, he looked over to Erika. To his surprise, she was staring back at him. Catching his eye, she gave him a smile. Her demeanor bolstered his sagging morale, and he gave her a smile in return.

Logan, flying a little forward of Erika, on her other side, nodded to Janus. The stoic gesture displayed a considerable degree of determination. Among the faults Janus found in Logan, resolve was not one of them.

Antonio, to Janus' left, was not doing as well. His eyes were closed, and foamy spittle covered his lips. He shuddered, and a forlorn gaze rested in his eyes as he opened them. It was apparent the hard strikes to his gut, compounded with the lofty altitude, had made him sick, and he showed no signs of shaking it. If anything, he was looking worse.

Janus turned away, unable to think of anything he could say to help Antonio out. The flight was going to be absolutely torturous for the poor young man. Janus felt sorrow and empathy at Antonio's plight, cursing the desolate specter of helplessness present in its cold, dark glory.

MERSHAD

Mershad slept soundly following the conclusion of another lengthy, active day. For him it was a deep, dreamless sleep, sorely needed by an exhausted body and troubled mind.

Just before dawn, a frigid wind whipped about the timbers of the small house. The wind flitted through every sliver of an opening. A few icy pathfinders of air penetrated narrow openings in the walls, stirring about the thick, fur covering draped over Mershad.

The cool air caressed his face much more gently than it did the outside of the building. Even if not brusque, it was still enough to rouse all three of the structure's occupants from the depths of restful slumber.

Mershad was the first of the three to get up. He pulled off the sheepskin covering, and slid out from the comforts of the feather-filled quilt resting atop the straw-stuffed pallet.

Yawning, he slowly cleared his groggy mind, and focused himself long enough to undertake his morning prayers in the gloom of the house. He would rather have faced the sun, and performed his prayers outside, but he was not yet sure how the Midragardans would take to his particular faith practices. A stranger to their lands and ways, he did not want to test the waters unnecessarily.

He then dressed himself, pulling on a tunic and trousers over his woolen undergarments. It took a moment to slip into the soft leather shoes, the feel of which he was unused to. Stepping quietly, careful not to disturb the others, he unlatched the door to their quarters and continued outside, gently letting it shut behind him.

The glow of dawn had just begun to outline the eastern horizon, beyond the sprawling settlement of King Hakon. Mershad moved off behind the timber house, and relieved himself in a pit dug for the purpose. He again felt very self-conscious exposed out in the open, even though no eyes were upon him. After he was finished, he adjusted his trousers and walked back around the house, striding into the heart of the settlement.

The sounds of animals, and the sight of several bond-servants and retainers moving about the rectangular, wooden structures, gave ample evidence that the tasks of the new day were well underway. Some lugged haversacks filled with barley and rye, culled from the storage granaries within the settlement. A couple of young women hauled wooden pails along with them, brimming with fresh milk taken from the ewes in their outdoor pens, and cows quartered in the nearby byres. Their arms were taut from the weight of the pails, and they moved slowly, so as not to spill any of the contents.

Mershad had already taken a strong liking to the salty butter the Midragardan's made, and the sight of fresh milk reminded him that his stomach was rumbling with a desire for breakfast. He hoped it would not be long before he could sate his appetite.

The blacksmith's workshop already echoed with the telltale clinking of hammer on metal, as smoke lazily rose from the structure towards the sky. A risk for fire within a large gathering of timber buildings, the workshop was set far from the main buildings by itself.

Mershad made his way towards the main longhall of the complex, noticing that Svein was standing just a short distance beyond its entrance. His back was to Mershad, as he was quietly taking in the sight of the rising dawn. His long, blond hair was caught up in a sudden gust of cool wind, tossing the locks all about.

"Good morning, Svein," Mershad greeted from a fair distance, a little anxious to make sure he did not inadvertently surprise a warrior like Svein.

Svein turned slowly to him. His face was at first pensive, as he seemed to force a smile. "It is a good morning, Mershad, though my heart weighs a little heavier today."

"Why is that?" Mershad asked, troubled at the other's somber tone.

"I am in the grip of a great apprehension, Mershad. And I do not know why," Svein replied heavily, his eyes turning to fix upon the golden sun, now a half-crescent on the boundary where land met sky. "There is something terrible behind us, not much different than what you can see now."

Svein turned and gestured towards the southern horizon. Lit up further by the sun's growing light was a dark, foreboding mass of clouds. The menacing formation looked to be approaching steadily, as if striding to obscure, and engulf, the beautiful sight unveiling to the east.

Svein cast a glance back to Mershad. He spoke in a melancholy voice, as he indicated the incoming thunderheads. "That represents what I feel. Like something is coming which seeks to destroy hope itself. The warm light of day is about to clash with a ravenous storm hungering to devour it. Have you ever felt a sense of dread, which you could not explain?"

Mershad nodded. "Yes, I have. And more than once."

"I have a very bad feeling, Mershad. Something is different in the air itself," Svein commented, as a deep frown lined his face. "It is just one of those things you somehow know deep inside, even if you do not know why you know."

"I have felt something like that before," Mershad replied, looking closely at Svein, whose sharp facial features were darkened with a plague of worrisome thoughts and dismay.

Mershad looked away at the distant vanguard of dark clouds, and then swept his gaze back towards the rising sun. It would not be very long before the oncoming storm clouds overtook the radiant vision. They would soon encompass the land with the darkness of thunder, shadow, and rain.

"It will not be long before that storm is here," Mershad said, grasping at anything he could say to break through Svein's morose demeanor. "But other storms may not be as imminent."

"Then it would be foolish to be caught out in the open," Svein remarked, with a small grin cutting through his shadowed countenance. He shook his head, as the grin widened further. "I am sorry for dampening your spirits this morning, Mershad. I find myself like this often lately. I just do not know what has come over me."

"Don't apologize, Svein. If you feel something, you feel it," Mershad replied. "It's not something you can really help."

Svein glanced towards the sunrise, and then back at the storm. "Come, enough of this dour talk. Let us get our first meal of the day."

"That sounds very, very good to me right now," Mershad agreed, chuckling as he patted his stomach. He was surprised it did not growl in response, as hungry as he felt.

A little spark of life arose in Svein's eyes, as he looked to Mershad. "Walk with me, and perhaps we have the good fortune to gain a welcome meal."

"Do you not get fed in the hall?" Mershad asked.

He did not think he had said anything particularly funny, but was glad his comment evoked a wide, warm smile on Svein's face. "We can, if we wanted. But we don't want to right now ... just trust me on that."

31

Svein winked at Mershad, and led him away from the main long hall. They entered an area where a few rectangular, timber houses were clustered. As Svein commented, they were the residences of some privileged, married retainers of King Hakon, who had not yet been assigned a farming homestead to look over.

"You are never late for first meal, Svein," called a very attractive maiden, from the doorway to one of the timber homes. Mershad could tell she was a maiden, as her long flaxen hair flowed freely, from underneath a blue, embroidered headband. "Would you honor us, by joining us today?"

Mershad looked up just in time to see the smirk and wink from Svein, before he looked back towards the maiden in the doorway. Now Mershad understood just why Svein had foregone a meal in the long hall, and taken a stroll among the outer homes in the settlement.

As Mershad was quickly coming to appreciate, the Midragardan maidens were a very bold sort. Though their marriages were normally arranged through their fathers, they could refuse the marriages outright. There was no mistaking their fiery, independent spirits, as the untamed look from the maiden before Mershad loudly testified.

The maiden was indeed beautiful. She wore a blue, pleated chemise that reached from her neck to almost brush the ground. On top of it was a red outer garment, which hung from straps over her shoulders down the front and back of her chemise.

The straps of fabric were clasped securely in the front, just under the collarbone, fastened on each side with two shiny, silver brooches in the shapes of turtle's shells. The brooches held two larger segments of red fabric together, the piece in back secured by the brooches to the piece hanging down in front.

The maiden exhibited a number of metal trinkets, from silver bracelets to a long silver necklace, from which a golden pendant hung. Her large, blue eyes appeared to drink Svein in, as the bridge of her sharp nose wrinkled cutely with the cheerful smile she greeted him with.

A plump, matronly-looking woman, her own hair tied back beneath a scarf, emerged in the doorframe behind the younger maiden. She had the young maiden's wide eyes, sharp nose, and strong-looking arms, visible from her short-sleeved dress, which was also dyed in blue. There were a couple of bright, twisting bands of silver about her right arm, no doubt a sign of stature within King Hakon's settlement.

"Looks like you are in danger, Svein," the older woman remarked, with a confident tone and warm grin. "But if you will risk it, we will set a good meal out for you, and the King's honored guest. Come, break your night's fast with us this morning."

As the maiden's face turned a shade of red, Svein grinned and replied, "It is probably the cure I need for the bad mood I woke up with today. Thank you, Sigrid. I will accept and risk the danger."

Mershad followed Svein, as they proceeded forward and passed through the doorway. It was a home that was partitioned inside, with living quarters sequestered beyond the main chamber by thin, timber dividing walls.

A prominent cauldron, made of soapstone, was suspended by iron chains from ceiling timbers over a long pit surrounded by small stones. A low fire was burning underneath the cauldron, and a favorable aroma wafted from the simmering contents within it.

Nearby, a long trestle table had been set up, around which several stools were set. Sigrid retrieved a couple more stools, one from where it had been resting by an outer wall, and another from where it had been placed before a vertical loom. The loom was set against the wall at the far end of the room. A half-finished length of woolen cloth was within the loom, and a series of circular stone weights held down the warp threads.

"Now Gunnhild, do not be shy," chastised Sigrid with a smile, as she looked towards her clearly-embarrassed daughter. Gunnhild stood a few paces away, near the cauldron, keeping her eyes down.

"It is good to see you again, Gunnhild, and you as well Sigrid," Svein commented cheerfully, as Gunnhild shot her mother a quick, hardened look. "How is Gardas? And where are the two boys today?"

Sigrid smiled at the inquiry. "At least they are away from mischief ... all of them. The boys are off with their father, taking a cart down to Hedirka today. Gunnhild and I have fashioned a good quantity of cloth that should yield us a number of things in trade that Gardas wants. As long as he brings me back a better set of weaving tools, especially a new whale-bone sword for this meddlesome loom, I will be happy ... oh, and some of the green rock-powder that allows me to dye my cloth in my favorite color. Never can have enough of that."

"I imagine the boys are excited to make a journey into Hedka. It is quite a place to be on a busy day, once the incoming merchants have all paid their tolls and begun their incessant haggling," Svein remarked, taking his seat upon one of the stools.

Gunnhild laughed, and rolled her eyes as she replied, "No, I fear not. The boys have taken very happily to Gardas' lessons in the use of the axe. They do not like long delays between their fighting lessons. I believe they already want to begin sleeping at night in the king's long hall."

"So I have suspected, as I have seen them practicing with Gardas. And they look to be learning their lessons well," Svein complimented. "Of course, that does not excuse them from helping their mother."

Sigrid beamed. "Gunnhild, I believe that Svein would like to break his fast on an ample meal, if you know my meaning."

Gunnhild and Sigrid then proceeded to prepare and serve a very satisfying meal. It included fresh fish, soft cheeses, a porridge made out of barley, some fresh butter, and a little rye bread. They also served a very delicious form of curds, which had a cheese-like flavor that was eminently to Mershad's liking. Finally, the two women joined the Midragardan warrior and his foreign guest for the sumptuous repast.

Though the meal tasted quite good, Mershad was still getting used to the general hardness of the breads, and the need to soften it in things like the porridge. He did not have to worry about drawing any attention. Gunnhild, and even Sigrid, seemed to have much more of their focus upon Svein, than they did for how Mershad was faring with the early meal.

He washed the food down with a limited quantity of ale, feeling some guilt for consuming the fermented beverage his faith disallowed. Yet there really was not anything else, as the ale was undeniably much safer to drink than water.

"Thank you, Sigrid," Mershad said, as he finished his portion of the meal.

"She will have you as fat as our home-field pig," Svein remarked with a carefree laugh.

"You are most welcome, Mershad," Sigrid replied. She then turned towards Svein, and asked, "And are you looking forward to the upcoming Great Gathering?"

"If I am still here, then yes. I never know where I might be sent these days, " Svein commented, with an abruptly somber edge to his voice.

"The Great Gathering?" Mershad asked, curious.

"Ah, yes … you do not yet know of an all-moot, do you Mershad?" Svein inquired.

"I'm afraid not yet," Mershad answered.

"It is a wonderful time for all who attend one, though a Great Gathering is not without a serious purpose," Svein replied. "Many contests of strength and skill, time for much trade, story tellers, music, the nectar of mead, and far more than I could ever hope to remember. It is a time of law as well, when we gather to hear the law-giver, and when all who attend will listen to disputes and grievances."

"And there is much time for rising young warriors and pretty maidens to dance and sing together, as the mead flows like rivers," Sigrid added mischievously, eliciting another noticeable blush from her daughter. She grinned as she added, "Even arrangements are made at such times."

"Indeed, there are such happenings at all-moots, and many at the Great Gathering, would not you agree, Gunnhild?" Svein added, plainly sharing Sigrid's amusment with Gunnhild's apparent embarrassment.

Mershad smiled broadly, barely able to contain a bout of laughter threatening to burst out. Gunnhild was most certainly outnumbered in the current exchange. "It sounds like a wonderful time."

"It is, and I wish we did not have all these tidings of war and other troubles," Svein said, his mood sobering a bit. "We will still have the Gathering, do not worry, for our people are not going to stop living the life we have always led. To do any less than continue forth in our traditions would to be embrace defeat willfully."

"A most wise answer," Sigrid commented, with no trace of jest in her voice.

At that moment, a strong-looking teenage boy came huffing into the doorframe of the house. He bore two loaded haversacks over his shoulders, which he appeared to be struggling with. Mershad recognized the boy from his first glimpses of activity in the early morning. The boy was now caked with sweat, his ruddy hair stringy and matted.

"I hope that we are not late, Sigrid", he blurted, as he trudged into the room.

"Over here, over here," Sigrid directed him hurriedly, gesturing towards the inner base of the wall running along the side of the house to their left. "I will be using a good amount of that today. I'm about out of bread, and we'll need more porridge when my boys and husband return."

The burly boy heaved and dropped the large sacks of barley down against the side of the far wall, right where she had directed. When he straightened up, he suddenly took notice of Svein and Mershad sitting at the trestle-table.

His eyes widened in surprise at the sight of the guests. The color lightened in his face, as the sweat of labor was suddenly a colder sweat of nervousness.

"I hope I do not scare you that much," laughed Svein merrily. "Do I look that frightening these days, Gunnhild?"

While Sigrid's daughter blushed again, the boy's mouth went agape, as if he was about to say something, before shutting tensely again. He bowed his head towards Svein and Mershad, eyes lowered to the ground.

"I am...sorry … for my ill manners…" the boy stammered.

"Come now, or Mershad will think me to be some kind of tyrant," Svein said in a light-hearted manner.

"Snorri has not yet had much of a chance to get to know Svein," Sigrid interjected. "The boy's got a good heart, but hasn't sharpened that which is between his ears just yet, though I still have hope. I would guess he's stumbled unannounced into the presence of a few Midragardans who have a little less good humor about them, am I right?"

Snorri nodded quickly.

Sigrid shook her head, and then looked towards Mershad. "Snorri's the boy of Naddod, one of the bond-servants on this farmstead."

"Do you have any porridge, or other food left still?" Svein asked.

"Yes, and perhaps a bit more bread and soft cheese, but I believe that Mershad cleaned us out of the skyr, " she said with a soft smile. She added quickly, noticing Mershad's confused expression at her last words, "The curds you obviously liked so much."

"Then sit with us, Snorri, that you may know Svein Thorsteinson is different from others you may have encountered," Svein invited, before adding, "If that is okay with Sigrid, of course."

"Boy's gotta eat," she said resolutely, having already moved to retrieve a stool from one of the rooms partitioned off from the main chamber.

She returned a moment later, setting the stool down close to Svein. Gunnhild prepared Snorri a dish of porridge, bread, and cheese, along with a full cup of ale.

"Now sit down, Snorri," Sigrid directed.

"Thank you, " Snorri replied, nervously, taking his seat next to Svein.

Svein gave him a hearty slap on the back. "A stout lad like you needs food to grow stronger."

The boy hesitated a little further. Mershad could sense that he truly felt anxious sitting in such close proximity to one of King Hakon's highest-ranking warriors.

"Go ahead, lad," Svein said, before adding a little more firmly. "If it makes you more comfortable, it is a command. But later you will speak to me of anyone who has been harsh with you. I strongly doubt you could have caused anyone genuine offense. That is also a command."

Snorri gave him a last, lingering look, and then began to eat heartily. As his sizeable body portended, he exhibited quite a substantial appetite.

"Naddod has provided King Hakon with a strong son," Svein commented.

Though the boy did not respond verbally, Mershad caught a flash of excitement within the boy's eyes. He drank deeply from his cup of ale, and listened to Svein's praise.

"Snorri is a very good boy, and a hard worker, even if he doesn't have the most grace going about it," Sigrid replied. Mershad could tell from her expression that she held genuine affection for the boy. "He obeys his father well, and obeys the retainers and household guards, often better than some of those louts deserve."

Snorri's eyes widened again at the last comment. He looked about, as if worried some of the ones Sigrid referred to were somehow listening, or watching.

"I've been around enough, Snorri, and I will say what I see with these eyes. They are not too dulled yet to miss much," she said with a wry grin. She patted the boy fondly on the shoulder, as she passed around the end of the trestle table to return to her stool on the other side.

"Perhaps you will have to speak to me as well about the things you see, Sigrid," Svein said in a low, more serious tone.

A look passed between Sigrid and Svein. Mershad could tell Svein was going to look into the harassment of the boy. Mershad was gladdened, having already taken a liking to the shy, awkward boy, even if he had not yet said very much.

"Yes, Snorri," Svein said, with another light slap on the boy's back. "Always look to the wisdom of women. You will be wise to know they are the highest of authorities in the Midragardan kingdom ... if you know what is good for your future health."

"So, Svein, you do know one of the main secrets of life, as to who is really in charge," Sigrid stated, laughing deeply. She turned towards Gunnhild. "See, he is already wiser beyond most any man in our land's long history."

Gunnhild reddened again, though this time the maiden could not hold back an amused grin.

"I hope to survive long, " Svein said, smiling. "And a man survives not just by the sword in his hand."

"With that kind of wisdom, you may survive a long time," Sigrid replied through bursts of laughter. "Hallgerd raised you very well."

"I admit my mother did, but my father also passed this wisdom on to me as well," Svein replied.

"Thorstein taught you that?" Sigrid retorted, with a look of mock surprise. "I will have to commend him when we next see him, at his farmstead or an all-moot. It appears we have a lineage of wisdom here … a true legacy."

Svein grinned. "I shall try to continue that with my own sons someday, as such wisdom will be instinctive with any daughters I may have."

Svein then turned towards Snorri, who was already about finished with his ample portions of food, "Maybe for now, I can pass some wisdom on to the sons of others. It looks as if great rain is coming today, so what I have in my mind may not be possible this day. If you can get your chores done, and if your father will allow, I will have Thorkell show you the use of a spear. A boy as strong as you needs to have some training, and I do not think your father will remain a bond-servant for much longer."

The boy's eyes enlarged, as if they were about to pop out of his head, as he looked back at Svein with surprise and eagerness at the sudden offer. Mershad could sense Svein had just fulfilled a large, unspoken wish in the boy's heart.

"Never have I seen such a look of dismay," Sigrid chuckled, with a strong current of sarcasm. "There is a little work yet to do in patching the outer barriers on a couple hay meadows, and I may need some help with grinding some grain. But I am sure I can ensure that Naddod will allow you to go when Svein calls for you."

"Really? … I can learn from Thorkell?" the boy asked, on the cusp of stammering.

Svein turned to Gunnhild. "And I would love for you to visit with me, at the next household feast of King Hakon, if you could attend with your parents."

"I would love to," she replied quickly, her expressive eyes rife with happiness.

"She has been a good girl, and put in more than enough time at the loom and tablet," Sigrid commented. "So I will make sure she is there. You will not need to ask Gardas, as you already know the truth about authority in a home."

"Thank you, Sigrid," Svein replied, with another laugh.

"It is an honor, Svein, son of Thorstein," Sigrid returned, in an entirely serious tone of voice.

"You have always been kind to me," he said, as he slowly began to rise up from his stool. He looked to Mershad. "I believe it is time we got going. I have to run some of the warriors through axe and sword drills today, if the weather allows it."

At the intimation, Mershad carefully got up, thanked his kind hosts, and accompanied Svein to the outside. He was glad to see Svein in a better mood than earlier that morning, but looking at Gunnhild it was not hard to understand why.

He admired how easily Svein was able to talk to Gunnhild. Mershad's nerves would have frayed long since in the presence of a female he had taken a deep liking to. He strongly doubted he would have been able to sustain a coherent conversation, much less the banter Svein had exhibited.

The wind outside was starting to whip about in greater strength, as the temperature cooled. The mass of dark clouds was spreading over the settlement, and there was no question a storm would be falling upon them at any moment.

Mershad hurried to keep up with Svein's long, brisk strides, as they walked back towards King Hakon's long hall. Svein had a content look resting upon his face, and Mershad chose not to interrupt the moment, as the tall Midragardan basked in the afterglow of his visit with Gunnhild.

Mershad's mind, left to idle, turned back to thoughts of Erika and the others left behind. Such thoughts brought an instant heaviness to his heart. He endured such pangs many times a day. Beyond Derek and Kent, they were his only links back to his own world.

The worst part was that their fates were unknown, heightening his anxieties without boundary, as his mind raced through hundreds of possible scenarios. Most of the possible outcomes he worried himself over were not pleasant or promising in the least.

He commanded himself to push the troubling thoughts deeper in the recesses of his mind, as he and Svein neared the great hall of King Hakon. Until he knew anything of their situation, he knew he was doing himself no favors by working his mind up into a frenzy.

Yet the uncertainty could not go on indefinitely. Sooner or later, some answers would have to be gained.

JANUS

No matter how hard he tried, Janus struggled just to keep his eyelids open. The journey to Avalos seemed to be unending, with hour after hour passing in uncomfortable monotony.

After the initial surges of energy derived from the stimulation of taking open flight had finally died down, the accumulation of fatigue could no longer be held at bay. Janus and the others began to doze, drifting in and out of the borders of sleep, and wavering at the edges of consciousness.

The discomforts of the saddle prevented the otherworld foreigners from falling into the mercy of full unconsciousness. Sores and aches gathered over the course of the long trek had now reached a point where their collective effects were an unyielding bane.

Pockets of turbulence, and sudden, brisk winds, stoked the captives' anxieties. But the Trogens escorting the prisoners skillfully adjusted the group's altitude or orientation from time to time, offsetting the worst of nature's discomforts. The Harraks were very strong fliers, and their demonstrated ability to handle the varying shifts in air currents elicited a rising confidence within the hearts of the captives.

With all of the uncertainties facing them, not one amongst the small party could afford to give in to the overtures of even a light sleep. As such, they all toiled in their own ways against the relentless onslaught of fatigue.

In truth, there was little for them to worry about, even if they did happen to fall into a deep sleep. The captives were all tightly secured to the saddles upon the Harraks. Even if the beasts flew upside down, the riders would not have fallen. The Trogen escorts flying at the sides of the band of prisoners, and those leading them, provided their steeds with guidance. There was no need to worry about drifting off on a wayward course. Yet the constant flow of cold air over their bodies, infused with the clean, invigorating essence born of a bright spring day, kept them from lulling into a drowsy state.

There had been two brief stops along the westward journey, taking place in large Gallean castles. On both occasions, following a sharp descending approach, the party landed directly within the outer baileys of the two imposing, stone fortresses. The two stops were conducted without much event, but Janus and his companions were able to glean a little more regarding the nature of the power holding them fast within its clutches.

On the second of the landings, a haughty castellan had manifested, appearing very miffed that the Trogens and their wards had suddenly alighted in the castle without having sent any advance word of their coming. He had begun to bitterly complain that the Trogens presumed far too much, and that his castle was not prepared to receive a modest party of guests.

The Trogens were not entirely fluent in Gallean, but they did not have to even know one word to bring the castellan down quickly from his lofty perch. All the Trogens had to do was display the seal of the Unifier they were carrying to the castellan. The sight of it transformed the man into the most compliant, concerned of hosts.

The stark reaction spoke volumes about how the Unifier was regarded. There was no hesitation, and the flare of genuine fear in the man was unmistakable. Janus took careful note of the response.

The two castle visits were almost identical in experience. Once dismounted, the prisoners were afforded only enough time to relieve themselves of their bodily needs, acquire a little portion of bread and weaker ale, and to stretch their increasingly aching, stiffened muscles.

Janus could get nothing out of the servants and attendants they encountered, nor even the few knights or castle staff that drew close during the interludes. If anything, the occupants of the two castles were careful to limit their interaction with the prisoners. Everything was watched over intently by the huge Trogens, save for the scant moments that the captives saw to the demands of nature.

During both stops, it seemed to Janus as if no time had passed when their Trogen escorts rounded them up to resume the trek. The Trogens gruffly aided the prisoners where necessary, as they got reseated in the saddles. After a signal from the Trogen's leader, they were all off into the skies once again.

Their journey took them over a wide array of landscapes, ranging from mountains, to plains, rolling hills, and sprawling, dense forests. Like veins running through a great, living body, broad creeks and swiftly flowing rivers coursed, branched, and joined in confluence all across the bountiful lands of Gallea. The light of the sun glittered, sparkling off of the meandering routes of water. Janus espied more than a few small vessels floating along the gleaming surfaces.

Capacious breaks in the forests revealed the locations of several villages, and their accompanying farmlands. Freshly plowed fields, with their telltale streaks of upturned earth, fallow fields covered in the stubble of wild growth, and sprawling meadows, dotted with the forms of grazing livestock, surrounded the simple, meandering dirt roads passing between the modest collections of timber residences.

Stone manor houses, with aggregates of attendant outbuildings, could be distinguished from the villages easily enough. From so far above, Janus could see the clusters of villages situated around each of the manor houses.

The orderly forms of monasteries, replete with large churches, encompassed cloisters, and wide swathes of cleared lands, were distinguishable in the landscape beneath the fliers. Some monasteries were much larger than others, their grounds permeated with ornate buildings fashioned of stone. Like the outlying villages gathered around a manor, many granges, with large rectangular barns, were arrayed about the more elaborate monasteries.

Other monasteries were much sparser in nature, located in more remote places, removed from the more abundant signs of civilization. Nestled almost imperceptibly into small mountain valleys, and encompassing woodland depths, the isolated monasteries harbored nothing more than a few simple, timber constructs.

Away from villages and manors, there were very few signs of anything that could be termed as a road. What routes could be identified looked to be nothing more than narrow, winding dirt paths.

Seeing the few lonely pathways cutting through expanses of dense wildlands, Janus surmised that land travel was a dangerous undertaking. It helped him weather the discomforts of flying a little better, as they soared over the terrain.

A few walled towns with associated castles appeared from time to time in the landscape beneath the fliers. A couple other towns cropped up that were attached to monastic abbeys, instead of castles.

A couple towns were little more than a singular main street running between an outer curtain wall and the gates of a castle. Other towns showed signs of a broader evolution, featuring large, open squares, filled with signs of activity amid a cluster of stalls, carts, and wagons.

The largest of the towns Janus saw had sprawling outgrowths of larger streets with narrow alleys, spreading outward from the simpler, elemental cores of the towns. These streets and alleys outlined more expansive plots of land than the cramped plots demarcated closer to the resident castle or abbey.

Arising within the heart of one of the larger towns was a huge, beautiful church of stone, set directly facing a great stone basilica. Flanking its western entrance were twin square towers of a lofty height, rising up in arcaded stages. The towers were surmounted by connical pinnacles, each topped by spear-point shaped finials.

The entire building formed the outline of a spear-shape that was visible from the upper air. High-set Clerestory windows lined its sides, and its lead-tiled roof had a steep pitch. A square lantern tower sat atop the area where the two slanting extensions converged at the spear-shape's tip. A squat spire, and another spear-finial, crowned the prominent lantern tower. Janus craned his neck to the side, as far as he could, to take in the sight of the remarkable structure.

The airborne party came across a few singular castles as well, perched on higher promontories, and often tucked into the folds of sinuous watercourses.

Eventually, the party came within sight of a wide, shining river, far larger than any waterway they had yet come across. The Trogens swiftly adjusted their flight path, shadowing the course of the westward-flowing waters. Janus soon got the impression that the river was like a silvery road, beckoning towards something much grander than anything they had yet set their eyes upon.

There was a greater frequency of castles along the path of the broad river. Its gleaming surface was traversed by both small and large vessels alike, traveling on the power of oar or sail. Flat-bottomed barges, sleeker galleys, square-sailed trading cogs, and two-masted, round-hulled ships shared the massive river with a number of tinier boats, some powered by as little as one pair of oars.

"Avalos! Avalos is here!" one of the Trogens loudly exclaimed, the exuberant words rousing all of the prisoners to full attentiveness.

Janus blinked, turning his neck from side to side, warding off the lingering stiffness generated where his chin had been resting for extended periods on the top of his chest. Wind beating steadily against his face, he brought his tired gaze up from the river below, taking in the sight now spreading out before him, filling the horizon.

Breath caught suddenly in his throat, as he beheld a vision instantly etched into his mind's eye. What lay before them was nothing less than a massive, majestic city.

The grand spectacle drew into increasing clarity as they approached on a downward-slanting course. The Trogens were taking them in at a lower level of altitude, affording Janus and the others a clearer view of the pieces comprising the living mosaic.

The crystalline weather around Avalos enhanced the vivid impressions. The beautiful spring day showered the city in brilliant, warming light, draping a deep aqua sky across the upper firmament, the latter ornamented with sporadic masses of immaculately white, puffy clouds. Like lavish accoutrements decorating the attire of a mighty king, the glorious state of the environment complimented the spectacular nature of the scene.

Avalos was vastly larger than the most extensive of the walled towns that Janus had recently observed. The great river flowing westwards ran through the very midst of the magnificent city. It joined its waters with the ocean lying just beyond, the mouth of the river emptying into a large bay serving as an extensive harbor.

Villages, a number of smaller enclosures, and some larger plots of cultivated acreage populated the landscape leading up toward the city. Sprawling far beyond the main walls surrounding Avalos were a kind of suburbs, which the skyward group was now about to pass over.

While there were so many interesting sights that it was difficult to focus upon any one of them in particular, his attentions were drawn towards a large multitude of horses. They were being quartered within a concentrated number of pens and long stables situated on the outskirts of the suburb area.

A fair number of people were strolling along the perimeter of the pens, and a few individuals could be seen riding within some of the larger enclosures. More than a few eyes turned upwards, watching the sky steeds and riders passing overhead.

Deeper into the suburbs, closer to the outer curtain wall ringing the city, Janus took note of some wide-open spaces in which sizeable, wooden frames had been erected. Upon the frames were stretched large swathes of cloth.

His attention then drifted towards the city's curtain wall. The rampart protecting the main portion of the city looked to be very formidable, with many elements giving ample evidence to potent defensive capabilities. Battlements ran all along the top of the stout enceinte. Supporting them was an evenly-spaced series of stone corbels, forming machicolations, through which the areas just beneath the walls could be covered by lethal missile fire.

At regular intervals were thick, semicircular mural towers, whose curved facings projected well beyond the wall itself. Placed high up from the ground, a number of cross-shaped slits graced the outer surfaces of the towers.

The slits availed well-protected defenders the ability to levy an enfilading barrage from either crossbow or bow. Janus had great sympathy for anyone unlucky enough to be caught within that kind of deadly hail.

The bases of the walls and towers were provided with an outward-sloping plinth, further bolstering the formidable nature of the barrier.

There were six main gateways visible in the walls ahead, matching six more on the other side of the river. Each was provided with broad, lofty guard towers flanking the entrances like stoic sentinels. Janus could see that the entryways were currently open, with iron portcullises raised.

A host of traffic was visible in dense clusters around the gateways, both without and just within the walls. A mass of pedestrians, carts, draft animals, and riders formed throngs anticipating admittance through the gates, whether entering or leaving.

A few prominent bridges spanned the great river, all but two of them fashioned of stone. On the stone-built bridges, massive, squat piers supported tall arches, which, in turn, supported the wide, upper surfaces of the bridges. Robust towers, pierced through by arched openings, sprouted atop several of the piers, with most of the high structures situated near the ends of the bridges.

It was clear that the bridges were not just a means of crossing the river. Running along both sides of a couple of the lengthy spans, a multitude of small buildings had been arrayed, most two-stories in height. Numerous individuals strolled and milled about the edifices, as if they were on just another street within the great city.

It was quite evident that the power of the great river was being extensively harnessed. The huge, churning wheels of many mills could be seen along the river's path. The mills were based upon the bridges, out on floating platforms in the water itself, or set into structures positioned along the shoreline.

More than one market area could be identified, dwarfing the ones that Janus had previously seen, in the other towns. A few ornate, gable-ended stone halls loomed over the markets, rising alongside the other buildings hugging the boundaries of the open spaces. Teeming stalls and carts, as well as a sprawling mass of individuals, congested the interior of the grand market squares.

Janus looked straight downward as they passed directly over a particularly stout, blocky structure, whose thick, square walls exuded an aura of strength. He espied the unmistakable sigil of the Order of the High Altar, flying prominently in the breezes atop the building's crenellated rooftop.

The harbor area was now spreading out beneath the group as they continued along the contour of the river. The harbor itself was no less impressive than the main body of Avalos. Around the perimeter of the great bay was an abundance of warehouses, quays, jetties, and docks, servicing a massive flotilla of waterborne vessels.

Three distinct channels had been cut into the land from the harbor's edge, looking from Janus' vantage as if the land itself had been pierced with an enormous trident. The three broad, lengthy channels were fitted with multiple quays.

Timber cranes on the long docks, and alongside the quays, rotated, dipped, and rose as they were utilized to attend ships at anchor. Wood-plank gangways connected the upper decks of many ships to the docks and quays.

An area of water and land along the northern side of the bay was cordoned off by a great stone wall. The wall shielded the landward side, and extended out in a wide, curving path to create a small private harbor farther out in the bay.

Within the enclosure was a complex of buildings. The edifices included a number of distinctive, elongated shed-like structures, set side by side down at the water's edge. A number of downward-sloping mud slips were cut into the soil along the shore.

Several arrays of wooden stocks had been set out in the open, a little higher up from the shoreline. A couple of the stocks provided support for the bodies of ships currently growing upon them.

Smoke drifted up from a few of the buildings, as the clanging of metal and thumping of hammers resonated. Supplies and materials were stacked in abundance, ranging from large assemblages of casks, to extensive piles of rough timber, waiting to be fashioned into shipbuilding materials.

The walls, the markets, the great harbor, and the bridges were all impressive elements in their own right. Yet more than anything else, it was the presence of religion that began to stand out most prominently to Janus, as he continued to eye the details of the vast city.

Signs of monastic activity were prevalent within Avalos. More than one enclosure held the telltale cloister garth and church of a monastery compound. A couple were placed adjacent to great hall-shaped structures, the nature of which Janus could not readily ascertain.

There were numerous individual churches situated all throughout the city, ranging from simple, hall-like structures, to highly elaborate edifices. Spear-shaped finials crowned the churches, from the gable ends of the smaller churches to the towering spires streaking upward from the more massive constructs.

One immense church stood above all the rest, soaking up Janus' attention as the group passed over it. In its sheer artistry and splendor, the remarkable building easily surpassed every edifice contained within the city's walls.

Two soaring, square towers, capped by the Western Church's spear-symbol, flanked great entrance portals set within the structure's western façade. A series of tall, exquisitely sculpted figures formed a line at the upper edge of the façade, which contained a carved mural in the center resting just atop a prodigious rose window of stained glass.

An array of flying buttresses supported lofty clerestory walls running the length of the church's main body, the eastern end of which exhibited a radial series of chapels beyond its chevet. Flying buttresses, like the spokes of a half-wheel, protruded at even intervals to brace the walls of the chevet.

Winged, muscular humanoid figures were set into elevated niches on the outer facings of the flying buttress piers. Ornate statuary, situated in two groups of six, rose atop the semicircular crown, a colonnade running between the stout piers.

The enormous church was not yet completed, evidenced by the open yards adjacent to it in which hundreds upon hundreds of laborers and craftsmen were heavily engaged. Prodigious accumulations of stone, timber, and other building materials were placed all throughout the vast construction site, amid simple, thatch-roofed timber shelters, with open, fully-exposed sides, and several enclosed hall-shaped buildings.

A symphony of industrious toil accompanied the small army of laborers, derived from hammers falling, men shouting, metal clanging, axes chopping, saws grating, and a mass of other noises. Numerous porters, using litters, or employing the assistance of hand or animal-pulled carts, ferried loads of material about the grounds. Other workers were concentrated around a series of long troughs, while teams of carpenters sawed wooden planks from the raw trunk segments of large trees. Several painters attended to the myriad figures and scenes depicted within the church's extraordinary western façade, and Janus' mind spun just trying to take in all of the activity.

The air around the massive construction site was marked with a haze, the latter formed by dust from lime mortar, stone, wood residues, and other substances. Extensive networks of scaffolding climbed the outsides of the great church, entailing a series of inclining ramps and platforms. Great windlass-powered hoists and simple pulleys were visible all along the upper levels of the towering construction. A considerable block of stone was being pulled slowly up the side of a rising tower with the turning of a timber wheel, located at the very top, powered by a couple of people treading steadily, enclosed inside the wheel itself.

Another substantial network of scaffolding reinforced the ribs of a great vault and the stone surfacing being put into place over the nave of the church.

No less than two cloisters could be seen off the north side of the church. The first cloister was accessed directly from one of the slanting wings towards the end of the church, while beyond the second cloister was a cluster of houses with small garden plots.

A house and a squat structure lay along the northern side of the church's nave. A larger hall-shaped building was being erected close to the northern flank of its western façade. The southern side of the giant church's nave was accompanied by something that looked like a small keep, with attendant garden plots.

Yet even the breathtaking religious edifice was far from being the most prestigious, elaborate structure within Avalos. That honor was reserved solely for a construct without peer. An awe-inspiring vision commanded Janus' attention, as they moved beyond the church and approached the edge of the city.

A looming colossus arose from the end of a small peninsula extending from the northern half of the city. The soaring wonder had been created from the efforts of both nature and skilled labor.

Nature had provided a lone mountain, forged of a dark kind of rock, reaching up to dizzying heights, as if seeking to pierce the sky itself. Sitting atop the conical mountain, like an ornamental finial gracing the top of a church spire, was a high, singular tower. From the top of the lofty tower fluttered a large standard, the details of which were still too far away to ascertain.

The tower was the apex of an immense, terraced fortress, an amazing construct built up the facing of the landward side of the mountain. The curtain walls and towers on each of the ascending levels rose up to the heights of the next terrace, positioned above and behind them.

Like the spokes of a vast, semicircular wheel, long, bridging walkways extended back from a few of the outer towers on each level. The walkways connected the curtain wall of one level to the lower lip of the next.

A variety of architectural styles were reflected in the towers. Circular ones with sharp-sloping, conical roofs were interspersed among mural versions with square, semicircular, or polygonal facings

At the angle at which they were flying, Janus was afforded a partial view of the seaward side of the mountain. Primarily a soaring facade of sheer rock, it was rife with jagged surfaces intertwined with broad sections of flat, largely featureless stone.

At the lower base, where the seaward facing touched the end of the northern arc of the bay, was another sea enclosure bordered by a thick stone wall. A few low sheds with arched openings set in the water accompanied several small buildings situated close to the water's edge. A pair of small, oar-powered boats and three elegant galleys rested within the wall, while a couple of large, two-masted sailing vessels bobbed at anchor just outside of the enclosure.

Drawing steadily closer to the mountain, Janus peered intently at the terraces rising up the landward side. At the bottom, a main road led up to the fortress-mountain, its path finally blocked by an imposing-looking barbican flanked with two stout towers.

A short distance past the barbican was a lowered drawbridge, spanning a moat accessing a gate complex piercing a series of three walls. A low, crenellated wall was positioned near the lip of the moat. Separated from the low wall by a short stretch of open ground was a much higher wall, provided with towers set at regular intervals. Beyond the second wall was yet another corridor of open ground, ending at another prominent wall designed with another sequence of towers, the latter positioned wherever open stretches existed between the towers of the second wall.

A large gateway, set into the third rank of walls, was protected with two huge, projecting towers. It provided access into a broad, open bailey, strewn with several timber buildings, fenced pens, and a few others fashioned of stone. A team of oxen was being unhitched from a wagon in one area, while dogs bounded down the length of another enclosure, shadowing the movements of a pair of strolling individuals.

Only one walkway bridged the curtain wall of the first level with the bottom of the second terrace.

A multi-storied keep crouched near the gatehouse on the second level. Past that structure was a stone hall of considerable size, basilica-shaped and provided with a sharp-sloping, lead-tiled roof.

A pair of smaller halls were situated close by. Smoke drifted upwards from a couple of isolated outbuildings, and a granary was easily identifiable by the short piles lifting it out of the reach of pests.

Close to the granary was a large, quadrangular cistern. A church, with spear-shaped ornamentation cresting one of its gable ends, rose up within the second level's bailey. Other buildings, a few quite elongated, were set along the inner side of the curtain wall.

Three bridges crossed from the towers of the second terrace to the edge of the third level. The structures visible on the higher level were not entirely different from the first, though a greater proportion of its buildings were fashioned of stone. A modest hall, another small church or chapel, judging from its spear-shaped finial, and an extended length that could enclose other chambers abutted the outer wall, set end to end.

Three crosswalks spanned the distance from the third level towers to the base of the fourth, which contained the only significant concentration of foliage. A lush abundance of greenery, augmented by a host of matured trees, held court around the sparkling surfaces of a few great pools of water.

Some taller edifices had been erected in the midst of the verdant growths, with some elements jutting into the gleaming water of the pools. Some small, roofed constructs were set in the midst of the water, accessed by narrow walkways from their edges. The dense foliage obscured much of the detail of the various buildings.

Like the two levels just beneath, three bridge-ways connected from towers to the lip of the fifth level, which contained a number of stone buildings forming an expansive, interior cloister. Most of the buildings were two stories in height, with the exception of a massive building rising above all the others, which served as the farther side of the perimeter surrounding the open courtyard.

Three walkways linked the fifth and sixth levels, the latter containing a particularly massive, stone keep that dominated the terrace. The four corners of the keep's upper level were each provided with crenellated turrets.

Only one spanning crosswalk connected the sixth to the seventh level, which beckoned with a vision of power and splendor. A huge, basilican palace of plaster-coated brick and marble was the centerpiece. Towering marble columns spanned the portico in the front of the palace. Fashioned out of porphyry, the rich purple hues of the columns emanated a regal aura. A singular, golden dome was set into the farther end of the rectangular structure's roof, strikingly resplendent in the embracing, afternoon sunlight.

The basilican palace was accompanied by a few other luxurious-looking constructs, three-story edifices fashioned of brick with white marble, the latter radiant in the light of day. Some of the stories were lined with an arcaded series of large windows, while others featured spacious, corbeled balconies. A group of covered, colonnaded walkways interconnected the various buildings to one another.

More foliage, statuary, a couple of small ponds, and several fountains ornamented the spaces around the palace and the smaller buildings. A thick, circular column of red porphyry, set atop a stout, square marble base, was placed a short distance before the steps leading to the palace building.

Set to the back of the basilican palace, a zigzagging ramp cut from the rock of the mountain ran up to where an imposing, round tower surged upward from the pinnacle of the mountain. The high tower was effectively a finial for the mountain itself, and its single banner flapped robustly in the winds.

As the party pulled within close proximity of the mountain-fortress, it became readily apparent that the Trogens and their escorted prisoners were far from alone in the air. The forms of several trios of Harraks, saddled with armed riders, drifted on the air currents above and around the mountain-fortress.

Most riders kept to a good distance, but one of the armed trios streaked directly towards Janus' group. Human warriors hailed the Trogens from a modest distance, showing no sign of alarm or tension towards the arriving party. Long kite-shields rested from guige straps at the riders' left sides, and their lances were gripped loosely, at mid-shaft, held close to the bodies of their winged steeds. The circular pommels of swords protruded from the mouths of scabbards affixed to their leather belts.

The riders were clothed in white surcoats, covering coats of chain mail of about knee-length. The mail coats were split up to the waist at the front and back, in the middle, to augment riding upon steeds. Their heads were covered in conical iron helms, fashioned with robust, downward-extending nasal guards.

The Trogens drew their steeds, as well as those bearing their charges, to a hovering stop. The Avanorans slowed on their own approach, bringing their Harraks to a halt just a few feet away from the Trogen-led party.

A brief exchange followed, in which the Trogens again displayed the Unfier's seal. Without further delay, the three sky riders sped off hurriedly towards the mountain fastness. The look of comprehension on their faces had been unmistakable, as they had gazed upon the seal and looked over to the four humans being escorted.

The Avanoran warrior positioned in their center took out a horn as they flew. He repeatedly blew a patterned signal upon it, consisting of several short, rapid bursts.

A slight nervousness and chill crept up Janus' spine, as they finally neared the cascade of walls; those above, below, and directly ahead. A great number of archers and crossbowmen were standing attentively on all the levels, as his eyes scanned up and down the terraces.

Their weapons were at the ready, bolts set and arrows notched. They eyed the newcomers diligently, as the Trogens guided the group into a sharper angle of descent. The fortress loomed ever closer, and Janus could increasingly feel the multitude of eyes intently shadowing the path of the incoming party.

He could only take solace in the fact that the Trogens were not slowing down, nor were they exhibiting any undue concern. Janus breathed a sigh of relief, loosing his inner tensions, as they finally passed over the outer wall of the second level without incident.

Once past the wall, the Trogens led them downward in a slower, wide-spiraling pattern. They descended methodically, until finally touching down behind the massive gatehouse of the fortress's second level.

A small assembly was forming up just past the shadow of the great gatehouse, clearly gathering for the arrival of the incoming group. There were several guardsmen at the ready, armed with long, broad-bladed lances, and tall, rectangular shields. Iron helms of a rounded shape and lower profile rested upon their heads, with broad nasal guards that had a descending flare to them that protected the mouths of their wearers.

The ends of extended blue tunics poked out from underneath their thigh-length mail coats. Cloaks of a similar hue to the undertunics were fastened over their shoulders, at the neck. Their leather-covered shields were divided in color directly down the center, with one half solid blue, and the other yellow. The blue and yellow pattern on the shield was repeated on pennons attached to a couple of the lances, tied just below where the socket of the blade was fitted to their long wooden hafts.

A smaller contingent of similarly attired and equipped guards was marching in from the direction of the second level's gatehouse. They escorted two notable figures, both of whom looked to be very prominent men, judging by their outer attire and confident demeanors.

The one to Janus' left looked to be in his early thirties. Tall and broad of shoulder, his narrow, deep-set eyes studied the new arrivals as he approached. His sharp nose and chin encased a small, thin mouth.

Save for a light growth of stubble, he was relatively clean-shaven. His thin, dark hair, flecked with random strands of gray, was trimmed neatly, falling straight down to the top of his shoulder.

He wore a sleeveless surcoat of blue, slit front and back from the waist down, over the top of an extended tunic of a darker blue shade. High boots of soft leather, folded over along their top edge, culminated his attire.

The man's companion exhibited a broader, more amiable-looking face. The appearance would have put Janus more at ease were it not for the hardened, piercing look coming from the man's slightly protruding eyes. He had a decidedly softer appearance than the man on the left, possessing the paunch and puffy face of a man who was anything but underfed.

Akin to the other man, he was also clean-shaven. His brown hair was styled in a bobbed cut, which hung down to lie evenly around his head, just below his ears, and was appended with high-trimmed bangs. Resting atop his head was a round cap of dark felt.

The signs of material luxury were prominently displayed, as he was dressed in a long-sleeved, green tunic of fine linen. The tunic was brocaded with swirling patterns of silver thread dancing along the hem, cuffs, and neck of the garment. Clasped by a silver brooch, a flowing cloak exhibited luxuriant white ermine fur along the hemline, boasting of the richness of the interior lining. The man's thick fingers displayed several rings, a couple pinching tightly on the man's ample flesh.

The Trogens saluted the oncoming ensemble with raised fists, lowering their heads in slight bows as the two well-dressed men approached. The Trogens unfastened their saddle straps, swinging down to the ground just as the two men came to a halt.

One of the Trogen's steeds gave a low growl, shuffling a couple steps backward as it eyed the two distinguished-looking humans. Its sudden agitation prompted its rider to move back, firmly taking hold of the mount's tether.

"You have come far. And you have brought most interesting guests along with you," the tall man to the left commented in an even voice, ignoring the uneasiness of the Harrak.

He had an articulate, cultured tone that matched his physical presence well. But the initial feeling that Janus gleaned from the man held no warmth within it.

"Escort of prisoners. From Five Realms. For the Unifier," the Trogen closest to the two men answered back, speaking in halting Gallean.

Another Trogen stepped forth, extending some rolled parchments, procured from a large hide pouch attached to the saddle of his Harrak. Janus could see that the parchments had wax seals affixed to them.

"From Bohemond. Of the Order of the High Altar," the Trogen with the parchments rumbled in a deep voice.

The man on the left nodded, taking the documents from the Trogen. He regarded the image on the seal briefly, before breaking the wax and straightening out the parchments. Silently skimming over their contents, his brow furrowed, and his mouth tightened.

"It appears we must not tarry here. Baalmon will want to see all of you, right away," the tall man replied calmly, looking up from the parchment. He turned to face the four prisoners. Though his expression was placid, his eyes were unable to mask his increased interest. "I am Jocelin de Lacy, Constable of Avalos. I regret that Sir Richard de Lusignan, our good steward, is currently attending to a gathering of nobles. Alberic Fitzhugh is here, on his behalf."

The second man tilted his head ever so slightly at the introduction, but continued to remain silent.

"You may dismount your steeds. Your travel is finished. You must be very tired of sitting in a saddle," Jocelin proceeded in a polite, almost friendly tone. "You will be provided with a good meal, and chambers to adequately accommodate all your comforts."

Janus and the others remained taciturn, slowly freeing themselves from the buckled straps holding them into their saddles. Wincing, Janus gingerly slid down, setting his feet back upon solid ground.

After the long flight, Janus found himself wracked with deep-seated aches and stiffness throughout his exhausted body. He was more than a little dizzy, keeping still as he concentrated on trying to regain his full equilibrium. Not wanting to seem impolite, he refrained from stretching his taut back, enduring the great discomfort as he awaited further directives from their captors.

Looking towards the others in his group, he saw that Logan carried a dark, pensive scowl upon his face. The look within Logan's eyes harbored sharp defiance. Antonio, standing close to Logan's side with slumped shoulders, appeared otherwise, having an expression of grim resignation.

Erika, as if sensing Janus' glance, turned her head and caught his eye. Her lips spread ever so slightly, into a small grin that was undoubtedly a gesture of reassurance. He held her gaze for just a moment, returning the expression before turning his attention back to Jocelin, Alberic, and the others before them.

Alberic then spoke to the Trogens, his voice articulate and full of authority. "Before returning east, you may avail yourselves of food and suitable quarters here in Avalos. Your steeds will be well attended. Once you have eaten and rested, you will receive your new assignments."

The Trogens rendered a low bow in response to his words. Alberic gestured to one of the guards nearby, who stepped forward from the escorting group of spearmen.

The guard turned, and waved in the direction of a long, rectangular structure set inside the gateway. A high-pitched roof crowned the building, which abutted the terrace's curtain wall lengthwise. The elongated side facing into the bailey featured two entrances at either end. Set at regular intervals down its length was a series of small window openings.

A couple of horses were being led by their tethers out of the left entrance. Emerging from the shadows of the other opening, three young men, wearing linen coifs, brown tunics, and hose spattered copiously with mud and other debris, came dutifully running at the signal from the spearman. The guard gruffly barked a few instructions to the men, who nodded and moved swiftly to attend the Harraks.

Once the Trogens had departed, and all of the sky steeds had been led off towards the stable, Jocelin signaled to the remaining throng of guards. He addressed them in a commanding voice, "Escort us to the Great Hall."

The blue-cloaked guards fanned out, surrounding the four prisoners. Once the prisoners were engulfed within their midst, the group started off in the direction of a large, stone hall structure.

Thick, wooden double doors in the gable end of the hall were swung slowly open by other guards at their approach. Above the lintel of the doorway was a stone arch filled with finely-sculpted floral designs. Higher up was a sizeable, arched window. The doorway and higher window were flanked by a pair of projecting buttresses, the first of a series of narrow buttresses running down the outside of the hall, set in between upper clerestory windows.

SPIRIT OF FIRE

Suspended from chains through the vaulted ceiling, a linear sequence of chandeliers went down the center of the hall. Each was of concentric circles of iron, rising from the largest circumferences at their bases, to the smallest at their tops. The iron circles held beeswax candles placed at evenly spaced intervals. At the moment, the candles were unlit, though their light was not needed, as there was enough natural ambience within the hall interior.

The ceiling itself was coated with a deep blue paint, dotted by a multitude of small, starry shapes, rendered in reflective silver. Plaster coated the stone of the inner walls while recessed fireplaces, dark and dormant, broke up the continuity of the walls' surfacing.

Several great tapestries were hung down the sides of the hall. Janus had no time to study what was depicted on them, as he and his companions were caught up in the flow of the group striding forward.

The guards continued down the center of the hall, heading across the rush-strewn, stone flooring towards a prominent dais rising at the opposite end. Light streaming through the narrow-arched clerestory windows formed alternating pools of light and shadow.

Out of the sunlight, Janus expected it to be much cooler inside the hall. But to his senses, the interior seemed unnaturally cold.

Whether a trick of his mind or not, it seemed as if there were movements occurring just out of the corners of his eyes. Yet whenever he chanced a direct look, there was nothing to see on the unoccupied sides of the hall. The spaces were empty, and the shadows were not so dense that anything could have hidden within them.

Inwardly, he admonished himself to snap out of his growing paranoia, feeling he was allowing his imagination to bestow undue stress. It was far more likely that fatigue from the extended journey, the uncertainty hanging over their situation, and the constant hollowness dwelling within him, since before the day he had stepped into this strange new world, had coalesced into a bitter, disorienting concoction. He knew he had to keep his wits about him, as letting anxieties roam unchecked would not avail him.

Atop the dais, a figure clad in a white, hooded habit of bleached linen sat upon a wide chair, fashioned of oak. The drawn-back hood revealed a man's face, cloaked with exceptionally pale skin. The pallid tone considerably enhanced the piercing nature of his deep-set, bright blue eyes.

57

His head was covered in thin locks of light blond hair, of a hue nearly white on a quick glance. The gaunt nature of his build gave his narrow face and sharp nose an elongated, drawn-out look.

A singular ring rested on the slender third finger of his left hand. A working of silver, the ring held a blood-red stone. Hanging from a leather thong about his neck was a distinctive silver pendant, in the shape of a five-pointed star.

His expression was unchanging as he laid his cold eyes upon the prisoners in the midst of the approaching mass of guards. Holding up his hand, the pale man brought the group to an instant halt.

With a wave of his hand, the guards at the base of the dais swiftly parted company, making way for the four newcomers. After a slight nod from the seated figure, the guards behind the prisoners moved forward, gripping the latter's arms and firmly guiding them to stand at the foot of the dais. The guards then stepped back quietly, as Jocelin de Lacy strode to the forefront of the assemblage.

"My lord, Baalmon," Jocelin addressed the figure upon the high seat, extending a bow. "Four outlanders have arrived, saved from the tumult in the east. They were liberated from the hands of the Midragardans. I have brought them immediately to you, as you requested."

There was a marked difference in Jocelin's manner from the way he had greeted the prisoners. His voice was subdued, carrying a tone undeniably deferential. His eyes remained lowered, staring towards the floor as he spoke. Janus caught a faint scent of fear emanating off the previously very authoritative man.

Neither Janus, nor any of his companions, dared to refute Jocelin's statement, even if was far from the truth of their ordeal. Janus felt deeply unsettled, as the eyes of Baalmon carefully examined the four outlanders.

A chill passed over Janus, and a clammy feeling crept across his skin, as the icy gaze of the figure settled upon him. Baalmon's ashen hue and white clothing only added to the effect, giving him a spectral cast.

Janus was relieved when the unpleasant feelings ebbed, as the azure gaze let loose of its hold on him, and moved onward. Almost immediately, his concerns switched to Erika, as the frigid stare engulfed her. He could see lines of nervous tension rise in her face, confirming the reality of his own strange experience.

"I believe you will want to read these, my lord," Jocelin intoned, holding up the parchments he carried. "They were sent from Bohemond, a brother-knight of the Order of the High Altar, upon whose ship these four were held."

At a nod from Baalmon towards his right, a man clad in a habit and coif of white linen strode into view. He wore a pendant similar in design to that upon Baalmon. Without a word or gesture of acknowledgement, he took the parchments from Jocelin's hand.

He walked slowly up to the top of the dais, and handed the parchments over to Baalmon. Like Jocelin had done, Baalmon read them in concentrating silence for an extended period of time, with signs of growing interest reflected along the lines of his face.

"I see that four very honored guests have arrived in Avalos," Baalmon finally said, looking down upon the quartet of prisoners. Devoid of the barest inflections of emotion, his voice nonetheless resounded with the air of authority in the expansive hall.

His face broke into a thin smile, exposing a set of long, bone-white teeth, not wholly unlike those in a sun-bleached skull. No trace of warmth was present in the expression, and his icy, hard eyes conveyed an even colder disposition.

"I believe the Unifier will be very pleased you have come to Avalos," Baalmon concluded, nodding slowly towards Jocelin, as if communicating an unspoken command. He looked to the prisoners once again. "You may now go to your quarters."

Jocelin, Alberic, and the contingent of lance-bearing guards then led the foreigners out of the great hall. The footsteps of the group echoed within the cavernous space, which was held in the grip of an uneasy silence.

They exited the hall, continuing across the grounds as they marched towards one of the high, square towers in the curtain wall. Drawing to a halt close to its base, they stood within the shadows of one of the great stone arches supporting a crosswalk to the third terrace level.

Jocelin and Alberic turned to face the prisoners with somber countenances. Jocelin announced, in a formal tone, "Alberic and myself will be leaving you, for now. The guards will escort you to your new quarters. You will be well-attended, for all of your needs."

Without another word, he gave them a curt nod, and strode away briskly with Alberic in tow. At a gesture from one of the guards in the lead, the remaining group then ascended a short flight of timber steps leading to an above-ground entrance into the body of the tower.

Once inside, they proceeded up a winding, stone staircase, finally exiting through a doorway onto the roof of the tower.

They crossed over to the bridging span connecting to the third terrace. The tower's battlements continued along with them, protecting each side of the span to the midpoint, where the removable wooden platform was placed. The crenellations resumed again where the wood came to an end.

Trudging across the high pathway, they continued forward to a small postern gate set into the wall crowning the next terrace. After the guard at their lead exchanged some words with a sentry on the other side of the gate, it was opened and the party passed through the large door in single file.

Janus stared intently at the shadowy outline of the guard in front of him, mindful of his steps as he navigated the unlit passage. The passageway let out into a wide expanse of open ground, forming the inner bailey of the terrace. Off to the left were several towers, and a long, rectangular complex of buildings situated along the wall. A spear-shaped finial rested atop the gable end displaying an entrance leading into one part of the ensemble of structures.

The guards led the group over to a set of stone steps climbing the inner side of the curtain wall. They slowly mounted the long flight, immediately turning left when they reached the top of the allure. A short walk ensued as they approached a great tower looming just ahead.

The circular tower rose from a sloping, plinth base, its skyward ascension culminating where two sets of battlements adorned its lofty summit. The first set of battlements was supported on projecting stone corbels ringing the tower, forming machicolations. The tower proceeded one story higher, where it was crowned by square merlons comprising the second set of battlements.

A small set of steps reached from the wall to a narrow doorway providing access to the tower. The doorway opened directly onto a spiral stairway running along the inner wall of the tower.

Opposite the entrance was an open doorway, leading into a large mural chamber. Standing within the portal was a slender man at the onset of his elderly years, with a pensive expression on his face. His gray eyes, thinning, light-hued hair, and high, pronounced cheekbones bestowed him with a tired-looking appearance. Seeing the prisoners, he clasped the long fingers of his bony hands together, at his waist.

SPIRIT OF FIRE

Janus' attention was momentarily distracted, as a rather plump, gray-furred cat suddenly brushed up against his leg. The large cat had a little white stripe running down between its green eyes, the stripe augmented by a conspicuous splotch of brown. The latter made it look as if the cat had gotten its nose smudged while rummaging around in chocolate.

Each of its four legs, ornamented with a pattern of narrow black stripes, culminated in white paws that conveyed the appearance of little socks. The amiable, clearly well-fed cat showed no tentativeness or inhibitions, purring deeply as it turned and rubbed against Janus' leg again, before finally sauntering off.

Janus watched the cat descend the spiral staircase. In the midst of all the anxieties swirling within him, the cat's greeting lightened his mood, and brought a brief smile to his face.

"Welcome to the Eagle's Tower," the older man addressed the group with a formal air, bringing Janus' focus back to the scene directly before him. The man had a gravelly, deep voice, deliberate and patient. "I am Guillame, in authority over the staff attending to honored guests such as yourselves."

As if an unspoken transfer had just taken place, the lead guard of their armed escort stated brusquely, "Guillame will show you to your quarters. Know that sentries will always be posted within this tower, and around it. There is a guardroom above. You are to be provided with escorts wherever you go in the fortress."

The message was not lost on Janus. While he and his companions had just been termed honored guests by Guillame, it was abundantly clear they were considered otherwise by the guards.

The hard-faced guard turned on his heel, departing through the doorway exiting the tower. The light in the stairwell dimmed, as the doorway was shut behind the guard.

"Do come into this chamber, for now," Guillame urged the four newcomers, standing back, and gesturing for them to enter.

Janus and the others filed into the wide room. Thick ribs of vaulting crossed the stone ceiling overhead. The dressed stone blocks of the room's walls were covered by plaster, brightening the overall ambience.

Skillfully embroidered panels of tapestry adorned the walls. A particularly vivid scene of a cluster of mounted warriors, charging forward with lances couched, attracted Janus' eyes for a few moments.

A fireplace had been cut into the wall, and provided with a small pile of firewood stacked in an orderly fashion, just to the right of the gaping, square opening. The fireplace faced the foot of a four-posted bed set against the opposite side of the chamber. The bed's heavy wooden framework supported three mattresses, and the canopy encasing it was currently drawn back.

To the far side of the bed, an armoire had been fashioned into the wall itself, with a tall, rectangular niche provided with a wooden door. Affixed by iron hinges, the door was pierced by a number of small, circular holes.

Three chests sat neatly along the base of the chamber's wall; one a long, narrow trunk, and two of a shorter, broader girth. They were all very solid in appearance, fitted with iron locks and banded with iron strips.

A couple of wooden stools completed the furnishings in the chamber. The floor was blanketed with thin mats of woven rushes, and there was a sweet edge to the scent of the room.

Guillame gestured towards a narrow passageway leading towards what looked to be a second chamber. Lining the outer wall of the tower, the other chamber was much smaller than the one they were standing in.

"Each chamber has its own latrine," Guillame commented. His voice carried a noticeable lilt, hinting at an exclamation of pride in his pronouncement.

Janus had not been in the new world for long, but he did not miss Guillame's meaning. In the culture surrounding him, a private latrine was very likely a great luxury.

"Conveniences. Wonderful," murmured Logan acidly, with obvious sarcasm.

Guillame looked towards Logan with a hint of nervousness, appearing unsure over how to respond to Logan's acerbic remark.

"I confess I have not had much time to prepare for your arrival," Guillame said politely, with a genuinely apologetic tone. "The rooms have been thoroughly cleaned. Fresh straw has been supplied to your latrines."

"Straw for the latrines? You don't say?" Logan quipped even more dramatically, with a look of disdain on his face. "You have spared no expense."

"By evening, we will have a full supply of clothing placed in each of your chambers," Guillame replied quickly, as if seeking to placate Logan.

"Thank you very much, Guillame" Erika interjected in a much friendlier timbre, before Logan had a chance to make another sarcastic remark. She added gently, "I confess we did not have much time to prepare for coming here either."

Janus knew Erika was likely as worried and irritated as the rest of them, but he was grateful she could exude such a warm response to the old servant at that moment. Janus knew that he was feeling distant himself, dwelling within his own thoughts. Logan was brooding and bodering on anger, while Antonio was silently wrestling with his own considerable fears and anxieties while echoes of physical aches played about his expressions.

Of all of them, Erika was the best suited in temperament for being congenial at the present moment, if not at most times.

Guillame gave a polite smile in return, visibly looking relieved at her contrasting response. "You are most kind ...Lady ...I confess, I have not been given your names yet."

"I am Erika," she replied. She then pointed over to the others, introducing them each in turn with a little hint of humor to her words, "The quiet, thoughtful one is Janus, the usually sullen one is Logan, and he is Antonio ... usually a little more extroverted, but not feeling that well after the journey. Our captors, and those that brought us to your city, were less ... accommodating ... than you are."

Logan shot her a dark look, while Antonio mustered a grin. Janus could not complain, as she had described him well enough. He was able to manage a smile and nod to the old man as he was introduced.

"It will be an honor to serve you, good Lady Erika," Guillame said with a slight bow. "And you, my new lords, Janus ... Logan ... and Antonio."

He gave similar bows to each of the others, pronouncing their names slowly and deliberately.

"And we are fortunate to have you helping us," Erika replied amiably.

"Of course, wherever would we get straw for the latrines," Logan said with a snicker. An irritable look was in his eye as he glanced towards Erika, as if daring her to make another comment about him.

Guillame smiled at Erika's comment, though his eyes flicked apprehensively towards Logan and back again. Janus almost felt an urge to intervene and tell Logan to take it easier on the servant, who was certainly not the cause of their troubles. He was definitely not the one that any of them should take their frustrations out upon. Guillame was as much tied to circumstances as they all were.

"This tower has been given over entirely to your stay within the Unifier's palace," Guillame said. "There are four chambers within this tower, one per level, set above each other, and each one furnished. You may each have your own chamber, if you do so wish."

Having a sense of the rather communal nature of living among the populaces of Ave, and the far lesser degree of privacy that its occupants enjoyed, Janus was rather surprised at Guillame's invitation.

"I wish," Logan said quickly, with a sharp edge to his voice that invited no argument or clarification.

Antonio nodded, and then ventured much more gently than Logan, "Some private space would be good … for all of us."

"We have not had much time for ourselves," Erika said. "Is that fine with you, Janus?"

"No disagreements here," he responded. "A private chamber would be fine."

"We will each have our own chamber then, if that does not put too much pressure on you, or those of your staff," Erika told Guillame. "We do not wish to unnecessarily burden you while we are here."

She then smiled brightly, even shooting a sideways glance towards the melancholy form of Logan. Her next remarks carried an underlying rebuke to Logan. "We are, after all, ambassadors of our own world. And we want to leave a good impression with you of our own people."

Logan scowled, not one to miss her meaning, though he remained silent and brooding.

A slightly confused expression came across Guillame's face, as if he was not used to such statements of polite consideration. "No …I am here for the needs of this tower. One to a chamber it will be then. You can decide amongst yourselves who will take each one."

Erika wandered over to the narrow, rectangular window looking out high over the world beyond the tower.

"Now, this is a sight to behold. I'm afraid everyone will want this chamber," she remarked.

"Not everyone," Logan retorted curtly.

Antonio shrugged. "I don't really have any preference."

The distribution of the four chambers was decided upon quickly enough. Logan wanted to be closer to the ground, and therefore chose the lowest of the available chambers. Not surprisingly, his close friend Antonio took the one just above Logan's.

Janus decided for the third, recognizing how Erika loved the view from the fourth chamber. He felt very rewarded by the glowing smile upon Erika's face as he readily conceded the fourth chamber over to her. He sensed that she knew that he had purposely done so out of consideration for her unspoken wish.

"I am sure that you are all quite hungry as well, what with your long and hard-pressed travels," Guillame then stated, the chamber issue having been settled. "I will leave you to yourselves for a short time, so that I can have the kitchen prepare all of you a plentiful and warm meal. I will return for you personally, as soon as it is ready."

"Thank you, that sounds absolutely wonderful. We will see you soon, then," Erika replied with enthusiasm, again responding before Logan could insert any biting comments.

Janus found that he was glad that she had pre-empted Logan, and that she was asserting herself to speak for the group. He much preferred her manner of representation, and he was not feeling like having open confrontations with Logan. It was not that Janus held any undue fear regarding him, it was simply that he had endured quite enough stress for the time being, and did not want to add to it unnecessarily.

Guillame bowed slowly to each of them, before striding out of the chamber. For the first moments in quite some time, the foursome was left alone to themselves.

"Now what?" Antonio said, as a tranquil silence settled over them.

Janus found himself immediately savoring the relative serenity.

"I, for one, am going to see my own chamber for a few minutes," Logan announced curtly.

"Not entirely a bad idea," Janus concurred, though in a much less acrimonious tone.

Antonio simply shrugged, and Erika nodded her assent.

Janus, Logan, and Antonio then departed to their chosen chambers for a few minutes, to begin acclimating to their new environs. Janus did not have far to go down the staircase, pausing before the wooden door to his selected chamber. He idly listened to Logan and Antonio's steps echoing off of the walls as they continued their descent.

The door was not locked, and Janus stepped slowly into the

room. Freshly strewn rushes shuffled under his feet, as he paused to shut the door behind him.

Janus's chamber was arranged almost identically to Erika's, with only a few minor exceptions. On the wall were different tapestries, and there was one less stool provided.

Instead of four posts, the bed that he found within his own solar had been provided with a prominent headboard and footboard, which each extended high up toward the rib-vault ceiling. The linen canopy that it helped to support only covered the top half of the bed, rather than the full encasement provided for Erika's.

The room was largely shrouded in a shadowy darkness. The shutters, set on the inside of the rectangular windows placed within the outer wall, were halfway closed. Only a small amount of daylight pierced the darkness of the chamber's interior. Janus moved over to each window and pulled the shutters fully back, letting both light and fresh air have full access into the chamber.

A soft breeze rustled through Janus' hair as he leaned forward to look outside one of the windows. The sight from his solar was simply breathtaking, taking in a panoramic view of the gleaming harbor and the sprawling city far below.

"Wow, now that is something special," he muttered aloud, as he continued to stare out in amazement at the incredible scene that his chamber's view afforded him.

Inadvertently, he heaved a rather soothing, extended sigh of relief, feeling the welcome caress of the warm sunlight upon his face.

After a few more idle moments spent relishing the expansive view, he turned away from the window. Janus crossed the floor over to the bed, pulling back the linen curtain near the headboard. He turned and flopped into a sitting position on the top mattress. While not uncomfortable, the bed was not nearly as soft as he would have initially guessed.

A little investigation revealed that the mattresses had been arrayed in order of softness, with a straw-filled, canvas one on the bottom, surmounted by two linen-encased ones. The middle one was filled with wool, and the top mattress stuffed with goose feathers. A linen sheet, quilted coverlet, and feather pillow completed the trappings of the bed.

Lying back upon the top mattess, Janus winced slightly as he felt the tightened muscles along his back slowly begin to settle down. Even if he and his companions were effectively captives, he knew that he could at least look forward to a good rest that evening. His nose filled with sweet scents wafting up from within the top mattress, an unexpected but pleasant surprise.

It was almost tempting to just close his eyes and indulge himself in a nap. Yet he knew that to do so would be a mistake, making him groggy and sluggish for the evening. With a light groan of objection, Janus summoned up his willpower, sat back up, and took a deep breath.

A couple of minutes later, he heard some steps in the outer stairwell, coming to a halt at his door. The door to his chamber slowly creaked open.

"On our way back up. You coming?" Antonio said, sticking his head into the doorway.

"Right behind you," Janus stated, hopping down from the bed. He strode across the room and followed Antonio back up the stairs to Erika's fifth story chamber.

Erika had pulled the canopy of her bed farther back. Like Janus, she had sprawled out on her back upon its upper surface. Unlike him, she had not gotten up from it just yet.

"I'm not wanting to get up right now, not at all …I shouldn't have tempted myself to begin with," she said, glancing out of the corner of her eye with a slight chuckle as Janus entered the room. "Are your chambers to your liking?"

"Just like this one," Antonio said from behind Janus, sitting down on one of the stools.

"He's right. Pretty much the same," Janus added, walking over towards one of the outer windows.

"These latrines are going to take getting used to, and I think I know what the straw is for," Antonio said with a grin. He then added, half in humor and half in pride, "Figured it out!"

The door then opened behind them and Logan strolled in, walking over to sit down on the remaining stool.

"Well, here we are. Doing really well, I might add," Logan commented in apparent frustration. "Surrounded by walls, and hemmed in by guards."

"Are you always so upbeat?" Erika remarked sarcastically.

"I like to have a handle on what I am doing, and I like to know a little about what is happening. Terrible ideology, isn't it?" Logan responded with a strong dose of thinly veiled sarcasm.

Erika did not give him an immediate response, though her hard stare locked with his.

"Logan, I can't really speak for everyone here", Janus stated calmly, deciding to interpose and give her a break. "But we can't change the overall situation we are in right now … just like we couldn't change the situation when we found ourselves in Ave in the first place …If we tried to get away, we would not get very far from this tower, much less the palace and city. We are here, and there's not a whole lot we can do about it. We might as well just try and get as much of a handle on things as we can."

"He's got a point, Logan," Erika mumbled wearily, having rolled over onto her stomach. Her words were barely perceptible with her face obstructed by the pillow underneath her face. "Might as well get rested up a little while we are here too."

Logan rose and walked slowly towards the window, shaking his head as he put his hands on his hips. "Rest? What about some answers?"

"That too," Erika said. "But just be glad that everyone in this world seems to have a lot of interest in us. Let's hope that's the way it stays. Things could be a lot worse. Let's be grateful for the positives."

"Positives? Be grateful?" Logan huffed, a look of incredulity splayed out across his face. "Maybe you like living in the dark."

"Well, Logan, maybe we just need to think about what's next for us," Antonio ventured in a cautious tone. "As in the next day or so."

"Yes … what's next? That is a very good question, but it looks like the answer is nothing," Logan retorted acidly, his agitation visibly rising. "In some ways, I would still like to be running around in the forest with the tribal villagers. At least we would have had a fighting chance if the interest in us suddenly waned …we're walled in now. There's no running anywhere, if you haven't figured that out by now."

Janus studied the dark-haired young man. He had not known him for very long, but Logan was clearly an introverted brooder in many senses. A situation like they were now in, held in an effective limbo, was not the ideal sort of existence for one who churned and rolled things over and over again within his mind.

Logan was also the kind of person who would probably snap out of his darker moods the second that they were offered a few longed-for answers. For the sake of having to deal with Logan daily, Janus hoped that time was sooner rather than later. Yet even so, he could not blame

Logan for his great frustration.

Janus gently countered, "There's no point to what if. There is a point to what will.... Think about it, Logan. At the least, that knocks down a lot of things to worry about."

"Oh, come on!" Logan spurted out, overtly exasperated. "Maybe when you all come out of your beauty sleeps you can offer me some better insights."

"You better get some rest, Logan, as it seems you are in need of it for your own attitude," Erika suggested curtly, raising up her head and glaring at him. Her amiable demeanor had departed, replaced by a sharp and iron-hard manner that indicated that her patience had been worn very thin.

"Speak for yourself," Logan snapped back, meeting her hardened look with an equal, unflinching resolve.

"I will speak for myself, and you will listen to what I have to say," Erika shot back.

Logan turned his back completely on Erika in an apparent expression of disdain. "I will listen when I choose, not that you likely have anything to say that will help answer any of this."

Janus could easily see the headstrong individuals escalating their conflict rather quickly into a torrent of shouting. Glancing towards Antonio, Janus saw him catch his eye and shrug his shoulders in a helpless gesture.

Causing a vitriolic commotion right underneath their new captors' roof would be anything other than advantageous to their situation. While Janus could not blame Logan for the frustrations at their general plight, as he shared them in his own way, he knew that the best that they could do was to be cooperative.

They had to lie low while they were under such extensive guard, held firmly within the daunting confines of many levels of high walls.

"Alright, enough ... enough," Janus interjected in a firm, steady voice, which held strong despite his heavy heart. His words were either going to encourage the others to simmer down, or they were going to be fuel heaped onto the burgeoning fire. "Let's keep it cooled off in here, at least among ourselves, I…"

He was then distracted by a welcome set of noises, which interrupted their precarious interaction. Janus took in a slow inhalation of relief, as he heard the sound of muffled footsteps outside of their chamber. They ended with the sound of someone gripping the handle of the doorway. The forthcoming intrusion had come just in time.

The door into the spiral stairwell outside swung open, and Guillame entered with a buoyant mien. He paused and gave them a bow. "My lords and lady, it is time for me to take you to the hall, so that we can get you some food and drink. While you are there, it looks as if we have gathered a good amount of clothing for you, which will be placed in your armoires while you eat."

Guillame then paused again and looked around the room, as if he had just sensed the great tension that had recently built up within the confined space. His eyes assessed the countenances of Janus and the others. The smile he had entered the room with faded.

"Is anything wrong here?" he asked in a lower voice, his eyes flicking nervously among their faces.

"Everyone's just wanting to know what's happening," Janus replied in a conciliatory tone, in the hopes of defusing the tension. He knew that despite the fact the interruption by Guillame had likely headed off an explosive moment, the pressures still lingered. "We've been kept in the dark about a lot of things, and simply want to get a few answers."

"I wish I could tell you … but I am just a mere servant. I am sorry I cannot help in this," Guillame replied apologetically, his answer again sounding entirely genuine.

"Well, what is happening is that we have a chance for some needed food and drink," Erika said, her expression softening, as her voice became more lively again. Janus was glad to see she was defusing things further. "Thank you for seeing to everything for us, Guillame. And thank you for taking care of finding us more clothes. It's not like we know what we're doing around here. We appreciate you, and please do not take offense if you catch us when our nerves are raw. We are very tired, and we've been through quite a lot."

She smiled warmly at him.

Guillame nodded, and paused before responding, again showing awkwardness in the face of openly expressed gratitude. "It is my duty, Lady Erika."

Janus stood up, stretching out his arms and back. A little food and drink sounded as good as an overstuffed bag of gold at the moment. The offer could not have come at more fortuitous time. "Guillame's gone through the trouble to take care of everything for us … then what say you all? Shall we go?"

Even Logan, in the midst of a new bout of silent brooding, gave a nod of consensus. Yet a scowl clung to his face as he accompanied the others out of the room.

MERSHAD

The sun's light remained overhead, but the day's work was finished for most on King Hakon's estate. Only those directly involved with the preparation of food, drink, and settings for the feast in the great hall still labored.

Held in honor of a visiting Midragardian Jarl, the feast promised to be a quite prestigious occasion. Mershad settled quietly onto a bench, with Derek and Kent seated to his right. All were speechless, as they looked about the hall, taking in the sights.

With cushions underneath, the three were placed on the side of the hall where King Hakon was located. The line of narrow banquet tables, trestles abutting each other, from one end of the hall to the other, faced a mirroring arrangement on the opposite side.

Svein took his seat on Mershad's immediate left. The three outlanders found themselves in a place of considerable honor, a few positions down to the right side of the king himself. Mershad noted that the lesser retainers and higher-ranking servants were seated at the farthest ends.

The hall itself was a work of exquisite beauty. The long, central hearth fire was blazing vigorously, augmented by an array of torches and whale oil lamps placed all around hall's interior. The light revealed an abundance of rich, magnificent adornments.

The pillars supporting the steeply-pitched roof, including a prominent quartet at the center of the hall, were covered in finely-detailed carvings. The images depicted intertwining animals, representations of great warriors, and other prominent symbols of Midragard's ancient heritage.

When filing into the hall, Mershad had noticed one image in particular. It was of a stout man, leaning over the side of a boat, dangling a line towards an enormous serpent. He had wanted to study the other carvings, but had not been given the time, as he and his companions were guided to their seats.

The illumination within the hall was enough to bring out the wood paneling lining the sides, behind the backs of the feasting guests. The panels were resplendent with further images of heroes, exotic creatures, and mythical legacies of Midragard.

Running just above the top of the wood paneling were a series of narrow, brightly woven tapestries. Set end to end, they formed an extensive frieze, which carried around the upper perimeter of almost the entire hall.

The tapestries portrayed many scenes, with numerous individuals represented. Seeing many figures repeated down the lengths of the embroidered tapestry, depicted in different acts and settings, Mershad concluded that the strips of cloth either told a tale, or recounted a part of Midragard's history.

The long benches by the trestle tables were draped with colorful, pattern-woven cloth. Most spaces towards the center, like Mershad's, had been provided with cushions.

King Hakon and the place distinguishing a guest of high honor, immediately facing him on the opposite side, were both located in the central area between the four ornate roof posts. Both locations were provided with padded wooden settles, the backs and arms of which were covered in skillfully carved designs. The King's place of seating was further demarcated by the two elaborately carved, shorter wooden pillars flanking his settle.

Adding to the richness of the atmosphere were the guests themselves. Tall, strong-looking men and women of proud bearing filled the hall to capacity. The firelight sparkled off an arsenal of arm rings, earrings, brooches, finger rings, neck rings, pendants, chains, and other jewelry wrought of gold and silver.

Hair on the men was neatly groomed, shining luxuriantly, whether cropped shorter, with a fringe, or loosely flowing to the shoulder or beyond. Still others wore braids, and some had donned decorative, embroidered headbands.

Most of the women could be identified as wives by their outward appearances, with their hair knotted at the back, or pulled up under a scarf. There were a few younger, unmarried women present, whose tresses flowed free, or were partially bound with headbands.

Gunnhild was one of the maidens, entering with Sigrid, and an older man of about Sigrid's age, who Mershad immediately assumed to be her father, Gardas. He had a paunch to his belly, and some lines of age were beginning to streak a kindly-looking, broad face. His full, black beard was combed slightly forward, and he wore an ornamental red headband, with diamond-shaped designs of yellow woven into it.

They paused briefly by a small table, which supported a washing basin, rinsing off their hands before making their way deeper into the hall. Svein rose and met them partway, embracing Gardas, and warmly greeting Sigrid and Gunnhild. Mershad grinned as he saw Gunnhild's pale skin noticeably flush in Svein's presence. Svein guided them to seats on the bench, just to Mershad's left, highly respectable positions even closer towards King Hakon. Gunnhild was placed to Svein's immediate left, with her parents sitting by her other side.

Mershad noticed that nearly all of the women, and a good number of the men, had quite luminous eyes, enhanced by the dancing firelight and the makeup they wore. Their bright eyes shone like precious jewels, vivid in contrast with the darker-shaded makeup around their eyes.

The clothes of the attendees displayed a bountiful cascade of bright colors and dazzling embroidery. An abundance of reds, greens, and blues colored the fabrics of the men's tunics and the two-part garments the women wore over their pleated linen chemises. Embroidered hems, necklines, and cuffs, many woven with threads of fine silver, graced most tunics.

The hard-packed earthen floor was thickly strewn with fresh rushes. After most of the guests were seated along both sides of the hall, a stream of females began crossing back and forth over its smooth surface. They bore platters of food, drinking vessels, bowls, and other containers, ferrying them in and out of the gable end of the hall, far down to Mershad's right.

Filling the hall with mouth-watering scents, both roasted boar and elk were served. The two meats were the result of successful hunts in the forested hills close to the estate. More than a few calls of adulation and raised toasts were given to the king's retainers identified as the hunters.

Spoons, bowls, and plates, primarily of wood, and many artfully decorated, were promptly set out before the guests. Mershad was glad he had not forgotten his own knife, which would be a handy utensil at such a prodigious feast.

The king's huge wolf, Heder, padded about the hall, as did a few of the big dogs kept on the estate. As the king was to the Midragardans, the black wolf was to the dogs, the latter giving respectful deference to their larger cousin. The dogs and wolf seemed to get along well enough, with plenty of tidbits and scraps to be obtained from the numerous guests.

Heder paused for a moment in front of Mershad and his companions. Wagging his bushy tail, Heder gazed at them with splayed ears, until Derek grinned and parted with a few choice slices of meat. Satisfied with the acknowledgement, or perhaps tribute, the wolf strolled onward.

A few of the estate's sizeable cats skulked about the shadows of the hall, obtaining a few rewards for their bellies. Mershad chuckled, as he felt one of the thick-furred, long-legged cats brush against his leg. He lowered his hand beneath the table to give the feline a pinch of roast boar, which was quickly received.

Serving women were constantly refilling wooden tankards and drinking horns with mead, from the ample bounty of a large container in the center of the hall. Most of the guests were given their own individual vessels, but Mershad did not fail to notice Svein sharing his own vessel with Gunnhild, reflecting many other couples at the feast.

Mershad's drinking horn was tipped on the bottom by an ornamental, silver wolf's head. A silver band, with a coiled serpent worked into its surface, circled the wider part of the horn.

Many other vessels of drink were brought in, and distributed among the attendees. A few other types of ale, and a fruity, rather potent beverage called bjorr, flowed freely alongside the mead.

After a little time had passed, recently-baked barley bread and fresh butter were brought to the feasters. Pickled and dried fish, soft cheeses, nuts, porridges, and seasonings such as cumin and horseradish were all included in the magnificent repast. Svein showed Mershad how to grace the dried fish with the butter, introducing him to a very tasty part of the Midragardan diet.

"Don't be shy," Derek remarked with a wink, as he carved himself a thick slice of roast elk from a platter, and moved it onto his own wooden plate.

"Your friend is very wise," Svein added with a smile. "Try everything."

Mershad carved a slice of elk and put it on his plate. Using his knife and fingers, he ate a small piece, feeling the flavors burst in his mouth.

"Just wait until you try the roast boar," Svein said, before turning his attention back to Gunnhild.

Roast boar was probably the one thing Mershad would not try, due to his religious dispositions. But he did not feel like he was sacrificing much, with the abundance of culinary options around him.

Kent leaned back, so Mershad could see him just past Derek. He raised his wooden tankard in a salute towards Mershad. "I think I can get very used to the cuisine around here."

"I can't argue," Mershad replied, with a chuckle.

He sipped sparingly from his horn of ale, and indulged in more of the buttered fish, elk, porridge, and other bounty. Mershad was content to observe the guests around him, looking across to the other side.

The mood in the hall was pleasant to savor. Everyone appeared to be in excellent spirits. Many bawdy jests intermingled with laughter, giddy and sometimes raucous.

Later in the meal, with a radiant smile, King Hakon called for the full attention of all the guests. Even the servants halted, as all heads respectfully turned toward the Midragardan King.

He began his address by reciting a six-line stanza, as he looked toward Jarl Skallagrim.

"Cattle Die
Kindred Die
Every Man is Mortal
But I know One Thing
That never dies
The Glory of the Great Deed"

The king paused, smiling warmly towards the occupant of the other principle seat of honor.

"That old verse is as true today as it was centuries ago, Skallagrim, my good friend and loyal jarl. A well-known verse for deeds proven true at all times. It is well-suited for you, who have done great deeds in past and present, and who will do many more for Midragard in the future. I am very pleased you are sharing our feast. I wish to bestow upon you a few tokens of my high regard, for you and yours."

The commendations began a very intriguing gift-giving portion of the feast. Mershad was astounded at the rich abundance of gifts exchanged between King Hakon and Jarl Skallagrim. Everything from twisted golden arm rings to gleaming new swords were given out, some gifts directly to each other, and many to individuals within the retinues of both men.

An axe, with an ornate, silver-gilt head, filled with a dense weave of patterns, was given by the king to Jarl Skallagrim. In response, an extravagant fur cloak was bestowed upon the king by the jarl, accompanied with great praise for Midragard's regent.

Jarl Skallagrim received a particularly interesting set of harness mounts in gilt bronze. The pieces were formed into the image of a dragon seated upon its haunches, with a forward-curving arch to its neck. The dragon's jaws were open wide, and swirling, artistic renditions of flames poured from within them.

Skallagrim also received an arching harness bow, in copper and silver. The ends of the bow culminated in snarling wolf heads on each side. Patterned designs were worked all along its length, converging in the central summit holding the hole for horse reins.

A spear with an inlaid, herringbone pattern of silver was given to Svein. Mershad could see that King Hakon's retainer was genuinely affected by the gift, as Svein's expressed gratitude and bow to the jarl testified.

One of the men near Jarl Skallagrim was then given a round shield, whose surface was painted with the image of a large, black wolf.

From the various compliments and recognition being given, Mershad gathered much more as to why Jarl Skallagrim was held in such high esteem by the king. Skallagrim and his warriors had been rooting out bands of raiders, preventing them from preying on the coastal settlements in the fjords. Cattle and sheep raids, the loathed strandhogg, had been brought to a complete halt in his region, a feat held in great regard by those gathered at the feast.

The feast was not without its business, though, as a few matters were put forward for discussion, or agreement. King Hakon asked Jarl Skallagrim to accept the son of one of the king's higher level retainers for fostering. The retainer was away, overseeing one of the king's other farm estates. Jarl Skallagrim solemnly accepted the request, promising the king to bring him up rightly, in the ways of Midragard.

A marriage was also arranged, much to everyone's elation. The betrothal was between one of the younger sons of Skallagrim, a bright-eyed warrior named Harthacnut, and a younger daughter of King Hakon, a particularly striking, raven-haired beauty named Gunnvor. It was apparent neither Gunnvor nor Harthacnut were opposed to the arrangement.

The marriage announcement brought heightened levity to the feast, and the mead accelerated its pace down the throats of the spirited guests. As it was looking to be a rather long evening, Mershad had to use the excuse of needing to go to the cesspit outside, to go attend to his evening prayers.

Begging his leave, he walked down the length of the hall and exited. A couple of guards were standing idle outside. They paid Mershad little attention, as he found a place around the side of the hall to conduct his evening ritual.

The walk outside exposed just how warm and smoke-filled the great hall had gotten. The open air felt refreshingly light and crisp upon his face, and clear to his lungs.

Once he had finished his prayers, Mershad decided to avail himself of physical relief at the cesspit. He did not yet know how late the feasting would go, and felt it would probably be uncouth to excuse himself again too soon.

Refreshed, he slowly made his way back to the gable-end entrance of the longhall. A huge, burly retainer, who had just made his own trip to the privy pit, caught up to Mershad, slapping him on the back as they were about to enter the hall again. Though the slap had been delivered in joviality, the sheer force caused Mershad to wince as he lurched forward. Mershad did not want to consider what kind of blow could come from such a man in anger.

The warrior had a rosy, beaming look on his face, a little glisten to his eye, and more than a hint of the sweet mead on his breath. His manner was far from inhibited.

"Hey there lad! You will have to tell me of the Silver Lands some time, while you are here. I have a few coins myself from your lands … though I've never been there myself," the giant exclaimed, amiably.

Mershad smiled, not really sure how to reply. He was becoming ever more curious about the 'Silver Lands' he kept hearing about. Everyone who did not know otherwise seemed to mistake him for being someone from those lands.

The retainer did not seem bothered over Mershad's lack of response. He leaned in towards Mershad, as if he were about to impart some vitally important secret.

He said, in a lowered voice. "You tell me your ways later. You better drink up the mead while you can. It will be the first to go. They've got plenty of ale and bjorr for later, when it won't matter what we are drinking … we won't know the difference!"

He boomed with laughter, giving Mershad another heavy slap on the back with his large, meaty hand.

"Thank you for the advice," Mershad replied, with a polite grin, keeping the new wince he felt inside from appearing on his face.

The warrior started up the back of the raised side, striding behind the length of attendees just ahead of Mershad. He paused for a moment, and turned back to Mershad, with a sheepish grin on his face.

"I forget myself, lad," he said. "I am called Grettir. Just be sure to ask for me when you want to know what's really important around here. I'll be sure to tell you what's best!"

Grettir did not have much farther to walk, taking one of the lower-ranking seats towards the near end of the hall. He grinned and laughed as he took a full drinking horn offered to him by one of the serving women. Holding his head back, he quaffed the entire thing in one extended swill. A modest amount of the horn's contents streamed around his mouth, becoming lost in his copious beard.

Grettir gave an exuberant shout, belched, and laughed again, as he sat down in between two other warriors. The pair clapped him vigorously on his broad back.

Mershad smiled, working his way back down to his own seat, where Derek patiently held his drinking horn. He had still not finished one round, and had opted for weaker ale over the potent mead, figuring it was less of a violation of the tenets of his faith.

There was plenty of entertainment throughout the feast, from musicians playing upon flute and lyre, to various renditions of poems. The music attracted a more casual level of attention during the main portion of the feast, while the men called upon for poems towards the end were given the most serious, focused attention.

The first poems recited were simpler in form, talking of legendary heroes and deeds, speaking of feats against monsters, and challenging incredible odds. Mershad found them rather melancholy, as tragedy intertwined with the fates of all the noble champions within the tales.

Another distinctive kind of poem followed the wondrous tales. The oration absorbed the rapt attention of everyone in the room. There was little mistaking the great reverence and status the final poem and its reciter held in the eyes of the audience.

King Hakon personally introduced his primary skald, or poet, to the feasting guests. Named Thorvald, he was a man of advancing years. He was of medium build, with no remarkable features, save for a booming, articulate voice, and a sharp, hawk-like nose that bequeathed a piercing mien upon him.

After a few moments of silence, when all eyes were upon him, Thorvald had launched into the poem. The lines mentioned individuals Mershad knew, such as King Hakon and Jarl Skallagrim. The poem was much like a short history lesson, speaking of the doings of the king and jarl, and what their deeds had accomplished for Midragard.

It was a much more confusing piece to follow than the earlier ones had been. There were many metaphorical references, some that Mershad understood, and others utterly foreign.

For every mention of something like the 'horses of the high heaven road', which he guessed to be the Fenraren, there was a reference to something stranger. He was particularly interested in a peculiar reference to 'wolves that walk on two legs, in the hour of Midragard's need.'

The enthusiasm and delight in the engrossed audience was overflowing, and Mershad soon noticed they had no trouble with the references that confounded him. He tried to remember as many of those phrases as he could, so that he could ask Svein about them later.

Evening matured into the fullness of night. Chill gusts whipped about the timber posts each time one of the guests exited the hall. The flames in the central floor hearth and others within the building's interior were batted about, as a heavier mood gradually filled the air.

The boisterous banter and jovial camaraderie filling the hall during the feast settled down, until only occasional outbursts of laughter and sporadic exclamations remained.

Only one minor incident occurred when one of the visiting retainers of Jarl Skallagrim, the man who had received the shield with the black wolf earlier, stood and gave a drunken boast. He claimed that Grettir could not hope to keep up with him, in either fighting or drinking. He was a young, stout-built man, who carried his head high.

As the guests witnessed, the young retainer carried his head perhaps a little too high. Grettir had promptly gotten up, trudged across the hall, and thwacked the man in the side of the head with a heavy ham-fist.

Mershad flinched, as the blow was painful to even watch. The young man's reaction had been far too slow to have a chance of blocking it. Seeing how fast Grettir's arm moved, Mershad's respect for the giant's formidable nature rose even higher.

Grettir doused the retainer with the remaining mead in the drinking horn gripped in his other hand. The man slumped down off his bench, and clearly would not be doing much more boasting for the rest of the evening.

Any potential tensions were defused when Jarl Skallagrim broke into uproarious laughter, exclaiming, "Now he has been well acquainted with Grettir, my good king. And he has gained a lesson to heed!"

Grettir added to the levity by striding over, dipping his horn deep into the thoroughly-depleted vessel near the hearth, and raising a vibrant salute to Jarl Skallagrim's honor.

"It will make the lad even better in service to you in the future. I gave him some fight, some drink, and perhaps he will awaken with a little humility!" Grettir declared, in obviously good humor, as he finished the salute. His words brought out another round of laughter, shouts, and table pounding from those still gathered at the tables. Even the Jarl's men seemed highly amused with Grettir's humbling of the brash, young warrior.

Eventually, King Hakon and Jarl Skallagrim retired from the hall, after some final words and a warm embrace. The jarl left through one end of the hall to the outside, while the king departed through a small door at the other end of the hall.

Drinking horns were diligently refilled, and the mead finally ran out. As Grettir had indicated, there were still ample quantities of ale and bjorr.

Mershad watched preparations being made for the rest of the evening. Servants cleared out empty platters and vessels, disassembling some of the trestle tables. Others began to roll out individual bedding along the raised sides of the longhall, converting the space from a feasting chamber to sleeping quarters.

Some men sat cross-legged on the sides, engaging in various

games involving wooden boards and carved figurines, while a few women set to embroidery, close to the warmth of the hearth fires.

Svein finally escorted Gunnhild and her parents out of the hall, disappearing for several minutes before returning. A mischievous smile broke out, as he looked to where Kent was leaning forward on the table board before him, his head face down, between his crossed arms.

"At least he has taken to mead, though he has a long way to go if he wants to keep up with a Midragardan warrior," Svein observed, chuckling.

Mershad looked around at several men remaining in the hall who were still functioning, despite imbibing a flood of the Midragardan elixirs. Kent would have a long way to go in matching up with those men.

"I will accompany you to your quarters, though you may have to help him," Svein said, indicating Kent. "Get him rested, I intend to take the three of you on a little journey tomorrow. You will be introduced to more of Midragard."

"He may be in for a rough morning then," Derek remarked, chuckling.

Mershad did not envy Kent's prospects for the morning, but was glad to hear they would be exploring more of Midragard.

After a little effort, Derek was finally able to partially rouse Kent. Kent's head lolled to the side, and he moaned while Derek heaved him up to a standing position.

Mershad moved in to help Derek support their wavering comrade before he toppled. He and Derek had to keep Kent braced on both sides to prevent him from falling over, on their way back to their quarters. Svein seemed highly amused with Kent's beleaguered condition, laughing and shaking his head more than once.

The night air was rejuvenating to the skin and lungs. Mershad breathed in deeply as they walked away from the end of the hall. A steady breeze wended through the looming buildings, bringing a shiver to Mershad at its first touch.

They made it back to the house without incident, whereupon Svein took his leave of them. Once inside, Derek and Mershad maneuvered Kent to his pallet, lowering him down slowly onto it.

Kent groaned as they pulled covering over him in the darkness. Mershad and Derek did not bother to disrobe him, agreeing it would be more effort than it was worth.

"First Midragardan feast," Derek remarked, as he and Mershad prepared themselves for a good night's rest.

"I definitely hope it is not the last," Mershad responded, pulling his leather shoes off while sitting on the raised earthen shelf his own pallet lay upon.

It was truly a wonderful night, perhaps the best he had experienced in Ave; and the next day already promised new explorations of Midragard.

SAXANY

The Arcamon utilized its arts to a degree far beyond the collective strength of many human Sorcerers. The baleful servant of the Lord of Fire maintained a state of entrancement upon the two massive Uktena, as they were brought back to consciousness.

Dismounted from his winged steed, the Arcamon stood alone with the enormous, elongated shapes. Far to the back of him, a large force of men and Trogens watched with growing fascination, and heightening fear.

For the witnessing throng, it was a cheerless environment. The presence of the Arcamon was enough to foster a nervous energy within every warrior. Just a single, direct look from the shrouded entity was enough to send slivers of terror racing down their marrow.

The Uktena, despite the Arcamon's rigid control over them, were creatures to be greatly feared. Instinctively, the mass of armed warriors moved back many paces at the first signs of the legendary creatures' awakening. They condensed more tightly, seeking to draw support from one another. The agitation normally manifesting between Trogens and humans evaporated almost entirely in the throes of their shared dilemma.

The Arcamon called out in a piercing, grating voice, which resounded with the discordant tones of an angered multitude. The language was undecipherable to the gathered warriors. Even had there been the most learned monks in all the world amongst them, collectively versed in the knowledge of every known speech used throughout Ave, the strange tongue would still have remained unknown. Ancient and forgotten within the mortal realm, the language belonged to another realm of existence.

Alertness crept into the eyes of the Uktena. First one, and then the other, the creatures sluggishly lifted their heads off the ground, swinging them around to gaze upon the Arcamon between them. The peculiar, crystal-like elements on their foreheads shone brightly, like diamonds receiving the sun's tribute.

Though the observing warriors were fully armed, and capably skilled, they knew they would be helpless if the horrific creatures attacked. Swords and spears would be useless against such monstrosities.

The light of day revealed the range of brilliant colors on the pair of creatures. Their glistening scales appeared to shimmer in the sunlight, refracting the light like an exquisitely jeweled array, nearly hypnotic to all who beheld the sight.

The Uktena dwarfed the Arcamon, but made no threatening moves towards the dark, hooded being. To all eyes, the Uktena appeared to be under a deep charm, continuing to stare placidly without regard for the surrounding multitude.

Again, the Arcamon spoke loudly in the ancient, otherworldly language. The massive Uktena heads lowered, as they turned their attentions upon a dead body laid out a few paces before the Arcamon. It was a large, muscular humanoid with a gray hide. The creature had a concave face, with a stout, outward-jutting chin.

It was an Unguhur corpse, culled from the blood drenched site of battle where the cave-dwellers had struck such an unexpected blow upon the Avanorans. Slowly, the Uktena brought their heads closer, converging in the space just above the still body.

The corpse provided the one piece of information that the Uktena needed for bringing the devastation that the Arcamon intended to unfurl within the lower caverns. Their forked tongues flicked out, deriving the essence of the Unguhur scent from the air around the corpse. Gradually, the distinct sensations taken from the roof of their mouths was fixedly ingrained within their minds. Finished with their serpentine assessment, the Uktena lifted their heads from the Unguhur corpse.

The Arcamon issued some final words in the ancient tongue to the Uktena. The words, augmented by the Arcamon's powers, conveyed a pure communication to the Uktena's minds, without need for translation. They compelled absolute obedience to the Arcamon's desires, binding the massive creatures to the infernal being's will.

Swerving away from the Arcamon, the beasts angled their great heads towards the lake waters. Flat upon the ground, the skin of their bellies grazed a furrow in the loam as they propelled their extended bulk forward, slithering towards the water's edge.

The two giant creatures moved out from the shoreline, heading towards deeper waters. Their heads disappeared below the surface as they began their descent, pulling the rest of their bodies after until no further sign remained, other than the ripples and rolling undulations of the water's surface.

The Arcamon strode back to where his nightmarish steed awaited. Seizing the reins and swiftly mounting it, the Arcamon prompted the creature to return to the sky. Black leathery wings flapped powerfully, wafting a nauseating, sulphurous stench over the nearest of the warriors.

The Arcamon took up a circling pattern over the lake's edge, gliding periodically over the mass of men, Trogens, and Gigans below. Even a few Atagar were now sprinkled amid the ranks, having returned from final scouting missions on behalf of the Arcamon.

After a few cycles, the Arcamon brought its steed lower, wings spread and holding steady as the air currents buoyed it. When the steed was drifting just above tree level, the Arcamon removed the great ebon sword sheathed at his side. There was no glint to its umber surface. Rather, the blade gave the impression that it absorbed light into its impenetrably black surface.

As the Arcamon held the black sword aloft, a strange series of markings, like glyphs, rose in a line running down the center of the blade. Each marking looked to be rendered with miniature rivulets of molten lava, coursing vibrantly along the contours of the distinctive shapes.

More than a few of the men standing below found themselves mopping sweating brows, in the ensuing wave of heat filling the surrounding air following the withdrawal of the blade. Trogens' mouths began to gape, revealing their elongated canines as they reacted to the thick, choking air with gasping breaths. The brawny chests of the Gigans began heaving noticeably, as the massive creatures also found the act of breathing a laborious effort.

All eyes were raised, staring towards the shadowy form gliding over them, a malefic corruption of the daytime sky. The runic inscriptions on the blade flared brightly, before settling into a steady glow. The thickness in the air dissipated, and the breathing of all the warriors returned to normal, fresh, crisp air flooding back into their lungs.

"Onward! Destroy those who would seek to destroy us. Give no quarter! Carry the victory on behalf of He who brings order to this broken world!" the Arcamon shrieked in the Gallean tongue, addressing the humans first. Without hesitation, the shrouded rider repeated the exhortation in the languages of the Trogens, Atagar, and Gigans.

All who beheld the display were greatly amazed at the ease with which the Arcamon could shift fluently between such vastly different languages. The Arcamon spoke their tongues with perfect articulation and inflection, as if a native speaker.

Each and every being felt a numbing dread pierce them at the mention of the Arcamon's own Master, and many were not certain that the rider was referring to the Unifier. Nevertheless, the terror-ridden feeling passed quickly, and all were relieved they were moving back into physical action.

A loud roar ignited amongst the warriors, a few moments after the exhortations. The cries continued to erupt with vigor from the ranks, as they channeled their frayed nerves and fears, girding themselves for impending battle.

The air was soon filled with the clinking of metal as the warriors picked up weapons and shields, and adjusted armor. The cacophany sounded sweet and harmonious to the ears of the Arcamon.

Like a tidal wave rushing towards a fragile, coastal village, the hordes of Avanoran warriors and their inhuman allies surged into motion. Striding swiftly, they flowed into the treeline.

Some warriors fanned outward, while the small band of Atagar scouts, a few guiding bounding Licanthers, ranged farther ahead of the vanguard. Maneuvering deftly amid the trees, they sought out any possible ambushes. While they were capable enough for such a task, the Atagar were not the only eyes looking out for the onrushing masses.

The Arcamon swept through the sky upon the hell-spawned steed, tracking the force's progress underneath the forest canopy. The shrouded entity waved the death-black sword overhead, loosing otherworldly cries and spurring the force onward with diabolic fervor.

It seemed the winds themselves carried foreboding sensations along their currents, sweeping unceasingly through the timber structures on King Hakon's homestead. The area was alive with activity, and the touch of the flowing air reached everyone going about the grounds.

Many of the bond-servants, retainers, serving women, and others outside ducked their heads, or pulled their cloaks tighter, with each sustained, robust blast of the chilly Midragardan air. Only the herds of livestock, having regained their strength following an arduous winter in Midgard, seemed not to care about the icy bite of the wind.

Mershad, Kent, and Derek stood idly, just outside the entrance to their dwelling. Kent groaned from time to time, suffering ill-effects from the bout of drinking at the previous evening's feast. He was alert, but complained of a throbbing headache.

Mershad leaned against one of the main posts of the house, immersed within his inner thoughts. As the hours passed, worries were growing regarding the unknown fates of their fellow exiles. Stranded in a strange land, within a strange world, Mershad found himself consumed with thoughts about the others they had left behind. He even felt a pang of guilt for having enjoyed the feast so much, though another part of him knew the evening's distractions were sorely needed.

An onslaught of anxiety plagued Mershad, as he knew well enough they could do nothing to either hurt or help the greater situation. There was little to do other than wait, a reality giving further life to the uncertainties swirling around them.

"Good new day, to you all!" Svein greeted exuberantly, his long blond hair billowing about in one of the sudden gusts of wind. His hair drifted back down in fairly good order giving off a bright, golden sheen. He gripped an ivory comb in his right hand. "I do not know why I bother to tend my hair so often … and most of all, on days such as this!"

He looked around at the glum countenances gathered before him, and a frown quickly replaced his smile. His next words were more subdued, tinged with empathy. "I do not have to look into your minds to know what burdens you. You think of those left behind."

"Has there been anything said? Anything at all?" Kent asked, with an undercurrent of impatience.

"No, it is still far too soon," Svein replied, shaking his head. "What ships are close will try to do what they can for the Great Sachems of the Grand Council of the Five Realms. Maybe they will help them seek out a position where a stronger defense can be made, and bring them some warriors to help in the fight."

"What if the force against the tribes is too great?" Derek asked. "Will they all become trapped with their backs to the sea?"

Svein paused, before tendering an answer. "I do not know. The people of the Five Realms are tough, proud people, and are very wise in their ways. We must hope that they will find a way."

"And we have no choice but to go on like we are," Derek said with a look of resignation, folding his hands together and squeezing them tightly before him.

Svein nodded slowly, his look sympathetic. "I am afraid so. Hopefully we will not have to wait much longer before we know more of what has happened in the north. Maybe your comrades will be brought back here, as you were."

"And what of these lands?" Mershad asked. "How vulnerable are they if the invaders cross the seas?"

"The one who holds the power of the sea holds the power of this land. King Hakon will not allow the sea to go unchallenged if the enemy dares to draw near to our shores. Have no doubt, Midragard will rise like never before if would-be invaders dare to come," Svein answered firmly, a hard look in his eyes.

"And the land?" Derek asked. "Will they be prepared?"

"Would you like to see for yourselves? It would be a longer foray than what I first planned for you today. We may come back tomorrow, or the next day. Who knows?" he said, a full-hearted, easy laugh suddenly emerging through somberness. "It would do me some good to take an extended morning ride, and it may help you rest more easily to witness the strength in these lands. So what say you?"

"I did not have any other plans for today," Derek responded.

"Me either," Kent said, as Mershad added his assent with a nod.

Svein turned and called to a couple of thralls struggling nearby with a simple barrow, made of boards lashed together and attached to long wooden poles. It was laden down with large clumps of what looked to be either sod or manure.

The men were quick to set the barrow down. They did not seem entirely ungrateful for the interruption, as they hurried over to Svein and the others.

A few more bond-servants and one retainer were summoned by Svein. All were sent down to the byre where the Fenraren were sheltered. The group returned a short time later, with four winged steeds, saddled and harnessed for flight.

Mershad and his companions mounted up. He was extra careful to tighten the leather straps holding him into the saddle. His breaths came shorter and quicker in anticipation of the flight, as nervousness spread through him. He willed himself to loosen his iron grip on the reins, awaiting Svein's coming signal.

When they were ready, Svein led them up into the heights of the sky. A rush of air coursed over Mershad as they ascended on the power of the Fenraren's wings. He kept his eyes set forward, fixed on Svein and the deep blue of the sky above, not wanting to spare even a glance towards the ground dropping away beneath.

When they reached an altitude where the air was markedly thinner to the lungs, Svein leveled out his steed, with the others following suit. Heading across Midragard, they passed over innumerable leagues of fjords, of varying lengths and breadths, with attendant crags, mountains, and cliffs. From the sky, it looked like a great maze cut through the rock and earth of the lands far below, a gleaming labyrinth working its way towards the ocean.

The Fenraren settled into a steady rhythm, their wings undulating in a uniform cadence that carried them at a modest speed. Occasionally, Svein guided the steeds into an extended glide, taking advantage of a strong air current.

Eventually, the fjords gave way to the waters of the open sea, as they reached the northern boundary of Midragard. The seas were highly choppy, with teeming white caps from the waves running along the surface.

Svein led them along the snaking contour of the northern boundary, straddling the coastline. Presently, they passed over land once again. The ground was far different than the craggy, fjord-laced lands they had come from.

The terrain below was level ground, and the presence of broad fields and rampart-enclosed villages soon manifested. The temperature was noticeably warmer, though the winds had picked up a little in strength.

SPIRIT OF FIRE

Following a downward gesture from Svein, Mershad looked to see a fascinating sight along the edge of the coast. The place was nestled at the tip of a short, curving finger from the ocean. Well-sheltered from the ravages of the seas, it offered easy access to ships.

Many vessels could be seen, including a fair number of warships. Most of the latter had been pulled out of the water, to rest along the shoreline. They were a short distance from where a huge, circular rampart, crowned with wooden palisades, surrounded what looked to be a host of great timber halls.

The rampart itself was faced with vertical, wooden planks, the circumference pierced by four main entrances passing through the high earthen embankment to the compound within. Square towers surmounted the gate openings, allowing access to the wall-walk at the top of the ramparts. A water-filled ditch surrounded the entire compound, with wooden bridges spanning to each of the four gates.

There was a definite order to the layout of the halls within. The interior grounds were organized into carefully arranged quadrants, marked by the two intersecting paths connecting the four gateways to each other.

Each quadrant contained four ordered groups of halls. Each group consisted of four halls, arranged into squares, for a total of sixteen in each quadrant.

Other smaller square and rectangular structures could be seen within the enclosure, most rising amid the hall-quartets. A couple of square, hut-like structures were placed just inside the gateways.

More halls, of a smaller size than those in the quadrants, were located outside the main rampart and ditch, arrayed in a curving row following the outer contour of the fortress. Another raised segment of earthen wall, also topped with a timber palisade, guarded the landward side of the outer line of halls.

Drawing closer to the fortress, Mershad observed that the halls were like upturned boats in their appearance. The halls' ends were straight, while their longer sides, and wood-shingled roofs, had a discernibly curving profile. Inward-leaning exterior posts were erected at measured intervals down the long sides of the halls. The gable walls had been fashioned with a vertical timber, stave-built construction. Crossing, wood-carved extensions were fixed atop the apex of each hall's gable ends.

Signs of life and activity were everywhere. Smoke was rising slowly in many places, forming several ascending columns, wafting slowly from central openings in rooftop ridges.

A host of people could be seen all throughout the large complex. A great many were clustered within the open spaces, drilling in martial activities ranging from sword combat, to spear throwing, to archery. Others could be seen along the wall-walks, the towers over the gates, or milling alone, in pairs, or small groups about the halls and other buildings.

Many ceased in their activities as Svein carefully guided the group of sky riders towards one of the open expanses. The Fenraren landed in the midst of one of the quartets of halls, in the fortress' southeastern quadrant.

All of the warriors within the open ground looked upon the new arrivals with great curiosity. Mershad could feel their collective stares, as if pressure was being applied all over his body. The scrutiny made him feel uneasy, even if he knew there was no imminent danger from the formidable-looking figures gathered around.

A large, blond-haired warrior, whose ample beard had been gathered into a single long braid hanging down to the middle of his broad chest, beamed a huge, welcoming smile as his eyes settled upon Svein. He had been standing in front of a throng of warriors when they had landed, and there was little question that he was a figure of authority.

"Hail, Svein! Maybe I can finally get some useful sword training now, since none of these louts will yet suffice," he exclaimed, roaring with laughter. He strode rapidly up to Svein, embracing him heartily.

The warrior was dressed in a blue tunic, the hem decorated with a bright brocade displaying an array of interweaving serpents, each woven skillfully with silver thread. A similar design graced the blue headband holding his shaggy blond locks in place.

"How fares the Fire Serpent, Ingvar?" Svein asked, when they had disengaged from the embrace.

"Resting on the shore. Fitting her with a new sail and mast, while I try to turn these baby seals into grown sharks," Ingvar replied, gesturing towards the younger warriors milling about, eyeing the newcomers as they talked low amongst themselves.

To Mershad's eyes, they seemed far more shark than seal, many tall and strong of build, and all with hardened visages. The warriors were armed with an assortment of axes, swords, and lances, and each had one of the large, circular wooden shields typical of Midragardan warriors.

Those with swords were standing in the forefront of the group. A few reflected evidence of recent exertion in their sweat-stained tunics, and matted, stringy locks of hair.

Svein proceeded to introduce Mershad and his two companions, informing Ingvar of the nature of their visit. Ingvar greeted each of the guests amiably, assuring them of the full hospitality of the fortress, before finally begging leave of Svein.

Ingvar returned to the waiting group of warriors. Svein made no move to depart, quietly watching Ingvar as he faced the sword-bearing men.

Ingvar picked up a shield from where it had been lying on the ground, and slid a longsword out of the scabbard at his waist. He then selected two fresh-looking young warriors, both a full head taller than Ingvar, and even greater in girth.

Within moments, it was readily apparent that Ingvar would press the young warriors to their limits. One after the other, the two men exhibited difficulty absorbing the heavy blows Ingvar levied upon them. The two warriors strained to deflect his strikes, while Ingvar easily repelled their own attacks.

It was not very long before the two looked much the worse for wear, while Ingvar had simply broken a light sweat. He finally called an end to the demonstration, looking back with a grin towards Svein.

"Still a ways to go with these lads, as you see," Ingvar remarked with a chuckle, before turning back to select two new combatants.

To the right of where Mershad was standing, a large activity, involving a sizeable throng, was about to take place. A long line of warriors was standing upright, shoulder to shoulder. Another similarly dense line knelt just before them.

All carried circular wooden shields, the facings exhibiting swirling or sectional patterns. The entire group faced a burly, older warrior, standing with two archers close by his side. Mershad noticed the arrows in the archers' hands did not end in metal points, the heads having been removed to leave the stump of the shaft.

"What are they doing?" Mershad asked Svein in a low voice.

"Training for the shield wall, a most important element in a warrior's training," Svein replied. "You have come in time, as they are just about to begin."

"A shield wall?" Kent asked.

"All warriors in Midragard of any use must know the shield wall. Want to try it out?" Svein asked them with a hint of merriment.

The trace of mischief tainting Svein's words caused Mershad to decline on his own accord, though Derek and Kent readily accepted the invitation.

"Let these guests of mine try the shield wall! They are new to our ways of war, and would learn faster by doing, rather than watching," Svein suddenly called out to the hardy-looking, veteran warrior.

The warrior looked over at Svein's words, without change to his expression. After a moment, during which his flinty glance flicked from Derek to Kent, he gave a curt nod back.

He then called over a young warrior, exchanging a few words with him. The man ran off, and retrieved two more of the large, circular wooden shields.

The warrior came over, handing one of the shields to Derek, and the other to Kent. Mershad's companions were then guided over to a place in the shield wall, where two warriors were temporarily dismissed to make room for the newcomers.

The veteran warrior took a few moments to show Kent and Derek how to position themselves in the shield wall. He also gave them some brief instructions regarding the proper holding of the shields.

The old warrior paid little attention to the fact that Kent was struggling to find a comfortable arm placement for bearing the heavy wooden shield, faced with alternating red and yellow swirls. Derek showed no such difficulty with his own, looking as if he was used to bearing such a device. He took his place next to Kent in the lower rank, which protected the knees of the standing rank, even as the latter protected the heads of the lower rank.

The two rows of warriors, standing and kneeling with overlapping shields, faced the veteran warrior quietly. The grizzled, burly warrior took several steps back, pausing for a few moments as he stared at the shield wall. His stern visage betrayed nothing of his conclusions.

The two archers were then ordered to come forth. After a brief gesture from the veteran warrior, the archers readied their headless arrows, notching them into their bowstrings and starting to draw them back.

The veteran warrior then looked over towards Svein, as if seeking some sort of final confirmation. Svein shook his head in the negative.

Raising his hand, the older warrior stayed the archers, who lowered their bows.

"Do not worry. Your friends are not ready for too painful of a lesson," Svein said in a low voice to Mershad, indicating the archers. "Those who do not take care to keep the shield wall tight, quickly learn the lessons that pain brings. Better that than death on the field of battle … for the man with the shield, or the warrior his shield should also be protecting."

The old warrior looked once again to Svein, who this time gave a slight nod. Svein remained silent, watching the proceedings with a focused expression.

The veteran warrior abruptly broke into a run towards the shield wall. The stocky warrior built up speed, and then launched himself upward, kicking out powerfully with his heel into the midst of Kent's shield. Mershad winced as Kent was bowled over in the thunderous force of the impact.

Kent slammed into the ground, losing his shield in the process. His sprawling form knocked the men behind him aside, creating a gap in the wall.

The seasoned, older warrior was evidently not impressed. He lowered the long broad axe he carried at his side until the edge of it lightly graced the surface of Kent's tunic, at the middle of his chest.

Though Mershad could not hear what the old warrior said to Kent, the look of disgust on the warrior's face, and the ensuing, dismayed look on Kent's face, told him all he needed to know.

"He has some work to do," Svein commented in a low voice, with a subtle wink to Mershad.

Mershad grinned at the understatement, unable to suppress his amusement at the remark. "I suppose I will need to try my hand at this too. Maybe another time … in a few years."

"Maybe you will learn the bow," Svein replied. "My people have always embraced the sword and the axe. Yet the bowman from ship, land, or sky is no less deadly. You look as if you have the blood of the Sunlands in you. If so, know that they are known for their skill with the bow, some even said to use a bow on a moving horse."

In front of them, Derek was setting himself with the shield again, as all of the others, including a sheepish-looking Kent, got back into position. This time, the chastened Kent was spared, as the older warrior tried to dislodge Derek with his next attempt. Overall, Derek held his place as the warrior's foot connected with his shield, stoutly repelling the old warrior backwards. He wobbled and tilted slightly in the aftermath of the robust blow, having to steady himself with his right arm.

Derek was given a much different evaluation as the veteran walked over, grinned, and slapped his hand on Derek's shoulder in unmistakable approval. The veteran then paused, a perplexed look on his face as he took note of the irritated countenance on Derek's face.

"You held strong for your first time in the shield wall. For one from the Sunlands, or even of Midragard," the warrior stated in obvious praise.

Derek glanced up, with his mouth set in a hard line. He responded firmly, "Not good enough, for my liking. To hold the shield wall, I must not move at all. My fellow warriors depend on me to be like a rock. Test me again."

The puzzlement faded quickly from the grizzly veteran's face, as a smile surged to replace it. Mershad could read both amazement and respect in the older warrior's gaze, as he stared at Derek.

The warrior then replied, in a voice loud enough for all to hear. "That is the kind of mind and right attitude that wins wars."

Derek was obliged in his request. He reset himself in the line, and the veteran warrior retreated before hurling himself against Derek's shield again. The warrior connected with an even stronger impact than before, having built up greater speed and delivering a heavier kick.

Derek's adjustments were such that he gave very little in response to the harder collision. The improved results prompted a vigorous commendation from the veteran warrior as he got up from the ground. Mershad could sense from the warrior's demeanor that he had not held anything back in the last attempt, and, unable to dislodge Derek, was genuinely impressed.

Derek and Kent remained in the formation as the testing of the shield wall was repeated several times. Most of the men along the line were able to maintain a firm standing. Those that did not elicited sharp scowls and remonstrations from the old warrior. He loudly upbraided the men wherever there were any flaws in their stances, or ability to hold up their part of the shield wall.

Kent was at the receiving end of a few more of those verbal barrages. Yet he almost succeeded in holding his position once, before buckling and crumpling to the ground. The close brush with success merely prompted mocking congratulations from the old warrior, shaking his head and rolling his eyes as Kent slowly got to his feet again.

"You look to be strong enough, so use it!" the old warrior growled. "You are not incapable!"

As they were undergoing the exercise, Mershad turned towards Svein. He was clearly enjoying the spectacle, his eyes glittering with considerable amusement.

"I suppose Kent won't be placed in the front of a shield wall anytime soon," Mershad remarked.

Svein laughed even harder. "Right now, I'd fear even more giving him a throwing spear or bow behind the shield wall. He would be much more of a danger to our wall than the enemy coming at it. He would probably be a danger to the dragons themselves, if they chose to come down and fight on our side."

"Dragons?" Mershad asked quickly, looking towards Svein with a piqued curiosity.

"Why yes, has no one told you of the dragons living to the south of our lands?" Svein replied, with an air of surprise.

"No, not yet," Mershad replied, a little incredulous at the statement.

He had seen the images of dragons everywhere he looked in Midragard. Among the people, there were an outright abundance of dragon depictions.

Mershad had espied their representations on everything from the carvings on the prows of longships, to the shining weather vanes at the top of their masts. Even a few of the designs on the crossing extensions atop the gable ends of the halls' rooftops were fashioned into pairs of dragon heads. There were dragon figures worked into the stout supporting posts in halls, the crests of women's whalebone boards, cloak brooches, memorial stones, and many other crafted items possessed by the Midragardians. Mershad had assumed it was all just fantastical symbolism, not unlike images used in his own world, but Svein was entirely serious.

"Then that is something all of you need to learn about," Svein stated. "It is one of the things our people can take great pride in, as the dragons found refuge in our lands."

"I have not seen any yet," Mershad said, becoming more fascinated by the moment.

"They live to the far south, in the Drakkar mountains that run across the lower edge of our lands," Svein said. "They are not the raging beasts others have made them to be. Fierce, yes. And to be respected. They can most certainly be dangerous, and not all of them are possessed of good nature. But I do not worry much over the Unifier's forces passing easily through their mountains."

"What are the dragons like?" he inquired. "We do not have living dragons in my world."

Svein smiled warmly before he replied, giving indication to deeper sentiments he held concerning the creatures. "Beautiful. Mystical. Grace. Strength. Intelligence. It is hard to describe everything about them. And it is a great honor to just speak with them."

"You've spoken to dragons?" Mershad responded in heightened amazement.

"Yes, you have to do that from time to time, as one of King Hakon's senior retainers. If only to make sure the herds of our people are not consumed when they are driven up to the mountain pastures in the middle of summer," Svein replied, chuckling lightly. "Dragons do have large appetites. It is good that the waters teem with fish, and the mountains are abundant in large game."

"You speak a dragon language, then?" Mershad queried.

"That, I cannot do. But they speak enough words in our own tongue. Some speak very well," Svein stated.

"Can we see one, sometime?" Mershad asked, his voice tingling with kindled hope.

"Why not? I have been bidden to show you these lands. But let our Fenraren rest this night. You would be hard task masters to the poor creatures," Svein chided him amiably, with a smile on his face. "There are several dragons that do not live far from the edge of this province, near to a village in the shadow of the Drakkar Mountains. I have been there more than once. A few ambitious dragons have taken to culling from our livestock herds from time to time. Yet that is a small price to pay for having friends ward our entire southern boundary."

"Friends?" Mershad asked, in disbelief.

"Yes, friends. And the majority are good ones. It will be beneficial if you and your companions meet them," Svein said, slapping his hand down upon Mershad's shoulder. "I shall tell Derek and Kent of our new plans for the morrow."

Mershad grinned, already feeling impatient for the sojourn. "In the world I am from, dragons are just myths. I find it hard to believe what you say. Maybe you should tell them what we are truly off to see, only as we are about to leave. I would like to see the looks on their faces."

"I can do that too," Svein said, with a deep, hearty laugh.

Their attention returned back to the shield wall, watching as the old veteran tested a standing warrior on the far right end. Fortunately, for the warrior's pride, he held strongly in place, and received deserved praise. It was hard for Mershad to concentrate on the activity, as his mind was churning with the prospect of meeting dragons.

ORANIM

The terraces of the Unguhur's stony, underground city ascended from where they began beyond the lakeshore at the far side of the vast cavern. A subdued atomsphere continued to reign over Oranim, as it had ever since the humans had departed.

The main entrances into the subterranean realm were being watched and warded carefully. Most family groups were gathered together within their dwellings, consuming their evening meals.

Knowing that all main approaches to Oranim were well-tended, the families did not fear immediate threats. If an attack occurred, all the Unguhur were confident there would be ample advance warning.

They had not accounted for the possibility of an attack coming from beneath the lake.

Several rafts were floating out on the lake surface when the terror commenced. An Unguhur male, who happened to be looking into the dark lake waters, was the first to witness the approach of the Uktena.

He lifted his long, two-pronged fishing spear above him, as he espied something moving deep within the water. At first, he believed it to be one of the larger breeds of fish populating the underground lake and adjacent streams.

Something sparkled amidst the shadowy, dynamic mass, looking like a small jewel at first. The Unguhur male had been to the surface world a few times during the course of his life, walking at night underneath starry skies. The unusual sight deep in the water was not entirely different

in appearance from those enrapturing, sparkling lights of the surface world, set into the black firmament of the night sky.

He began to wonder what the strange phenomena exactly were, peering intently towards the expanding light, growing larger with great celerity. He knew it belonged to no fish he had ever encountered, or even heard tales of. Mesmerized by the glittering sight, the Unguhur was unable to plunge his spear down at it.

The Unguhur did not have enough time to cry out when the enormous body of the Uktena broke the water's surface. Torrents of water burst violently upward, like the onset of a geyser, spraying far and wide in every direction. The raft pitched high out of the water, flipping over and casting the hapless Unguhur into the air.

In a controlled, precise movement, the vast jaws of the Uktena widened, and clamped down onto the unfortunate Unguhur. The rows of backward-curving teeth on its upper and lower jaws held the Unguhur in place, as the leviathan rapidly swallowed its prey whole.

The other Uktena emerged in a similarly explosive, lethal fashion, upending another raft and consuming its occupant. The pair of monstrosities swiftly proceeded to attack several other Unguhur caught out in the open upon their rafts.

The mammoth forms of the serpentine Uktena looked both garish and surreal in the bluish light emanating from the sprawling fungus growths in the cavern. They erupted out of the dark waters again and again, levying their deadly assaults. Their actions were etched all too clearly by the dim, dispassionate luminescence. The brutal visions were horrific to behold for the nearest witnesses, who were doomed to become victims themselves.

The Unguhur surviving the first torrent raised a panicked outcry, calling desperate, forceful warnings at the top of their lungs towards the shore, as they hurried to get their rafts moving. Slithering with dizzying speed along the surface, the Uktena swiftly chased down the fleeing rafts.

The commotion on the lake evoked urgent alarms along the shoreline, as many from the Unguhur warrior class raced down to the water's edge. All looked out in horror upon the scene of catastrophe out on the lake, unable to lend any kind of help to their imperiled brethren.

Once their quarry on the lake had been eliminated, the Uktena whipped towards the shore, and its beckoning, terraced structures. The pair of Uktena shot forward, cleaving through the lake surface as they streaked towards Oranim. The crested portions of their upper heads were lifted high from the water, as the monstrous creatures hungrily eyed a bountiful harvest.

The mass of Unguhur warriors forming at the shore gripped their spears tightly, watching the Uktena slice through the water on their relentless approach. The bright spots in the middle of the great serpents' foreheads were like harbingers of death, marking the onrush of the waterborne juggernauts.

Narrowing their approach towards one section of the shoreline, where most of the Unguhur warriors had mustered together, the Uktena reached the boundary of the lake. Breaking free of the water, their momentum carried them far past the shore's edge. Their bulk smashed into the gathered Unguhur, with the full, battering force of their massive bodies.

For their part, the Unguhur warriors bravely tried to resist the huge Uktena, quickly discovering that their spears had little effect upon the thick, colorful scales of the extensive beasts. The Uktena lashed their heads about, snapping at a few Unguhur, consuming others, and crushing many under their enormous girth.

The tips of the legendary serpents' fangs dripped with venom as the carnage mounted. The dead and broken bodies of Unguhur warriors rapidly piled up, their corpses strewn about in a chaotic jumble along the rocky shore.

The bitter struggle was not pursued without an ultimate purpose, even if the warriors involved had not consciously intended the purpose. Awareness of the mortal danger was spread all throughout the terraced buildings by the time the warriors on the shore were deeply engaged in combat with the hulking nightmares. Where the stone edifices had shown little activity only heartbeats before, they were soon teeming with the forms of Unguhur.

A chorus of frightened screams and cries broke out amongst the structures. Unguhur on the terraces espied one of the Uktena suddenly break free from the dwindling fighting along the shore, and slither menacingly towards the rising terraces. A blood-chilling hissing emitted from the baleful creature, as its gaping jaws exposed its extensive, glistening set of fangs to the terrified Unguhur.

Yet the Unguhur were not alone in their agitation. The monstrous intruders elicited a response from more than just the humanoid

SPIRIT OF FIRE

inhabitants of Oranim.

Very few of the Unguhur noticed the strange development occurring out on the lake. Their attentions were fully fixed upon defending their fellow creatures, or helping the members of their family groups to escape.

The sudden storm of violence, filling the waters with reverberations from the thrashings and immense splashes of the Uktena, heralded the presence of the invaders all throughout the cavern. The sensations roused a considerable number of gallidils into action. Their territory had also been intruded upon in the brutal attack besetting the Unguhur, and they were not creatures accustomed to shying away from threats to their own dominion.

The shining reflections from a host of staring, reptillian eyes drifted along the waters, just a short distance out from the shoreline. Farther across the cavern gigantic shapes of some particularly massive bulls began cutting a sharp path through the water's surface, leaving a rippling wake trailing behind as they headed towards the Uktena.

Though a few Unguhur had fallen prey to gallidils over the multitude of years that Oranim had existed, the two races shared a long, and relatively peaceful, co-existence. The same could not be said of the Uktena, who the gallidils viewed as an intrusive threat, as well as being a very promising source of fresh meat for their gullets.

The fighting along the shoreline drew to a stark end. The few remaining Unguhur warriors, who had gathered to form a sacrificial line of defense, were slain to the last.

The final Unguhur warrior breathing at the water's edge shuddered and fell silent. Punctured through with massive fang wounds, a flood of lethal venom had been injected into the warrior's body.

The second Uktena was now freed to concentrate its attention upon the terraces of the Unguhur city. Yet it did not proceed immediately towards the structures, as it was well-aware of the creatures massing in the water behind it.

Whipping around, the Uktena hurled its wrath upon several gallidils that had strayed close to the shoreline. A brief, one-sided battle ensued, with one smaller gallidil getting swallowed whole. The Uktena coiled and constricted around several more, crushing them mercilessly, while driving its venomous fangs deep into others.

The remnant of younger, smaller specimens retreated, the water

101

near the shore now cluttered with their dead companions. As if stirred into euphoria by the frenzied slaughter, the triumphant Uktena filled the cavern with its eerie, blood-curdling hisses. With an explosive movement, it struck out for the terraces of the city.

Both of the Uktena aggressively beset the mass of structures, exacting appalling losses from the Unguhur population. The titanic predators were indiscrimminate in their murderous savagery, slaying youth, hale adults, and elderly alike.

Many Unguhur blundered unwittingly into the direct path of the attackers, several meeting horrific fates as the Uktenas' heads lanced forward with incredible speed. Some were swallowed in their entirety, others were skewered by fangs, and a few were crushed by the enormous creatures' bodies.

The onslaught became a harrowing contest pitting the wiles of predator against prey, as the Unguhur struggled to escape and evade the huge serpents. The actions of many brave warriors, and several non-warrior males, helped to enable many mothers to escape higher or deeper into the terraces. The mothers needed no urging, anxiously shepherding cowering, terrified offspring along with them.

During one such incidence, an Unguhur warrior put all his might into a downward spear thrust over the edge of one of the upper terraces. One of the Uktena had just brought its head up and over the lip of the next lower level, its body supported by the bunched coils of its extensive length.

The warrior had intended to strike the monstrosity directly in the head, but the spear missed his intended target. Nonetheless, the quick movement of the Uktena was an immense blessing. The sharp spear blade drove right into a seventh spot in back of the creature's head. In a stroke of incredible fortune for the Unguhur warrior, the creature's own swiftness carried its most vulnerable area directly into the path of the plunging spear.

The great serpent stalled in its assault, quivering, and then collapsing, within moments. Its body extended all the way down to the ground level, its length draped over the next two lower levels of the terraces. The warrior froze in place at the abrupt development, stunned in sheer disbelief, before realzing what had transpired.

About twenty other Unguhur, including ten children and four mothers, moved out of hiding to join the warrior, as he regained his senses. He guided them as they edged past the limp, lifeless body of the

Uktena, leading the group away from the carcass.

The peril facing the denizens of Oranim was far from over. The remaining Uktena roved with lethal abandon around the terraces of the cavern-city. The creature slew each and every straggler it came across, gorging itself with a seemingly limitless appetite.

At the far ends of the city, flotillas of rafts were being hastily assembled. More and more escapees from the stricken metropolis made their way to the two areas. Several stout warriors surrounded Khan Treas, Khanum Vuriant, and a few surviving members of the Elder Council.

The warriors were almost compelled to force their own leaders forward, as the Unguhur rulers and council elders showed reluctance to abandon the terraced city, while so many were vying desperately for their lives. Several of their number blanched, warrior and leader alike, their faces paling as they witnessed the ongoing massacre.

Khan Treas clutched an ancient, wooden chest, the rickety timber banded with rusting iron. The old chest was not the work of any Unguhur craft or design.

The inner thoughts of the venerable Unguhur leader were consumed with worry. The security of the chest and his beloved Vuriant held full precedence, far transcending any worries over the matter of his own survival.

The Unguhur boarding the rafts did not take notice of the strange absence of gallidil eyes out on the lake's surface. Just moments before, their huge bodies could be seen converging in number as they advanced towards the shore.

Shrieks and wails rife with terrified urgency surged among the Unguhur, who had just begun to drift out on the rafts. The lone Uktena had broken away from the beleaguered city, and was now slithering quickly down the shore, towards the water. The Unguhur on the rafts were inviting, hapless targets, far too tempting for the ravenous, serpentine monstrosity. The massive creature plunged into the lake, its gaze fixed hungrily upon the slow-moving rafts.

Lurking just below the surface, where the Uktena had entered the water, the other principle race living within the underground world of the Unguhur moved to defend their territory. Having submerged and taken up a silent, patient wait, older, larger, and savvier gallidils reacted to the Uktena swimming above them. Retribution loomed for the slaying of so many of their kin.

The Uktena had barely gotten its full bulk into the water when a multitude of gaping jaws exploded up and down the sleek, scaled length of the creature. With tremendous strength, the gallidils snapped their jaws together with full force against the scaly hide of the Uktena.

The largest bulls, with their devastating power, were able to rip out several of the Uktena's scales. The gaps created in the beast's natural armor provided vulnerable openings, allowing large chunks of exposed flesh underneath to be torn out in ensuing strikes. A few of the gallidils exploiting the scaleless patches clamped down fiercely upon the Uktena's now-trembling body.

The explosive, condensed assault caused the Uktena to thrash violently within the blood-frothed waters. The creature felt its considerable girth being pulled downward, gradually being forced under the surface by the gallidils gripping onto its flesh.

A fair number of smaller gallidils further exploited the wounds created by their larger brethren, tearing ever deeper into the Uktena's body. A crimson lather formed in the churning waters around the struggling monstrosity.

The sorely beset Uktena was still far from defenseless, and several penetrating bites injected its deadly venom into many of its underwater tormentors. Its long, spiky fangs flashed with lethal abandon, stabbing downward and piercing the tough hides of the gallidils with ease.

Yet the Uktena, wounds mounting fast, as its lifeblood flowed steadily out of a multitude of areas, was eventually worn down. The beast's remaining life force ebbed out, and the creature finally expired amid the swirling, foaming waters. When its great bulk ceased to thrash, laying still atop the dark waters, the triumphant survivors began to reward themselves with a bountiful feast.

The Unguhur on the rafts looked upon the scene in both bewilderment and relief. Many uttered supplications of gratitude, astonished at the intervention by their reptilian allies.

Yet a soul-wrenching sorrow loomed beyond the moments of thanksgiving. The vibrant Unguhur city had been reduced to little more than a sprawling, colossal tomb. Bodies broken and torn littered the expanse of stone terraces, rendering the formerly wondrous sights of Oranim into something cold and horrific. In many places, blood glistened in rivulets slowly making their way down lengths of stone steps.

Continuing onward, and reaching the far side of the cavern, rafts from the two main flotillas began converging, on the outskirts of a broad channel leading out from the lake. A few small rafts, each with just a pair of warriors, broke away from the massing formation, and steered towards the tunnel leading to the underworld forests.

Dreadful tidings would be taken to those possessing the good fortune to be out of the city during the attack. Additionally, the Unguhur in the outlying fungal groves would be summoned to join their comrades in the terrible exodus unfolding.

The grief-stricken Unguhur on the cusp of the broader tunnel looked back sorrowfully upon their beloved city of Oranim. The metropolis had been both home and haven for so many generations of their ancestors before them. For long ages, it was the only world that they, and those before them in their extensive lineage, had ever known. The Unguhur could barely even believe what was happening, as the rafts began slipping into the great tunnel, one by one.

The rafts containing the khan, khanum, and several members of the Elder Council were among the last to leave the cavern. They hesitated as long as they were able, lingering on the edges of the tunnel with haunted, forlorn expressions as they faced back towards the abandoned city. Finally, even they had to depart, and go forward into an uncertain, foreboding future.

The tempests of the surface world had laid bare the underground sanctuary harboring generations of Unguhur for centuries. The khan and khanum, and very member of the Elder Council, understood that there would be no letup on the part of their adversaries in seeking to uproot Oranim and the Unguhur inhabiting it.

The pair of titanic, serpentine monsters was only the vanguard of darker forces that could not be ignored or resisted by the underground-dwelling race of beings. Only fools would remain to face an enemy that could send such devastating horrors into the heart of Oranim.

Perhaps one day the Unguhur could return to Oranim, but things precious and irreplaceable, from the lives of the Unguhur themselves, to a sacred charge they could not waver from, had to be safeguarded without delay. An evacuation prepared for by every generation of Unguhur, and dreaded by every khan and khanum of the population of Unguhur living in Oranim down the ages, had befallen Khan Treas and Khanum Vuriant.

Only the gallidils were left afterward to witness the later emergence of a dozen brawny warriors, from the innermost section of

Oranim. Bidden with a momentous duty, the twelve chosen warriors looked around cautiously, and did not come into the open until they were fully satisfied the Uktena were dead. They moved with heightened alertness, wary of potential threats.

Two of their number carried large hide pouches, while the rest were armed with the traditional spears used by the Unguhur warriors. As a few of their number readied a pair of rafts, two warriors made their way to where the first Uktena had been slain on the terraces.

Wasting little time, the two warriors climbed up to where the great beast's lifeless head lay slumped upon an upper terrace. They quickly proceeded to carve out the crimson streaked, crystal-like object set into its forehead. One of the Unguhur warriors carefully wrapped it in layers of gallidil hide, handling the freed shard gingerly. The two warriors then hurried back, without further delay, and rejoined their brethren at the shoreline.

The last Unguhur within Oranim thus departed on the final two rafts, trailing in the wake of the main armada, as they glided silently into the channel mouth on the eastern side of the cavern.

The losses were staggering to contemplate, with nearly four Unguhur dying for every one going forth from the cavern. Not one survivor had escaped the stricken city without enduring the agony of great individual losses, forced to leave behind the bodies of mothers, fathers, brothers, sisters, children, or friends. The once-vibrant home of the Unguhur had become a hushed necropolis.

A maelstrom of emotions shook even the greatest Unguhur warriors to their core, as the two final rafts passed underneath the rough, stony arch of the tunnel. Cast in the blue light from the fungus patches, tears stained the cheeks of the last twelve evacuees. The unknown reared menacingly ahead, and the known was left in woeful desolation behind.

Many centuries of a strong and proud civilization, and the fruits of an entire culture, had almost been brought to utter ruin; in a pitiless sliver of time.

MERSHAD

Dawn arrived with a clear sky and soft touch, a calm atmosphere beckoning favorably for impending flights into the heavens. The flowing breezes were light and invigorating, far from being the kind of gusts that stoked worries of difficult turbulence.

After packing a few provisions into small leather pouches and haversacks, the foursome led by Svein saddled up shortly after first light. All were well-rested, refreshed after enjoying the generous hospitality of Ingvar and the other Midragardans in the fortress.

It took a little effort to rouse Kent from his deep slumber, as he had partaken copiously of Midragardan ale. It was one area where he drew compliments from the old warrior who had berated him in the shield wall training.

Aside from Kent, the others quickly awakened. Mershad slipped away quietly to perform his morning prayers outside the long hall, and returned eager to embrace the coming day.

The Fenraren lifted off, and headed towards the south. The fortress compound of Trellkat was soon well behind them. The coastline and ocean beyond Trellkat diminished into the horizon, until finally indistinguishable.

The last words Mershad and Svein exchanged, shortly before they set to flight, lingered in Mershad's head as they soared over the flatter Dahnmar territory. He smiled, calling to mind the amusing events occurring just prior to their departure.

Svein had been packing cloth-wrapped dried fish and some wedges of hard cheese into one of the haversacks. He had turned towards Mershad, as he drew the drawstrings tight on the sack, before securing it to the saddle of his Fenraren.

"Today, Mershad, you will see dragons!" Svein exclaimed. "The creatures' appearance might intimidate one that does not know them, so I feel bound to tell you more of their wisdom and knowledge. Their own language is said to be very complex. They have few needs, and live simply in their own manner ... long of life, and few in number."

The myths and legends from Mershad's own world had painted one predominant image of dragons. They were normally deemed horrific creatures, primal and fierce, far different from the kind of creatures that Svein was describing.

Old legends had them taking maidens and warding treasures, and only in the eastern regions of Mershad's world were there any different kinds of tales. The mental images were not something easily driven from the mind, having had over twenty years to become ingrained.

"What are you all talking about?" Derek had called out, working to secure the lobed brooch on his long woolen cloak. Whether or not a stroke of great coincidence, the brooch was a silver piece artfully crafted into the form of a curling, winged dragon.

Keeping his expression serious, Mershad had answered back over his shoulder, "Svein was just telling me that we will have to keep an eye out for dragons, when we near their territory … before we meet them, of course."

Neither Svein nor Mershad could keep back the burst of laughter culled from the ensuing expressions on both Derek's and Kent's faces. Derek's look was one of complete disbelief. Kent's skin had turned a whiter shade of pale.

Mershad and Svein had exchanged knowing glances.

"Better tell Kent before he runs off," Mershad suggested in a low voice, eyeing his anxious-looking companion.

Svein grinned. "Yes, there is that to consider."

Looking back, Svein gestured for Derek and Kent to come over and join them. He wasted little time, quickly filling them in on what he had told Mershad earlier. Like Mershad, their eyes had widened as Svein relayed the fascinating information.

In turn, they had explained to Svein the notions of dragons from their own world, echoing the things Mershad held in his own mind. The things they related brought forth a few incredulous laughs from Svein.

Svein reassured them there would be no danger from the dragons they were to seek out that day. Derek and Kent were both in states of eagerness by the time Svein finished talking.

Ingvar, as well as the old warrior who had drilled the shield wall, whose name Mershad finally learned was Thormod, had arrived shortly thereafter. A number of other warriors from the surrounding halls came with them.

Many warriors clustered around Derek, several having shared ale with him the previous evening. He was given a few gifts, including a pair of intricately carved pendants, and a finely-wrought ivory comb. It was undeniable that Derek had gained respect from the warriors, and had already formed a bond with many of them.

Kent was not left out of the generosity, having acquired a little more respect himself after demonstrating his abilities to consume prodigious quantities of ale. When they departed for the skies, Kent was wearing a red headband given to him by a burly warrior he had befriended during the evening's bout of drinking. Mershad could tell that many of the warriors had warmed to his comrade, his infectious, likeable personality winning out over his shortcomings as a warrior.

During those moments, Mershad felt a little regret that he had not bonded with any of the warriors. He had chosen to keep to himself during the evening meal, sitting with Svein, and had then retired at the earliest opportunity, to take advantage of as much sleep as he could.

The chance to see living dragons made the several hours of travel pass by much easier. The lands to the south of Trellkat were very flat, broken by sparse woodlands and gently rolling, windswept plains. There were many signs of life visible within the landscape, including broad, cleared fields, meadows, and several villages, of various sizes.

As the hours rolled on, one blending uneventfully into another, a jagged, violet outline gradually came into view in the distance. Growing slowly, and coming into greater focus, the distinctive shapes of a host of lofty mountain peaks soon spanned the horizon.

The mountains kept expanding ever larger and taller, as Mershad began to sense just how enormous the mountain range really was. A chill passed through him, and his heart nearly skipped a couple of beats. Lightheaded, and breathing rapidly, Mershad drank in the stunning sights as they steadily drew closer.

The majesty and grandeur of the summits ahead were beyond his wildest expectations. Snowcaps covered most of the silent giants. Great expanses of rocky, barren slopes rose up from the darker edges delineating treelines.

The forested areas below those boundary lines were immense in scope. He could only imagine the vast precipices, ravines, and valleys contained within the colossal mountain range. Mershad's eyes constantly scanned the skies, looking for any signs of dragons, wondering if he just might be able to catch an early glimpse of the living legends.

Svein guided them along a course banking directly to the east, running parallel to the mountain range. Nearly an hour later, Mershad espied the form of a village ahead and below, enclosed by what appeared to be an earthen rampart.

While not exceptionally large, the village contained a number of timber, thatch-roofed buildings arranged in clearly demarcated groups.

Some involved a cluster of several buildings, surrounded by lines of fencing, while other plots were little more than a workshop building and a small home.

The Fenraren slanted downward on the guidance of Svein. They descended lower and lower, until finally alighting on an expanse of open ground, within a few hundred feet of the timber-gated entryway for the village. The group's approach had evidently sparked some commotion within the village, as by the time the Fenraren set their paws upon the earth, an assemblage of excited children had gathered, with others trotting and running out from the village entrance. From their energetic gestures and expressions, Mershad could see they were familiar with Svein. They still maintained a modest distance, curiously, and cautiously eyeing Svein's three foreign companions.

"Hello young ones!" Svein called to the throng of diminutive forms, after he had dismounted, and set his own feet upon the ground. He trotted over, scooping a little girl up in his arms. She squealed and giggled in childish delight, her scant weight little impediment as she flew up effortlessly in his grasp. He hoisted her high above him, and twirled around in a circle. He lowered the little girl to his chest, as she wrapped her arms tightly around his neck. "Little Borgny, my little Shield Maiden, have you been a good girl since I was last here?"

"Very good! Ask my mama," the girl replied enthusiastically, in her high pitched voice.

As if they had all been asked the same question, a chorus of affirmations arose from the other children, eager to gain the visitor's attention. Several adults began to emerge from the village, as Svein bantered with a few of the children.

One boy, about eight years of age, boasted loudly that he could show Svein why he would someday be the best swordsman in the village. Of all the children, he had moved the closest to Svein's companions, as if testifying to his bravery. The boy beamed with excitement when Svein said he would indeed like to see his skills demonstrated.

Svein set the little girl down gently, as his eyes came to rest upon one of the adults approaching them.

"Svein! You have finally come back to us. It has been far too long," proclaimed a tall, stout-built woman.

Her kindly visage overcame the evidence of a harder life. The lines of age about her eyes and mouth enhanced her smile in a way that took the observer's attention from the weathered nature of her skin.

Her long, silvery-gray hair was pulled back underneath a type of cloth scarf. Its blue color matched the hue of an outer garment hanging down from shoulder loops over a white linen chemise with short sleeves.

The shoulder loops were fastened with two silver brooches; both resembling the back shell of a tortoise. A third brooch was affixed a little lower, with an assortment of sundry items dangling from thin chains, ranging from several keys to a small knife. A light gray shawl-like garment was draped loosely over her shoulders, fastened by yet another brooch.

Her hands were decorated with several finger rings of silver. A pendant of smooth, greenish glass hung from a festoon strung gracefully between the two shoulder loop brooches. A couple of silver bracelets rested on each wrist, above hands holding a spindle and distaff. A necklace strung with beads of colored glass circled her neck. As she drew nearer, Mershad saw that she wore eye makeup, which effectively shadowed, and brought forth, the brightness of her blue eyes.

She walked briskly up to Svein, taking him into a firm embrace, a movement evidencing considerable strength. "Would that my husband were here to greet you as well, Svein. Is it king's business that brings you here this day?"

Her eyes roved over to the trio standing in back of Svein. Her gaze lingered, both appraising the newcomers, and seeking to prompt Svein for explanations.

"I am sure your husband is busy drinking ale in the halls of the All-Father, Bergthora," Svein replied, with a trace of gentleness. "And to your question, I am on King Hakon's business."

He turned towards his three companions. "These are my honored guests, named Derek, Kent, and Mershad. I will tell you much more of their tale soon enough. They are from a faraway place, and we have had the good fortune of them being brought into our lands."

Bergthora looked over three, eyes narrowing as she closely studied them. She nodded back to Svein, announcing, "At Glittering River, any guest of yours is a guest of ours."

She straightened to her full height, letting a luminous smile brighten up the air about them. "You have come a long way, and must all be hungry. Come into our humble village, where what we have is yours. You may sleep under my own roof, if you stay this evening."

Svein nodded. "Thank you Bergthora. I will speak with you on a way to repay your kindness."

"Stay around over the next month or two," she replied, with a grin hinting at mischief. "We will have plenty of sheep sheering, lamb weaning, and the great drive to the highland pastures for the mid-summer. We could always use an extra hand."

"I fear I am no farmer," Svein replied with a laugh, shrugging his shoulders.

Bergthora laughed warmly. "I thought as much, Svein. Yet I felt inspired to ask."

"Summer is for warriors, is it not?" came a resonant voice, belonging to a man tall enough to look Svein eye to eye.

A simple round cap sat atop his head. His broad shoulders were draped in a green, knee-length tunic, brocaded at the end of its long sleeves and hem with circular patterns fashioned of silver thread. Below the tunic, untapered trousers descended to the top of his leather shoes.

His dark, well-combed hair culminated in a fringe just below his ears, flecked with gray. The man's rounded face was broad in proportion to his head, graced with a thick beard and moustache. The ends of his ample facial growth rested on the top of his chest. His dark eyes held a notable level of sternness, as well as a perceptible measure of kindliness.

He stood with his thumbs locked into a narrow leather belt, secured about his waist by leather strap ends and a metal buckle. A couple of small leather pouches, one metal-framed, hung down from the belt on his right side.

"Aye, Thorgils, summer is for warriors," Svein replied, moving over and embracing the man.

"To the longships we'll go then! Leave the sheep for others," Thorgils chuckled in reply. He glanced over towards Svein's three companions, clearly evaluating them.

Mershad felt uncomfortable under the appraising stares of the villagers, but did not feel anything other than inquisitiveness within their gazes. He knew that Svein's presence and reputation allowed it to be so, blunting any hostile reflexes that might otherwise have arisen.

"To the longships, then, Thorgils … But before this day ages too far, I would speak with our friends from the mountains," Svein said. He added after a pause, "My guests have never seen live dragons before."

"Return swiftly, and bring the Summoning Horn," Thorgils stated, to a slender man nearby.

He looked to be of the same age as Thorgils, and was clad in a plain brown tunic and breeches, both of rough-spun wool. Lacking the color and décor of Thorgils, and spoken to in such a blunt manner, Mershad presumed him to be a thrall like those at King Hakon's homestead. The man turned, and hurried back towards the village.

"A man of few words, but a good worker, and a loyal man nonetheless," Thorgils remarked, with an undercurrent of genuine fondness, as the man disappeared through the gateway to the village.

The older thrall soon hustled back, with a large horn in his right hand. He handed it to Svein without delay, who accepted it respectfully with both hands.

"Let there be no delay, if you seek to summon our winged mountain friends, for the day is growing older," Thorgils commented.

Svein, Thorgils, and Bergthora then led the guests and others, adults and children alike, farther from the village. A tall memorial stone, with well-worn markings, stood sentinel at the foot of a wooden bridge they approached. It crossed over the wide stream meandering lazily by the north side of the village, leading to a cleared field, now sitting fallow at the onset of spring.

Mershad saw they were well away from the marked fields, surrounded by wattle-and-daub fencing, as well as the open meadows filled with cattle, goats, and sheep. Svein looked back towards his guests, as the group drew to a halt in the open field.

He winked as he slowly raised the horn up. "The three of you are about to meet dragons."

Svein made the statement with such casual confidence that Mershad knew, if a small part of him still was in doubt, it was truly no jest. He was about to witness something he would have deemed impossible in the world he came from.

A long, single note blared from the horn. The sustained, smooth noise cast its reach towards the distant mountains. A hushed silence was upon the crowd, as Svein loosed a horn blast every few moments, the length and resonance of each sounding similar to the others.

Several minutes passed, and nothing happened. Each horn blast died away into silence, as chilly breezes bathed the gathered crowd. A little of Mershad's initial fervor began to dampen, opening the door to his previous doubts.

He watched Svein's chest expand, as he inhaled a deep breath, releasing it powerfully through the horn a moment later. As with the other blasts, it dissipated into silence.

A murmur rippled through the gathering, and a few cries erupted at the first sightings of motion in the distance. Most of the villagers were focused intently in the direction of the mountains. The village children clustered close to their parents, a few little girls and boys nearly taking shelter within the long, sweeping over-garments and chemises the adult women wore.

Following their collective gazes, Mershad rested his eyes upon a group of three winged creatures heading directly, and swiftly, towards the village. Lofty and distinct, their forms were outlined distinctly against the backdrop of sky and mountain.

Mershad felt his heartbeat quicken. There was no denying what he saw.

Dragons.

The creatures flew with elegant grace, their movements appearing effortless. They glided smoothly upon the air currents, beating their broad wings sporadically to maintain altitude.

To Mershad, the approaching creatures were like hallucinations conjured from the depths of a vivid imagination. He realized no artist's conception he had ever seen captured the essence of the incredible beasts. He found he could hardly trust his own eyes, looking away just long enough to see that both Derek and Kent's faces were filled with looks of sheer astonishment.

Mershad put out a hand to steady Kent, who was beginning to tremble. Kent mustered a nervous smile in return, as Mershad gave him an encouraging smile of his own.

Were it not for the abundant calm amongst the villagers, Mershad knew he would have shared Kent's fears. As it was, he took confidence from the villagers' ease.

The creatures angled downward, starting their final approach to the village area. They were close enough for Mershad to assess their sizes more accurately.

The dragons were easily large enough to grasp a fully-grown cow securely, in the wide talons of their two long, front legs, lowering from their sides as they neared the ground. A matching pair of rear legs also descended into sight, from their tucked positions against their bodies.

Powerful gusts of air were thrown across the crowd as the three dragons touched upon the ground. Steadied by the sustained labor of their membranous wings, the landings were remarkably smooth.

All the dragons possessed elongated necks and tails, coursing smoothly into bodies long and narrow in form. Their bodies noticeably thickened near the front, with robust chests and iron-like cordings of dense muscle flowing in and around the bases of their great wings. Their legs were of a moderate length, sinewy and lean.

The dragons, as individuals, manifested notable differences in their appearances. The dragon to Mershad's left was the largest of the three, in height, breadth, and wingspan. Its surface was of a very dark, reddish hue, covering both skin and scale.

The dragon's neck was a little thicker and shorter than those of its companions, and ended in a head bearing an elongated snout, narrowing from a wide base into a small, curved tip. Its mouth was lined with huge, conical teeth. With its massive jaws closed, several teeth were visible sprouting from both upper and lower jaws.

The dragon's back was dressed with a prominent array of scutes, the raised scales like individual, thin keels, descending down its back in varying degrees of formation. Four orderly rows of scutes ran along its back, shifting to two on the upper part of its tail, and finally changing to just a single row atop the lower part of its tail. The five digits of its forelegs, and the four of its hind-legs, ended in claws, the three inner toes of each appendage hosting talons of very substantial size.

A ridge ran from the orbits of each of its eyes, extending along the center of its heavy snout. The speckled, golden orbs of each eye held a dark, slit-like pupil within their center, narrow in the brightness of the day's light.

The center dragon, though a little smaller, was no less formidable in appearance. The shade of the beast was a deep, rich blue.

The creature's great, triangular head was graced with a host of short spines, arrayed along the sides, and its throat was a little puffed out below the lower jaws. The dragon's skin took on an even darker shade along the underside of its head and throat, such that in appearance a comparison to a beard was evoked.

The dragon's dark, round eyes were positioned a short distance from the end of its upper jaw, just behind two nostril holes. Its wide mouth was filled with a host of short, serrated teeth.

A singular row of spines ran along the top of its back. Its tail was the shortest of the three, while each of its legs ended in five short, sharp talons.

The last beast, to Mershad's right, was the oddest in appearance of the three. The dark green creature was comparable in height to the dragon in the center, though it was of larger girth and wingspan.

Where the other two had jaws armed with formidable sets of teeth, there were none to be seen along the bony jaws of the third dragon. Its head was triangular in shape, ending in a sharp, hooked beak.

Small, fleshy outgrowths extended in a ring around the dragon's eyes. Round pupils were ensconced within a dappled yellow and brown orb.

The dragon's body was more rounded in its vertical profile, with a back covered in large, raised scales, arranged along three primary ridgelines. A long, muscular tail, the thickest of the trio, completed its length. Like the reddish dragon, it had four claws on its rear legs, and five on each of its forelegs.

The three enormous creatures continued gazing at the humans. Standing almost as still as statues, they made no sounds other than their pronounced breaths.

"Who summoned?" the red-hued dragon queried at last, its voice deep and resonant. The words were spoken in Midragardan, the human audience showing expressions of comprehension as a good number of them looked towards Svein.

Svein stepped forward, holding the summoning horn aloft within his hands. "I have summoned you, my friends. I also bring you tidings. We have travelers with us, from another world."

Mershad looked to Svein, and then back at the dragons. His mind was still struggling to reach equilibrium, vacillating between a sense of normalcy and the stark reality before him; of creatures he formerly consigned to legend and myth.

"Otherworlders, stand forth. No harm to you. We would see you," boomed the middle dragon, its voice was a little higher in pitch than the first.

Derek stepped forward, his jaw line taut as he stared at the dragons. Kent shuffled forward, staying close to Derek's side. Mershad commanded his legs to move, contending with a wave of dizziness as he peered up at the dragons looming over them.

"My friends, if you should choose to speak with them in your own language, they will be able to understand, and speak back to you. The Wanderer has given them great gifts, to help with understanding languages in this world," Svein told the dragons.

"You can understand us, Otherworlders? Then give us your names," rasped the third dragon.

To the ears of Svein and the villagers, the words of the dragon were little more than a series of growls. But to Mershad, the words were easily understood.

One by one, beginning with Derek, the three otherworlders introduced themselves. At first, the eyes of the dragons widened in undisguised amazement, as they heard words perfectly rendered in their own tongue by humans.

There was an extended pause, as the three dragons looked to each other. Mershad perceived the dragons regarding them with much greater interest, and considerable caution.

"It is true. You speak dragon tongue. You wear the gifts of the Wanderer," the reddish dragon said, in Midragardan. The creature swiveled its gaze towards Svein. "Where found?"

"They were found in the Five Realms, east of Gallea," Svein responded. "There were more otherworlders, seven in all. Some were taken captive by the Unifier. His forces have invaded those lands."

"Seven?" the middle dragon queried. "If prophecy, more in world."

"I have heard of no others," Svein replied.

The three dragons had a somber, pensive air about them as they looked to each other. After a few heartbeats, their heads turned back towards Svein.

"Battles come. Dark words come," the blue dragon said.

"All-Father warriors seen in skies," the red dragon stated.

"Elder have come to us," the dark green dragon added. "They speak of great wars. They speak of prophecy."

Whispers and low conversations broke out amongst the villagers at the mention of the Elder. Mershad had little idea of what the Elder were, or why the mention of them caused such a spirited reaction. Whatever the Elder were, they were clearly of momentous importance, and commanded substantial reverence among the villagers.

"If Elder come again … we will speak of otherworlders," the dark green dragon continued.

"Maybe others from otherworld, known in world," the red dragon added.

"Will bring word ... to village, if others in world," the blue dragon said.

Svein gave a slight bow. "I thank you, our good brothers of the mountains, and the All-Father."

"Are there more tidings, brother in Midragard?" the red dragon responded.

Svein shook his head slowly. "These are the only tidings I have to bring to you. I wanted for you to witness these three, with your own eyes."

"Then we will return ... we will take tidings now," the blue dragon said.

The dragons shifted about, stepping back and outward, creating greater space between them with each stride. Mershad could feel vibrations from each heavy step, as the three huge creatures moved. The dragons drew to a halt when there was enough distance between them to fully spread their wings, without danger of obstructing each other.

"Must be ready, brothers and sisters of All-Father," the red dragon pronounced in a grave tone, stretching its wings, and looking back to Svein. "War comes. Even ... for dragons."

With a furious flapping of their wings, stirring up an intense wind around the villagers, the great dragons launched themselves with powerful thrusts from their back legs. Lifting off the ground, they tucked their legs snugly into their sides. Climbing higher, they headed onward, towards the great Drakkar Mountains in the distance.

All eyes remained fixed on the three dragons until their forms were tiny specks on the horizon. They were finally absorbed into the expanse of soaring mountains and cloud-filled vistas.

Mershad was lost in a swirling tumult of wonderment and uneasiness. He knew Svein had not summoned the dragons for the sole benefit of his three foreign guests. It was now quite apparent that Svein desired to convey information to the dragons themselves.

His eyes stayed fixed on the line of mountains, long after the dragons were gone from sight, until Derek gently tugged at his arm. Quietly, they filed into the throng of villagers, as all turned back towards the bridge.

NEAR ORANIM

A couple of small rafts, packed with Unguhur warriors from the abandoned city, reached the edge of an underground forest. It was the one situated near the tunnel leading up to the human woodsman's abode. The warriors brought with them the terrible word of the ill-fortune befalling Oranim and its occupants.

The warriors shouted quickly for the Unguhur in the vicinity to hasten down to them, whether laborer, warrior, or raft pilot.

The Unguhur warriors watching over the fungal forest, and the blocked passage to the woodman's abode, swiftly relayed the summons. A few laborers from deeper within the tall growths hurried to join the rest, as all streamed towards the river's edge.

Apprehension built swiftly, as they came within sight of their summoners. They knew in the very moment they laid their eyes upon the forlorn expressions of the warriors on the rafts that something horrifying had transpired.

Gathering en masse at the rocky edge where the rafts were tethered, the Unguhur from the cavern-forest formed a semi-circle around the reluctant heralds. The guards that had been watching over the fungal forest, and the few laborers with them, listened to the grisly tale of the catastrophe with horror written across their faces. For many, it would have been more desirable if the cavern itself had then collapsed upon them.

More than a few of the tall, muscular beings sank down to their knees, sobbing with torrents of grief as the shock of the atrocity gave way to a gaping abyss of inner pain. The warriors upon the rafts had just begun to gently urge the others to gather themselves together to depart, when the warriors of Avanor harshly interrupted their lamentation.

The timing of the attack was impeccable, as if guided by an otherwordly intelligence. Breaking through the blockages in the passageway to the surface, the Avanoran warriors poured down from Gunther's dwelling with shields and weapons raised. There was no room for subtleties, as the Avanoran cries of "The All-Father's Way!" blasted forth from the narrow rock passage, and swelled to fill the cavern.

"We are under attack!" cried one of the Unguhur warriors, whirling about with spear in hand, where he stood a little farther away from the river's edge.

Though their vision was still obstructed by the tall mushroom stalks in the forest, the Unguhur knew the attackers were part of the same cataclysm that had just been levied upon their beloved Oranim. A few of the grief-laden warriors hefted their spears, roaring with fury and madness as they charged to meet the rush of Avanoran warriors.

The Unguhur laborers from the cavern listened to the exhortations of warriors on the rafts, barely restraining their more raw impulses. After incurring so much loss, every remaining Unguhur was invaluable to the future of their kind. The laborers boarded the rafts, heeding the warriors who had witnessed the horrid downfall of Oranim.

Pulling up the tethers and pushing off, a small cluster of rafts began pressing farther up the river. The Unguhur warriors watched the water closely, with great trepidation, not wanting to encounter another of the giant serpent-monstrosities that had beset the city.

Behind, the forces of Avanor flowed through the stalks of the cavern-forest. Numerous mailed warriors engulfed the few Unguhur warriors charging to embrace their approach. The final, enraged battle cries of Unguhur warriors echoed throughout the cavern. Weapons slashed and stabbed with a desperate, savage frenzy.

The skirmish was brief, as the Unguhur warriors were slain to the last. Taking several enemy fighters down with each one of them that fell, the Unguhur warriors both paid and exacted a heavy price in blood. Their ill-fated fight contained a greater value than personal vengeance, enabling their brethren on the rafts to gain some precious momentum, and distance on the river.

The Avanoran fighters, ignited with the blood lust of battle, swarmed towards the river's edge in a mood awash with deadly intentions. A few archers among them raced along the edge of the water, eyeing the escapees.

They drew out arrows from their quivers, notched them, and hurriedly pulled their longbows back, right as the small flotilla neared the far edge of the cavern. The loosed arrows fell just short of their intended targets, landing harmlessly into the flowing, dark waters.

Other Avanorans hovered about the water's edge, impatient, and eager to press the attack onward. Some excited cries rang out, as the Avanorans discovered a few rafts not used by the departing Unguhur. In their haste to retreat, the Unguhur had failed to scuttle them, giving an unintended boon to the invaders.

Archers, spearmen, and a few knights boarded the great rafts, taking care to test their balance and weight on the floating platforms. They were delayed for a few moments, as others quickly hacked down a few mushroom stalks, in order to fashion several crude paddles.

The knights barked out orders, as a few crossbowmen, clad in padded gambesons, trodded down to join the others at the shore. The crossbowmen were assigned evenly to the various rafts.

The archers kept arrows at the ready, some testing the pull on their longbows as they waited. Several of the idle spearmen gripped their weapons securely, looking anxiously towards the mouth of the tunnel where the Unguhur rafts had disappeared. A few exchanged nervous jests with each other, awaiting the command to set in motion.

The commanding knights positioned those who would serve as paddlers, while the crossbowmen leaned over, and braced their feet against the bow end of their weapons. With muscles taut from the strain, they pulled the chord spanning the two wooden bow arms upward, bringing it along the weapon's wooden shaft to lodge against the trigger release. With deadly quarrels set in place, they waited.

The knights issued the command to move out. Hide ropes securing the rafts to the prominent stones perched on the natural quay were lifted free.

Using their newly-fashioned paddles, the Avanorans pushed the rafts away from the moorings. At a unified cadence, the warrrios of Avanor started after the fleeing Unguhur rafts.

Thoughts were concentrated fully upon navigating the underground stream, as the paddlers put everything they had in their back, shoulders, and arms to the task of accelerating the rafts. The rafts began picking up speed, as the pursuit of the Unguhur commenced.

The Avanorans were caught unaware, and wholly unprepared, by the ambush occurring a few moments later, when they were in the midst of the waterway. A sudden storm of aggression exploded from directly beneath them. Massive bodies and jaws of huge gallidils slammed into the rafts, with tremendous force. It was as if the creatures hurled themselves into the attack with uninhibited wrath, one last tribute to the race of beings that had shared their territory for so many generations.

An enormous, older bull came up under a small raft, near its direct center. Having built up speed, the reptillian monster snapped the watercraft in half in the force of its thunderous impact. The proud

Avanoran warriors were instantly condemned to hapless fates, crying out and flailing, as they tumbled into the waters.

Those wearing heavy chain mail and helms, such as the knights, and many of the infantry spearmen, sank quickly into the murky depths. Their desperate cries were choked off abruptly, as their forms faded swiftly into the merciless blackness beneath.

Some unarmored archers and crossbowmen were able to tread water. A few even had the presence of mind to try to swim for the shore.

Had there been few gallidils, they might even have had a chance to survive. But the waters were filled with the carnivorous reptiles.

Helplessly strewn amid the frenzied gallidils, the Avanorans at the water's surface met nightmarish ends. One by one, the survivors were dragged underneath the surface in the iron grips of clenched jaws. A few of the larger gallidils had jaws so immense they engulfed doomed Avanorans in one bite.

Three rafts were able to hold their structural integrity following the initial attacks. Of these, one was subsequently smashed by larger gallidils, while the pair weathering a second bucking cast several terror-stricken occupants into the dark, frothing waters.

The surface of the river was shredded apart, sending plumes of blood and water everywhere, as the horde of gallidils whipped themselves into an orgy of devastation. Avanoran warriors along the shore, having already begun to fashion crude rafts from felled fungal stalks, watched the proceedings with horror and dismay. Macabre sights were burned into their memories, forming the essence of nightmares that would haunt them for a long time to come.

A few Avanorans scrambled to their feet, and hurried back through the underground forest, a couple tripping over their own feet in their terrified haste. Shoving themselves back up quickly, the fallen resumed their flight through the tall stalks, as fast as their legs could carry them.

Without pausing to catch their breath, they made their way back up the rock tunnel. Their abrupt emergence from the passage startled a few warriors loitering within the abandoned timber home sheltering the underground entryway.

Stumbling out of the structure, they looked around at the assemblage of warriors gatherered there. All eyes fixed upon them, and there was no mistaking the bared look of fear upon the men.

While still gripped in terror, the men had enough presence of mind to alert the higher-ranking knights to the calamity underground. Their stammered, rushed reports were met with looks of alarm and consternation, and even a little disbelief, as they told of the blood-soaked ambush.

The commotion attracted the attention of the shrouded Arcamon. The menacing figure silently watched the men from the saddle of its baleful, winged steed.

Warriors hurriedly parted and spread outward, giving a wide berth to the Arcamon as it flicked the reins on its steed, and spurred it to walk towards the fright-riddled messengers. The men shivered in increasing dread as they gazed into the darkness of the Arcamon's hood. The knights who had been interrogating the messengers wordlessly edged backwards, their own eyes filling with fear.

"You run ... from beasts in the water?" the Arcamon hissed, using the Gallean tongue, with accusation permeating its acerbic tone.

A cold, icy pall saturated the air, as the Arcamon remained still, staring down upon the messengers. The air grew thick with tension, and a rising sense of threat.

"A knight? Of Avanor?" the Arcamon uttered, in a voice barely above a whisper, the words themselves like icy shards.

One of the men, whose sleeveless surcoat, chain-mail shirt, and mail leggings identified his stature plainly enough, slumped to his knees before the Arcamon. The knight was too terrified to speak, his face twitching as rivulets of sweat coursed from his forehead and ran down the sides of his cheeks.

A soul-wrenching shriek emitted from the umber depths of the Arcamon's hood, stabbing into the hearts of all hearing the eerie sound. It was a cry of undiluted rage, focused singularly on the cowed knight.

With blinding speed, the head of the Arcamon's steed shot forth, jaws gaping wide. The knight did not even have time to react, as glistening, spiky teeth drove down with tremendous force into his skull.

One of the creature's broad claws slammed into the knight, pinning him to the ground. The winged abomination abruptly wrenched its long neck upward, teeth firmly clenched on the knight's head. The headless body lay before the steed, twitching, and blood pouring into the soil, as the Arcamon gazed upon the shocked, terrified witnesses.

"This was no knight of Avanor. Not even worth being food

for my steed," the Arcamon announced, as its steed spit out the head gripped within its mouth. The thump of the head onto the hard ground resounded in the pensive silence.

The Arcamon took up the reins, guiding the steed towards the opening of the timber home. Using axes, and other implements, the Avanorans had already enlarged the entryway from its original size, for the smoother conduit of men and material into the underground passage.

The Arcamon swung down from the saddle at the entrance, keeping hold of the reins as it led the winged beast forward. Tucking its wings in, as tightly as it could, the Arcamon's steed barely fit through the opening. The mottled, scaly skin of its sides and back scraped harshly against the structure's timbers.

The loud, shrill cry of the Arcamon's infernal beast soon filled the underground forest. The aberrant sound sent an immediate, immobilizing chill through the spines of the Avanoran soldiers waiting below, near the river.

They looked with apprehension towards the rocky ceiling of the sprawling cavern. As another cry rang out, the shadowy form of both steed and rider glided above the tops of the mushroom stalks, far above their heads.

The gathered forces gave the malevolent entity and its steed a wide clearance, as they landed upon an open stretch by the shoreline. Dismounting the hellish steed, the Arcamon slowly withdrew its long, black blade.

Completely ignoring the men surrounding it, the Arcamon strode to the edge of the water. Its eyes burned fiercely, living torches within the darkness of its hood. The reddish orbs surged in intensity, as if an inferno was welling up from within.

The Arcamon brought the great sword up towards its hooded face, the sharp tip pointed rigidly upright. Its fiery gaze locked fixedly upon the ebon blade, bringing it closer until the top edge of the entity's hood pushed lightly against the surface of the blade. The Arcamon then leaned forward slightly, pressing the leathery skin of its thin, dessicated lips upon the dense, light-soaking substance forming the blade.

The Arcamon then pulled the blade away from its face, while continuing to hold it in a vertical position. A white-hot fire sprouted from the runic inscriptions on the blade's surface. Spreading, and working their way down its ebony length, the eruption of fire inundated the sword thoroughly. In moments, nothing could be seen of its black, inner core.

It was not the fire of purification or cleansing, but rather of destruction in its most elemental form. All the men standing within the cavern could have sworn they all felt a searing blast of heat wash over them, the instant the sword burst into fiery life. .

"By the power and authority of the Lord of Fire, the True Prince of the World, I set these waters to the embrace of the flame. Destroy those who dare to oppose the Will of the One I serve," the Arcamon hissed menacingly, in its ancient tongue.

The eerie sound of its sibilant voice caused many of the human observers to tremble, held captive within the suffusion of fear. The flaming sword crackled and sparked with an unholy energy, as the Arcamon lowered the fiery weapon down to touch the surface of the water.

Upon contact, a blue circle of pulsing energy, rising tongues of living fire, formed swiftly and raced outward. The spreading cerulean flames brightened, and shifted in color, changing first to a reddish hue, and then finally to a blinding white.

As the colors transformed, the waters they covered began to bubble and churn. The Avanoran warriors felt the waves of heat wafting thickly off the waters. Steam rose in dense masses of vapor, filling the air.

A clammy sweat broke upon the faces of the Avanoran force. Their clothes dampened as the mist clung heavily to them, forming droplets on their weapons and armor. The air itself became ever more difficult to breath, thick and choking to the lungs.

A chorus of hideous sounds, ranging from hisses to noises like deep barks, sprang in abundance from among the frothing waters. Through the blistering mists and boiling surface, the Avanorans could see the huge forms of their water-bound adversaries. The gallidils tossed and thrashed about in their inescapable perdition, condemned prisoners of their own environment.

The Arcamon waved its burning sword in the direction where the Unguhur had fled on their rafts, loosing more utterances in its ancient tongue. The blue energy at the far edges of the liquid inferno began to creep onward, as if the sprawling mass of fire was an entity that could be commanded. The edge of the flaming mass marched towards the far tunnel, with a steadiness almost like sentient obedience.

Soon, the tumultuous waters around the mouth of the nearer

tunnel, which led to the abandoned underground city of Oranim, ceased gradually in their violence. The white flames changed into shades of red and orange, continuing in the sequence of transition to blue. When the hues had shifted to their original color, the flames lowered, and settled down into the water's surface, vanishing completely a few moments later. Only the ripples and creases from the motion of the slow river current could be seen.

The bodies of a large number of slain gallidils now floated along the surface, bobbing and drifting in the current. Their great jaws were still, never again to snap down upon any creature within Ave.

The Arcamon turned slowly towards the watching Avanoran warriors. Many flinched, as its gaze encompassed them. The Arcamon commanded them to resume their pursuit of the Unguhur.

The Avanorans wasted no time responding to the Arcamon's desires. No questions were asked regarding whether any dangers yet lurked in the river. Within moments, hempen ropes brought down from the surface were being tied, as lengths of fungal stalks were secured together. Axes rose and fell, as the construction of crude rafts resumed all along the rocky shore.

More paddles were formed, and piled up near the rafts, awaiting the completion of the vessels. The construction advanced steadily, as the Arcmon watched impassively. As rafts were completed, they were lugged down to the water's edge.

Relatively light for their size, and quite sturdy, they were not difficult to maneuver for the teams of Avanorans forming to man them. The newly-fashioned rafts were then shoved into the river, secured for the moment by ropes to the rocks on the riverside landing.

The dead bodies of gallidils littered the surface of the water. A few jarred the new rafts, shaking the nerves of the men attending to the floating watercraft.

Some of the Avanorans with weapons at hand angrily skewered the bobbing forms out of sheer spite. They drove their spears and swords deep into dead reptillian flesh, in thrusts fueled by vengeful anger. They needed no reminders that the bellies of the dead creatures contained the flesh of many of their comrades.

The work was conducted with diligent efficiency, and a good number of rafts were soon readied for use. Another contingent of spearmen, knights, crossbowmen, and archers then boarded the rafts, in an orderly fashion. While wary of the dark waters, and the threats that the depths might hide, they were not frightened enough to contradict the desires of the Arcamon.

The mass of rafts started out for the far tunnel, the one the retreating Unguhur had gone into. Using spears and paddles, the Avanorans shoved gallidil bodies out of the way, methodically working their way through a maze of carcasses.

The flames at the tunnel's mouth had finally died down, and disappeared, so that by the time they reached the far exit of the cavern, the rafts passed over water alone. Some tendrils of mist still drifted through the cavern, but the air had thinned considerably, becoming much easier to breathe. Weapons at the ready, the flotilla of rafts entered the tunnel.

MERSHAD

Bergthora smiled warmly at Mershad, though he did not see the kindly expression. She walked up behind him, as he stood silently in the open ground, just a few paces outside the doorway into her home. The assortment of keys, small knives, a comb of carved bone, and other diminutive objects, hanging from several thin chains connected to one of her tortoise shell-shaped silver brooches, clinked softly together with each stride.

Mershad was looking off towards the horizon, casting his gaze over and beyond the simple earthworks bordering the outskirts of the main village area. Having eaten his fill, and finished his evening prayers, he found himself in a very peaceful, relaxed mood as night fell.

The distant sounds of music, muffled within one of the timber houses, carried delicately through the air. A mixture of playful and strident barks could be heard from dogs farther off, towards the opposite end of the village. The sounds of spirited conversation and laughter rose up from yet another dwelling. The village was settling down for the evening, but was not in full slumber just yet.

"Did you enjoy the evening meal?" Bergthora asked Mershad in a low voice.

Her words did not catch him by surprise, or startle him, as he had easily heard the rustlings and janglings of her chains and other implements. He turned his head slowly towards her. The older Midragardan woman looked at him with soft, almost motherly eyes, mirroring the kindliness of her smile.

Bergthora had donned a long woolen cloak in the cooling evening air. It was secured around her neck by yet another silver brooch, of a three-lobed variety.

A thin silver chain lined with several glass beads was suspended between the brooches holding together the two pieces of her woolen over-garment, the latter under the cloak and atop a short-sleeved, linen chemise. Becoming more familiar with Midragardan clothing, Mershad knew the layers had to be effective in fighting off the night's chill.

Bergthora's hair was still tucked up under a wool scarf. As earlier, she wore an assortment of decorations, including an arm ring of twisted silver, several finely etched silver finger rings, a necklace with beads of green glass and an amber pendant, and a couple of silver bracelets. Mershad did not find the display ostentatious in the least; they were simply beautiful adornments, on a very generous, warm lady.

Mershad turned towards her, and grinned broadly. He quietly acknowledged his bloated stomach with a gentle pat. He had partaken of far more food than he previously thought he could handle. Bergthora, aided by her daughters and female bond-servants, had overseen the outlay of a prodigious repast.

The large soapstone cauldron over her hearth had produced a bounty of sumptuous porridge. A stone slab at one end of the hearth proffered a goodly number of honey-sweetened oat cakes. An assortment of rich cheeses, warm barley bread, dried herring, and a freshly roasted sea bird, of a type unfamiliar to Mershad, rounded out the bountiful meal. He had emptied his wooden bowl more than once, though he was still getting acclimated to eating with the usage of just spoon, knife, and fingers.

He had sipped only as much ale as would keep his thirst at bay, once again hoping the Divine Creator would forgive him in his necessity for drinking the fermented liquid. Those to whom he passed the drinking horns expressed surprise at his limited consumption.

Mershad did not fail to notice they were more than happy to quaff the rest of his share, as well as their own, before summoning one of the attending female bond-servants to refill the horn. By the end of the meal, he was relieved that he had not imbibed enough to affect his senses to any significant degree.

"Yes, and a feast it was," Mershad replied, with all sincerity. "I thank you for your hospitality, Bergthora."

"Do they have food like we have, where you are from?" she queried, curiosity sparking in her eyes. "Your lands sound very interesting. Even if I cannot imagine some of these strange things you speak of in my mind."

It was not the first question he had heard that evening. He had fielded many inquiries during the meal about his homelands, trying to describe them as best he could. Most had listened to his account with a high degree of incredulity displayed on their faces.

Mershad did not begrudge them in their disbelief. He understood his home world seemed like a place of magic to the Midragardans. In their view, his world was more fantastical than even the most boastful and fanciful of the sagas they told to each other from generation to generation. He was conscious of the fact that had he not witnessed the things of Ave with his own eyes, he would have regarded stories of their world with just as much skepticism and astoninshment.

Mershad shook his head. "No, and yes. A few things are similar, but the kinds of food you have here are new to me in many ways. I like a lot of it much better, to be honest with you. And there are other differences about your world ... that I do take note of. They are not as hospitable to strangers in my former land, as your people are here."

Bergthora smiled, looking visibly pleased with the outward compliment, but her brow furrowed as his last words reached her ears. She ventured another question, her voice tentative with the asking. "Do not take offense. I am curious about something you have just spoken of. Do you often find yourself a stranger in your own lands?"

Mershad glanced back at her, not entirely surprised with the substance of her question. She was a mother, and his own mother had always seemed to know what he was really saying, underneath the words he spoke. Bergthora had honed in on something intangible underlying his reply. Her perceptiveness was a skill common to mothers, whether they resided in his former world, or in Ave.

There was little he could do to make her understand the world he came from, but there were other things that could transcend all times and places. "I have felt more at home among these new and wonderful lands, even with all of the danger I've been through, than I ever did in over twenty three years back in the world I am from," he replied in an even, low tone. It was almost like giving a confession to his own self, as much as it was an open admission to her.

The answer was one Bergthora had not evidently expected. A quizzical look spread across her face, and her surprise was further echoed in her voice. "More at home here? More than your own lands? I wonder how that can be. Is it because of wars?"

"A part of it, yes," Mershad answered, nodding in the affirmative. "When I found myself here, there was a war occurring between the country I lived in, and the country of my ancestors, and many relatives. I had lived my whole life in my country, but many there treated me as if I was a foreigner. And worse, some made me feel like I was an enemy."

He shrugged, looking over to her with a resigned expression on his face, "But there are some things I've taken from that whole experience, as far as being a stranger in my own land. It has made it easier to be a stranger in a strange land."

"As wars will do, turning a people against themselves, for many reasons," Bergthora replied, with a clear tone of sympathy. She looked him in the eye, the wrinkles at the corners of her eyes accenting the gentle look held within them. "I have lived my entire life in this village, but wars have always been with my people. I have seen men leave in the summers for every manner of ambition … from cattle raids on our own shores, to wars between jarls and lesser kings, to raids in distant lands, where younger sons went often to seek their fortunes. Under Hakon … bless his wisdom … this has quieted much over the last twenty years.

"I have never seen the sense in these wars. It would seem that most of those who carry the sword and axe do most of the bleeding, for the one who will see the most silver and gold bands placed upon his arms in the great halls."

"At least your leaders do go and fight in the wars of these lands," Mershad replied. "It is more than I can say for the lands I lived in. Where I am from, those that send others off to war remain home, and never fight in battle."

Bergthora looked mystified by his words. "Why would any fight for such a chieftain? There would be little honor in asking others to fight, and not being willing to share the same risks. How is such a thing possible?" Bergthora responded, as if she could not comprehend a reality such as the one he described.

"Like I said, some things are different … very different. But other things are not so different. We have individuals in our world who gather power to themselves. Like this Unifier that plagues your world. How does one man gain so much power?" Mershad asked, knowing he had never been able to answer similar questions regarding the powerful world leaders of his own time and place.

"Again, I know little of the lands beyond, in our world, and nothing of the lands of your world, but it may not be so different between your world and mine," Bergthora answered.

Her eyes drifted upward, staring off into the night sky, as she drew into herself in thought. After a few moments, she looked back to Mershad.

"A man has only to make others feel they are serving their own desires by following his. Men will always do what they believe is best for themselves, no matter what they might proclaim. They may claim allegiance to others, and swear their swords to them, but they would likely not do so if there were no prospects for gain of some kind. Could be silver. Could be women. Could even be spiritual rewards, such as in the old world, when warriors proved themselves worthy for a place within the Great Hall of Valhalla in the afterworld.

"The powerful simply marry their own wishes to the desires of men and women, until the two seem to become one. It is an illusion for most, but as long as there are those who believe their road is the same as that of the leader, that leader will grow stronger. If there are many such people, the leader will grow very strong.

"Do you understand? It is that way with all things. It is the way a village chieftain, or a great Jarl, or even a mighty king, brings power behind them. And I believe it is the way the Unifier brought king after king under His influence. All see a greater gain, or protection from loss, in serving this Unifier. In the end, they are all thinking of themselves."

"I never have understood it, in that way," Mershad replied, as the wisdom in her words dawned on him. Her rationale rang with truth and clarity, though the words were anything but soothing. They were hard truths, seen in a cold but accurate, light.

The forces moving the world seemed so vast and complex, baffling to behold, and even more bewildering to comprehend. Yet a mother on the edge of a faraway land, who had barely seen anything beyond the immediate surroundings of her riverside village, could keenly understand the forces moving kingdoms and lands, in both Mershad's world and her own.

Her mention of spiritual rewards in such a light made him feel a pang of guilt. The self-interest of survival through eternal life, or the avoidance of everlasting torments, were undeniably the primary forces behind the bowed head of many a religion's supplicant, if not the overwhelming majority of them. Remove the hope of heaven and the threat of hell, and all places of worship would empty overnight.

Taken further, any willful act or choice was ultimately a derivative of self-interest, whether of a concrete or more abstract nature. It could be anything from the sacrifice of the worshipper desiring to follow the teachings of a god, to the warrior choosing to defend the land and people he valued. In a sense, the opposite of self-interest was the cessation of the individual, and existence itself.

"Few good men ever strive for great power over others, but I do not mean to condemn all who hold power," Bergthora continued, after a pause, as if she had forgotten to add a final element. "We must not forget the good fortune that comes with a kind, able leader. There are indeed a few who truly seek the betterment of their people. I believe King Hakon is one such man."

"I think he is too … from what I have come to know of him," Mershad concurred.

Like a candle flame bursting to life in the midst of darkness, the thought of King Hakon countered the somber, disheartening reflections on the nature of most leaders, and the majority of humankind itself. Mershad was grateful for the sense of balance Bergthora had just provided.

Her lips turned up in a winsome smile. "It is good to know you feel that way, and it reminds us you can never judge one for the behavior of a hundred others. It is that way with raising children. You can learn a lot of things about life, if you take the lessons offered you every day."

"There you are," called a soft voice from behind.

Mershad turned about, and beheld a silhouetted figure emerging from the shadows of the timber structures. He could not make out the features of the young woman's face, framed by long, silken hair, a few strands of which floated gently upon the crisp evening breezes.

"Asa, you are still up and about, " Bergthora remarked jovially, looking to her daughter. "I thought you would be finding rest by now."

At the mention of the name, Mershad thought back to the young lady he had been introduced to at the evening meal. Her features flooded back from his memory.

Sparkling blue eyes in the firelight, creamy skin glowing with a youthful sheen, and snow-white teeth that flashed with her broad smiles, Asa was an elegant beauty. Her luxuriant blond tresses had been held in place by an embroidered blue headband, intertwining curves and shapes woven into it with golden thread. She had laughed in a carefree manner, and had spoken with confident assertiveness, traits Mershad was finding to be rather prevalent among Midgragardan women.

"No, mother," Asa replied, coming to a stop at her mother's left side. "Your home is prepared for the night. Everything has been attended to, from the hearth to the bedding. I am finished with weaving and spinning for this day, and we have no saga tellers staying with us tonight. I simply wanted to find you."

"I must confess it will not be long before I will be seeking some sleep," Bergthora replied.

"Nor will it be long for me, but not just yet," Asa responded. She looked past her mother, towards Mershad. "I regret I did not get to speak to you much during the meal. You spoke of wonderful things. Did you get enough to eat?"

"Yes … I did," Mershad replied, feeling a choking nervousness welling up within. With Bergthora alone, words were not a problem, but with Asa present, it was as if an inner balance had been upset.

"It may not be what is served in the hall of King Hakon, but I am glad you enjoyed it," Asa stated.

"Have you spoken with Magnus?" Bergthora asked her daughter.

Mershad could tell from Bergthora's inflection, and the instant tensing in Asa, that the subject was both familiar and a source of contention for the two women. In a single moment, it seemed Asa forgot Mershad was present. She turned, and squared her shoulders towards her mother. Of equal height, the women looked at each other eye to eye on the same level.

"He is away, though not with the herds, trappers, or ore finders," Asa said tersely. "He is out courting the wolves again. Seems he likes those that walk on four legs better than those who walk on two. It is not like Njal, who is ever more likely to become one of Jarl Guttorm's men. A warrior among our people."

Mershad could feel the strain thickening between the two

women. He felt deeply awkward witnessing the confrontation, as it was a family matter he had no business in.

"It is just Magnus' way," Bergthora responded in a calm tone. "Not every person is destined for the life of the village. He brought us much food through the winter, and many good hides to the men living here. He is no idle man, and he has not made his gains on a sword blooded far away."

There was a noticeable sharpness to her last words, which drew a harder, edgier look from Asa.

"If he wanted to marry me, then he would have to love the village and its people more than beasts," Asa responded with a defiant lilt. "If my father was still here, he would know Njal Thorgilson can provide a strong bride price, and a worthy Day After Gift."

"As your father once brought bog ore down each year for the smiths, Magnus provided food and hides in abundance since he left to seek the wolf packs," Bergthora said, her face and eyes like iron. "Love for the village is shown in many ways."

"Hides and food," Asa said dismissively, ire sprouting within her eyes.

"Hides and food … not so different from bog ore, and you would be wise to learn why. All of it helped the people of this village. Maybe you need to open your eyes to the wonderful things of our land. Magnus is still out there, alive, so you know he has been judged worthy by others. And those judges are harsh judges indeed on the inner character of a man," Bergthora retorted, more than matching the intensity of her daughter's glare.

Asa locked her eyes with Bergthora's. The sparkling blues seen at the feast now seemed like steely orbs in the shadows of night. After a few moments, without another word, she stormed away, striding in the direction of the house.

Watching her daughter heading off, Bergthora shook her head, a grin forming as the rigidity ebbed from her face. She glanced at Mershad. "It is not that she does not like Magnus. It is that her favor for Njal grows. She is as headstrong as I was, when I came of age to marry."

Mershad did not feel comfortable in the slightest degree discussing matters of family and marriage prospects for Asa. Yet he felt prompted to respond, choosing what he believed to be a safe observation, "You seem to favor this Magnus."

"I do,' Bergthora replied quickly, and confidently. "If Asa's good father was still here in this world, she would be proven right in one matter. He would likely favor Njal. Yet as he knew, and as I know, Asa will not be married against her wish. She knows the way of our people. A wife can break a marriage she is not happy in, even if she could somehow be forced to marry against her wishes."

"And this Magnus?" Mershad queried, curious about the young man Bergthora favored.

"A good young man. His father was declared an outlaw after committing a terrible crime, and was made to flee this land when Magnus was just a boy of twelve. All his father's property was taken. The boy had nowhere to go … his mother had died three years before, lost to illness.

"Magnus was allowed to live under the roof of Thorgils. This makes matters very difficult now. Magnus grew up in the house of Njal's own father, and now both Magnus and Njal would marry Asa. Magnus has great courage, and would be devoted to Asa. I fear Njal desires arm rings of silver, and Jarl Guttorm's favor, more than Asa's favor. As a mother, I favor Magnus for my daughter … though many in this village would disagree with me."

The firm declaration came without any shred of doubt or hesitation. A wider smile spread across Bergthora's face, even as a haunting, melodic music suddenly filled the night air.

"It may be that Magnus heard of my approval," Bergthora remarked, the smile lingering upon her face, as she looked off into the night. "The voices of the pack he sought serenade us now."

Mershad's attention was drawn by the resonant sounds reaching out to him from the depths of the surrounding night. Their nature was unmistakable.

Howling.

The howling was buoyant and varied, filled with a variety of rich tones. Some notes were deep and sonorous, and others sustained at a higher, sharper pitch. The manifesting night chorus piqued his curiosity even more concerning Magnus.

"What do you mean by the 'pack he sought'?" Mershad asked.

"You know nothing of the Seekers, or the Ulfhednar?" Bergthora asked, an eyebrow raised.

"No," replied Mershad.

"Then you shall learn something more of our people. The

Ulfhednar is sacred and rare among the people of Midragard. Long has the wolf walked alongside our people, ever since the days of the old gods," Bergthora commented, falling silent. A look of amusement came to her face, and she laughed softly. "Now that I speak openly of this, I suddenly find it is all hard to explain."

She looked at the ground for a few moments, as if searching for the best words to convey a clear explanation of the issue to Mershad.

Finally, she brought her eyes back up, and resumed. "There are some … very few … who can seek a special gift of communion between the blood of the wolf, and the blood of man. Some fail, some are frightened off, and some are even slain … it is not known how the Seekers are judged, but it is said the wolves perceive the truest nature of a human. A Seeker cannot hide what is truly held within the heart. Those who are accepted, are adopted, in a way. There is never more than one Seeker, for one pack. Then, they become one of the Wolf Kin. There is something much like this involving the great bears of our lands as well, as I have heard from tales told on many a wintry night.

"There is a time … and I do not know how … when the pack gives a final gift to the Wolf Kin. A dying member of the pack offers its own skin to the Wolf Kin, giving that individual the gift of the Ulfhednar.

"The Ulfhednar and the Berzerks have oft risen to serve the cause of Midragard. They are warriors of unimaginable fury, and, if the tales are true, they are much alike to the wolves and bears they have grown iron bonds with. They are not foes any man would eagerly face in battle."

"Sounds as if Magnus could be the warrior Asa sees in Njal, in that case. Maybe even more so," Mershad observed, entirely fascinated by the strange story.

"If Magnus becomes a full Ulfhednar?" Bergthora laughed heartily. "Njal would soak his breeches before they could even fight."

Mershad smiled politely, not entirely understanding the humor. He wondered what kind of warrior could give another such a high level of fear. The sounds of the howling off in the distance reminded him that any man brave enough to willingly seek out a wolf pack, and then somehow be accepted into it, must be an incredible sort of individual.

As for himself, he preferred to stay within the rampart-enclosed village, under the same roof as several other humans. For once, he did not mind the communal nature of the Midragardan households.

"Do not worry, the wolves do not ever come into the village," she said, as if seeking to soothe any worries he harbored. "There is plenty of game in these lands for them."

"That is good news," Mershad stated, continuing to feel a tingle of fear at the sustained howling. His mouth opened in a light yawn.

"You should perhaps get some sleep," Bergthora suggested, watching him closely.

Another yawn rippled across Mershad's face, and he noticed his eyelids had indeed grown heavier, as the young night had drawn onward.

"You may be right," he admitted, through yet another yawn, wider and longer lasting.

"Day always comes soon enough, and you will be traveling back in the early morning," Bergthora said. "I'll guide you back to where your friends are likely sleeping. The bedding is already set out, awaiting you."

Mershad stood up straighter, arching his back as he stretched out for a few moments. Loosing a long exhale, he turned to follow Bergthora back towards the house.

He smiled to himself, thinking of the tale of the Ulfhednar. He suspected he had not likely even scratched the surface of the surprises lying in wait for him, along the pathway of the future. The world he now lived in was simply incredible to fathom.

NEAR ORANIM

The Unguhur had cultivated only a few patches of luminescent fungus along the walls of the outgoing tunnel. The passage was decidedly smaller, and much more meandering, than the tunnel leading from the cavern-forest to the underground lake and city.

The Avanorans passed slowly through the dim channel on rafts, a palpable tension emanating from the wary passengers. Few words were spoken, and those that were uttered were delivered in whispers and hushed tones.

The lower ceilings and narrower sides pressed in all around the Avanorans with a ponderous weight. The principle sounds filling the men's ears were those of water lapping against the rocky sides of the channel, and the splashes of paddles, as the Avanorans dipped and pulled in rhythm.

The fires from the Arcamon's dark sorcery had fulfilled their lethal purposes. There were no further attacks from the gallidils, though a few dead bodies cluttering the way caused a few momentary delays within the constricted channel.

The Avanoran warriors felt a collective sense of relief when they finally exited the passageway, rounding a final bend and emerging into another sprawling cavern. Another underground forest had been cultivated within the cavern, which looked to be roughly half of the size of the previous one. Like the other cavern, this one was also sufficiently illuminated, with the ambient blue glow from a number of fungal patches.

A host of matured stalks soared up in well-ordered ranks from a thick bedding of refuse, amply built up over the rough, stony flooring underneath. There were a few narrow stalagmites shooting up amid the stalks, echoing the small number of stalactites reaching down from the rock ceiling far above.

Another smooth-surfaced, flat landing area stretched along the riverside. A multitude of rafts was present, empty and tethered to a few heavy-looking boulders.

There was no sign of the former occupants of the rafts, and an unsettling silence hung in the still air. The Avanoran knights directed those engaged in propelling the rafts to land by the rock platform. Arrows and crossbow quarrels were trained fixedly on the forest of stalks.

There was no immediate challenge to the Avanorans as they tied up the rafts and disembarked. The spearmen and knights moved to the fore, forming a protective line in front of the archers and crossbowman, as they filed away from the moored rafts and started across the solid ground.

They proceeded in an orderly, controlled fashion, approaching the growth-filled expanse looming before them. Once they were among the thick, tall mushroom stalks, and other large fungal growths, the Avanorans strode with ever more caution.

The first paces into the shadows of the towering stalks went without incident. A few of the knights even began to surmise the Unguhur had all fled far onward.

In an instant, huge spears were embedded deep into five Avanorans in the front line, as Unguhur warriors exploded out from their positions behind a few bulky fungal stalks. The Avanoran spearmen did not even cry out, as the puncturing weapons drove them from their feet, brutally knocking the wind from their lungs.

Attacks occurred at several different points along the Avanoran line. The sudden strikes threw immediate chaos into the Avanoran force.

A few spearmen and knights scattered out in confusion and panic among the stalks, looking frantically about for other enemy threats. Many remained fixedly in place, several recovering from their initial shock to begin assailing the Unguhur warriors.

A number of disciplined spearmen and knights dropped back, to reform a solid line as the fighting spiraled. Shields held up, the Avanorans tightened their screen for the line of archers and crossbowmen just behind them.

Several archers and crossbowmen sought cover, peering around the edges of stalks with their weapons at full tension. Their eyes darted about, frenetically searching for available targets among their assailants.

The Avanorans finding themselves caught out among the stalks, forward of the regrouped line, gripped their weapons tightly. A nervous sweat broke out as their gazes searched for Unguhur.

Two Avanoran spearmen were looking straight ahead, shields up and weapons extended forward, when an Unguhur warrior manifested right behind them. With its stone-gray hide, and balled-up position at the base of a stalk, its body looked like nothing more than a large rock.

The spearmen had barely sensed the hostile presence behind them when they had their iron-helmed heads smashed together thunderously, within the Unguhur's massive hands. Their lifeless bodies flopped down heavily, shields and spears falling uselessly to the ground.

A knight standing nearby saw the attack and rushed forward. Coming from behind the Unguhur, sword raised up, he slashed down and across with all of his might, striking at the back of the Unguhur's right knee. The blow instantly crippled the large humanoid, buckling it, and sending it sinking to the ground. The enemy warrior emitted a gutteral cry of shock and pain, and reached out for its spear.

The knight yelled as he crashed the iron boss of his long kite shield into the side of the creature's broad head, stunning it temporarily. The dazed Unguhur fumbled with its spear, crying out in fury and pain.

Three other Avanorans arrived in time to drive their spears into the wounded Unguhur, right as the knight brought his sword plummeting down upon the creature from overhead. They tugged and pulled their weapons free from the tough hide of the slain creature, just in time to brace for the next threat.

The killing of the Unguhur drew two of its huge brethren out from their places of concealment. The tall, muscular beings bellowed raucously, bearing down upon the three Avanoran spearmen and the knight. They leveled their great spears at the Avanorans, building up speed.

A cluster of arrows, and a couple of quarrels, cut the charge of the Unguhur warriors short. The accuracy of the arrows and quarrels was exceptional, killing the two Unguhur almost instantly. Only a few missiles thudded into stalks, or hissed harmlessly into the space beyond.

Four more Unguhur were flushed out from their hiding places by the latest slayings. Barreling into the scattered Avanorans, the brawny creatures delivered several swift blows. Battered and broken, a few Avanorans toppled to the ground.

Avanorans came at the four Unguhur from all sides. Effectively encircling the Unguhur, they sealed off any possibility of escape.

A short, ferocious span of combat ensued, leaving the four Unguhur dead with a multitude of bleeding wounds. The bodies of a dozen Avanoran soldiers were strewn about the fallen Unguhur, a testimony to the creature's incredible strength.

No other Unguhur warriors came forth in the aftermath, as an uneasy silence settled once again throughout the rocky chamber. The more battle-hardened of the Avanoran knights took advantage of the respite, rallying the dispersed Avanorans together.

Their sharp voices echoed loudly in the huge chamber, as they brought together all the other knights, spearmen, archers, and crossbowmen, forming everyone into orderly ranks. The previously scattered Avanorans looked extremely relieved to rejoin their comrades.

The knights then led a slow, methodical sweep forward, looking among the high fungal growths for any remaining Unguhur. They led the war parties throughout the cavern with a restrained caution, eyeing each and every feature in the area carefully.

The search narrowed towards the far end of the cavern, on the side opposite the river. Knights and infantry prodded and poked tenaciously at any shadow or mound large enough to possibly conceal an Unghuhur warrior, but none were discovered.

The leaders of the small force assessed their options. The river passing through the rocky chamber continued onward, into another tunnel. The knights knew the Arcamon would be ordering many more Avanorans down into the caverns, to conduct a full, thorough search of every passage, nook, or cranny.

There was little doubt the Arcamon intended to completely eradicate the presence of the Unguhur. The Avanorans were delivering the severest of punishments, one that would not end until thorough extinction had been achieved.

The underground environment was unfamiliar to all of them, far from a simple matter for warriors used to the surface. The horrific incident with the gallidils, demonstrated the grave dangers that lurked in the subterranean depths.

The Unguhur could not be taken lightly, even in small numbers. They were formidable opponents, having proven themselves to be masters of concealment. Immensely stronger than even the most physically gifted of men, a few Unguhur warriors could contend with many Avanorans.

The knights' ruminations were interrupted by excited shouts, coming from beyond the end of the cultivated formations of fungal growths. There were no sounds of ringing steel, or telltale cries of battle, but the energetic calls were filled with urgency.

Hustling to the area, the knights in authority found a group clustered around what looked to be a vertical crease in the rock facing serving as the cavern's far boundary. After a brief assessment, the narrow crevice was revealed to be a passageway, leading from the cavern's interior.

The Avanorans more experienced with the nuances of cave environments detected drafts of fresh air coming through the opening. The discovery was encouraging, indicating a pathway running all the way to the surface.

While pleased to find a passage to the surface, the veteran knights eyed the tunnel with great caution. The passageway was lightless, having none of the bluish light generated by the strange fungal growths found within the caverns and river channels. Pitch black and foreboding, it almost seemed to be daring the Avanorans to enter its maw.

One determined knight raised his long shield up. In his other hand, he carried a round-pommeled sword, with a tapering blade. He took a few deliberate steps forward, moving boldy into the waiting darkness behind the extended shield.

His body quickly disappeared from sight, enveloped by the impenetrable blackness a few paces inward. A couple of spearmen filed in nervously behind the knight, holding their weapons in sweating, tentative grips. Their fears were soon justified.

The lead knight had no warning when an Unguhur spear lunged out of the abyssal darkness. The spear was driven downward with incredible force, plunging over the wide, round-ended top of the knight's shield, penetrating through both mail and flesh.

The spearmen behind tried to turn back as the knight's impaled body crumpled to the ground. They had heard the sickening impact, shattering iron links, and tearing through bone and flesh.

Quickily abandoning reason, the spearmen discarded their shields and spears in a panicked act of folly. While turning to run back to the entrance, both were run through mercilessly, lanced through their backs.

The knights and other warriors at the entrance backed up several paces at the distressing commotion erupting within the dark passage. They gave the opening a wide berth, as several crossbowmen and archers trained their eyes and weapons firmly on the black crevice.

One nervous archer loosed an arrow, which pierced the darkness, and clattered harmlessly a short distance inward off the curving, rocky side of the passage.

The lone shot exposed the principle strength of their enemy's position. The bends in the passageway served to prevent the loosing of missiles, to clear the way for the Avanorans.

A tense standoff developed rapidly. The enemy warriors defending the passage made no move to come forth. None of the knights, or other Avanorans, were about to go into the passageway, well-aware of the mortal danger lurking within.

The veteran knights began to see a relation unfolding between the tactics being conducted in the passageway and the fighting in the cavern behind them. The Unguhur warding the passageway, like those in the cavern, were likely acting as a sacrificial rear-guard for the main body of escapees. They were purchasing time with their blood, gaining precious moments for the others of their kind to gain distance from their attackers.

In the constricted, rocky tunnel, only a miniscule number of determined Unguhur warriors would be necessary to hold a much greater Avanoran force at bay, and force a lingering stalemate. Yet an impasse was entirely unacceptable, even if addressing the obstacle led the Avanorans to a course of action all of them dreaded; informing the Arcamon.

The knights knew a force on the surface could be sent to search out the opposite end of the passage, but a sweep of the woodlands could take a considerable amount of time. A delay was exactly what the Unguhur sequestered in the passageway were seeking, and by the time the opposite end was found, the aims of the Unguhur could well have been achieved.

No knight wanted to be responsible for making a decision to conduct a search above ground, only to find out later that the Arcamon would have chosen a more effective means of dealing with the Unguhur from below. For all the leaders in the Avanoran force, only the Arcamon could determine whether a foray on the surface, or some action underground, would be the most viable path to take.

While knowing the Arcamon's anger would grow with every moment of needless delay, the Avanorans hesitated. None wanted to bear the message regarding the dilemma with the passage. All had witnessed their comrade getting his heard torn off, for simply delivering unwelcome news.

But there was no choice other than sending a report of the impasse to the shadowy being. Anxiety-ridden, the knights dispatched a group of men to carry word of the standoff back to the Arcamon, in the first, larger chamber. The tension thickened as all awaited the response.

Archers and crossbowmen kept their weapons aimed at the passage entryway, while several knights and a throng of spearmen remained alert near the crevice. Sentries in pairs and trios were posted all around the perimeter of the cavern, making sure any threat emerging would have a minimum of advance warning.

After some time had passed, several rafts emerged out of the tunnel connecting to the first cavern. The sentries did not envy the men assigned to work the paddles on the foremost raft, which held the Arcamon.

As soon as the raft pulled alongside the small quay, the Arcamon stepped off, and walked briskly forward. All of the Avanoran warriors near the crevice reflexively grouped closer together, when the Arcamon strode into sight. The entity's movements made little sound, other than the faint swish of its dark attire.

The Arcamon did not bother to consult with any of the knights gathered close by. It walked resolutely towards the opening, coming to a stop on the edge of the jagged sides flanking the entryway.

As all had witnessed in the larger cavern, the Arcamon spoke once again in the strange, unknown language. Its utterances were made with the ghostly quality of voice that had been used when bringing the river to a flaming boil. Also as before, the Arcamon withdrew its great black sword.

The Arcamon called upon deep reserves of inner stamina, and any who could have understood its last words could have proclaimed what was about to happen. "By the fires burning within all who serve the Lord of Fire and the Infernal Abyss, I cast forth living flame, to consume the enemies who resist the Will of Jebaalos."

The Arcamon brought the black sword up and outward slowly, as the white flames burst into life once again from within the ebon blade. The flames, once loosed from the runic inscriptions on the blade's surface, raced up and down the length of the sword, in rapid succession. Their movements appeared barely restrained, as if the fire was very impatient to be set free.

Bringing the sword down methodically in the crevice, the Arcamon began tracing a conspicuous outline with its tip. Starting a couple feet above the Arcamon's head on the left side of the passage, the hooded entity drew the sword down the length of the rocky edge. The Arcamon did not hesitate in continuing the motion across the leveled bottom of the opening, before finishing upward, along the uneven right side.

The purposeful movements were accompanied by the faint sounds of metallic scrapings on stone. Wherever the sword's fiery end touched, blue flames abruptly ignited. The flames began their cascade into pure white, swiftly matching the intensity of the flames on the Arcamon's sword.

The gradients involved were dazzling to gaze upon, as the white-hot stage was reached first on the left side of the passage. The bottom section, and then the right side, followed in sequence, blending smoothy through the spectrum.

The Avanoran warriors watched entranced, as the segments unified into a white-hot fire outlining the bottom and sides of the passage. The Arcamon then lifted its sword up high once again, letting the blade tilt forward slowly, until it was on a level plane with the ground.

The white flames surged in strength, growing until they formed a permeating channel of fire, which began moving forward into the depths of the passage. The mass of flame was now so bright it was difficult for the surrounding Avanorans to even look upon it.

SPIRIT OF FIRE

As the fire proceeded deeper into the passage, the areas behind it were released from its touch. The ensuing stretch of flames was similar to a long, fiery serpent, the length of the snaking flame-channel about six paces long, if measured in human strides.

The flame-channel turned with the contour of the passage, traveling along the rocky path until it was gone from view moments later.

"Follow the fire, now!" the Arcamon ordered one of the knights, in the Gallean tongue. The flames on its own sword ebbed, until the original, black blade was all that remained.

The mailed warrior nodded wordlessly, his visage hidden by the iron facing of his flat-topped half-helm. No Avanoran envied the knight, caught between the fear of what was in the passage, and an even greater fear of the one commanding him. He gripped his shield and sword, striding into the passage, in the wake of the moving fire.

The Arcamon's posture slumped a little after the channel of fire had moved forward. It was evident to all observers that the second use of the flaming sword had greatly weakened the shrouded figure. Yet none of them moved forward, whether to inquire as to the Arcamon's condition, or to venture any assistance. The men's terrible dread of the entity formed an impassable barrier.

Where the Arcamon had held the great sword as if it weighed nothing moments before, the enigmatic being exhibited difficuly bearing its weight when returning the dark blade back to rest in its scabbard. The tall figure remained in place, facing the entrance to the passage in silence.

A few seconds later, agonized cries and throaty screams erupted deep within the passage. The tones were inhuman and guttural, and all the Avanorans knew the fire was rooting out their enemies, without hesitancy or discrimmination. Many listening to the terrible cries shuddered, as the deadly power of the Arcamon exacted its brutal toll.

Several more knights moved to enter the passage behind the first, who had already progressed well into its depths. They moved with greater confidence, as the passage resonated with the anguish of the beset Unguhur, somewhere beyond the advancing fires just ahead of the knights.

With the dense, blistering flames moving ahead of them, the knights had no fears of encountering sudden suprises. The only discomforts came from the tremendous swell of heat within the narrow passageway. Though the knights were battle-hardened men, a couple

145

even felt a shred of sympathy for their beleagured enemies, writhing in a horrific doom.

Outside the passage, the Arcamon turned towards two of the highest-ranking knights within the force. Holding their helms in the crooks of their right arms, they had opted to let their faces cool, while watching the Arcamon work its dark magic. The fear manifesting on their faces was bared to all, as the burning eyes of the Arcamon fixed upon them.

"Cleanse these caves of the Unguhur filth," the Arcamon ordered, in hissing tones. "Drive onward until you find no more. Show no mercy to these beasts. I trust I do not have to do everything myself. If I do, then you all become unnecessary."

The Arcamon kept its penetrating gaze directed upon the knights, letting the full implications take root, and sprout within their minds. Both of the stalwart men turned several shades paler.

Without another word, the Arcamon turned away, and started in the direction of the river. As if momentarily paralyzed, the two knights remained in place until the shadowy form passed from view into the host of fungal stalks. Only then did the color gradually begin returning to their drained faces.

section 11

MERSHAD

Panic spiraled among the bond-servants, retainers, and children on the grounds of King Hakon's homestead. Even the animals laboring or feeding in the open air were hurled into distress, as a vast shadow sprawled across the numerous buildings.

A young maiden's hands slumped listlessly to her side, barely holding onto the spindle and distaff she had been spinning wool with, since the first meal of the day. An older stonecutter, working on a small runestone, dropped the sharply pointed hammer he had been using to inscribe with. In a moment of great irony, his half-finished design included a few stylized, interwoven dragons, but nothing like the mythical shape now flying over him.

Retainers practicing diligently with sword and axe on an expanse of ground ceased their activity, as the dark shadow cloaked them. Among their number was Derek, whose fingers nearly let slip the long-hafted broad axe he had been wielding.

A couple of bond servants, following behind an older woman with a jingling set of keys dangling down in front of her, stopped in their tracks. They had been helping the woman bring a goat towards the cookhouse, but ceased cajoling the animal. The goat emitted sounds of great agitation, despite the reprieve it had unwittingly been afforded. At first, the older woman looked back with a scowl, but then saw why the bond-servants tarried, and why the goat was suddenly anxious, as the enormous shadow engulfed them.

Those inside buildings poured forth, into the open, emerging from the various byres, workshops, cookhouse, and other structures around the estate. A blacksmith paused only long enough to set his hammer and tongs down, on the edge of his turf-built forge, responding to the commotion rising outside the open facing of his workshop. His assistant followed closely behind, and both men's jaws spread wide in amazement, following their fellow Midragardans' gazes up into the sky.

Several women hurried out from a weaving shed. They left behind their tablet-woven braids, newly-made cloth, and other work without an afterthought, gasping and calling to one another, as their chemises swished along with their quickened strides.

Just outside one of the cattle byres, a few men had been engaged in harnessing an ox to a cart loaded with dung. Their intended chore, of taking the organic cargo out to the home field beyond the great hall, was indelibly cut short for the day. They did not even bother to finish harnessing the ox, and broke into a run as a cool shadow blanketed them.

When the clamor was breaking out, Mershad and Kent were in the company of a pair of King Hakon's retainers. The retainers had gone to one of the outer fields, to oversee the construction of one of the four-posted, square structures used for hay storage.

The site was located just beyond a bordered meadow, where a large herd of sheep had been grazing idly upon the fresh spring grasses. The sheep were now gripped by a wave of terror, bleating and milling about in confusion. Workmen, overseers, and sheepherders alike shouted to each other, as a massive form passed above them.

The men working on the hay storage edifice grabbed up their weapons from where they lay, as no Midragardan working in the fields left himself naked in arms. They ran towards the central cluster of buildings, with Kent and Mershad following behind.

Mershad glanced upwards several times, eyeing the oncoming juggernaut, as he hurried to keep pace with the others. He had to skirt the wattle and daub fences of a couple meadows until finally drawing near to the Great Hall, where many Midragardans were now gathering.

Mershad looked just in time to see Svein trotting out from the near end of the great longhall. His eyes sparkled with excitement, and his face was a mask of sheer astonishment. Many men streamed out beside him, as a feverish energy rippled through the air.

"An Elder! An Elder!" Svein cried out, staring towards the cause of all the commotion. He darted a glance towards Mershad and Kent, who were finally able to reach him through the storm of people running to and fro. "I never thought these eyes would look upon one … never!"

The people were not cowering, or running for cover, even if many seemed apprehensive at the dragon's presence. The reaction did not surprise Mershad in the slightest, having already seen the congenial interaction between humans and dragon-kind outside of the village at Glittering River.

The monstrous beast continued to circle around and descend, wings spread out fully in a graceful, looping glide. The dragon's course lowered further and further down, towards the open ground just outside the estate's principle cluster of buildings.

The closer the great dragon approached, the larger its form was revealed to be. By the time the talons of its massive rear legs finally dug into the hard earth, the creature's stature could only be described as colossal.

Mershad drew a breath deeply into his lungs as he felt the tremor of the beast's impact. He stared in wonder, beholding a living creature that towered high over the buildings around him, dwarfing the dragons he had seen before.

Svein had already started forward, heading towards the space where the giant dragon had landed. Mershad broke into a trot, seeking to catch up to him.

His eyes widened, and he almost tripped over his feet, stopping as he saw a number of bulky, four-legged shapes filtering through the crowd of people around him. The cattle in the vicinity of the landing area had been scattered in all directions, disrupted by the dragon. The bellowing, terrified creatures presented a momentary danger, as they barreled through the people heading the other way.

Other than making sure to avoid the cantering bovines, the people paid them little heed. Mershad resumed his forward progress a moment later, as the last of the cattle passed by.

A reverent hush had fallen upon those gathered at the edge of the field, under the sweeping gaze of the great dragon looming over everything and everyone. Mershad slowed down, and came to stand near the front of the semi-circle of Midragardans.

Kent put a hand on Mershad's shoulder, taking a place next to him. "Brave people. I wanted to run," Kent confessed in a lowered tone, in between strained breaths, winded from the long jog.

Mershad's heart raced, but his voice was a little steadier as he whispered back, "These people have no fear of dragons ... but I think if this dragon was a danger, we would have known long before we got here."

His neck craned back as he focused his attention on the immense, silvery dragon. Oddly, the Dragon was standing upon only three of its stout legs.

Its right front leg was raised off the ground, the claws curled tightly, as if holding something carefully within. Mershad's brow furrowed, as curiosity welled up regarding the clenched talons, wondering what might be held inside such large clutches.

King Hakon walked forward to stand before the dragon a few

moments later, his approach heralded by a swelling murmur running throughout the awed crowd. He was accompanied into the open ground by a small throng of armed warriors, as well as the great black wolf Heder, who loped along at the king's side.

"On behalf of the lands of Midragard, I, King Hakon Olafsen, hail and welcome you, great Elder," the king shouted, loud enough for all to hear. The old king's voice was strong and resonant, ringing out clearly in the stillness.

"It is an honor to be among those who saved so many of our little brothers and sisters," the dragon responded, in the Midragardan tongue. Mershad could not imagine anything sounding as regal as the dragon's tone with its fullness of depth, a voice harmonious and resonating with authority. "I, Bevriedak, of the Elder, come to you as a dark age looms over this entire world. I have little time myself, as even now the Ban takes its effect."

"I know that only the gravest of dangers would provoke you to transgress the Ban, great Bevriedak. What is it that we may do for you?" King Hakon stated. "The Elder have not strode upon the surface of Ave since the First Age."

"I have with me Wulfstan of the Saxans, who will speak of the need that brings me into your lands," Bevriedak replied.

The dragon slowly extended his right claw forward, turning it carefully, to lay the backside against the ground. In a delicate manner, his talons unfurled, revealing the occupants carried within.

Within the Elder's grip was a dark-haired, young man, clad in a coat of mail, and wearing an iron helm. Accompanying him was a winged steed, of a type Mershad had not seen before. To his eyes, the creature held a keen resemblance to a large dog, as much as the Fenraren's form was reminiscent of a wolf.

Overall, it was a little shorter at the shoulder, and stockier in girth, than the Midragardan steeds, while being of approximately the same length. The beast had four lean, sinewy legs, ending in sizeable paws equipped with sets of black claws. Sprouting from its back was a pair of dark wings, expansive in proportion to the rest of its body. Rounded ears rose up slightly, to where the loose end-folds flopped over and downward.

The creature was predominantly covered with a shiny coat of short, ebony fur, from its large head to the tip of its extended tail. Patches and smaller markings of a lighter brown hue could be seen on its well-muscled chest, thick muzzle, lower areas of its legs, and around the eyes. The creature displayed a distinctive white patch in the middle of its chest, as well as a few other white spots running along its underside.

"Bevriedak, I will need someone to speak my words in their language," the helmed man called up to the great dragon.

Though Mershad understood everything, he realized many of those around him were looking to each other with perplexed expressions. Before the dragon replied, Svein stepped forward.

To Mershad's great surprise, Svein ventured the idea of having one of the three otherworlders come forward, to translate for the Saxan warrior. As the dragon looked on, Svein then gestured for Mershad, Kent, and Derek to approach, and stand next to him.

Mershad walked forward slowly, with Kent at his side, while Derek emerged from where he had been standing with a number of King Hakon's warriors. Mershad felt a wave of lightheadedness wash over him, as the dragon's attention was drawn towards him and his companions.

The revelation of the three otherworlders brought a stark shift to the proceedings, as the dragon lowered his head, looking closely upon the three men. The Elder's eyelids narrowed, as if in intensive concentration. Mershad could feel the weight of the dragon's scrutiny bearing down on him, the large round pupils looking as if they could absorb his very thoughts.

"Where did you receive the jewels born of Drauenir?" Bevriedak asked firmly.

The three outlanders looked to each other with mystified expressions. Mershad could only think of one possible thing that the dragon was referring to.

"Drauenir?" Derek finally asked. "I am sorry, but I don't understand."

"The great jewel from which yours sprang," Bevriedak replied, as if reluctant to offer more information.

Kent looked down to his chest, and fingered the luxuriant blue stone hanging from his neck. "This? We got these from a blue-robed man called the Wanderer, in the forests of the Five Realms. Before we were brought here."

"The Wanderer? You spoke with him, and received these from him?" the Elder asked them pointedly.

All three of the others nodded, though only Derek spoke in reply. "Yes, and they help us to speak various tongues, and understand them."

"Do you understand what I am saying now?" Bevriedak stated. The Elder looked up, sweeping his gaze over the crowd. "Do any others of you here understand my words? Speak up and say so, if you do."

Mershad looked around at the silent Midragardans. Expressions of puzzlement met his gaze, and it was obvious that none of them understood the dragon's words. He glanced back at the Saxan held within the upturned surface of the dragon's great claws, and found no sign of comprehension.

"Walk forward, seven paces from where you now stand, if you truly understand me," Bevriedak continued.

Mershad and his companions took several steps forward, all of them stopping at the seventh, as instructed.

"I am now speaking in an ancient tongue. It is one not used in any realm of humankind. Only the fruit of Drauenir could bring you understanding of these words," Bevriedak said. "You have been given great favor."

The Elder looked back to King Hakon. "And they were in the Five Realms? Why have they come here?"

Mershad perceived that the dragon had shifted languages, as King Hakon responded without hesitation, "The Unifier would have hunted them down if they had not been brought here. For they are not of Ave."

"Not of Ave?" the dragon asked of King Hakon, a lilt in the Elder's voice reflecting surprise at the king's words.

"Not of Ave. They are from another world," the king replied gravely. "The storms of the enemy fall over the Five Realms, and the otherworlders were brought here for their protection."

The dragon looked back to the three otherworlders. "Tell me something of your journey."

Derek did most of the speaking, as the three told of their arrival in Ave, and everything that followed. Though they did not go into great detail, they spoke of the encounter with the Wanderer, the sighting of the huge force marching along the forest's boundary, their discovery by the warriors of the Five Realms, and the horrific assault on the Onan village from the skies. They finished with the escape from the island when the enemy ships attacked, and the subsequent journey to Midragard.

Mershad could sense the growing interest in the Elder throughout the rendering of their account. When the telling was concluded, the dragon grew silent for several moments.

"I regret that we cannot speak more," Bevriedak said at last. "The Ban takes hold of me, and the Saxan lands have little time. Though I can speak in the language of Wulfstan, and also that of the Midragardians, all will understand the words if you allow him to use the Wanderer's gift."

Before Kent or Mershad could respond, Derek nodded and stepped forward, looking towards the Saxan warrior. "You may use my pendant. Place it around your neck. You will understand them, and they will understand you."

The Saxan hesitated for a moment, eyeing the pendant with a look of great curiosity, and a little apprehension, before walking over to the edge of the claw. Slipping the amulet off his neck, Derek reached up and offered it to Wulfstan. The Saxan crouched down, and stretched his right hand out, taking the pendant from Derek.

Wulfstan stared at the stone for a moment, before slowly hanging it from his neck. After speaking a few words, and confirming that the Midragardans understood him, the Saxan warrior proceeded to address King Hakon.

Mershad listened with increasing dread as Wulfstan related dire tidings regarding a massive invasion that had been hurled into Saxany. An enormous battle was taking place on the western plains in Saxany, at a place called the Plains of Athelney. Wulfstan spoke of more than one realm involved in the invasion of his homelands.

Wulfstan spoke of treachery, as a freeholder on the westernmost edge of the Saxan Kingdom had first tried to conspire with the enemy, only to lose his fortress and land to enemy occupiers. Mershad saw a sliver of justice in that part of the tale.

Wulfstan continually emphasized the immensity of the invading forces, and how desperate the Saxan plight was. Most troubling, there was no way of knowing whether the Saxan lines still held, despite having resisted two days of direct assaults.

He spoke a little about his dreams, seeing a strange, white cloud, and making the choice to hazard a skyward journey. Wulfstan described the incredible flight to find the Elder, including the moment he believed he had forfeited his life. Relating the following encounter with Bevriedak, he spoke of how the Elder dragon had agreed to assist him in the Saxan Kingdom's hour of need.

The Saxan warrior's story was incredible to fathom. Mershad wondered if he could ever have been able to find the courage to truly risk death, in pursuing something so uncertain. Wulfstan had been driven by desperation, with only a dream of legends to hold onto, but his faith had been justified a hundred-fold.

Wulfstan's last words explained that the enemy menace was something that would eventually seek out the Midragardan lands, whether sooner or later. He explained that there was a true common cause between Midragard and Saxany, in the face of the Unifier.

He ended with a plea for any kind of assistance that King Hakon could offer the Saxans. Mershad was profoundly moved by the impassioned supplication, and hoped that King Hakon would give it the most careful of considerations.

As his words concluded, Wulfstan looked around at the Midragardans. His gaze seemed to hold each of them for a moment, as if he were entreating with every one of them personally.

When the Saxan's gaze touched upon him, Mershad could feel pain, fatigue, sorrow, and desperation emanating from Wulfstan. Not one of the Midragardians stirred, as a heavy air hung over all gathered.

Mershad's eyes traveled over to where the old, white-haired king was standing. He could only conjecture from the king's appearance that the words struck powerfully, the weight of them bearing down upon King Hakon's body, such that his posture noticeably sagged. The king looked visibly drained in the wake of the Saxan's tidings, weariness replacing the lively expression on his face when he had first approached the dragon.

Night was approaching, and to Mershad's imagination it seemed as if the old king might well have perceived a sunset occurring across his own world. The king stood silently, with a deeply troubled expression, lost in the shadowy depths of inner thoughts.

As if the debilitating grip empowered by the dark tidings and long-harbored fears suddenly loosed its hold, King Hakon finally straightened up, a determined mien blossoming across his face. The haggardness reflected in his face and body simply fell away, as the king raised his eyes to render an answer to Wulfstan.

"You speak with heartfelt truth, brave Saxan, and you are a great blessing to your people," the king pronounced, in a steady, strong voice. "The battle will come to all of us. Of that I am certain.

"Midragard must be prepared for the coming of this storm. We cannot wait, frozen by inaction, until we are standing alone. The choice before us is clear. The fight will come to each of us later, one by one, or we can fight together, now. All of Midragard must do what it can to help resist the enemy that faces us all.

"We will help you, and Saxany, in any way we can. I will call for a fleet to be assembled … summon what my people call the Leidang … This fleet will be sent forth to Saxany, without delay, once it has been gathered."

Mershad looked back to Wulfstan. The Saxan closed his eyes for a few seconds, and Mershad could see faint movements of the warrior's lips. The man was speaking words not intended for any human ears to hear.

Opening his eyes again, Wulfstan bowed low towards the Midragardan King. "Thank you, great King … thank you. This is beyond all my hopes."

"It will be an honor to any Midragardan to stand at the side of a man such as you," King Hakon replied.

Wulfstan nodded, and looked up to Bevriedak. He called in a louder voice. "You need not suffer the Ban any longer."

The great talons forming the boundary of the living platform for Wulfstan and his steed slowly began to close inward. The Elder dragon began to shift its considerable weight, beginning to turn its vast body towards the open stretch of land behind.

"Hold for a moment, Great Dragon!" the king shouted, suddenly.

The dragon looked back to King Hakon, the talons halting their closure over the Saxan and sky steed. Bevriedak responded. "Speak, King of Midragard."

"If I may ask, great Bevriedak, why does your kind remain so idle, in the face of such a great evil?" King Hakon asked. His voice held no sense of accusation or judgement. It was simply a humble petition, for an answer to a troubling question. "Why do they not intervene in this fight?"

The great dragon did not appear to take offense at the query. If anything, the creature seemed burdened by unspoken regrets, as he answered the Midragardan king in a melancholic tone. "It is not that many of us do not wish to. Our kind took a great oath long ago. We are strongly bound by this oath. Its power can be invoked by Wizards, or others who have been taught how to call upon it.

"The Oath drains us from the moment we come down into the lower areas of Ave. It can slay us if we stay here for very long. If we use our own strength, as we would in war, we merely hasten its grip. The invocation by a Wizard or sorcerer is very dangerous to us. It can bring us to death ere we can reach the Forbidden Dominions far above.

"Yet a terrible choice lays before my kind. We took an Oath to prevent a great darkness, and it may be that we must break this Oath to prevent one now. It may be that by breaking this Oath during this age, we remain loyal to what the Oath truly meant. That is a matter for each of my kind to decide, for their own part. I have chosen for myself."

King Hakon listened to the Dragon's words with a knowing look upon his face. Mershad appreciated the horrible dilemma facing the Elder, and found that he respected Bevriedak all the more for it. The Dragon was enduring the debilitating effects of the mysterious Ban, while not knowing for certain whether the right choice had been made.

"It is indeed a risk you have taken, and a suffering you have embraced for our sake," King Hakon replied gently, empathy laced within his voice. "Do not mistake my question for ingratitude. I fear we need all the help that can be found in this hour."

"And I will try to bring you such help, as much as I can," Bevriedak responded firmly. He then added, more lightly, "Though I hope I will find forgiveness for my violation of an oath kept for thousands of years, if I have chosen wrongly."

Mershad looked a little more carefully upon the dragon. The very surface of Bevriekdak was duller, having lost much of its luster since the winged monstrosity had landed in the field.

The dragon was also exhibiting a more labored manner of breathing. Bevriedak's nostrils flared broadly at the end of its rounded snout. For every few normal breaths, a couple were quicker and tenser, as if a growing pain was taking hold within.

"You test the Ban's power far too much, my friend," King Hakon replied. "Do not tarry here any longer. Go in haste to the Saxans. As I have said in reply to Wulfstan's tidings, let the Saxans know I will summon a fleet, to send to their port of Landahn … as soon as this fleet can be assembled, and set to sail on the seas.

"My thoughts turn to the Five Realms as well, where our people fight alongside the tribal peoples against our shared enemy. There are perhaps a great many others in need of aid that we cannot give in time, from this land. Therefore, I have but one petition for you, great Elder.

"If the Saxan fleet is still beyond their eastern shores, and is not engaged in the war, ask the Saxans to send a few ships to the shores of the Five Realms. I fear that the fighting there will fare badly for those courageous people. They do not have the numbers to resist the great power the western kingdoms can send against them.

"The ages of history carry a strange testament indeed. All of our peoples warred against each other once, Midragardan, Saxan, and the tribes of the Five Realms. We all survived, endured, and learned to respect each other's will. Now, we are all attacked by an enemy seeking to place us under a binding, dominating authority, seated on thrones of power far from own lands.

"It is a power claiming that those in Avanor know what is best for the people of Midragard. That knows what is best for Saxany, and what is best for the Five Realms. I defy such a great, devious evil. Each land must determine its own destiny. It is not for others to impose their will upon a sovereign people. We must now stand together as one, or most certainly each of us will fall into a formless, rootless void, which is little better than nothingness."

Listening to the words of the venerable king, Mershad was filled with a feeling of sheer gratitude towards the place where he and his companions found themselves. Midragard was a most worthy place to take a last stand, if it ever came to such a finality.

The dragon nodded deliberately, looking down upon the Midragardan king. "You speak wisely, good king, with wisdom greater than many who have lived since the dawn of this world. I will seek to do as you wish, though I must rest above for a short time. It becomes clearer that my kind have remained deaf to a cry for justice, but the Ban has not relented in its hold upon us."

"I humbly thank you for coming to us, Bevriedak of the Elder," King Hakon replied.

"May the Almighty be generous to you always, in this world and the next," Bevriedak said, nodding his head towards the king. "May your faith guide you, good king."

Slowly, Bevriedak closed his claw, fully enveloping the Saxan warrior and the sky steed. He turned the claw over slowly, while spreading his beautiful wings out wide. The sight of the dragon with wings unfurled formed a breathtaking image.

Bevriedak crouched back a little on his hind legs, and then thrust forward powerfully, the vibrations from the dragon's heavy steps felt under the soles of Mershad's shoes. The Elder propelled off his front leg for one stride, before leaping upwards on the power of his back legs.

His wings beat down mightily, before reaching up gracefully to clutch at the air again. With a blasting gust of air that toppled a number of the observers onto the ground, and staggered and jostled most of the others, the dragon's body lifted from the ground. The Midragardans who had been bowled over watched from wherever they lay or sat, as the astounding creature swiftly ascended towards the high heavens.

The light of day was indeed ebbing now, as the aqua sky had taken on a deeper blue shade. It formed a beautiful backdrop as the august form of the Elder grew ever smaller, passing towards the northern horizon. Finally, the immense dragon was gone from sight.

A somber, subdued atmosphere predominated among the Midragardans as they quietly turned away from the field, and started back towards the buildings of the homestead. Kent, Derek, and Mershad remained together, well after most of the others had turned back. Wordlessly, their gaze lingered to the north for a few last moments.

Mershad was not surprised at the hushed silence enveloping the estate. There was little doubt that something of monumental importance had just transpired, and the fate of every single person hung in the balance.

WULFSTAN

Equaling the arduous journey would have debilitated the hardiest of the Himmerosen, even in a cooperative mode conserving stamina, and optimizing their rate of flight. Traveling in hard-pressed intervals, one following after the other, with a fresh, fully rested creature taking off where the tiring one could keep up its accelerated pace no farther, the Himmerosen as a team could not have even come close to matching the journey taken by the ancient dragon.

As it was, it only took several hours for the massive Elder to span the incredible distance, traversing the highest reaches of the sky itself. Even more extraordinary, that relatively modest time period included a short respite.

Within the sightless dark of the great dragon's claws, Wulfstan settled himself back into the coarse outer fur of Spirit Wing. Several times during the journey, Spirit Wing shuffled about, modifying the position of its body. After the last adjustment, the Himmeros' curled body position finally allowed the creature to lay its wide head comfortably in Wulfstan's open lap.

After that point, the sustained restlessness that had plagued the winged creature finally ebbed. Wulfstan idly scratched the beast's head, as if it were merely one of the dogs running about his village, on a lazy, mid-summer's eve.

There was little else to do to pass the time, though a full drinking vessel filled with Saxan ale would have been very welcome. The shifts, jostles, and bumps that the dragon's flying incurred, in the winds and turbulence of the upper skies, were not quite as terrifying as before. Like most new experiences, the longer that Wulfstan was around the sensation of flight, the more familiar he became with it. With familiarity came an increased ease to his tender nerves, a development that the Saxan highly welcomed.

He was quickly becoming desensitized to the less abrupt changes in motion, which contrasted greatly with the state he had been in not long before. Frayed and skittish, he had panicked at every dip, lift, swerve, or other undulation, from the moment they had first left the dragon's lofty abode and set out for the lands of Midragard.

Admittedly, there were a few sharp plunges and lurching rises when he had felt his gut seemingly go through his throat. Yet for the most part, he was acclimating better to the unanticipated movements, content to sit in silence, even to the point of relaxation. He was even able to take a few light naps, though after awhile his aching back and stiff legs begged for stretching.

It was truly an incomparable experience, being carried by the dragon. Wulfstan could hear the wind whistling about the clenched talons of the beast, even as he felt the consistent, rhythmic flaps of the creature's massive wings. The outer air beating into every crevice, and the reverberations of incomprehensible muscle power, touched Wulfstan's senses, testifying to an underlying urgency.

The dragon was not content to glide along easily, soaring upon the lifting air currents. Rather, the creature was pressing forward with a notable degree of haste.

The upward climb to those lofty heights had seemed to go on forever when they had left Midragard behind. Wulfstan had keenly felt the force of the sharp climb, pulling strongly upon his body for an uncomfortably extended period. He had been very relieved when he felt the tell-tale shift, as the dragon straightened its flight path out. There was little doubt in Wulfstan's mind that they were now, at the very least, at the altitude of the dragon's snow-white haven.

Such incredible truths were still difficult for Wulfstan to fathom. Everything now transpiring was awash with a surreal aspect, which made a firmer grasp of it all elusive.

Throughout his entire life, he had never traveled as far as he had when the General Fyrd of Saxany had been summoned to defend against the impending invasion. The tiring sojourn from his home village to the Plains of Athelney had certainly been an incredible enough experience. On its own merit, the trek to the Western Marches of the Saxan Kingdom was a tale to last a lifetime. Yet now, it was mind-boggling just to try and comprehend what had happened over the course of the past day alone.

It was sobering to think that he had stood upon the surface of the Plains of Athelney in the morning, and upon the land of Midragard that very evening. Nothing less than an Elder could have accomplished such an astonishing feat, at least by purely physical means.

Yet even the mighty Elder had their limitations. It was something that Wulfstan was coming to appreciate more fully, as the debilitating nature of the Ban was being brought into a clearer perspective.

Just a few hours into the flight from Midragard, they had stopped to take refuge upon one of the floating, white masses hovering within the heights of the Forbidden Dominion. The stay had lasted a couple of hours, during which time Bevriedak had left Wulfstan and the Himmeros to themselves, claiming the need to heal and regenerate from the harmful effects of the Ban.

The changes that had come over the dragon during their descent into Midragard, and the subsequent audience with that land's king, were stark. The creature's vitality had worsened noticeably, over a relatively short amount of time. Bevriedak's breathing had become markedly labored, and the previously luxuriant sheen of the dragon's body had transformed into a clammy, duller gray.

Seeing Bevriedak's condition steadily degenerating was a startling, troubling thing to witness, especially in a creature that appeared so outwardly powerful. Witnessing the Ban's effects inculcated a deep concern, and keener awareness, within Wulfstan.

The dragon had not been the only being for whom the halt in the Forbidden Dominion was beneficial. The respite had afforded Wulfstan a chance to finally stretch his legs and walk about in the crisp, open air. He had marveled at how easy it was to breath the air within the haven, knowing how utterly thin the air had felt to his lungs when flying to the upper elevations on the Himmeros. Like the atmosphere within the interior of the dragon's claws, he knew there was some strange, powerful essence at work around the haven.

While he had felt good about getting out of the confinement of the dragon's claws, he had not been tempted to stray far. He was in an entirely unfamiliar environment, and did not want to take any risks. While he had soon found that he was ravenously hungry, he knew that such discomforts would have to be endured for the time being.

There were some consolations to be had in the midst of the uncertainty and hunger. The sight revealed to his eyes, when Bevriedak had opened up his great claws to let Wulfstan and Spirit Wing dismount, helped immensely to keep his mind off of his empty stomach.

The firmament and stars above had never looked more vibrant or richer than they had when Wulfstan's eyes were drawn up towards the clear, undiluted sky. It was an intensely magical, inspiring sight, wholly unobstructed by clouds, and presented in the purest manner he had ever seen before.

He wondered what the twinkling, shining bodies up above truly were. They filled the deep black firmament surmounting Ave itself, surrounding the gleaming moons making their nightly sojourn across the sky.

Looking around, he had beheld only a slightly less extraordinary view. It was like gazing out over a deep winter's night, with snow-covered lands brilliantly illuminated by silvery moonlight.

The rolling formations spread out before him looked like low hills to his eyes. Turning around in place, he realized that the dragon had flown well into the interior of the haven. The white masses spread out to the horizon, in all directions. In that moment, Wulfstan had felt like he was standing on top of the whole world.

"This does not happen every day, does it?" he had remarked to Spirit Wing, smiling as he basked in the embrace of wonder. The creature had whined in response, and fluttered its wings. "Sore and hungry I bet?"

The Himmeros had replied with a curt bark.

"So you do speak," Wulfstan had quipped, laughing in a carefree manner.

He had then walked a short distance from the Himmeros, continuing to look around. Though he was hungry, his bladder had become full over the length of the journey. Conscious of the fact, he knew he had to answer nature's call and alleviate the discomfort.

Though feeling guilty about blemishing the unsullied white surface of the haven, he had then copiously relieved himself, with his back turned towards Spirit Wing. The sense of guilt was soon replaced by a feeling of great relaxation, unburdened by the discomforting pressure inside of him.

Walking back towards the Himmeros, he had lowered himself down into a seated position, letting himself sink into the soft, comfortable surface underneath. After a few moments, he had lain onto his back. Stretching out with a sigh, he had eased his mind and let the expansive vision of the night sky envelop his senses. Shortly afterward, his eyelids had grown heavy, and he had drifted off into a relaxing sleep.

A timeless darkness and the host of stars embedded within it were still draped across the sky when Wulfstan finally woke up. He had given a little start, as his eyelids spread apart, as the dragon's towering form blotted out nearly all the sky just over him.

"I trust you got a little rest?" Bevriedak had asked him.

Wulfstan had then smiled, as his jittery heartbeats began to settle back down into place. It certainly was not every day he woke up on a hovering surface far above the clouds, with an Elder dragon leaning right over him.

"Yes. I am fine. I am more worried about you, as you are the one flying and carrying us. I hope you received some rest as well," Wulfstan had called back up.

As the dragon loomed above him, his thoughts had roved back to the vibrant image of the dragon, prior to their descent into Ave's lower regions. That memory had been emblazoned within his mind, and the contrast with what his eyes had beheld since was considerable.

Yet the worrisome changes coming over the massive creature had been rolled back since Wulfstan had last seen Bevriedak. The Elder was no longer breathing heavily, and a vibrant sheen had come back over the dragon's body, silvery in hue, and reflective once again. The restored appearance brought the small red circles, scattered all about the dragon's girth, out more prominently, a particular characteristic Wulfstan had noticed on close proximity to the Elder.

"I have recovered enough to endure more of the Ban's grip, for a little while," Bevriedak had replied stoically.

Wulfstan had felt a sharp pang of sympathy in that moment. He had known the dragon had merely renewed his strength just so he could suffer the erosion of his life-force once again, the very second they crossed the unseen boundaries from the Forbidden Dominions into the world below.

"Do humans no longer have a good sense of smell?" Bevriedak had then asked him. There had been an odd timbre to the dragon's voice as the words emerged, conveying an air of amusement.

Wulfstan's attention had been so engaged with the dragon's condition that he had not taken notice of the thick scents of roasted meat saturating the air all about him. Looking downward, just a few paces away, he had seen the partial carcass of some manner of creature laid out. He could still feel the last vestiges of heat from the fires that had thoroughly removed any easy means of identifying whatever kind of creature the section of carcass had once belonged to.

Peering a little closer, with greater scrutiny, and taking careful account of its overall shape, Wulfstan's eyes had widened considerably, as a feeling of shock had passed over him. Realization dawned upon him, bringing in its midst a rather unexpected divulgement. What he had thought was the greater part of a full carcass was a singular, very large leg bone, with ample amounts of flesh still attached to it.

"Bird meat is acceptable with your people, is it not?" Bevriedak had asked. "I know some of your kind, like many in the Sunlands, do not like the meat of swine ... but I have not heard of any human groups who object to the meat of fowl."

"Fowl?" Wulfstan had repeated, still incredulous at the sight before him.

If Bevriedak was hinting truly, the giant leg had belonged to a kind of bird that Wulfstan had never known to exist.

"I devoured much of it, and the other leg was given over to your steed," Bevriedak had then replied. "I believed that you would be hungry. You must eat now, for we must be on our way again, before the dawn breaks. I wish for the Saxans to be well aware of my coming before I land in their midst."

Wulfstan had nodded, comprehending the dragon's intentions, while still working to shake his startled condition. Looking off to the left, he had seen that Spirit Wing was fervently indulging in the meat on another giant leg bone, about twenty paces from where Wulfstan stood. His steed had already consumed a significant amount of the meat down to the bone.

The sight of freshly cooked meat, even if highly unorthodox in its preparation, combined with the succulent aromas wafting off it to swiftly arouse his appetites. Wulfstan had hitherto been extremely hungry when he had fallen asleep, and the condition had not gotten any better since.

Drawing his seax out from the sheath at his waist, he had risen up from the ground, and strode over to the warm, roasted flesh. Setting the single, sharp edge of the blade to the meat, he had carved himself a large slice.

The unusual meat was luscious and tender, each mouthful heavenly to the taste, the juices dribbling copiously off his chin and onto his hands. The meat would have been deemed well-suited for a thane's feast in a great hall, and was like nothing Wulfstan had ever eaten before. He had sliced off several more pieces, and quickly wolfed them down, before his hunger had finally begun to be sated.

Knowing they had little time to waste, and not knowing how long it would be before they stopped again, he had cut off a couple more broad slices to save for later. Returning his seax back into its sheath, he had straightened up, and turned to face the dragon with his lower face amply smeared with the meat's juices.

"Is that better?" the dragon had asked.

"Much, much better," Wulfstan had replied, patting his newly-replenished belly. "Thank you."

"I am sure few from Saxany have ever eaten the meat of a Roc before," the Dragon had stated casually, with another perceptible hint of mirth.

"Never heard of it, this … Roc. But whatever it is, its meat is delicious," Wulfstan had replied.

The dragon had then put his upturned claw forth, speaking a few words to the Himmeros in the strange, unknown tongue that had calmed the sky steed when Wulfstan had first encountered Bevriedak.

Spirit Wing pulled away from the other leg bone with a little visible reluctance, and had trotted back over. The Himmeros leaped back up into the open claw, landing deep within its midst.

Wulfstan had then scrambled up after the steed, careful to cradle the large slices of meat he had salvaged. The Himmeros had already moved further towards the center and lain down, and Wulfstan had taken his own place next to the creature.

He had eased into a crouch, as there was not any sense sitting until the claw was turned into its final position. The Himmeros' big brown eyes had looked up at him, while sniffing eagerly in the direction of the slices of Roc meat.

"Why do you think I cut off a few hunks, and brought them along?" Wulfstan had asked Spirit Wing with a smile.

He had given the Himmeros a playful rub on the head. The dazzling, star-filled sky was dimmed, and then completely closed off, by Bevriedak's long talons, as the Elder brought them together. It had felt a little disconcerting as the dragon gradually rotated his claw over. Bevriedak moved slow enough, so as to give the two travelers ample time to shift their weight and turn, until they were settled in the curve where his talons bent back in and over.

Wulfstan had given his head a little shake to clear the momentary disorientation that suddenly came upon him. Sliding down close to the Himmeros' body, nestling against its warm fur, he had taken in a deep breath as he waited for the expected lurches, thrusts, and crowning leap that he knew was imminent.

Getting fully acclimated to the sensations of flying in the dragon's grip would undoubtedly take more time, but he had felt he was well on the way. The dragon had gone into motion proceeding into its awkward initial gait just after Wulfstan had time to take a few drawn-out breaths. Bevriedak had left the solid surface of the high haven behind as he gave himself to the sky, producing the disconcerting, sharp leap in Wulfstan's gut that the Saxan was quickly coming to dread.

They had leveled out almost immediately. Wulfstan had leaned back as the dragon flapped its great wings, and rapidly built up its speed, focusing on relaxing the tension within him.

Wulfstan's thoughts returned to the time that he and Spirit Wing challenged the heights where they now flew. He recalled the ensuing descent into an unconscious oblivion that had rendered him entirely helpless, and the memories had sent an icy chill snaking down his spine. He had come perilously close to death, as had his courageous, dutiful steed. The animal had pressed upward, even when its instincts for self-preservation had undoubtedly screamed for it to cease its climb.

After some time, the general monotony of the journey helped cause the fearful memories to fade, until Wulfstan had finally dozed off into a light slumber. He returned to a half-awake state, after about an hour, before swiftly falling into sleep's embrace again.

He repeated the entire cycle a couple more times, before coming back into a state of full awareness. He quietly passed his waking moments in calm idleness, devoid of any significant stimulation to his senses, other than the fluctuations of the dragon's flight.

After awhile, his hunger began to beckon, and the extended period of inactivity facilitated a desire to do something, even an endeavor as simple as eating. As he had promised the stalwart Himmeros earlier, he shared one of the remaining slices of Roc meat with his winged companion, while consuming another by himself.

Within the impenetrable dark, he had extended the slab of still-juicy meat forward. It was not long before he heard the probing sniffs of the Himmeros, as he felt the sky steed lift its head up, and shift about in response to Wulfstan's movements and enticing offering. With a gentle tug at first, Spirit Wing firmly gripped the meat in its jaws, and took the contribution from Wulfstan. The creature gulped the meat down quickly, well before Wulfstan was finished with his own smaller piece.

Wulfstan then divvied up the remaining meat between himself and the steed, proceeding slower by breaking off smaller bits of the food. He fully mollified his hunger by the time he was finished with the last bite.

The cold wet nose of the sky steed brushed across Wulfstan's cheek, right before he felt the rough, damp edge of the creature's tongue licking his face. Wulfstan endured a few more passes of the broad tongue as the Himmeros affectionately expressed its gratitude. Wulfstan rubbed the creature's head gently, smiling in the dark, and settled back against its warm body.

At long last, Bevriedak finally began a long, downward descent. The sustained drop in altitude created a very queasy sensation, which welled up steadily within the depths of Wulfstan's gut. The feelings almost threatened to spoil the contents of his recently consumed slices of meat. It was all that the Saxan could do to keep from retching, as he fought against the surging waves of dizziness engulfing him.

His breathing came in quick, short gasps, as his nerves hurriedly frayed. The great dragon was dropping down far quicker than it had on the descent into Midragard. That approach had been conducted in a gradual decline, smoothed by extended periods of gliding. To Wulfstan, the current descent felt more like a plunge.

Even though he could see nothing from within the impenetrable blackness, Wulfstan closed his eyes, praying that the horrid feelings would end soon. Pressing even tighter against the Himmeros, he wrapped his right arm around the creature's neck to steady himself. Thankfully, Spirit Wing did not protest, its own nervous whines and fidgety movements announcing that the creature did not feel confident with the sensations of rapid descent either.

Mercifully, the descent transpired for much less time than the one into Midragard had. Bevriedak sharply leveled his flight out, and continued forward at a slower, cruising pace. Wulfstan breathed a deep sigh of relief as he felt the quick change, slowly regaining a more normal level of breathing. Disheveled, and more than a bit nauseous, he worked to collect his thoughts.

There was only one reason why the great dragon would have come down out of the Forbidden Dominion, and left the sanctuary that shielded the creature from the wasting effects of the Ban. The sharp decline signified they were now coming into the skies over Saxany itself, or were already well into the lands of Wulfstan and his forefathers.

There was a part of the Saxan ceorl that sorely wished he could look out at the lands they were now passing over. We wanted to see the breadth of his homeland in a way he had never imagined being able to do, before being introduced to the act of flight.

He knew that under the dragon's talons was a vista of rolling hills, thick forests, cleared fields, villages, rivers, and towns, passing by in abundance. Wulfstan made a silent promise to himself within the dragon's claws. If he were to somehow survive the terrible war that had befallen his homeland, he would seek to do anything he could to secure a sky steed, for one long ride across the skies over Saxany. Perhaps such an excursion could be undertaken with the adroit steed that had already accompanied him so faithfully, and successfully, on his current journey.

Yet he knew that personal desires would have to wait. First and foremost, he had to finish his task, and then he needed to survive the war. The first goal was within sight, but he did not want to ponder his chances at the latter.

As the dragon diligently soared towards the western reaches of Saxany, Wulfstan expected to soon hear the cacophony of drums, horns, and furious combat, heralding the final approach to the battlefield. Yet nothing but the sounds of rushing, whistling winds, and the occasional grunts and whines from Spirit Wing, entered his ears.

Worry gradually rose within Wulfstan, and he wished more than ever he could see what was happening outside of the dragon's claws. They might still be far from the battlefield, but there was also the dreadful possibility that they were too late in returning. Impatience and speculation tormented him, as he did not have the answers that could ease his mind.

He did not know what he would do if the Saxan lines had been broken, and the invading horde was now spreading into his beloved homelands. The mere thought of such a disastrous development was far too horrid to even contemplate.

He tried to console himself with the notion that they were too high for sounds coming up from the surface of Ave to reach him, especially encased as he was within the dragon's claw. But he doubted strongly that he would miss the din generated from tens of thousands of warriors and beasts embroiled in heated battle.

His nerves on edge, the Saxan warrior could do little but listen anxiously for anything that would indicated the presence of battle, as the dragon flew steadily onward. After a little more time had passed, an abrupt lurch in the pit of his stomach alerted him that they were going into another descent. This second one was much gentler and more gradual than the prior one had been, and Wulfstan fathomed they were drawing near to the place where the dragon had decided to set down.

Muffled sounds reached through the dragon's talons to his ears. As he focused upon the new sounds, he realized they were from horns, blaring resonantly.

The sounds were instantaneous reassurances to his troubled mind, testifying that the fighting on the Plains of Athelney had not ended. With the battle still ongoing, Wulfstan reasoned, the enemy had not penetrated farther into Saxany.

He could not tell whether the horns were Saxan, Avanoran,

or any other, but, in a strange way, the continuing blasts from outside spurred his flagging hopes. The mere fact that the dragon was landing also indicated something favorable, bolstering his morale further.

A chorus of excited cries erupted, though Wulfstan could not make out any individual words, which might ascertain the nature, or source, of the voices. Just one momentary glimpse on the other side of the dragon's talons would have immediately given him an answer, but he had no choice but to remain mired in the darkness of the claw's interior.

A couple of discernible words would have been a godsend in that tense moment, as they spiraled downward on the dragon's outstretched wings. The dragon gave a few more powerful flaps, adjusting his downward course, as Wulfstan girded himself. The answers he sought would not be much longer in coming.

Wulfstan felt the brief, momentous jolt as Bevriedak finally landed his bulk upon solid ground. The dragon's back legs were the first to touch the surface of Ave, just a moment before his one free foreleg set down firmly, bracing and balancing his massive body.

The Saxan warrior felt Bevriedak extend his right talons forward, and place them lightly against the ground, as the moment of truth arrived at last. The Elder turned the appendage slowly and delicately, so Wulfstan and his steed could again adjust themselves to the rotation.

Now standing on the palm of the creature's broad forefoot, Wulfstan took in a long, slow inhalation, letting it out in a similar, controlled fashion. Light then poured in to chase out the dark, as the great claws separated, falling away all around Wulfstan and the Himmeros.

Masses of Saxans filled Wulfstan's vision, a dense sea of jubilant, curious, and attentive faces. The sight exhilarated the ceorl. The Saxans were still standing strong in the great battle; unbowed, and unconquered.

To the crowd's eyes, there was no mistaking the garb of the man emerging into sight from the dragon's opened talons, or the nature of the winged steed with him. Those nearest to the titanic dragon, though still keeping a modest field's length of distance between themselves and the enormous beast, started to break out into a zealous, euphoric cheer.

Almost immediately, those in the foremost ranks started to surge forward, as those arrayed behind took up the raucous cheering. The adulation swelled into a mighty, deafening crescendo, rippling back like a great, rising wave.

Wulfstan was nearly dumbstruck, having no idea why he was

receiving such an incredible reception. The eyes of the men, thanes, ceorls, and peasant levy-men alike, were filled with excitement, wonder, and unmitigated joy, as they drew nearer to Wulfstan.

They looked expectantly at Wulfstan, and up at the great dragon, as the boisterous overture was sustained. Others were running in towards the marshaled throng from all over, adding swiftly to the widening mass gathered before the Elder dragon.

From what Wulfstan could tell, Bevriedak had landed close to the palisade-enclosed encampment. They had set down in a position roughly between the camp and the frontal battle lines.

Yet there were absolutely no signs of active battle or the enemy. A deep-seated hope tugged at him then, as he wondered at the enemy's conspicuous absence.

Spirit Wing then tugged at its tether with vigor, evincing eagerness to set its paws on Ave's soil once again. Wulfstan focused himself, and walked over with the tether in a firm grip to where he and Spirit Wing could drop down together.

Wulfstan let his grip on the tether go, and the Himmeros alighted gracefully, after a short leap. The Saxan then turned around, crouched, and then slid down to the grassy surface just beneath the dragons' claw.

When his feet touched the ground, Wulfstan gazed upon the wide line of warriors encompassing the perimeter around him. They were all armed and dressed for war. From their attire, he could tell there were many warriors of notable rank near the front, whether thanes or more affluent ceorls.

The cheering slowly died down, although there was still a low hum from innumerable murmurs, as the Saxans talked amongst themselves within the vast crowd. Wulfstan's chest swelled, as he drew a full breath in to begin addressing them.

"I am Wulfstan, son of Ealdred, of Sussachia. I serve our great King Alcuin of Saxany, and his majesty's loyal ealdorman, Byrtnoth, of Sussachia," he called loudly to the surrounding warriors, bringing a complete hush to the crowd, as his voice carried out over them.

"Wulfstan, son of Ealdred," one of the men in the front ranks, garbed in chain mail and most likely a thane, called back. "You have quite powerful allies, it would seem. Our hopes have been with you."

"Your hopes?" Wulfstan replied to the brawny, mailed warrior, surprised at the words. He had not expected to hear that any others' hopes lay with him, especially from one he did not know.

"Word of your flight to the heavens has spread all throughout the camp, tidings given to us by one of the sky riders, a man named Ulfcytel," the man answered.

As the warrior quickly explained the rest of it to Wulfstan, it came to light that Ulfcytel had witnessed the direction in which the daring Saxan had gone, following their separation. Ulfcytel had evidently watched Wulfstan for some time, judging by the conclusions the veteran sky rider had spoken of upon his return. It would not have come as a surprise to Wulfstan if Ulfcytel initially regarded him as a rash fool, but clearly a shred of hope had taken root, and grown swiftly among the Saxans.

"Ulfcytel spoke much of your flight. He watched you go well beyond the boundary where the sky steeds dare not go," the thane stated. "Your bodies never fell back to the world, even though no creature from the surface of Ave could possibly survive in such heights. He swore that something massive moved with great speed at the edge of his vision, beyond the place where he could no longer see you, or your steed."

Wulfstan could not blame the Saxan skyrider for having a keen interest towards his strange mission. His procurement of a steed had not been the most ordinary of requests.

"Ulfcytyl, and others here, believe that such a reckless ascent could only mean that you sought after a creature of legend. This was a thought and hope held by many in our encampment ... and evidently not one rooted vainly. A creature of legend you have indeed brought back with you," the thane replied. A euphoric tinge present in his voice, a look of unbridled wonder shone within the thane's bright eyes as he gazed upward.

Wulfstan could only imagine what the sight of his return, with an Elder dragon harboring him, could have meant to the thane and many others at that moment. Yet he knew that he did not have much time. There was one burning question he needed to push off the edge of his tongue, before things went any further.

"Tell me, what has happened here? There is no sound of battle ... have we won?" he asked the thane.

"No," the thane replied ruefully, shaking his head. "The enemy camps are still over the horizon. They did not array for battle this morning. There is talk they are trying to send forces through the forests, bordering the neck of the Plains. But they will find that area far less promising than the fighting here on the plain itself."

While not bringing the relief that word of a full retreat would, the news that there was a sustained cessation in the hostilities was a welcome tiding. The enemy might be regrouping, and readying for another assault, but a precious gift of time had been given to the hard-pressed Saxans. Such a respite promised to be very favorable to Wulfstan's ongoing endeavors with the Elder.

"Then I fear I should waste no more time. Perhaps more can be done to aid our homeland. Our new friend before you, Bevriedak of the Elder, cannot remain here for long. The power of an ancient Ban assaults his strength even now. He has taken me very far to seek help for our lands, and I bring good tidings to all Saxans," Wulfstan replied quickly, and wasted no time in tendering the news he bore to all listening. "The Midgragardans will be sending a fleet to our shores … to the city of Landahn itself. Their king, a great man named Hakon, has agreed to aid us in this war."

There was another low murmur, as the Saxans looked to each other with expressions of surprise. All of those that had understood Wulfstan spoke quickly amongst themselves, passing the news onward to the ears of those in the ranks behind. Wulfstan's tidings rippled swiftly back to the farthest edges of the still-growing multitude, and the air buzzed with a vibrant energy.

"This is welcome news indeed! What of the Midragardans?" a lean southerner then questioned Wulfstan. "How long will it take them to reach here?"

"I do not know the answer, as I know little of travel upon the seas. Their King is sending a fleet of ships as quickly as he is able. I do not know the distance from Midragard to here. A more learned man could tell you that," Wulfstan replied.

"What of these … dragons? You spoke of this dragon as of the Elder. Is your friend truly one of the fabled, ancient dragons?" asked another warrior tentatively, a tall man clad in chain mail.

He had spoken in a low, hushed voice, almost whispering the word 'dragons', as if for Wulfstan's ears only. The word 'Elder' was spoken so lightly that it was barely audible to him.

All the while, the man stared upwards at the towering dragon, who was peering out over the assemblage. Wulfstan could not stifle a smile, as it was still beyond his own comprehension as to what his desperate notion and effort had accomplished. He could only begin to imagine what it was like for the beleaguered Saxan warriors to have an Elder show up suddenly on the battlefield, with one of their own fellow Saxans accompanying the mythical creature.

"This great dragon is indeed one of the Elder, and I know what many of you would ask," Wulfstan orated, raising his voice as much as he could muster. "Many of you may not even know of the Elder, but I have learned much in a short time. What I tell you is true, much by my own experience.

"This great dragon has violated an ancient oath, one that comes with a grave price, to help us. We can ask no more than what he is able to give. I could not ever have hoped to get to all the lands, such as Midragard, even were I to have several of the swiftest Himmerosen that ever lived.

"There is terrible risk being taken by Bevriedak. An enemy Sorcerer can bring this Elder to great harm, and the longer he stays on the surface of this world, the more his strength is drained."

Wulfstan wondered why the great dragon had said nothing as of yet, and he turned to look up at Bevriedak. The dragon was still gazing out over the area, his body so motionless that it was like an enormous statue.

Wulfstan could not yet tell how much the Ban had effected Bevriedak. The dragon's scales still held their silvery luster, but he knew they did not have very long. As Wulfstan had come to appreciate, time was a very delicate matter to an Elder held within the grasp of the Ban.

"And there is one more thing I have been asked. There are others oppressed by the Unifier, even now," Wulfstan continued, looking back to the assemblage. "The tribes of the Five Realms, to the north of our lands across the sea, are also under an attack and invasion, as we are here.

"Their warriors and many Midragardans that went to fight by their side may become trapped, from what I have been told. The King of Midragard, Hakon, asked about our own fleet of ships. If our own fleet is not yet in the fighting, he asks that we send a few ships to the north, to help those that may have survived to gain a chance to leave those lands before all is lost."

Those that looked to be of the rank of thane, or were prominent household guards, looked to each other. Several spoke quietly together, for a few moments, as Wulfstan awaited some manner of response. Mounting anxiety built in Wulfstan as they deliberated, his thoughts fixed to the condition of the Elder.

Looking back at Wulfstan, the first thane who had spoken to him after he had landed replied, "We need to summon one of the rank of Count, or Ealdorman. This is not a request any of us have the authority to address."

"I do not think you will have to issue any summons," a tall, lean fellow behind the thane interjected. The warrior was looking over his shoulder, towards the back of the gathering.

The assembled ranks behind had already begun to part, clearing a pathway, as a few men mounted on horseback approached. The lead rider was seated upon a midnight black horse, a regal-looking warrior whose steady, confident gaze rested squarely upon Wulfstan. A rider just behind carried a high standard rippling in the robust breezes, colored entirely in black, with the image of two golden moons woven into the fabric.

All but the lead figure wore helms of iron, and every one of the riders wore coats of mail. They did not come to a stop until the black horse was drawn up right before Wulfstan.

The horses in the entourage snorted and pawed at the ground nervously. Wulfstan could sense the riders' mastery over their agitated steeds, simply to keep them in place.

Wulfstan did not know exactly how he should respond. He had recognized the man on the black horse right away. He had already addressed Wulfstan, in a way, as part of a large group of warriors in the encampment. Yet Wulfstan had never been the sole object of the man's attention, as he was right then.

Somewhat awkwardly, Wulfstan lowered his eyes, gave a low bow, and said in a deferential tone, "My Lord." He raised his eyes up expectantly, not quite sure how to proceed.

"You have done an incredible, brave thing, young warrior … and it appears your great risk has met with considerable success," Aelfric said to him, glancing up for emphasis at the dragon looming over them both.

Aelfric then dismounted, letting a nearby Saxan hold on to the tether. He brought his stoic gaze back to focus upon Wulfstan, and continued.

"Byrtnoth should be most proud to have men like you in his province. You well know I am Aelfric, Ealdorman of the Wesvald, and commander of King Alcuin's army. You were among those sent by me to the traitor's fortress just a day past. I am not one to easily forget faces, though I admit I was not expecting to see yours with an Elder standing behind.

"Rise up, you must not delay in telling me what word you bring to us in these evil times."

Wulfstan slowly straightened back up, looking into the man's face. The noble warrior had a strong countenance, with a well-formed chin, wide forehead, and large nose set in front of hazel, deep-set eyes. His light brown hair hung down straight, to end just underneath his ears, and his beard and moustache were trimmed to a shorter fringe. He was not a particularly large man, being of a relatively modest build and height.

Resting on the outside of his mail coat was a lone silver pendant, in the shape of the Western Church's Sacred Spear. He was wearing a deep green woolen tunic underneath his mail coat, the ends of the sleeves poking out, displaying the decorative woven bands of yellow at their cuffs.

The signs of his noble, high status were everywhere upon his person. A leather belt, mounted with a triangular-shaped buckle girded his waist. The buckle was gilded in gold, etched with intricate symbols too small for Wulfstan's eyes to make out, and mounted with garnets.

In a similar fashion, the leather baldric slung down and across his chest also featured a golden-gilt buckle, to fasten the ends together in front. The scabbard hanging from the baldric was decorated with silver fittings, including the mouth and the chape at the end. Sitting secure in the scabbard was the finely-crafted hilt of an exceptional sword.

A three-lobed iron pommel, with gilded silver bands wrapped around the base of the pommel and running in between the crevices in the lobes, rested at the top. The hilt had three silver bands, inlaid with patterned designs, ringing it. One was in the middle of the grip, with the other two at the edge of the pommel, abutting the downward-curving iron crossguard.

As if a smaller cousin, the three-lobed end of a seax rested in a folded leather sheath, the latter suspended horizontally from a couple of bronze loops at Aelfric's waist belt, opposite the sword. The pommel was graced with silver décor closely matching that of the sword, and rested up against the simple silver fitting at the sheath's mouth. The sheath ended in a stylized, silver dragon's head, which curved outward from the leather body.

Even the round shield hanging from its guige strap was ornate. The raised, conical shield boss of iron culminated in a silver-inlaid disc finial. Golden discs were set directly atop the places where rivets ran through the wood to secure the ends of the shield's central grip. A long strip of artfully etched gold ran along the top of the shield, covering the rivets for the guige strap itself.

Never comfortable in the presence of thanes, Wulfstan found that he was extremely nervous before Aelfric, indisputably one of the greatest men in all of Saxany. He hesitated, remaining silent for an extended moment, as his heart beat noticeably faster.

"Tell me of what you have done, and learned," Aelfric urged him more firmly.

Slowly, Wulfstan began to relate his incredible tale to Aelfric, gaining more confidence with every moment of the telling. He briefly covered his prior dreams, and the sighting of the white patch during the journey to Godric's fortress.

Several times, he feared Aelfric would perceive him to be stricken with insanity. He forgot the immediately apparent fact that the gigantic, living proof of his endeavor was there for all eyes to see, soaring up from the ground level just behind him.

Aelfric listened calmly to the full story. The Saxan Ealdorman interrupted on only a couple of occasions to clarify a small point, or to ask for a little more elucidation from Wulfstan on a particular aspect of his incredible account.

Wulfstan finally relayed the request given to him by King Hakon, regarding the use of the Saxan fleet to aid the Midragardians and tribesmen of the Five Realms. Aelfric's eyes narrowed, his brow furrowing as Wulfstan conveyed King Hakon's wishes.

When Wulfstan finished rendering the account, Aelfric nodded slowly back to him, and then looked up to the dragon. Wulfstan followed Aelfric's gaze and saw that Bevriedak's attention was now fully turned upon them. The dragon's deep, wizened eyes were honed upon just the two of them, to the exclusion of all others.

"Everything is as he says, Aelfric of the Wesvald," Bevriedak suddenly boomed.

If there ever was such a thing as an audible gasp coming in unison from thousands of people at once, the sound that emerged from the subdued, observing crowd could only be described as such. Even

Aelfric's intensive demeanor could not hide the outright astonishment upon hearing the dragon speak succinctly in the Saxan tongue. Only Wulfstan himself was not surprised.

"I thank you … Great Elder," Aelfric replied in a reverent voice, giving the creature an extended low bow, as if a commoner rendering obeisance before a king. "I understand what you have taken upon yourself, for our behalf, Great Elder."

The crowd grew quiet, listening intently for the dragon to speak again. After a moment, the Elder responded.

"I will do as much as I may. As you have heard, there are great dangers to our kind when we are upon the surface of this world," Bevriedak stated.

"Then know I will have word sent right away, to see what transpires with Aethelhere of Wessachia, who commands the fleet of Saxany," Aelfric replied. "It is doubtful the enemy would try to contest the seas off the northern shores of our lands. The waters in this time of year are far too rough for passage by even one ship, much less a fleet of vessels.

"It may be that we can send some ships to the help of the Five Realms, and to those Midragardans who have gone to their aid. Great Elder, I cannot leave this army myself, as the enemy's intentions here are not yet known, and my King has placed the responsibility for this army into my hands.

"But I can send a few riders now. And there is no better man to go forth as an emissary with you, than the one you have already carried with you. His courage has earned that right, more than any man among us."

The Saxan ealdorman paused at the conclusion of the words, giving Wulfstan a brief, pointed glance, before looking up again at the dragon. Wulfstan was both pleased and encouraged, able to remove the last vestiges of anxiety over the matter of whether he would be regarded as insane, or a great fool, for having attempted to reach the Elder.

"I will help Wulfstan convey this message," Bevriedak responded resolutely.

Aelfric nodded. He turned towards one of the mounted men by his side. "Bring me one of the priests, or monks, with some parchment, ink, and a seal. Make haste on this."

The warrior turned his horse about, and headed away quickly.

All of them waited until the man of Aelfric's household guard returned at last, leading a priest on horseback just behind him.

He was a round-faced man of average height in the prime of his years. While possessing a broad mouth and nose, both of which looked to be quite conducive to merry expressions, the priest's mien was now one of sheer incredulity, as the horses drew to a full halt. He craned his neck far back to look all the way up towards the dragon's head. For a precarious moment, it looked as if he were about to topple backwards out of his saddle.

The priest could not take his eyes off the dragon as he slowly dismounted, tightly gripping the writing materials requested by Aelfric under his arm, and in his hands. As the cleric trod closer, Wulfstan could see telltale signs that the priest had been very involved in the bitter events of recent days.

His face was streaked and grimy, and his long, rough-spun, brown woolen tunic was stained and tattered in many places. Even the silver spear amulet hanging from a leather chord at his neck was dull and smudged.

Wulfstan recognized the dark hues of dried blood copiously blemishing the priest's garments. The priest had a drawn-out, highly fatigued appearance, as if sheer willpower alone, or some other outside power, was keeping him standing upright. Wulfstan was halfway surprised that the priest did not trip over his own feet, as he was almost dragging them across the ground.

"Amazing," the priest muttered in a low, detached voice. His eyes remained fixed upon the dragon, as he made his way towards Aelfric and Wulfstan.

"Father Dafinus, we live in very dark times, but there are yet some wonders," Aelfric commented, with a brief chuckle, as the highly-distracted holy man continued over to them.

"An Elder? Truly? One of the Elder?" the priest queried.

"Yes, good priest, an Elder," the dragon replied. Wulfstan could detect that Bevriedak was more than a little amused at the priest's awed reaction.

"Father Dafinus, I could use some assistance," Aelfric said. "I need to send word to the northeast, to Aethelhere, with the Saxan fleet. I must send this word in writing, under my seal."

"Of course, of course," Father Dafinus replied quickly, as if snapping out of his haze, though his gaze still remained squarely oriented towards the dragon.

"I believe you will need to actually look at the parchment, to see what you are writing," Aelfric suggested with a warm smile. Wulfstan could perceive the great familiarity the Saxan ealdorman enjoyed with the priest.

"Oh yes, of course, you are absolutely right, Aelfric," Father Dafinus replied, though his eyes did not move.

"You will need to look upon your words, good Father, to write them clearly," the dragon then added from above, with a slight nod, as the Elder's eyes focused in on the writing materials in Father Dafinus's hands.

Wulfstan had to catch a laugh in the back of his throat, not quite sure whether letting it free would be considered improper. Aelfric evidently saw no such problem, as he was already laughing heartily at the dragon's admonition.

The priest gulped, and he finally took his eyes from the massive beast. He blinked rapidly several times, as he collected himself. "Yes … yes, of course. Just tell me what you need for me to put in writing, Lord Aelfric."

"Let us first create a surface for you to write on," Aelfric said.

The priest looked back up to the dragon, as Aelfric conveyed instructions to the men around him. There was a little fear in the priest's eyes as he cleared his throat.

"I … thank you for coming … good Elder. I am truly sorry for what happened to your smaller kin … in these lands long ago," the priest stated apologetically.

As Father Dafinus spoke, Wulfstan comprehended there must have been truths to the old dragon legends he had heard as a youth. Some of the creatures were said to have been real terrors to humankind, but a stronger suspicion was growing within him that he had not been given the full story. He could now imagine dragons that had had no quarrel with mankind, who had still been sought out in remote places, simply to be slain, or driven even farther off.

Wulfstan did not believe that Bevridak could ever be an apologist for the aggressive, violent dragons that had menaced humans in some of the old stories. Yet neither could Bevriedak countenance at any level what had been done to dragons in the central and western lands.

Wulfstan knew that Bevriedak held a great affinity for his lesser kin. The dragon had made his inclinations very clear, openly honoring the fact that the Midragardans had provided a haven for the lesser dragons, within the midst of the latter's harrowing persecution.

"You were not even alive to commit any offense when the last dragons were slain or driven away from these lands. You bore no part in it, and need offer no apology," Bevriedak replied in a somber, sincerity-filled voice.

The reply by the dragon was something of a comfort to Wulfstan. It was good to know that the Elder who was helping Wulfstan's people harbored no grudges, especially against some of the very descendents of those that had chased Bevriedak's smaller kin out, or hunted them to their destruction in distant ages.

Wulfstan committed the response to memory. It was a golden piece of wisdom born out of the process of ages of experience.

Often had people accepted the idea that children answered for the sins of parents or even ancestors, whether it was the matter of a child born with a deformity, or even a royal lineage that had run into some grave misfortunes. Wulfstan had never rested easily with such pervasive beliefs, and the words of the Elder resonated clearly with his truest, heartfelt feelings.

The priest nodded back to the Elder nervously, though looking visibly relieved at the dragon's response. "Thank you, good Elder. Thank you for coming to our help."

By then, a makeshift table had been formed, involving a couple of ale casks and the surface of an undamaged shield. Father Dafinus shifted a bit uncomfortably, as he sat down upon another cask brought forth to serve as his seat.

He placed a few sheaves of parchment down on the shield's surface, setting a small erasing knife alongside. He whetted his quill with ink from the horn carefully held in his left hand, and looked expectantly to Aelfric.

Aelfric then dictated the specific words of the request for Father Dafinus to inscribe on the parchment. He paused periodically, so that the priest could finish writing each segment of the words upon the sheaf.

A couple of times, Father Dafinus had to ask for a momentary pause, in order to scrape away markings he was not satisfied with. He would then brush the surface of the parchment with his hand to remove any shavings, and resume writing.

The wording given by Aelfric to Father Dafinus was direct enough. The missive requested that if Aethelhere was not otherwise engaged to immediately send vessels to the eastern coast of the Five Realms.

The suggested landing site Aelfric put into the message was a place located on the far southeastern coast of those lands. It carried an unusual name, called the Water Head-Cradle.

When Aelfric was finished, and Father Dafinus had rendered all the words to parchment, they incurred another small delay as a brand of fire was procured to heat the wax used to seal the parchment. Folding the parchments over, Father Dafinus dribbled the melted wax into a glob on the parchment's free edges, and then firmly imprinted Aelfric's personal seal, before allowing the wax to cool and harden.

Aelfric accepted the sealed parchment from Father Dafinus, and turned to a couple of men standing at the front edge of the gathering.

"I will need you to convey these parchments to Aethelhere with haste. If the fleet is able to send some vessels, we will need some relays of sky steeds set up … both to help coordinate the ships, and to keep me informed here, with our forces in the west."

A young, fair-haired warrior with a strapping build nodded dutifully to Aelfric. "There should still be a few fresh steeds remaining in burhs along the way."

"Then saddle yourselves, and follow the great dragon to the northeast," Aelfric ordered him. He then added, with a wry smile, "I am sure it will not be difficult to follow the dragon's form in the sky."

The young warrior nodded again, showing no mirth at Aelfric's lighter comment. "At once, my Lord."

Aelfric handed the parchments over to the keeping of the younger man. A couple of other warriors accompanied the blond-haired Saxan, the trio picking their pace up as they hurried off swiftly, heading in the direction of the nearby encampment.

"I deem that you must depart immediately," Aelfric stated, looking to both Bevriedak and Wulfstan.

"That would be best," Wulfstan replied firmly.

The dragon's breathing was starting to change. Though the light of day had not shifted, the surface of the Elder was undeniably duller, as the Ban exacted its terrible price.

Reaching out, Aelfric clasped the outside of Wulfstan's left arm tightly. His hazel eyes flared, a fiery look surging within that bore deeply into Wulfstan's own gaze.

"My prayers have been with you since word came to me of your daring flight. It is indeed a good thing to believe that one's prayers have been answered in a way much hoped for. I thank you for that ray of light in the midst of such darkness. In men such as you, Saxan blood still runs strong," Aelfric stated resolutely, for only Wulfstan's ears to hear.

"I am very honored," Wulfstan replied, bowing his head.

A feeling of awkwardness encompassed him. Speaking with a great ealdorman was one thing. Receiving such outward, high praise from such an individual, especially one with the reputation and authority of Aelfric, was another matter entirely. Wulfstan hoped he did not suddenly lose his wits entirely, finding it difficult to decide how to respond to the high-ranking Saxan.

Looking upward, Wulfstan spoke loudly to Bevriedak, "Let us go to the northeast, to find Aethelhere's fleet."

"A fleet of vessels upon the water, near to the coast, will not be difficult to see from the skies," Bevriedak responded.

"I should leave this good steed behind," Wulfstan said, looking back to Aelfric, and indicating Spirit Wing. "This brave creature has risked far enough already."

Guilt still wracked him for having driven the animal to such extremes, in desperately trying to reach the white, skyward patch he had gambled everything upon. Had Bevriedak not chosen to save them, Wulfstan was very conscious of the fact that the Himmeros would have suffered certain death.

In the short time he had spent with Spirit Wing, he had become aware of a deeper bond forming with the brave steed. It only made the feelings of guilt that much worse.

"The steed stays with you. It is clear this noble animal favors you," Aelfric replied, with a small grin, looking back at the Himmeros. His countenance then grew stern. "Anything may happen on your journey. It would be good for you to have a means of moving about on your own."

Wulfstan nodded, but was surprised by the answer. He knew he had been more than a little deceptive in convincing Ulfcytel to let him take the steed into the skies.

He glanced back at Spirit Wing, and caught the creature's eyes. As if reflexively, the Himmeros' tail swished back and forth, as it whined excitedly. There was little mistaking the interpretation. The steed was stating its own intentions to remain with Wulfstan.

"Thank you, Lord Aelfric," Wulfstan replied, stunned by the great regard being shown to him.

A sky steed was one of the more rare and valued things in all of Saxany. Wulfstan knew that to be bestowed with one was a high honor; especially for a ceorl of lower rank.

"May he bear you safely to journey's end, Wulfstan," Aelfric said, before bringing his eyes back up to Bevriedak. "Is there anything more I can have done for you, great Bevriedak?"

"Only one thing more must I ask, before we depart. I will need to have a clear path of land, so I may take to flight without risk to any of yours," the dragon requested.

The ealdorman nodded, and the request was swiftly relayed to a number of thanes and others of rank, the missive racing through the sprawling crowds. As if a parting sea, the mass of Saxans split, pulling to the sides and creating a widening channel of open ground.

Aelfric remounted his black war horse. With a little coaxing, he brought it close to where Bevriedak's claw was still held open. Wulfstan and Spirit Wing were settling themselves back into its center, readying for the impending flight.

Aelfric quietly regarded Wulfstan for a moment. He then nodded, and said, "May the Almighty's favor embrace you always. You have given an entire Kingdom a chance to live onward, Wulfstan of Sussachia."

"Thank you, my lord," Wulfstan replied, as Bevriedak slowly brought his talons together.

The great dragon shifted about, before lurching forward. Wulfstan knew the Elder was starting down the open channel created through the gathered Saxans.

Bevriedak thrust upward, with a prodigious spring. The ensuing sensations of a sharp incline, and then a steep curve, pervaded Wulfstan, as the Elder flapped, glided, and brought his huge body into alignment with the direction they were to go.

Wulfstan's ears caught the sounds of a horn blast, which he judged to be originating close in proximity. He knew without having to see beyond the dragon's claws that the Saxan sky riders commissioned by Aelfric were near, following in the wake of the massive dragon. The signal heralded that the next part of his incredible mission was firmly underway.

THOMAS

The sun beat down ceaselessly upon the timber market stalls near the docks and quays, soaking them with its rising heat. Scattered patches of clouds lent occasional shade to the sprawling area, each respite far too brief for the city's inhabitants.

The aroma of fish permeated the oceanfront air, as Thomas accompanied his mother through the throngs milling about the fishmonger's section of Avalos. Rows of flat wooden displays rose up to about a table's height, holding a prodigious bounty from the sea, rivers, streams, and ponds in the vicinity of Avalos.

More than a few kinds would inevitably fetch delicacy prices from higher level buyers, those that supplied the tables of the great merchants and city officials. A particularly huge pike caught Thomas' eyes, likely destined to be a prime component of some noble's feast. Such were items of mere curiosity for the likes of Thomas and his mother.

Yet the prices of even the most choice catches could not be too extravagant, nor could they be bargains. Like most business concerns, even the fish sellers were under the firm yoke of their guild rules. The governance of the guilds encompassed the rarest sea delicacy provided for a noble's banquet, to the more common perch, trout, and cod often finding their way to the tables of artisans and laborers.

Thomas casually eyed an ample batch of eels harvested from one of the mill ponds outside the city, before strolling past some carp, and a small allotment of crabs and shellfish.

"Thomas, be sure to come back out of your day dreams when I need help in carrying," Alice said gently.

"Yes mother," Thomas replied, looking up at her.

She had a broad smile on her face, as she gazed down upon her energetic, twelve-year-old son. She shook her head, and looked back towards another fishmonger's display, leaning closer and scrutinizing the offerings.

Abruptly, and without a word, her grin faded into a tense expression. She pulled up and moved on to the next seller. Thomas knew his mother's tendencies well enough to know she suspected the previous fish seller of using blood to give a fresher appearance to aged fish. It was not an uncommon practice, but guild rules strictly forbade the offering of spoiling stock.

The basket she carried was still empty, and it was not certain how long it would be before it contained anything. Alice Weaver was anything but a hasty buyer.

Thomas kept up with her, his thoughts returning to the tidings he had recently heard. Disseminating around the city, the news concerned the war with the Kingdom of Saxany, a land farther to the east and south from where Avalos was located.

The conflict was part of a larger war to end all wars, as the people of Avalos understood it. The Kingdom of Saxany had rebuked the Unifier, openly denouncing the alliance spreading across all of Ave. The kingdom had thus declared itself a threat to all.

A state of war had soon ensued. Forces long since marshaled by the Unifier, in response to the inevitability of conflict, had finally thrust forward into the defiant Saxan kingdom.

As Thomas was well aware, the people of Avalos had been mystified by the Saxans' hardened resistance to the Unifier. They believed Saxany should have followed the course of so many others, including widely varying realms such as the Sacred Empire, the city-states of Lambar, the Kingdom of Norengal, the Sultanate of Saljuka, the Kingdoms of Eberias, the lands of Andamoor, and the empire of Theonia.

Everyone knew the peaceful vision of the Unifier, which could only be made possible in the comprehensive alliance He advocated. The Unifier promised an end to the age-old struggles between realms, and within realms, for power and dominance.

Proclaiming peace and then starting wars made little sense to Thomas, but he had heard the reasoning for the ongoing wars explained by many adults in Avalos. The Unifier could not allow for wars to be prosecuted by realms outside the alliance, against those who were a part of it. Nor could realms be allowed to stand in the way of the wondrous, peaceful new age envisioned by the Unifier.

According to what was said, there were not many holdouts left within Ave. The barbaric Midragardians, the hostile Saxans, and the heathens of the Five Realms were perhaps the only sizeable realms standing in the way of the unity and peace offered by Avanor's great ruler.

Thomas found some aspects about the wars to be curious. Very little debate went up among the populace over the wars themselves, even as they griped incessantly about the demands being made upon them. Taxes and tolls had risen significantly, eliciting discontent from incoming ships, carts, and wagons. The guilds of Avalos had been put under even greater pressures to respond to the voracious needs for the ongoing war efforts.

From what Thomas had heard on the streets, it was the same all over the land. Representatives from other towns in Avanor had come bearing copies of their town charters, protesting the increasing requests, only to leave with the burdensome financial demands still in place.

In most times, such heavy demands, and clear transgressions of granted charters, would have quickly resulted in open resistance. But the overall mood in the populace was one of tolerant passivity regarding the wars.

Yet some things could not be denied. The Unifier's rise calmed the incessant tumult long plaguing Avanor, which so often found itself caught in the middle of struggles between the rival kings of Norengal and Gallea.

A few skirmishes occurred now and then between individual lords, but, overall, peace had taken hold in Avanor. Trade had proceeded in a largely uninterrupted state, far from a bad thing for Thomas' own family, and all weavers in general.

His grandfather had spoken to Thomas of older times when wars had broken asunder the stability of the cloth trade in Avalos. During such wars, merchants, who were the lifeline for the city's weavers, had been unable to employ or contract the weavers. The church doors had been quickly filled with begging, desperate weavers, left without work, and wholly unable to feed their families.

Regular bread on the table outweighed most other concerns when it came to the average family, but Thomas' thoughts were rarely concerned with something as mundane as bread, except when his stomach rumbled in emptiness. For him, the prospects of seeing other lands, and finding adventure, was the stronger force tugging at the core of his soul.

Thomas wished he could find a way to be of service to the Unifier's army, perhaps as a squire to an Avanoran knight, so that he could visit the exotic lands spoken of by the storytellers. Visits to fish markets could only elicit so much excitement for an imaginative, twelve year old boy.

"Thomas, let's concentrate for a few moments … I could use your help now," urged his mother, snapping Thomas out of his wandering thoughts.

She had concluded a transaction with one of the fishmongers, and was now holding a basket filled with five silvery fish, of a long, narrow variety. The Silver Runners were not Thomas' favorite taste, but they were very inexpensive, the most primary concern for the family of a weaver.

He was not about to complain. On fasting days set by the Western Church, when one could not eat poultry or other meat, there were not many other options.

"Yes mother, of course," Thomas replied agreeably, moving over to assist.

She grinned, handing the basket over, and relieving herself of the burden. "You are ever the dreamer, Thomas."

Thomas laughed merrily, as she playfully ruffled his thick auburn locks. He eyed the contents of the basket. "Looks like you've got quite a lot here, mother."

"It is fortunate word came swiftly of the good catch of Silver Runners, or I am afraid it all would have been gone, before ever we got here," Alice replied. "Now let us return home, so that your father is not too burdened with work."

They set off together, making their way down the narrow, crowded streets. Overhead, it looked as if the houses, most of which doubled as shops, using their ground floors, were leaning forward to touch each other. A cacophony of voices filled the air, ranging from idle chatter to craftsmen barking instructions to their workers and apprentices.

Clad in a long brown, woolen tunic, a priest walked by Thomas and his mother, with a pensive expression etched upon his face. Two cloaked members of the city garrison's men-at-arms walked a few paces behind the priest. The guards strolled at a relaxed gait, showing they had no urgent place to get to. Beyond the guards was a cascade of other men and women.

Some exhibited the richer colors and expertly embroidered clothing indicative of wealthier standing. Others wore plainer, earthy attire, common to those of lower stations, these being the majority of the crowd.

Thomas' eyes widened when three strong-looking, bearded men strode purposefully through the crowd. Two were clad in long black mantles, with red spear-like emblems resting upon their left breasts. The third was attired in a white mantle, with a similarly placed red spear-symbol.

Excited, Thomas recognized them immediately, as members of

the heralded Order of the High Altar. They were the warriors of the Creator Himself, the brave, faithful ones protecting the pilgrims, and fighting the unbelievers in the distant Sunlands. Their massive, keep-like commandery loomed not far from where Thomas' own home was located.

He turned his head in wonder as they passed by, his eyes pulled by the sight of the men. Thomas wished he could ask them about the Sunlands, and perhaps how a person of lower means could become one of their order. It was said those initiated as a brother in the Order of the High Altar had to be of some means, like a knight, though it was also said it had not always been that way.

Thomas could not stop thinking of the famous order of holy knights until he found himself walking through the front door of his family's multi-level home. As with most houses of the sort, the spacious front room on the street level was where the daily work of the artisan or craftsman was conducted.

A thin man with a hawkish appearance sat upon a high-backed chair, working the horizontal loom before him. Thomas grinned as he set his eyes upon Nicholas, a journeyman by status, who had been working steadily for Thomas' father, William, for several months.

Nicholas was well beyond the time and skill needed to become a master weaver, but had not pursued the acquisition of the official rank, as he wanted to continue living in Avalos. With the steady stream of work flowing into the city, and a full number of master weavers, the guild was not permitting new master weavers in Avalos as of yet. For the time being, it meant that Thomas' father was availed of some very effective, skillful help.

The sounds of jovial laughter came from the back room, just a moment before two men emerged. One was Thomas' father, and the other he recognized as Hervee of Delshire. Hervee was a man of short physical stature, but of large wit and esteemed reputation, one of the more successful cloth merchants in all of Avanor.

Hervee was well-liked by all in the household, and not just because he was the source of William's employment. Thomas' father considered the merchant a fair and just man, and Hervee was always cordial to their family.

For his part, Hervee had often expressed his sincere appreciation of William's considerable work ethic, and keen focus on producing quality work. William was, by far, one of Hervee's most productive, consistent weavers.

Thomas greatly wanted to visit Hervee's huge house of stone situated close to the harbor. It was said to be furnished in an opulent manner, rivaling most any lord of a castle. Thomas could not imagine what such a place might look like, as the sons of weavers rarely found themselves in the houses of rich cloth merchants.

"Hello Thomas Weaver, and hello to you, Alice," Hervee greeted cheerfully, in the clear, confident voice that had conducted so many successful negotiations and sales. "I am glad I got a chance to see you before I leave." He punctuated his greeting to Thomas' mother with a bow, the gesture having a natural smoothness and elegance.

"Thank you, Hervee," Alice replied, with a warm smile. "And I trust all is well with your lovely wife?"

"As long as I labor to keep her coin purse well supplied," laughed Hervee, amiably. "Thanks to the good work of those such as your husband, I may have a chance yet to continue to do so."

He turned back towards William, with a resigned look on his face. "I would enjoy talking further, but before time escapes, I suppose I need to go meet with the others of your esteemed guild… The day is truly getting away from me, as it always seems to do when I have a pleasant visit. I wish a good day to all of you, as I need to go meet with Simon … Unlike yourself, Simon is far behind schedule, and I am still well short of where I need to be for the upcoming fairs. Simon is a good man, but he could do with a little more of your efficiency."

After a brief exchange of parting pleasantries, Hervee strode past Thomas and his mother, with a swish of his blue supertunic of fine linen. He proceeded out of the front room, stepping into the thoroughfare outside.

"It looks like we will be very, very busy for some time. The great summer fairs in Chamarais seem to have no end to their appetites for new cloth," William announced with a smile. He had the look of contentment that came with the promise of long-term, guaranteed work. "This year will be our busiest yet."

"That is very good news, my husband," Alice commented, with a pleased look upon her own face.

"And it looks like the word of the good catch was true. A basket full of Silver Runners, of large size too," William commneted, looking down at the basket Thomas cradled.

"Yes, and for little expense," Alice responded quickly, as if to head off another question.

"How did your lessons go?" William asked of his son.

Unable to afford the expense of the Cathedral school, William had managed to work out an arrangement with their parish priest Anselm, to help Thomas gain an understanding of letters. It had resulted in Thomas having to do a few regular chores around the church, but his father insisted that Thomas had the better end of the bargain by far.

Thomas knew his father wanted him to follow in the footsteps of his brother Hugh, who had managed to attain church support to go to the University at the Island City in Gallea. Thomas was not sure how he felt about the idea, as he did not yet share the same enthusiasm for letters, as did his brother. He wished his father would be interested in seeing him become a brother-knight in one of the holy orders, like the Order of the High Altar, or perhaps the Order of the Healers.

"More of the same, father. Over, and over, and over again. And then the next day I repeat things again, and again, and again," Thomas said with a wearisome sigh, before hastily adding, "But do not worry, father. I cause Father Anselm no trouble. I do all he asks."

"You will find yourself learning yet, my son," his father replied with a grin. "I wish I could have done so when I was your age."

"Father Anselm could talk a little more about the wars of Avanor, or the Sunlands, or even Theonia," suggested Thomas, feeling a little bitterness towards the boring lessons he regularly endured.

"I am afraid we have not come to the end of all wars," William said, the mirth fading from his face. "So many wars, and so many things happening in these times. It seems time itself is moving far too fast."

"Since I am only twelve, I have little to compare it to," retorted Thomas.

"We certainly have more and more of them," William remarked, nodding past Thomas in the direction of the street, visible through the open doorway.

Thomas followed his father's gaze through the open door, to where a quartet of blue-cloaked men-at-arms strode down the street. It seemed they were cast by a metalworker, from the same mold, at least to Thomas' eyes. All of the lance-bearing men had squared jaws, stone-like expressions, and hardened looks in their eyes.

They were not the men of the guild-supported city watch. The men of the watch were derived from the members of all guilds, at least those not specifically exempt from providing for militia service.

The blue-cloaks were from places like the keep tower, the prison and administrative center set over the Grand Bridge spanning the Saina River. Many were known to be quartered at the dreaded Tomb Hall, as well as the Seneschal's Castle, and the Unifier's immense mountain-citadel.

As his father indicated, it seemed like the soldiers from those garrisons were visible everywhere. Either something had changed, or Thomas was simply noticing them more often.

"It is no wonder the tolls and taxes have steadily increased. We have so many of their kind among us, and so many of Avanor's men are being sent off to war," grumbled William. It was clear to Thomas his father's ire had been ignited by the sight of the men-at-arms. "We may have more coins flowing into the city, but we have less and less real freedom in Avanor."

Alice shot him a sharp look. "You know what I said about speaking your mind in public. It is not good to cause a disturbance that will benefit us nothing. I have warned you … if you have a habit of outbursts at home, you will have an outburst out there. We are now in good standing with the guild, and you are in good standing with Hervee … if I need remind you again."

"Yes, my lady," William replied gently, giving her a grin, while winking at Thomas. Turning aside, he remarked to Thomas in a lower voice, "Survival, my boy. Survival."

"You know so," Alice laughed, "And, Thomas, if you find yourself a wife someday, you will learn that most important lesson too."

"It is what keeps me happily single," Nicholas piped in, from where he sat at the horizontal loom.

A mischievous grin rested on his face, as he continued working the two treadles underneath the flat plane of warp threads with his feet. He passed the weft thread through, with a newer style of shuttle, which had a contour reminiscent of a boat's general shape.

"Now Nicholas, consider yourself lucky you are not an apprentice, or I would have you working to clean clothes right now," Alice responded, in a light-hearted fashion.

Thomas knew the comment was fully in jest. His mother had

never been one to take advantage of apprentices, as the wives of other Masters tended to do.

"Nicholas, you play with fire," smirked William, winking again at Thomas. "I won't be able to save you."

"Ah yes, it is always trouble when one speaks the truth, is it not?" Nicholas chided, with an impish grin, as William laughed boisterously.

"You go too far, Nicholas, as do you, William, for supporting him with your laughter," Alice retorted, in mock indignation. The stern expression she forced onto her face quickly crumbled into merry laughter.

"I have gone too far indeed, sending you into such a bout of laughter," William teased.

Alice shook her finger at him, shaking her head, as she shook with more laughter. "You tread on dangerous ground, my husband!"

"Very contentious household, this is," Nicolas quipped, smiling wide. "It is why I stay a journeyman. The entertainment is like another share of pay."

"I'll give you some pay," William commented, laughing loudly, as he strode over towards Nicolas. Nicolas paused just in time for William's large hands to rest in a semblance of a choking grip on his neck. "There's your extra wages … for getting me into trouble with my wife."

Thomas chortled at the sight, as Nicolas made an exaggerated expression of gasping for air.

"Now don't drop our meal, my boy," Alice said, her eyes sparkling in amusement. "Best take those on back to Emma … she should still be back in the kitchen."

Thomas nodded, as William released his hold on Nicolas, slapping him amiably on the back. Life in Thomas' household was not always idyllic. There were times of unhappiness and conflict. William and Alice had their fair share of arguments, and Thomas and Emma had both misbehaved often enough, and been made to endure stout punishments. Yet the atmosphere in such times never reached the level of tensions or outbursts other boys and girls had to withstand in their households.

A few of Thomas's friends had been badly scarred by a vile kind of darkness that William and Alice had always held at bay. Evil acts, rooted in multiple forms of violence, were given life in the struggles of poverty, the grip of excessive drink, and angers born of resentment and envy.

A couple of boys Thomas knew had become very withdrawn in the time since he had first met them, and he was not sure that he ever wanted to discover the true nature of what they had been through. Their silence, distant eyes, and multiple bruises warned him strongly enough. It also made him appreciate his own situation all the more.

Walking to the back of the house, to the kitchen separated from the front areas by a small, open air space containing a cesspit, Thomas set his eyes upon his sister. Younger by a year, with long auburn locks matching the hue of Thomas's own hair, she looked towards him through her wide, expressive brown eyes. Her brow furrowed, in slight irritation.

"All having yourselves a good time out there, I see," she remarked, working to cut up some vegetables, to add to a stew heating within a pot suspended in the hearth. She gave a long, wistful sigh. "I suppose it is the lot of a girl, isn't it?"

"Is it?" Thomas grinned. "When I get sent out in downpours to attend to one of father's chores, or to do one of mother's errands, while you relax in the solar."

Her hands closed into fists, and rested on her hips. "Relax? You refer to spinning wool endlessly as relaxing? At least you get to see that oaf friend of yours Tristainus, and some of the other louts when you run about the city."

"Before you get too angry, where do you want these placed?" Thomas asked, holding forth the basket of Silver Runners.

She glanced within, a look of resignation crossing her face. "I wish eel would one day be priced the same as these. Oh well, it is better than what many have on their table this day. Put it here, on the floor for now."

Thomas set the basket down where she indicated. He asked her in sincerity, "Is there anything I can help you with, before mother or father come up with a new task for me?"

A grin came to her face, as the look in her eye softened. "I suppose it is not altogether bad to have a brother such as you. But I think I am managing well enough back here. Go on, and maybe you can check to see that your oaf friend hasn't fallen into a dyer's vat. He is skilled enough to do something like that."

Thomas chuckled, shaking his head, not entirely disagreeing with her assessment of his friend Tristainus.

"Well, just remember, I offered to help you," he said, as he turned to leave the kitchen.

"I shall," Emma confirmed, shaking her own head and smiling, as she turned back to her cutting. "See you shortly, for our grand feast of Silver Runners."

Thomas hesitated in the doorway.

"Between you and I, I wish it were eels as well," Thomas answered, before continuing out through the doorway.

Behind him, Emma shook her head again, as a cheerful laugh escaped her.

DRAGOL

Dragol scooped water from the creek, and splashed it across his increasingly leaden face. The cleansing waters removed the caked sweat clinging onto his cheeks, brow, and neck, while refreshing eyes grown heavy with the long sojourn. About ten paces away, Dragol's older companion stood silently, and patiently. Incredibly, the elder human still showed no outward signs of fatigue.

"Do you ever grow weary?" Dragol inquired, marveling at the other's extraordinary stamina.

The two had been marching through the woodlands at a brisk pace for several hours, covering numerous leagues of rolling forest lands. As the day wore on, it was not the hale Trogen warrior in his prime who led the human looking to be in the dusk of his days. Rather, it was the old man who often had to slow his pace, to allow the Trogen's strides to catch back up with his.

Dragol always felt great pride in the durability and rugged endurance of Trogen warriors, even more so as he spent increasing amounts of time in the midst of humans. Even more was expected of a Trogen leader such as himself. To truly command the respect of his warriors, it was imperative to be of exceptional ability among his own kind.

Besting a fit, hardy young human in a contest of stamina would have been an afterthought. Outlasting an aged human did not even warrant a flicker of a thought as to the outcome. What Dragol was now witnessing defied all logic and experience.

"Do you grow tired?" Dragol pressed, repeating his query with impatience and a trace of exasperation.

The older man's lone eye glinted with obvious amusement. "More tired of the way the world has become, perhaps. It is the price of gaining wisdom in this world. If you see things as they are, it will indeed make you weary. Knowledge is often the greater of burdens. So, yes, I do grow tired, in a manner of speaking. Beyond that, I feel very good in my body. You would not be tiring now, my Trogen friend, would you?"

The old man's countenance sparkled with mirth, as a harsh chuckle escaped Dragol. He took the gentle chiding in good humor, reluctantly conceding he could not prove the man otherwise. He was exhausted, and the old man was yet full of vitality. The old man's buoyant demeanor was not mocking, as an acerbic braggart would have quickly drawn heated scorn, or a more forceful manner of response.

"A mystery ... you are, human, or Wizard. My Trogen brethren would not believe me if I spoke of you to them. They would feel I have greatly weakened somehow, to struggle to match an elder man," Dragol said, looking to his traveling companion. "But I know my body well. At the outset of this journey, I know I could have contended with any of my brethren. Let us continue forward, for I will not let it be said a Trogen was a burden to an older man's travel."

The old man smiled, and extended his right arm. "Then take the first step, as we resume, good Trogen."

The invigorating creek water had given some renewal, and Dragol's face felt fresh, as a cool woodland breeze caressed him. At the very least, his eyes felt less weighty.

The condition of his legs was another matter, still feeling like two pillars of rock. He had to concentrate to keep pace with the old human, whose light step brought him alongside the Trogen after only a few paces.

"I would hope your future tales among humankind, if that is indeed what you are, will not speak of the Trogen who hindered your travel," Dragol remarked dourly.

The sense of embarrassment was returning, as he noticed the swish of the man's blue-hued robes slow. He was adjusting his pace to a level Dragol could more easily sustain.

"Be consoled, good Trogen. It would not be the first time I have heard a complaint from one I have journeyed with ... I have heard similar things uttered often from the lips of another. It has been this way with many who have known my kind," the old man replied.

Despite his jovial expression, he appeared resolute on safeguarding his mystery. He offered nothing in the way of explanations, and the continued murk about the old man was beginning to become maddening.

"And I do not even know what your kind is," Dragol said, with a sharp, inquisitive glance. "You may look to the eyes like a human, yet my spirit tells me that you are not. Are Wizards not human?"

Again, the old man merely smiled, and irritatingly offered nothing in reply.

Dragol shook his head. "Still mysteries, old one … still mysteries. You neither answer me, nor do you deny me."

Just ahead was a shallow, gracefully meandering creek. It sat low within its bed, not hurried or fattened by any season of rain. The calm weather of recent weeks had afforded it a little rest, and its current state complimented the tranquil atmosphere. In such an environment, Dragol found it very difficult to believe a war of immense proportions was ongoing within the same forest lands.

The high banks of the narrow stream were close together, such that a modest jump would easily carry Dragol over it. Without hesitating, Dragol thrust off his right leg with a small grunt of exertion, landing a moment later upon the soft earth on the opposite side.

Seeing that the old man was neither beside nor ahead of him, he looked back to see what was keeping his strange companion. The old man was still on the other side, but it was not due to any inability to cross. He was steadying himself, as he climbed down the bank on the other side.

He drew to a halt at the edge of the clear waters, and paused. Leaning over, he formed a little bowl with his cupped hands. He then dipped his hands into the light-flowing creek waters, growing silent and closing his eyes, as if deep in reflection.

Easing his cupped hands back out of the waters, he rose up, and turned towards Dragol. "Do not get too far ahead of yourself, good Trogen … I don't want to spill much of this. Would you mind jumping back over here?" the old man inquired, in a casual voice.

Though bewildered at the development, Dragol obliged the strange request. He perceived an opportunity to learn something more of his traveling companion, and intended to take advantage of it.

Dragol leapt back over to the side of the creek the old man stood on. Crouching, and bracing himself with one arm, the Trogen made the short drop down to the creek bed.

With slow, purposeful strides, the old man approached the curious Trogen, a few drops of water falling to the ground from his cupped hands. "Here …drink of this water. It will fill you with a new energy."

Not really knowing why he assented so readily, Dragol accepted the water. He cupped his own huge hands so that the old man could pour the water into them.

Most of the contents pooled into his dark palms, with very little lost in the transfer. Dragol's eyes looked into those of the old man as he raised his hands to his lips, drinking of the cool liquid.

Whether a trick of his mind or not, Dragol felt as if the water was vibrantly tingling as it cascaded down his throat. It felt as if the water was spreading a deeply permeating sensation of warmth as it traveled into his body.

Dragol did not fear the feelings, continuing to drink the remaining water cradled in his hands. As he finished, he carefully noted the manifestations within him.

The incredible sensations extended from his hand, to his mouth, throat, stomach, and gradually to all areas of his body. To his further surprise, in the very moment when he believed his mind was finally going awry, losing its hold on reality, a tangible energy rippled throughout his veins.

Almost the instant he perceived the sensation, he felt completely rejuvenated. The flowing sense of power and renewed strength coursing through his body was like nothing he had ever experienced. It was like he was well-fed, well-rested, and in the most optimal physical condition.

"Go now to that fallen tree, Dragol. Lift it up for me," the old man gently directed the Trogen, as if reacting to the pronounced disbelief displayed upon Dragol's face. "We will see if you are still tired."

It took a moment to break away from the incredulity gripping him. Again, without knowing entirely why he did so, Dragol acquiesced, following the old man's directives. He clambered up the bank, and walked over to the fallen tree lying just a short distance to the left.

It was an old tree that had finally succumbed to the force of a mighty storm. The great trunk was split, rendered into a jagged mass at its sundered ends. The tree's fall had opened a wide hole in the forest ceiling, letting a channel of warm light pour through.

In height, the fallen part of the tree was at least twelve times

Dragol's own. Its trunk was almost too broad in circumference for Dragol to even get an outstretched grip around it. If the tree had lived a few years longer, he likely would have found it impossible to follow the old man's wishes, simply being unable to wrap his arms around it.

He looked back towards the old man, who nodded and stated, "Lift the tree back up in the direction that it fell. Trust me, and try to do this. Do not consider what you believe you can or cannot do."

Dragol was astounded at what he was agreeing to do, given the apparent absurdity of the directive. Had it been any other figure suggesting such an action, he would have been sure it was a ruse to make a fool out of the Trogen.

Yet it was no ordinary man that spoke to him, and Dragol knew the behest had not been given frivolously. As such, he was curious to see where the old man was going with all of this.

At first, Dragol started towards the farther end of the tree, with the intention of picking up the higher end, and then walking back, bracing the trunk and pushing it upwards. The old man quickly raised a hand to stop him.

"No, as I said, do not consider what you think you can or cannot do. Lift from the lower, base end, so that you are able to lift the full weight of the free portion of the trunk, from the onset," the old man instructed.

Dragol stopped, and wondered why he assented so easily, as he turned and headed back to the base of the tree. He carefully gauged where it had fallen, positioning himself with his back facing the direction that the large tree had fallen from.

He straddled the trunk in a broad stance, just beyond the exposed base with its jagged arsenal of shards, crevices, and fragments. He leaned over and squatted, feeling his steely leg muscles bracing for the coming effort. Just barely, he clasped his arms around the lower part of the tree trunk, locking his fingers together.

As his shoulders, back, and arms tensed, he blocked out the thoughts pouring into his mind regarding the seemingly ridiculous attempt he was about to make. The old man had admonished him not to ponder what he thought he was capable of, and Dragol decided to see the mysterious event through.

With a grunt and vigorous heave, his muscles flexed as he put his full strength into the act. Though the tree was heavy, he felt the sensations of movement almost immediately. Dragol kept his mind as still as possible, trying to stifle the new thoughts arising swiftly within. He slowly lifted the entirety of the fallen trunk up into the air, to a chorus of small branches snapping, a host of leaves rustling, and close-by stretches of brush being disturbed.

He knew there was no way in all of Ave he should have been able to lift the fallen tree trunk, no matter how strong the race of Trogens were. Even a Gigan did not have the strength to make such a prodigious lift, nor did any of the enormous Mountain Trolls living east of Gigan lands.

As the tree gradually rose upward, it wobbled slightly. Dragol struggled to control the tree, and hold it upright. His back, legs, and arms strained, and he had to concentrate hard, but he found himself able to keep control of the long trunk until the opening in the forest canopy was plugged by the fallen treee's upper branches. It was all he could do to refrain from gawking in sheer amazement, as he gazed up the now-vertical length of the tree trunk.

"A little tough, yes?" the old man asked, with a slight grin. "I expected it would take a little exertion. Trees are not light objects, you know … You can let the tree go now. If you hold on to it for very much longer, I would feel guilt, as this initial surge lasts but a very short time … and it would not do your body well to exceed that brief period, believe me."

Dragol needed little impetus to heed the warning, finding the whole experience bizarre enough. He leaned a little forward, so the weight of the tree would be controlled as it fell back towards its original resting place. As soon as he felt the momentum of the tree's fall, he let go and fell backwards, coming down hard upon his posterior.

The long mass of trunk, branches, and foliage crashed noisily to the ground. Some nearby birds shrieked and flapped into the air, while a few small animals skittered anxiously from their hiding places, and scurried hastily away.

Wide-eyed, Dragol slowly turned his head to gaze at the old man. Not surprisingly, his companion was laughing, the bridge of his sharp nose crinkling, and his expression undeniably merry.

"This is unbelievable," Dragol exclaimed, knowing that what had transpired was anything but illusory. His muscles still felt the burning aftermath of the strain he had incurred in lifting the tree. "What is in that water?"

Standing up, brushing himself off, and feeling no lasting effects of the hard fall onto his rump, he strolled over to the bank. He scrambled back down its facing, to where the old man stood, feeling wholly nimble and refreshed, despite the incredible effort he had just made.

"I hope this can last for a little while," Dragol commented, savoring the energized condition of his body. "I have never felt this kind of strength before."

"It is not the Water that another One, One who is much greater than I, can give to you, but it will heal your body's weariness nonetheless," the old man replied. "Much can be gained from the gifts we have available to us in the world … more than most would recognize."

The old man paused, and turned slowly from side to side with his arms outstretched, indicating the full forest surrounding them. "These lands are the body, and the waters the blood, of what is given to us in this world of matter. Some Powers work to cause weakness, or even destroy, by these things … while other Powers work to build strength in and through them.

"Each Power has a purpose, as such purpose will effect those who move through this deep and fleeting shadow of time. That purpose is governed by a greater War, one that was in motion before time even existed.

"The momentary surge that helped you lift the tree will pass quickly, as I have said. But what is left should make our travel a little easier for you to bear, so we can enjoy conversation, and worry less about tired, aching muscles."

Dragol rested his hands upon his hips, and stared down into the lazily flowing waters of the creek. Again, he shook his head slowly in response to the riddle-like, cryptic answers rendered him by the old man.

"Perhaps we should start forward again, Dragol. We are both on our own journeys, and would that we both reach a good destination," the old man commented, with a jovial wink. The old man jumped nimbly across the stream, with a grace that far belied his seeming years. He pulled himself up on the far bank with no trouble, and looked back to Dragol. "I know you are not tired now … what are you waiting for?"

Dragol sighed, sprung across the stream, surmounted the opposite bank lithely, and started off after the old man. His head was spinning with thoughts.

He found himself wondering whether the words of the old man

contained a double meaning. He had to hustle to catch up with the dexterous old man. This time, he found the task effortless, the bounce returned to his step with full abundance.

"You mentioned destinations. So where are we going?" Dragol asked, keeping pace.

The old man looked over briefly, and Dragol thought he caught a glimpse of a vivid sparkle within the man's deep blue eye. "Get you away from danger. The destination is something for both of us to find out in good time. Let us worry more about the journey."

Again, the strange manner of speaking perplexed Dragol. Only Trogen Shamans' speech reminded him a little of the old man's. He was thinking about the right question to ask his secretive companion when a rumbling growl abruptly filled the air.

Emerging from the forest growth directly before them, without any regard for stealth or surprise, was a most fearsome-looking creature. Walking upon six sinewy legs, the beast carried an arsenal of weapons in its very step.

Each of its legs ended in broad paws, armed with an array of nestled claws, each like deadly blades unto themselves. The natural blades were partially unsheathed, the spiky ends protruding as if to herald the beast's deadly capability.

The creature stepped with a silence hard to believe for an animal of such girth. Boasting exceptional height, its large round head was level with the middle of Dragol's chest, even in a relaxed posture. Dark, silky fur covered the surface of its long, chiseled body, giving a rich sheen to its muscular contours.

Piercing, feline eyes gazed upon Dragol, narrowing in the daylight to thin ellipses. The predator's lips curled back as it emitted an eerie hiss, revealing gleaming daggers of white set into its upper and lower jaws.

A foreboding tension coalesced, setting off alarms at every level of instinct the Trogen possessed. The hairs at the back of his neck stood on end. A veteran hunter, Dragol had no illusions about what the situation before them presented. His body statue-still, Dragol made no sudden movements, but he prepared himself to dive to the side the moment the predator before them lunged.

"My friend, have no trouble with us. We intend you no harm," the old man addressed the beast, his easygoing timbre cutting through the stillness.

For a moment, Dragol thought the old man had lost his wits, but the look in the eyes of the creature in front of them softened at the old man's words. Its lips closed, shutting their exposure of the lethal weapons within. The sense of coiling threat Dragol had felt dissipated rapidly.

"Come over here, my friend," the old man invited, holding his hand out towards the large predator.

Deliberately, the cat-like monstrosity sauntered over to Dragol and the old man. Despite every instinct to run off or draw his blade, Dragol kept control of himself, and remained in place.

The old man reached up, and stroked the creature on the side of its head, just behind one of its triangular ears. He worked his hand up gradually to rub the space between its eyes. The creature closed its eyes as the old man scratched, emitting a sound reminiscent of a small, purring cat, only much more resonant.

"He will not bite, or try to maul you," the old man said, inviting Dragol over to pet the creature. "I have two wolves of my own … big fellows, and sometimes irascible curmudgeons. But they are good lads who, though they both look monstrous, can be as gentle as lambs. Appearances do not always reflect that which is true, I have long come to realize. There is nothing to fear from this one right now."

Following the incident with the large tree, Dragol knew that reality was not being governed by the same rules he had been used to throughout his life. Though admittedly nervous, Dragol reached forward and touched the soft fur of the creature.

To his surprise, the beast lowered itself to the ground, rolling over onto its back. It folded its legs underneath, fully exposing its belly for rubbing. Dragol noticed the claws of the beast were now entirely retracted.

The old man reached out both of his hands, scratching and massaging the creature all along its belly, eliciting sounds of gratification from the huge carnivore. Dragol did likewise, though still riddled with tentativeness. He ran his hands along the fur of the creature, feeling the steely muscle lying underneath.

Dragol could not assuage his worries whenever he looked upon the creature's wide paws, containing the host of deadly knives that could emerge in a flash, and be wielded with blinding speed. The thoughts kept his heart rate quickened.

The Trogen glanced over at the old man several times, as the mystery surrounding his companion grew. The event with the stream water, the lifting of the tree, and the peaceful interaction with a deadly predator were undeniable examples of deeper powers harbored within the enigmatic figure.

Dragol was a hunter and a warrior. He had spent many days and nights tracking game back in his homeland, with others of his Thunder Wolf clan. His instincts had been acutely honed through war and hunts fraught with peril, such that he could recognize the confidence that came with exceptional martial capability. There was no question the elderly man with him had that sense about him; in abundance.

A part of Dragol deep inside, which he called his spirit, told him the old man would have protected them, if the creature had attacked. It also told him the old man could have driven the creature off with little trouble or disruption to their travel. Instead, the old man had chosen to invite the creature over, to have its head and belly scratched as if it was merely a tame animal.

Dragol knew he had gained further insight into the nature of the mysterious wanderer. While his curiosities were not satisfied by far, every glimmer of understanding helped make the man less of an enigma.

"You are quite large, my friend. A very big one of your kind," the old man remarked to the beast. "Night comes in a few hours, and you will be seeking food. And this is the time of year for you to be seeking your mate. Good luck to you on that. Females can be very formidable, of any kind."

The old man chuckled lightly. Dragol could not dispute the old man's last statement, humoring himself with a brief remembrance of the way his own father, a fearless warrior, was cowed into meekness in one moment by his stalwart mother.

The old man laughed more heartily, rubbing the creature vigorously on its belly. He patted the creature solidly a few times near its haunches and stood up. Though Dragol felt more secure, he took the movement as a cue and rose to his feet with him.

The creature slowly rolled over with a final, contented purr, getting slowly back up to its broad paws. It turned about, and extended its large head to the old man.

The old man looked proportionately miniscule. The creature's massive jaws could easily engulf the skull of a human within them. Instead of threats, the creature leaned forward and rubbed its face affectionately

against the right cheek of the old man. Merry laughter came from the old man as the creature brushed its fur on him.

The creature then turned to Dragol, and did the same. Dragol saw that his exposed neck was just inches away from glistening teeth that could end his mortal existence in a flash of time. He could feel the hot breath of the beast upon his skin.

Before the Trogen could worry himself too much, the forest predator then casually turned and walked off, to be lost amid the trees after a few strides. Dragol remained in place, staring in the direction the creature had gone. He kept silent for several long moments, as if transfixed.

"There is a gentle nature in all of us, great or small," the old man said reflectively.

"You have a way with beasts, " Dragol observed, a wry grin coming to his face. "I am fortunate you were here."

"He just wanted to greet us, have his belly rubbed and scratched, and go attend to his own concerns," the old man replied with a shrug, chuckling. "Humans and Trogens always expect the worst."

"The worst is usually the way things occur, as the creature's concern could have been turning me into a meal," Dragol replied. "Not all of us are gifted with the kind of touch you possess."

"The ... touch ... as you call it, can be possessed by everyone," the old man replied, with no trace of exaggeration. "You just have to open your mind and heart to things that would not seem logical to you ... to accept another reality as your reality, without a taint of doubt."

"You sound like a messenger for the One they call the All-Father," Dragol responded, memories coming to him. "Their type came through my lands before, traveling up from Kiruva. I admired the strength and courage those men had, to brave lands they did not know, and risk their lives ... just to bring tales of this All-Father and try to persuade others to believe in them."

"How did the Trogens react to them?" the old man queried.

"Those men came to no harm in our lands. They left in disappointment, as Trogens do not commit themselves to tales brought by humans," Dragol answered, in a lower tone.

"But you know of something bad that happened to them," the old man pressed.

Dragol nodded. "The men were slain trying to take their tales of this All-Father to the Elves. We warned them of the Elves, but they did not heed us. And they had no magic with the Elves, as you had with that beast."

"A great many have lost their lives, in many lands, for just such as that … merely wishing to speak of the All-Father," the old man commented. His countenance grew downcast, as if the Trogen's words had dredged up darker remembrances.

"I would guess you have come to know many of these messengers, or followers of the All-Father, in your travels," Dragol ventured.

"Yes, and many became friends," the old man said, with a heavy timbre.

Dragol's eyes might have deceived him, but he thought that he caught a flickering glint of sadness within the old man's eye. The look made a vivid impression upon the Trogen. The sorrow contrasted with everything he had heretofore witnessed regarding the old man, and he knew his story of the messengers had touched upon something profound and heartfelt.

"You are right, Dragol," the old man continued. "They showed great courage. They believed so strongly. And most of them did not experience anything out of the ordinary to gain such strength of belief. They were fully willing to give their lives for the All-Father.

"Courage does not always come from the sword and shield. There are times when the greatest courage comes not from feats of arms, but from the very restraint of using weapons in the face of the gravest of dangers, and facing one's fate, come whatever may."

Dragol nodded. "Something in the manner of those men was a lot like you. They were not warriors, but they all had strong resolve and bravery. Akin to that held in a warrior's heart."

"I was often with them, and they with me," the old man replied softly. He looked to Dragol with a serene expression, and asked pointedly, "What do you think of the All-Father? What have you thought of the things you have heard?"

Dragol glanced downward, feeling a little discomfort at the question. After a moment's hesitation, he answered, "If it were more than a tale, it would bring me joy … But I do not know whether it is just a tale, or not, and I will not accept the words of humans. I must see and experience what I am to believe, if I am asked to believe tales that did not come from the tesitmony of my own kind, who I know well. It is the way of most Trogens. We are a wary race. We believe in the present, which we can grasp. We remember the past … and we prepare as we can for the future.

"You must understand we have always had to rely upon ourselves. No other has ever aided us, or given us reason to make ourselves vulnerable in trust. That is why we emphasize the longblade. It is the way by which we are always prepared for the dangers that may arise. We may not always gain victory in a battle, but at least we are always able and willing to fight it."

Dragol watched the old man closely, hoping he had delivered the answer clearly and respectfully enough. The beliefs spoken of by the priest-men of the All-Father appeared to be healthy in nature, but they were in the form of words Dragol could not hope to verify for himself.

"Were it not for the All-Father, perhaps that would be the wisest path of action to follow in this world," the old man responded, thoughtfully. "Just keep your mind, heart, and eyes open, Dragol. See what there is to see, and hear what there is to hear; for many in this world refuse such, when it is given openly to them."

"I will keep my eyes and ears open, as I always have," Dragol replied in sincerity, glancing over to the old man.

"That is all I can ask of you," the old man replied. A grin then came to his face, as he nodded towards the trees. He was looking in the direction they had previously been heading in, before the encounter with the forest predator. "So, shall we resume our journey?"

Dragol nodded in agreement, starting forward. He found himself wondering what sort of new encounters and strange experiences might be lying just ahead of them.

Lifting up the better portion of a matured tree, and petting a wild, carnivorous beast, especially one unfettered within its own environment, had certainly not been experiences he could ever have seen coming when he had arrived in such great fatigue by the creek waters. Yet despite the uncertainty as to what might transpire, in even a few scant moments, Dragol had a calm state of mind. With the mysterious and undeniably powerful companion at his side, Dragol discovered a great confidence dwelling within. With his new friend, Dragol trusted that things would turn out well enough.

AELFRIC

There had been no messages of hope since the younger ceorl departed from the Saxan encampment with the ancient dragon. The respite in the extensive fighting was now at an end. Vast enemy forces were drawn up in their massed ranks once again, arrayed for battle on the open plain.

The only consolation was that the woodlands had proven to be largely impassable to the enemy, as Aelfric had thought. It left little mystery as to how fighting would resume. Saxany's adversaries were going to come right at them again with blunt, and likely overwhelming, force.

Both sides had incurred heavy losses in the sustained fighting, but losses were something the combined armies of Avanor, Ehrengard, and Andamoor could absorb. Saxan losses were mounting dangerously, with many irreplaceable, courageous warriors having already fallen.

Riding with his thanes and household guards towards the Saxan center, where the proud standard of Prince Aidan yet stood defiantly, Aelfric thought back upon many inspiring moments since the titanic battle had first begun. From the stalwart leadership of Count Einard, saving the Saxans from rout after tearing into the Andamoorans, to the insightful use of pits by Count Gerard, thwarting an Avanoran advance in the center, decisiveness and ingenuity had deflected greater might time and time again. From Aldric the Stormblade's brave and desperate strike into the enemy reserve from the skies at daybreak, to the brave flight of Wulfstan to seek out the enormous Elder dragon, courageous acts, with tangible threads of hope woven into them, had countered the seemingly overwhelming advantages the enemy possessed.

There were countless individual moments involving all manner of bravery and wit, that Aelfric had not personally witnessed. Nothing else could explain how else the Saxans had been able to withstand days of fierce enemy onslaughts, and continue resisting against all reasonable odds.

Astride his black stallion Midnight, he cantered towards the billowing dragon standard of Prince Aidan. The prince was sitting tall upon his great war stallion Starshine, whose luxuriant coat was as pure white as unsullied snow. Aelfric reached down, patting the neck of Midnight, as he approached the noble prince.

The two horses had probably known each other long before,

perhaps even sharing common origins. Midnight had been a gift of the king to Aelfric, and was about the same age as Starshine. Both horses were from the storied Burton Monastery, which excelled above all others in horse breeding amid the many capable studfarms across Saxany.

The prized coats on the two respective horses, one of the deepest black, and the other unblemished white, were what enamored most observers. But Aelfric found Midnight's durable bearing and steadfast temperament most to his liking. He had no doubts Prince Aiden's love of Starshine was based upon similar qualities, rather than the particular shade of the horse's coat.

The sun had just started climbing in the east behind them, burning away the cool morning dew, and unveiling relatively clear skies. Aelfric was grateful for the promising weather, as much as he was for a reconciled spirit and a full stomach.

He had taken his morning meal alone, in quiet, partaking of a side of bacon, fresh cheese from the milk of sheep, and a portion of fresh wheat bread. Aelfric had also indulged himself in a single cup of mead, as well as a bowl containing a variety of woodland nuts, both personal favorites of his. On a day with great uncertainty as to whether or not he would still be drawing breath when the sun next set, such seemingly small things were rich treasures.

A melancholy mood weighed heavily upon him as he ate, and then prayed to the Almighty in the shadowy silence of his tent. He had felt an urge to seek confession from one of the priests within the encampment, desiring to clear his conscience with the accompanying absolution before donning his mail, helm, and weapons. To his view, a sincere confession was the most important element of his preparation, even more so than his weapons and armor.

In truth, there was little to confess, mainly simple, ordinary transgressions that most others would not likely even pause to regard. Yet if he was to fall in battle, he wanted to face the next world with as few blemishes on his soul as possible. The matter of the next world held far greater implications than the one he was now entrenched in.

Word had finally come to him that the enemy was massing on the horizon, marshaling their ranks with the full intention of offering battle. Aelfric could only smile ruefully as he began to gird himself for the battlefield. Slipping on his mail-coat, he wished that the report would have been of the enemy disassembling their encampment, and heading back to the west, but he had known such thoughts were only an exercise in wishful thinking.

Summoning a priest, he had delayed long enough to engage in a confession. He had felt an ensuing sense of peace when he left the tent, and surmounted Midnight's saddle.

The ground had not yet begun vibrating with the approach of the enemy formations as Aelfric had worked his way down the rear of the Saxan lines. The uneasy stillness hovering beyond the assembling Saxan ranks told him he still had a little precious time left before the invader's assault began.

Aelfric had not been surprised at the delay in the attack, highly skeptical that the enemy ranks would start their forward march with their eyes staring directly into the rising sun. Aldric the Storm Blade's daring attack had undoubtedly helped in that regard, dissuading any other impulses the enemy commanders may otherwise have entertained.

Aelfric's pace had been slowed by the masses of Saxan warriors heading towards their various placements along the extensive lines. Flags and pennons carried high among the various contingents served as markers for those following behind.

Drawing upon Midnight's reins, he had been forced to halt as a large throng crossed his path. He watched a number of levy men, bearing bundles of javelins and quivers filled with arrows, hurrying by with anxious faces. He had hoped that many of the arrows nestled in the quivers were tipped with the four-sided, mail-piercing variety of heads. It was a specific directive he had adamantly ordered to be dispersed among all groups involved with defending the Saxan center.

The Avanorans were well-armored, and Aelfric knew any failures to heed his dictate would result in much greater losses of life. For each and every Avanoran knight felled before the enemy reached the shield wall, Saxan lives were inevitably spared.

Avanoran knights were wolves among sheep when opposed by any Saxans other than ceorls and thanes of the Select Fyrd. Seeing those knights break through the shield wall, set loose to rampage through the deeper ranks of levymen, was one of Aelfric's greatest fears.

Prince Aidan quietly watched Aelfric as he approached. He gave the Saxan Ealdorman a smile that was one part amiable, and another part bittersweet. The lines of his face were noticeably taut. Aelfric sensed great inner turmoil behind the stoic façade of the prince.

The elderly King Alcuin was in his sunset within the world of Ave, and Prince Aidan had been well-accepted as his crowned successor. There were not likely to be any difficulties with the transition of rulership.

Yet the timing could not have been worse. The storms of war were breaking right as the young Prince was coming of age.

If one looked carefully enough, there was still some boyish ebullience left that had not yet been doused by the trials of maturity. The prince still had a rather thin beard, though it framed his face well, with the thick, curling black locks hanging freely to about an inch above his shoulders. His facial lines were strong and defined, with a squared, protruding jaw, and a prominent forehead.

His forehead was graced with dense eyebrows, lending favorably to stern expressions. Aelfric thought the natural feature an additional boon for the prince, as a single firm look, backed by honorable authority, was far more efficient than any long rants or tirades by lesser men.

The Prince's body was like a sword whose weaponsmith's name had just been etched into the fuller of the blade. Not yet scarred with the nicks and scrapes of battle, or needing the whetstone, his tall, broad-shouldered frame supported a body that was neither too lean, nor too bulky. He had large, strong hands that had proven very capable in wielding sword and spear in training, though they had yet to draw blood in war.

On his head, the Prince wore a most stunning helm, which represented a trove of Saxan symbolism and legacy. It had been worn on many battlefields, by many of the prince's ancestors.

A chain mail neck guard affixed to the helm's lower rim in the back augmented the ornate headpiece. The rim itself had a golden edge spanning the full circumference, from the back and sides, to up and along the arching brows over the wearer's eyes.

The helm was provided with two forward-curving iron plates, which hung down on the sides of the wearer's face, serving as protective cheek flaps. The plates, like the helm's lower rim, were also bound with a golden edge.

A low ridge crest arched right over the center of the helm, continuing past the brow into a nasal guard. The golden crest was stylized, exquisitely fashioned into the long neck and head of a dragon. The nasal projection was shaped into the form of an upright spear, representing the Western Church, with the uppermost tip fitted perfectly into the dragon's open mouth.

The ridge-crest was bisected at its apex by a narrow, golden band. The transecting band complimented the motif of the crest, crafted into the form of dragon's wings. Words in the ancient Reman tongue were worked into both the low ridge-crest and the transverse band.

The helm intrinsically recalled an older, valiant age, a bygone era when steadfast courage forged vibrant new realms out of a foreboding wilderness. Those days were long gone, and the helm had been passed down the ages, an heirloom in the royal line. Nonetheless, the storied helm sat very well upon Prince Aidan's head, something Aelfric readily noted. He considered it a favorable harbinger in regards to the future sovereign of Saxany.

Beyond the fitting of a cherished helm, there was much to be hopeful about regarding the prince. Where another young man on the edge of kingship might have let prideful arrogance interfere with better judgement, the prince had demonstrated wisdom and restraint. Aelfric knew the Prince wanted with all of his heart to risk himself as much as any thane, count, or Ealdorman.

To Aelfric's relief, the Prince had remained steadfast with the Saxan reserve, which included most of King Alcuin's vaunted King's Guard. The great warriors were gathered all around the Prince. Though they rode well-bred horses to a battlefield, they were men who fought with their feet firmly planted on Saxan soil.

Their long shields were not unlike those of the Avanorans. They had an extended, triangular shape, with a wide, rounded top that narrowed gradually inward as it descended on both sides to culminate in a small, rounded bottom. The leather-covered shields were painted with bright white backgrounds, with the image of a red dragon rendered on top. The winged beasts reflected the windsock battle standard now hovering proudly above the throng of veteran warriors.

All of the royal houseguard carried finely-crafted swords, the multi-lobed pommels of which rested against the mouth of scabbards attached to baldrics. They wore long coats of mail, split in the front and back up to the waist, the protective lengths extending down to just above their knees.

The most fabled element of their equipment was now in plain view, secured in iron-strong grips. The weapons were wielded two-handed in battle, possessing thick hafts of over three feet in length. The vaunted Saxan broadaxe, carried by the houseguards of the king and greater thanes, had long ago garnered its renown of devastating effectiveness on fields of battle. Wielding the deadly axes with ferocity and keen skill, and backed by an unshakable courage, the royal housegard had proven many times over, during the reign of numerous kings, why they were unrivaled within the greater Saxan force.

To a man, the warriors had hardened, resolute looks to their eyes. Aelfric knew they were all prepared to fight to the very last, if they were called to do so. If the one they served fell in battle, such warriors looked for only one end; to avenge the death of their beloved leader. They would not abandon the body of the one holding their loyalty, warding it fiercely against any attempt by an enemy to mutilate or otherwise desecrate it.

"Hail to you, Prince Aidan," Aelfric greeted the prince as he drew closer.

"May victory shine brightly upon you this day, Aelfric," Prince Aidan replied warmly. His voice carried a resonant, reassuring quality. It was confident and authoritative, but not domineering or patronizing.

"The men's spirits look strong today," Aelfric commented, his eyes scanning those gathered close to the Prince. "I felt it as well ... from the moment I walked outside my tent, before the dawn broke."

"They will need have strength of spirit," Prince Aidan replied more firmly, as his smile dimmed. "I fear the heaviest blow yet will fall today. My question to you is where do you think it will fall?"

The Prince's eyes narrowed, as he awaited the response. Aelfric had already given his assessments during the previous evening's war council, but the Prince's question indicated that he wanted to know whether anything in Aelfric's thinking had changed, after acquiring a little food and sleep.

"They could hit at us anywhere. They have strength in numbers on both flanks, and in the center. There is no weakness anywhere in their lines," Aelfric replied dourly, not one to soften the realities facing the Saxans. "My greatest concern lies in the right flank of the enemy."

"The rulers of Ehrengard?" the prince asked, his eyes reflecting a little surprise at the response. His voice then lowered, "Or the mercenaries ... the Halmlander?"

Aelfric held the prince's gaze, and did not hesitate in his reply. "The Halmlander. You and I both know what is at stake if those reavers should break through our lines."

The Prince nodded, with a darkening countenance. He stated

evenly, "My own men are fresh, and guilt is steadily rising within all of them. They see the men from all the other provinces bloodied and battered, and yet they stand in place, without a single drop of blood wetting their own blades. They know what the Halmlander are, and the savagery that would fall on the Saxan people if those ruthless beasts were to survive this battlefield."

The way in which he spoke the words implied strongly to Aelfric that the Prince had more than an idle notion as to where to commit his personal force. He wanted to hurl the royal houseguard into the mercenary ranks.

"It is no easy thing to hold back, Prince Aidan. But if the reserve is committed, then there is a great danger to the entire Saxan line," Aelfric replied. "You must keep a strong reserve maintained, a place of strength to rally around if all else should fail. We must have a force that is not weary and depleted, to throw back any sudden breach threatening to collapse the Saxan line. I counsel you to keep your force steadfast, and ready to face any crisis."

"As I will," Prince Aiden responded somberly. "Though words mean nothing, until I can prove that to you."

In the prince's response, Aelfric heard the plea of a young man coming into his own, who knew he was yet unproven in war. The prince had shown growing maturity, but there were likely strong impulses within him. Aelfric did not think that the Prince would likely give himself over to those impulses, but he still felt that it was best to maintain a firm perimeter surrounding the Prince's decisions for the time being.

Yet Aelfric still held a strong feeling of compassion within his heart for the Prince's dilemma, though he left the sentiments unspoken. He could plainly hear the unvoiced desires of the young man to assert himself before those who would soon be his people. It was born of the Prince's hunger to show his people the measure of his leadership, to gain a chance to demonstrate his mettle, and let all see that he would share fully in their own risks.

Not lost on Alefric was the recognition that the Prince also wanted to gain the full confidence of the Saxan army commander. Aelfric had few doubts that the Prince would gain the opportunity to address all of those desires, and likely much sooner than even Aelfric anticipated.

"Listen to me, my prince. You may not believe it, but you have already proven much. You have succeeded where many in your place would have failed," Aelfric said, wanting to soothe the young man's chafing disposition. "Your restraint and discipline, in the face of the forces pulling at you from all sides, and within you, show the makings of a great leader."

He could see the Prince straighten up a little in his saddle at the sudden compliment. Aelfric knew Prince Aidan was well aware of how much his father, King Alcuin, trusted and valued the Ealdorman of Wesvald. Any commendation coming from Aelfric was one the Prince would likely regard with high esteem.

"I will not hesitate, should you need me to commit," Prince Aidan said, a glint of steely determination flaring in his eyes.

"Or should you see the need, and judge it to be such a moment, without any doubts. Know that I have trust in your judgement as well, my prince," Aelfric replied.

Aelfric was not offering empty platitudes. He had a rising degree of trust in the Prince, even if the young man did not possess much experience in war. At the court of King Alcuin, Prince Aidan had always impressed Aelfric with his more subtle qualities; including the ability to patiently listen, when others would speak, to attentively observe, and to hold impetuousness at bay.

Aelfric wished with all of his heart that the Saxans could somehow strike a decisive blow, so that Prince Aidan could progress into the fullness of what he would be inheriting soon enough. A ruler such as Prince Aidan promised to be a great blessing to the Saxans, as King Alcuin most certainly had been. If the prince's chance to rule Saxany were forever unrealized, it would be a terrible tragedy in itself.

"We will strike a fatal blow to the Halmlander when the opportunity presents itself. That I promise you", Aelfric said firmly, sharing the prince's concerns regarding the blood-lusting mercenaries. "For now, I shall position myself on the Saxan left, with Count Leidrad. Know well that I will be positioned directly opposite the Halmlander, and that they can make no move without my taking notice of it.

"Hold the reserve with you, and remain vigilant. If the Avanorans come again in strength, the center must be held. I have made certain the numbers of mail-piercing arrows were bolstered among the contingents in the center. The Avanorans will be greeted with a different manner of rain from that normally falling out of these skies."

"Then let a downpour break upon the Avanorans," Prince Aidan said, as his face eased with a knowing grin.

"Let them come, and the rain will fall," Aelfric replied, exuding conviction. "And may the blessings of the All-Father be on you, my prince."

Giving Prince Aidan a salute, clenching his right fist to his chest, he bowed in the saddle. Aelfric then guided Midnight away from the Prince and his attendant houseguard.

Aelfric rode with the warriors of his own houseguard down the back of the Saxan lines. They headed towards the far end of the shield wall where Count Leidrad was positioned on the Saxan left flank.

He listened to the hooves of the horses streaming behind him, as they progressed at a full canter. The low rumbling bolstered his spirits, the strong reverberations like living symbols of the potency still remaining to defend Saxany on the great battle plain.

The sun now shone a little higher in the sky, and most of the men looked to be set in their places along the great shield wall. A few messengers galloped by on horse, or ran to and fro on foot, but the bulk of the Saxan ranks were now settled into their designated positions.

A forest of spears and lances jutted up towards the morning sky, the backs of many thousands facing Aelfric as he continued along the length of the massed Saxans. At long last, Aelfric and his houseguard finally reached the far left of the shield wall, where Count Leidrad had gathered a sizeable host of cavalry.

Aelfric and his houseguard dismounted without delay, gathering up their shields and weapons. A cluster of camp attendants quickly materialized, and led most of the horses away, to remove them far back from the battle lines. Aelfric could see the nervous energy coursing through most of the camp attendents, who kept casting worrisome glances back towards the western horizon.

As far as Aelfric was concerned, it felt good just to get his feet under him again. Like his houseguard, he preferred to fight on his own two feet, rather than horseback.

A cavalryman always faced the grave risk of having his mount cut down from under him. Devoid of a mount, Aelfric took a little comfort in the fact that the enemy had one less target to strike when fighting him.

Aelfric did not have long to adjust, or savor the feeling of being on the hard ground again. When he started walking towards Count Leidrad, he felt the first distant vibrations underfoot. The light tremors coursing through the ground were unmistakable, signaling the beginning of the enemy's thunderous approach.

Nothing was visible yet, as Aelfric glanced to the west. It would still take the enemy ranks some time to march over the western horizon.

The final arrangements of their vast multitudes, conducted within clear sight of the Saxan lines, would present its own worries. Aelfric understood well enough what the mere sight of their approach entailed, in terms of how the vision was received by the defenders. Widened eyes, blanching faces, and trembling hands within the Saxan levies reflected the raw feelings invoked by the enemy advance.

The new day made such reactions even more worrisome to Aelfric. With the heavy losses already incurred, men from the General Fyrd were being pressed into gaps within the shield wall. Most of those replacing fallen veterans at the forefront were farmers and simple tradesmen.

Aelfric could not entirely blame the levy men for their extreme anxiety. The sight of the Unifier's immense forces was enough to cause the hearts of even the strongest warriors to flutter momentarily.

He pushed the concerns back in his mind. Nothing more could be done than what had already been undertaken to address the realities of prolonged fighting. The men filling the front ranks had many veteran thanes and ceorls interspersed among them, to stiffen their confidence and provide close leadership. It would have to be enough. There were no other options.

Aelfric turned his thoughts to the moment at hand. He strode up to Count Leidrad, who was conferring with some of his senior retainers while they sat idly astride their mounts.

"Hail Aelfric," Count Leidrad greeted, looking up to see the Ealdorman approaching.

"Hail, Leidrad," Aelfric responded amiably.

"What thought is foremost in your mind, as this day begins?" Count Leidrad asked him. His senior retainers ceased their discussions, and all looked towards the Saxan commander who held King Alcuin's confidence.

"Today we must look to break the Halmlander," Aelfric answered.

Poitaine, the count's lands, was one of the closest provinces to the Plains of Aethelney. Aelfric knew Count Leidrad had read the horrific accounts of the Halmlander and the hapless villages they had ravaged. He knew very well what the barbarous mercenaries indulged in. Murder, wanton destruction, and rape were the sustenance the Halmlander had an insatiable hunger for.

They were a force of brutal, merciless men, vagrants, criminals, and other miscreants, whose very survival had lain in staying together as a feared mercenary company. A scorn to their own lands, they were reviled by the very individuals who hired them. There was a cold logic to the Halmlander presence in the opposing army, as Aelfric knew the enemy would much rather have the barbaric horde sating themselves on Saxan blood and women, rather than Ehrengard's own.

As Aelfric drew close, he took note that the characteristic roundness in the Count's belly and cheeks were noticeably reduced. His deepset eyes had dark patches emerging underneath, a development betraying the man's significant lack of sleep in recent days.

Yet the Count's eyes reflected full alertness, despite the signs of hardship. His golden-starred, purple pennons snapped and fluttered in the robust breezes flowing across the battlefield. The men bearing up the standards carried them proud and high, reflecting the determination of their respected Count.

"The Halmlander must be broken," Count Leidrad replied, with inflexible determination in his voice. "Broken absolutely asunder. Shattered to pieces and ground into the dirt."

Aelfric looked out over the massed levies on the Saxan left flank. They appeared much denser than on the previous days, indicating a shift to heavily reinforce the flank.

Infantry from the Select Fyrd of the southern provinces of Saxany, such as Count Leidrad's Poitaine, and Count Arnulf's Rouenum, were arrayed in force behind the shield wall. Their positions were easy to detect, with their simple, nasal-less round helms, pairs of extra throwing javelins, and large round shields serving to identify them.

Scraggly and rough in appearance, a good many having no shoes upon their feet, the host of peasant levymen bore a motley mix of weapons. War-scythes, hand axes, short flat bows, spears, shorter, single-edged scramseaxes, and many other implements suitable for combat, whether simple farm tools or intentionally crafted for war, were held in the callused hands of the unarmored men.

"Have more levies arrived this day?" Aelfric asked, keeping his eyes on the levymen. "Or have great numbers been repositioned here."

"All know what terrible danger is at hand. Every man in camp was begging desperately to stand at arms today. No matter how frightened many undoubtedly are, they would use the ridge poles of tents as weapons, if nothing else was available," Count Leidrad replied. His tone reflected sincere admiration as he spoke of the courage of men who were largely villagers and farmers. "Count Arnulf and I could not deny them a place on the left. If the Halmlander break through, there will be nothing waiting for any of the levymen back home. They are all that stands between those mercenary hellspawn and their beloved families. Who could deny them the right to stand and fight under such circumstances?"

"I cannot disagree with you, and will not dispute you," Aelfric said. He had some misgivings, as an unwieldy, untrained mob on a battlefield, especially one driven by great fears, could present its own new problems to contend with. "But make sure that enough veteran men are in place amongst them. Men who can lead, and hold them back in good discipline until they are needed. I advise that you place even more veterans than you think you might need to do this."

Count Leidrad nodded. "That we will, Aelfric, as you advise. The Almighty Willing, perhaps they will not have to see battle this day."

"Let us hope, and pray, that they will not," Aelfric responded somberly, as he brought his gaze back onto the western horizon, the vibrations growing stronger underfoot.

The horizon was now filled with the massed ranks of the invaders, as they poured over the crest of the land into full view. War drums boomed faraway among the Andamorans anchoring the enemy's left flank. Masses of stately pennons and gonfalons flapped and undulated where they were carried forward once again, throughout the Avanoran center. Yet as foreboding as those two principle formations were, it was to the advance of Ehrengard that Aelfric's scrutiny turned.

He carefully searched the oncoming right flank of the enemy for the distinctive black banners, displaying their blood-red blades. He soon eyed the loathsome sigils flying in great numbers among the sprawling mass of pikes carried by the vile mercenaries, as they tramped steadily forward.

The Saxans on the left end of the shield wall also took notice of the Halmlander's appearance on the battlefield. A defiant roar erupted spontaneously from the Saxan ranks spread before Aelfric. The Saxans vigorously beat their weapons upon their shields, as a couple of distinctive, boisterous chants swelled above the rising din.

"Hail to the Almighty!" thousands of voices called out, in unison.

"By the Sacred Spear!" followed soon after.

Aelfric could feel the confidence surging, like rippling lightning, through the clouds of apprehension and fear lingering over the Saxans only moments before. It ascended in waves of spirited defiance that had the potency of a dragon's roar.

Aelfric knew that the determined reaction was not born of misplaced hopes. Having resisted the enemy forces for a few days already, the Saxans knew they could resist the invaders.

Aelfric watched the enemy lines drawing closer. He could not see well enough to tell exactly what was happening on the far right, but in the center, the movements were clear enough. The Avanorans were in the process of bringing large contingents of archers and crossbowmen, intending to shower the portion of the Saxan shield wall arrayed in front of them.

Thick lines of infantry were arrayed just behind the deploying missile troops. In the space between the Avanorans in the center, and the orderly contingents from Ehrengard on the enemy's right, Aelfric recognized the hulking shapes of Gigans lumbering amid a force of brawny Trogen warriors. He knew a similar formation warded the Avanoran left, separating it from the Andamoorans.

Aelfric was relieved that the posture of the smaller Trogen and Gigan forces had been largely defensive so far in the battle. The Gigans were terrifying to witness in combat, wielding their huge war axes and maces with mind-boggling strength. The Trogens, with their tall shields, heavy blades, and long lances, were ferocious warriors.

Aelfric could only hope the restraint continued to hold with the non-human allies of the Unifier. If they were unleashed fully, the Saxans would find themselves facing a terrible onslaught.

The Halmlander screening the forces of Ehrengard on the far end of the enemy's right continued advancing. They marched forward until they had reached a position a short distance beyond the Saxans' effective arrow range. Horns sounded loudly, and the rythmic cadence of their steps ebbed.

Once they had fully halted, the mercenaries shored up their dense, prickly hedge of pikes. The hated black banners with their cruel red blades rippled in the winds above the dark ranks, boldly proclaiming the mercenaries' position to Saxan eyes.

From the defender's perspective, beginning from the right edge of the mercenary contingent, and continuing throughout the rest of the Ehrengardian lines, kettle-helmed archers and crossbowmen made their first appearance of the day. With more horns sounding, they advanced to the forefront of the enemy ranks, in loose groups scattered up and down the facing of Ehrengard's multitudes.

Once in the open ground, they slowly proceeded many paces forward, halting at positions just within range of the defenders. Without delay, arrows were notched in longbows, while belt-hooks were employed in setting bolts and triggers on the crossbows.

Following a long, sustained blast comprised of many signaling horns, they loosed a torrent of lethal missiles. Great volleys of arrows arced over the defender's shield wall and into their massed ranks. While many arrows drove into the hard ground, many struck Saxan bodies. Thick clusters of bolts tore across the open space between the two opposing battle lines, embedding in shields, or punching through mail and flesh.

The archers were quick in retrieving new arrows from their quivers. Bracing their feet apart, and pulling their bowstrings back, they sent more clouds of arrows towards the defenders.

The slower-loading crossbowmen did not hesitate either. Using one foot placed into a stirrup-like piece of iron affixed at the bow end, with the crossbow string in the belt hook, they gradually pulled the string up until the trigger was again set into place.

Frequent volleys of arrows interspersed with periodic waves of bolts harried the Saxan lines. It was not long before numerous Saxan shields bristled with embedded arrows and bolts.

While the deadly rain continued pouring down on the Saxans, Aelfric hurried over to where a throng of peasant levymen with bows stood. They were southerners, with bows a little shorter than the longbows of Saxan northerners. Aelfric knew the bows of the southerners did not have the range to duel with their Ehrengardian counterparts. Even so, the Saxan archers could be utilized in another way, concerning the enemy's non-human forces situated between the ranks of Ehrengard and Avanor.

"Watch the Gigans …the huge brutes, there!" Aelfric called forcefully to the levymen.

He gestured towards the gigantic forms looming over the Trogens. Scattered amongst the dog-faced warriors, the tusked monstrosities bellowed and roared as they glared at the Saxans, brandishing their massive weapons in the air.

"Concentrate your arrows on the Gigans, if they move to attack this line. Bear down on the Gigans, and loose as many arrows as you can towards them!" Aelfric shouted.

While fear reflected in the eyes of the levymen, as they glanced at the hulking beings, the peasant archers nodded towards him. Aelfric had no doubts the archers would want to fell the Gigans as quickly as possible, long before the fearsome creatures could bring their heavy maces, axes, and spears into striking range.

As the defenders continued absorbing further volleys of missiles, the Saxan left flank stoutly fended off a few initial sorties conducted by heavily armored knights of Ehrengard. While they did not break through the shield wall, the knights took very few casualties in their grazing, probing forays. With both horses and riders thoroughly armored, the knights seemed almost impervious to Saxan weapons.

Aelfric could not deny that the knights of Ehrengard and their steeds were impressive sights to behold, both colorful and imposing. The encompassing trappers adorning the war horses were fashioned in hues matching the particular elements of the knights riding them, whether shield, surcoat, pennon, or a combination thereof. A few horses were encased in trappers of chain mail, looking like chargers made of iron as they thundered onto the battlefield.

Aelfric espied a low mitre crowning the helm of one particular knight, located in the midst of one cluster wheeling away from the Saxan lines. The warrior was wielding a long, flange-headed mace, even though a longsword was plainly visible in a scabbard at his side.

Hearing of the warrior-prelates of Ehrengard was one matter. Witnessing one in person was quite another. The bishop from Ehrengard was a vision in stark contrast to the men of the clergy, including bishops, residing in Saxany. Armored, wielding weapons, and commanding contingents of warriors, the low mitre was one of the only ways the bishop could be differentiated from a secular lord.

All the while, Aelfric kept an eye trained on the dense throng of Halmlander. For the time being, they were keeping their extensive thicket of pikes set firmly in place. They seemed content forming a haven for the Ehrengardian knights, as well as providing a deterring presence on the enemy right flank.

The Ealdorman sorely wished the battle would somehow remain in its current form, as the Saxans could maintain their defensive position without undue stress. Yet he knew that was too much to hope for. He waited for the marked shift in the enemy ranks that he knew would be coming, wondering what new methods the enemy would unveil.

Pennons then began to wave and surge forward in the distance, as horns brayed a sonorous, unified signal. An Ehrengardian tidal wave then rolled forward, heading right towards the Saxan shield wall.

A great force of knights emerged from the Halmlander's protection, starting forth at a slow trot across the field. Approaching the Saxans' far left, the rumble of hooves filled the air, sending powerful vibrations running through the ground underfoot.

Further inward, past the Halmlander screen, the crossbowmen ceased loosing bolts lest they harm their own fighters. A dense throng marching up from behind quickly engulfed archers and crossbowmen alike. A line of heavy Ehrengardian infantry emerged into the forefront, tromping across the open ground towards the Saxans, followed closely by a line of mounted knights.

To Aelfric's great concern, the Trogens moved in cohesion with the humans. They carried their tall rectangular shields close together, each one an individual mantlet. The few Gigans sprinkled amongst the Trogens roared as they trudged forth, shaking their maces, axes, and lances menacingly at the Saxans.

Aelfric's eyes roved towards the Avanoran center, to the right of the Trogens and Gigans. His dismay rose further, as the enemy center was unfurling a mass of infantry, and sending it towards the Saxan center. Idenfitied by their visored helms and swords, numerous Avanoran knights had dismounted to fight on foot, considerably reinforcing the advancing lines of heavy infantry.

Though he could not see far enough, Aelfric had no doubts the ominous trend continued all the way down to the far end of the enemy left flank. The enemy was hurling its full weight upon them, in a unified, tremendous surge, seeking a decisive moment in the titanic battle. It was a bludgeoning hammer blow intended to shatter Saxan resolve to pieces.

Aelfric took a deep, cleansing breath, collecting his thoughts as the ground shook underneath. The massive advance was like nothing he had ever beheld before.

The gap between invaders and defenders shrank steadily, and a deafening din erupted as the two lines came together at last. Iron cracked thunderously against the wood of shields, and thousands of cries filled the air.

"The Gigans!" Aelfric shouted urgently towards the peasant archers. "Bring the Gigans down!"

Though the men were undoubtedly filled with terror at the monstrous wave heading towards them, the archers set their feet, and drew their bowstrings back. They hesitated a moment, as they aimed towards the huge Gigans, before loosing their barrage. The bevy of Saxan arrows coursed over the front ranks of the shield wall, plummeting down around the Gigans and any Trogens surrounding them.

Aelfric watched as several Gigans staggered and fell in the first wave of arrows, stricken by many shafts. A few Trogens howled in pain, or dropped to the ground. The discipline of the peasant archers was encouraging to Aelfric, as he saw many retrieving arrows from their quivers for the next hail of missiles.

The archers would need to keep the volleys going. The Gigans had not all been brought down, and he could see the rage on a few of the brutes lumbering forward with arrows sticking out of their bodies. Pushing aside Trogen fighters with ease, the Gigans sought to reach their Saxan oppressors more quickly, their strides picking up speed.

Aelfric could not remain transfixed on the Gigans. Moving forward, surrounded by his own household guards, he watched the furious engagement breaking out along the shield wall. Broadaxes arced down and cleaved into horse and man, while spears and swords slashed and thrust in a relentless, martial tempest. Weapons clanged together loudly, and footing quickly became treacherous, as bodies of the slain and grievously wounded piled up along the contested line.

From what Aelfric could tell, the shield wall was jostled all along its considerable length, buckling a little in some spots, and wavering tenuously in still others. Yet it was still holding.

Saxans stepped up to fill any gaps created by those falling in front of them, and any punctures were quickly driven back and sealed. Such intensive combat was exhausting, and Aelfric knew the enemy assault could not remain at its current, feverish pace for long.

Aelfric watched for breaches, and waited, looking for the opportune moment he sensed was coming. Trading blows, the two condensed sides continued to strain and bleed. Knights were toppled from horseback, and men on foot from both sides fell, but the pace of the fighting gradually ebbed along the shield wall.

Arrows continued to fly in both directions. A heavy storm was being loosed from the Saxan center. Aelfric hoped that more than a few of the mail-piercing arrowheads were finding their way to dismounted Avanoran knights.

At the moment, there was very little Aelfric could do but wait and keep his wits about him. The cacophonous sounds of fighting enveloped the Saxan commander. He dismissed the tumult to the back of his mind, keeping his concentration rigidly focused ahead of him.

He could not help but admire the endurance of the knights of Ehrengard, watching their swords rising and falling as they hacked at the Saxans below them. Their powerful war destriers bit and lashed out with their hooves. More than a few Saxans found their chests or skulls shattered in the thunderous force delivered by Ehrengardian mounts.

Just when Aelfric feared the enemy could fight on forever, he finally heard the signals he had expected, coming from the mounted knights of Ehrengard. The knights began to bring their horses about, disengaging wherever they could from the close combat at the left end of the shield wall.

Aelfric knew the knights would be crossing back to their lines in a state of exhaustion. He was also aware that the knights were far too valuable of an asset to the enemy to leave them completely exposed to the mercies of the Saxans.

There was one move the enemy could make to protect its vaunted knights, and it was the very move Aelfric was now counting on. Aelfric glanced towards Count Arnulf, and then at Count Leidrad, who was a little farther down with his force of cavalry gathered all around him. Both had held back from striking at the force of knights, letting the shield wall stymie them, and waiting for the same moment Aelfric anticipated.

After a few moments, the two counts looked back towards Aelfric. He gave them a slow nod, and was met by resolute nods in return. Count Arnulf and Count Leidrad were of grim countenance, and a fire burned within their eyes.

Aelfric then looked to the men immediately around him, seeing a reflection of the determination he harbored. He turned to his signaler, and gave the order to begin the counterattack.

The man's chest swelled, and he loosed a few short bursts on his horn, which were matched a moment later by one of Count Arnulf's men. Horn blasts rose from within Count Leidrad's mounted force just a few heartbeats later.

The enemy had to be kept off balance. The greater the fear was of losing a large portion of their vaunted knights, the more things might well result in hasty, shortsighted moves to protect them.

Raising their swords high, reinforced by a strong contingent of their own household guards, Aelfric and Count Arnulf led a large force forward beyond the shield wall. A loud roar filled the air as the Saxans tramped forward, shields and weapons in firm grips. An aura of smoldering anger accompanied the warriors, finally allowed to end their restraint and go on the offensive

The cavalry under Count Leidrad cantered forward, and the ground resounded with hundreds upon hundreds of hoofbeats. The tremors increased as the mass of well-rested Saxan cavalry sped up.

The throng of horsemen warded the ends of the Saxan left flank, harrying the knights now falling back from their concentrated sortie. Javelins were soon being hurled from experienced hands, though most did little damage to the heavily armored knights.

The forward riders throwing the javelins wheeled sharply away from the edges of the retreating mass of knights. The riders from Poitaine drew their close-combat weapons out, as they came back around to rejoin the main body of Saxan cavalry.

Sword and lance-wielding Saxan riders overtook a few of the slower-moving knights. An ensuing flurry of vigorous thrusts and bludgeoning sword blows downed several of the weary Ehrengardians. The enemy knights laboriously tried to defend themselves, but the heavy Saxan blades were delivered with crushing impact upon their mailed bodies.

Count Leidrad's force now threatened to swallow up a majority of the retreating knights. Then, the moment Aelfric was hoping for arrived.

Numerous horns blared from the enemy ranks, with a tenor of urgency. The broad, spiky hedge of pikes, which had previously served as a fixed haven and flank guardian, lurched into motion. The Halmlander finally committed their strength to full battle. The waving black banners flowed forward, as the thumping steps of several thousand mercenaries marched to meet the oncoming Saxan warriors.

The Halmlander moved to halt the pursuit of the retreating

knights. While undeniably laced with risk, it was a chance to engage the vile mercenaries with full force, and strike a heavy blow upon them.

Aelfric, with his household guards in his immediate wake, charged forward with zealous fervor. The men around him broke into a run, shouting various challenges and insulting epithets towards the hated mercenaries.

"Cut through them! Hold nothing back, this is our chance!" Aelfric shouted, as the Saxans came face to face at last with the venemous Halmlander. "Fight them like the All-Father's Archons! Drive these devils back to the hell from where they came!"

"Hail to the Almighty!" was the predominant cheer filling the air over the Saxans, as the first blows were exchanged.

The axes of the houseguards flashed in the sunlight, shattering spear shafts into splinters. The Halmlander jabbed, parried, and slashed back with their long pikes, using the advantages of range the lengthy weapons afforded them.

The houseguards chopped and hacked furiously, tediously forging holes in the Halmlander's line. A few grew wide enough that a number of Saxan warriors were able to infiltrate the wall of pikes, and begin to engage the mercenaries at close quarter.

While very little chain mail was present among the Halmlander, their leather jerkins and padded gambesons turned aside many kinds of blows. Yet they could not turn aside all attacks, and several began succumbing to the ferocious Saxan assault.

Aelfric wetted his blade more than once as he slashed at the Halmlander with a passionate fury. Thoughts of vulnerable Saxan villages lying beyond the defensive lines spurred Aelfric towards a frenzy. He knew well enough what the black-hearted mercenaries would do if turned loose in Saxany, and used that knowledge to empower his sword arm to a fearsome level of martial ardor.

He hacked downward, severing the haft of one mercenary's pike. The man's eyes filled with fear as Aelfric lunged down the length of the broken haft, bringing his sword blade plunging down into the mercenary's exposed neck.

Aelfric did not bother wondering whether the mercenary had ever regarded the fear in his own victims, as the man had probably savored terror in others. All that mattered to Aelfric was that the dead Halmlander would never rape a woman again, or laugh while running his spear through an old man too frail to flee a doomed village.

Aelfric then looked up in surprise, just as he heard an oncoming mass of shouts, and unified horn calls. He glanced back just long enough to see an elevated, windsock dragon standard advancing rapidly in back of him.

Prince Aidan was throwing his weight into the battle on the Saxan left flank. At the least, he had committed a large number of the reserves.

Aelfric's blood raced in his veins at the sight, both exhilarated and anxious. He knew the Prince's move was timed fortuitously, as far as the Saxan left was concerned. He just hoped the commitment of the reserve force was not out of balance with the things happening at the center and right of the Saxan lines. He could only trust in Prince Aidan's judgement.

Released at last from their prolonged, tormenting inactivity, the royal household guards with Prince Aidan, the King's Guard, descended rabidly upon the Halmlander as if they were fighting a lifetime's worth of battles in one day. They were like starved lions, maddened by cavernous hunger.

Though the tempest chained within them was finally loosed, the veteran warriors did not forget their discipline and training. Shield bearers worked closely in tandem with axe wielders. They protected the axe-swinging warriors as the latter brought up their feared undercuts, or sent the axes chopping down in arcing, overhead motions that achieved devastating results.

Men from the Select Fyrd and garrisons of the burhs, accompanying the elite contingent of royal houseguards in the reserve, were equally vigorous with their freedom to attack. Exploiting every new opening in the mercenaries' wall of spears, the warriors relentlessly widened them.

Driving their combat spears into the Halmlander ranks, they demonstrated expert skill with the heavy, long weapons. They dexterously caught enemy shafts and blades with the iron extensions flaring out at the base of the spear blade's metallic socket. With deadly grace, the warriors worked off their defensive catches to deliver lethal counterstrikes, whether slashing or thrusting.

The great round shields carried by many of the warriors were fitted with substantial iron bosses at their center, whose conical forms tapered to narrow points. The shields were as much weapons, as they were defensive implements, when in experienced hands.

SPIRIT OF FIRE

A few Saxans bore a unique type of seax that was sword-length, and provided with a very sharp end point. The weapons were, in essence, elongated versions of the single-edged knives commonly carried by Saxans. While not outright swords, such langseaxes were effective enough for the bloody tasks at hand.

Those still fighting on the outside rim of the fracturing pike-hedge caught enemy pike blows on their shields. The impacts of iron on wood cracked the air loudly, and repeatedly. The Saxans labored to hack apart ever more of the pike hafts with their heavier swords and axe blades.

Those accessing the widening openings pressed hard to enter the interior fray, rife with an abundance of targets. The Saxans pummeled, cut, chopped, and slashed at the enemy, spreading a growing chaos among the Halmlander.

Prince Aidan waded into the Halmlander with nothing but death to offer the enemy. One after another, the prince's bloodied sword claimed mercenary lives. Seeing the prince break like a thunderstorm into the enemy, all the Saxans around him were inspired into a martial delirium.

Once a considerable portion of the long, unwieldy pikes had been reduced to uselessness, the most effective element of the mercenary defenses was eliminated. In terms of weaponry, most of the Halmlander resorted to using daggers, placing them at a severe disadvantage in the widening melee.

Not all the Halmlander wore leather curies and padded gambesons. A fair number had nothing but tunics covering their upper bodies, and few carried shields.

The addition of Prince Aidan and his men swelled the Saxan ranks, injecting an energy that was like oil poured onto a blazing fire. The Halmander, so used to being predators, had been transformed into prey.

The ensuing course of battle weighed down heavily upon the invaders, as the momentum swung rapidly in the Saxans' favor. The knights formerly protected by the host of pikes now found themselves fending off attacks from Saxan warriors. Ever more Saxans reached the knights warded by the pike-hedge, breaking deep through the collapsing mercenary ranks.

Aelfric slew more than eight Halmlander as the mercenary ranks crumbled. He called up every last vestige of fury within as he delivered strike after strike, cleaving into their midst. He did not worry for a moment about being cut off, or surrounded, for such was his single-minded effort to slay every Halmlander mercenary possible.

He was immersed within the frenzied passions of raw battle-rage; primal, reactive, and unshakeable. Aelfric was so consumed by the inferno he did not even hear the corresponding horns, as both Ehrengardian knights and heavy infantry shifted over to resist the mounting threat to their right flank. They moved with desperation, seeking to prevent their increasingly exposed flank from being rolled up and put to rout.

Aelfric obtained a particular gratification as he hew one of the mercenary's standard bearers down, sending one of the black banners with its blood-red blades toppling to the ground. He then smashed the multi-lobed pommel of his sword into the face of the warrior next to the standard bearer. Blood sprayed as the man fell heavily.

Before Aelfric could finish the dazed warrior off, he came face to face with one of the mercenary company's leaders. He recognized the man's special nature, the very moment he set his eyes upon him.

Though it was a matter of sheer circumstance, Aelfric's right foot stomped down upon the fallen Halmlander banner as he squared to face his prominent new foe. Armed with a tapering sword of excellent quality, and clad head to toe in links of mail, the knight was one of the leaders of the bloodthirsty mercenary company. As with most of their number, his disreputable past was probably unknown to most, even his fellow men, but it did not make his skill at arms any lesser.

He was a very powerfully built man, whose face was hidden behind his iron helm's visor. His long kite-shield was covered in solid black, the same color as his sleeveless surcoat. The knight moved with an icy coolness, making no verbal exclamations as he took measure of Aelfric.

Picking his moments, Aelfric traded several blade strokes with the huge knight. He felt the ripples of energy coursing through his arm and body, whenever he caught one of the knight's weighty sword strikes on the edge of his own sword. A few of the knight's hits were caught on Aelfric's shield, breaking off chunks of wood, and sending a host of splinters outwards.

It quickly became apparent that the knight equaled Aelfric's skill at arms, and exceeded his strength by far. The Saxan knew he would have to find an opening very soon, or he would wear down fast in the exhaustive nature of extended sword combat.

He swayed to the side just in time, hearing the swish of air caused by the knight's sword passing within a handspan of Aelfric's right shoulder. Bunching himself behind his shield, Aelfric barreled forward. He rammed the shield into the knight with all the strength he could muster, knocking his opponent backwards and eliciting a heavy grunt. Knocked off balance, the staggering knight teetered for a moment, struggling to regain his footing. His troubles gave Aelfric a prime opening.

Coming back across his body with a downward, diagonal slash, Aelfric brought his sword blade cutting into the back of the knight's shoulder, just above his sword arm. A muffled outcry erupted within the knight's encasing helm, a sound filled with shock and pain.

The blow caused the knight's hand to open briefly, just long enough that his sword fell to the ground, but the knight did not lose his presence of mind. Reacting fast, he brought his own shield around, just as Aelfric shoved his shield forward to catch the move.

The wood of the shields slammed together with a resounding thwack. Shields engaged, and no longer having to worry about the knight's sword, Aelfric put his strength into a low, sweeping strike. His blade smashed into the mail links covering the knight's left ankle.

Links broke and flew outward in the crushing impact. The knight crumpled to the ground, shrieking out in agony from behind his dark iron visor.

Aelfric rained blow after blow down as the knight collapsed. Though many of the hits struck chain mail, the heaviness of their impact, enhanced by the wider, heavier style of Saxan blade, untapered for most of its length, exacted a brutal toll from the fallen knight.

When Aelfric was finished, his chest heaved as he gasped for air. He gazed down at the still, broken body of the knight, but only for a moment, as he regained his bearings and took account of his surroundings.

Saxans swirled all around him, having overrun the ground where the knight and the standard bearers had been. Traversing the ground was now a hazardous task, with many wounded and slain from both sides lying all about.

The enemy's wounded were not necessarily harmless, even if they were prone. Aelfric had to be wary, lest an enemy fighter muster enough strength to lash out as he passed by. The chaotic nature of large-scale battles riddled the contested terrain with threats to even the best of warriors.

Though still in the midst of his battle-fever, Aelfric restrained himself from charging onward. He was immensely fatigued, a stark fact becoming ever more apparent with each moment he labored to catch his breath again.

An angry sea of melee surrounded him. It was one of the most dangerous environments a warrior could be in during a battle, with friend and foe swarming in every direction. Allies made grave mistakes in such circumstances, just as easily as an enemy landed a killing blow from behind on an unwitting opponent.

A number of mounted Ehrengardian knights who had been sheltered within the hedge of mercenary pikes finally broke free. They fought their way towards the massed Ehrengardian ranks to the inside of the Halmlander. Other Ehrengardians from the edge of the mercenary ranks joined their numbers with the knights. Together, they began forming up a new line of defense, just beyond the splintering Halmlander.

Very few knights of Ehrengard remained in the thick of the fighting. Most were subsequently encircled, caught in small pockets as the Halmlander's pike wall collapsed entirely. One small cluster of entrapped knights was fighting very close to where Aelfric now stood.

Pillars of iron, they were seated upon their majestic warhorses, the latter garbed in colorful, protective trappers or bards of chain mail. The surrounded knights fought vigorously, and desperately, from horseback, aided by the thrashing hooves and bites of their inflamed war stallions.

Saxan household guards with their long axes cut a few of the knights' mounts out from under them, pinning a couple of unfortunate knights underneath their fallen horses' heavy bodies. Another few knights were slain as they tried to scramble back up to their feet, no minor task under the ponderous weight of their armor.

Aelfric watched as another knight was toppled from his wood-framed saddle, leaving only a handful of knights remaining in the diminishing pocket. A Saxan broadaxe rose and fell in the space over where the unhorsed knight had fallen, leaving few doubts that the prone knight was caught flush and defenseless by the plummeting blow.

Aelfric found he was grateful that the most heated areas of combat were now a short distance away from him. His limbs felt absolutely leaden in the aftermath of his sustained assault into the Halmlander ranks, taxed especially hard by the intense engagement with the rogue knight.

Turning his head, and looking to the direct north, right down the line of the enemy, he saw the Ehrengardians coalescing into a robust, protective line. Heavy infantry, and knights both mounted and on foot, were fashioning a new wall on their outer flank. A few knights and mercenaries straggled in amongst them, escaping the maelstrom on the enemy's tattered right flank.

A sharp cry caused Aelfric to snap his head back in sudden alarm. He relaxed his guard, seeing that it came from an Ehrengardian knight who had tripped and fallen backwards on the corpse of a slain mercenary. A powerful, overhead swing of a household guard's two-handed broadaxe silenced the hapless knight.

Aelfric knew it would not be much longer before the enemy would be positioned to muster a counterattack. They would use their vaunted knights as the spearhead of such a thrust, against which Count Leidrad's cavalry would be no match in a head to head fight.

Searching for the Prince, he found to his relief that the young man was now esconsed within a large group of royal household guard. They were engaged in fighting a small, surrounded group of Halmlander.

Working his way over to the prince, he stepped over several dead bodies, keeping his senses alert for any sudden attacks. He finally reached the young warrior. Grime and blood were caked upon the prince's face, and spattered all over his beautiful helm. His eyes were filled with an inferno as he looked towards Aelfric. His jaw set firm, the prince's face was a mask of sheer resoluteness.

Looking upon the prince's face, there was not even an echo of the buoyant young man Aelfric knew so well. It was the mien of a determined warrior, one whose sword's thirst had been slaked with mercenary blood.

"Prince Aidan, we have done what we can, and it is time to fall back to our lines," Aelfric said. "We will soon be vulnerable to being routed ourselves. Our destruction of the Halmlander could become our own end in moments."

The prince, a dark scowl spreading on his face, looked back over to where the King's Guard and other warriors were whittling down the remaining Halmlander. He nodded to Aelfric, though it seemed as if he had to force the gesture through the fire of the battle-fury encompassing him. Aelfric knew how hard it was to pull back from such an edge, and hoped the prince's discipline could override the blistering war passions within him.

The prince then nodded to one of the men with him. The man

dutifully raised a horn to his lips, and sounded a long, sustained call for retreat.

Aelfric let out a breath of relief. In the scorching heat of combat, the prince was still in control of his most important faculties. The young prince had passed another important test in the ealdorman's eyes.

Aelfric held his own men up for a moment, as the prince started back towards the Saxan lines accompanied closely by the King's Guard. If it were the very last thing he did in the world, Aelfric would create a solid buffer between his prince and the enemy forces.

Seeing the Prince making good progress across the open field, Aelfric finally gave the signal to his men to begin their own fallback. In a most welcome development, the infantry of Ehrengard showed little inclination to break from their lines and pursue the Saxans. Occasional arrows and crossbow bolts cut through the air around them, but in nowhere near the volume to constitute a grave danger.

Cautiously backing up at first, Aelfric and the other Saxans presented their shields towards the reformed Ehrengardian line. When the arrows and bolts diminished further, he slung his shield across his back, before turning and hurrying across the open ground.

Aelfric's chest heaved as he gasped for air, watching his strides to avoid tripping upon the many bodies littering the grisly battlefield. He called out whenever he recognized the movements of a wounded Saxan on the ground.

Men with him hurried to assist any surviors, though a few had to be nearly dragged through the grass and gore, due to the grevious wounds they had suffered. Their chances of living were slim, but they had no chance whatsoever if they remained stranded in the no-man's land between the great armies.

Aelfric and the other withdrawing Saxans then heard one of the most dreaded sounds possible on a field of battle; the heavy thuds of hoofbeats thundering up from behind them. Looking over his shoulder, his heart sank, as he beheld a throng of Ehrengardian knights charging in their wake.

"Run! With everything you have left!" Aelfric shouted.

There was still a fair distance between them, but the galloping warhorses would close the gap quickly enough with the Saxans on foot. Aelfric hoped desperately that Count Leidrad's retreating cavalry, exhausted, and much lighter armored than the pursuing knights, did not wheel about. Matched against the heavily armored horses and knights, Count Leidrad's riders would be overwhelmed and decimated. The losses would be devastating to the Saxans.

Aelfric risked stumbling on the cluttered battlefield and looked around for the count. He espied the mass of cavalry under Count Leidrad, just as they neared the Saxan lines and were about to filter into the shield wall.

Aelfric kept his legs moving through sheer force of will, despite being sorely winded, and feeling a rising burn in his overly strained muscles. His mail-shirt, helm, and shield felt heavier than ever before.

He was tempted to cast whatever he could aside, as the items would be entirely useless if he was caught in the open ground. He knew he could no longer wield his sword or maneuver the shield with any effectiveness in his drained condition.

Alternating glances between Count Leidrad's force and the enemy pursuit, he saw the span between his Saxans and the mounted Ehrengardians shrinking rapidly. His hopes fled, as his best estimations offered no favorable prospects. Even if he threw his encumbrances aside, he would still find himself well short of the shield wall when the knights overtook him.

Aelfric gripped his sword firmly, readying to acquit himself as well as he could in his last moments. He whispered a prayer to the All-Father, girding himself for the crossing of the veil between life and death.

As he finished his prayer, more horns blared, just up and to the right of Aelfric. He looked to see the cause of the commotion, and found himself grinning at the incredible sight meeting his eyes.

"The All-Father be praised!" he gasped exuberantly, through his strained breaths, heart pounding in his chest.

Coming from the end of the Saxan left flank, a broad formation of cavalry charged in towards the Ehrengardian knights. Swords and lances at the ready, and shouting war cries, the riders' determined faces were fixed hotly towards the onrushing enemy.

The scale-armored horses from Bretica streaked in, and Aelfric watched the heavier Saxan cavalry smash into the pursuing riders. The timing of the intervention was extraordinary, and everything inside Aelfric said it was no mere chance.

Count Gerard II had positioned the heavy cavalry from Bretica to counter any pursuits in the inevitable fallback from the Saxan attack on the Halmlander. He had waited until the enemy committed themselves in full, and had expended their horses' stamina further in the pursuit, before signaling his own strike. The knights of Ehrengard were in no position to evade the Bretican force, as the momentum of battle shifted once more.

Though he kept moving forward, Aelfric espied the burly, bearded leader of Bretica as he felled one of the enemy knights. The stunned Ehrengardians broke off their pursuit, and struggled to rally themselves, to stave off the Bretican attackers. They fought back furiously, claiming the lives of several Bretican riders. Nevertheless, numbers and morale were with the Saxans on that part of the battlefield, and the knights were driven back towards their own lines.

"Keep going! Keep moving with all your strength and do not stop!" Aelfric yelled with urgency. He saw many tired warriors slowing down, as they no longer heard or felt the rising storm of hoofbeats that had been closing in on them just moments before.

The returning Saxan warriors roused themselves to haste, stumbling and staggering back to their own lines. Passing through the shield wall, they received a host of jubilant accolades from ecstatic levymen that had witnessed the daring attack on the Halmlander. Many raced forward to assist the wounded and others in a state of complete exhaustion.

Aelfric stood under his own power when he reached the shield wall, though he was out of breath, and his legs felt like two stone pillars. He was barely able to sheath his sword, and he sloughed off his shield, to lie on the ground for the time being.

The Saxan ealdorman felt the hands of some of his men patting him excitedly on his back and shoulders. Their weary faces were lit up by euphoric smiles. The Halmlander had been devastated, and the enemy right had been sorely wounded.

Aside from a total routing of the enemy, it was the best possible outcome the Saxans could have sought. It assuaged one of Aelfric's greatest worries.

"Aelfric!"

He turned his head and saw Prince Aidan. His helm and armor had acquired more filth and blood, and his shield exhibited many gouges, but the Saxan prince was hale, and none the worse for wear. The prince trotted over towards Aelfric, and gave the Saxan ealdorman a tight embrace.

He took a step back, putting his hands up in a gesture of protestation. "I know, I know, I took a risk. But the opening was there for the taking, I promise you. I had no doubt. I took full account of the fighting in the center and on the right, and we were holding strong. I left two of every three men to keep a reserve in place. And I really believed you would have told me to make a move, with what I saw before me."

Aelfric initially feigned a dour look, but was unable to hold the facade for long. A gleaming smile dawned on his face, as he chuckled and shook his head in amazement.

"You took a well-calculated, well-timed risk, one that has broken the Halmlander beyond hope," Aelfric praised the young prince.

A little of the youthful glow in the Prince radiated through the elation emerging on his face.

"You are acquitting yourself quite well, Prince Aidan," Aelfric added.

"I have had a great mentor," Prince Aidan replied, throwing his right arm around Aelfric's shoulder.

"And I, a good student," Aelfric responded in full sincerity.

"Just good?" the prince replied, with a laugh.

"I cannot allow you overconfidence," Aelfric replied, smiling.

The two warriors stood together in silent camraderie, listening to the cheers of the men all around them. They watched as the warriors of Ehrengard retreated towards the Western horizon.

Continuous horns were being sounded all throughout the enemy ranks. An orderly withdrawal was already well underway with the Trogens, Gigans, and the Avanorans.

The Saxan shield wall had bent, and was battered in many places, but it had not broken. The dragon standard still flew proudly where it was now held aloft towards the end of the Saxan left flank.

Even so, it was not a cause for outright celebration. The greater battle was not over, and attrition was mounting steadily, towards a level Aelfric knew could result in only one outcome.

He pushed the darker thoughts out of his mind, savoring the moment of triumph alongside his prince. Life itself was a series of moments, a great many sorrowful and burdensome, and Aelfric had long ago learned to cherish the good ones.

Knowing the Halmlander could not possibly harm one Saxan village made for a wondrous moment in time. Aelfric's smile at the thought held a level of contentment which had not been present in his expressions for quite some time.

No matter when the final blow came, this day could not be taken away from the Saxans. They had risen to meet a tremendous challenge, had spared many innocents a horrid fate, and would live to fight for at least another day. The ealdorman's smile broadened even wider.

THOMAS

Thomas' stomach was full from an ample repast of fish, wine, bread, legumes, and nuts. The meal also included a little fresh fruit his mother had procured for a low price at one of the market stalls, a welcome surprise Thomas had enjoyed very much.

As it was the mid-week, the fast day of the Church was honored, but Thomas did not mind having fish as much as he did going without some good cheese or eggs. It was still difficult for him to reconcile why the fasting was even necessary, if the spirit was what was important. But he knew better than to argue the matter with his parents and Father Anselm.

The day was moving by quickly enough, but it had already been rife with activity and chores. Thomas had spent a few hours helping his mother and Emma spin yarn, and had dutifully attended a reading lesson with Father Anselm. Neither activity invigorated him in the slightest, but they had occupied his attention during the early hours of the day.

Thomas joined Emma in assisting their mother with bringing the empty wooden platters, cups, bowls, earthenware wine jug, spoons, and knives back downstairs, after resetting the solar room. Thomas discarded what few scraps remained into the open-air cesspit behind the kitchen. Once back inside, he helped clean off the various dining implements, returning them to their proper shelf spaces.

"Thomas, my boy, please go down and draw some water for us," Alice asked in a pleasant voice, as he replaced the last of the platters. She grasped and then handed over the handles of two familiar, medium-sized wooden buckets.

"I will, right away, mother," Thomas said brightly, taking the buckets from her. The timing of the chore was fortuitous. He was feeling eager to get out of the house for awhile, and go for a walk about the city.

He passed back through the lower level of the house, unnoticed by his father and Nicholas as they remained engrossed in discussing their approaches to a few new pieces of cloth just ordered by Hervee of Delshire. Clutching the handles of the buckets tighter in each hand, he took a deep breath, and stepped out into the street.

It was perhaps the brightest sky he had seen since the winter had passed. The sky was virtually cloudless, a tapestry woven entirely of opulent turquoise. Even the best man of the Dyer's Guild, a fellow named Jacques who his father said was of exceptional ability, would have been hard pressed to even come close to equaling the dreamy hue spread across the firmament of the upper skies.

There was a buoyant mood to the pedestrian traffic moving along the streets. Thomas carried the two wooden pails, setting off briskly for the spring-fed pool, located near the Healing House run by the black-robed monks of the adjacent Beniac abbey compound.

"Thomas! Thomas!" a voice cried out, grabbing his attention and bringing him to a sudden stop.

Looking back over his shoulder, he saw his friend Tristainus wedging past a couple of well-attired men, who cursed the youth's clumsiness as he bumped into them on his approach towards Thomas. Tristainus hurriedly offered apologies, which did little to assuage the deep scowls on the irritated men.

Nearly the same age as Thomas, he was a lad blessed with size. A few inches taller, with a thick mop of red hair, the boy's stout build advertised a considerable strength that seemed to increase daily as he labored alongside his father, who worked as a porter within the city of Avalos. It was a fortunate attribute in other ways as well, as it prevented peers that found Tristainus to be a lout from trying to bully or harass him.

Tristainus was carrying a large basket cradled in his right arm. Like Thomas, he was also about some chore for his family.

"A good day, Thomas!" he exclaimed, finally drawing near his friend. He glanced down at the basket, which he adjusted to hold by its handle in his right hand, and rolled his eyes dramatically. "Working with dad is hard, but I like it better. Mom has me out today to collect manure for the kitchen garden."

He wrinkled his nose and laughed as Thomas made his own face, catching the first scent of the pungent contents occupying much of the basket.

"Sounds like a fun task," Thomas replied, sarcastically.

"She wants a full basket, and I mean to take my time about it. Definitely careful not to spill it out," Tristainus said. His timbre then became markedly more excited. "And wait until you hear what I have to say!"

"Walk with me, and tell me then, I have to get some water for mother. I dare not risk taking my time about that," Thomas replied, chuckling. Tristainus fell in alongside Thomas as they resumed their walk down the narrow street.

"Did you hear the word? It has spread all around the city … Baron Osbern of Rocheston, of the Kingdom of Norengal, has arrived with a large retinue of knights and warriors who have taken the Spear Oath," Tristainus said excitedly. "They are said to be embarking today for the Sunlands at the water's edge, down in the harbor!"

Thomas hesitated for a moment. He greatly wanted to see the knights for himself. They were much more interesting than weaving wool, laboring to read parchments, or gathering up water from pools.

A frown then crossed his face, as he wrestled internally with his desires versus the duties given him. The temptation was not a light one, but Thomas's conscience was not merciful when it came to matters of obedience to his parents.

"Why don't you ask your father? I'll walk with you to bring the water back now, so you'll not disregard your duties. I'll even carry a bucket for you!" Tristainus exclaimed.

"Worth a try," Thomas remarked, embracing the alluring invitation.

They proceeded to the spring-fed pool, stone-bordered and kept in the open for easy access by the city's inhabitants. Thomas lowered the buckets, filling them up to the brim with the cool waters flowing from below to collect abundantly in the stone-fashioned reservoir.

Another fountain fed by lead pipes was located a little closer to their home, but he always walked the extra distance. Thomas' grandfather had once talked to a reputable healer, who had admonished them strongly to take the extra effort to go a little farther to partake of the better waters of the spring-fed fountain.

He had cited more sickness among the families that took their water from the pipe-fed fountain, than among those that drew water from the spring-fed pool. Water was water, and Thomas suspected the man was probably superstitious, but there was something about the healer's firm insistence, and his grandfather's endorsement of the man's position, that had impressed itself strongly upon Thomas.

Handing one of the filled buckets over to Tristainus, with a sincere feeling of gratitude at not having to lug the two heavy containers back by himself, Thomas set off for his home with his brawny friend. The water in Tristainus's bucket sloshed and spilled a little more generously than did Thomas's on the journey, but they both managed to retain most of the water by the time they reached the Street of the Weavers.

Thomas and Tristainus strode through the front door and into the house. Without pause, they carried the water down the left side of the front workroom, and out into the open courtyard. Thomas paused there, and prompted Tristainus to set down his basket, as manure was never a very welcome addition to a kitchen. The pair then continued into the kitchen, at the far back of the house.

Emma looked up as they entered, giving a little wince as she forced a smile. She was standing by a cluttered table surface holding several storage vessels, readying to prepare the contents of a stew for the evening meal. Thomas knew she regarded Tristainus as a bit of an oaf, and was simply glad his friend was entirely oblivious to the disdainful expression on his sister's face.

"Seems like you have gained in number since you left," she remarked.

Thomas could hear a faint edge to her voice, as she shot a furtive glance towards Tristainus. Bogged down in her chores, Thomas could sense she was not in the best of moods. She was not enthusiastic about having a youth she considered a buffoon as company.

Thomas placed his bucket down against the wall to the right, and gestured for Tristainus to set his down just next to it. "Did mother leave?"

"No, she's upstairs. Working on some spinning at the moment … there's always a need for that," Emma replied, letting the implication hang in the air for a moment. She glanced at Tristainus. "I'm sure he is not here just to help you carry water, or to learn spinning. What mischief calls to the two of you?"

"Many knights are leaving for the Sunlands, ones that have taken the Spear Oath, down at the harbor," Tristainus blurted out.

"And I suppose you two want to see it," Emma said with thinly masked distaste. "It doesn't take much to excite boys. Men wearing metal and prancing around with colorful pennons."

"As if you wouldn't like to see a host of handsome knights," Thomas retorted, smiling. "All in fine clothes, being cheered on by the crowds, on a bright and sunny day."

Emma paused for a moment, a light grin emerging. "Okay, there is that. But I have too much work to do now. And you had better ask father before you do anything, if you value your life."

"I planned to do that," Thomas replied.

"If I were you, I would not leave that lout to ask for you," Emma said.

Thomas's brow furrowed quizzically.

"It would seem he has already wandered off," Emma said, nodding towards where Tristainus had been standing just behind Thomas.

Thomas looked to his side and saw that Tristainus had already exited. He rolled his eyes, as he looked back to Emma.

"See you later," he said, feeling a sudden urgency.

"Tell me all about it, if you get to go. I would like to hear," Emma admitted, as Thomas turned to leave the kitchen. With an audible sigh, she turned her attention back to her tasks, moving over to retrieve the water buckets to fill the empty iron kettle that would soon be warming in the hearth.

Thomas went back to the main workroom, in the front of the house, where his father and Nicholas had been working the loom. Tristainus was already there, and, as Thomas feared, he was in conversation with his father. The recognition made Thomas inwardly cringe.

With all of the duties needing attending to on any given day, a request to indulge in the sights of a departing host of knights had to be approached most delicately. Tristainus was not one who was known for such skills.

"Baron Osbern, you say?" his father was asking Tristainus, upon Thomas's return.

"Yes, from Norengal, and there are many knights of the Sacred Orders joining with them for the sea journey," Tristainus replied, his voice briming with enthusiasm. "A fleet of ships has gathered, many of great size."

William turned towards Thomas as he entered the room. "And I would suppose the two of you probably want to get a closer look. Lucky for you I still remember being your age."

"You would not mind?" Thomas asked with guarded hope, a little hesitantly.

"Just another muster for more wars, " his father commented, shaking his head. "Such extravagance, for a grisly business. Yet you may go. See what you wish to see. Just do not find yourself boarding any of the ships. The weaver's loom may not fascinate like the sword, but I assure you it is much friendlier to your life and limbs."

Thomas grinned, excitement welled up within, "Thank you Father!"

"Just do not take too long. Your mother will need some help with things, and do not forget she will hold me to account for giving you permission," William remarked, smiling, and shaking his head as he turned back to the loom.

The two boys almost tumbled out the door, hurrying past the streets of the cobblers, tailors, a public bath, and a number of other familiar landmarks marking the pathway down to the harbor's edge. The salty scents of the sea, and the presence of long, low warehouses, told them their destination was imminent, spurring them forward even quicker.

Thomas ignored several annoyed curses from pedestrians, including a particularly colorful barrage from a man with a two-wheeled cart. His horse had been startled, rearing up as Tristainus and Thomas nearly ran into them when turning a corner by one of the large warehouses. Fortunately, the youths were well past him before he could react, as the look on his face clearly showed his desire to throttle the two.

A substantial crowd had gathered around the shoreline, docks, and quays located on the southern crescent of the expansive port. A few sizeable tarides had been beached on the shore, the portals in their rear open wide as horses were led up the gangways and into their dim holds.

The docks and jetties, of wood and stone, reached out into deeper waters. They now were servicing the needs of several massive, round-hulled transports. The huge sailing vessels were being loaded with supplies and men, using a number of pulley-driven cranes and gangplanks. Some of the sailing vessels, like the beached tarides, also harbored wide openings in the sterns large enough for horses. A number of sleek war galleys were also in the process of being loaded, some pulled up on the shore, and others resting alongside timber-faced quays.

It was a massive undertaking, with numerous sacks, barrels, pottery containers, chests, and other items piled along the jetties and quays. Tended by pensive-looking men, flocks of livestock herded close together, waiting to be ushered onto the idle ships. A small army of crewmen and porters, with sweat-stained brows and burdened strides, kept a continuous current flowing from the piled stocks onto the ships.

Thomas and Tristainus milled about in the crowd, working their way gradually to a vantage point giving them a solid overlook of the harbor. For nearly an hour, they watched the incessant stream of the ships being loaded, relieved to hear from bystanders that the main force had not yet boarded for departure.

Finally, a great cry went up from the crowd, as a host of sky riders flew into sight, just overhead. The graceful steeds circled the area a few times before their riders landed them at the base of one of the extended jetties.

The narrow-bodied flying steeds tucked their broad wings tight against their bodies as they touched the ground. Their riders prodded them to step forward, as space was cleared for the other descending riders behind.

A fair number of warriors from the city's garrisons, and a strong contingent of Avalos' watch, labored diligently to keep the throng of spectators far back. Unimpeded, the sky riders maneuvered their winged steeds, now riding them much like horses, down the length of the jetty towards one of the larger sailed transport vessels.

Thomas looked upon the magnificent winged steeds, called Harraks, marveling at their powerful builds and fearsome appearances. The Harraks were not often seen at so close a proximity in Avalos, largely staying to the upper skies, or the towering, multi-terraced citadel of the Unifier.

Thomas had often stood in the midst of a narrow city street, gazing skyward as two or three of the steeds passed overhead on their forays from the Unifier's great mountain citadel. To see so many of the creatures from so close was a rare, exhilarating experience.

The wave of sky riders was just a prelude. A few moments later, an excited murmur rippled through the crowd. Looking back, Thomas and Tristainus watched as a long, orderly column approached down the winding road running along the water towards the southern side of the port.

Pennons fluttered proudly from a host of upright lances. A larger gonfannon flew from the lance of a squire near the front of the column. The squire rode just behind a very noble-looking man of proud bearing, who Thomas could only believe was Baron Osbern himself.

The man radiated confidence from his stoic mien. Nodding and giving an occasional wave, he acknowledged the bevy of cheers and excited cries from the enraptured crowd. To Thomas, he seemed a living embodiment of determination and authority.

The nobleman was wearing a blue surcoat of fine linen, whose sleeveless design displayed a long-sleeved blue linen tunic of a darker hue underneath. The snug-fitting sleeves ended in cuffs embroidered with gold thread, as did the triangular opening just visible under the squared collar of the surcoat.

Having been around his father's trade, Thomas knew that the dyes used to produce the exquisite hues of the surcoat and underlying tunic were quite expensive. The grade of material used to fashion the surcoat and tunic was simply of the highest quality.

The man had an angular face, with a long nose that aligned with his sharp chin. He exhibited only a light stubble on his face, almost as close as one could get to a fresh shaving. Locks of dark brown hair were cut in a perfectly even line at the cusp of his collar, parted in the middle on his forehead. The fine locks sprouted from underneath a dark cap of soft felt, whose narrow brim was turned up slightly at the outer edge.

High boots of soft leather, with a down-turned upper rim, ran up his legs to end just below his knees. Intertwining lines of some unrecognizable design, likely a geometric pattern, were etched into the leather of the boots.

The knights following in the wake of the nobleman were imposing, strong-looking men, with robust builds and fierce countenances. They were largely attired in the surcoat and tunic style of their lord.

The knights rode nimble palfreys, each of the equines elegant and sleek in form, stark in contrast to their draft brethren that Thomas encountered laboring around Avalos. The mighty destriers of the knights followed just behind. The treasured war stallions bore no riders, instead being led forward by attendant squires. A sturdy cluster of stout packhorses brought up the rear of the column, heavily laden with bulging saddlebags and waterskins.

The riderless destriers caught Thomas' eyes in particular. The tall stallions were well-muscled, exalted beasts, carrying within them rich bloodlines originating from Eberean lands. They were the kind of horses rarely seen in the streets. Destriers were the pinnacle, and most lucrative, of the offerings at the horse markets held outside Avanor's walls.

Other weapon-bearing riders followed the formation of knights. Of a greater number, they rode upon a noticeably lesser quality of horse, with far fewer attendants interspersed among them. Thomas's trained eyes noticed the lower quality of their attire, fashioned with rougher fabrics and more common dyes.

A wide column of iron-helmed foot soldiers followed the secondary group of riders. The column featured a large faction bearing long, heavy crossbows. Others carried great, unstrung longbows of yew. Many bore extended lances and high shields, the latter rectangular in form. As a whole, they had the professional look of garrison men, marching with cohesion.

As the knights and others passed, Thomas noticed all of them had large red spears of Emmanu stitched over their left breasts. He recognized the badges, given to those who had taken the Spear Oath. Going to fight in the Holy Wars was also referred to as Taking the Spear, reflecting the receiving, and wearing, of the cherished symbol.

Thomas picked up the conversation of a couple of sailors, standing idly nearby and watching the procession. One was a tall, blonde-haired man with narrow features, while the other was a stouter, dark-haired man, with a round face and broad nose. Both were clad in simple tunics and breeches, and were barefoot in the manner of many who worked around the docks and quays. They had the leathery, weather-beaten texture to their skins common among sea-faring folk.

"I wonder what sights could be seen during the great Holy Wars," the dark-haired man stated. His accent told Thomas he was a Gallean man. "Now the Sunlands are much more settled, with only small outbreaks between lords and emirs, and the usual raids upon pilgrim caravans."

"This is very small," the other man remarked. His sharper accent indicated he was from the southern lands of Erengard, as his slightly slower, more deliberate cadence evidenced Gallean was not his native tongue. "Over a hundred thousand men alone left in the Third Holy War, with the king who is now the King Under the Mountain."

Thomas listened to the claim with a little skepticism. He could hardly imagine a sight being more impressive than the one now spread before his eyes.

"Ah, the rich and imaginitive tales of Erengard," the dark-haired man replied, with a strong undertone of incredulity. "Your legendary King Under the Mountain."

"In the darkest hour of our land, he will return once again," the other responded curtly, showing a hint of annoyance in his furrowed brow.

"No offense meant, I just have a hard time believing such incredible tales," the Gallean replied, in a more placating tone.

"Do you know much of this Baron Osbern?" asked the other man, tension ebbing as he changed the course of the conversation.

"Little, other than he will likely fight against a renegade among the followers of the Prophet," the dark-haired man answered. "A man named Ibn Amal."

"I have heard the name of this Ibn Amal spoken of before, in the ports," the Ehrengardian replied. "Does he not fight among the followers of the Prophet?"

"Ibn Amal is an upstart. He is a lord among their kind," the Gallean stated. "It is said the Khalif in Caiandria now shakes with fear of him, as does the rival Khalif, and the Saljuka Sultan, who I assure you won't move a step beyond the great walls of Madinat al-Salaam. Word of Ibn Imal's rise spreads, for they have not been able to stop him."

"It is hard to believe that times are such that a lord of Norengal goes to aid the Khalifs ... in a fight against this upstart," the other man said, with apparent distaste. "For that is what is truly happening here."

"He won't be fighting alongside the Khalif in Caiandria, in the Fahtamid lands, or the Kalif and Sultan in Madinat al-Salaam, in the lands of Saljuka, and I am sure he does not see it that way. For Baron Osbern, it is simply a call to defend the Holy Kingdom," the dark-haired man answered. "But the irony is there ... ahhhh, the irony. You are right, my friend. He will truly be fighting the war of the other Khalifs and the Sultan."

"So where do you suppose this fleet will go ... from here?" asked the Ehrengardian.

"They will sail for the Monk's Mount, I expect, for a vigil. To pay respects to the Sacred Lady and the Great Archon of the All-Father. Then they will sail to the north, following the coast, and crossing the Sword Sea to the Sunlands," the Gallean answered.

"I suppose it is appropriate. They have taken up the Spear of Emmanu," the other man observed.

"Were I them, I would start for the Sunlands with no delay. I do not have such regard for religion," the dark-haired man commented, in a more subdued tone.

The Ehrengardian shrugged. "It depends on the day with me … but it is no small thing that moves such men as these."

The dark-haired man shook his head. "I don't understand them at all. These men leave without a silver penny to their name. And for what? So many die before they get there, and many more, once they are there.

"Aye, there are tales of men who have gained lordship and land, but for most it is a much different end … Penury at best, most likely death.

"Nothing is the same for all men, but for most, it is a faith I do not know or understand that sends them to clutch such folly … from rich to poor, from alive to the tomb. Sending them into scorching foreign lands, ripe for the men of the Prophet who fight with the fury of demons."

"No, it would seem this is not a road paved with gold," the Ehrengardian replied, in apparent agreement. "But surely something powerful keeps men taking up the Spear of Emmanu … generation after generation."

"You spend most of your time sailing between Erengard and Avanor, my friend. I know of what I speak, and if you doubt me, travel to the ports of the Maritime Republics, and Gallea, Paleria, and elsewhere. You will see that the roads of the kingdoms are filled with penniless knights returning after such perilous journeys. They return to a life of struggle and hardship, after risking so much."

"I have seen many such in the heart of Erengard," the other man stated firmly.

The dark-haired man shook his head. "What reward is that? The Great Vicar himself says their offenses are forgiven, and that they go to the All-Father's lands if they die. Perhaps that is a reward, though I know of no man who has seen such a place, and returned to tell of it."

"And nor I," the other said. "But I will find out whether or not there is such a place … if I linger long here. Our captain desires to depart for the south … soon after this fleet leaves."

"Do you not have time for one more round of ale at the tavern?" the dark-haired man asked.

The Ehrengardian smiled amiably. "Maybe one more."

The two men laughed as they headed away, striding towards the area where the rather grimy, waterfront taverns serviced ship crews and others laboring around the harbor. Thomas had never been to the waterfront in the depths of night, but some of the places were said to serve fully cooked meals at all hours.

Thomas' eyes drifted towards the great ship the Baron had boarded, at the end of a very long jetty. It was a majestic, round-hulled vessel of enormous size. Two huge spars were affixed to towering masts, the sails currently furled. Two extensive forward-curving timber spurs, whose ends had been carved into an orb shape, flanked a lofty stern castle, like the horns of some great beast.

The majestic destriers were already being loaded into a portal set into one of the lower decks of the vessel, at the stern. The Baron and the knights had already boarded, and some had already gathered in the square forecastle at the bow of the ship to watch over the proceedings.

Thomas turned his attention back to the procession as three new contingents arrived, to a new eruption of outcries from the enthusiastic crowd. His breath caught in his throat as he saw the banners at the forefront of the first contingent. He realized he was about to witness a large mass of knights from the fabled Holy Orders defending the Church in the Sunlands. He gazed upon them in wonder as they passed by, taking in every moment.

The first contingent bore the well-known half-black and half-white standards of the Order of the High Altar. The symbol was the very one Thomas saw fluttering against the sky whenever he passed the fortified keep serving as the order's commandery within Avanor. The men leading the contingent wore white mantles displaying a red Spear of Emmanu. On their heads, they wore dark circular caps, fashioned of soft cloth. To a man, they wore their hair in a length cropped evenly just below the ears, and all of their faces were covered in full moustaches and beards.

Others in the first contingent, following closely behind the group in the lead, were clearly of a lower status, though greater in number than their white-mantled brethren. These were distinguished by their long black mantles, with red spears of Emmanu stitched into them.

The second large contingent followed at a good distance from the first. Their flowing banners featured a red background, inset with a pure white Spear of Emmanu. The men at the forefront were garbed in long black mantles, with white spears of Emmanu worked into the woolen fabric over their left breasts. Their heads were covered in simple white coifs, surmounted by round skullcaps of felt. The men of the second contingent were noticeably clean-shaven, to a man. The length of their hair was also presumably short, as nothing of it could be seen, hidden by their skullcaps and white coifs.

Like the first contingent, there was a more numerous faction within the second group, following just behind the leading brother-knights. As with the Order of the High Altar, the larger subgroup was clearly of a different status, with brown outer mantles demarcating them from those in the forefront.

Thomas knew the second contingent was of the Order of the Healers, named as such for the extensive hospitals they were known to maintain throughout the Sunlands. They had a convent house within Avanor that Thomas had walked by on a few occasions, though it was nowhere near as impressive as the Order of the High Altar's stout commandery.

The third contingent followed closely behind the second. The attire of their leading brother-knights was almost an inverse of the second group, with large black spears of Emmanu set against white tunics. The design was replicated on the multitude of banners they bore along with them.

Nearly the entire third group was composed of exceptionally strong-looking men, hardened of countenance and proud of posture, with blazing looks in their eye. The men exhibited a great diversity of facial appearance, some with full beards and moustaches, some with moustaches only, others clean-shaven, and even a few with just trimmed, pointed tufts of hair extending downward from their chins.

The third group's number was significantly lesser than either of the other two contingents, and they had no presence in Avanor that Thomas was aware of. Were it not for comments from the surrounding crowd, Thomas would never have recognized them as being warrior monks of the Order of the Sacred Lady. He had heard of them before, the heartland of their order being within Ehrengard and the Sacred Empire.

A throng of lesser-status individuals accompanied the brother-knights. Their mantles were gray, and the black spears stitched upon them were truncated in the haft by nearly a third in comparison to the brother-knights in the front of the formation.

It took quite some time for the contingents from the three holy orders to file by. Each group headed towards different jetties, clearly traveling separately.

Thomas noted that the men of the Order of the Healers would be traveling on some of the most prominent vessels among those gathered in the harbor. The realization surprised him, as the Order of the High Altar was known to be in control of far greater wealth and holdings than any order in allegiance to the Church. Thomas had even heard they handled the royal treasure of the Gallean King himself.

Following the various Holy Orders and the main force with Baron Osbern was a motley, diverse throng. Some of the surrounding crowd began to disperse at that juncture, as the final mass of travelers did not elicit any noticeable excitement. Thomas watched nonetheless, still enthralled by every element of the extensive procession.

A good number were simple men that had taken up the call to the Sunlands, with crudely-fashioned cloth Spears of Emmanu affixed to their rough woolen tunics, the latter primarily of earthen colors. They carried an assortment of weapons, mainly long-bladed knives, spears, and simple bows. Little armor was in evidence, other than an occasional old wooden shield, simple iron cap, or padded gambeson.

Others in the last group wore the distinct garb of priests and Sisters of the Western Church. Most of the priests were by themselves, while the Sisters were gathered into a few small clusters sprinkled within the throng.

Many of the priests and Sisters nodded, smiled, and spoke brief words with bystanders wishing them well. There was a very serene look on most of the men and women of this number, a contrast to the anxiety-ridden faces exhibited by the commoners around them.

The content look on the priests and Sisters did not surprise Thomas. They were all heading to the fabled lands of the Sacred Kingdom. To serve the Western Church in the homeland of Emmanu was something that little else could rival in the eyes of an ordained priest or vowed Sister.

It also did not surprise Thomas that they moved among the poorest, most disheveled elements of the disembarking force. He had seen how dedicated Father Anselm was to the commoners of his own parish, and guessed that many of the priests were likely journeying alongside the commoners from their own home parishes.

The Sisters, Thomas surmised, were probably going to the Sunlands to tend to medical needs. It was the Sisters that largely staffed the various charitable institutions throughout Avalos, whether for widows, the crippled, or hospitals for the poor.

Others in the rear mass looked to be simple pilgrims, clad in plain wool tunics and wearing sandals. They carried the tell-tale walking staffs and pouches of a pilgrim heading to the Sacred Kingdom. A few of the men and women in this group were evident veterans of pilgrimages, their pouches displaying several badges of the kind given out at the famous pilgrimage sites of the Western Church.

Mixed among the pilgrims and various religious individuals were a number of others whose express purposes Thomas could not begin to identify. Men who bore no weapon or signs of pilgrimage, and several highly attractive women, whose purpose in war or religion Thomas could not fathom.

There were even a few that seemed to be of better means, with finer caps and attire, and walking in small groups. Yet nearly all the multitude following the stately procession of warriors looked to be of poorer means, carrying only a few possessions within simple cloth sacks.

Thomas realized a good number of them could not be any better off than the condition of his own household. It kindled a flame of hope within him for the future; that he might one day be able to undertake a great journey like that he had always dreamed of.

Were it not for his family, he knew he would have tried to leave right there and then. The excitement of a great fleet streaking across the seas for the Sunlands, to defend the faithful, and to see the sacred lands where Emmanu Himself once walked, was enough enticement and reward for Thomas. He wondered if all the people boarding the ships knew just how fortunate they were to be taking on such a bold, extraordinary adventure.

The dark-haired sailor had spoken ill of those who had taken up the Spear of Emmanu, but wealth and lordships were not what inspired Thomas about the idea. It was the adventure, and the purpose itself, and it was apparent the dark-haired man did not understand such things.

"To be going on those ships," Thomas mumbled aloud.

"No way," Tristainus replied quickly, shaking his head. "Just think of the storms at sea. I've heard about 'em. What would you do if you were shipwrecked?"

"It would be a risk," Thomas agreed. "But think of the adventure you would have. Do you want your whole life to be Avanor?"

"If it keeps my limbs on my body and breath in my lungs till I'm old, then yes," Tristainus replied. "I'll look at the knights gladly … and hear the stories, but I don't want to set my foot on no ships."

Thomas shook his head and grinned. "You are hopeless."

"You'd be hopeless if your ship got caught in a storm," Tristainus retorted. "And we'll both be without hope, if we wait around much longer here."

Thomas smiled, knowing that no explanation would penetrate the barriers in Tristainus' mind. "Then let's return," he said cheerily.

With a last glance over the teeming ships, being loaded with the great force going to the Sunlands, he turned with a reluctant heart towards the streets leading back into the heart of Avalos. Reality beckoned for the time being, but he held fast to the idea that reality could also change.

MERSHAD

Mershad's own harrowing experiences within the Five Realms had been debilitating enough. The tidings brought with the Elder dragon and the young Saxan warrior, regarding the colossal war now underway, had been nearly overwhelming to digest.

He was far from alone in his dread, as it was evident the dark words had been daunting to hear for many among the Midragardans. The conveyance of foreboding news through the efforts of a living, breathing creature of legend only served to enhance the importance of the message. Terrible storms were now on the horizon of Midragard itself.

A hushed, subdued spirit pervaded King Hakon's estate in the wake of the dragon's departure, even down to the normally boisterous animals. The usually playful, spirited cadre of Midragardan dogs living on the grounds was nowhere to be seen. Even the large, thickly-furred breed of cats, so often visible as they lounged and stalked the estate's buildings and fields for small game, had evidently gone into hiding.

Late on the evening following the great dragon's unexpected visit, Derek and Kent caught up with Mershad in the main living space of their dwelling. They sat together for quite some time in extended silence.

Only the sounds of the wind beating around the posts, roof hole, and the vertical planks of the side walls broke the heavy stillness. A low fire burned in the central hearth pit with a haphazard series of crackles.

Derek and Kent looked somber as they sat across from Mershad, on the raised earthen side. The air was perceptibly thick, and not just in a physical sense. The trio of outlanders had much more to think about than the average Midragardan in regards to the huge dragon's visit. None of the three had failed to notice the intensive interest given to them by the massive creature.

"The word of us may spread," Derek finally remarked, his voice as dour as his expression.

His arms rested on his knees, hands clasped tight between them. His tensed forearm muscles pushed through the skin to form taut ridges, which disappeared beneath the sleeves of his woolen tunic.

"And that is not necessarily a good thing," Derek added curtly, after a few more moments of weighty silence passed.

"Believe me … I would like it if very, very few people knew of us. Especially that we are here in Midragard," Mershad replied, in a low voice.

Kent just shook his head, with no verbal response. His feelings on the matter were easy to tell by his countenance. His furrowed brow and pensive lips were devoid of the carefree joviality normally pervading him.

War had broken through like a long-restrained river through a collapsing dam, explosive and voracious. As the three otherworlders sat quietly, within the stillness of the small timber home, the Five Realms were under a horrendous assault, as was the entire kingdom of Saxany.

All roads and routes of the enemy would eventually lead to Midragard. Mershad, like his companions, realized well enough that the place would not likely remain a secure refuge for long. All of Midragard would be cornered, with them trapped within it, by a relentless enemy seeking after them with rapacious vigor.

There had been little to discuss, as there really were no other options to consider at the present. For the foreseeable future, they would have to remain in Midragard, bide their time, and learn whatever they could. After brooding for a little while longer, the three had finally given themselves over to their pallets for the night.

The evening brought little rest, as Mershad struggled with a troubled sleep. For long stretches of the night, he pulled the sheepskin covers closely about him, while staring up silently at the dark roof.

The wind whistled through the cracks between the posts, beams, and planks, and Mershad concentrated his thoughts upon the sounds. He grappled with himself, to blank his mind in the hopes that his eyelids would eventually grow heavy. All he wanted was a little temporary oblivion, to escape thoughts of the horrid plight facing so many people in Ave. While he finally did fall into a light sleep, for a few short stretches, he spent most the time tossing about restlessly on the goose-feather stuffed mattress.

Though drowsy, he was very relieved when he trudged outside to perform the first of the new day's prayers, at the cusp of daybreak. The familiarity of a well-practiced routine, one connecting him to his own world, was like a cup of cool water to severely parched lips.

It did not take long for him to notice the heavy pall hanging over King Hakon's estate. Bondsmen heading out towards the fields and byres were shrouded in a brooding silence. A small cluster of women, heading towards a small storage building, walked quietly with their heads down, exchanging only a few words in low, tense voices. All seemed occupied within the sphere of their own thoughts, speaking only when necessity demanded it.

Thinking a good Midragardan steam bath might refresh him, Mershad started toward a square timber building set a little distance away from the main longhall. An older bondsman aided a couple of retainers there, attending to the peat fire heating the pile of stones set in the center of the unique building. Like the others around the estate, the men were all pensive, and short with words.

The bondsman gave Mershad a curt greeting as he entered, and bid him to join the others, as he was just in time for the heated stones. Mershad kept to himself, as he stripped down and stepped across the stone-flagged floor inside. He took a seat in a free space on the raised timber ledge surrounding the central hearth, with its high pile of hot stones.

The bondsman poured cool water on the heated stones, and Mershad sat down quietly, letting the hot, rising steam that gushed forth fully envelop his body. The warm vapors draped generously all over his bare skin, and the dense, moist air filled his lungs. He waited patiently, as the droplets from the steam formed a thorough layer over every exposed surface of his body.

As he had been instructed before, he took up a small bundle of twigs the bondsman provided for him. Repeatedly, he whipped it lightly against his steam-dampened body. The technique was designed to loosen up any dirt or grime that clung to his body, but the action also felt soothingly good.

When he and the retainers were finished with the bundles, he stood up and followed them out. Once they were all outside the building, the bondsman proceeded immediately to pour large buckets filled with cold water on the bathers.

The extreme contrasts between icy water and hot steam provoked a vibrant, clean feeling all over Mershad's body, as he was rinsed off. He shivered at the initial icy touch of the water, but felt far more awakened when he dressed himself once again.

The refreshingly cool, soothing sensations he felt as he strolled through the estate in the open air were pleasureable enough, but his inner morale was still low. In the clarity of alertness and thought, he found he simply wanted to get away for awhile from the deep tensions permeating the estate. He strode towards the main longhall, with the singular purpose of finding Svein.

Mershad smiled in polite greeting to a few passersby, almost bumping into a pair of outcoming warriors as he stepped into the dimmer interior of the longhall. Like most of the senior retainers, Svein was where Mershad had expected to find him, within the environs of the king's great hall.

He had had to walk deep into the hall to identify Svein clearly, as there were far fewer lamps and torches alight than there were at a feast. The dim, hazy interior of the hall capably reflected the ambiance cast by the men now assembled there, standing about and talking in low, hushed tones. There was none of the characteristic boisterousness usually so evident among the Midragardan warriors.

The air inside was thick, and much warmer than the crisp outside, but the heaviness accented the dour countenances silently beholding Mershad as he walked into their midst. He found Svein engaged in an intense discussion, which he was loath to interrupt. Svein was likely to have a host of new worries bearing upon his mind in the aftermath of the new developments.

As Svein had not taken notice of Mershad yet, he decided to wait until a more opportune moment presented itself to approach. He passed the time by looking closely at the many narrow tapestries lining the walls, as well as the painted, ornate carvings worked into the stout main posts holiding up the gable-ended rooftop.

He honed in on the dragons represented in the various images, artful depictions taken from Midragardan sagas and legends. A couple of them he now recognized, from a tale that he had recently heard.

The story told about a bold hero who had fallen deeply in love with a daughter of one of the greatest old gods of the Midragardan's rich lore. The dragon shown on the tapestry referring to that legend had been slain by the hero in the telling Mershad had heard.

Other images were from tales that still remained to be told to Mershad. Judging by the creatures and other figures rendered, Mershad knew he would find the other stories quite fascinating, at the very least.

Extending his arm, he idly traced his finger along the skillfully-etched contours of a dragon-head staring back at him, from the wood of one of the main posts close to the rear of the long hall. The reptillian visage was not wholly unlike that of the enormous beast witnessed the previous day.

When Svein finally pulled away from the men he had been speaking with, Mershad moved to intercept the senior retainer. Svein smiled amiably at recognizance of him, though Mershad could see the warrior's face was heavily laden with worry.

Mershad spoke with Svein about the prospects of him and his companions soon taking another journey by air. When asked the reason, he told Svein he personally hoped to return to the village by the Glittering River, in the shadow of the great mountains.

To his great surprise, Svein had readily assented to the request, though not without the firm stipulation that two experienced warriors from the king's homestead would accompany Mershad and his companions, if they wanted to join in such a foray, all the way there and back. To Mershad's surprise, Svein turned aside and begged leave of some others who had evidently been waiting a few paces away to speak with him, and indicated he would see to the otherworlder's request without delay.

"I did not mean to interrupt your important business," Mershad stated apologetically, noticing the sharp surge of agitation on the other Midragardans' expressions. "I didn't see those other men waiting for you."

"Do not apologize. Getting away from here is the one thing I would like to do right now," Svein remarked, with a rueful grin, as they walked back into the light of the rising sun. "I need some clean air in my lungs. And it would not be right to prevent you from doing what I would want to do myself, just because I cannot go myself at the moment."

He then added, with a hearty laugh, "And who knows? I just might decide to accompany you anyway. Let us call the next few moments a great test of my willpower. Let us see together if I can pass it."

"I promise I won't make it harder and try to persuade you," Mershad said, with a smile. "I won't try to push my friends into going either, but it's only right to see if they want to go."

"I appreciate your mercy in not seeking to sway my mind, as I do not wish to neglect my duties. I fear I could be counseled into doing so far too easily," Svein said, laughing as they walked together.

Not far from the longhall, Svein paused at an open yard, where several warriors were practicing diligently at arms. The air was filled with the clamorous impacts of weapons, and grunts of exertion.

"Let us ask your friends now if they wish to accompany you," Svein asked, eyeing Derek and Kent where they were taking part in the martial activities a short distance away. "At least we did not have to go very far to find them."

A large Midragardan warrior was exhanging sword blows with Derek, who looked balanced and powerful in his movements, blocking and countering in a steady rhythm. To Mershad's eyes, Derek carried his sword and shield with as much poise as the man sparring with him, and it was very evident the outlander fit in well with the field full of hardened-looking warriors.

Another Midragardan, with a plainly consternated expression, was demonstrating to Kent how to grip the hilt of his sword properly. To say that Kent looked out of place among the men surrounding him was an understatement.

Svein called for a respite in the action, summoning Mershad's two companions over. Before breaking away, Derek exchanged nods with the warrior he had been working with, displaying clear signs of respect between the two fighters. The warrior who had been assisting Kent looked relieved at the interruption, almost drawing a smile of amusement from Mershad.

"Mershad wants to go to the village of Glittering River," Svein announced when the two drew near. "I cannot go there today, as duties on the king's estate bind me here, though I am going to provide a pair of warriors to serve as guides. We came here to see if the two of you desired to join Mershad and go to the village today."

Derek looked towards Mershad. "I am getting some very good instruction in the use of Midragardan blades. If you don't mind, I want to stay here and keep working at this, and get more used to these weapons."

"That's no problem at all Derek. I just didn't want to leave without asking you and Kent," Mershad replied. "And don't let me keep you from what you are doing here. I'll catch up with you later."

"Sounds good!" Derek said, spiritedly. He grinned and nodded to Mershad, before turning and heading back towards the sword-bearing warrior he had been training with, leaving the others behind.

"And you?" Svein asked, turning towards Kent.

"Want to go?" Mershad added.

"Not today," Kent said, looking to Mershad. He indicated with a furtive glance from his eyes a couple of beautiful maidens lingering close to where Derek and he had been practicing. "I need more practice too."

"I am sure that gaining skill with our weapons is all that occupies your mind," Svein responded, with a chuckle. Plainly having caught the gesture Kent intended for Mershad, the Midragardan cast a brief look towards the blond-haired young women watching the warriors practice at arms. "Or perhaps there are other motives."

Bearing a sheepish grin, Kent looked a little embarrassed at Svein's words. But he did not deny the implication.

"Yet I do not blame you, as I myself enjoyed such attentions when I was first training in the arts of a warrior," Svein said. His voice then took on a weightier tone. "Just be sure to focus on your training. It can make the difference between living and dying."

Kent's expression grew more somber as Svein's last words flowed into his ears, and he nodded back. His tone rang with sincerity. "I will, Svein. I'll do my best to learn."

"Good, and as long as you keep your focus, and work hard on your skills, you can enjoy the rest too," Svein said, with an air of levity.

"You don't mind if I stay, do you Mershad?" Kent asked, as if feeling some guilt at turning down the invitation.

"Not at all," Mershad replied amiably. "Like Derek, we all have things we want to do. Go ahead, I'll be seeing you soon enough too."

"Thanks, Mershad," Kent said, with a wink, before turning and trotting back towards his waiting instructor.

Mershad strongly suspected that the veteran-looking warrior would have greatly preferred it if Kent had decided to go to the village. The thought brought a slight grin to his face.

"So, shall we proceed on this path?" Svein asked, with a grin.

Mershad nodded, as Svein called over two particular warriors who had also been exercising in the open yard. He commissioned the pair to serve as Mershad's escorts for the developing excursion.

The warriors assigned to Mershad were men that he had not yet been acquainted with. One was a burly, shaggy, blond-headed warrior, with a deep scar running along the left side of his face. The other was a sinewy, lean man, with a braided beard, and flowing dark locks.

Both were quite tall, and Svein had introduced them as being very seasoned, capable sky warriors. Mershad could sense both men enjoyed Svein's full confidence, which was by itself a great reassurance.

Bondservants were subsequently dispatched to retrieve the two warriors' Fenraren, as well as another for Mershad's use, from the byre where the creatures were quartered. The warriors took a short leave to gather up supplies and additional clothing, during which time Mershad procured his own cloak, and a few other items from his guest quarters.

Svein wished them all well when they gathered back together. Mershad and the two warriors mounted the steeds, and prepared to set off. Svein remarked that he had barely passed his own test of willpower, in the face of the great temptation to take to the skies with Mershad.

As they took off from the ground, Mershad took account of the fact there was more cloud-cover above than on the previous day. Though the clouds were tinted gray, imminent rain did not yet threaten.

Though Mershad wanted to be alone, the escorting warriors were of little disturbance to his desire for solitude. Aside from guiding him in the right direction, as they left the craggy, fjord-filled region where King Hakon's homestead lay, the two warriors were just about unnoticeable. Taking up positions on either side of Mershad, they settled in just a little forward of his own steed.

The crisp, biting air of the higher altitudes broke upon Mershad's face. He was glad he had donned the thick, fur-lined cloak, clasped at his shoulder by a trefoil brooch. He only hoped the silver brooch held strongly enough, as his elbows kept the heavier cloak pressed closely to his sides.

Mershad's thoughts remained decidedly melancholy, as he reflected on the bitterness of wars, and how they swept so many innocent people up within their fury. Unwilling majorities were plunged mercilessly into conflicts that only tiny minorities of elites desired; such was the ugly, resounding truth of wars.

Countless leagues separated Mershad and his two remaining companions from Erika, and the other few also from their world. There was absolutely nothing he could do within his power to help them. With everything raging to the north of Midragard, he had little doubt they were probably even more caught up within the tumult related by the hulking dragon than he was.

The vivid images of his parents, two brothers, and sister passed through his mind. The visions were welcome, warm remembrances, while also being ones tinged with growing sadness and despair. More and more, Mershad was beginning to face the dire notion that he might never see them again.

He had no physical images of them along with him. Only the halls of memory remained to his access. More than once a day, and often within the course of his five daily prayers, their faces passed before the eyes of his inner mind.

His mind and heart were increasingly the likely places where they would forever remain, at least in the years left to him in the physical world. Mershad would have given anything just to know whether he would see them again in his mortal life, even if it were only one more time. It was the abiding feeling of uncertainty, and the fading of hopes, that were the most brutal aspects of the undesired transference into another entire world.

Emotions invoked by the contemplations finally overcame him. Like a storm breaking upon a still landscape, he wept bitterly, and openly, as they continued over the Midragardan lands far below. His shaking, trembling body appeared to unnerve his steed, as the creature seemed to sense the depths of sadness wracking the rider seated upon its back.

Several times, the steed turned its wolfish head to look back towards him. There was a softened aspect to its gaze, as if the winged creature wished to comfort him. If Mershad's mind had not told him otherwise, he would have found the expression to convey sympathy.

Leaning forward, he patted the creature gently on the neck, choking back sobs. Mercifully, the two escorting warriors did not take notice of his distress. The tensions, worries, and debilitating feelings gathering within him for quite some time tumbled as a waterfall over a cliff-side. When the flood of emotions finally subsided, Mershad found himself beset with an encompassing fatigue.

Keeping one hand clenched to the reins of his Fenraren, he raised his free arm up to wipe his face and eyes with the woolen sleeve of his tunic. His eyelids felt like monstrous boulders in their weight, and he gradually slumped down in his saddle. Nestled in the arms of an emotionally drained exhaustion, Mershad's head lolled to the side. The winds coursing over him were hypnotic, soothing and mesmerizing, as he slowly fell into the embrace of a dreamless sleep.

The tight leather bindings from the harness and saddle ensured there was little personal risk in having fallen asleep. Mershad was secured well enough that his Fenraren could have flown upside down without any significant threat to its rider.

When he finally came to, he realized he had been asleep for quite some time. The looming mountains he espied on the horizon signified they were drawing close to the lands containing Bergthora's village.

His neck was a little crimped and tight where it had arched to rest his chin against his chest. He turned his head slowly from side to side, carefully working the stiffness out.

The two escorts kept pace next to him, as he noticed they had dropped back to his immediate right and left. They had enabled him the luxury of rest during the flight, choosing not to disturb him, but had remained close enough to rouse him, and help guide his steed, if any sudden threat presented itself.

Staring ahead, a part of Mershad felt an urge to fly straight into the heart of the mist-covered mountains lining the far horizon. He felt a pull within to go as high and far as he could, to seek to reside among the majestic dragons dwelling within that lofty refuge. Perhaps they would even know a way he could return to his own world.

The sleep refreshed him, as the cobwebs of drowsiness fell away to reveal a renewed vigor underneath. His body continued to ache from the normal toll of a long time spent in the saddle, added to some lingering stiffness from the slumber. There would undoubtedly be a manifestation of pronounced saddle-soreness from the extended journey when he finally landed and dismounted.

He kept peering at the towering mountains for any sign of the dragons occupying the elevated domain. A few times, he glanced towards the tree-blanketed, undulating ground far below, to see whether Bergthora's village was drawing near. As the Glittering River had not yet come into view, he knew they had farther to go. Nonetheless, he knew it would not be much longer, and his spirits rose as he continued alternating his gaze between the horizon ahead and the landscape beneath.

An alarmed snarl emerged from his sky steed, as it abruptly slowed. The gutteral, reverberating sound reminded him of a dog finding itself cornered and threatened.

Mershad looked upward, and an icy terror gripped him by the throat. The two warriors by him shouted in alarm, raising their long lances. It was as if time and space were askew, as his mind struggled to cope with the horrific vision meeting his eyes. If only what he saw could have been a hallucination.

The flying steed rushing towards him was hideous in appearance; a reptilian, serpent-like beast over three times as long as his Fenraren. The creature's sulphurous eyes appeared to burn with a sustained fire, and its extended jaws were lined with rows of dagger-like teeth. The surface of its scaly hide was a sickly, mottled green, evoking thoughts of death and corrupting disease.

As terrible as the appearance of the leathery-winged nightmare was, the rider upon the steed's back was the primary source of the choking, paralyzing fear enfolding Mershad. An inhuman, horrid form sat upon the winged beast's saddle, with a taut, elongated face covered with dessicated skin mottled gray and black.

From the depths of its eye sockets blazed a pair of baleful, fiery orbs. Its lips were pulled back in a sneer, revealing disproportionately long, sharpened teeth. The figure was a mockery of physical life.

Mershad sensed the odious being was an emanation of something far more vast and wicked. He knew implicitly that the figure upon the steed was no mere mortal creature. Rather, it was an entity transcending the things of the world, shrouded in a dark aura hearkening to powers not entirely bound by time and space. The understanding swelled within Mershad, bringing a cold terror in its wake.

Beyond the hellish rider, Mershad gained a distinct cognizance of a looming, incorporeal Presence. As he sensed the Presence, a weighty dread came over him.

One of the infernal rider's long-fingered hands, like skeletal talons, clasped the reins of its steed. The other held what looked at first to be an extended, sword-shaped series of flames. As Mershad looked upon it, he realized the flames shrouded a dark blade within their midst. Though encompassed by the fire, the rider's leathery hand did not burn as it gripped the ebon hilt.

"Otherworlder! Do not test the bidden servant of the Unifier!" the rider thundered from a distance. Its voice had a haunting, mesmerizing quality, hypnotic from the first spoken syllable. Mershad listened to the words as if entranced. "Come with me now, or feel the embrace of the unending flame!"

The abhorrent entity's attention was focused squarely upon Mershad, to the exclusion of the escorting riders. He felt abject despair under the burden of the rider's penetrating gaze. A clammy chill saturated him, of an encompassing nature he had never felt before.

The fires of the being's eyes appeared to flare, as it lowered its infernal sword towards Mershad. In the flash of an instant, he felt the searing bite of fire, looking on in horror as his steed screamed and reared up, beating at the air furiously.

Both Mershad and his Fenraren had erupted in tongues of flame, covering their entire bodies as if bursting out from the surface of their skin. Anguished cries and screeches from nearby revealed the two escorting warriors had been likewise stricken.

As suddenly as the torturous feeling lashed into him, it departed, leaving neither trace nor sensation of its consuming embrace. Though his steed cried out, and continued flailing its wings as if to shed a burning affliction, the cause of its torment had likewise vanished.

In helpless sorrow, horror, and fury, Mershad then saw that the two Midragardan warriors and their steeds had not been released from the flames. Riders and steeds alike tumbled downward, delirious in their unyielding agony.

Writhing and contorting in blinding pain from the hungry flames, they lost all control, plunging towards the land far below like dead weight. Only the solid ground freed them from the gruesome, fiery bondage forced upon them.

Mershad looked back to the malefic rider, his heart racing, and his thoughts embroiled in the blackest chaos. He knew he was helpless against the ghastly being.

"You have tasted the unending flame, and they have been claimed by it," the being hissed malevolently, guiding its steed in a tight circle around Mershad and the Fenraren as they continued flying slowly forward. The hellish entity threatened, "Deny me, and no water will quench the flame I will cloak you with!"

Mershad's mind was locked, shut down with paralyzing fear in the deadly pageant played out by countless figures of prey over the long ages of his own world, and his newly adopted one. The silent, frozen response by Mershad was the timeless, haunting litany serenading the impending few moments left to hapless prey, just before the final killing blow of the predator.

His adversary ceased its circling pattern, drawing up abruptly, to hover directly in front of Mershad. The wings of the steed snapped out wide, as if to coerce the Fenraren into halting.

The Fenraren then opted to take its own course of action, in light of the threat arrayed in front of them. Submitting to a freefall, the Fenraren folded its wings into its side. Rider and steed both went into an immediate, rushing descent, the sensation terrifying and exhilarating as they plummeted.

The choice made by the Fenraren was most opportune. The air occupying the space they had just vacated was filled with deadly fire a moment later, as the entity whipped its fire-sword through the vicinity. It was like the flame-sword set fire to the air itself as it passed through the space, pulling an ever-increasing mass of flames along with it. Mershad and his steed would have been engulfed by an inferno had they waited but a single moment longer.

With exceptional speed, the unholy aggressor reacted to the bold evasion by taking its steed into a breakneck dive after Mershad. The Fenraren snapped its wings out, catching the air, and swooping into the bottom of a brisk, looping arc that turned back up towards the sky. The elusive, dexterous maneuver caught the pursuing entity by surprise. The demonic being shrieked in rage as its reptillian mount raced past them.

The Fenraren continued upward, and a pit formed in Mershad's stomach as he realized what his steed was doing. The small leather pouches tied at Mershad's belt fell upward, into his stomach, and his cloak flapped

down past his head in the direction of the ground far below.

Mershad's eyes widened as he looked upside-down at the entity streaking below, laboring to get its own steed turned about. Sky was now beneath Mershad, and solid land above, at least to his perspective. The saddle held him securely as the Fenraren completed the loop, and flapped its wings vigorously.

Mershad glanced back, and saw that the dark entity was curving back around to resume the chase. Its steed emitted an ear-splitting cry, as if to vent its own wrath.

The Fenraren had gained some distance on the adversary now hastening in their wake. Mershad did everything he could to spur the Fenraren to go faster. In the midst of the frenzied pace, a cascade of ear-shattering, raging cries erupted, threatening to fracture the sky itself.

The deafening cries had not come from either the steed or its baleful rider. At the edge of his field of vision, Mershad perceived two large forms plunging down from the upper heights. At a dizzying speed, they were bearing directly towards the entity and its scaly mount.

Their shadows blanketed Mershad and his steed for a fleeting moment. He jerked his head around to try and make some sense of what was happening. Panic swirled around him at the presence of the new intruders in the sky with them.

Finally, he recognized their forms. The jaws of the nearest dragon were open wide, exposing a cavernous maw. A torrential blast of fire erupted from deep within the creature, shooting forth to engulf the dark entity.

Both rider and steed were bathed in the swathe of flames. Cloaked in dragon-flame, their own cries of fury turned swiftly to sounds of agony.

The second dragon spewed another thick wave of flames. The jet of fire saturated the diabolic figure and its steed such that Mershad could only see a cloud of fire for several moments in the place where they had been.

Hunter now hunted, shrouded in flames, the dark entity screeched in pain and rage. A shrill, piercing cry erupted from the hellish steed, creating an unholy chorus of torment within the Midragardan skies.

With the flames feeding off their bodies, the entity and its steed looked as if they were composed of dragon fire. The fires clung steadfastly to them, rippling, flaring, and licking upon every inch of their bodies, sparing them not even one moment in its withering intensity.

The entity broke off from its pursuit of Mershad, as the reptillian steed banked sharply to the right. Despite the clinging flames, a darker power was at work, as the flames consumed neither the entity, nor its hellish steed. Neither lost control of their senses, or governance of their physical forms, despite the extreme agony they were suffering.

Picking up speed, the winged monstrosity sped forward, trailing flames in its wake. The two dragons conducted a tight arc, bringing themselves around in the aftermath of the winged beast and the dark rider. Their focus honed upon their quarry, they paid not even a glance towards Mershad and the Fenraren.

Mershad, nearly at the brink of his mental breaking point just scant moments before, could barely believe his eyes. Fortune was with him, as his adversary was unceremoniously routed from the vicinity.

His steed hovered in place, as Mershad watched the dragons thundering after the fleeing entity. The forms of both pursued and pursuer swiftly diminished as they raced towards the far horizons, shrinking in their pressing haste.

Mershad could not bring himself to stop watching until the still-flaming entity and steed finally disappeared entirely. He forced himself to relax his tension on the reins, guiding the Fenraren into a slow, forward drift. The creature was breathing calmly, its manner in marked contrast to the frantic pace it had just endured.

A vast, dark shadow then crossed over Mershad, causing his heart to skip a beat as he snapped his gaze towards the sky above. Partially hidden by the vapors of the lowest level of clouds, the form of an enormous dragon soared just above Mershad and the Fenraren.

A great awe filled Mershad as he observed the dragon, its wings stretched wide and beating slowly as it navigated the high air currents. Swathes of the low cloudbanks' cottony vapors were cast awry, buffeted by the sheer force of the dragon's passage.

There was no mistaking the dragon's size, far larger than the two besetting the dark entity. Mershad had no doubts it was of the exalted kind that had visited King Hakon's estate. The winged giant's body had a distinctly reddish hue, the light of day reflecting off its gleaming body.

The Elder lifted upward, its great form obscured by the low cloud masses as it bore itself towards higher altitudes. It passed into another cloudbank, ascending rapidly. Mershad's eyes remained fixed on the area. His mind was a mixture of anxiety, wonder, and a little fear.

He knew there was really nothing to fear, as such an enormous creature, if it had intended harm to him, would have long since destroyed him. The Elder had not threatened Mershad, though its purpose, and appearance near the two rescuing dragons, were intriguing mysteries.

Whatever the answers were for the presence of the Elder, and the intervention of its smaller kin, Mershad was simply grateful. He had undeniably been saved in the brink of time from the malevolent rider.

Alone in the sky, Mershad turned his focus to the realities of the moment. Having endured more than his fill of unwelcome airborne encounters, he did not want to linger in the area.

Mershad quickly noticed a problem as he steered the Fenraren towards the mountains, in the hopes they would soon come across sight of the Glittering River. The Fenraren was obliging his desires, but the manifesting dilemma was far from insignificant.

The Fenraren was drifting slowly for reasons other than the fact they were free from imminent threats. Panting audibly, the Fenraren was exhibiting signs of deep exhaustion.

Its sorely depleted condition was of little surprise. Mershad knew a heavy price had been incurred in the blistering pace undertaken during the desperate evasions of the dark entity. Following a flight of long distance, the Fenraren had exerted itself to the utmost limits of its body, and had no reservoirs of energy left to draw upon.

The movement of the creature's wings was becoming very labored. The Fenraren sagged sharply in altitude each time it pumped its broad appendages.

The series of curt drops evoked a hollow pit deep in Mershad's stomach, accelerating his own trepidation. Instinctively, the creature began to descend, gliding for extended stretches before mustering enough energy for another beat of its wings.

Mershad spurred the Fenraren to land, without undue worry about the location. The wearied steed was all too eager to cooperate, angling its wings in a faster, smoother, descent. The tempered glide was much less taxing upon the Fenraren, and the passage was much easier for Mershad to endure.

They landed shortly within a broad expanse of grassland. The Fenraren mustered enough energy at the end of the descent to alight in a steady, controlled fashion, its legs still containing a little strength following the skyward odyssey.

The grassland held a sprinkling of lighter brush, which contrasted with the high, wild grasses forming the overwhelming majority of the foliage. Off in the distance, to all sides, Mershad espied dense boundary lines formed by trees. Looming beyond one side was the echelon of great, snow-capped mountains that captivated the depths of his imagination.

Now safely upon solid ground, Mershad slowly began to loosen his saddle straps, and work to dismount. He did not want to burden the weary Fenraren a moment longer than he had to. He paused for a few moments, regaining further equilibrium after the riveting plummet, before finally setting foot to the hard earth. His head was dizzy, his emotions drained, and his physical body lethargic.

"Can we take a rest for a while?" Mershad asked the Fenraren in a low voice. While the creature was not conversant in language, the act of speaking helped to gird him. "I could use a break right about now, and I know you could too. I just don't want that thing, whatever it was, to return to attack us."

He gazed skyward, and his heart fluttered as he feared seeing the dark entity somewhere on the horizon, bearing towards them again. Fortunately, much to the relief of his frayed nerves, the skies remained entirely clear and open.

Perhaps the Fenraren understand his words, as the creature walked around for a few moments, sniffed the air, and then sank heavily amid the grasses. The steed's energy was beyond spent, and it fell asleep almost instantly.

"Well, if you don't sense danger … and it clearly looks like you don't … then we're likely okay," Merhsad whispered, more for his own reassurance, though he did not want to disturb the sorely-depleted creature.

He then dropped where he stood, within the high grass. Soft and adequately padding, the grasses formed a capable pillow that he could rest his head upon, as well as providing cushioning for the length of his body. He stared back up at the unblemished, blue-green canopy of the sky, framed by the surrounding grass above his head.

The breezes through the grass serenaded gently, even as they brought sweet scents of wildflowers to his nose. His eyelids were quick to droop, and it was not long before he joined the Fenraren in a deep, dreamless sleep.

DRAGOL

"Still, you remain strong," Dragol grumbled in irritation. His legs were on the verge of giving out from the nearly complete lack of energy remaining within them. "I have never seen anything like this. Never before."

Still as limber as he had been when the march began, the startlingly hale old man stepped up on the trunk of a fallen tree, and continued smoothly down to the other side. He had barely broken a sweat, and his breathing was regular, unlike the labored breaths coming from the Trogen warrior.

A part of Dragol wanted to ask the old man if he could perform the strange working with the water again, recalling the act that had instantly rejuvenated his body earlier. Yet he restrained himself from doing so, largely because he wanted the old man to know his own determination, and ability to transcend weakness with sheer willpower.

"Much of what you think is physical is often in the mind itself," the old man replied, grinning as he looked upon the consternated expression splayed upon Dragol's face. "Not all things old in years are awaiting death. There are times when better things come with age, Dragol. You may find that out in your own life, if you allow it to happen."

"To have a better life when I am old?" Dragol responded in disbelief. "Could I have made this journey, or fought the battles I have fought in, if I were a frail, old Trogen awaiting the mercy of death?"

The old man just smiled, and shook his head slowly, with an air of amusement. "Dragol, not all journeys are of a physical nature, and not all battles are fought with the sword."

Dragol exhibited another look of confusion at the old man's aggravatingly cryptic, evasive words. "I do not understand. Can you not speak more plainly?"

The old man gave Dragol a warm, reassuring smile, much like a human parent would to a younger child. Strangely, Dragol was not offended by the patronizing expression. "When you question the warriors under your command, about anything, what do you want out of them?"

"I expect them to give me the truth," Dragol replied quickly.

"And as for you, when you question those in command of you, what do you want from them?" the old man questioned.

"I wish for them to answer me in truth," Dragol said firmly.

"And what of the world? Where it came from. Where it is going. And where you are going," the old man continued. "What do you want in these things?"

"I wish I could know the truth about them all," Dragol admitted.

"Then everything is centered upon what is true, and what is false," the old man said, nodding towards Dragol.

Dragol agreed. "Yes, that is no great mystery. That is how a Trogen always lives. What is true is that which we stand by, and what is false are things we do not wish to be around. What is real, and what is not real. I hold to such thoughts."

"Then you have to see for yourself what is true, and what is false. A time is coming to you imminently. All I ask is that you keep your mind open," the old man stated.

"I have just said that a Trogen lives by what is true. If something is shown to be true, then a Trogen takes in that truth. If it is shown to be false, then a Trogen is set against it," Dragol replied curtly, a little more tense at having to reiterate the Trogen philosophies.

The old man reached inside his blue robes, retrieving a small pendant mounted on the end of a long, looping leather strap. "I did not wish to anger you, Dragol. Here is a gift you may find very useful in the future."

He extended the pendant forward. Though reticent, Dragol grudgingly accepted the gift. It was an outright insult to refuse a gift among the Trogen culture, showing outright dishonor to the giver.

The old man had undeniably helped him, and had not yet shown himself to be of any threat. Dragol was not anywhere close to the point where he would even want to dishonor the old man, so he extended the courtesy of his own kind towards the proferred gift. Without a word, Dragol quietly slipped the pendant over his neck, though he barely glanced at the blue stone embedded in it.

The two traveled onward in silence, Dragol brooding over the old man's continued references to being open to truths. Though confounded by the old man's ways, the Trogen warrior was not fooled. He could see, as clear as by the light of an open, cloudless day, that the old man meant to either teach or guide him towards some supposed truth. Further reflection told him that the old man must have found something missing within Dragol, something that needed to be added.

Dragol, like most Trogens, was not overly favorable to being informed he was lacking in some area, at least without the alleged shortcoming being discussed openly. Nonetheless, his convictions regarding Trogen values were very strong. If a truth was shown to be a truth, then he was willing to accept it without rancor.

He knew there was something deeply mysterious about the old man traveling with him. The mesmerizing power demonstrated over the woodland carnivore, and the unconquerable stamina the seeming human continued to exhibit, were just two of several hints pointing to a supernatural nature.

If the old man was an enemy, then Dragol was certain he would have already discerned it. He had to admit it was bolstering to have such a companion in the unfamiliar land.

Dragol wondered what the end of the journey would bring. He might yet find a way to escape the cluthces of the enemy, but he knew he would part with the old man at some juncture. Where the old man's intended destination was served as yet another mystery for the Trogen to fathom.

"Sounds are coming from up ahead," the old man stated abruptly, sounding entirely calm, even nonchalant.

Dragol stood still, straining to listen as the old man drew to a stop. In the silence of the forest, Dragol waited several moments.

"I do not hear anything," he finally replied, knowing fully well that the hearing abilities of a Trogen were exceptional in comparison to those of a human.

"Listen carefully," the old man answered him.

Dragol was just about to express his frustration when the faint sounds of light steps through the brush reached his sensitive ears. Glancing quickly towards the old man, he motioned to take cover behind some trees close by.

The old man looked at Dragol, and slowly shook his head. Even more maddening, the man's lips were turned up in the beginnings of a smile. Dragol's ire sparked in the same moment that another voice reached his ears.

"Do not move!" a sharp, purposeful voice commanded, in perfectly rendered Trogen.

Dragol turned his head slowly, while keeping the rest of his body rigidly still. About fifteen paces to his right were four enemy warriors bearing bows, arrows already notched and aimed directly at him. Their painted, tattooed bodies were tensed, muscle contours etched along the surfaces of their mostly bared skin. Flinty and hardened, their dark eyes offered no sense of welcome.

Dragol was amazed that one of the warriors had spoken in perfect Trogen. Looking carefully back to where the old man stood, it was as if his companion read his thoughts. Reaching up slowly, lightly patting his chest, and then pointing back to Dragol, the old man signaled the pendant Dragol had just donned.

In that moment, Dragol understood the significance of the old man's gift. The timing and foresight were particularly extraordinary. He knew in his heart the old man had been aware of the approaching interception by the group of tribal warriors, and he had prepared Dragol better for it.

The presence of enemies was immediate, though, and had to be dealt with very cautiously. The situation facing the Trogen was tenuous at best.

Dragol looked back towards the tribal warriors, who now stepped a few paces closer. Five others emerged from the trees a short distance ahead, and a couple more walked into sight from the other side of the old man. Like the first four, all were armed with bows and arrows.

Still others manifested from the trees, shadows, and brush, in all directions. Some carried long wooden clubs, whose balled ends looked heavy and lethal. Others bore short hand axes, and some gripped long spears. Most displayed knives in fur-covered sheaths, worn at their hips, or hanging from their necks to the center of their chests.

He took a moment to study the tribal warriors more meticulously as they emerged from their cover, trying to glean what he could from their appearances. Their faces and bodies were covered in red and black body paint. Much of their bodies were exposed, save for what was covered by their short hide kilts and leggings. They were lightly equipped, with belts or sashes tied about their waists, pouches on hide straps slung from their shoulders, and moccasins on their feet.

They were heavily adorned, with rings of silver or shell decorating either ears or noses, and in many cases both. Necklaces and wristbands of shell, and armbands fashioned of hide or shell were displayed on their lean, chiseled bodies. A few had kneebands tied over their buckskin leggings.

Dark images of a variety of types had been worked into the surface of the warriors' skin. Tattoos displaying images of the natural world, such as turtles, lightning, arrows, eagles, bear claws, and other elements were mixed in with circular, swirling compositions, the latter representing no discernible object or creature. Their legs, arms, shoulders, chests, and backs displayed a wide array of figures and images, ranging from just a few on some warriors, to a great many on others.

Their heads were largely shaven, with the exception of a tuft of hair sprouting up from the crowns of their heads, often graced with feathers. They all had the wary, poised look of capable warriors.

Dragol sensed from their appearances that there were likely many close similarities between the Trogens and the tribal humans. To wear the images of the natural world on their skin showed a reverence for the things of their world. Trogen clans held a similarly close association with their surroundings, even if the veneration was displayed in different ways.

"What are you doing in these lands, Trogen?" the one who had first spoken to him questioned.

"My steed was slain," Dragol replied. "I was left in these woods, alone, before meeting him." He nodded towards the old man.

The speaker's eyes widened momentarily, as if something about Dragol's response surprised him. Dragol realized it was the fact that the speaker understood Dragol's words, and had evidently expected not to.

"And who are you?" the warrior addressed Dragol's traveling companion, glancing over cautiously towards the blue-robed man.

"One who is not of this world, but is simply in it," the old man replied, his face shining with a warm smile. Not one trace of concern was on his face. Dragol drew a little further confidence from the old man's untroubled demeanor.

"If you are of the One Spirit, then what are you doing with this Trogen?" the warrior questioned, making an inference that was not lost on Dragol.

"All are invited," the old man replied amiably. "But some have simply never been shown a different way. Only one path will suffice, and I chose to help this Trogen find it."

The warrior looked between the old man and the Trogen, appearing to be taken off guard by the old man's answer. He eyed the Trogen more assiduously.

"Disarm yourself," the warrior ordered Dragol stiffly. "Place the weapons before you. The old one may retain his walking staff."

"Why should I?" Dragol replied hotly, his temper rising sharply. He girded his resolve, and his words rumbled out with determination. "I am simply going to be your prisoner. You will torture or kill me. I would rather die with honor."

"Trust that they will show you honor," the old man interjected.

Dragol turned to look at the old man. "Why should I trust them? Have you forgotten they are at war with my brethren? I have heard much of these people."

"These people sought no war with your kind, nor gave the Trogen clans any cause for provocation," the old man said, loud enough for all to hear his words. As he spoke, his gaze moved slowly, and deliberately, from the Trogen to the leader of the tribal war band. "But we cannot change what has happened. Just know that not all that is spoken of a people is necessarily true, Dragol. Much is said about Trogens that is not true. And if the tribal people are truly of the One Spirit they revere, then they will show you the honor they claim to hold to."

It seemed to Dragol that the old man was subtly presenting a type of challenge to the war band's determined-looking leader. The tribal warrior nodded slowly towards the old man, as if comprehending the old man's meaning. He turned his attention back towards the Trogen.

"We do not desire to kill you. We will show you honor, as a living creation of the One Spirit," the leader stated firmly. "If you do not contest us, then no harm will come to you. The choice is yours to make, Trogen warrior. That is my word to you, in the witness of the One Spirit. But we cannot let you go free, not when your kind are joined with those warring against our people."

Dragol paused for several moments, considering the words of the leader. His instincts did not sense any sign of treachery. It was undeniably true that the Five Realms warriors could have cut them to pieces if they had wanted to. A number of arrows, from multiple directions, were honed in on him at that very moment.

Dragol and the old man were sorely outnumbered. While the old man possessed mysterious powers, Dragol had only his skill at arms. Those skills were formidable enough, and he might well take several warriors with him if combat erupted, but he knew he would not prevail against over twenty hale tribal warriors.

He thought carefully of the appeal made by the old man to the tribal warriors' spiritual convictions. The warriors in front of him were undoubtedly steadfast in their religious tenets and traditions, above everything else. The things the tribes adhered to were the very reasons they had taken a stand against the Unifier, a fateful choice that brought war upon them. As such, the oath given Dragol by the tribal leader, in reference to their One Spirit, was one Dragol decided he could take full confidence in.

Reluctantly, and slowly, Dragol withdrew his great longblade. He tossed it down, to land on the ground in front of him. He then proceeded to tediously lay down his longbow and dagger, as well as his leather-encased quiver of arrows.

"There," Dragol stated darkly, when all of his weapons were displayed on the ground, out of easy reach.

The stoic tribal leader nodded towards a couple of the warriors at his side. The two moved in, and hurriedly collected up the discarded weaponry.

Dragol cursed inwardly. Watching the tribal warriors carrying off the arms of a Trogen warrior was a kind of humiliation, even if there were no other Trogens to witness the travesty. Simultaneously, the feeling of helplessness surged within him. He now had no chance whatsoever to fight his way out of the encircling group.

He had willfully placed himself into a very vulnerable position, entirely at their mercy. The old man truly had gained an incredible amount of influence over the Trogen, as Dragol's response would likely have been unthinkable not long beforehand.

"Come with us," the tribal leader intoned. "We will leave your hands untied, until you should prove to us otherwise. Your weapons will be kept with us for now."

The leader glanced purposefully between Dragol and the old man. Dragol knew that a gesture of some kind had been delivered to the old man within the statement.

A feeling of total disbelief struck Dragol at the development. He was a prisoner taken in the heat of a war, and they were going to let him keep his hands and legs entirely free. It would have been an unheard of act within the Trogen clans. Any surrendering enemy warrior caught was tightly bound, without a second thought.

"Come," the leader stated, gesturing for Dragol to move.

The old man had already started forward, as three warriors moved near to him, keeping their arrows loosely notched in their bows. Likewise,

Dragol was escorted closely by three warriors, with the addition of the war party's leader moving closer and walking just a few paces to his right.

"You speak the words of our language, as well as one of us," the leader said, his eyes regarding the Trogen warrior with great scrutiny. Despite the pledge, and the relative freedom extended to Dragol, the Trogen could see that the tribal leader was far from comfortable with him. "You seem different from other Trogens. Few would allow us to take their weapons."

"We are not fools," Dragol replied sharply. As if in way of justification to the tribal leader, and to himself, he added, "With a dozen arrows trained upon my body, there is not much I could do."

"True enough, it was the only choice to make, in order for you to survive," the patrol leader agreed readily. He then asked another question, after walking in silence for several more paces, "How long have you been in these lands?"

"Since our steeds were driven from the skies by Midgragardan warriors," Dragol replied. "I have spent nights and days moving through your lands."

"Then you have done well. It is very dangerous for a lone traveler in certain parts of these woods," the patrol leader said, evidencing some genuine admiration for the Trogen's survival in the forests of the Five Realms.

"The old man helped me a few times," Dragol grudgingly acknowledged, pointing ahead to where his robed companion was walking at his usual, brisk gait.

"And what of him?" the other queried. "Did he come to these lands with you?"

Dragol shook his head. "He joined me after I had already spent some time in your lands …our paths crossed, very unexpectedly for me. He has strange powers over the animals, and seems to possess a vast wisdom."

The Trogen grew silent for a few heartbeats, and then looked into the eyes of the tribal warrior. "I thought you might know something of him, for he appeared to me as a stranger, though he seems very familiar with your woodlands."

The tribal warrior grew silent, focusing ahead on the form of the old man. His eyes squinted, as if he was trying to see something no one else could see. His face, in a slight grimace of frustration, gradually relaxed, and he turned back towards Dragol.

"Yes, the old man is unusual. That much is very clear to me as well. You say that you encountered him within this forest, and never before?" the leader asked.

"Yes, I felt his presence following my trail for some time, and then he asked to join me," Dragol said. "You will find he has an incredible stamina, and his knowledge seems to have no boundaries. He is not very good at answering questions clearly."

The tribal warrior had nothing else to say, walking on with a pensive countenance. Dragol noticed that he looked to be increasingly consumed with the mystery regarding the identity of the old man.

Dragol knew exactly what was going through the tribal leader's mind, even if he could not read the other's thoughts. If the old man was said to have powers over animals, a vast knowledge, and an inhuman level of stamina, then the old man was likely not as he outwardly appeared.

Dragol himself was probably an enigmatic figure to the tribal leader. The enemy warrior probably could never have imagined, not in a thousand years, a Trogen warrior acting as acquiescent as Dragol. The tribal warrior likely expected Dragol to claim a few enemy warriors' lives while fighting ferociously to the death.

Dragol was about to question the tribal leader further, when a couple of warriors from farther ahead abruptly yelled out, "Enemies! Upon us!"

In the next few moments, the forest came alive. The air filled with the whistling sounds of arrows and bolts, as Gallean fighters streamed into view. It was an ambush, as the Galleans were in positions all around the contingent of tribal warriors. Dragol flattened out instinctively on the ground, as an arrow whizzed through the air just above him.

"You betrayed me!" the tribal warrior cried out, looking to Dragol with eyes wide in shock and accusation.

Dragol hated the accusation that he had violated the honor shown to him. He made no move to attack the tribal leader, who had dropped to one knee after scooting behind the cover of an oak tree.

The leader grunted in pain, as an arrow lodged into his upper back. A moment later, a crossbow bolt drove deep into the back of his right leg, and the tribal leader fell forward to the ground. Pierced twice, the tribal warrior was effectively rendered helpless. Dragol quickly crawled over to the leader, who was still alive.

"I did not betray you. I did not know of these fighters. I will show you the honor that you showed me," Dragol related quickly to the injured warrior.

As efficiently as possible, Dragol dragged the wounded tribal leader further behind the tree. The warrior winced, and clenched his teeth in the pain wracking him with the rough movements.

The crossbowman and archer who had stricken the tribal leader no longer had a clear angle on him. Dragol reached down and took a bow from the tribal warrior, as well as an arrow from his quiver. He clutched both in his left hand.

He could feel that the simple bow would be far less strenuous to pull than a Trogen one. The arrows were significantly lighter as well.

He gripped the long wooden haft of the tribal warrior's war club with his right hand. Dragol could feel the dense weight of the wooden ball carved into the opposite end. He knew it was a formidable weapon at once.

"You … will … kill me? After … I … showed you … dignity?" the tribal warrior gasped, between sharp outbursts reflecting raw pain.

"I will protect you," Dragol said firmly, staying low, and looking alertly around.

The sounds of stringent combat filled the air about them, flowing through the trees in a sustained, deadly serenade. He could hear the clash of steel, and the thuds of arrows and bolts, as the battle sprawled through the trees.

The Trogen warrior glanced in every direction for a sign of the old man, but there was none to be found. Dragol's woodland companion had vanished again, or was obscured by the surrounding trees.

The tribal warriors were now heavily intertwined with those who had attacked them. The battle was widening ever deeper into the surrounding trees, with each and every passing moment.

Dragol could see the shapes of combatants from both sides flitting in and out of view all around him, as they moved amongst the trees. A melee such as the one at hand was a very dangerous environment, and Dragol had to keep his wits and senses primed without even a moment's respite.

A tribal warrior, running with war club upraised, and a bellowing cry, charged into sight off to the left, bearing down upon some unseen opponent. Out of his peripheral vision, to his right and deeper in the woods, Dragol espied three iron-helmed Galleans with shields and spears stalking forward.

Each time that he turned his head, he saw the quick blur of racing shafts loosed from crossbows and longbows. Heavy thwacks sounded as shafts embedded deep into the bodies of trees. Sharp outcries of agony burst out wherever the missles buried into flesh.

It was a chaotic, unpredictable situation, unceasingly requiring Dragol's full vigilance. He readied for any sign of attack, from any source, as the fighting swirled around him. A wrong calculation at any time could mean instant death.

A couple of knights, heads encased in full, flat-topped helms, trotted directly towards Dragol out of the dense underbrush. Both were very strong-looking men, who moved with confident bearing. Clinks and metallic rustlings, from their chain mail shirts and leggings, accompanied their steps.

Dragol slowly rose to his feet, making no sudden moves. He gripped the haft of the war club firmly in his right hand, and kept the bow clenched in his left. He kept his body relaxed, not wanting to send a provoking signal to the two warriors by taking up any semblance of a combat stance.

Dragol recognized the two swordsmen from their surcoats as warrior-monks of the red spear. The white, sleeveless surcoats vividly displayed the red symbol over their left breasts. He knew the men were to be taken with great caution, members of a human order who intertwined their religious passions intimately with their considerable skill at arms.

Each carried a triangular shield, and steel-edged longswords that tapered to sharp points. The facing of their shields was half-black and half-white, in the manner of their order. Dragol could feel the iron weight of their gazes through the horizontal slits in the facings of the cylindrical, flat-topped helms.

"Trogen, you are free. Stand aside, as I lay waste to this infidel betrayer of the Unifier," the warrior to the right addressed Dragol, in a deep, commanding tone. He gestured sharply as he spoke, indicating for Dragol to move over to the side, away from the wounded tribal leader.

"No, he stays alive," Dragol replied sharply, remaining in place. "He let me live after capturing me."

"A Trogen that speaks fluent Gallean? Now that is a rarity," responded the warrior-monk on the left, exchanging a glance with his comrade.

"And as for this infidel, he spared you just to get information from you, or to torture you," the other warrior stated coldly, refocusing everything on the issue before them. "Are you not aware these savages have been known to eat the flesh of captives? Now, move, and let us destroy him ... This is a war, and he is an enemy to us, to the Trogens, and to our faith."

"No," Dragol challenged them, his ire spiraling at the humans who dared to question his judgement. The more typical Trogen temperment was quickly returning to the fore, and this time there were no mysterious old men in blue robes around to blunt it.

Trogens and humans in the forces guided by the Unifier interacted no more than was absolutely necessary, but Dragol knew the Trogens were well understood to be steadfast in their stated intentions. A part of him hoped it would suffice, but a rising part of him also hoped that the two warrior-monks dared to transgress him. The arrogance exuding from them was particularly rankling, and begged for a thorough humbling.

"I am a commander in the ranks of the sky steeds of the Unifier's army," Dragol continued, his lips curling back on his short muzzle to reveal his lengthy set of canines. The snarling expression accented his words strongly. "I am a chieftain in the Thunder Wolf Clan, of the Trogen race. I demand that you recognize my authority, and spare this man."

"Have you forgotten the enemy is to be imprisoned or destroyed, not protected?" the warrior to the left asked, his tone incredulous, and plainly caught off guard by Dragol's resolved response.

"I cannot afford him any less than he afforded me," Dragol responded, his anger continuing to grow. "That is a warrior's code. A true warrior understands honor." He let the implications of his words hang ominously in the air between himself and the two warrior-monks.

"The command of the Unifier goes above any code!" the warrior-monk on the right shot back at him. A fell tone crept into his words, as he spoke in a low, growling voice. "There is no law in all of this world that can supersede the Unifier. This is the Unifier's world."

"Even religion?" Dragol asked, somewhat taken aback by the warrior-monk's reply. He had believed that the warrior-monks would never display any ambiguity regarding the priority of their god's authority. He had previously believed it to be at the very center of everything they were, but it was unmistakably obvious that it was not. The Unifier held their truest loyalty.

Dragol then posed another question. "And what if sparing this man is part of my own religious belief? Of the Creator who founded the world?"

"You speak to us of matters of religion, Trogen? We, who are warriors of the Western Church itself?" the warrior on the right replied disdainfully, patently growing iritated with Dragol's reticence to hand over the injured tribal leader. "Remember that you are an infidel to us as well … and keep that closely in mind, Trogen."

A threat manifested from the warrior-monks with those words, and clung heavily to the air as the tension coiled between the humans and the Trogen.

"Your Church does not proclaim to slay prisoners," Dragol ventured in the way of argument, though he admittedly knew little of the particulars of their strange faith.

Some assumptions could be reasonably made. Founded as it was by a sacred Man who had submitted to a violent and cruel death, after being made a prisoner Himself, Dragol doubted strongly that the religion would ever advocate the abuse, or murder, of other prisoners.

"The Unifier decreed that none who resist are to be spared in this war," the warrior-monk to the left said, his knuckles whitening as he clenched the hilt of his sword tighter. Sunlight refracted off of the blade, hitting it through a crease in the tree canopy and creating a starry burst, as if the sword was empowering itself.

"I see. Then the Unifier is a religion, put above all others," Dragol said. He added, with the edge of a hiss, "Even yours…"

"Enough of this debate, Trogen! It is over! Now step aside!" the warrior-monk on the left snarled, patience clearly exhausted. He raised his sword so that its tapered point was aimed right at the Trogen warrior.

"Yours is no religion I ever wish to serve … and I speak of your true religion. Your true religion is not the one you claim to profess," Dragol roared back at them.

All semblances of formalities fell immediately by the wayside. Dragol dropped the bow and war club he had taken from the tribal leader, letting the weapons fall to land on the ground.

The other two reflexively backed up. The warrior-monks were not fearful, simply not reckless, remaining disciplined and taking a firmer combat stance. They eyed the Trogen warily.

Dragol hurriedly rolled up the tunic sleeve from his left forearm, exposing the small symbol that had been burned into his flesh when he and his other fellow Trogens had sworn their allegiances to the Unifier. He had given the star-shaped symbol little thought at the time, seeing it as nothing more than a body marking signifying an alliance.

Yet he knew the marking held some monumental importance to those who were most fanatical about the Unifier. He now had little doubt that the two warrior-monks were such men.

He crouched down, leaned over and took a short knife from the sheath worn by the injured tribal leader. Deliberately placing it against the edge of the symbol, he looked straight into the iron visages of the two warriors. He winced momentarily, as he sliced through the area of skin, a burning pain lancing through his arm as he severed the mark completely off.

The piece of flesh fell to the ground. Dragol raised up his right leg and stamped down upon it, grinding it into the soil. The pain he felt drove his fury as he worked the symbol-ridden flesh into bloodied pulp.

"Traitor!" shouted the warrior-monk on the right, his discipline evaporating as he charged right at the Trogen with murderous intentions.

Dragol ducked at the last instant, as the adrenalized warrior-monk slashed down, burying his sword deep into the wood of the tree just behind the Trogen. The Trogen countered with a thrust of knife in his hand, straight upwards, catching the warrior-monk solidly underneath his chin.

Though the knight's head was further protected with a mail hauberk worn beneath the helm, the driving force of the blow pierced the links, and broke through into flesh and bone. An eerie gurgling came from behind the iron visor of the warrior-monk, just before he slumped over, falling lifeless with the knife buried to the hilt.

Out of the corner of his eye, Dragol saw the second warrior-monk closing in, preparing to send his sword forward in an impaling thrust. He had no time to try and snatch the knife free, lodged as it was in his other opponent. Arching his back at the last moment, Dragol felt the blade spearing the air where his body had just been. He rotated slightly, gaining his balance on his right leg.

With his left leg, he kicked into the knee of the warrior, catching the human squarely. With a sickening crack, the warrior-monk was sent heavily to the ground. Twirling about, the Trogen laid his grip on the hilt of the sword stuck in the wood of the tree. He dislodged it with a powerful jerk, his amply muscled back, arms, and shoulders flexing in urgent unision.

Bringing the sword about without delay, he swung it mercilessly down upon the fallen warrior-monk. His opponent's feeble attempt to raise his own sword to block Dragol's attack was far too slow to counter the descending blow. The plummeting strike cleaved deep where it landed beneath the man's helm, shattering chain mail links and burying the steel edge into the man's neck.

Dragol left the blade there, the battle finished. He turned his attention towards the tribal leader, who had pulled himself over to the left of the tree during the torrential burst of fighting. He was on his left side, propped up, and keeping his weight from further antagonizing his two injuries.

The tribal leader had a baffled look upon his face, and Dragol was not surprised. The man had just watched the Trogen willingly cut off the Unifier's mark, and then proceed to slay two elite warrior-monks who were supposed to be fighting on the same side as the Trogens.

"You showed me honor. I cannot serve those who cannot return honor," Dragol explained in a tense voice, his teeth clenched with lingering anger in the immediate wake of the confrontation. He glared hotly at the two prone bodies of the warrior-monks. "It would be better to be dead, than to be a dishonorable warrior. Those two are both dead and dishonorable. As they deserve."

"Thank you, Trogen," the tribal leader replied. He then added, in a lowered tone. "They would have killed me."

"I know," Dragol replied firmly, keeping his eyes out for any new dangers.

"I wish to learn your name, Trogen warrior," the tribal leader responded.

"I am known as Dragol, of the Thunder Wolf Clan," answered the Trogen. "I would learn yours as well."

"I am Ayenwatha, of the Firaken Clan, of the Onan tribe," the Five Realms warrior replied.

"I will stay here, Ayenwatha of the Firaken Clan, until the outcome of this battle is known," Dragol said, taking a couple of steps to where the bow and war club had been discarded. He bent over and

picked the weapons up, moving to take up a position by Ayenwatha's side.

His senses keenly alert, he began a new vigil over the wounded tribal warrior. The sounds of fierce fighting throughout the area continued, but diminishing steadily as opponents were gradually elminated by one side or the other. No new threats emerged to challenge Dragol or the wounded warrior he stood guard over.

Dragol peered around the tree, and listened attentively as the furious combat fizzled to an end, leaving the woods wreathed in an uneasy silence. The cessation of violence did not come as a relief to the Trogen, as there was no way of telling who was the victor, or how many warriors might yet remain nearby.

As he tried to assess his situation, he heard a crunching footstep and shuffle alerting him that some survivors were near. He waited patiently, coiled and ready to act, no matter what side the approaching survivors were on. Armed, free, and no longer badly outnumbered, his choices had expanded considerably.

A couple of slowly moving tribal warriors stepped into view. Their eyes fell on Dragol and Ayenwatha almost immediately, and they angled towards them. Their sweaty, sullen faces showed no alarm at the Trogen, seeing him with their leader. Ayenwatha's back was to the Trogen warrior, and it was abundantly clear that Dragol was warding the tribal leader.

One of the two approaching survivors was badly injured, judging by the warrior's pronounced limp as he approached. The warrior's companion lent him a shoulder to brace upon, bleeding from a few light cuts himself. The injured warrior leaned heavily upon the stronger man, hobbling along with great effort.

Two other Five Realms warriors then came into view, from behind Dragol. He did not see them at first, as their steps were silent. Only a faint sense of their movements brought his head whirling about.

Neither of the two was the worse for wear, emerging practically unscathed from the fighting. Recognizing the Trogen, and not taking full assessment of the rest of the scene, they swiftly raised up their bows, setting arrows into place with smooth precision.

"Halt!" Ayenwatha cried out immediately, and forcefully, mustering up some strength. "The Trogen is not to be harmed! He saved my life, harm him and you harm me!"

Instantly, the two bows were lowered. The warriors returned the arrows to their quivers, and made their way over to where the others were. As they reached the others, Dragol could see the distress reflected within their dark eyes. Their faces were taut as they stood quietly.

"All are dead, both of the enemy, and of ours," the warrior shouldering the badly wounded fighter reported glumly.

"It is a sorrowful thing indeed," interrupted the voice of the old man who had traveled with Dragol. "What must take its course, must take its course, though it brings us much loss and sadness."

Trogen and tribal warrior alike looked abruptly towards the elderly figure in the blue robes as he walked out of the brush. They made no moves to obstruct or intercept him, as he kneeled down to Ayenwatha's level.

Dragol eyed the old man with heightened curiosity. Now that the fighting was over, he wondered what the old man had been doing during the swirling melee.

"You have been wounded badly," the old man said to Ayenwatha, before turning his head to eye the tribal warriors gathered around. "Get the arrow and the bolt out of him, and then I will see to him."

The two healthy warriors stepped forward, and methodically rotated Ayenwatha onto his belly. As swiftly as possible, with focused care, they examined the wounds closely.

They were able to work the arrow free from Ayenwatha's back, pulling the fletched shaft out with little further damage to the site of the wound. Then, they worked the bolt carefully out of his leg, pushing it forward a little so that they could break the tip off first, before removing the main portion of the shaft. Both of the extended series of movements elicited a few sharp cries of excruciating pain from Ayenwatha. The two warriors then took a step back, making space for the old man to maneuver.

The old man edged closer, and then reached forth, laying his hands on Ayenwatha's back over the first of the bleeding wounds. Then, he moved his hands down, and placed them gently over the second. Each time he performed the action, he closed his eyes momentarily, and his brow furrowed, as if in a state of intense concentration.

As he withdrew his hands, the others watched in sheer amazement as the wounds visibly healed themselves. The glistening, oozing blood faded from sight as the punctured areas steadily closed. The flesh sealed itself, until there was only smooth skin on the back of Ayenwatha's right shoulder and right leg, where the wounds had been.

The strange art the old man had employed with the stream water, which had renewed Dragol's sapped energy during the woodland hike, was astounding enough. What Dragol now witnessed was nearly incomprehensible.

"Come around, and bring him here," the old man ordered, gesturing towards the injured warrior propped up by his comrade, standing just a couple of paces behind.

Obediently, the healthier warrior helped the injured man move around, to stand before the old man. The limping warrior's face was a mask of incessant pain, sweat pouring down his grimy face. His eyes had a light glaze to them, and his breath came in staggered, labored intervals.

His right thigh had suffered a wide, deep gash from the stroke of a sword, or perhaps an axe. He had already lost a lot of blood. It was the kind of grievous wound that would almost certainly fester over the coming hours and days, leading to a debilitating sickness, and subsequent death. Dragol was well aware that such a wound was often as much of a death sentence, if not an even worse one, with all the ensuing agony incurred, than an abrupt death on the battlefield.

As he had done with Ayenwatha, the old man set his hands over the ugly wound, and closed his eyes. As before, the wound proceeded to heal fully. The skin appeared to knit itself back into form, the healthy tone of fresh, clean skin soon covering the place where the mangled, cleaved flesh had been. The man's pallor improved considerably, his breath growing steady, and his alertness returning in full to his eyes. The healing of arduous and precarious weeks had condensed itself into mere moments.

Both Ayenwatha and the warrior looked up to the old man and expressed their gratitude, calling the blessings of the One Spirit upon the old man. The old man accepted the accolades humbly, with a kindly smile as he lightly patted each of the two newly-healed men.

The warrior with the deep leg wound was almost feverish in his thanksgiving. Dragol could see that the man consciously realized he had been miraculously spared from an all but inevitable slide towards a terrible death.

Dragol doubted he would have felt any different if he had been in the man's place. He gazed upon the scene in awe, and even a little fear, as he wondered further about the strange old man.

Gradually, the tribal warriors turned their attentions back towards their surroundings. After a short conferral, they agreed to spread out, and search the area, to see if there might yet be some other survivors amongst the trees.

The healed warrior and the companion who had aided him formed one searching pair, and the two other warriors formed another. Dragol remained with Ayenwatha and the old man, as they formed up a third group.

After the potent healing display, the warriors did not bother to question Ayenwatha about the wisdom of being left alone with the Trogen, or the mysterious old man. Dragol knew they already took it for granted that their leader would be physically safe in the company of the unusual pair of allies.

The three groups moved out to begin the grisly, and rather debilitating, search. As they started out through the woods, Dragol and the others laid their eyes upon the carnage strewn all about the woods by the fight.

The battle had been fiercely contested, and the vicious evidence was everywhere. Broken bodies, shattered shields, cleaved hafts of weapons, blood-stained swathes of ground, and arrow shafts embedded in cold, lifeless flesh were among the host of gruesome sights testifying to the ferocious nature of the clash.

Seeing the dead bodies of his tribal companions, Ayenwatha's eyes glimmered with sadness, a deeply emotional response that surprised Dragol. The man had displayed an undeniably steadfast courage all during the battle, keeping his composure, and Dragol had no doubts about what his instinct told him; the tribal leader was a great warrior among his people.

To see the man beginning to weep was an uncomfortable and even disconcerting, sight. The Trogen chieftain almost averted his eyes, though the raw, emotive response touched something deep within Dragol's own spirit.

"Always take refuge in the One Spirit, the All-Father," the old man then said, looking upon Ayenwatha's mournful disposition. He smiled compassionately towards the tribal leader, the kind expression conveyed further in his gentle tone. "Many of those who died in this fight are now better off ... far more so than either you or Dragol have been in your entire lives. If you only knew by experience of the place where they went, then it is very likely you would not be thanking me for doing anything to extend your own life, for even a moment longer, within this world."

"I cannot see it as you see it," Ayenwatha replied forlornly, looking to the old man with a little confusion showing through his mask of grief. "But if you are certain of the better fate of those who have passed on, then why did you extend my life?"

"As it is, my new young friend, you and Dragol both have much more work yet to do in this world. Of that, I am quite certain," the old man replied, with his characteristic lack of clarity on the matter.

Dragol stifled the complaint that came to his mind. The old man then patted Ayenwatha consolingly on the shoulder, and glanced towards Dragol briefly, with a nod and a slight smile. He then looked forward again, resuming his pace.

Dragol slowed his pace, staring silently at the old man ahead. He had just spoken with an unmistakably sanguine tone, rife with surety about transcendent things that Dragol could barely even imagine. The Trogen warrior longed more than ever to know the man's true identity, especially in light of the ever-increasing examples of his mystical nature. The stranger was unquestionably a man of great, hidden power, but he was also one who either genuinely respected, or viewed himself as in friendship with, the One Spirit that the tribal warriors' recognized and revered.

After visibly healing the tribal warriors, and his following discourse with Ayenwatha, nothing would readily suffice to assuage Dragol's growing hunger for answers. Somehow, Dragol had to learn who the enigmatic man really was, even if he was a man at all.

"Good stranger, tell me one thing," Ayenwatha suddenly remarked to the old man.

"Yes?" the old man replied, looking back to the tribal warrior.

"Do you sense that we have the time and the peace to spare those fallen in the battle, of the ravages of beast, weather, and time itself?" Ayenwatha asked, in a low voice. "I do not wish to ask for what you do not choose to offer us, but can you tell me this much? It weighs very heavily on my heart."

A soft look came to the old man's eye. He paused for a moment, growing very quiet and still, without a word of reply to Ayenwatha.

Dragol stared hard at the old man's face, as his focus seemed to detatch itself from their immediate surroundings.

To Dragol, it appeared that the old man had fallen into a kind of deep trance. It was of the kind where he did not appear to be fully present, even if his body was right there in front of them. Several moments passed before clarity and awareness returned back to the old wanderer's expression.

"You are safe to do what you wish, when you are finished with your search," the old man replied.

"It is not asking too much, then?" Ayenwatha queried softly.

"No, and it is the right thing to do," the old man replied gently.

Ayenwatha looked hesitant for a moment, before asking, "Do you have any suggestions? Our tribal ways to honor the dead may be inadequate for the time we have availale to us. We cannot fashion platorms, or a great pit, or even a great mound as in past times."

"Commit their bodies to the pure flame, as many have done in many lands, including your friends in Midragard," the old man suggested.

The tribal leader grew very quiet for a few moments, before slowly nodding. "That is a good way."

Ayenwatha continued the search for a short while. Among those found lying on the ground, there were no survivors. They presently came across one tribal warrior straggling in towards them, who spoke of a hard pursuit of some fleeing Gallean warriors. Several had evidently gotten away in the aftermath of the main fighting, though the tribal warrior claimed to have downed a couple of the retreating Galleans with his bow.

At Ayenwatha's behest, they turned their efforts to locating the other two groups. To the tribal leader's evident gladness, the other two groups had fared a little better in their explorations.

The first pair had found four other warriors, two of which had incurred light injuries. The second pair discovered two largely healthy warriors, and one mortally wounded one, who expired before they could even ask the old man for any aid.

"It is a boundary that I cannot cross, in such a way, though I wish it were otherwise," the old man had said softly, when they were informed of what had just happened.

Dragol realized the old man had addressed the unspoken question hovering in the air, as the others looked to him following the announcement regarding the man who had died only moments before.

SPIRIT OF FIRE

At that juncture, Dragol would not have found it entirely surprising to discover that the old man could call the recently deceased back from the Elysian Fields. Yet evidently, there were some limits to what the old man could do.

Once assembled back together, they now numbered a full dozen tribal warriors, in addition to the old man and the Trogen. None of the newcomers required any sort of special attention from the old stranger.

Ayenwatha then explained his desires regarding the slain warriors to the other tribesmen, and not one of them offered so much as one complaint. The faces that Dragol could read reflected a consensus of great relief at their leader's wish. They even did not take any exceptions to the proposed fiery method, one that the tribal people apparently did not normally employ towards the dead. Though they looked to be heavy of heart as they set out to gather the bodies of the fallen tribal warriors, Dragol could sense their firm determination to carry out the melancholy task.

A range of unspoken thoughts flowed through Dragol's mind, as he quietly joined in and helped the tribal warriors in their efforts. While the gathering of the slain took place, a couple of the tribesmen set about clearing space and building up a rough pyre for the makeshift funeral of their tribal brethren.

A significant and unexpected addition then occurred, one that added substantially more labor and time to the endeavor. As they gathered the bodies of their fellow comrades, the tribal warriors came to a most surprising agreement amongst themselves; at least to Dragol's eyes.

They made the decision to add the bodies of the slain Gallean fighters to the pyre.

In the aftermath of their choice, Dragol made sure to personally drag the bodies of the two slain warrior-monks who had fallen by his own hand over to the pyre. With a vigorous lift and heave, he lumped each body onto the growing pile of the fallen. For no real reason that he was cognizant of, he paused to remove their helmets, and looked down upon their still faces.

One of the thickly bearded men looked to be simply asleep, while the second stared out of glazed, lifeless eyes. Dragol passed his broad hand over the second man's face, closing his eyelids shut before moving away.

Dragol had fought in defense of himself and Ayenwatha, and had

297

no misgivings about slaying the two men. The two warrior-monks had both been willing to commit a treacherous act in killing a helpless man, but he knew that they also had a homeland, had been born to families, and had a purpose in life. They had fallen as warriors, and in doing so died with the Trogen's genuine respect, even if they had become enemies hellishly bent on the Trogen's own destruction.

In a sense, looking upon their faces without any regrets, unflinching and without rancor, was a quiet salute in its own right. It was an unspoken tribute to their better qualities, such as the warriors' courage they undeniably possessed.

It became clear that the tribal warriors had fought back their own grave misgivings and bitter feelings in extending the funerary ritual to the fallen enemies. Dragol watched with growing respect for the tribal warriors as they proceeded to offer up prayers of intercession for the slain enemy warriors to the One Spirit, after they had piled all of the bodies together.

It was not long before thick tendrils of smoke were rising up through the tree's canopy, and the acrid smell of burning flesh filled the air. The flames rapidly consumed the bodies of friend and foe alike, as the small group of tribal warriors, the old man, and the Trogen stood by in silent witness.

As Dragol suspected that he would, the old man congratulated the tribal warriors and the Trogen on the wisdom shown by their efforts. The old man seemed to have an almost fatherly pride about him, as he commended each man, and the Trogen, individually.

Dragol did not exactly know what wisdom the old man was referring to, especially regarding himself. Yet he hoped it would all become clear in time, along with the identity of the old man. The latter question was becoming utterly maddening, as all seeming opportunities to fathom more met with sheer futility.

Shortly thereafter, as the flames died down, the small party left the pyre behind. Not a word was spoken as they filed through the trees and headed onward.

MERSHAD

Very slowly, Mershad's eyes opened. Above, the bright, blue-green of the late afternoon sky had been replaced with a ripe harvest of stars, set into the deep violet firmament of silken night. The lush beauty of the unsullied night sky took his breath away at once, as his eyes drank in the expansive magic of the scene far above. Everything held a dreamlike, mystical quality, beckoning with a sense of timelessness and infinite horizons.

The sight hinted of greater realities, reminding him that he had slept right through more than one of his five daily prayers. He felt a sense of guilt, and especially regretted missing the sunset prayer.

Where many others may have seen just the lights of distant stars, Mershad saw the hand of the Creator. Remembering his simple prayers was the least he could do to honor the One who had brought everything before his eyes into being, out of sheer nothingness. A dynamic tapestry of existence encompassed Mershad at all times, where each and every thing, great and small, had an ordained place.

In that moment, he wondered why anyone in his own world, or Ave, could ever choose to subject themselves to the things of the world, and not the Creator of them. The distinction seemed so clear and evident; reverence belonged to the Creator, not the creature.

He wondered about the tale of the first man and woman, in the eternal Garden before their fall from grace. They could easily have chosen to revel in the life given to them, and grown into each of their own best potentials.

They had been given the foremost of environments, living within an abundantly flowering, harmonious atmosphere that had been bestowed on them by the Creator. It was an environment entirely devoid of death and ruin, sadness and disease, and it had been theirs for the taking. It had also been the world their descendents would have inherited, to enjoy right alongside those that came before them.

The thought of the stupidity of humankind brought a rueful smile to his face. The first man and woman were far from the only ones willing to exercise their free will in a patently misguided direction.

He was no different himself. He had made his own choices, and there had certainly been times when he had acted, or failed to act, in relation to the knowledge of the right thing to do in a particular instance.

He had been guilty of the same tendencies plaguing the first born of humanity.

With a sigh, he exhaled a long breath, and stared deep into the night skies. Every living thing, in every flawed world, in a sense, spent a lifetime in exile. Perhaps one day, every living thing, within all the possible worlds, could reach the state originally intended.

Faint sounds of movement in the brush caught his ears, the sounds snapping him out of his contemplations. Surmising the Fenraren was foraging about, whether stretching out its limbs or searching around for some kind of food, Mershad decided to sit up.

Reluctantly, he leaned up and over slowly, detaching himself from the comfortable, natural bed he had slept soundly upon for many hours. He groaned a little in response to the tightness and aches in his muscles and joints, taking a few moments to limber up his arms, arch his back, and twist slowly from side to side.

Rubbing the sleep out of his eyes, he chuckled to himself as the rustling sounds approached a little closer. Now rested, the Fenraren was likely impatient to get going again.

Flying at night would be an engaging experience, and would provide a whole new spectrum of sights to enjoy. It would be a welcome distraction from the turbulence buried just under the surface of his heart and mind.

The village was not likely to be very far, and the Glittering River certainly would not be hard to see under a clear sky. Sparkling like a vein of silver under the light of Ave's two moons, it would serve as a beacon and path to follow.

The light falling over the field was comparable to a bright full moon within Mershad's world. Looking around, he could not locate any sign of the Fenraren. His brow furrowed in concentration, as his gaze drifted across the top of the grasses.

The rustling sounds occurred again, from just behind him. He turned his head in time to see a portion of the tall grasses shift for an instant, before becoming still. Another swishing of the grass reached his ears, coming from the direction he had previously been looking in.

Whirling his head about, Mershad bit his lip as he clenched his jaws, trying to avoid making any inadvertant sounds. He stared into the cold night, his muscles within tensing, and his nerves set on edge. About fifty yards away, to the right, another clump of grasses swayed.

He wished he knew where the Fenraren was, as a seed of fear sprouted and grew rapidly. The rustlings then resumed, this time coming from multiple directions at once. The sounds prompted him to crouch below the tops of the grasses.

Scolding himself for being so foolish, having landed in a wilderness he knew nothing about, Mershad hoped whatever good fortune keeping him alive in a foreign world had not finally run its course. He lamented that he had not forced himself to stay awake, and pressed onward after giving the Fenraren a short period of rest.

Whatever choice had been made in the past, he had to face the present. He knew he had to find the Fenraren, if he was to have any chance of escaping a possible threat. Yet he did not want to move, knowing his clumsy passage through the grasses would be swiftly detected by anything in the vicinity.

After several pensive moments passed, he risked one more look. Slowly raising his head, he peered over the top of the grasses.

The Fenraren was standing about thirty yards away, having also risen up. It made no sound, but its ears were perked up, orienting for a moment in one direction, and then another. The animal was well aware of the presences Mershad was sensing within the grasses.

With no time to waste, Mershad cautiously brought himself higher, so the Fenraren could see him. He hoped it would move towards him, as he moved in its direction.

Fear and alarm clenched his gut. A number of dark shapes were with them in the open. If they had wings, and a more elongated, thinner body structure, they could have passed for smaller Fenraren.

As it was, they were the largest wolves Mershad had ever beheld. About ten in all, the creatures stood silent and still. Ears pointed straight up, the wolves watched Mershad and the steed with alert, fixed gazes, shining dangerously in the moonlight.

The Fenraren now seemed impossibly far away. In some ways, the predicament facing him was even worse than the one endured with the dark entity in the sky above. An evasion could not even be attempted, as they were entirely surrounded.

Careful not to make sudden movements, he looked slowly to his left and right, assessing his position. As his gaze panned farther to the right, he came to an abrupt stop, taking in an unexpected aberration within the scene.

The unmistakable silhouette of a human figure rose up about a hundred feet away, standing near two of the great wolves. The presence of a bipedal figure brought instant relief, representing a slim hope to Mershad's panicked mind.

As he recognized the shadowy outline of a human figure, a fragment of memory pertaining to his visit with Bergthora jarred loose. He remembered her speaking to him outside of her house, following the evening meal, talking about the rare Midragardans who dwelled among wolves. According to Bergthora, one of the two young men courting her daughter Asa was one such person.

Mershad knew he was close enough to the Glittering River and the village for the possibility he grasped for during the next moment. It still took a great act of will to mouth the words, and break the heavy silence. "I am a friend of Bergthora and the Midgragardans," he called out, in an anxiety-laden voice.

The wolves remained motionless. Although only a few moments passed, it seemed like a hundred thousand years to Mershad.

"Who are you, then? And what are you doing here?" the figure standing near the two wolves finally called out, in the clear voice of a man.

Mershad could tell nothing about the man's intent by his tone. At best, there seemed to be no sense of threat or hostility within the stranger's timbre.

"I was just getting my steed some rest, following some danger we encountered in the skies. I am a guest of King Hakon," Mershad responded, slightly tentatively.

"And of the Unifier?" the man questioned him firmly.

For a moment, a shard of fear lanced through Mershad. He wondered whether the man was another minion of the Unifier's, as the dark rider in the sky had been.

Keeping an eye upon the man, he looked out of the corner of his vision towards the Fenraren. He began calculating a course of action, if there was to be any desperate attempt at escape. Fully surrounded by huge, poised wolves, he harbored little hope of even reaching the winged steed.

He decided to give the man the benefit of the doubt, thinking upon what Bergthora had said to him. "My loyalties are to Midragard, and to those that serve King Hakon. They have been friends to me, and my companions."

"And you? Do you serve the All-Father?" the man asked.

"With all my heart," Mershad replied, without hesitation. It was no lie, as he had come to find the All-Father revered in Ave to be the same as the Creator in his own faith, transcendent and eternal.

The man brought his hands up to his face, making a curt sound resembling a growl or bark. Understanding came to Mershad, even though the sounds had not been definitive words. The man was calling for some kind of judgement, which Mershad assumed referred to himself. A flurry of movements erupted around Mershad, as the wolves standing in the field slowly began trotting inward.

Mershad almost jumped straight up in the air. Right behind him, a wolf rose up from where it had been quietly monitoring him, less than than five feet from where he stood.

Four other wolves were positioned around him in like fashion, in extremely close proximity. He realized he could not have even begun to try and attempt an escape, even if he had wanted to.

The huge wolves crept in deliberately, sniffing the air about Mershad, and watching him intently. Hemmed in on all sides, and still unsure of the situation, Mershad sweated out several burdensome moments, his heart racing ever faster.

He flinched as a few of the wolves gave off excited yelps and barks. Mershad forced himself to take a deep breath, his body rigid in fear, with his tension at the heights of strain.

"I am Magnus," the man said, in a decidedly more relaxed tone. "A Wolf Kin of Midragard. The wolves around you are of the pack that has accepted me among them."

Mershad saw the posture of the wolves ease further as Magnus spoke. A couple of the stout-bodied, gray beasts turned to watch Magnus approach Mershad across the open ground.

"And I am Mershad," he replied. "I am not from your lands, but Midragard is a haven for me."

He struggled to hold his voice steady, as wavering tones emitted from his mouth. Even if he had wanted to convey a sense of confidence, as some sort of defensive bluff, his quavering voice betrayed him.

"Then you are the one Bergthora spoke of to me," Magnus stated, drawing closer. There was a definitive shift in Magnus' manner, as he engaged Mershad on a more familiar level.

Magnus was a man of tall stature, his height reaching around six and a half feet. He had a noticeably rougher appearance than the predominantly well-groomed Midragardans Mershad had dwelled among.

His thick, shoulder-length locks of dark hair were banded about snugly with an undecorated, black headband. Broad shouldered, with long, powerful limbs, and a proportionately narrow waist, his appearance exuded great strength. His movements were imbued with a graceful ease, lithe and balanced.

His piercing, light blue eyes, close to having a gray hue, were slightly recessed. The look carried within them was firm, but not cold or hardened.

He had a stout, squared face, with finely chiseled highlights and a sharp, prominent nose. It was not an unfriendly face, but it was one that spoke of many hardships endured. A coarse growth of stubble sprawling across his face revealed the contours of an emerging beard and moustache.

Clad in a simple woolen tunic and close fitting trousers of earthen hues, he blended well with the shadows of the night. Mershad had little doubt Magnus could melt into the trees and foliage whenever he wanted to. His outward posture and demeanor spoke volumes about how little he was worried about Mershad's presence.

Magnus carried a longbow in his left hand, his right hand hanging loose and free. The feather-fletched tops of many arrows filled a cylindrical quiver suspended at his waist.

Affixed to a leather belt around his waist was a scabbard, of a sturdy wood and leather construct. The hilt of a broad-bladed seax of moderate length protruded from its mouth, fitted with a rather simple, triangular pommel.

"Then you are the Magnus that she spoke to me about … the … Ulfhednar, was it?" Mershad ventured cautiously, finding he was able to bring a little more steadiness into his voice.

He remembered Bergthora's desire to have her daughter choose the man now standing before Mershad as a husband. Judging from his impressions of Bergthora's character, and his own interior inspirations, Mershad found his fears about Magnus subsiding.

"Now, only a Wolf Kin, a Seeker who has found a pack. I have not yet been given the great honor of becoming one of the Ulfhednar," Magnus corrected Mershad, in a gentle manner. "However, I am the same Magnus that you heard of from Bergthora."

Magnus extended his hand, and Mershad reached out his own in response. The moment was awkward, as Magnus' hand slipped up to clasp Mershad about the forearm. Mershad mirrored the action, clutching Magnus' forearm, maintaining the grip until he felt the other man release his hold.

"It is good to meet you, Mershad," Magnus stated. "Bergthora spoke well of you. I trust her as I would my own mother."

"She spoke very well of you too," Mershad replied, mustering a grin.

Magnus smiled broadly, brightening at Mershad's words. "Those are wonderful words to my ears, Mershad. And you met Asa? The love of my dreams and life?"

"Yes, I did," Mershad answered.

Try as hard as he might, he could not bury the comments welling up in his memory from Asa, concerning Njal and Magnus. The biting words lingered darkly in his mind, as if wanting to be given release to cause harm to the tall, young man before him. Though Mershad had just met Magnus, he knew such words would wound the man deeply, and he decided to restrain them, where they were bound within his mind.

Striving to keep his expression calm, a part of him fearing Magnus could perceive his inner thoughts and conflict, he replied, "She is very beautiful."

"And so much more," Magnus said wistfully, evidently not reading Mershad's thoughts. Nevertheless, he shook his head slowly, and his mood turned a tinge darker. "I just wish she would understand the ways of my life. She is so swayed by Njal ... I am sure that you heard of him."

"Yes ... I did," Mershad said hesitantly, his anxiety rising quickly.

He hoped Magnus would not ask him any specific questions about Njal, and what he had heard. He did not want to start his relationship with Magnus off through lies. Yet he hated the idea of relating what he knew of Asa's feelings. Mershad could sense the pain harbored inside Magnus, in the quick shift of mood at the mere mention of Njal.

"I thought so," Magnus replied, his eyes looking away, into the night.

Mershad's heart sank further, as he watched the sparkle in Magnus' eyes dull. Eyes glistening in the moonlight, Magnus' voice dropped even lower, laden with a burden that increased with each word he spoke.

"Njal moved into her mind with his charm, and his high esteem as a warrior among the villagers. I do not deny he holds better prospects than I do as a future husband. He will have the favor of Jarl Guttorm. Of that I am certain. I do not deny he can fight better at arms … and he is the son of the man who took me in, when my own father lost honor, and left me with nothing. There has been much for me to struggle with … sometimes it seems far too much to bear…"

Mershad could feel the sorrow emanating from within Magnus, rising with a potency that evoked the waves of heat off a building fire. The fact that Magnus and Mershad had just met, and were standing in an unpopulated wilderness during the dark of night, did not matter in the least.

As if Mershad provided his first opportunity to give vent to his inner torments, Magnus continued. "Why does a woman seek the qualities that they do in a man? Why does Asa not see that I would place her far higher in my life than Njal ever will? Why will she choose him, when he will choose many other women to share his nights over the years, as he already has? Why should a woman look upon whether a man has a Jarl's favor? Why should she be swayed by how many metal rings he may put on his arm? What does that have to do with what he feels about her? Should women listen to such things? Should they choose silver over this?"

With his clenched right fist, Magnus gave an audible thump to the middle of his chest, emphasizing his final query. The words carried into the night, as his faraway gaze slowly returned back to fix upon Mershad.

A few weighty moments of silence transpired between the two men. The air felt thick, permeated with the sorrows and regrets Magnus had openly manifested.

The last question, a subjective one, was one Mershad did have a firm opinion on. He was also not convinced his answer was anything other than objective in nature.

"No, they should not," Mershad said, feeling an obligation to respond, and try to offer some form of comfort in the face of the man's terrible burdens.

Ill at ease, he had always found it difficult to give voice to the emotions runnning through him during powerful experiences in his own life. He could not imagine what Magnus must have been going through, to speak so openly to a stranger, and immediately felt a great sympathy for the man.

He looked directly into Magnus' eyes. Though he repeated his words in a near-whisper, the connotation held within his voice was resolute. "No, they should not."

A smile broke through Magnus' shadowed mien. The expression was a thin ray of light piercing the melancholy thickly shrouding him. "Thank you, Mershad. I have only met you this night. Yet you already seek to soothe my mind, and the strains of my spirit. You remind me of the healing Redeemer the Church-men speak of … here to bring hope against the world's sorrows."

Magnus paused, as his smile grew a little wider. He then added, "Such a man as yourself could become a true friend."

"A friend is one of the greatest gifts you can get in this life," Mershad replied, smiling himself. "After speaking with Bergthora, and hearing the way she spoke of you, I can say I already feel it is an honor to meet you."

Magnus glanced towards the sky, loosing a warm-hearted laugh. His mood appeared to brighten a little further.

"You are too kind, and so is that good and wonderful woman. I once looked forward to having her as a kind of mother … through marriage … though long has that hope been growing greater in doubt," Magnus replied, his tone lowering at the end.

His eyes then lowered, and looked past Mershad. The fledgling hopes Mershad had that Magnus' disposition was on an upswing were blunted. Whether a figment of his imagination or not, Mershad thought that he caught another glimmer in Magnus' eyes.

Mershad looked on with a small degree of disbelief. Knowing what he knew of the Midragardan people, he found it hard to think such a tough-looking man could be on the verge of allowing tears to fall freely before a stranger.

Mershad turned his eyes away from looking upon Magnus. He knew there were no words he could then say to ease the man's torturous inner burdens, and preferred to extend Magnus a moment of privacy.

"What a fool I have been just now," Magnus announced, after another extended length of heavy, discomfiting silence. "What has any of this to do with you, and what you have been through?"

Magnus' voice took on a more lively timbre. "Enough of me. Here I am, speaking about all my troubles when you are alone out here, and not from our lands. You need food and rest, and it is not safe for you out in these wildlands. I am sure you will tell me what brought you here."

"I will, and believe me, you don't have to remind me how dangerous it is. I am very aware of the risks out here," Mershad replied, reflecting upon his harrowing travails in the skies. "Thank you for being willing to help me."

Magnus looked towards a large wolf that had settled down at his side. Reaching down, he casually scratched the wolf between its ears, with a familiar ease. He shrugged, and grinned. "It is no great risk on my part. My companions do not lie to me. They sensed no darkness in you."

"A good thing they didn't, or I think I would have had a very bad night," Mershad replied in good humor. His words and grin masked his own simultaneous, inward shudder at the thought of provoking such formidable creatures.

Magnus nodded, and another short laugh escaped him. He rubbed the wolf's head firmly with his hand. The creature's tongue lolled out between a set of large, gleaming fangs. The wolf turned its head, giving the back of Magnus' other hand, still gripping the longbow, an affectionate lick. Mershad could not help but think how easily the wolf's great jaws could have engulfed Magnus' entire forearm.

"I cannot argue with that judgement, Mershad," Magnus said. "You probably would have had a very bad night of it."

The two shared a moment of laughter, which relaxed Mershad, even as it lightened the air around him.

"You need not worry. I believe they even favor you! Come now, we should get going," Magnus stated, suddenly straightening up. He patted Mershad a couple of times on the back as he strode past him. The wolf rose to its paws and broke into a trot alongside the Midragardan.

Mershad turned to follow, desiring to keep his own person as close to Magnus as possible. He could see no other viable choices in the midst of all the huge wolves.

A few paces ahead, Magnus cupped his hands over his mouth, and made a few more barking, growling sounds. Mershad understood the sounds as a call to move out. The wolves sprang up, almost in one motion, immediately fanning out to surround the two humans.

Two of the largest bounded ahead, looking as if they were taking up advance position. Realizing he had slowed to watch the wolves lope ahead, Mershad's heart skipped a beat, as he looked for Magnus. Seeing the tall man continuing forth, Mershad spurred himself forward after him.

Magnus had not gone very far, walking straight up to Mershad's idle steed. He was gently stroking the beast's long muzzle. He glanced over to Mershad as he made his way to them. Though the Fenraren's eyes flicked occasionally to the wolves around them, it showed no signs of fear.

"It is not often I have had the honor of standing before one of the great Fenraren, lords of the skies," Magnus remarked, in evident admiration. "One of the All-Father's most wonderful creatures. Do they have Fenraren in your own lands?"

Mershad shook his head, feeling regret at the answer. "Nothing such as this."

"Does he have a name?" Magnus asked.

"He is called Baldor," Mershad replied, looking appreciatively upon the snow-white creature, which appeared to be taking a strong liking towards Magnus.

"You already know well you have nothing to fear from your cousins here, Baldor, my new winged friend. Both of your kind will bound alongside Fenris, when he is found and freed at last," Magnus said, speaking to the Fenraren.

"Fenris?" Mershad asked.

"Who the Fenraren are named after. You have not learned of the Betrayed One yet?" Magnus asked, with a hint of incredulity.

"No, not yet," Mershad replied.

"Then there is much for me to tell you, though the tale of Fenris is not a happy one. But we do need to get going," Magnus said. He looked into the Fenraren's eyes, and asked the creature, "Ready to come along with me and your cousins, Baldor?"

Magnus gave the creature a couple of firm pats on the neck, and strode onward. As if the winged steed understood what was expected, it took a few steps after Magnus and the wolves. Baldor cast a glance back towards Mershad, pausing briefly, before continuing in the wake of the others.

Mershad sensed the Fenraren was tacitly encouraging him to go along with the Wolf Kin. Not wanting to be left behind, he started after the group. Having to quicken his strides considerably just to catch up, he found himself bordering on a slow jog to match the pace of the others.

The limber wolves, and apparently Magnus, were well-suited to a faster pace of travel on foot. Mershad, having spent years in cities, and very little of that time engaged in strenuous physical activity, was ill-prepared.

Magnus cast occasional glances from time to time towards Mershad. He did not slow his stride as they entered the treeline, and headed into the light-dappled forest interior. Silvery rays tumbled down into scattered pools of luminence, spread all throughout the terrain.

Baldor also looked back every few moments, in a manner uncannily echoing Magnus' behavior, as Mershad pressed hard just to keep up with the group. As if recognizing that Mershad was struggling too hard, the creature suddenly slowed, dropping back towards him.

Drawing to a halt after a few more paces, Baldor lowered down to a prone position, and waited. The creature gazed into Mershad's face as he reached the Fenraren's side.

For a moment, Mershad was held in amazement at the Fenraren's action. He carefully climbed into the saddle, and patted Baldor on the side of the neck. "Thank you. I wasn't going to ask you about carrying me on the ground."

Baldor merely stood back up in response to Mershad's words, and broke into a forward trot. They soon caught back up to the wolves and Magnus, who had continued farther onward.

Mershad could not help marveling at the ease with which the creature adapted to travel by land. Baldor moved with a grace that echoed its majestic aptitude at flight. The Fenraren padded with silent steps, and a smooth gait equaling the canter of horses.

As the Fenraren kept pace, Mershad took in a deep breath of the night air. He relaxed his mind in the consolation that he had not been stranded all alone in the foreign, dangerous world. As he saw things, the creator of his former world was the creator of this one, and was just as present in both. Baldor was a shining reflection of that realization, and Mershad felt the Fenraren's presence in his life was no coincidence.

After they had traveled approximately another league under the trees and stars, Mershad began wondering as to where Magnus was taking him. Curious, he spurred Baldor forward, the Fenraren picking up speed with light, springing steps as they swiftly closed the ground separating them from Magnus.

Magnus cast rider and steed a brief, sideways look as they trotted alongside.

"Sometimes I forget … I live like this every day," the Midragardan remarked, after a moment. "I am sorry for not thinking of whether you lived like this or not. There are times when even I need a ride myself. Humans may be capable of many things, but we are not unlimited. It is the way of the All-Father, to keep us from growing hearts too filled with arrogance. Perhaps I need a ride even now."

He had barely broken a sweat, and his breath and speech were steady. Mershad highly doubted that Magnus needed any ride, and suspected the man was simply trying to make him feel more comfortable.

Smiling, Magnus gestured towards one of the larger wolves, walking a short distance to the side of them. As if some communication passed between them, the sizeable creature trotted over to Magnus' left side. Placing his hands at the base of the wolf's broad neck, Magnus leaped up, swinging his left leg around in one smooth motion.

He landed perfectly on the wolf's back, and tucked his legs up against the creature's sides. The wolf barely broke stride as it proceeded forward at a steady gait.

"Now that the humans are no longer slowing the rest of the group down, we can pick up our pace a little further. They will probably appreciate not being held back by our limits of having two legs, and weaker endurance," Magnus commented, a sparkle returning to his eyes.

He chuckled in apparent amusement, signaling again to the wolves in another bark-like call that Mershad understood to be an invitation to move faster. The group of wolves loped across the debris-strewn ground, moving with a level of swiftness that only the ardent quadrupeds could achieve and maintain without undue strain.

The Fenraren kept stride easily with Magnus' wolf, and the two riders were able to exchange a significant volume of conversation before they reached their destination. It did not take long for Magnus' own curiosities to arise regarding his newfound traveling companion, and Mershad was glad to oblige the Midragardan.

Magnus was acutely inquisitive about Mershad's origins, prompting him to speak at length about the ways and things of his own world, as best as he could describe them. Mershad found the telling getting a little easier, as he had already related the story more than a few times to others within Midragard.

He told Magnus in precise detail of the strange mists covering him in his world, and how the vapors had dissipated to reveal the world of Ave all around him. He hoped Magnus would have some insights regarding the reason the mysterious phenomenon had occurred. To his mild disappointment, the Midragardan showed no particular reaction, merely continuing to listen with rapt interest.

Mershad related all of the events bringing him up to the current moment. A range of emotions ebbed and flowed within him, as the vivid recollections prompted him to relive experiences both awe-inspiring and frightening.

His tale ranged from the first trials of the bewildered exiles in the forests of the Five Realms, including their witnessing of the large army marching along the outskirts of the woodlands. Mershad told of how the Onan warriors had confronted his group soon after, and taken them back to their large hill-top village.

He talked about the devastating nighttime assault on the Onan village, conducted by the flying monstrosities from Avanor, and the storms of war gathering over the tribal lands. He described meeting the Midragardans, and the eventual transfer of the exiles to the island settlement for their safety. Recounting the near capture on the island, Mershad spoke of the ensuing, harrowing escape using the Fenraren.

He proceeded with great detail, speaking at length of his introduction to Midragard, his first journey to the village at Glittering River, and the visit of the Elder and Saxan warrior to the King's homestead. At Magnus' insistence, he related every last bit of the news brought from afar, regarding the wars abroad, and the request for King Hakon's help.

Mershad continued his telling right up to the terrifying encounter with the Arcamon just hours ago, in the skies over the very landscape they were traversing. He concluded the lengthy account of his exploits with the unexpected intervention by the two dragons, the appearance of the larger, Elder dragon, and the desperate need to land his hard-pressed, exhausted steed.

He could see Magnus' great fascination with the incredible tale, even though the Midragardan's face remained somber and intense for the most part. During the entire time, Magnus only broke in with a few questions, seeking clarification about a few particular things within Mershad's account.

Most of the queries centered upon the dour news conveyed by

the Elder and the Saxan messenger, regarding the wars in the tribal lands and Saxany. Mershad noted that the Midragardan appeared especially troubled when he told him of the king's decision to call for a Leidang.

Telling the most current version of his story, Mershad found himself becoming more cognizant of just how incredible his path in life had become. His own story would have fit in well with the mythical tales from the Thousand and One Nights he had enthusiastically listened to many times over as a young boy.

A part of him then mused, if only for a slight moment, about the true nature and origin of those boyhood tales of magic and adventure. Having lived through astounding events, Mershad felt that perhaps not everything fantastical was just an exercise of imagination.

Following Mershad's oration, Magnus then spoke at length about his own life, in and around the village of Glittering River. He recounted his upbringing in the village, smiling as he spoke of more golden, warmer memories. His face shadowed over as he talked of other, colder events during his life, times that Mershad knew marred the present.

His path from childhood had started with Magnus knowing both of his natural parents. He had lost his mother to illness before being separated from his father, who had formally been declared an outlaw at a regional all-moot.

To Mershad's understanding, it was as if Magnus' father had died following the Moot. The man had been forced to leave the territory, or face the harsh reality that he could be killed by anyone, at anytime.

As Magnus explained it, the killer of a declared outlaw did not have to fear any retribution, or risk paying a wergeld fine. An individual designated an outlaw was precisely that; a person cast outside the bounds of law itself.

According to Magnus, some declared outlaws took up refuge with loyal friends, or had enough strength of their own in the form of family members to protect themselves. But Magnus' father was no such man. With nobody willing to stand at his side, and nowhere to turn, Magnus' father had only the choice to vanish, or die a violent death.

As such a path led to nowhere a young boy could be taken safely, Magnus had been left behind when his father had departed. It was then that Thorgils had taken Magnus in, to live under his own roof and provide for his upbringing.

From what Mershad could infer, Thorgils had been a capable

surrogate father. Thorgils had evidently treated Magnus like a son, in terms of both firmness and affection. Looking upon it, Mershad could see Thorgils' genuine acceptance of Magnus likely adding to the tensions with Njal, if not setting them into motion in the first place.

Magnus described a life filled with hard labor, in the fields just outside the village. His chores had extended to tasks involving livestock, wood-cutting, and the upkeep of Thorgils' home. Magnus claimed he had demonstrated little aptitude for either woodcraft or metal-working as the years transpired, but had gradually discovered an affinity and skill with animals.

He spoke fondly of taking to the surrounding woods whenever he was afforded some moments to himself. He had come to love being under the open sky, whether he was out hunting with Thorgils and Njal, or taking a short, solitary hike by himself. Magnus said the feeling was as natural as drawing breath, and he spoke of feeling more at home in the wilds than he ever had in his life within the village.

Yet there was still one strong force pulling at him from within the village. He and Asa had grown up together, like all of the children in the village, but the feelings between them had changed as he had grown to become a young man, and she a maiden. From the first moments that his transition from boyhood to young adulthood had taken place, his thoughts and desires had increasingly turned towards Asa, far and above any of the other young women living in the village.

Like his feelings within the surrounding woodlands, he talked about having a sense of inner peace around Asa, as well as a vibrant inner fervor he had never encountered before. The latter was like a constant flame burning within him, at times surging with an exhilarating feeling of excitement. Magnus remarked that during other times it took on a very different quality, becoming all-consuming and painful.

At first, Magnus claimed Asa had returned the feelings he held. He recounted what a glorious experience it was to have such powerful emotions reciprocated. Yet in a manner as profound as the change from summer to winter, the warmth and brightness manifesting in his life did not last, the decline bringing a growing chill along with it.

As time had gone on, Njal had also begun to take an interest in Asa. Like Magnus, he had openly revealed his affections to her.

According to Magnus, the revelation had come as a surprise, as Njal already enjoyed the affectionate glances of virtually all the attractive maidens within the village. He even enjoyed glances from a number of the most desirable maidens living in the surrounding villages.

As Magnus explained it, Njal had never shown an inclination to give himself to just one woman. To Magnus' view, the shift in Njal's disposition was as if a lightning bolt had lanced down out of a cloudless sky. At the very least, it was a harbinger of dark storms arriving in Magnus' life, as he saw it now.

As he listened to the recollections, Mershad found himself beginning to wonder whether Njal had taken to Asa simply because Magnus desired her, and was finding true happiness. It was a notion that was nothing more than just a hunch, yet it radiated with the bright luminence of truth.

Whatever the reality was, Magnus had soon found himself in a rising state of conflict with Njal. To Magnus' further dismay, Asa's attentions had begun to discernably shift, as Njal began taking up more of her time and attention.

Magnus lamented that he headed into a winter of his spirit as he felt Asa's feeling for him ebb. Magnus had increasingly lost himself within his labors whenever he was around the village, gradually drawing away from interactions with others.

He told of how he sought every opportunity that he could to flee to the beckoning solitude of the forest. The forest had become more and more of a refuge, if not becoming the only place in which to cool the burning flames that were now entirely consuming, and tormenting.

It was in those times that he had first encountered one of Midragard's wolves. As Mershad was well aware, wolves were an intrinsic part of life in Midragard, deeply woven into their traditions and lore. He had seen their images in the art of the Midragardans, and heard several stories featuring them. The tales were varied, ranging from accounts of large, ravenous packs crossing iced waterways to plague entire villages during seasons of harsh climates, to stories of the two great wolves said to accompany the father-god of Midragard's older faith.

It was no mistake King Hakon's cherised Heder was a wolf, as the creatures enjoyed a prominent place in the cultural fabric of Midragard. The lupine occupants of Midragard's wilderness were a living, iconic symbol of strength, community, resilience and fortitude.

For Magnus, the wolf was much more than a symbol. For a select few out of each generation, the boundaries between wolf and human were resolutely sundered. As Magnus told it, the pathway that brought wolf and human together was one of healing for the great betrayal of Fenris.

Magnus spoke reverently of how the pathway had existed throughout the centuries, set into motion from the time of Fenris. Ever since the great tragedy befell Fenris, a unique order of Midragardans had evolved over the ages.

This order, Magnus claimed, served as a powerful sign of redemption, even if there was so much still unrealized. The order was striving towards a sacred state of being, of a kind that had existed within the first age in the world of Ave.

Magnus had smiled then, talking of how the church-men sermonizing in his village had talked of a future time when the wolf would lie down with the lamb, in an eternal age of peace. Such a vision was not, in his view, so markedly different from the world he desired as member of the mysterious order of Midragardans.

Magnus had then looked Mershad directly in the eyes as he spoke further of his order, and the more dour aspects its adherents willfully accepted. He had described it as a terribly lonely path, fraught with danger, and often met with scorn and fear from many among his own people.

Mershad listened with intense interest as Magnus then described the way in which a person evolved into fullness within the strange, fascinating order. A person who felt a calling to the order became what was known as a Seeker, which was the most dangerous stage of the person's evolution. A careful discernment on the part of the individual was critical, involving close examination of the self, before setting off into the wilds.

Magnus commented that an encounter with wolves in the wild could be a purely random event, or it might be a sign of a deeper, more significant connection. A human could not afford misinterpreting such an event, as doing so brought great peril to a Seeker.

Once a wolf pack had been found and approached by a Seeker, a momentous judgement was soon rendered. A Seeker who harbored true evils within the heart, and was gripped with a strong will to control others, was quickly set upon by the pack and slain. The seemingly harsh judgement was the outright rejection of one who would betray the very soul of the Midragardan people, employing purposeful deception in doing so.

A Seeker accepted by the pack, while not perfected of heart by any means, was one who reflected the embracing of a journey of atonement and self-growth, of a kind taken by the Betrayer of Fenris in long ages past. In choosing such a direction, a Seeker was like a torch becoming lit, giving radiant light in a world of shadow, and serving as a beacon of a wondrous age to come.

The acceptance brought with it the elevated path of the Wolf Kin. Wolf Kin were tacitly invited to walk along this higher path the moment the pack's members assented to take in the former Seeker.

Magnus stated that the Wolf Kin were individuals in full communion with the things of nature. They developed over time into a unique kind of warrior, one that would go to the defense of Midragardans without hesitation.

Wolf Kin did not abandon the world of mankind. They were a fusion of the natural order, and the individual consciousness given to humankind. While the Wolf Kin spent most of their time among their adopted pack, an individual who became a full-fledged Ulfhednar often dwelled for extended periods within the halls of kings and powerful jarls.

Exactly how a person was initiated or became one of the Ulfhednar, Magnus did not say, or even hint at. It was an intensely intriguing question that Mershad placed in the vault of his mind for a later, more opportune time. Not the least of Mershad's new curiosities concerned the differences between one of the Wolf Kin, and the Ulfhednar. He suspected the answer would be extraordinary, at the very least.

Mershad did learn that the strange and mysterious path taken by the Wolf Kin had a parallel order in Midragard revolving around the great brown bears of the land. These latter kind, in a comparable stage to the Ulfhednar, were known the "Bear Shirts", or Berzerks.

Though fewer in number, and much more solitary, the berserks had amiable relations with the Ulfhednar. Both orders responded to the call of Midragard, whenever needed by its people.

The longer they talked together, the more Mershad came to realize that in some ways he and Magnus were not so very different. As Mershad often felt he was a stranger in his own country, he perceived Magnus as harboring similar feelings. While it was true they came from two separate worlds, Mershad's laced with inventive technologies, and Magnus' flowing with magic and mysticism, the two young men shared a kindred spirit.

Both walked a lonely and difficult road, each searching for a path to something transcending the world itself. They were restless spirits traversing a world that could never offer satisfaction.

DRAGOL

His strange human companion had disappeared once again, as Dragol walked with Ayenwatha and the band of tribal warriors. They were heading towards a rendezvous point Ayenwatha had spoken of earlier, where they expected to meet up with many other tribal warriors, and possibly some of their Midragardan allies.

A few moments of irony occurred during the course of the travel. Dragol and the others froze in place near the trunks of trees, or used other cover to conceal themselves, as Trogen sky patrols passed overhead. Dragol never could have imagined he would be hiding from his own kind. Yet in order to keep his freely given word to Ayenwatha, he would not reveal the presence of the tribal warriors to the sky riders above.

The prevailing mood within the group was somber, and few words were exchanged during the trek. Dragol did not yet know what to make of the overall situation, other than the fact he implicitly trusted the stalwart war sachem.

That the noble Onan warrior was a war sachem was one of the few things Dragol had learned about the warriors escorting him. The designation of a war sachem was one of the ways in which the tribal people delineated their leaders. From what Dragol was able to glean, the tribes appeared to have three main types of authorities; male village sachems, sachems for war, and matriarchal females who headed their various clans and held the responsibility of choosing village sachems. There also appeared to be some sort of Grand Council, comprised of a set number of special sachems derived from all of the tribes.

He had learned the names of the five primary tribes. They were the Onan, of whom Ayenwatha was a member, the Kanienke, the Onondowa, the Onyota, and the Gayogohon. The former three were considered the Older Brothers, while the latter two were seen as the Younger Brothers.

The Onan were also the Keepers of the Sacred Fire. It was a piece of knowledge raising a lot of curiosity within Dragol, as to the tale behind the intriguing designation. For the moment, he had to be content in simply knowing the fact, as it had been slipped in among the few things that had been offered to him.

Dragol hoped Ayenwatha did not harbor too many worries about his intentions. The Trogen warrior had spilled the blood of vaunted warrior-monks on the side that his kind was supposed to be allied with. He had willfully removed the Unifier's marking from his skin. Both acts had been done right before the Onan war sachem's eyes. Dragol knew Ayenwatha was far from naïve, and doubted that the tribal warrior failed to realize the many easy opportunities the Trogen warrior had to slay the war sachem if he had wanted to.

There was also the reality that Dragol crossed a perilous line when he had removed the marking. The act would result in swift death if he were ever recaptured by Avanorans. Removing the mark was akin to having declared irreversible opposition to the Unifier.

At times he had felt like explaining that to Ayenwatha, as he was not quite sure whether Ayenwatha understood the full magnitude of the action. Yet at the present he found he was still content to remain silent on the matter, as he accompanied the tribal warriors through the woods.

Coming to the edge of a small brook, the party encountered a large number of warriors. Dragol appraised them quickly enough, even as their eyes took regard of him.

Most of the warriors were tribal men, armed with bows, hand axes, or heavy wooden clubs. A few carried simple shields made of rods of wood lashed together, but there was little else in the way of protective gear.

Their skin was bared for the most part, save for their shoes, referred to by them as mocassins, short hide kilts of buckskin, and the pouches, shell-bead arm bands, and other minor adornments. A number of the warriors additionally wore buckskin leggings.

Their skin was covered by the black and red war paint that Dragol found to be common amongst the tribal warriors. Dark tattoos of many diverse designs, from geometric shapes to representations of natural elements, were etched into a variety of areas on their bodies.

A few Midragardans were also present among the throng. Tall, sharp-eyed, and possessing iron-hard gazes, they carried a broader assortment of weapons. Dragol found the Midragardan weapons to be much more to his own liking. Several carried wicked-looking, long, two-handed axes, with variations in the types of blades affixed to the end of their hafts. There were also several swords, lances, smaller hand axes, and bows in the weaponry of the Midragardans.

A few wore shirts of mail, a couple wore jerkins of hide, and others had either quilted-tunics or simply woolen tunics. All wore iron helms and carried large round shields, the latter faced with swirling, checkered, or other types of multi-colored patterns.

Dragol noted that a majority of the shield designs were rendered in black and white. He realized that the shapes and mixed colors on the shields had a particular purpose. They prevented an opponent from easily assessing the arrangement in the planks of wood composing the shield. It was a clever aspect of the shield design, as knowledge of the direction and layout of the wood planks could enable an experienced attacker to shatter a wooden shield with the right kind of blow. Such a design would undoubtedly be of great benefit to warriors like the Midragardans, who liked to array for battle by forming up walls comprised of overlapping shields.

Despite the relaxed demeanor of Dragol's escorts, a number of the warriors in the other war band expressed initial shock at the sight of him. The rustle of feet upon the debris-strewn forest floor, the scratching of clothing upon bark resounded, as all rose quickly to their feet, turning towards the newcomers. Several gripped their spears, bows, axes, war clubs, and other weapons firmly as the small party neared the banks of the sparkling brook.

A ponderous silence wiped away the low murmur of conversation prevalent when Ayenwatha's party had approached. Seeing their alarmed reactions, Ayenwatha quickly held up his hand. "It is okay! Ease yourselves, all of you, and listen to my words. This Trogen fought for us, and saved my own life. I, Ayenwatha, war sachem of the Onan, vouch for this Trogen warrior. You must trust my word that he is a friend. I shall explain more to you in time, but know that his actions spoke truly during an ambush we endured earlier this day."

The dark, hardened looks did not fade, but the grips on the weapons relaxed slightly as postures eased. Dragol could still feel the weight of the scrutinizing gazes bearing down upon him, but he kept his head held high and his shoulders squared. He would not intentionally provoke anyone, but neither would he allow himself to be cowed by any attempt at intimidation.

"Sky Arrow, how far to the people?" Ayenwatha asked one of the tribal warriors, a tall, hawk-faced man whose eyes glared hotly at Dragol. The warrior clearly held no liking for Trogens, and given that Dragol's kind was at war with them, he could not fault the man. Even so, Dragol calmly held the warrior's stare, without blinking. "Do you have word of Deganawida?"

"He is now with the people, moving east with them," the warrior replied, finally breaking his gaze from Dragol and turning his full attention to Ayenwatha. "They are no more than a league's distance from here."

Dragol could sense the inquisitiveness burning within the man. Ayenwatha volunteered nothing to satiate the unspoken curiosity, though the war sachem certainly could not help perceiving Sky Arrow's great unease.

A strongly built, blue-eyed Midragardan, a portion of whose long blond hair was fixed into two braids, one on each side of his head, eyed Dragol carefully as he walked up to join them. He had a confident stride, and exuded the distinctive essence of a formidable warrior. It was an air that a lesser man could not hope to imitate, and one that a veteran warrior like Dragol recognized immediately.

"Gunnar!" Ayenwatha greeted the man amiably, a warm smile coming to his face.

"Ayenwatha," the Midragardan responded, though his face remained impassive as his eyes kept fixed to the Trogen. "It would seem you have brought an interesting new guest with you … but know that I will honor your word, as I always have."

Much was said underneath the man's words, revealing many things about the warrior's relationship with Ayenwatha. Dragol found himself wondering whether the Midragardan was speaking in the tribal tongue, or whether Ayenwatha was speaking in the Midragardan's, as he understood them clearly enough with the stranger's pendant around his neck.

Ayenwatha nodded. "I will tell you my tale as soon as I can, Gunnar. Know that this Trogen is a warrior with honor. How fares our fight?"

The Midragardan's expression became grim. "We can harass them, and we can slow them, and bleed them, but we are not going to stop them, Ayenwatha."

Ayenwatha nodded again, drawing into a discomfiting silence.

"More arrive?" the war sachem asked a few moments later.

Gunnar's voice was steady and even as he answered. "The scouts say more keep arriving. Many are common men, not the skilled knights, but their great numbers allow them to push forward along a wide front."

After a tense pause, Ayenwatha replied, with a hint of exasperation. "Is there no end to their army?"

"For our purposes, there does not seem to be," Gunnar stated. "The forces of the Unifier are driving ever deeper into this forest. We will not have much more time to get the refugees to the coast safely."

"We have no choice but to remain strong in our efforts to hold the enemy back, at least long enough for the main body of our people to reach the shore," Ayenwatha said, with a trace of despair that was not lost on Dragol.

"And we will be, Ayenwatha, we will be," Gunnar replied reassuringly, though his expression remained inscrutable.

Dragol caught the distinctive sense of a man resigned to a dark fate. He also perceived a warrior that would not bemoan such a reality, and who would stride forth to meet it with his war axe firmly in hand. The Midragardan gained more of Dragol's respect by the moment.

"How long will it be until the tribal people arrive at the Water-Head Cradle?" Ayenwatha asked, turning towards Sky Arrow, who had remained in place during the discourse.

"About three days time, Ayenwatha, if they are able to travel at the pace they have been going," Sky Arrow responded. "Most of the very old and the very young are now being carried upon hide pallets. The full number of refugees are now able to move much more quickly."

"That is at least a little light in this horrible darkness," Ayenwatha responded dourly.

"We will take all the light that we can get," Gunnar replied. He then added a moment later, "And we will create our own, if we must."

With his right hand, Ayenwatha clutched the left upper arm of Gunnar. "Friends to our people, such as you, bring such light."

Ayenwatha then let go of Gunnar's arm, and looked back towards Sky Arrow. "I need to reach Deganawida, and I will take the men ambushed with me. If you, and those with you, were to come with us, we can form up a war party and gain some supplies."

Sky Arrow looked over the men gathered around Ayenwatha. "None were injured seriously in the ambush?" Sky Arrow asked, with a hint of surprise. "Fortune has smiled warmly upon you."

Ayenwatha had a slight grin come to his face. "That will be a story for us to share during the walk. We have unexpected friends wandering these forests, in the midst of all this madness and bloodshed."

"Then I would like to hear this story," Sky Arrow replied. "Are you ready to go now?"

"A drink of water, and then we go," Ayenwatha said, starting over towards the edge of the brook.

At Ayenwatha's beckoning, Dragol joined the war sachem by the waterside and proceeded to slake his own thirst. He did not talk as he drank handful after handful of the cool water.

There was little to say. He was simply relieved that the current encounter had ended without incident, though his thoughts were already engaged in speculation regarding the next one. He could still feel the pointed stares coming from all around him. Dragol knew Ayenwatha was all that stood between him and disaster.

MERSHAD

By the time they finally reached the outskirts of the lands around the village, a few hours later, Mershad felt that a true bond of friendship was being forged between himself and Magnus. Daybreak was just starting to crest the far horizon, heralding the arrival of something new and pure. The approach of a bright new day, unveiled in a fresh, clear sky, reflected the buoyant feelings within Mershad. Though he had gotten little rest, he nonetheless felt refreshed as the first rays of dawn graced him.

The wolves came to a sudden halt where the woods came to an end, and the rising sun's light revealed an expanse of cleared land. A short distance ahead, a rough dirt pathway, cut through with the deep lines of wagon tracks, meandered through the open ground leading up to the earthworks and timber palisade surrounding the village. Not much farther beyond, a wide, glittering channel of water wound its own course through the land, crossed over by a lone wooden bridge.

Mershad recognized the place well enough. He glanced towards the wolves, wondering at their sudden hesitation at the boundary of the timberline.

"This is where my friends end their journey, for the time being. They will go no farther," Magnus stated. "They carry a natural fear of most humans, and it is not without reason.

"Even the great Wizards betrayed the mightiest of their kind. These wolves would not harm the villagers, and the villagers understand not to harm them. But my friends are much better off staying within their own world."

He laid his right palm down between the two erect, triangular ears atop the head of the wolf he was now astride. Staring out towards the village, he caressed the dense fur of the huge wolf.

The wolves surrounding them milled about the edge of the woods. Not one of them set even one paw past the point where the trees ended, and the broad, fallow field began.

At Magnus' cue, Mershad and the Midragardan dismounted their respective steeds. Mershad gave affectionate pats to the creature that had borne him so capably.

The Fenraren continued onward with the two humans as they stepped out from the trees, as the wolf pack melted deeper into the underbrush with nary a sound. Mershad did not have to ask his new companion as to whether the wolves would go far or not. He knew they would be attentively watching from the obscuring shelter of trees and brush, awaiting the human member of their pack. Mershad could feel the weight of their piercing gazes even now, as he and Magnus started across the open ground.

The two men and the Fenraren had not gotten far before they espied a group of men heading towards the enclosed fields in the lands outside the village. Most were bearing farm implements, including iron-edged timber spades, and picks and hoes of wood-hafts fitted with iron heads. A few were leading a couple of burly, plodding oxen.

Some amongst them, including two appearing young enough to be construed as boys, were trudging with the listlessness of individuals not enthusiastic towards their looming tasks. Mershad could not stifle a grin, remembering getting roused in the morning by his own father for chores when he was a teenager.

It was only a few moments before several heads turned in the direction of Mershad and Magnus. Words were swiftly exchanged among the laborers, and soon all were focused in the direction of the two newcomers.

One of the men came to a full halt, squinting with an intensive expression. He spoke a few quick words with his comrades, and gestured for them to continue onward. He then broke into a loping run towards the new arrivals. The man's narrow face was aglow with a wide smile, his bushy locks of flaxen hair flowing back in the morning breezes.

He was on the smaller end of the spectrum, in terms of the average size of Midragardan adult males, having a rather lean body to go with a stature of about five and a half feet. Attired in a faded blue tunic of roughspun wool, brown trousers, and leather shoes, he displayed little adornment. Only a small silver amulet hanging from around his neck, fashioned in the shape of a warhammer, and a single silver ring on the first finger of his right hand, were visible.

"Magnus! I thought that was you! My eyes did not deceive! You have come back again, after more journeys into the far reaches of Midragard, creating tales that will be tomorrow's hall sagas!" the man cheerily greeted, with a flare of delight in his eyes.

He planted the end of the iron-edged, wooden spade he carried into the ground with a vigorous thrust. Leaving it behind him, he strode forward and gave Magnus a warm embrace. Mershad remembered seeing the diminutive Midragardan on his previous visit, though the man was one of many he had not personally interacted with.

The man recognized Mershad as well, as he disengaged from Magnus. "I can see you have found one of our most recent visitors. I hope he did not get lost going home. Surely not, with a steed such as yours!"

His eyes gazed approvingly upon Baldor, who favored the Midragardan by stepping forward, and lowering his head for the man to stroke.

"It is good to see you, Sturla, my friend," Magnus replied. "I trust everything has gone well since I last was here?"

"Yes ... and no," Sturla responded. He gave the Fenraren a final rub, and straightened back up. "The fields require much work, so there is little difference to each of the days that pass here. But this village has always had women who bless us with the nectar that is a greater treasure than a chest full of silver ... ahhh, good, heavenly, mead!"

"Our village's mead has long enjoyed an excellent reputation throughout these lands," Magnus interjected.

"Yes, we have heard from many a trader how exceptional our

mead is," Sturla remarked. "To everyone here, it is normal, but I do listen to what the traders say. Their words have helped me gain a greater appreciation for the skill of our women in preparing mead. So, Magnus, the going is drearily the same with our daily labors, but it is always made sufferable with steadily replenished mead!"

"I could use a horn of mead myself," Magnus remarked, with a grin. "Been drinking nothing but water lately."

Sturla gave a dramatic cringe. "Sounds horrible."

Magnus laughed. "I've survived."

"Not me," Sturla said. "No, I couldn't live like that."

Magnus smiled. "Believe me, it is not a life for everyone."

"I'll not argue. Your woodland friends put a scare into me. I'll admit it," Sturla retorted.

"They would like you, if you would ever come out with me for a day or two," Magnus replied.

"How they would like me is the right question. Would they like me as you intend, or as a fresh hunk of meat?" Sturla queried, chuckling. He then shook his head. "No, no, I'm fine here. Even if it means more furrows to prepare, and ever more need for barley." He rolled his eyes with another grin, and gestured back towards the men and the plough team he had been walking with.

Magnus clapped him on the back. "Maybe someday."

"Even you'll put fear into me, my friend, when you become an Ulfhednar," Sturla said, his words sounding only half-rendered in jest. "Will I be able to tell you apart from your other companions then?"

Mershad found the cryptic comment intriguing. For a brief moment, he sensed discomfort in the air between Magnus and Sturla.

"Yes, you'll be able to tell me apart from my friends," Magnus answered, in a firm voice. His face grew more taut, as his tone lowered, and softened. "And Asa? How is she?"

Sturla looked away, almost as if in reflex, before turning his head back with his eyes rooted to the ground. The half-smile on his face faded swiftly, like a dark storm cloud crossing over the face of the sun.

"Perhaps we should speak of that later, my friend," Sturla replied gently, casting a flicking glance towards Mershad.

"Then we will speak of it later," Magnus responded, his voice heavier. He took a deep breath, and clapped his right hand down on Sturla's shoulder. "Retrieve that spade, and let us find old Thorstein. If they can spare you from the fields for a short while, that is."

"We've got Ingolf's two young lads with us today. It will not make up fully for me … not even five men could," Sturla stated, with the flair of a humor-laced boast. "But they'll get by well enough. Can't say they're very excited about today's quest."

Mershad smiled, thinking of the two groggy-looking youths he had focused on just moments before.

"You saw the ones I am speaking of? Yes, they radiate their excitement, do they not?" Sturla solicited, looking to Mershad with a chuckle. He took a couple of steps, and yanked his spade out of the ground. "Come, let us see what old Thorstein is up to at this early hour."

With the haft of his spade resting on his shoulder, Sturla turned and accompanied them towards the village entrance. As they drew nearer to the open gateway, Mershad could gradually see more of lands to the farther side of the village, an area previously obstructed by the village's high earthen embankment and palisade crown.

A large number of cattle and sheep were already out to pasture, with several herders tending to them. In one glance, the surrounding lands and village formed into a gentle, pastoral vision. It was a tranquil sight evoking the more settled, rustic side of the tough Midragardan folk.

As Mershad anticipated, a number of village children rushed upon them in a tumble of laughter, wide-eyes, and gleeful shouts as the group entered through the timber gates. Though the children gave the white Fenraren a wide berth, they were plainly thrilled by the winged steed's presence. Baldor showed no alarm, or even agitation, at the youthful cacophony its presence generated.

A number of the village's womenfolk, from older wives with accessories jingling on thin chains, to lustrous, hale young maidens with hair flowing free, emerged into view following the swirl of excited children. Mershad noticed a wary edginess to the wives' gazes as they saw Magnus, a few even forcefully calling their offspring back.

A couple of tall, blond maidens, holding spindles and distaffs, smiled amiably towards Magnus, showing no such reticence. Magnus nodded his head towards the maidens in polite greeting, while showing no acknowledgement of the less friendly reactions.

Mershad could do little but concede to himself how wonderful it would be to have such beauties display warm overtures in his direction. His eyes lingered upon them, as they continued looking at Magnus.

"The daughters of Hallad are coming into full bloom, indeed," Sturla muttered low, under his breath, to Mershad.

Mershad grinned sheepishly, inwardly reproving himself for becoming so distracted. Such thinking could not result in anything good, even if it was hard to resist. Alas, it was impossible as a man not to take notice of the daughters of Hallad.

"Magnus, you must grace me with a visit later," called Bergthora from the left, where she had just emerged from her dwelling. Magnus' attention moved immediately from the two radiant young ladies Sturla had named, and snapped towards the stout Midragardan matron.

She rested her hands on her hips, and gave the visitors a warm smile. "And I suppose you have returned for another of my meals, young Mershad of the out-world?"

"Hello Bergthora! It would be wonderful to visit with you again," Mershad replied, knowing she had to be curious about his presence alongside Magnus.

"There is much to tell, maybe even the start of a scaldic verse, with what he's gone through since he last was here," Magnus added, with a glance towards Mershad. "If we can, we will visit with you. Please carry my greetings to Asa."

"I shall," Bergthora said. Her face remained the same in expression, but Mershad could see a layer of shadow fall over the look in her eyes. She glanced towards the door of her home. "She is engaged at the loom now, but I will speak to her, Magnus."

Magnus nodded, as Bergthora turned and went back inside, disappearing into the darkness of the entrance. Magnus stared after her for a moment, and Mershad did not miss the longing reflectedd in his eyes.

Magnus, Mershad, and Sturla continued onward, following the winding path through the fence-demarcated properties of the village. Mershad winced, overhearing another woman just before she came into view. Loosing a fierce verbal tirade, she was berating two adult women who were hurrying towards the front gate of her property, bearing empty wooden pails. He was instantly glad he was not the target of her ire.

"Worst thing that happened to the thralls here was the passing of her husband," Sturla commented with a chuckle, as they neared the property. "I believe the village fears Oddrun more than the strongest of its men."

He laughed, and moved as if in afterthought to cover his mouth, when Oddrun's hard eyes fell upon him. Not looking her in the face, Mershad did all he could to avoid the eyes of the flush-faced, matronly woman, a little older and more ample in build than Bergthora.

"Sturla! You are fortunate I have no time, or I would have a few words with you!" she barked out, in a harsh voice. "And a few more for that idiot's grin you wear!"

"I will get you the carving. It will be soon done, I promise, Oddrun," Sturla replied quickly. He turned to Mershad, leaning in and uttering, "Good thing she doesn't have her new whalebone loom-sword in her hands, or I fear we'd all be well on our way to being bruised up good and thorough, my friend. She'd whack you just for being in my company. And she probably wouldn't spare your good steed either. She is indeed possessed of a merciless streak."

"Don't scare him too much," Magnus commented, with a roll of his eyes and an amused grin.

Oddrun frustratedly threw up her hands, turned around in a cloudy huff, and stormed back towards her hall-house.

"Seems we are fortunate today," Magnus observed, laughing, before adding, "unless she returns to beset us with a weapon in hand!"

"I've been slow in getting dragon heads carved on the top of her new bed posts. Though I might say there's more dragon in her than any image I can ever carve," Sturla offered to Mershad, in the way of further explanation.

Sturla's tone betrayed that he was only half-joking, as he continued eyeing the entrance to her hall-house. When a few moments passed, and she had not crossed the threshold of the open doorway, his shoulders visibly relaxed.

The two women with the pails scurried through the gate to the large property. Both looked relieved and grateful to have gained the diversion.

"You can both thank me later," Sturla called after them, with a mischevious smile.

They glanced back with haggard smiles, and gave a quick wave. Neither paused, their feet carrying them hastily forth, as if Oddrun was right on their heels with the whalebone loom-sword Sturla had spoken of.

Magnus turned towards Mershad as they passed one of the

329

largest plots of land within the entire village. It was on the side opposite Oddrun's land, located just a little farther up the pathway.

"This is where I grew up, when my father left. "This is Thorgil's land, and will one day be Njal's, as it should be," he said, in a reserved voice, sweeping his left hand in a broad motion from side to side to indicate the expansive plot. He did not stop, nor did he look interested in speaking further about the place.

The sprawling plot held a number of timber buildings, from a pair of larger byres to square roofed hay-stores. There were also a couple of gable-ended structures, whose considerably low height revealed they were edifices half-sunken into the ground.

What looked to be several small sheds, workshops, and two small hall-house buildings stood near the frontal fence-line. There were a few men working on the beginnings of what looked to be another hall-house structure. At the moment, they were setting one of the main support posts into place.

Though he had a stoic expression, Magnus kept his face oriented rigidly forward as they walked along the facing of the property. Mershad knew a swarm of thoughts were whirling through the Wolf Kin's mind. His pace even quickened a little, further betraying the nature of those inner reflections.

Mershad noticed a number of glances in their direction, from the men laboring on the property. None were old enough to be Thorgils, and he doubted from what he knew that Njal would be the sort of man to engage in the raising of a small timber house. Njal, from the accounts Mershad had heard, sounded like a man who would not easily deign to perform menial labor, leaving it solely to those such as the thralls.

The trio continued past two more of the fence-marked tracts. They finally approached the far end of the village, where the outer earthen rampart encircling it rose just beyond the boundaries of the last properties. Walking up to the waist-high gate of the last plot on the right, they drew to a halt. Magnus and Sturla scanned the open ground and buildings carefully.

It was a much more modest plot of land than that of Thorgils and several others in the village. The grounds held just a small hall-house, and a few wooden outbuildings.

The immediate area beyond the gate was not unoccupied. There was a lone figure standing a short distance within, a rather stocky boy of about twelve years old, with a shaggy mass of dirty blonde hair set atop a wide, round face.

The boy was tending to a number of hens inside a small penned-in area, within clear sight of the front gate. His back was initially to Magnus and the others, and he flinched in apparent surprise as he turned around, seeing them looking right at him.

Recognition echoed on the lad's face, and he recovered quickly enough. He reared up straight, his face beaming with joy. Leaving the pen, he ran with heavy steps down towards them.

"Thorsleif!" Sturla called out, shaking his head with a grin. "Chickens taking up your time? What are our people coming to?"

"Sturla, you know my mother very well! Chickens are no choice of mine!" the boy answered excitedly, looking towards Mershad, Magnus, and the winged steed behind them. "Hail, Magnus! It is good to see you!"

"And you as well, Thorsleif," Magnus replied. "And that brother of yours is around?"

"Loafing at the bellows, most like," Thorsleif replied, with a mischievous grin. He opened the gate from the other side, and swung it open for them to enter.

"Then we'll announce ourselves ... take the Fenraren and keep him with you for now. If you have any food around, he will be a little hungry," Magnus said, walking through the gate, and tousling Thorsleif's mop of hair.

"We've got a side of bacon, and maybe some stockfish," Thorsleif said, before his buoyant demeanor dimmed. "But mother will not be wanting to have any of it given to steeds."

"Give Baldor some bacon. Don't worry, I'll hunt up some meat for your mother right away. Maybe some fresh elk soon would be agreeable for some bacon now?" Magnus replied, in the way of an offer.

"She won't mind that at all. And me neither. I'll take care of your steed," Thorsleif readily agreed. The youth's eyes widened, and Mershad could see the anticipation of Magnus' offer taking root already.

As Mershad and the Fenraren walked inside the gateway, Magnus patted Baldor lightly on the neck, and handed the tethers over to Thorsleif. Like a pet dog, the Fenraren wagged its tail, and nuzzled the young boy in a friendly greeting.

"Let's go wake Thorstein up. Want to make a quick wager that he's sleeping?" Sturla asked Mershad.

"Have you no honor?" laughed Magnus. "Taking advantage of visitors now, are you?"

Sturla grinned, and shrugged, winking mischievously towards Mershad. "Never hurts to try!"

Making their way deeper into the open yard, they walked towards the dark opening of a timber workshop. The structure was set well off by itself, isolated from the other buildings, the nature of the work conducted within always a threat for birthing destructive fires.

Led by Sturla, the trio entered through the open facing, which led directly into a gloomy interior lit only by a small, singular flame. The meager light emanated out of a metal vessel set atop a thin pole, the container provided with a supply of fish oil and a wick. The trio paused for a few moments to allow their eyes to adjust to the shadowy environs. Further details of the room's layout began to emerge more clearly.

A sizeable, triangular-shaped leather bellows was fitted into a semi-circular piece of soapstone, where blasts of air could be channeled into the heart of a layered turf forge. The forge itself rose up to a height just over Magnus' waist.

The space was quite cluttered, with small piles of slag, charcoal, a cluster of ingots, a rough timber table, a large cooling bucket filled with dirtied water, and other various implements of Thorstein's trade and craft. A couple different sizes of hammers and a long pair of tongs rested idly on the edge of the forge. Many other objects, such as a ladle, a couple of soapstone molds, an unbroken clay mold, a couple of files, and a small, hand-sized saw were displayed on the surface of the wooden table. An open chest, with its lid leaning back and resting against the back wall, was filled with a variety of tools.

A broad tree stump set on the ground had been fitted with two anvils; one a stout iron block, and the other formed into the shape of a right angle. A larger surface, in the form of a flat-topped rock, against which leaned a long-hafted hammer, stood just a couple of paces in back of the dual anvils.

In all, the workshop was significantly smaller than its counterpart on King Hakon's estate. There was barely enough room for the primary craftsman to manuever, much less any assistants. While the space was arrayed in a generally similar fashion to the one on the king's land, the workshop did not hold any displays of metal wire for making mail, nor did it exhibit rows of weapons, or any other distinctive warrior implements.

A couple of spades were lined up to the right of the low chest, with new iron edges fitted to their digging ends. A sickle blade and a set of wool shears completed the entourage of recently-fashioned tools.

Another small wooden table abutted the corner where the first table ended. It held a cluster of iron rivets and a pile of nails on the left side. In the middle of the table was a broken clay mold with its offspring, a bronze ring-brooch used for pinning a cloak. To the right was an elongated metal plate, pierced with a row of holes arranged in ascending sizes, lying by a simple set of horse's stirrups.

At the moment, the bellows were still, and the tools all resting idle, but the room was attended. A mountain of a man sat upon a small stool set near to the larger wooden table. He was looking closely over a protracted soapstone mold of rectangular shape, into which three wells had been fashioned to create small pendants.

The shapes of the wells were uniform, and evenly spaced. Each was comprised of two short diagonal lines, of equal lengths, converging at the apex of a longer shaft. Mershad recognized them immediately, as the symbol of the Western Church, though he paid the mold only a passing glance as his eyes marveled at the figure holding it.

An extensive, bushy beard tumbled down to rest soundly upon the middle of his great chest. A prodigious growth of straight brown hair framed the sides of a broad face, falling to where it had been trimmed evenly at the shoulder level.

When the trio had first entered, the huge man's expression was set firmly, into an intensive countenance. His deep-set eyes peered studiously from either side of a large nose, which had a pronounced, rounded slope to it.

His arms had the requisite, granite muscularity of an active blacksmith; steely, rippling, and ending in massive hands. His brawny chest and pronounced shoulders also reflected the strenuous nature of his work. Yet his belly betrayed a rounded paunch, one testifying loudly that not quite all the hours of his days were laborious.

"Thorstein!" Sturla proclaimed, loud and sudden, a devilish grin spreading wide across his face.

The giant man started instantly, rearing back wide-eyed, and dropping the mold as he nearly fell off the stool in surprise. The mold clattered unharmed onto the table's surface, coming to a stop where it perched right on the edge.

The discombobulated expression on the big man's face cast Mershad's two companions into raucous laughter. Their mirth increased as the blacksmith joined with them, laughing at himself.

"Sturla, when I get my hands on you," he said, in mock anger. Picking up the mold, he set it farther back on the table, and rose slowly to his feet.

Almost a full head taller than Magnus, he positively towered over Sturla. The ceiling had just enough clearance for his full height, giving just a few inches to spare.

While Thorstein rivaled the king's warrior Grettir in shear mass and loftiness, Mershad perceived substantial differences between the two massive men. The blacksmith had a noticeably more earthy, gentler ambience than did the intimidating retainer of King Hakon.

Sturla backpedaled, making as if he was going to bolt out of the workshop and into the open yard behind. "You will have to catch me first, you bumbling oaf."

Thorstein dismissed Sturla with a wave of his wide hand. "Bah! Then run! Amuse yourself. I will use the wits you do not have. There are other guests for me to visit with!"

He looked to Magnus with a warm, engaging smile. "So, Magnus! You are back with us!"

He stepped forward and embraced Magnus, who winced and chuckled, patting his sides as Thorstein finally let him free of the tight hug. "You wouldn't need to become a berserker. You have the strength in you, as it stands right now."

"Ah, but I like mead too much. And if I ever get through all these requests for brooches, farm tools, and horse's tack, I might get to make a few weapons, for once," Thorstein rumbled, with a slight hint of annoyance.

He looked past Magnus, towards the opening of the workshop where Sturla was still hovering. The corners of Thorstein's mouth twitched, and threatened to turn up into a grin.

The blacksmith kept his voice steady, as if making a serious inquiry, as he asked, "And speaking of berserkers, and Ulfhednar ... I am curious, Magnus ... Is there a path for those who would fit well with rabbits?"

A waggish grin spread swiftly across Magnus' face as he glanced back towards Sturla. He gestured towards the opening and indicated the small man, as if seeking some sort of confirmation, looking back to Thorstein with a raised right eyebrow.

Thorstein nodded. "Yes, Sturla. He has the fierceness of a rabbit, and the talent of taking to flight at the first sign of danger. Perhaps you could guide him to the rabbit-skins, though I have heard of no such legends in the sagas I know of. I am sure they must be in our tales somewhere, as Sturla is such an obvious addition to their ranks."

"Hey! You forgot about the talent of a rabbit to mate," Sturla called back, with an impish smile of his own.

Thorstein guffawed. "Ha! Yes, there is that. It is good you are man enough to recognize your shortcomings. Thank you for the reminder about the nature of rabbits. I guess you are not fully prepared to join the rabbit-skins after all."

Mershad held back a bout of laughter at Thorstein's barbed teasing, though Magnus did not, his spirited chortles showing his great amusement with the deprecating comments.

"Rabbit-skins. You think you are really clever, don't you, Thorstein?" Sturla riposted, with a wry grin.

"I am, and before you bravely run off again, it so happens I did something here other than just fill village requests. And it might make you feel better for your shortcomings in relation to mere rabbits," Thorstein quipped, almost snickering through the words.

Mershad could see in Thorstein's face that he was barely constraining a full outburst himself. The bearish man was undeniably well-pleased with his wisecracks.

"Come over here," Thorstein called in feigned impatience, rolling his eyes at Sturla's hesitancy. "I won't hurt you, even if your wergild would only cost me a tiny piece of copper."

Thorstein paused, as if making a reassessment, and then shook his head. "No, not even that much, I'm afraid to tell you. But maybe a small pile of slag."

The big man shook with laughter. Sturla shook his head and took a couple of steps inward, taking himself from the bathing rays of daylight into the deeper shadows of the workshop.

With one long stride away from Magnus and Mershad, Thorstein drew back up to the edge of the larger table. He leaned over, and picked up three items lying towards the far back of the table's surface.

The items had been obscured from Mershad's view by the

blacksmith's substantial body when they had entered. Thorstein turned and extended them towards Sturla in his enormous hands, gripping them by one end.

"Here, see what you think. This should improve your wood hacking," Thorstein remarked. His momentarily serious expression crumbled quickly into a beaming grin.

Sturla looked down at the three pieces Thorstein held forth and slowly emitted a cherubic smile. The buoyant mien was accompanied by an excited gleam within his eyes, which flared into an ecstatic brightness as he looked over the items further.

The three items were tools of a sort used for woodcraft. The first was a small adze. In some ways, it resembled an axe, though the sharpened edge of its downward-curving blade was horizontal to the short wooden haft it was provided with. The top end of the haft disappeared into a socket formed in the crowning iron piece.

The second tool featured a small iron piece, made of a narrow, downward-bending iron loop. The two ends of the loop were traversed and secured in place by a fitted wooden handle, designed for holding in the midst of palm and fingers. Held in such a way, it was intended for working out mouldings in wood.

The third was an auger, whose sharp, narrow bit was fitted vertically into a wooden grip. The wooden grip had short, protruding extensions on the sides, placed for gripping by the fingers when the wider, flaring base of the auger rested firmly against the palm. Held in such a manner, and rotated with some force, it could effectively drill holes into, and through, pieces of wood.

Sturla glanced up expectantly towards Thorstein, looking barely able to hold back a rising tide of exuberance. There was the faintest trace of disbelief on Sturla's face, which Thorstein honed in on immediately.

"So, what do you think, rabbit-skin? Of course I made them for you, you dim-wit! Who else would want these? Though, I must admit sorrowfully, it will have been a waste of my time to fashion these, with the barbaric hacking you will be doing with these finely crafted tools," Thorstein jested sarcastically, with an expansive smile.

Though the words themselves said otherwise, Mershad sensed the genuine, deep friendship the two men held. It was reflected further in the person of Magnus. Summoning a youthful playfulness to the surface of the three Midragardans, it was a camraderie built on familiarity, trust, and a shared history.

Though he was loath to recognize it, Mershad admittedly felt a chilly breeze of envy in the presence of such eminently warm, abiding friendships. He had often wondered what it would be like to have such friends, with whom he could be completely at ease.

"The first piece I hack out using these, and that is your word ... hack ... will be for you then, my friend!" Sturla exclaimed. "I must say I am nearly without words. No, I am speechless."

"The All-Father be praised. Sturla silenced at last!" Thorstein retorted, with a thunderous laugh.

"We can only hope," Magnus added with a deep chuckle.

"Hey, that is enough from the both of you," Sturla riposted, his face still radiant. He looked back to Thorstein, and his expression grew serious for a fleeting moment. "I am most appreciative for this, my friend."

"I thought you might enjoy those, being that you dig at wood so much," commented Thorstein with a laugh. His eyes then rested upon Mershad, with a glint of curiosity. "And who is your companion?"

"Mershad, of a land very far from here," Magnus replied.

"Ah, yes, I heard of your visit, though I was working here to fill the interminable requests I get. Welcome to my home, Mershad, friend of Magnus," Thorstein greeted. He then clasped Mershad's forearm.

Thorstein's eyes widened, with a burst of excitement, evidently recalling some inner thought or remembrance. He glanced towards Sturla and Magnus. "Oh, and there is one more thing I have not shown either of you."

He looked back towards Mershad, smiling. "Mershad, friend of Magnus, you have come here on a very good day."

He glanced again to the other two, before he turned and walked back to the smaller table set along the end wall. With a little effort, he kneeled down and retrieved a sizeable leather object from beneath it.

"I am about to try my hand at copper wire, on the stirrups on top of this table. But there is something else I have already put my hands to," he said, lurching back up to his feet and turning to face the others.

The object in his hands was a spacious pouch, out of which he withdrew a linen-wrapped object. He slowly unwrapped the covering, and withdrew an axe head of a quite interesting shape.

From the upper portion containing the socket for the haft, the top edge of the axe curved upward in a gentle incline. It culminated in a sharp point, forming the apex of a substantially broad blade. The lower edge of the blade arched into a very pronounced, and extended, downward curve. The curve ended abruptly, where the extending, bottom portion had been cut flat, as if sheared right off. The cutting edge of the axe was finely honed, and the metal had been tenderly oiled, reflecting jewel-like glints of light.

"A bearded axe, by an amply bearded man, no surprises there," Sturla remarked, though only half in jest. The look within his eyes did not mask his pride in his friend's achievement.

Thorstein handed the axe-head over to Sturla, who took it carefully into his hands. He looked at the axe for a few moments, nodding and grinning at Thorstein, before passing it on to Magnus.

Magnus turned it over slowly in his hands, seeming to look at every minute section of it. Like Sturla, a fervent smile crossed his face as he looked up to Thorstein, before passing the axe-head over to Mershad.

Knowing virtually nothing about the work of blacksmiths, or of the quality of axes, Mershad could only marvel at the unusual shape of the axe head. He handled it gingerly, sensible enough to respect the sharp blade edge. At the very least, he could understand why Magnus called it a bearded axe. Even to Mershad's untrained eyes, the axe head truly had a profile evocative of a bearded individual.

"That is excellent work, Thorstein" Sturla remarked, with manifest sincerity.

"Well done, Thorstein," Magnus added. "That axe could pull any shield down, or a longship's side closer."

"I did get time to make one weapon, as you see," Thorstein announced. "And it felt much better to labor on this than any number of nails and rivets."

Mershad could see the pride blooming on Thorstein's jovial face. He slowly handed the axe head back to the blacksmith, who reverently wrapped it up, and placed it back into the large leather pouch. He returned it to its former place, underneath the smaller table.

"No words about this, I want to make a few more pieces before I claim to be a weapon maker," Thorstein stated.

"You can always trust a rabbit-skin," Sturla retorted.

Thorstein waved his hand dismissively again towards Sturla, as if shooing a fly away.

"My cousins, and my friends, old and new," exclaimed Magnus. "Are we going to stand here, and exchange jests and barbs throughout the rest of the day?"

"If they are hurled at Sturla, I will never grow weary," laughed Thorstein. "But for the sake of our guest, and my own, let us see if my kind sister has met with success in her own craft."

"At last, a good idea from you," Sturla retorted.

"It was what I was hoping you would suggest," Magnus said, with a wink towards Sturla.

Thorstein removed the thick leather apron protecting the front of his body, hanging it up on the wall from an iron peg. He then led them out of the workshop and across the grounds, towards the hall-house whose main door was propped open.

The hall-house was arranged in a like manner to other Midragardan dwellings, gable-ended and thatch-roofed. Its sides were provided with timber posts, forming a frame for the wattle and daub siding comprising the bulk of the wall space. Slender posts were set at intervals along the outside of the building, slanting in and serving as bracing for the side walls.

A greater portion of the interior was taken up by a principle living room provided with an elongated central hearth. Timber screening partitions broke up the space. From what Mershad could judge from his first glances, there were small chambers situated at each end of the rectangular structure.

An upright loom leaned against the wall on the far side of the main room. It held a half-finished piece of cloth. Mershad's eyes traveled from the series of circular stones holding the warp threads taut over to where a few extended weaving implements leaned against the wall at the loom's base.

It was relatively dim and shadowy inside. The ambience was boosted a little by a couple of small, bowl-shaped lamps, made of clay and filled with oil. The room received some additional light from the fire in the central hearth. But there was not any further luminance available, beyond whatever light filtered in through the main door, or the sheltered smoke hole in the center of the upper roof.

Mershad could see there was at least one figure inside the house. His nose filled with a most succulent smell, which immediately whetted his appetite, and reminded him that he had not eaten anything in quite some time.

"Thordis, we have some guests!" boomed Thorstein, after they had all filed into room.

"We always have guests. Seems to be the curse of making good ale," came the firm reply, with a distinctively feminine hue. "But I have recently set up a table, and you are welcome to it for the moment, unless you have brought a full raiding party with you."

A tall young woman turned as they stepped deeper into the interior of the hall-house. She had been attending a soapstone cauldron, hanging by a chain from an iron tripod suspending it over the hearth. It was the source of the pleasant aromas, as something cooked steadily within it.

Mershad could immediately see Thorstein, and the young boy, Thorsleif, reflected in the young woman's physical features. She had the deep-set eyes and more prominent nose of her brothers. Yet her features were more gracefully proportioned, in a face that was a little more narrow and oval than it was broad, as opposed to the structure of the two related males.

She was certainly an attractive woman in her own right, even if she was not one of the stunning beauties Mershad encountered so regularly in Midragard. Long-limbed and wide-shouldered, she had a decidedly strong appearance, but it was one without the overly masculine bulk of her stout brothers. Well-combed and carrying a lustrous sheen, her long golden hair fell free and loosely about her shoulders.

She was wearing the type of overgarment worn commonly by Midragardan women. Held up by straps over the shoulder, and secured by two oval brooches, it revealed a pleated chemise underneath. The chemise was secured at the neck by an additional circular brooch.

A thin chain between the two brooches fastening the overgarmnet was strung with several amber beads, and a singular, circular metal pendant in the center, which looked to be silver. A small leather purse was affixed to a narrow belt bound around her waist.

"Just four, and you know three of us already," Thorstein said.

Thordis nodded, and replied, "That we can accommodate."

Thorstein guided Mershad and the others over to a long trestle-style table, on one side of which was a bench and a pair of low, three-legged stools. Thorstein took a moment to rearange the stools and bench, with the two stools on one side of the trestle-table, and the bench set on the other.

There was plenty enough space for the four arrivals to sit and face each other. Mershad took a seat on one of the stools, as the young woman looked the group over.

"Sturla … No surprise to see you, I still do not know what it takes to get rid of you," Thordis pronounced, with a mischevious chuckle. A comely smile then broke across her face, as her eyes settled on Magnus. "But as for you, I do not know what it would take to keep you around more."

Magnus smiled. "I like to give you a challenge."

"And I would like to meet it," she replied evenly, and Mershad did not miss the sparkle within her blue eyes.

"You are indeed a force of nature, Thordis, one that could overcome any challenge," Magnus replied, and Mershad could tell he was flattered by the maiden's obvious attraction.

Yet he also knew that Magnus' heart was chained to another, one who no longer reciprocated. Such was the misfortune and tumult involving attractions between individuals.

"And who have we here?" she then asked, her mood changing as she looked amiably upon Mershad. She peered at him closely, with evident interest.

"Reminds you of the people of the Sunlands," Thorstein interjected. "This is Mershad, who has come with Magnus. He is one of the men who stayed with Bergthora, when the dragons were summoned by Hakon's man, Svein."

"A Sunlander, or, as I prefer to think, one from the Silver Lands," Thordis said, plainly intrigued by Mershad's presence. She fingered the coin-sized pendant hanging down in front of her. "I once met a traveler from the Sunlands, in a market town of Midragard. I thought that this silver coin the traveler gave me, which I later had made into this pendant, was the only thing from the fabled Silver Lands that I would ever have under this roof. I certainly never expected to have a guest from the Silver Lands visit here."

"I have been told I look like I come from there, these Sunlands, or Silver Lands. But I am afraid that I do not," Mershad replied politely, with a smile. "I would very much like to see those lands for myself, given that everyone seems to believe I am from there."

Thordis's eyes widened in apparent surprise, and her face showed a little puzzlement. She then exclaimed, "You are not from the Sunlands?

You do have the look of a Sunlander. Well, you do speak our language much better than that traveler I met did, with his handful of words."

"There is much to tell, and much that I don't know yet," Thorstein interjected. "And we hope Magnus and Mershad will tell us much over the course of several rounds of ale!"

"You would do everything over a round of ale, if you had the chance," Thordis said, rolling her eyes.

"Take it easy on the poor lout, Thordis," Magnus said in jesting supplication, chuckling amiably.

"For you, Magnus, I will, and for our new guest, Mershad," Thordis said. "But be sure it is not for that rascal Sturla, or for the … as you say … poor lout, who is unfortunately my own brother! Nevertheless, I will be right back."

Mershad watched as Thordis strode briskly towards the far end of the room to his right, disappearing into the small chamber through a door in the partition. She returned with four wooden cups a few moments later, making her way over to a large wooden tub standing a short distance from the hearth.

A ladle rested across two points of the tub's upper edge. She picked the ladle up, and dipped it into the tub. Thordis proceeded filling to overflow a couple of the wooden cups, with a liquid Mershad surmised to be the requested ale.

She walked over to the trestle-table where the four men were seated. Setting down cups before Magnus and Mershad, she returned to the tub and filled up the last two. Mershad rested his right hand in a loose grip on the cup in front of him, determining to drink sparingly of the strong fluid.

"It is not long till evening meal. Will you all be staying?" Thordis asked as she returned, looking around the group.

Thorstein nodded.

Thordis sighed. "My work is never done. Nor does it get any easier. But I think we have enough wooden trenchers for everyone, though."

"Thordis, where is Ragnhild?" Magnus asked.

"She is down visiting with Bergthora, most likely. Those two try to find every excuse they can to visit with each other," Thordis replied.

"Two wonderful women," Magnus commented, though Mershad saw something akin to a faint shadow pass across Magnus' face at the mention of Bergthora.

Thordis wrinkled her nose dramatically as she stood next to Thorstein. She bent forward and set the second pair of filled wooden cups down on the rough table surface before Sturla and Thorstein. She leaned closer towards her huge brother, with her melodramatic expression still lingering upon her face.

"You seem to aspire to be like the men from the foreign lands in the west," she said. "You have certainly achieved their potent scent. And, just so you are not confused, I am not giving you praise."

"Bathing once a week is too much. And I do not care for what our custom says," Thorstein replied adamantly.

"Not unless you want yourself a good wife someday, you oaf," Thordis shot back, with equal insistence.

"May you soon find a good man to suffer your onslaughts, so that I may be left alone in peace," retorted Thorstein sharply.

"Perhaps soon, but then will you not miss my brewing skills?" Thordis inquired of her brother, with the hint of a triumphant grin. "What if your new wife makes weak ale?"

Thorstein threw up his hands, looking utterly exasperated. "You are impossible."

Thordis looked back over at Sturla, Magnus, and Mershad and flashed a winsome smile. "I suppose I will show mercy to my brother now, and we will get some food prepared for you in a little while. But please do not be too easy on him."

"You do not have to worry about that," Sturla replied, grinning.

"Keep trying. You may yet redeem yourself, Sturla," Thordis retorted, as a laugh escaped her.

A grin dawdled on Thordis's face as she turned away from the four men, and headed back to the soapstone cooking pot. "And I am sure you can decorate something in our house, with those new tools my brother has provided for you," she called out to Sturla, over her shoulder.

"You should not have told her anything!" Sturla growled accusingly at Thorstein, as he turned back to the others around the trestle-table.

"You are on your own, on that one," Thordis said, tittering in great amusement.

Sturla shook his head and then looked towards Mershad, before glancing towards Magnus.

"I suppose you might now tell us why Mershad has returned to the village," Sturla stated, his voice growing decidedly serious. Curiosity flitted in his gaze, as he looked towards Mershad. "It is not often we receive visitors, and very seldom do we receive visitors from such distances as he has come from."

"It would seem that the servants of the Unifier are prying about," Magnus replied. "He was set upon by a very powerful minion, saved only by dragons, from the Drakkar mountain range. Mershad also espied one of the great Elder flying far above, though I do not know for what purpose one of the ancient ones might have been there."

"An Elder?" Thorstein replied swiftly, in open amazement. His eyes wide and mouth agape, he made no efforts to subdue his look of astonishment.

"That cannot be a good sign. An Elder? Truly? They have not been seen since the earliest ages of this world," Sturla remarked with a grim face, looking towards Mershad with a little anxiety woven into his countenance. He took a long draught of ale, and followed it with a deep breath. Sturla looked around gravely at the others before continuing, "I do not remember everything about the tales of old, but I believe the Elder are not supposed to ever come down to the surface. They are said to live in some kind of exile, in some faraway place … til world's end. Was it really an Elder? Are you sure?"

The weighty question hung in the air for several moments among the four men.

"The creature Mershad described cannot possibly be anything else," Magnus commented dourly. "There was no comparison between the creature he saw to those that live in the Drakkar Mountains. I am afraid there is little in the way of good tidings in our days. For even Mershad is a living sign to those with eyes to see. Heed what I now tell you, for he is not just from another land. He is from another world."

Thorstein's eyes widened further.

"Then that was no tale in mere jest? We heard it from some in the village after his last visit, when he arrived with King Hakon's warrior, Svein, but I did not believe it. I thought it an outlandish claim born from fellows drinking too much mead. Who could believe such a thing? From another whole world?" Thorstein asked, his last words trailing off to the edge of a whisper. He looked ever more astonished, as he gawked at Mershad.

"It is true," Magnus responded evenly. He looked Sturla and Thorstein squarely in the eyes, conveying unmistakable sincerity that negated any possibility of humor or exaggeration.

Mershad felt the subsequent looks from Sturla and Thorstein, as they turned back towards him. Their faces were full of fear and apprehension, and not a little confusion.

"Axe, Blade, and Shield are now mustering strength at the order of King Hakon," Magnus stated, after a few moments of pensive silence.

"The whole land of Midragard? A full war muster?" Thorstein asked, in a tone rife with incredulity.

"Yes, the whole land. Every power of sea, sky, and ground. A full levy of our sea forces have been called up by King Hakon," Magnus said. "A Leidang invoked throughout all the coasts, rivers, and fjords. And the Elder that Mershad saw above him was not the only visit from one of that most ancient race. Another descended into Midragard, not long before Mershad left to come here, to speak directly with King Hakon. It was even bearing a messenger from Saxany itself."

"Then the war that all feared would come has come. For no mere war between men would compel one of the Elder to descend," Sturla stated woefully. "No, this is something much greater. Perhaps much worse for all, a clash of powers like nothing we have ever seen before."

"And I also thought the Elder were an old legend before these days," Thorstein muttered somberly, half to himself, as he looked down morosely at the tabletop.

"I cannot bring comfort to either of you regarding this. The tribes of the Five Realms have seen their lands invaded, as has Saxany itself. The Unifier brings the forces of many, many lands to bear on those still refusing to bend knee to him," Magnus said.

Thorstein shook his head, and a palpable agitation rose up to the surface. When he spoke, his deep voice was heavy with regret and resignation. "Otherworlders ... Elder ... and now the last free lands being invaded. If that is not a sign of what war this is to be, then I do not know what is."

"The war to end all wars," Magnus replied, with a melancholic edge.

Sturla murmured a strange word under his breath. "The Ragnarok..."

There was no mistaking that the news was galling to Magnus' two companions. Mershad was glad only for the fact that he had been spared the onerous task of being the one to tell them of the dire portends.

"Is this all indeed true?" Sturla asked, as if in a suspended state of disbelief.

"The Five Realms and Saxany? Invaded? A Leidang over all of Midragard?" Thorstein echoed, as if he needed another clarification.

Both of the men looked towards Mershad. He slowly nodded, "I witnessed the Elder and the Saxan messenger myself, when they came to the King's settlement. That is the word they carried."

The men at the table were lost in silence for several long moments.

"This is most dire news indeed," Thorstein remarked at last, the first to break the cheerless hush.

"Yes, it is terrible news," Magnus replied somberly. "We cannot deny that. Yet we must face that reality, as it is something we cannot even hope to avoid. This is a war waged not just for land, but for the soul of the people.

"As I see it, there are only two paths to take. It is either surrender our beliefs, and everything that we are as Midragardans, or stand and fight against a tyranny seeking to take away our self-determination. No matter the outcome, you both know well what path those of my order will choose."

"And you know what path a true Midragardian will choose. We have no real choice left to us, Magnus. You know that. Only an illusion of a choice," Thorstein iterated, solemnly.

"Very true, Thorstein. There is no real choice for any of us," Sturla said. "Then it is simple. We all will have to turn our thoughts to the coming fight. So be it, the end of all things it is."

Sturla's melancholy words trailed off into thick silence. He seemed to be drawing deeper into himself. His leaden stare, set within a stony expression, erased all traces of the lively, good-humored man Mershad had met on his way into the village with Magnus.

A brooding unease coalesced around the table. Mershad could not read the minds of the others, but he surmised a few things about the two village men. It took little to conjecture that the two men preferred a life pursuing their interests; one as a metalworker, aspiring to be a weapons-maker, and the other as a highly skilled woodworker.

Sturla and Thorstein were the kind of men who were the salt of the world, with ambitions of simply living life. They were not of the type given to hoarding up every last scrap of silver, but rather men devoted to the art of living, and letting others live. It was men such as they who made the approaching maelstrom of blood and fire so tragic.

"I know your feelings, my brothers. I know them all too well. Do not forget I have a lot of time to think upon things, in the seclusion of the woodlands," Magnus said, after a lengthy stillness.

"But we know where we stand," Magnus continued. "And we know where we will be standing when the time of the world is brought to a halt, even here, in the far reaches of Midragard, right here in Glittering River."

The others slowly nodded their agreement to his bolstering statements.

"We do," Thorstein said resolutely, raising his cup of ale upward. He repeated, in an even stronger tone, "That we do."

"Yes, we do," Sturla followed, confidence returning to the tone of his voice, as he lifted up his ale cup.

Their eyes all turned towards Mershad. One by one, they nodded towards him, as if to encourage him.

"Yes, we do," Mershad concurred, with a half-smile, raising his own drinking vessel.

Led by Thorstein, the group proceeded to make a drinking salute to brotherhood, to loyalty, and to the treasure of newfound friends. Though still not comfortable with drinking ale, Mershad had absolutely no misgivings about honoring the virtues of the men with him.

Strong, abiding friendships were indeed jewels so very rare, whether in Mershad's own world, or this new one. Slugging down his ale, till his own cup was drained, he looked to each of the others and smiled contentedly. Wherever sentiments had dampened their spirits moments before, recognition of friendship, and the promise that they would move forward together, brought with it a renewed, invigorating spirit.

Three new friendships, Mershad reflected, was a wonderful cause to celebrate on a personal level, even in the midst of such a dark time. For once, he did not feel any guilt about imbibing the ale, even when his head began feeling a little lighter. His conscience was at ease with the fact that he was simply within a different culture, and was not pursuing drunkenness. When Thordis came around again, and offered to fill their vessels, Mershad even allowed himself to indulge in another full cup.

section iii

BEVRIEDAK

As Bevriedak expected, the Saxan fleet was not difficult to find from the skies. Once they had reached the northeastern coastline of Saxany, the escorting sky riders led them towards the area where the fleet was thought to be.

Their judgement proved quite accurate, as Bevriedak's eyes focused upon a number of distant sights dotting the surface of the ocean, a short distance off the northern coast. The various timber-crafted objects became more distinct in form as the Elder approached.

Crawling down the coastline was a considerable force of vessels. Spread out over several leagues, there were easily over a hundred and fifty ships plying the waters of the sea below. Seen from such a high altitude, the formation had the appearance of an enormous sea serpent, winding its way slowly along the glittering surface.

Bevriedak was relieved to see the large mass of ships, as there was little chance it was anything other than the main Saxan fleet. A long search would have exposed him to the debilitating powers of the Ban for a more prolonged period, and he knew he had to conserve every last bit of strength. There was no guarantee the strength remaining in him would be enough to complete the increasingly grueling task he had chosen to undertake.

The force of Bevriedak's wings was such that he had to keep a considerable distance between himself and the sky riders flying farther below. Spurring himself ahead, he continued down the coastline, towards the west.

Glancing down and back, Bevriedak saw that the sky riders had broken away, beginning a descent towards the fleet. The dragon proceeded onward, rapidly gaining distance on the Saxan fleet, seeking a favorable place to set Wulfstan and his steed down.

The contours of the land rose substantially as the dragon flew west, finally becoming a line of towering, majestic cliffs. Sea birds drifted in and out of the numerous crevices and caves riddling the cliff faces. The birds looked like tiny white specks as they glided and soared throughout the rock formations. The open ground that Bevriedak eventually landed on was close to a cliff edge, bordering an imposing drop of jagged, light-hued rock.

Bevriedak carefully turned his huge talons over, opening them to expose the Saxan and sky steed cradled carefully within. Looking down, he watched Wulfstan and the steed stretch their cramped muscles, and work their way onto the solid ground a few moments later.

Far below, the ocean's waves thundered against the rocky bases of the immense cliffs, beating relentlessly as if striving to break through them. The sound of the crashing water battering against the rocks soared to fill the air where Bevriedak, Wulfstan, and the steed now stood. The Saxan warrior looked towards the open sea, before gazing back up at the Elder with an inquisitive expression.

"The riders of your people have already descended to the ships of the fleet … to the east of here," Bevriedak informed Wulfstan, glancing back up the coastline, to indicate the general direction. "You should catch up to them on your steed, learn what you can, and say what you will."

Wulfstan nodded quietly, and moved over to climb into the Himmeros' saddle. The Saxan warrior glanced more than a few times towards the vast panorama of ocean waters provided by the high overlook.

"Fly up the coast, towards the east, and you will come upon the fleet very soon," Bevriedak stated. "They are not far from here. Do not waste more time than necessary, as you know what I face with every moment I am down here."

"I will return as soon as I can," the Saxan replied firmly.

Wulfstan lifted the reins of the sky steed, readying to spur it into action. The human's chest rose and fell with a deep breath, and then he snapped the reins, digging his heels into the Himmeros' sides.

With a burst of motion, the Himmeros surged towards the cliff's edge, and made a prodigious leap. Spreading its wings, the steed's body dipped sharply at first. Its wings gripped the air, before lifting the Himmeros upward with a few vigorous flaps. After a moment, the creature went into a graceful arc towards the right, starting on a path of flight straight down the coastline, towards the east.

Bevriedak grew still as he watched the Saxan depart. He wanted to expend as little energy as possible, as the Ban's shrouding power continued working its onerous effects upon him. His eyes watched Wulfstan become a speck, which finally blended into the far horizon.

Though his senses were keenly alert, for any disturbance or sign of danger, the huge dragon looked like nothing more than a gigantic, silvery statue, perched on the cliff's edge like some titanic monument. Only the most careful of observers would have been able to discern faint movements on the dragon's underside, and the slight distending of its nostrils, as the Elder took in slow, periodic breaths of air.

The dragon kept his head rigidly positioned facing east, knowing the Saxan would eventually be returning. Bevriedak waited patiently, blocking out all thoughts of the energy slowly ebbing from his body. The effects of the Ban did not cease their withering governance, but the rate at which they drained him slowed considerably, as he assiduously refrained from significant bodily movements.

After some time had passed, his far-reaching sight finally picked up the sight of Wulfstan and his steed coming back up the coastline. The speck emerged suddenly out of the horizon, before growing into the distinctive form of rider and steed.

When Wulfstan's Himmeros landed on the expanse of ground before the Elder, Bevriedak sensed immediately that the Saxan was in an elated mood. Without delay, speaking while he dismounted, Wulfstan related the newest tidings to Bevriedak.

After finding the Saxan fleet, Wulfstan had flown lower, passing over the line of ships. One of the riders from the delegation sent by Aelfric emerged shortly after from the surface of one of the ships, gaining Wulfstan's attention. The sky rider directed the incoming Saxan to the vessel of Aethelhere, the fleet commander. The other sky riders dispatched by Aelfric were already aboard the ship, having delivered the sealed parchment over to Aethelhere.

Aethelhere had informed Wulfstan that there had not been any signs of the enemy, at any time, in the waters off Saxany's northern coastline. After listening to Wulfstan, the other sky riders, and reading the message from Aelfric, Athelhere's response had been quick and decisive. He had determined that a significant force of ships could be sent across the waters towards the north, to the southeastern tip of the Five Realms.

The distance was not unduly far, according to Athelhere's judgement, and the fleet commander had rendered his best estimation of the journey's length. He promised Wulfstan and the other sky riders he would proceed without delay, and divert the fleet onto a hastened course towards the Five Realms. He had cautioned them that he would be making a couple of brief stops along the coastline, to gain some additional foodstuffs, barrels of water, and casks of ale, from burhs situated along the northern coast.

Wulfstan had then taken leave of Aethelhere, having received the answers he sought. Aethelhere had bid him well, before turning his attention back to the cadre of sky riders.

"Now, it remains for us to take a message to the Five Realms. We must let them know a fleet goes to aid them," Wulfstan said, finishing his account of the promising meeting with Aethelhere.

"Then it shall be without delay," Bevriedak replied, offering his upturned claws for Wulfstan and the steed.

The Saxan and the Himmeros brooked no delays, situating themselves once again as they prepared for the dragon's takeoff from the cliffline. Bevriedak steadied himself, as he turned the claws of his right foreleg back over. He felt his passengers' slow, careful movements within his grasp, as they adjusted to the rotation.

Bevriedak made use of the cliff's edge, thrusting off from its edge, much as the Himmeros had done. He knew the sharp drop at the onset of his launch was likely very unsettling to the pair within his charge, but the method was much less strenuous than taking to flight from a stretch of flat ground. His broad wings snapping downward, Bevriedak lifted up towards the sky, continuing in a steep incline that did not flatten out until he had once again gained the comforting heights of the Forbidden Dominion.

A soothing relief flooded over the dragon as he crossed the lofty boundary. He felt the grip of the Ban dissipate, like some ephemeral fog dispersed by potent gusts of wind. Released from the arduous bindings, Bevriedak swiftly gained speed, as the fullness of his strength was freed up.

Finding his bearings, and eyeing the course of the sun overhead, Bevriedak oriented his flight towards the northeast. Cloud masses on several levels below prevented any clear view of the surface of Ave, but he knew they were crossing the open stretch of ocean separating the north of Saxany from the southern borders of the Five Realms.

He passed a couple of havens during the flight to the north. Bevriedak knew his passage would undoubtedly arouse more than idle curiosities, in any of his ancient kind that might happen to witness his spirited flight to the north.

Bevriedak was not traveling with the relaxed gait of an Elder going between havens. Furthermore, he was not in a region that held any good hunting prospects, of desirable prey such as the highly-coveted Rocs that Elder often fed upon.

League after league passed, and the journey continued without interruption until he saw a great landmass just ahead, through a few breaks in the clouds. The Elder slowed down considerably, after covering the main portion of the distance at a pressing rate of speed.

Though reluctant to court the Ban's effects again, he began his descent, approaching the outskirts of the Five Realms. As he slanted downward with his great wings outstretched, the dragon was buoyed along by the stout air currents.

Like clammy droplets quickly spreading to form a thin layer over his entire body, the Ban reasserted itself. Bevriedak passed down through a bank of clouds, and then through another, a short distance beneath. He girded his resolve as the unwelcome sensations manifested with alacrity, narrowing his focus until the bitterest edges of the Ban's effects were pushed from his thoughts.

A distinctive boundary, marked by white-capped waves breaking upon the shores of a rugged coastline, passed by underneath. A sprawling landscape of densely forested hills radiated beyond the shore, in all directions. An abundance of oak, maple, conifer, elm, and several other types of trees flourished everywhere Bevriedak's farseeing eyes looked. Like veins of glittering silver, he saw rivers and streams crossing through the midst of the copious, lush expanses of foliage.

It was a beautiful, harmonious sight, evoking many distant memories of great joys Bevriedak had once known, in ages past, when he had been able to fly unhindered across the surface of Ave. Pangs of biting sorrows struck, as he was vividly reminded of what he had left behind so long ago, after taking the Oath.

While he wished he could take a few moments to bask in the vibrant sights of sun-bathed forestlands, he knew he was there for a singular purpose. Engaged in an outright war for survival, the tribes of the Five Realms would not be too difficult to locate. Bevriedak just hoped to find them before the enemy was fully aware of his presence. It was far from implausible that the enemy would have a sorcerer present among them, one who could skillfully invoke the Ban's powers on Bevriedak.

Bevriedak's keen vision scanned the forest sedulously, looking for any vestiges of movement indicating a large number of people on the move. Despite his immense size, little could be spared his notice when he chose to concentrate his exceptional powers of sight. Fully focused, an Elder could make the most exceptional hawk seem more than half-blind by comparison.

Bevriedak kept pushing the expanding strain brought on by the Ban to the far recesses of his mind, disciplining himself to ignore the creeping sensations as much as possible. He knew there would be little time to do what he needed to do.

There was certainly no allowance for bemoaning a plight he had known to exist since the first day of his accepted exile from Ave's surface. Furthermore, there was nothing that he could do to alter the situation.

Turning his head to the left, looking due west, he saw that the forest's unbroken tapestry came to an abrupt end on the edge of the horizon. Open plains dotted with thick copses of trees ran onward from the forest's boundary, demarcating Gallean land.

He judged that he was flying just inside the westernmost border of the Five Realms. He angled his path a little more towards the central region of the forest, territory that he knew contained the core of the tribal lands.

It was not long at all before he came across the sights of emptied villages, perched on the cleared tops of sizeable hills. Caustic bitterness, and not a little righteous anger, welled up inside Bevriedak as he recognized the destroyed condition of the villages.

The wooden, bark-covered structures within the high palisades had been smashed into hosts of fragments and splinters. Many massive stones, and a great number of mid-sized ones, were strewn all about the broken husks of the village structures.

Bevriedak saw at once that the shattered villages were entirely deserted. There was no sign of the tribal peoples, even in the land surrounding the villages. The discovery of one ravaged village after another brought a swiftly mounting anger, fueling ire rising far faster than the debilitating effects of the Ban.

The sheer power wielded by the enemy, starkly evidenced by the widespread, indiscriminate, and wanton destruction inflicted on the villages, was terrible to even contemplate. The dragon knew that no mercy had been extended to the hapless villagers. He also knew that the ways of people who had lived in the woodlands for generation upon generation had been hurled into chaos and misery almost overnight. The shock the tribal people had been made to endure was horrible to ponder.

Bevriedak's body trembled with the boiling rage coursing through him. He caught himself just in time from clenching his talons, preventing a disastrous tragedy from occuring to the human and Himmeros in his care. Girding his resolve, he maintained his composure, despite the inferno blazing within.

Dropping lower, the Elder's wings hurled the force of a small storm towards the ground below. The turbulence caused even the strongest trees to sway like stalks of wheat. His low passage stirred up a tempest of leaves and snapping branches, coating the forest floor with an abundance of new debris.

The Elder kept glancing off towards the left. He looked with great interest towards the outer borders of the forest, where the easternmost plains of Gallea began.

A part of him greatly desired to take a closer look along the edges of that frontier, though he knew full well that he would be increasing his chances of a hostile encounter with a sorcerer or Wizard. The invading forces had come from the west, and would most likely have encampments in place just outside the forest's edge.

The dragon sorely wanted to see if he could discover the methods by which the terrible devastation had been wrought upon the tribal habitations. There was an air of mystery about the ruined villages.

Bevriedak knew much about the war engines used by humans, having taken an ongoing interest in the affairs of Ave since the day of his exile. The stones dispersed throughout the village wreckage had not been discharged by any type of siege engine he was aware of. There was no possible way that large trebuchets, mangonels, or catapults could have been used against the hilltop villages.

The forests surrounding the missile-ravaged villages were devoid of favorable clearings in which to set up, or use, stone-throwing devices. The land around the villages lacked pathways with which to bring in carts carrying the components for larger engines of war, of the kind capable of levying such sizeable missiles.

Considering the destruction further, eyeing yet another of the doomed villages, Bevriedak ascertained that the stones had plummeted on a direct, downward trajectory. He came to the judgement as he scrutinized the shattered section of a particular longhouse. Its frame was still standing, displaying the gaping, jagged hole in the bark-paneled roof where a mid-sized stone had crashed through.

Bevriedak knew that a very dangerous, unprecedented art of war had been used to assault the villages. Despite a burning desire to learn the cause of the villages' destruction, the dragon knew his first priority was to locate the surviving tribal people and their leaders. Above all, he had to deliver the vital message concerning the Saxan fleet.

Even so, he hungered to gain at least an insight into the means by which the assault had been conducted. He also wished he could deliver some justified recompense to the oppressors.

The feelings grated within him, tugging one way and then another. One group of impulses finally surged to the fore, compelling him into action. Tilting, he banked sharply to the left, and spurred himself forward with powerful flaps. The forest rushed by below, as the western boundary line sped forward to meet his swift approach.

His sharp sight took account of significant signs of movement beneath the treetops. A few human voices broke out in excited outcries, fading into the air behind after he darkened the skies over them. Bevriedak knew they did not have the time or position to get an adequate look at him, as fast as he was flying. As close as the voices were to the western edge of the forest, he also knew they were not likely to be coming from any of the tribal people.

There were a few further indications of a great many individuals lurking within the trees below, but Bevriedak paid them no heed, speeding across the forest's outer western boundary. An expanse of low, rolling hills, and stretches of open ground, sprinkled randomly with groves of trees, beckoned.

Off to the north, the dragon observed a considerable number of tents arrayed on flatter ground. Enough to quarter a small army, the tents were located close to a sparkling river. The river was one of many such watercourses crossing the plains, delving into the rolling woodlands on their meandering journey eastward, towards the open sea.

The images on the banners flying from the tops of the tents were varied, but they were identifiable, even from such a great distance. A few of the sigils were to be expected, but others conveyed foreboding implications by their mere presence.

The three-bladed, flower-like sigil of the Kingdom of Gallea, golden upon a blue background, was the most common symbol within the encampment. It was far from the kind of image that could bring dismay to the dragon.

Rather, the banners flying from a large cluster of tents set distinctly apart from the majority were what troubled the Elder. Billowing proudly in the winds, the banners were rectangular in shape. Their longer side was vertically oriented, running along the stout poles they were affixed to.

The banners displayed two distinct, but complimentary, styles. Both were composed of stark separations of black and white, rendered in two even halves. On one kind, the black portion surmounted the white, both halves left plain, with no décor on their surface. On the other type, the white portion was on top. On several of the latter types, black lance heads were woven into the upper, white half.

It took just a moment to analyze the black and white sigils, but Bevriedak knew where they came from; and just who they represented. He had heard of the symbols often, over the most recent hundred years. They had a prominent place in many of the tellings rendered by the ravens that brought him regular word of the comings and goings in the lower world.

The black-winged messengers had oft spoken of a very powerful order of monk-knights, who used half-white and half-black banners. Known in Ave as the Order of the High Altar, the order had risen swiftly in prominence over the course of the past century.

Bevriedak knew much more about the Order of the High Altar than merely the look of their banners. He realized the lethal threat they represented to their enemies.

The people of the Five Realms worshipped the Creator in a manner diffcrent from the austere orthodoxy held by the brother-knights of the formidable order. As such, the tribal people represented nothing more than a population of unbelievers, ripe for a bloody harvest using swords wielded with great skill.

The Order of the High Altar was not the only dedicated brotherhood of monk-knights within Ave. Bevriedak knew there were other eminent orders who were dedicated to the Western Church, such as the Order of the Healers, and the Order of the Sacred Lady. Yet among all of them, the Order of the High Altar was the very one he most wished was absent, and not flying its banners on the borders of the Five Realms.

The Order of the High Altar had long ago achieved prominence and wealth of a magnitude far surpassing other orders. The concentration of worldly power gave birth to dark rumors that swirled thickly around the order.

Ostensibly formed to protect the pilgrim routes to holy places in the Sunlands, the order had unearthed something of tremendous importance during their earliest years. The discovery occurred during an excavation on the old site of a great temple in the Sacred City, and had prompted an immediate delegation to be sent to the Great Vicar of the Western Church. Ever since that time, the Order of the High Altar had enjoyed a strange, dizzying rise in power, which had seen a host of nobles bequeath them land and sizeable donations.

Though the order still fought in the Holy Wars in the Sunlands, and maintained a significant presence there with a strong network of castles, their focus, in Bevriedak's eyes, seemed to be growing ever more ambiguous. The Order of the High Altar was handling increasingly vast sums of wealth and land, and in Gallea, they directly handled the wealth of the king himself. Such endeavors did not seem to be the kind of tasks expected of a simple holy order, of disciplined monks.

Bevriedak found some profound ironies in the differences between the Order of the High Altar and other orders. The main rival orders, the Order of the Healers and the Order of the Sacred Lady, both had their initial roots in hospitals, and tending to the sick and infirm. The Order of Healers foundations hearkened back to a hospital institution that existed in the Sacred City before the Holy Wars had even begun. The Order of the Sacred Lady's origins reached to makeshift field hospitals of the Third Holy War.

Like the Order of the High Altar, they also fought in the Holy Wars, those in the Sunlands, and even assisting the efforts of smaller orders in other territories, such as Iberias. Their activity extended to lands bordering on Ehrengard, involving a series of conflicts the Order of the Sacred Lady had prosecuted successfully.

Yet the donations and other material support to the other orders always seemed balanced with the undertakings they were engaged in. Bevriedak suspected strongly there was something very wrong, hidden deeply, within the mysterious Order of the High Altar. Their activities and associations were always caculated and precise, and most often centered on prominent areas of worldly power. He felt the latter was no mere coincidence, deepening his mistrust of their true intentions. Those following in the footsteps of Emmanu did not congregate so ardently around the fountains of worldly power, seeking to drink the crimson nectar of its golden cup.

Even more disturbing, despite their affluence the knights of the Order of the High Altar were not soft men, indulgent in the usual trappings of luxury. Whatever passions they indulged beyond the eyes of others, as more than one rumor attested that the embrace of women was not unknown to them, they were hardened, well-disciplined warriors. They had carved out a bloody reputation as elite fighters, merciless to those they deemed enemies. Bevriedak held no illusions that the monk-knights would have few qualms about massacring the tribal peoples.

Beyond the dismaying knowledge of the Order of the High Altar's presence, the location of the mass of tents gave some useful information to the dragon. There was little doubt the invaders' encampment was situated well-behind the fighting. The invading force would be advancing within a general pathway connecting to the camp. Bevriedak had only to search to the direct east of the encampment to find where the invaders were pressing their advance.

In the woodlands, the invasion would proceed more slowly than on open ground, but it was likely the assault was well-underway. Judging by the swathe of destruction levied upon their villages, the tribal people had doubtlessly been pushed deep into their lands.

Bevriedak knew the ones he sought would be farther east, but before he turned to seek them out, he set his mind to causing some disruptions to the enemy. If done quickly, it was unlikely any sorcerer or Wizard would be able to fully invoke the Ban upon him. Any potential practitioner of arcane arts would barely have time to register his presence, much less identify his nature, and muster a response.

The muscles powering his wings surged with energies borne of his inner tempests. The trees to the right, on the perimeter of the forest, swayed like thin blades of grass at the onset of a storm, under the might of his passage.

He inhaled deeply, his lungs swelling with torrents of air, and then loosed a deafening roar, saturating land, water, and sky for many leagues with its resonance. His enormous shadow cast a pall over the ground he flew over, engulfing sentry posts in an icy, dreadful darkness causing the normally stalwart men to quail and shudder.

His sudden, onrushing appearance, overpowering roar, and blanketing shadow combined to have the desired effects. Countless shouts of alarm and terrified screams accompanied a frenetic scramble in and around the sprawling encampment. Disarray and chaos flourished within the erupting atmosphere.

Grazing herds of sheep and cattle, brought with the invading forces in the wake of their long supply trains, were thrown into a frenzy of maddened terror. Located just to the west of the encampment, the herds scattered, bleated, bellowed, and bolted in every direction.

Even many of the vaunted monk-knights of the Order of the High Altar scrambled hurriedly away from their select gathering of tents. Without hestitation, they left behind both weapons and armor in their frightened haste.

All were seeing an Elder for the very first time in their lives. Even more terrifying, they were beholding the massive creature at close proximity, and the result was undiluted upheaval.

Turning sharply, Bevriedak skimmed back at an even lower level, risking a pass that would take him just above the tips of the highest banners. A part of him greatly desired to spew a river of searing fire into the heart of the encampment, but reason won out over his roused emotions.

Setting a great fire into motion, surging beyond control so close to the woodlands, could easily become a greater danger than the invaders to the retreating tribal peoples. A woodland fire could spread rapidly, and catch the tribal people well before the Saxan fleet had a chance to reach their shores.

Bevriedak contented himself with another ear-shattering roar, fueling the chaos in the horrified ranks running aimlessly below. The blunt force of his close passage toppled more than a few tents and banners, sending debris and equipment tossing about within the wing-generated maelstrom.

Extending his rear claws, he raked them through the camp, ripping a broad pathway down its midst. Uprooted pavilion-tents were thrown far and wide, crashing into smaller tents, carts, horses, men, and other camp items. Trestle tables and a great quantity of food went flying, as Bevriedak tore through a sizeable mess-tent.

A few cook-fires would likely disperse their flames as everything was flung around and toppled over. Such fires were not a grave concern to Bevriedak, as they would be nothing the encampment could not extinguish before they became the kind of threat that loosing his hellish dragon-flame would have been.

With a deftness few would have believed given his tremendous size, Bevriedak dexterously changed directions and streamed eastward. He kept his flight path low, a little above the sea of treetops. It took several moments for the biting edges of the rage he felt within to begin subsiding.

Despite his storm of emotion, his eyes did not miss the small war parties, larger clusters of enemy warriors, and other signs indicating the front lines of the battle. The clash of arms, shouts, and cries of pain wafted up to Bevriedak from directly ahead, and he slowed his pace.

As he approached, he passed near a huge throng of lance and shield bearing Gallean warriors, marching east in a column wending its way through the woodlands. Their helms and lances were like a host of gleaming sparks flickering beneath the branches of the trees. He could hear the rhythm of their heavy steps, and the rustlings of cloth and metal.

Bevriedak turned sharply, and came back around so that he could fly right over the extensive column. As he did so, the dragon emitted another thunderous roar, and draped his shadow over a good portion of the column's length. The previously orderly warriors dispersed instantly in all directions, several flinging their weapons down, and a great many crying out in panic.

Craning his head around, and arcing about, he levied another great roar, which spread the pandemonium even further. It would be some time before the scattered column could regroup. At the very least, Bevriedak's bellows had purchased a small respite for the sorely pressed defenders.

Bevriedak continued onward towards the east, knowing the main body of people who had recently occupied the destroyed villages, non-combatants such as the children, mothers, and elderly, would be moving away from the lines of battle.

MERSHAD

The new day's light had not showered upon the village for very long when an excited commotion broke out. For the second time in just a few days, important events were taking place in the little village by Glittering River.

Two dragons approached through the skies, descending to land within the open fields on the outskirts of the village. It did not take very long at all for the village inhabitants to cast aside menial tasks. They hurried from the cares of morning labors to gather outside the village, coming together to stand before the pair of dragons.

Mershad, Magnus, and the others at Ragnhild's homestead trundled out with the rest of the villagers. Mershad had been talking with Magnus, Sturla, and Thorstein in the hall-house when word of the dragons arrived.

While engaged in a leisurely morning, all were roused to their feet by the unexpected tidings. They strode at a quick pace down the main pathway, out of the village, and into the fields beyond.

Once he set his eyes upon them, Mershad recognized the pair of dragons. The two, along with one other, had been the ones who responded to Svein's summons.

To the right was the larger, reddish-hued one with the prominent scutes running down its elongated back. The black slits within the golden pools of its eyes were exceedingly thin. The dragon cast an intensive scrutiny upon Mershad as he drew near with Magnus, Thorstein, and Sturla.

On the left was the silvery dragon with the rounded body, the one with raised scales running down its back in three distinctive lines. Mershad could feel the penetrating gaze from the rounded pupils in the midst of the dragon's yellow and brown eyes.

The two dragons waited in patient silence, their bodies seeming like enormous, intricately fashioned statues. When all of the villagers were assembled, the red dragon broke the heavy stillness.

"Enemy seeks … the One-Not-of-Ave," the red dragon stated in the Midragardan tongue, its resonant voice decidedly somber as it carried over the villagers. The dragon's stare bore down on Mershad. "We watch the sky. Elder have asked much of us. Maraghen came to us. Also watches. Darkness grows without."

Mershad's brow furrowed, and he wondered whether the name Maraghen referred to the Elder who had manifested during his altercation with the Arcamon.

"He must go … back to King," the silver dragon then boomed, also looking straight at Mershad. "Arcamons come from great darkness. Have been sent from the darkness. Our kind battle Arcamon from sky. Arcamon seeks One-Not-Of-Ave. One-Not-Of-Ave now here. Village not safe. Arcamon may return. One-Not-Of-Ave must go."

Their words were as unerringly direct as their gazes. There was one possible individual the dragons were referring to. Only one person in the throng from the village qualified to be addressed as the 'One-Not-

Of-Ave', and just one had attracted the attention of an Arcamon.

The dragons' looks and words were far from lost on the villagers. A breathless silence fell upon the crowd, and a multitude of eyes slowly looked towards Mershad. From young to old, woman to man, Mershad felt the pressing weight of the villagers' thoughts as they concentrated upon him. A cold feeling of isolation washed over him.

A palpable fear filled the air at the open mention of the Arcamon. As Magnus had explained to Mershad during the previous evening, as they sat together and unwound by the hearth fire, there were many legends of diabolic spirits returning to the mortal world among the Midragardans.

Most often, the fell spirits took on the raiment of a physical body, of one previously deceased. The more common tales had these spirits, called Draugr, haunting desolate areas, or old grave mounds from former eras. The vile entities appeared in many sagas, wickedly powerful beings often requiring heroic efforts to subdue.

To the Midragardans, an Arcamon was something like one of those malevolent spirits, only of a kind with a much more specific purpose than hauntings, or preying upon an unwitting passerby. The reviled Arcamons were understood to be infernal spirits of tremendous power, with origins shrouded thickly in mystery.

An Arcamon was said to be a darkened soul who had willingly chosen to reject the life-sustaining light of the All-Father, whole-heartedly embracing the stygian realm of Jebaalos. They were abominations to life itself, a sentient mockery of creation ardently committed to the service of evil. That, in itself, was enough to make the spirit of any person of conscience shudder, and Mershad was no exception.

Whether true or not, some tales said the hellish entities were dispatched into Ave straight from the deepest pits of the abyss, empowered by the Lord of the Fire Realms, Jebaalos, the Great Adversary. Accounts mentioning the dark spirits were evidently ancient among the people of Midragard. Magnus said they were used most often in the form of morality fables, to frighten unruly children towards better behavior.

That an Arcamon was in the skies directly over the lands of the villagers would be more than enough to stir up a tempest of worry. The fact that the Arcamon was intensely interested in Mershad was enough to spur that tempest into a maelstrom of terror and anxiety.

"Walk forward, Wolf Kin," the red dragon intoned.

None of the villagers moved at first. It took a few moments for

Mershad to register exactly who the red dragon was addressing, as his mind was swirling with concerns.

"Wolf Kin, come," the silver dragon gently added, as the dragons turned their stares towards Magnus.

A look of surprise on his face, Magnus took a couple of cautious steps forward. After a moment's hesitation, he took a few more, until he was standing several paces in front of the gathered villagers. He was at a point just in between the dragons towering high over him.

"Honor to you … from dragons. You helped One-Not-Of-Ave. You help land. Land of Man and Dragon. Seek others. Protect village … protect land," the red dragon said.

"Age of Fenris will come. Healing will complete. Do not fear. Much to be asked. Elder have spoken on this. Maraghen comes to us … in mountains. Stand now, all brothers … and sisters … of Wolf and Bear," the silver dragon said. The dragon's head lowered a little, and its voice carried a hint of urgency as it added, "Heed us … Wolf Kin. Heed us."

The words were quite specific to Magnus, and the mention of sisters was very deliberate and purposeful, as much as it was intriguing. Mershad noted that it provoked an immediate look of confusion on Magnus' face.

The eyes of the spectators had shifted towards Magnus, and Mershad was able to study the villagers with some anonymity. He peered around at their faces, seeking to read their responses. Some reflected mild surprise, while the miens of others grew darker and colder, as they looked upon Magnus. Mershad noticed that those in the latter group were gathered around a very strong-looking man.

"Time is short. One-Not-of-Ave step forward," the silver dragon invited, pulling Mershad's attention forward and upward, to look into the huge visage overhead.

Willing himself forward, taking confidence from Magnus' ease before the dragons, he took a few tentative steps. He consciously reminded himself it was dragons such as the ones before him that had saved him from certain doom, whether capture or death, at the hands of an Arcamon.

"Bring steed. Go with us. We take to King," the red dragon stated. "Sky not safe …for humans. We protect."

Mershad stood silently in place, not knowing how to respond.

Magnus came to his rescue, turning around towards the crowd behind them.

"Thorsleif, bring Mershad's Fenraren, and hurry!" Magnus called out. He turned back, and looked up to the dragons. "He will bring Mershad's steed here now, good brothers of Midragard."

"We wait," the silver dragon replied firmly.

Within a moment, the younger brother of Thorstein was bounding across the ground, racing off in the direction of the village. For a stocky build, his legs pumped with exceptional swiftness as the twelve-year-old hurried to fulfill his delegated task.

"Do not fear the dragons. They are our family in Midragard, as are the wolves, the ravens, and the other creatures of the Axe, Sword, and Shield," Magnus said in a low voice to Mershad.

"Do I have much of a choice in this?" Mershad responded, in a voice just above a whisper. "I heard them, and believe them. I cannot stay in the village a moment longer. I would never want these people in danger because of me."

"It is better that you are taken back to the king. It is for good reason, I have trust in that," Magnus said. "Dragons would not bother to come otherwise."

"But don't the dragons all live in this region? What will save the king if the Arcamon goes there?" Mershad asked nervously.

"There are other powers, also ancient and loyal to Midragard, and to the One who gave us this land. It would not surprise me if one of these have drawn close to the king during this dark time," Magnus replied. He smiled warmly. "Did you not speak of the Wanderer? Did he not help you, as soon as you came into this world?"

As if to emphasize his point, Magnus glanced down to Mershad's chest, where the mounted stone pendant hung from its leather cord. Mershad would not have been able to speak with Magnus, much less the dragons, were it not for the Wanderer's gift.

"Yes," Mershad replied, thinking of the wizened old man who had manifested so soon after his arrival in Ave, within the forests of the Five Realms.

"Then I believe that other forces are at work for you, even if you do not always see them," Magnus stated confidently, patting Mershad lightly on the back. "Do not lose heart, my new friend. Wickedness is not the only force at work in this world."

"I will try not to," Mershad replied, with a small, rueful grin, the best he could muster in the face of all the uncertainty.

"It is good to have made a friend this past day," Magnus said. "I will remember you well."

"And I will remember you," Mershad replied, with a hint of melancholy, wishing he had more time to spend with Magnus.

A pang of regret hit him, as he realized he would likely never see Magnus again. The possibility was very tangible, and looked more like a coming reality, especially with the looming dangers to the village necessitating Mershad's departure.

Mershad was once again caught within a tumult not of his own choosing. He knew he could not rest assured that he would reach King Hakon's estate, even with dragons escorting him. For all he knew, the unpredictable winds of fate could blow him off course again, taking him away to another distant, unfamiliar land without warning.

Magnus was someone Mershad had finally been able to understand on a personal level; a man alone to himself, a stranger among his own land and people. Mershad had not reached that kind of understanding with any of the other inhabitants of Ave he had met.

Yet despite Mershad's great disappointment, there was absolutely no doubt over the need to leave. To stay would only endanger the village and its inhabitants. As Mershad saw it, he could not depart the village a moment too soon.

The time passed in tense silence, with only the sounds of the winds flowing through the gathering. The villagers and dragons waited quietly for Thorsleif to return with Mershad's sky steed.

Thorsleif finally emerged from the village gates with Baldor in tow, having saddled the noble sky steed competently enough. Thorsleif jogged towards them, with Baldor trotting along at his side.

The throng of villagers parted quietly to let the burly youth through. Thorsleif's eyes darted between Mershad and the lofty pair of reptillian figures behind him. The look within the lad's eyes was a mixture of fear and awe as he eyed the dragons. He extended the reins of the Fenraren to Mershad, his gaze remaining on the dragons.

"Thank you, Thorsleif," Mershad replied in a low voice, taking the reins from the boy.

Thorsleif just nodded in response, slowly backing away with his eyes continuing to remain steadfast upon the winged giants. He edged over to the side of his mountain of a brother. Thorstein placed a hand down on Thorsleif's head, and gave the shaggy mass atop it an affectionate tousle. A little of the anxiety faded from Thorsleif's face.

Taking a couple of breaths, Mershad stepped into the stirrup on the left side of the Fenraren, and hoisted himself up into the saddle. He took a few moments to buckle and tighten the straps holding him in place, now knowing from direct experience how important the leathery anchors could be. After situating himself, with his back set comfortably against the raised cantle, he held the reins in a loose grip before him.

Ready for flight, he looked up towards the dragons. Both of their gazes were on him, as he nodded back at them.

"One to guide you above. Go now. Follow dragon above," the silver dragon said, gesturing with an incline of its head towards the upper sky.

Mershad looked upward. Far above, he espied a distant, winged form circling about slowly. He understood immediately what they wanted.

Mershad gripped the reins of Baldor more tightly, and looked back over the people from the village. He knew he was doing what they all wanted, villager and dragon alike, but he had not wanted to leave so soon.

He found Bergthora among the villagers, nodding and smiling to her as he did, saddened that he had to depart before he even had a chance of visiting with her again. She returned his smile warmly, and gave him a slow wave of her hand. Whether imagination or not, he perceived Bergthora's own expression as melancholy.

Mershad then turned his attention back to Magnus, Thorstein, and Sturla. "May the Great God watch over all of you. May the Great God ... the All-Father as you say ... be a light to you."

He spoke the words intently, meaning them with the utmost of sincerity. Mershad was conscious of the likely finality of the parting. He wished with all his heart that the Creator would watch over his newfound friend, his companions, and the village.

His eyes then flicked towards the hardened faces he had noticed earlier, gathered around the tall man of strong appearance. Mershad had more than an inkling who the man was. He sensed that all of the men, especially the one in their midst, bore ill-will towards Magnus. Though a part of him found it hard to say the words, he spoke again, as he looked upon their antagonistic countenances.

"May the Great God protect and guide you in all things," he said, willing for some light to shine into the men's hearts. It was hard for him to accept that anyone would harbor ill-intent towards someone like Magnus.

He then looked back to Magnus, and smiled again. "Thank you, my friend, for everything."

Magnus nodded. "Go with the All-Father, Mershad. If we do not meet again in this world, we will resume our friendship in another … one that will last much longer than this current wisp of breath."

Giving a slight bow and stepping back, Magnus created a path for Mershad's steed. Mershad took a deep breath, and prompted the steed to move forward, and take to the skies.

With a nimble spring, and mighty flexing of its wings, Baldor reached for the sky. Given leave to fly again, the creature exuded eagerness, its energy solidly renewed by a full night of rest and ample quantities of food.

Within moments, climbing steadily, rider and steed passed well beyond the village boundaries, which grew ever smaller behind and below them. It was not much longer before Baldor reached the lowest level of clouds.

Catching movement to his right, Mershad turned to see a dragon approaching from the side, the gliding figure he had espied from the ground. It was the blue dragon that Mershad had seen once before, the one with the bearded appearance to its face.

Without the need to evade an Arcamon, he was able to take in the sight of the flying dragon at his leisure. The creature glided with graceful majesty, a living wonder out of the mists of legends.

The cool winds buffeted lightly about Mershad's face. He took in a deep, crisp draught of the clean air into his lungs. The moment was magical, far beyond anything he would have believed even possible not so very long ago.

The oncoming dragon swiveled its great head to look upon Mershad as it neared, passing him by in a swoop. Mershad was grateful the dragon kept to a glide as it went by him, feeling the powerful rush of air in its wake. If the huge creature had pumped its broad wings even once, Mershad had little doubt the ensuing turbulence would have engulfed and overwhelmed his Fenraren. He did not want to find out how long it took for a robust Fenraren to regain control over its flight out of a tumbling freefall.

"Follow!" the dragon boomed, neck curved back towards Mershad.

With a few tugs on the reins, a little sharp pressure from his heels, and some verbal cues, Mershad induced Baldor to swiftness in the wake of the blue dragon. The Fenraren responded very capably, as Mershad felt the air rushing over him increase in force with the steed's powerful surge. The familiar dips and bumps from navigating the air currents accompanied Baldor, as the creature steadily built up more speed.

The dragon settled into a restrained, easy pace that Baldor matched without undue exertion. Maintaining a higher altitude than the Fenraren, the dragon set its course as a guide and escort, heading off in what Mershad was sure to be the direction of King Hakon's homestead.

With the journey underway, Mershad turned in his saddle and squinted, trying to gain a last glimpse of the village at Glittering River. Far below and behind him, at the outermost edge of his vision, the red dragon and its silver comrade could be seen climbing into the skies. Their huge forms looked so small, from such a considerable distance, as they ascended. Orienting themselves, the dragons leveled out as they streaked across the skies, heading back towards their mountain homesteads.

Mershad could no longer distinguish the village out of the landscape behind him, a realization that weighed heavily upon his heart. He thought of Magnus, Bergthora, and the others, consigning their images to a special place within his memories, hoping fervently that his mind would not be the only place he would revisit them in the future.

AYENWATHA

Deganawida, Ayenwatha, and Gunnar strained to keep up with a mountain of tasks, as the sprawling, hasty retreat began. Outfitted with refilled pouches of roast cornmeal, and a little dried fish salvaged from the villages, a number of warbands had been dispatched within the forest.

The individual warriors moved like shadows within the woodlands, covered with their distinctive red and black body paint. They had all been sent to harass and slow the pursuing enemy forces, as much as possible.

Most carried longbows of ash or oak, as well as a full compliment of arrows. Emerging suddenly from hidden positions, they sent arrows into flight from deep shadows, and disappeared just as quickly. They moved with the seasoned, nimble step of veteran hunters, alternately sallying forth and withdrawing amongst the concealing trees and undergrowths. To the enemy, it seemed as if the forest itself was alive, lashing out violently, before settling into an uneasy stillness.

Gunnar's Midragardan warriors were arrayed wherever the enemy's largest thrusts occurred. They were aided in their efforts by a fair number of tribal warriors. Those most familiar with every rock and tree within a given area were called upon to help Gunnar gain every advantage.

With their distinctive, large shields fashioned of wooden rods lashed together, many tribal warriors fought side by side with their Midragardan allies. Several of them donned a lengthy type of timber body armor, fashioned in a similar method to the craft of their shields.

With such indigenous guidance, even the Midragardans were able to fade like receding mists into the woodlands. They thwarted heavy pursuit time and time again, only to unexpectedly reemerge to strike potent blows on the enemy.

The multitudes hailing from the five woodland realms were urged to press onward, to the east, with as little delay as possible. The smattering of packhorses still available to the tribes were pushed to their limits. Not a few of the weaker individuals in the retreat, those who suffered from infirmities of old age, physical disabilities, sickness, or the limitations of small children, had to be assisted as well as possible. Crude litters were hastily fashioned, and quickily used to assist the more incapacitated members of the tribes.

There was no hesitation in assisting the weaker ones, despite the great anxiety and desperation pervading the masses of tribal people. Everyone pitched in their skills and strength to make certain that all were tended to, and none left behind.

The nights provided a few badly needed respites, for everything from physical rest, to morale, and even the traditions that helped so effectively to bind the tribes together. Yet not every practice could be maintained.

Even though some village sachems, including a few war sachems, had recently died, there was no time for the elaborate condolence rituals involving the clan matrons to honor the dead. Neither was there any time for the proper treatment of the dead, such as the building of high platforms to hold aloft the traditional bark coffins, or for burial within large earthen mounds.

The dead were hurriedly buried, at least when the bodies could be retrieved. Many hearts agonized over fallen comrades whose positions had been overrun by the advancing enemy, before the bodies could be taken away.

Yet whatever could be salvaged from the tribal culture was diligently attended to. The wise among the tribes knew well that every familiarity held onto would serve the people well in the baleful trial they were enduring.

Best of all, the Sacred Fire of the tribes, kept and maintained by the Onan, had not been extinguished in the attack upon Deganawida and Ayenwatha's village. Easier to maintain at night within an encampment, taking the Sacred Fire along with the mass of people was a laborious and delicate process. Carried on large firebrands, at the head of the throngs of tribal peoples, the Sacred Fire's survival and continuity produced a reassuring undercurrent. The sliver of hope represented by the Sacred Fire resonated throughout the multitudes of beleaguered, harried souls, who trudged forward in its beckoning wake.

The Faithkeepers were also doing their best to uphold the people's spirits. Giving words of reassurance and encouragement, they enjoined the people to focus their hearts on prayer to the One Spirit.

The clan matrons, and members of the Healing Societies and other sacred mask fellowships, for their part, drew upon seemingly inexhaustible pools of energy. They labored unceasingly throughout the dark hours of night to administer aid or healing, wherever necessary.

The matrons' aged hands worked the various fellowships' masks diligently with oil from sunflowers. The masked followers of the many fellowships cordoned off areas near to halting points, where secretive rituals could be performed as properly as possible.

It was not an uncommon sight to see men wearing headdresses fashioned of the pelts of Firaken, panthers, wolves, and bears. Moving through the moonlight-cast shadows through the trees, they looked as mysterious as their clandestine arts to huddled tribal onlookers.

The medicine fellowships were bracing themselves for the coming days, even as they performed their tasks, as the need for them was rapidly mounting. A large number of injured warriors were brought to the warded, relatively secluded areas for the ancient rituals. Carrying wood staves and timber-handled rattles made from gourds, hickory bark, or turtle shells, and wearing the distinctive wooden masks carved from living trees, the masked men of the medicine fellowships made their preparations, and exercised their secret arts. Again and again, they blew their sacred ashes into the faces of the injured men, in order to resist and heal sicknesses that open wounds often brought in their wake.

Additionally, the existence of the same animal-associated clans within more than one tribe proved to be a source of great strength. Members of a particular clan, encompassing multiple tribes cooperated to attend the needs of all the people during the grueling exodus.

As clans within each tribe were permanently paired with another specific clan, represented by a different animal, the system of clans provided yet another invaluable benefit. The associative pairings formed a solid foundation for mutual assistance within the people of each tribal village. In normal times, the system ensured that there was always support in times of suffering and death. With the ongoing deluge of struggle and tragedy, the system was pushed to an extreme. Despite all the darkness assaulting the tribal people, the strengths of the clan system still prevailed, with widespread, sustained reciprocation, as clans labored to aid their counterparts within the context of a particular village group. Consoling even as they were themselves consoled, no clan, within any tribe, had gone unscathed in the early stages of the terrible assault.

The nights were undeniably difficult to get through, but the tribes had so far managed to regroup enough in spirit to meet the dangers and demands arriving with the coming of dawn. Normally a source of uplift, the sunrise was a cause for trepidation, the moment the horizon began to lighten. It was after one such arduous, worry-fraught night, just after the rising sun burned away the morning mists, that the great dragon suddenly arrived.

The people had been traveling for only a few hours, having started in the chilly, damp period before first light. For the movement of so many people, the relative silence of their travel was extraordinary. Even the dogs trotting along with the mass of humanity were unusually subdued, perhaps sensing the anxieties of their human comrades.

Tribal sachems, both war and civil, continued to be very busy, and few had gotten any significant amount of rest. Mentally exhausted, and physically drained, they perservered onward without pause until the momentous arrival occurred.

Ayenwatha had concluded yet another extended session among the Onan warriors the previous night, including conferring with a number of war sachems from the other tribes and villages. Concerns regarding arrow supplies, and sustaining food supplies, were just starting to become more than an idle concern. Keeping up the strength of the warriors, as they were driven beyond all endurance, was of the highest priority.

He had been pushing his own stamina to the far limits, and when the morning arrived he was still fraught with a multitude of apprehensions. Adding to his concerns were some misgivings of a more personal nature, especially regarding Deganawida.

The old sachem had traversed the sprawling encampment throughout the night, conferring with several of the fifty exalted sachems of the Grand Council. Like Ayenwatha, a number of deep concerns were burdening him as the light of the new day was unfurled.

Both of the Onan sachems were heading back towards the west, as their people headed eastward. They were striding right in the direction of the oncoming hordes from Gallea, as the sunlight drove back the last vestiges of night, and filtered down through the overhead branches. The two were hoping to reach the forward-most warbands set to defend the retreat, when the first roars reached their ears.

Gunnar had joined them in their hike, just shortly before. His soiled, stained appearance, and throughouly gouged round-shield, testified to the unrelenting nature of the fight. Only his sword, which had evidently been tended to during the night, looked freshly primed for the new day.

Like Ayenwatha, the Midragardan carried his weapons at the ready, as they moved through the unpredictable forest region. In the silence of the woods, they listened for the slightest snap of a twig or rustle of undergrowth. Several armed tribal warriors accompanied them, fanned out wide and stepping forward with caution.

At first, the terrifying cacophony above caused Ayenwatha's heart to sink. The thoughts of another diabolical weapon being hurled against them by the Unifier was nearly too much for his constitution to take. The remembrances of the giant, flying monstrosities, unloading a storm of heavy stones onto the hilltop villages, were far too raw.

Another ear-splitting roar ensued, which was shortly followed by a frenzied outcry off in the distance, where the vanguard of the enemy was. Ayenwatha slowed down, discerning the nuances of the sounds far ahead.

The cries interested Ayenwatha greatly, and not just because they marked the position of a large enemy force. Rather, it was the nature of the cries' tenor that Ayenwatha focused in on. The cries were not those of battle, but of sheer terror.

In that moment, Ayenwatha's eyes took in the wide grin breaking through the sweat, dirt, and grime caking Gunnar's face. The smile showed under the iron half-helm on his head like the sun coming out from behind a dense thundercloud. His bright blue eyes glittered spiritedly, to either side of the helm's nasal guard.

The Midragardan chieftain shook his sword in the air vigorously, in an ebullient gesture. Ayenwatha stared at him with a feeling of puzzlement, not knowing the reason for the warrior's cheerful demeanor. He hoped the Midragardan was not falling into madness.

"I'm not mad, do not worry," Gunnar said quickly, seeing the perplexity spread across Ayenwatha's face. "That sound you hear shaking the heavens is one I know very well, from my own homeland. That is the sound of a very large dragon, or I have never heard such before."

"And this is good?" Ayenwatha asked, even more confused.

It was true that a fire dragon had once aided the World Mother, in the creation stories of the tribal peoples. Yet that had been the only dragon he could relate with his own people's history. Ayenwatha had heard many tales from the western lands, which had long since driven out all dragons from their domains. Dragons were said to be ferocious, highly dangerous creatures, and precious few were said to be benevolent; at least if the western tales could be trusted.

Ayenwatha knew of the great presence of dragon images among the Midragardans. He had long since attributed it to a warrior's association with something fearsome, or possessed of some admirable attribute worthy of adoption. In that way, he related dragons to the Midragardans, somewhat as tribal clans did to the particular animal they were associated with.

While his fellow members of the Firaken clan reverenced the many powerful characteristics of the woodland beasts, a tribal warrior would not necessarily be joyful at the prospects of an intimate encounter with a Firaken. He had long assumed the Midragardan's pervasive reverence for dragons to be much the same, but Gunnar's overjoyed expression shattered the inference. The warrior was clearly elated to perceive the sonorous roar of a living dragon.

"I do not know what one is doing here, but they have no love for Galleans, or other western folk, that I can say," Gunnar commented, though his brow furrowed slightly. "Even so, it is very odd one is in the skies over your land. They have long since been confined to the south of Midragard, in the Drakkar Mountains as far as I have ever known."

He then looked at Ayenwatha and shrugged. "Whatever the cause of this is, our ears tell us the dragon is no friend of the invaders. Their cries hail no ally. I say we try and find out what kind of mayhem our flying friend is causing."

The Midragardan's great confidence and excited demeanor served to kindle a sudden hope within Ayenwatha, though it was tempered by lingering worries. A dragon could be a danger to humans on all sides of the ongoing conflict. Even as he desired to join with Gunnar in seeking out the dragon, he was already thinking of the need for the tribal people to take cover, and to conceal themselves, until the dragon's disposition and purpose could be fully determined.

MAGNUS

"You have heard the dragons," Bergthora stated forcefully, at the top of her lungs, attracting the attention of the other villagers.

Her voice summoned the villagers out of their subdued reverie. They had remained silent for many long moments, as the forms of the red and silver dragons shrank to mere specks on the distant horizon.

"There is trouble about, and we must be nothing less than vigilant!" she continued firmly.

At that moment, a tall, strong-looking figure moved forward to stand in front of the group. Like attendant shadows, several of the younger, stronger men of the village moved in his wake, taking up positions towards the front.

"You have spoken well, Bergthora," the figure said, in a low, smooth voice.

He was nearly equal in height to Magnus, though noticeably more robust of build. His flowing blond hair accented his thin, angular face, set with piercing blue eyes evoking the steely look of a predator. His short beard was well groomed, descending into a point beneath his chin that added to the sharpness of his countenance.

He was dressed in much better attire than were most of the other villagers, with a green tunic graced with tablet-woven bands of red and blue at the hem and cuffs, and a headband of similar fashion. The knee-length tunic was belted at the waist, fastened with a simple bronze buckle. From the belt hung a leather pouch set within a metal framework, as well as a langseax sheltered inside a well-crafted scabbard.

A black woolen cloak was fastened at his right shoulder by a silver, penannular brooch. The lower part of his trousers extended below the cloak's hem, to touch the top of his ankle-high leather shoes. A couple of gleaming silver pendants and a few ornamental amber pieces were strung together in a necklace, and his hands were decorated with several rings of silver.

Noticeably absent were any neck or arm rings, items that Magnus knew Njal craved. Nonetheless, Njal carried himself with the air of a man whose neck and arms were laden down with many such momentous awards. His mouth was drawn small and tight, in a petulant expression setting his otherwise strong appearance a little off balance.

"Much must be done," Njal stated firmly, "And I will ride immediately for Jarl Guttorm. A watch must be kept, and the beacon sites must be seen to."

"But do you even know what we are looking for? The Sunlander-looking one's gone sure enough," snapped Oddrun, from the forefront of the crowd. "Work enough to do around here. Nobody's going to have interest in a little village, Njal. The Sunlander one was who anyone had an interest in. You heard the dragons."

There was much murmured consent to her comments among the audience, bolstered further in the form of several nods and a few short, outward declarations of assent. Oddrun appeared quite pleased by the extensive agreement, acknowledging the others with inclines of her head. Mangus knew the crowd's reaction irritated Njal to no end, watching the man's eyes narrow as he stared coldly at Oddrun.

Right when Njal sought to project himself as a quick-thinking leader, she had effectively diminished the importance of the entire village, which included him. While she was correct that the village was not the focus of Midragard's enemies, Magnus knew Njal would rather entertain the illusion that he and the village were indespensible to Jarl Guttorm and Midragard.

"And did not the dragon ask Magnus to seek others?" thundered Thorstein.

All mutterings ceased, and a taut silence gripped the air. Inwardly, Magnus cursed Thorstein's inadvisable timing, coming right when Njal's ego had been rubbed raw.

Njal's face whipped, casting a heated glare towards Magnus' massive friend. Though almost imperceptible, Magnus noticed that Njal's right hand, thumb hooked in his belt, twitched in the direction of the langseax's leather-bound hilt. The subtle movement spoke volumes about Njal's true feelings towards Thorstein.

"If there is any seeking of others, I shall do it, as I am going to Jarl Guttorm anyway," Njal responded icily.

Magnus placed a hand on Thorstein's arm, clutching him firmly to silence the retort that the large man was about to loose. Magnus looked back towards Njal, replying cooly, "I do not seek to interfere with your own dealings, Njal. Going to Jarl Guttorm was not what the dragons were speaking of."

"Then who was it Magnus? Your feral beasts?" Njal said mockingly, a humorless smile cracking his face.

"I do not know," Magnus responded. He could feel the tension coiling within Njal, probing for an opportunity to release itself, and strike out.

"What good have your beasts been to the village? We can do our own hunting," Njal continued stridently.

Magnus did not respond to the barb, knowing that to do so would provide the excuse Njal sought to sharply escalate the situation. His restraint once again proved stronger than that of his comrades.

"You'll get your arm-ring soon enough, Njal. Go to Guttorm, and be about your business," Sturla interjected testily.

While Magnus appreciated the loyalty demonstrated by his friends, he was less than impressed with their discretion. He could not blame them entirely, as Midgardard was not populated by men or women inclined to inhibition. His own self-discipline was a bit of an anomaly.

"I will earn more than one, little woodcarver. Go back to your whittling, as tiny blades are all that you can handle," Njal replied in a near growl. He then looked to Magnus, his icy smile broadening. A sharp glint came to his eyes as their gazes met. Looking back over the assembled villagers, he continued in a casual tone, "While everyone is gathered together, there is one more thing I wish to say. Asa, my love, come here by my side."

The crowd shifted to create a channel as Asa walked from where she had been standing near to Bergthora. She strolled with a relaxed gait to Njal's right side, and looked for a moment towards Magnus. For an instant, he thought he saw a faint trace of sadness come into her eyes.

In the next moment, the hint appeared to be nothing more than a cruel illusion, brought about by Magnus' wistful heart. A bright, beaming smile lit up her face, and her eyes sparkled with joy as she looked at Njal.

"Asa and I are to be wed. We will be married in just a few weeks. I can promise all of you there will be a celebration and feast like this village has never seen," Njal announced, looking pointedly at Magnus. He then eyed Sturla with a glacial expression. "I expect those rings will be coming soon. Jarl Guttorm will be coming in person to the marriage and feast."

Magnus watched the transpiring scene, and heard the terrible words, as if detached. It was like he had been abruptly cast into a dream state, one where he could not move his limbs, even if he had wanted to.

There was no mistaking the hateful intent contained within the cold smile Njal then gave him. Magnus' burdened heart was now bereft of the last shreds of hope he had tenaciously clung to. His spirit felt as if it had been ripped asunder. He had thought it probable that Njal was eventually going to marry Asa, as Magnus was not one to deceive himself, but now that the reality manifested, he found himself wrapped in a cocoon of disbelief.

Most of the villagers erupted in a raucous cheer at the pronouncement, and Njal stood a little straighter, basking in the fervent accolades. Only Bergthora appeared subdued, other than Thorstein, Sturla, and those from Ragnhild's home. Magnus' two closest friends had darkening miens that could only be described as resentful scowls, bordering closely on hostile anger.

Summoning all the resolve he could, Magnus slowly turned to walk away from the assemblage, resigned and heavy hearted. He had not taken more than two steps when Njal's voice cut across the air. Keeping his back to Njal, Magnus came to a halt, knowing salt was about to be rubbed in his inner wounds.

"Everyone will be invited to eat and drink their fill. Nearly everyone, that is. No mangy curs allowed. If you want to come, Magnus, you will have to leave your dirty companions in the woods, where they belong," Njal said, in a barbed tone dripping with insult.

"When has Magnus ever brought wolves into the village?" Sturla snapped. "He has always respected the feelings of the people of the village. And he has always done right by us all."

Magnus did not say a word, backing up a step, and quietly bringing his arm out, to grip Sturla's firmly. Sturla looked perplexed, his expresssion revealing his expectation of Magnus to act or respond in a forceful manner to Njal's biting insult.

After a moment, Magnus let go of Sturla, and took a step forward with his right leg. His blood ran scorchingly hot through his veins, but his mind still governed his feelings as he lifted his left foot up, and took another conscious step onward. He willed himself to walk away, and leave the area in peace, though the effort involved was laborious.

"I suggest you clean yourself, and comb your matted hair. Running around in the woods, you may have forgotten the manner of the men of Midragard," Njal stated, his face glowing in triumph, as his eyes bored through Magnus' back. His voice became a near hiss, as he added, "Maybe that is why I stand here today, with Asa at my side."

Magnus stopped suddenly in his tracks again, swinging about, and locking his gaze with Njal. There was no give to Njal, as he met Magnus' glare with equal force. Neither man was about to budge, as a nervous silence fell over the crowd.

"You go too far, Njal," Magnus said, in a low, even voice.

He knew Njal was baiting him with each belittement. Despite his inner anguish, and mounting rage, he continued to hold himself back. He loathed giving Njal the satisfaction of any kind of response.

"Not far enough. Go on to your mangy curs, Magnus," Njal said dismissively. "Animals are your kindred."

Out of the corner of his eye, Magnus noticed a number of Njal's companions fanning out, until there was a semi-circle facing him. Thorstein and Sturla stepped over to flank Magnus on either side, but they were outnumbered over three to one.

"Enough of this, Njal, there is no need for any conflict here," Bergthora interrupted, taking a step out from the crowd.

Magnus' gaze did not waver from its clutch on Njal's, but his heart grew heavier as he listened to her intervention. He could hear the great disappointment within her voice, and knew that among the villagers she was one who had not received Njal's announcement with any joy.

"Bergthora, there is no better time to finally resolve this," Njal replied, keeping his eyes on Magnus. "What of his kind? They hide in the woods, and come to a few battles every now and then. What are they in relation to those who are here every day? Those who see to the fields, the herds, and who truly serve Midragard. What has he brought you, but some meat we could well have gotten by ourselves? Do not be fascinated by his kind. Nor fear it. He seeks to be an animal. Nothing more than that."

"Now you go too far!" Thorstein roared at Njal. The brawny man's fists clenched tightly at his sides, the corded muscles of his forearms bulging.

"Enough, Thorstein," Magnus said, in a controlled voice. "Do not give him what he wants."

Slowly, commanding every last ounce of willpower he had left, he turned, to once again try and make his way to the forest's edge across the cleared fields. He ignored the cackling laughs from Njal's companions, as he steeled his thoughts towards the singular goal of physically crossing the open ground. The trees, streams, and meadows beyond offered him a promise of haven, where he could try and find succor for his interior wounds.

He drew to a halt yet again, and shook his head slowly. Turning back, he strode up to Thorstein and Sturla. Ignoring Njal and the others, he asked Thorstein, "Does your sister still have some mead in your house?"

Thorstein nodded, though his broad face was still brimming with tension.

Magnus forced a smile. "Then let us share some together. My visit with you should not end like this."

"Go into the woods, wolf-boy," Njal snapped, with the lofty air of a command.

"When I choose to return, on my own time," Magnus replied, his timbre icy and unyielding. "I am not finished visiting with my friends."

Njal chuckled malevolently, and slowly unfastened his cloak, letting it fall to the ground behind him. He lined himself up so he was directly in Magnus' path. "There is no need for any further talk, wolfling.

We need no more disruptions from your kind. I order you to leave this village … or must I throw you out of it myself."

"He does not need to leave. He is welcome anytime under my own roof!" Bergthora interjected, with an aura of defiance. "No matter who Asa chooses to marry."

"Bergthora, please do not upset yourself over this," Magnus addressed her gently, casting an affectionate glance in her direction. It pained him to see her obvious distress. "This is between myself and Njal only."

"That is correct, Magnus, just the two of us," Njal added. "So do this village some good, and leave."

"Yes, Magnus … listen to Njal, and just leave. Your animals are waiting for you," Asa added derisively, her words driving into Magnus' spirit like the cold iron point of a spear.

"I do not have to leave," Magnus responded, keeping his eyes from Asa, as he looked back to Njal. He had no desire to provoke Njal, but neither was he going to concede a most basic right. "This is my village as well. And I will stay here if I please."

"You will not!" Njal shouted, his eyes erupting with malice as he left Asa behind and advanced on Magnus.

The semi-circle of Njal's companions then moved in, to converge on Magnus and his two friends. A number of shouts and cries broke out from the throng of villagers, as supporters of Njal, including Asa, voiced their encouragement to the attackers.

With a bellowing cry, Thorstein barreled forward and slammed into three men to Magnus' left. Sturla darted forward and sent a fist crackling under the jaw of one of the men to his right.

Njal hurled himself at Magnus. The barriers restraining Magnus finally gave out, as the instincts to defend himself took over. The two men tumbled down heavily, arms and legs twisting and grappling as they wrestled upon the ground. Magnus was undeniably at a disadvantage, as Njal was the most skilled and well-trained warrior in the village. There was also the fact that he was physically quicker, and stronger.

Njal rolled on top of Magnus, and took advantage of an opening to send a heavy right fist crashing into the side of Magnus' face. A searing pain flashed through Magnus, even as he took advantage of Njal's right-handed punch to bring up his own left leg. Hooking it around Njal, he toppled his opponent backwards.

Magnus lunged inwards as Njal scrambled to get his feet under him. With a nimble spring, Njal leapt up as Magnus arrived, bringing his right heel chopping down in the middle of Magnus' back.

The powerful blow knocked all the wind out of Magnus' chest, and he gasped as he rolled to the side. He kicked hard up and outward, as Njal swiveled towards him, catching the other man squarely in the stomach. Njal grunted in pain, as the impact landed with full force.

Asa cried out furiously, and started to move forward until Njal shouted to her, "Stay back, Asa, this is my fight! … It ends here and now."

As she halted in her tracks, Magnus could see Asa's desire to come to the aid of Njal. Her face was a vision of antipathy as she looked upon Magnus.

Njal then grabbed the hilt of his langseax, freeing the lengthy single-edged knife from the scabbard. The sun's light glinted off the blade, its edge freshly honed and at its sharpest.

A murderous, feral look blazed deep within Njal's eyes, and Magnus knew the struggle would culminate in a deadly finality, one way or the other. Calming his mind, Magnus waited for Njal to make his move.

"I'm going to enjoy cutting you, and gutting you, wolfling. This has been a long time coming," Njal said. "Things get set to rights this day! Maybe I'll decide to wear your skin!"

At that moment, a loud outcry rose up amongst the villagers. The shouts and screams carried a strong element of panic and fear within their tones.

With his peripheral vision, Magnus saw a number of huge, bounding gray forms racing across the open fields towards them. Njal cast a glance over his shoulder, and froze for a moment. The hatred in his eyes was replaced swiftly by sheer terror.

"To me!" Njal called loudly, hustling back several paces, and summoning his friends over to him. Her eyes also reflecting raw fear, Asa hurried to Njal and took up a position at his side.

Several of the villagers had already taken off running for the village, though several stopped abruptly, as three of the great wolves moved in and placed themselves directly between the villagers and the entrance. Magnus felt the righteous indignation and thirst for vengeance pouring out of the wolves, and knew he had only a heartbeat to act.

"Brothers! Sisters! Hold yourselves!" Magnus shouted powerfully, emptying his urgent desire for restraint into the force of his voice.

Ears erect, hackles raised, and lips pulled back from arrays of deadly fangs, several of the large wolves formed a semi-circle of their own, facing Njal and seven of his companions. All of the men had knives or seaxes drawn, save for one gripping tightly onto a small hand axe. Nearly all of them bore newly-acquired sigils of combat, in the form of busted lips, bruises, and noticeable limps.

His head throbbing, and choking in gulps of air, Magnus looked around for Sturla and Thorstein. Sturla lay unconscious, likely knocked out by a heavy blow to the head. Thorstein groaned, crawling laboriously across the ground.

A couple of Njal's comrades lay prone where they had been rendered unconscious, in close proximity to the heavy-fisted man who had delivered them there. But the weight of numbers had gotten the better of Magnus' big friend. His lip was split and bleeding, one of his eyes was already swelling shut, and there was a deep gash higher on his head.

To Magnus' dismay, he saw that Thorstein was lurching toward the still form of Thorsleif, who had evidently tried to intervene on behalf of his brother. Magnus' sharp eyes caught the shallow heave of Thorsleif's chest, which was a great relief, though the boy's nose had been bloodied badly.

The low, rumbling chorus of growls continued emanating from the fearsome wolves nearby. Their huge teeth gleamed with saliva, as the looks in their golden eyes lanced hotly into Njal and his companions.

Magnus could feel their burning desire to leap to the attack, but he knew it would be an action that could never be forgiven by the village, or by himself. No matter how angry, wronged, and humiliated he might have been, the core of everything he stood for meant he could not condone a slaughter.

"Hold, friends," Magnus said, in a gentler voice, slowly regaining his focus, despite the continued pain resonating in his head.

"Is this how you serve Midragard?" Njal growled, through clenched teeth.

Magnus had to respect Njal's courage. Above all the others, he could see Njal was resolved to fight, and expected the wolves to attack at any moment. He was not looking to run, or to shield himself amongst his comrades. If anything, he had edged forward a couple of steps, separating himself further from them.

The villagers had gathered tightly together, a short distance past Njal and his companions. Magnus saw where the three large wolves continued to obstruct their path, holding them all at bay.

"What are you waiting for, Magnus? Protect the village!" Njal mocked. He looked towards the wolves, and challenged them. "What are you waiting for, beasts? Would that I had a broad axe with me, to bury in your hides. But this langseax will cleave through your filthy coats well enough. I swear I will send more than one of you out of this world before you bring me down!"

The men around Njal, feeding off his defiance and bravery, stood a little taller, and their faces grew harder. There was no question that Njal would be an asset to Jarl Guttorm, as he carried strong warrior's blood in his veins.

An unexpected voice then sliced through the rising tension. Now, it was Magnus' turn to freeze in place. Distracted by the battle, the heavy feelings bowing his spirit just moments earlier rushed back in full force, causing his heart to sink once again.

He turned and beheld the approach of the beautiful, blond-haired maiden, who had once shown him a glimpse of what could only be described as a full state of happiness. As elating as that experience had been, so now was the pain and deep sorrow flooding over him.

Asa walked forward from where she had been standing with Njal, a grim expression chiseled upon her face. Her words were unrelenting, striking him to the core. "Let him go, Magnus! What are you going to do? Destroy the village? Set your wolves upon women and children too? You hold my mother and our families like this?"

"Would you even have shed a tear if I had died, Asa?" Magnus asked her quietly, an abyss of sadness reflected in his eyes.

"Let him go!" she repeated, unmoved by his demeanor, with anger saturating her voice.

She cast a glance in the direction of Njal, and Magnus could see the deep concern she held for him. There was no question regarding whose heart she had given her own to. There was no sense prolonging a wisp of a dream any longer.

"I will go," Magnus answered softly, enduring a maelstrom of thoughts and emotions. "I meant no harm. They came in to protect me. I did not start this fight."

He turned back to the wolves, but as he did so, a realization welled up within him. It was as if something hidden, a long-suffering reality lurking under the surface of his innermost self, had finally been given release.

The sorrows remained, and he knew they would still be there for a long time to come. Yet the sudden light of reason that freed itself from the chains of his faint hopes was a welcome development, coming to the fore in the face of fiery emotions.

While so beautiful on the outside, Asa was simply not as comely on the inside. It had taken him a long time, and a deeply wounding experience, to see what should have been obvious before.

She knew what Njal was, yet she hurried after him for reasons that had nothing to do with love, loyalty, or the things transcending the visible world. Asa was getting exactly what she wanted, a path to stature and wealth. As far as Magnus was concerned, Njal and Asa wanted to marry each other, then they could have each other.

"Have him, Asa. I will trouble you no more. You get what you deserve," Magnus stated, in a stronger, more resolved tone. His face held no humor in it as he looked directly into her eyes. "You were never what I was looking for. I saw you for what you never were. I loved an illusion. I can see now what you truly are. It is nothing I desire."

He slowly shook his head, laughing ruefully to himself and wondering how he could have been a fool for so long. When he looked back to her, his head was held higher.

"Stay back, and stay far out of my life, from this day on!" Magnus said hotly, his words more authoritative than a Jarl's battle command.

A surprised, dumbfounded look sprawled upon Asa's face. Magnus had never so much as raised his voice once to her in all the years they had known each other. He could see she was stunned, and did not have any idea how to respond.

"Thorstein and Sturla merely stood with me as friends. They have no part in what I am, or what path I choose to walk upon," Magnus continued, in a steady tone, looking upon Njal and his companions. "You have my word as a Midragardan that my next visit here will be much different in nature if you should do anything to harm them. By the All-father, I swear that any injury to them will be brought back to you a hundred-fold. You will become my prey, and will be hunted to the ends of Midragard, if that is what it takes."

He walked over to Thorstein and leaned over, placing his hand upon the huge man's shoulder. Thorsleif had been revived in the interim, breathing slowly, and dazed from the heavy hits he had suffered. The boy was very brave, and had been unflinchingly loyal to his brother, enduring several blows from full-grown men trained for fighting.

"Be strong, the two of you. And tell Sturla what I have said here. You should be fine. Do not follow me," Magnus told him.

"Magnus…." Thorstein began, wincing as a tremor of pain wracked him.

Magnus held his hand up, to cut off his friend's next words. Despite the firm, quick gesture, he spoke softly to Thorstein. "You must take care of Ragnhild, Thordis, Thorsleif, and those on your land. I will be fine. Do not make this any harder. Go, get some rest, and tend to your wounds. Your friendship is one of the greatest of honors I could ever have in this world. As is Sturla's."

Magnus then turned to face the rest of the villagers.

"Do not hold Thorstein and Sturla responsible for what you may feel toward me. If you do, I promise all of you that I will give you reasons to truly dislike me," Magnus said to them with a fierce expression, his voice carrying a sharp, threatening edge to it.

He turned his back on the villagers, and walked towards the semi-circle of wolves facing Njal and his comrades. He did not even give Njal and Asa so much as a single look as he passed by them.

Looking forward, he called out loudly, "Come, my brothers and sisters! Let us return home."

The three wolves standing between the assemblage and the village entrance growled and snarled at the intimidated men and women. Breaking out from their stasis, the wolves removed themselves from the path of the stymied villagers.

Giving the humans a wide berth, the three lupine forms skirted the mass of unnerved villagers, loping around to rejoin Magnus and the other wolves. The combined group crossed the open fields, heading briskly towards the welcoming shelter of the forest. The wolves clustered in closer to Magnus, padding alongside their friend and brother, as if seeking to lend him support during his time of deep burden.

"Magnus!"

Magnus slowed, and then came to a stop, though he did not turn his head. His name had been called by perhaps the only voice that could bring him to a halt at that moment. He listened to a hurried series of footsteps thumping on the ground, as Bergthora approached from behind.

The wolves accompanying him also stopped, and turned, though they made no threats toward the oncoming figure. They sensed Magnus' feelings clearly enough to know Bergthora was not an enemy. If anything, they could sense a great, abiding affection dwelling within Magnus towards her. Their gazes lingered on her as they waited patiently.

"What is it, Berthora?" he asked her softly, turning slowly. "I hold nothing against you. You had no part in any of this."

"I am sorry ... so sorry, Magnus," she replied, her voice choking up.

The sound caught him by surprise, as he had never before witnessed her in such a distraught condition. She had always put forward a strong face in the midst of onerous burdens and troubles. She was always the immoveable rock in the storm, and he knew it took a lot to shake her up in the manner he was witnessing.

"Few have courage, when it matters," she continued, looking as if she was gathering herself back together. "Do not hold anger in your heart against all in the village. Many are just simple people, who seek to avoid any part of a conflict. It does not absolve them of their cowardice, it is simply the reality of the world."

"But their craven reality does not include you. Nor Thorstein. Nor those under Ragnhild's roof. Nor Sturla. No, I do not hold anger against everybody," Magnus said firmly, looking upon the tear-stained face of the middle-aged woman standing in front of him. "As for the others, it remains to be seen if they can leave those I care for alone. I hope for their own sake that they can muster enough discipline to heed my warning."

The implications of his last few words hung forebodingly in the air between Magnus and Bergthora. Though she was not among those implicated, he could see she was very unsettled by his response.

"You know what I feel," Bergthora said, in a low voice, her tone at the cusp of shaking. "I am not my daughter. But she is still my daughter. Do you understand where I am placed?"

Magnus nodded. He then replied gently, "I know, Bergthora. And this does nothing to how I feel towards you. I will always value your friendship, Bergthora. Always. You have been one of the few who has always been kind to me, and one of the few who made any effort to understand the truth of me. I will never forget that. Not ever."

Without another word, or waiting for any reply, he slowly turned his gaze away from her, continuing forward on his way towards the woods. The surrounding wolves broke into motion, and settled in alongside him once again.

Bergthora made no response in the wake of his departure, nor did he hear the sound of her footsteps. She remained quietly in place, sadly watching him go onward.

Magnus and the wolves continued farther and farther away from the village. The wolves gradually spread out wider, and kept a vigilant eye to all sides, as Magnus let the powerful emotions within him finally begin to simmer down.

The day's light was broken up by an intertwining continuum of branches and leaves as he moved into the trees. The coolness of the woodland shade washed over him, embracing his return. He looked over to a couple of his lupine companions, padding along by his side. Their golden eyes looked up into his, reflecting strength and loyalty.

The sight of them brought a smile to his face, and a spark of joy to his heart. His traumatic ordeal was over at last, a needed resolution had been gained, and it was simply good to be home once again.

BEVRIEDAK

It greatly bothered Bevriedak to hear the new chorus of frightened, shrill cries rising from just below him. His eyes carefully scoured the broad tract of undulating hills, filled in between with a dense mass of movement that the trees could not adequately mask.

His keen ears differentiated the timbre in many of the cries. The intonations were not those of seasoned warriors taken by surprise, but rather of human children gripped by terror. The cries announced that he had found what he was looking for; the main body of the tribal peoples, now refugees forced into fleeing their own lands.

The amorphous, widespread mass of tribal refugees was heading towards the southeast. Bevriedak flew past them, and went into another wide, looping arc to come back around.

He wanted to dampen their fears as soon as he could. The tribal people had been through far too much already. Even if inadvertendly, Bevriedak felt great distress at the thought of adding to their burdens.

When he opened his giant maw again, it was not to roar and cause fright, but rather to speak in the very tongue used by the refugees. "Tribes of the Five Realms! A friend flies above you. Have no fear! I would speak with you," the dragon boomed, in a clear, articulate voice that all within the woodlands below could hear.

The presence of understandable words did little to assuage a great number of the people. Some scattered, fleeing in several directions, while others cowered, under whatever cover they could find. Many hugged themselves close to the base of trees, even as they clutched children tightly to themselves. Still others were paralyzed in their fear, eyes wide with fright and riveted towards the hulking shape gliding over the trees just above them.

The venerable dragon espied a large hill rising just ahead of the main body of refugees. A broad stream wound around its base to one side. The hill's unoccupied summit presented no possible risks of landing and unintentionally hurting any of the humans.

The dragon made a couple of short passes above the hill-top, doing his utmost to ascertain that there were no tribal scouts upon its crown. He then lowered down to a position just above the summit, flapping his wings fast and powerfully to hold him in a hovering pattern.

Using the claws on his rear legs, he clasped and wrenched trees free from the ground, in their entirety. The deep roots clung to the ground in futility, meeting an irresistible force in the enormous dragon's strength. Throwing up showers of dirt and other organic debris, he pulled the trunks up, and deposited the uprooted trees haphazardly on the far side of the slope.

In a short time, the crown of the hill was cleared and laid bare, looking utterly ravaged with its upturned soil and tendrils of roots. Bevriedak did not enjoy rending the blighting scar on the hilltop, but it was a necessary mar on the landscape given the desperate moment. He knew well-enough that nature would eventually reclaim the hilltop, and restore it to fullness once again.

Bevriedak was now feeling a marked pain with each inhalation of breath, knowing very well that it was not from the exertion of clearing the hilltop. Time was noticeably waning in his favor, accelerating with his increased activity. It was certain he would soon need to return to the havens above, or he would be too weak to reach them, in which case he would die.

   With a few powerful flaps, he lowered his back legs down first, bringing his free front claw down afterwards to help balance as he came to stand upon the summit. He knew that the mass of refugees, even those who had dispersed in panic in the wake of his unexpected appearance, were within the expanse of trees directly before him. In the aftermath of his landing, he heard the sustained crying of many children coming from beneath the trees on the other side of the stream, the tiny sounds piercing his heart. He could also hear the sharp whispers of adults, as they admonished the children, and struggled desperately to quiet them.

   "I come as a friend to the tribal people of the Five Realms! I will do you no harm! Send one to speak with me, people of the Five Realms!" Bevriedak called loudly towards the refugees, trying to inject as much of a non-threatening tone as he could into his resonant voice.

   He set his last claw down carefully, rotating it slowly until it was upturned. Wulfstan and the Himmeros were then let free from their dark confines. Bevriedak peered outward towards the trees before him, feeling the steed and the Saxan getting down from the midst of his talons.

   Glancing down a moment later, he saw that the human warrior was looking around in stunned amazement at the uprooted, gouged surface of the hill's apex. The Himmeros was less impressed with the stark testament to an Elder's strength, being far more interested in simply stretching its cramped wings out.

   From his elevated vantage, and with his acute sense of hearing, Bevriedak sensed the tide of refugees had come to a full stop. While they had not moved away, they were keeping a wary distance from the hill. In effect, he was now singularly blocking their forward path.

   The great dragon called out towards the tribal people a few more times, striving to convey his peaceful intentions. He started to worry about causing them to head straight back in the direction that the invasion forces were coming from, by far the very last thing he wanted to do.

   The thought nagged at him on many fronts, raising his concerns about being unable to convey the important messages from the Saxan Ealdorman Aelfric, and the Saxan fleet commander Aethelhere. Yet there was no other way for the dragon to reach out to the tribal peoples than to do what he was now doing.

The situation was rife with irony, and not in a pleasant sense. After waiting for thousands of years, he found that he could not afford to wait for even a couple of hours more.

He could not bear learning that his presence impeded the tribal peoples' passage or, even worse, reversed it, allowing the invaders to catch up and fall upon them. There was also the stark reality that he could not physically endure the effects of the Ban for much longer on his own. Even further, waiting raised the possible chances of the enemy bringing up a sorcerer or Wizard, to wrap Bevriedak thoroughly in the chains of the Ban.

His hopes sinking fast, he tried to stave off the dour feelings. His eyes carefully scanned the horizon for any signs of enemies coming through the skies. Fortunately, as of yet, there were none to be seen.

His heart was beginning to pound more rapidly, compounded by worries as well as the relentless progress of the Ban. The dragon could now do little to mask his labored breathing, and knew without looking that his scales were now dulling in hue, a harbinger of advanced regression.

Bevriedak's piercing eyes finally noted a small figure slowly approaching the base of the hill, flanked a few steps behind by two others. There was no sign of fear or hesitation in the approaching humans' movements, which gave Bevriedak a spark of comfort.

He saw that the lead figure was an older human male, garbed in the distinctive dress of the Five Realms. Despite his advanced years, the older man moved with a supple step, and still carried himself with good posture.

The man wore a pair of leggings and a long, robe-like garment descending well past his knees, the clothing fashioned out of buckskin. A wide buckskin pouch hung at his right side, from a strap slung over his head and extending diagonally across his chest and back. The pouch had a continuous outer fringe of deer-hair tassels, as well as a colorful array of quillwork fashioned into its surface. The quillwork featured an inner sun-like image, surrounded by outwardly spiraling floral patterns.

His moccasins were skillfully adorned as well, displaying an intricate quillwork image of flames that flowed along the central seam on each foot. The ankle-flaps on the mocassins were decorated with a fringe made out of short tufts of deer hair.

An elegant type of headdress topped his wizened, leathery face. Upright eagle feathers sprouted from its summit, and a pair of broad, prominent deer antlers flared up and outward from the sides. His dark eyes were alert and studious, seated deeply where they peered out from behind his large, sharp nose.

He clutched a special item in his hands, extended out before him. It was a wide, rectangular belt, which seemed to be constructed entirely out of small shells, of purple or white coloration.

There was a specific design within the predominantly purple belt. White shells formed the outlines of five connected images, two open squares to either side of what was unmistakably a tree shape in the center.

His right hand was also gripping a peculiar, elongated bundle. Upon closer inspection, Bevriedak saw that the bundle consisted of five arrows tied together at the top, middle, and bottom of its length by hide thongs.

The two men standing a pace behind the old leader, set close to his right and left, were also of interesting appearances.

On the old man's right was another warrior of the Five Realms, wearing little more than buckskin leggings, moccasins, and a short hide kilt. A sash was tied securely around each of the leggings, just below the knee. Bare of chest, his exposed skin was covered in red and black war paint. The swirling patterns of several tattoos formed natural, dark armbands etched into his body.

His high cheeks, pronounced nose, firm jawline, and flinty eyes were fixed into a particularly taut expression. His visage could have been sculpted out of solid rock, as rigid as it looked. Only the strands of black hair comprising the tuft at the top of his head showed any movements, swayed about by gentle breezes.

Many years younger than the first man, and exhibiting exceptional muscle tone, the warrior carried a simple bow in his right hand. A cornhusk quiver filled with arrows was visible over his left shoulder, hanging from a strap that went down and across his chest. A wooden war club was looped into the hide belt around his waist.

The warrior also wore a few additional accoutrements. He had a couple of upper armbands, as well as a necklace, all crafted out of the small, multi-colored, shells.

The image contained within the armband gracing his right arm was particularly interesting, enough that the great dragon took note of it. On a purple background, it displayed the outline of a white circle with four short, ray-like extensions. The latter emerged at even intervals marking the top, bottom, and sides of the disc. The circle itself was filled with several white, diamond-shaped images.

The warrior carried a shell-belt in his right hand, one a little smaller in size to that held by the older tribal man. The second belt displayed a repeating image down the length of its center, portraying the recognizable figures of humans standing side by side, connected from hand to hand. The people were rendered in carefully arranged purple shells, set against a host of white shells forming the background.

Bevriedak then studied the last figure, to the left side of the older tribal male. The man was clearly not a member of one of the woodland tribes.

A large, thickly built individual, he was clad in chain mail, and wearing an iron helm. A long plait of golden hair extended down on each side of his head, alongside locks of free-hanging hair flowing out from below the lower rim of the helm. He bore a large, circular wooden shield, whose leather covering was painted with a swirling white and black pattern.

The shield, Bevriedak noticed, was splattered with dark stains, and a number of chunks and divots had been gouged from its surface and edges. A closer look at the man revealed that his hair was matted and stringy, and his face was caked with grime and sweat.

There was little question as to the origin of the man. He would easily have been absorbed into the gathering Bevriedak had so recently witnessed with King Hakon. That a Midragardan stood with the two tribal men came as a mildly unexpected surprise.

Bevriedak did not doubt the blond-bearded man could invoke a fearsome visage in the heated face of battle. Still, the gawking, amazed expression currently on the man's face was a little humorous to behold.

"I am Deganawida, a Sachem of the Onan, the Keepers of the Sacred Fire, and member of the Bear Clan," a voice finally called up to the dragon, the words rendered in the Quoian tongue.

The voice belonged to the tribal elder standing at the forefront of the trio. The older man spoke the words with clarity and patience, conveying the vibrant, deliberate tone of a leader.

"I was chosen as First Sachem on the Grand Council of the Five Realms, and First Sachem of the Bear Clan," Deganawida continued. He turned, and indicated the two with him. "With me is Gunnar, of the Midragardans, a friend to our people. And Ayenwatha of the Onan, War

Sachem of our village, and a member of the Firaken Clan."

Bevriedak took an immediate liking to the old tribal sachem, seeing great bravery within the expression on the wizened old leader's face. He knew it took no small degree of courage to walk out into the open before a hulking monstrosity, such as an Elder dragon. The dragon was well aware that the populations of Ave had no prior experience with his kind, a fact that he was very sensitive of.

Bevriedak perceived the warmth of generosity and kindness within Deganawida's deepset eyes. Such a genuine look was impossible to feign in the face of an Elder, creatures not easily deceived by beings whose full lives spanned just a handful of years.

The great dragon paused for a moment, giving a slight incline of his head to respectfully acknowledge the introduction. He hoped the tribal elder read it as such, as Bevriedak had no experience in interacting with the tribal people. It was simply fortunate that all Elder possessed a gift of tongues.

"Well met, Deganawida, First Bear Sachem of the Onan, Gunnar, Midragardan and friend of the Five Realms people, and Ayenwatha, War Sachem. I am Bevriedak, of the race of the Elder," the dragon stated in a formal tone, responding in Quoian, his cadence intentionally similar to Deganawida's.

The dragon continued, after a brief pause. "Though I wish otherwise, I do not have long to speak with you. I bear with me Wulfstan, of the Saxan kingdom to the south, across the waters. I have already taken him to speak with King Hakon of Midragard, only a day ago."

Bevriedak wondered if there would be a need for translation regarding the third figure, but the Midragardan reacted as if he understood every word said by the dragon. Gunnar exchanged glances with the other two, especially at the overt mention of the Midragardan king. When he looked back up to the dragon, his expression was filled with astonishment and awe.

"Then let us delay ourselves no further, though some traditions I must try to hold onto. I have brought a special item to offer. It is one that signifies our intention of true relations with you, great dragon. And we extend this to you, Wulfstan of the Saxan kingdom," Deganawida proclaimed, addressing both Bevriedak and the Saxan warrior.

As he spoke, he turned and extended the wide shell-belt he carried over to the keeping of the younger warrior. The war sachem looped his bow over his shoulder, freeing his right hand to hold both of the elaborate shell-belts.

"It is told in our ancient legends of the help a Fire Dragon once gave to our Great Mother, the World Mother" Deganawida continued, speaking in a reverent timbre. "We extend you our hope of friendship, the light of day to shine during this night of darkness holding all of my people."

The old sachem then brought forward a small medallion, pulling it out from the ornately fashioned buckskin and quillwork pouch hanging at his right side. The medallion was made of the same shell-beads that the belts were constructed of.

The medallion was in the shape of a purple disc with a white circle in the center. Like the circle on the younger warrior's armband, it had four evenly placed projections radiating from its outer edge.

Deganawida walked forward slowly, continuing all the way to the base of the slope and up it, until he stood before Wulfstan. The old sachem extended his right arm, and handed the shell-medallion over to Wulfstan. Wulfstan gave the sachem a slight bow, as he accepted the proffered medallion. The Saxan glanced up to Bevriedak after a moment, as if needing a cue for how he was expected to respond.

"Be assured that our intention is of the truest nature. We bring you some hope, if you will have it," Bevriedak replied, in a low voice.

Deganawida looked back up to the great dragon, with heightened curiosity on his face. His eyes narrowed, focused and keen, around his large, sharp nose. "What would you have of us? What tidings do you bear us? I fear you will have to be quick, as we have little time here. Our enemies close in with each passing moment."

"As I also have little time. An ancient Ban weakens me with every moment," Bevriedak replied somberly, intimately feeling the tremors of pain escalating inside of him. As if to punctuate his words, his next breath had the quality of a wheeze. "We bear a message from Aelfric, Ealdorman of the Saxans, and from Aethelhere, a northern thane of their people, and commander of their fleet, as well as one from King Hakon of Midragard. Wulfstan can speak to you of what we have learned. Do any know the Saxan tongue?"

Deganawida shook his head. "We know the words of Midragard, and some among us know words of the Galleans, but only those in the southern and easternmost settlements may speak the words of Saxans.

And it may take us too long to find one who can."

"Very well. Then I shall give his words to you, and yours to him," Bevriedak said, proceeding to inform Wulfstan in the Saxan language of the need for translation.

With Bevriedak's assistance, Wulfstan conveyed the details of the various meetings with Aelfric, Aethelhere, and King Hakon to Deganawida and the other two men. All three listened intently, as the Saxan concluded with the promising tidings gleaned from Aethelhere, right before the dragon had flown to the Five Realms.

Wulfstan described how a sizeable fleet of Saxan ships had been freed up to cross the sea, to come to the help of the people of the Five Realms and their allies. He spoke of the urgent need for the tribal peoples, and any Midragardans with them, to proceed to the southeast; to the place known as the Water-Head Cradle.

Bevriedak was relieved to see the hopeful looks welling up on the faces of Deganawida and the younger war sachem. The blond-haired Midragardian still looked at Bevriedak and Wulfstan with an expression of sheer disbelief, but a brighter spark had come into his weary eyes. The Elder could see Wulfstan's message resonating amongst the trio, as if a saturating, life-giving rain soaking into a parched, withering land.

"Wulfstan, of the honorable Saxans," Deganawida replied in a deep voice, after the Saxan had finished his oration with Bevriedak's help. The sachem nodded his head respectfully towards the Saxan warrior. "You bring us renewed hope, and most wonderful tidings. We deeply thank you for keeping us within your hearts, coming to a land far from yours, at a time when your own families and peoples are in such danger."

Bevriedak conveyed the sachem's words to Wulfstan. The Saxan hesitated for a moment.

"We may come from different lands, but we know what it is to love our land, and our people," Wulfstan replied slowly, through Bevriedak's assistance. His words came a little stilted at first, but as he spoke, they began to flow smoothly. Bevriedak knew the Saxan warrior was speaking from his heart. "As Saxany is for the Saxan people, so is the Five Realms for the people of your tribes.

"Now, all are under attack, and we must stand together against a common enemy. We would dishonor everything we believe if we were to abandon those in need. If we did not honor your right to your lands, then we could not expect for any to honor our rights to our lands. If we do not honor your ways, how could we expect any to honor ours?

"As Midragard answers your call and ours, so we answer yours and theirs. We must stand together, so we can defend our own lands and ways."

The old man listened attentively to Bevriedak's rendering of the words in Quoian. When the dragon had finished, Deganawida gave a deliberate, slow nod towards Wulfstan. Bevriedak sensed the sachem was highly impressed with the words of the much younger Saxan.

Likewise, the war sachem and the Midragardan's expressions had altered slightly, as a different look seeped into their eyes. They too had regarded Wulfstan's response in high esteem, and the dragon could tell a nascent respect for the Saxan had taken root within them.

"You speak with much wisdom, young Saxan," Deganawida said. "We will guide our people to the Water-Head Cradle, as you have asked of us. With the use of scouts from the air, you will be able to know where our people are, so that you can bring your ships in. We can only hope and beseech the One Spirit that there will be enough time left to all of us."

Pausing, Deganawida looked towards the war sachem at his right. He retrieved the belt he had been carrying at the outset, and his eyes then lowered to the second belt of shells, the one Ayenwatha still held onto.

"I asked Ayenwatha to bring this belt with us, when you called to us, as you called out in terms of friendship. I wish to send you with a sacred symbol of our own trust and friendship, in the manner of my people. We may not be able to do all things regarding the ceremonies and customs that are time-honored among our people. We may not be able to give you honor in the way we would truly wish, but please accept this further symbol from us. Please know that what it represents is given to you in the truest spirit."

At a nod from Deganawida, the younger war sachem walked forward slowly. Ayenwatha presented Wulfstan with the predominantly white belt, holding it forward with two hands, such that the purple human figures lining the center stood on an even level as they faced the Saxan. Though a little gingerly, the Saxan warrior accepted the belt.

"The white speaks of purity, and the figures in purple show a symbol of alliance, and mutual friendship," Deganawida explained, through Bevriedak.

Wulfstan continued holding the shell-bead belt before his

eyes, staring with a look of wonder at it. Deganawida then gazed up at Bevriedak, with a genuinely burdened expression.

"I deeply regret that we do not have one with a symbol of one of your kind upon it," Deganawida said, in an apologetic tone. "We have not yet had the great honor of having a friendship with one of your kind. Please understand I would have made sure that one would have been fashioned, if I knew this day was to come."

The words were not necessary, as Bevriedak understood that the belt applied just as much to the Elder as it did to the Saxans, whether or not his own particular form had been worked into the images. "I humbly thank you, honored Sachem of the Five Realms. I know much of the ways and paths of your people. Know that it is a great honor to have the friendship of the people of the Five Realms, and that you have my enduring friendship."

"I have heard something of the old tales, and know something of this … Ban … that you speak of," Deganawida then stated. "You have brought your message of hope to us, and it has been gratefully received. Do not suffer any longer, Bevriedak of the Elder. Go now to your refuge in the skies."

Deganawida then turned his attentions towards Wulfstan. "May the great Creator, the One-Spirit, light your pathway. My people will meet yours at the Water Head-Cradle, if all is not yet lost."

Wulfstan gave a low bow in response. At Bevriedak's additional prompting, he hustled to gather the loitering Himmeros. The Himmeros had wandered a short distance during the conversation, more interested in nosing about than in listening to the conversation.

Wulfstan led the steed back by its tether, and they climbed back up into the open claw of the dragon. Bevriedak closed the claw gently, securing his passengers once again.

Carefully turning the claw over, to face towards the ground, he nodded towards the old sachem below. "We will meet again, honorable Sachem. Nothing is more certain than that promise, when you know the true nature of the Creator's world, the One you know as the One Spirit," he said, drawing upon a truth built upon his own living witness, hearkening back to the very first rays of life's light within Ave.

The old sachem paused, with a curious expression welling up on his face. The look remained for a few moments, before relaxing into a peaceful, even joyous, countenance. The change was accompanied by the emergence of a lively glimmer within his eyes, and the spread of an exhuberant smile not entirely unlike that of a young human child.

It was as if all the burdens, cares, and sorrows weighing down upon the old man had lifted, if but for a few brief, merciful moments. Bevriedak innately knew the old sachem had garnered the dragon's intended meaning, a message of reassurance and encouragement.

"Farewell to all of you, my new friends," Bevriedak added, pleased with the sachem's understanding.

Tensing into a crouch, and tightening his muscles, Bevriedak turned carefully to face towards the far slope. He thrust off the top of the hill in an upward leap, and pumped his wings vigorously. Trees swayed, leaves swirled, and branches cracked, broke, and were cast all about in the tempest churned in his wake.

The dragon was just high enough off the ground that his wings were able to catch the air and bear him aloft. Bevriedak was soon streaking in a sharp incline towards the Forbidden Dominion, motivated by his urgency to get free of the Ban's clutches.

Wulfstan would soon have to be returned to his own land, and Bevriedak resolved to take him there. The time involved would be welcome, as the Elder had much to think about. As he began to ponder his encounter with the tribal sachem, Bevriedak found he had a peculiar feeling that there was something strangely familiar about the old man.

Bevriedak could not yet discern just what it was about the tribal sachem that elicited the sense of an elusive memory, one currently beyond reach of his mind's grasp. But he meant to give the matter some thorough, extended reflection.

For the moment, he had other hurdles, as his breathing was now reaching a very precarious state. Pain wracked his body, and he felt much weaker physically, but at least his spirits were rising faster than his body was ascending. A part of him felt with certainty that he was beginning to make up for ages of lost time.

MAGNUS

The main body of the pack loped farther ahead, disappearing amid the trees. While they were out of sight, they had not passed beyond the senses of the mind. Magnus, acutely attuned to their presences, could feel them with the clarity of a purely physical sensation.

He had put several leagues between himself and the village. Another day had risen, and matured, and Magnus was growing weary after enduring much of the previous night in a state of restlessness.

It did not even occur to him that he had eaten nothing since he had left the village. Nor did it strike him that he had only consumed a few gulps of water, out of a stream that he and the wolves crossed in the chilled mists of the early morning.

Even those minimal handfuls were imbibed more out of ingrained habit than conscious desire. Magnus felt utterly numb on the inside, even as his legs bore him ever deeper into the forest. His thoughts were fixed on new horizons, and leaving the past in the past, but he slogged forward with the heaviest of hearts.

The wolves sensed his plague of despondency from the outset, and had empathically given him space, as the gray, cloudy pall fell over his spirit. They exhibited none of the animated playfulness they usually displayed, intimately feeling Magnus' state of sorrow, as much as he could feel their own dispositions.

For Magnus, the trek into the forest was a journey filled with inner travails and painful memories. The stark feelings of loss were still agonizingly fresh, like open wounds bleeding from his body, mind, and soul. It was virtually all he could do just to continue forward.

Nearly all the people of the village, who formed the only community he had ever known, had essentially rejected him, whether overtly or tacitly. He had lost his natural family long ago, and now the roots of any sense of fellowship with his own kind had been harshly torn out from beneath him.

In a way, the affair related strongly to the banishment of his own father, designated an outlaw and cast out from his home so many years ago. Magnus was under no indictment that would openly allow anyone who might wish to slay him, but the effects of his recent expulsion were undeniably similar. Magnus felt, in all truth, like an outcast.

The burdensome rejection was tempered somewhat by the bonds he felt with his two closest friends, Thorstein and Sturla. They had boldly stood forth in the face of the torrent of animosity, defiant and loyal. It was readily apparent the pair had been willing to shoulder what Magnus was being faced with, in the process risking far more than Magnus ever wanted them to.

Even had each of Magnus' arms been lined continuously, from shoulder to hand, with silver arm rings, it still would not match the true riches of having two such friends. There was no question wealth could be measured in ways other than silver and gold.

A long, undulating howl suddenly pierced the still air. Magnus quickly brought himself out of his dour reflections. Looking around, and snapping back into focus, he realized he had likely traveled far beyond the territory he normally roamed with his pack.

He recognized that the howl indicated an alarm towards intruders, and it had not been emitted by one of the wolves from Magnus' pack. As other howls poured in from the surrounding area, the wolves with Magnus emerged from the trees, grouping themselves around him. Magnus cursed his foolishness, as he had placed his pack needlessly at the risk of a confrontation.

Another howl then came from just ahead, though it had a slightly different tonal quality. Only the refined sharpness of Magnus' ears caught the subtle distinction.

"Another of the Wolf Kin," Magnus whispered, as much to himself as to his quadrupedal companions. He was a little relieved, as it decreased the chances of conflict, as might have occurred in an encounter with a large, wild pack.

Magnus proceeded forth cautiously, as did the wolves with him, who kept him close within their midst. He periodically cupped his hands and made distinctive howling sounds of his own, which uniquely identified himself as one of the Wolf Kin.

He listened earnestly for the expected response. It was not very long before an answering call filled the air.

Magnus peered farther ahead, through the narrow trunks of the younger trees all about him. His eyes caught some wisps of movement, and in moments another group of large wolves silently padded into view, heading directly towards his pack.

Jumping down from the lower branches of one of the trees ahead, landing deftly in front of the approaching wolves, was a tall, slender figure with flowing black hair. Walking with purposeful, lithe steps at the head of the other wolves, the figure strode directly towards Magnus.

When Magnus got a closer look at the figure, his heart almost stopped beating within his chest. Thick, waving locks of raven-black hair tumbled down around a set of strong, gracefully rounded shoulders. A set of wide, piercing blue eyes regarded Magnus carefully, emanating alertness, confidence, and intelligence.

While a unique kind of beauty, the woman coming towards him had an untamed, unpredictable air swirling about her. Her full lips were set into a stoic expression just above a narrow chin, aligned symmetrically with the higher lines of her cheeks. Her nose was aquiline, well-balanced with the proportions of her face. Her dark eyebrows were now pulled closer together, in a sign of pensive scrutiny.

She was clad simply, in a rather snug-fitting, brown woolen tunic, and leggings of a similar hue. She had a leather belt with a couple of pouches, and a small, sheathed seax, affixed to it. There were no shining rings decorating her hands, the left of which gripped a strung longbow. A cylindrical quiver filled with fletched arrows hung securely at her waist from a leather strap running across her body and around her right shoulder. Her only distinguishable ornamentation was a small amulet, crafted into the spear-symbol of the Western Church.

"I did not expect visitors today," she said, in a relaxed voice, middle-ranged in tone. "And definitely not one of my own Brethren."

Suddenly, her face broke into a carefree smile, though her eyes remained alert. "You look a little surprised to see me, so I suppose I should introduce myself, to my fellow Brethren. I am Brynhild, and you might say, most correctly, that I am Wolf Kin."

Magnus stared at her for a couple of moments longer, as if she was the only being existing in all of Ave.

"I am Magnus, from the village at Glittering River," he finally replied, breaking out of his momentary entrancement with awkwardness. "Yes, and one of the Brethren."

"I had guessed that, with all of the wolves standing around you," she replied with a mirthful smile, and an amused sparkle within her blue eyes.

He found himself mesmerized by her comeliness, in wonderment at the sudden, unexpected encounter with a female member of their ancient order. There were long-established traditions regarding the Shield Maiden Wizards, who were like daughters to Wodan. There were also sagas heralding strong, courageous women, who led their families amid times of great trial and uncertainty. Such women forged celebrated destinies in the chaotic wakes of their husbands' deaths.

Midragard had always had a sincere, deep respect for the strength and prominence of its women. They had always been a significant part of the land's enduring legacies, and had never been taken for granted. As such, Magnus was not entirely surprised to discover the reality of a female member of his order. His amazement was simply due to the fact that Brynhild was truly a great rarity among their kind.

"Yes, the others, whether Kin, Ulfhednar, or Berzerkers, find me to be a little uncommon," she replied in good humor, with a slight shrug. "It is not a simple story, but then nobody's story is ever truly simple."

"It is just as much of a surprise to encounter another of our order out here now, as I was not thinking where I was headed," Magnus admitted to her, as there was little use pretending otherwise.

"Such a lack of thinking can get you into danger quickly, wayward Magnus. It is very fortunate that you wandered to my pack's territory," she responded, the admonishment within her words rendered lightly in tone.

"It is fortunate," Magnus agreed, knowing the various kinds of dangers he could have blundered into within the wilds of Midragard. He knew that his wolves would have been wary towards most threats, but there were dangers in the world of kinds going far beyond physical senses, lurking in dark haunts, and mist-shrouded swathes of untamed wilderness.

"Know that a Draugr inhabits an area not too far from my own boundaries. And while I have an understanding with a Huldra whose territory overlaps my boundary in another part, I doubt she would have a similar disposition towards a man like you," Brynhild stated, as if seeking to instill a deeper caution back in Magnus.

"I am glad I have someone with me who knows these lands, who can warn me of such dangers," Magnus replied.

Brynhild's warnings regarding the locales of the two menaces were very sobering. He hoped he never encountered a Draugr, a wicked terror that only the mightiest could even hope to overcome.

Huldras were a different kind of threat entirely. The lusts of some Huldra were known to be insatiable, often of a predatory nature, which met with lethal ends for the hapless men they lured into their embraces.

"Now you know, so take your next steps governed by a better wisdom," Brynhild pronounced, with a grin.

"Count me as one who is well-reprimanded, Brynhild. And I

thank you for not being too harsh in doing so," Magnus responded.

"I must look out for one of my fellow Brethren," Brynhild said amiably. "It would be very amiss for me not to do so."

"I must admit I am not entirely myself, and am not always this reckless," Magnus confessed, mustering up a grin.

Though his face displayed a friendly mien, his eyes could not mask the heaviness of his deeper feelings. His inner turmoil pressed outward, the wells of sadness within him reflecting in the look of his eyes.

She gazed at him intently for a moment, her eyes narrowing, as her face grew decidedly more somber. Her voice was low and gentle, and her words showed her recognition of his deeper state. "You have just been through a great and terrible pain, one that is not of the body?"

Magnus nodded slowly, and the open acknowledgement brought up a little more of the emptiness and sorrow like a black bile. The effect was mercifully fleeting, as he stared into her eyes, the deep, blue pools filled with the presence of compassion.

"Part of my own story, and also not very simple, I am afraid," Magnus replied, in a subdued voice.

Brynhild's smile slowly returned, spreading across her face. This time, the expression conveyed a different message; one of solace, rather than any merriment.

"Then perhaps we should travel together for a time, and swap our own sagas with each other," Brynhild responded lightly, in a tone of invitation. "It would be good to have some company with my own kind, as much as I love my other companions."

A gentle peace soaked into Magnus at her generous smile and proposition. At last, standing right before him was someone who could really understand what he was, as one of the Wolf Kin. She was also someone who would know what drove him to pursue such a solitary, difficult path in life. It would undeniably be welcome to have the company of a kindred spirit, one who was not tied to his former life within the village.

"I would like that, very much so," Magnus replied, without a shred of doubt. His eyes then looked slowly towards either side, taking in the sight of the lupine forms gathered all around. "And it would seem our other companions are already getting along well enough."

While Magnus and Brynhild had conversed, the two groups of wolves interspersed amongst each other. Unlike a normal pack of wild wolves, none seemed to have any urge to stand up to each other, to vie for any degree of supremacy. It would have been impossible to bring two wild packs together in a manner like that now taking place around Magnus and the raven-haired Wolf Kin.

Members of the ancient order tended to absorb some characteristics of wolves over time, culminating in the deeply mystical transition of becoming a full Ulfhednar. In a similar manner, some human characteristics transferred to the wolves that the Wolf Kin lived among.

A tranquil harmony reigned in the air, even as the leading males from the two packs walked directly up to one another. The two males were particularly massive wolves, of nearly equal stature.

The one with Magnus' pack was covered in rich silver fur, and the one with Brynhild's had a luxuriant coat of midnight black. The silver wolf was edging forward in age, but was still savvy, and strong enough to remain at the top of the pack's hierarchy. The ebon beast with Brynhild looked to Magnus' eyes to be considerably younger than his silver counterpart, ascendant in the full bloom of strength and vitality.

Neither bared its fangs towards the other, even though neither made any sort of move to crouch, lower their head, offer to lick the other's muzzle, or any other manner of deferential lupine gesture. There were none of the timeless behavioral nuances involved in the identification and ranking of wolves in a pack.

The silver and black wolves kept their heads held high, their respective amber and golden gazes regarding each other confidently. Magnus noted the two wolves were careful to avert their eyes from locking too firmly with those of their counterpart. Their mouths were relaxed, looking to be hanging just barely open with the lips pulled partly back.

Unexpectedly, Magnus witnessed an unusual phenomenon occur between the two pack leaders. Almost in the same moment, both of the pack leaders lowered their heads slightly, and their previously erect ears splayed out to the sides of their great heads. A couple heartbeats later, each leaned forward, and gave a delicate nip under the chin of the other.

The majestic wolves had acquiesced to each other. The outward sign could only be interpreted that the two pack leaders regarded each other as equals. Magnus glanced over towards Brynhild, who had the same look of wonderment upon her face, as he now had on his own.

Around the two pack leaders, the other wolves engaged in sniffing, nuzzling, and gently nipping each other in a manner that both reflected and expanded the sentiments expressed by the two leaders. It was an astounding display that Magnus knew would have never occurred in the wild, especially if a pack crossed the demarcated territorial boundaries of another.

Magnus suddenly realized that another human-like trait had filtered over to the wolves with him and Brynhild. There was a propensity within many humans to engage strangers in a spirit of goodwill. While the noble quality was not universally exhibited in humankind, it transcended the strict pack bonds of the wolf.

"They are getting along very well, Magnus," Brynhild remarked, grinning as she looked upon the black wolf. "It is not a sight I ever expected to see, not to this extent. I expected them to keep their distance, at best. Their reaction heartens me greatly, and is a good sign, even more so, as Nightheart is a very headstrong, fiercely proud male."

As if sensing her thoughts, the great black wolf turned its radiant golden eyes toward her. The front of its body crouched down playfully, as its ears splayed out once again.

"Not yet, Nightheart," she replied, in an amused tone.

"And Sky Star is a very cautious, careful one, wise among his kind, as much as he is yet strong," Magnus added. "Not one prone to ever take unnecesary risks."

The large silver wolf's amber eyes then turned in Magnus' direction, at the mention of the name he had personally given to the pack leader. Magnus felt an effusion of warm affection from the wolf's gaze, as it regarded him quietly for a moment, ears splaying, and open mouth resembling a human grin.

"Then I would say we have all started out very well together," Brynhild said, reaching her right arm forward. "A good and favorable meeting, Magnus."

Magnus returned the proferred clasp about the forearm, immediately feeling the strength coursing through her arm and grip. "Yes, a favorable meeting," he replied contentedly, a full smile breaking out on his face.

"Should we walk towards the territory that you and yours live in, or should I take you around my own?" Brynhild queried.

"I do not feel ready to return to my own area, not just yet. It is too near the place where I am no longer welcome, and my spirits have already been lifted here, within your boundaries," Magnus confessed, a melancholy edge creeping back into his voice.

"Then the matter is decided easily enough," Brynhild replied swiftly, and intently. She then asked him, "Have you had much to eat lately?"

Magnus shook his head. "No, and it is because of the last part of the story, which I have not told you yet."

"As it happens, I was just about to go on a hunt when we detected the approach of your pack. There is a large herd of great elk moving through this area. They are not far from here. If your pack would choose to join us, there will be more than enough to feed all," Brynhild stated. After a moment, she added, as if an afterthought, "More than enough for a Jarl's feast."

"I would be very glad to join you," Magnus replied, knowing he was in need of food. His appetite, dampened in his recent solitude, was already showing signs of returning. "Though I fear that in the tempest of my anger I left my belt with my knife, and my own bow and quiver, back in the village."

"The last part of the story?" Brynhild asked sensitively, with a sympathetic timbre.

"Yes, the ending of that tale," Magnus confirmed in a low voice.

"All is not lost then, Magnus, though we will have to first pass close to my father's estate. I believe the good Jarl can spare us a belt, a knife, and another bow," she replied encouragingly. "My father is a demanding man, but he is fair and generous. Just do not ask for ax or sword. I fear he will not part with such so easily, even if he could arm the warriors of ten large estates."

"Guttorm?" Magnus ventured cautiously, his eyes widening in incredulity. There was only one Jarl that could be located nearby. He asked, "You are the Jarl's daughter?"

Brynhild tilted her head back slightly, looking upward, and laughing vibrantly. She then gazed back toward Magnus, with great amusement spread across her face, her blue eyes twinkling in merriment at his expression of stunned amazement.

"Yes, I suppose it would take a Jarl's daughter to chance a road such as the one I have chosen to take. Though I would say he was probably expecting something much different out of his daughter. Yet he does not begrudge me, as he loves to think that his daughter is like one of the legendary Shield Maidens of the First Age.

"Still, it was no easy thing for him, as he had many interested in marrying me. Luckily, I had a couple of strong, attractive sisters that chose to marry the ambitious sons of his closest allies. And my brothers distracted him enough with their own squabbles and mishaps. He has been able to suffer me taking this path, and has lived with it quite well, better than I ever expected, knowing the usual concerns of Jarls. In truth, I feel guilty that I do not visit him often enough."

Magnus could not suppress a chuckle, imagining the look on Njal's face if he knew that a daughter of Jarl Guttorm now walked with Magnus, and that she was a member of the very same order he was. It was a coincidence of staggering proportions.

"You are very amused by all of this, yes? So, Magnus, do you know my father?" she asked, grinning amiably.

"No, I have not met him. I just know someone who would be more than surprised that I've met you, and that the Jarl's daughter is Wolf Kin," Magnus replied.

"There are always surprises in this world. It is what keeps life interesting," Brynhild commented.

"To say the least," Magnus responded, shaking his head in bemusement.

Brynhild smiled, and took a few strides forward, before pausing, and looking back. "Well, what are you waiting for? There are more surprises to be found, and a bow, belt, and knife to be obtained."

Shaking his head again, and marveling at the abrupt turnabout in his fortunes, Magnus started after her with a feeling of rejuvenation. The wolves of both packs fell in alongside the two, as the combined group headed briskly through the trees.

Magnus was merely grateful, as he glanced over at Brynhild. He was content to remain in the moment, forgetting the past, and not worrying himself about the future. He certainly was not about to question his sudden change in fortune, as he had walked alone long enough.

BEVRIEDAK

As each and every moment endured in the world below drained Bevriedak's vitality and strength, every moment spent within the lofty sanctuary renewed him. After the sorely taxing flight from Saxany to the Five Realms, and making the laborious climb back up to the Forbidden Dominions, it was necessary to gird his depleted strength as much as possible for the last part of the journey.

In the present, he would spend only as long as it took to recoup his strength adequately. While he did so, there was one other individual he wanted to seek council from, in addition to harboring hopes of a more distant nature. Once that was accomplished, no matter the outcome, the burdensome onus he had so willfully taken upon himself would continue.

Wulfstan and his Skiantha steed were left for the moment within Bevriedak's own primary dominion, to partake of a needed rest themselves. The Elder was well aware that the mode of travel they had bravely endured inside his claws was far from comfortable.

Rest was about the only thing that the Elder could offer them. Bevriedak did not have the time to hunt them down any more food. He knew their only sustenance during the course of the entire journey had been the Roc meat he had earlier provided for them. It was not a minor concern, as the energies of both the human and the winged beast were undoubtedly lower.

Fortunately, in Bevriedak's domain, as in all the havens of the Elder, there were several small pools containing the purest water that could be found in all of Ave. The two visitors could drink aplenty of the invigorating fluid, but as food was something that was hunted, and not stored within Bevriedak's realm, they would still be left hungry.

The behemoth form of Bevriedak safely within the renewing confines of the Forbidden Dominions, he soared across the highest edges of the sky. His strength slowly returned, and the motion of flying was no longer laden down with the collective, debilitating encumbrances brought on by the Ban.

He was now flying far above a solid, sprawling mass of dirty-looking gray clouds. It was a portion of an extensive formation gliding above the world below. Featureless and flat in appearance, the distant cloud plain was rich with gathering, condensing moisture. The clouds portended a significant amount of rain for the lower surface of Ave.

SPIRIT OF FIRE

Their presence was not a worry for Bevriedak, as the gray cloud masses would not come even remotely close to threatening the unsullied environment of the Forbidden Dominions. The icy air he now flew through was soothing to the outer surface of his own body. It was a welcome relief from the compressing, tightening sensations riddling him mercilessly in the lower skies and ground below.

Another of the many havens provided for the Elder throughout the Forbidden Dominions came into view, filling the horizon just before him. As he gazed upon it, he knew it was the specific haven he sought.

In many ways, it felt markedly better to be in places where he was no longer a giant among his immediate surroundings. He had forgotten just how large the bodies of the Elder really were, in comparison to the things of the world's surface. His perspective had shifted somewhat after the many long ages spent living far above Ave.

He felt a sense of relief that he had not yet stepped on any of the diminutive humans. As he had been surrounded by thousands of humans close to the Saxan encampment, that feat alone was a small miracle in itself.

A thin formation of white, misty vapors was buoyed forward by soft winds crossing over the haven's ivory terrain. The pure white masses of the haven formed what looked to be a wide plain, going on for many leagues before rising into an expanse of rises akin to low hills. Just beyond the low hill-like formations rose a line of towering, mountainous forms.

The milky, evanescent tendrils of the delicate mists wafted over and around him, as he descended lower. The dragon stretched his legs out to their farthest reach, easing them forward slightly to absorb the initial impact of his landing.

This time he did not have to worry about bearing small travelers. Having the complete use of all four limbs once again made the landing much smoother, and far more natural. Landing with three limbs had been a cumbersome act requiring great concentration. He gave a couple of strong flaps to help steady his body, just before his talons sank into the spongy, snow-white surface.

It was the same haven he had taken momentary refuge within recently, namely during the night of the returning journey from Midragard. The thought of his condition following the departure from Midragard almost made the giant dragon wince in remembrance. The effects of the Ban had rendered the Elder into a harrowing, tormented state of being, before he brought a cessation to the Ban's enervating power by lifting himself into the safe confines of the Forbidden Dominions.

The other Elder he now sought was the very same one Bevriedak had spoken with during those few short hours of healing. That stay within the Forbidden Dominion had seemed altogether too short, but the circumstances demanded that they continue onward, far before Bevriedak wanted to.

A great brightness filled the unobstructed sky above, where the direct light of the sun shone down with its full brilliance upon the iridescent dwelling places of the Elder. The unfiltered, warm rays of light reflected in their purity off the immaculate whiteness forming the substance of the extraordinary Elder sanctuary.

At a springy bound, Bevriedak traversed the surface of the snow-like plains. His sights were set upon a cavernous opening, beckoning from high in the side of one of the mountain-like shapes overlooking the stretch of smaller hills and flatter lowlands. His wings tucked into his sides, it felt good to have his leg muscles pulse and relax in a consistent rhythm. As he limbered up, and a buoyant spring flowed back into his every step, the great dragon trotted more swiftly towards the high peak with the yawning entrance.

The formations rising ahead formed an extensive line sharply demarcating the boundary area where the ivory plains ended, and the host of ascending highlands arose. Some of the towering formations located deeper into the range were large enough to be akin to the greatest mountains on the face of the world below. The lofty sentinels loomed mightily over the broad, cottony plain, surmounted themselves by the unmarred radiance of the turquoise sky, spread elegantly above their exalted pinnacles.

The Elder havens within the Forbidden Dominions were the last significant elements before reaching the uppermost edge of the world itself. Seen in the unveiled glory of a bright, shining day, Bevriedak always found they were an incredible sight to behold, even after so many centuries spent living in their midst.

As he approached the outward line of hills, his destination rising a little farther beyond, he picked up his pace further. The height of the opening in the slope of the cloud-mountain appeared to expand ever higher and wider. By the time he closed the final distance on the great plain, drawing up to the base of the first of the hills, the magnitude of the approaching opening's size could be truly appreciated.

Picking up even more speed, Beviedak sprung upward. He snapped his wings out to the sides, flapping them vigorously, and feeling the renewed strength coursing within them.

The great dragon used his wings to carry him up the long slope of the first hill. He crested it in mere moments, continuing out over the crowns of several other rises as he flew towards the greater summit ahead.

His broad wings pumped and pulled him higher and farther, until he passed over the bevy of hills and right into the foreground of the cavernous opening he sought. His clawed feet pressed deep into the surface as he landed once again, touching down just within the sprawling shadow of the immense passageway.

Even as enormous as he was, the gaping entrance towered over Bevriedak. It was easily wide enough that five Elder of Bevriedak's size could walk comfortably side by side into the colossal passageway. Folding his wings against his body once again, he stepped forward slowly, into the opening.

He instantly sensed the presence of the one he was seeking. A little apprehension tugged at his mind, as he thought about what he was there for, and what he hoped to accomplish. Momentous implications hung over the forthcoming audience. Coupled with the uncertainties concerning the matter at hand, the result was an unsettled disposition as he continued forward.

The entryway shortly narrowed down into a channel about twice Bevriedak's width. The ceiling of the passage lowered only slightly, remaining well above the top of his head, at the dragon's fullest height.

The passageway curved gradually to the left for several paces, before opening suddenly into a magnificent cavern, of immense scope. The powerful essence of the Elder that Bevriedak sought radiated throughout the capacious enclosure.

The cavern itself was truly gigantic, large enough to fit a small horde of Elder within its environs. It reached at least a thousand feet high, at its most elevated point. A small, roughly circular opening was set within the center of the snowy canopy overhead. Streams of bathing light poured down through the aperture, reflecting brightly off a cascading multitude of shiny, near-translucent particles. The mote-like particles methodically swirled and drifted about in a spiraling fashion, forming a column of light.

The light and its attendant twinkling particles touched softly upon a familiar form. The creature the light caressed was leisurely basking in the gentle warmth of the luminescent beams, lying in a posture of repose.

"Gerasen!" called Bevriedak exuberantly, his booming voice multiplying like a chorus within the mystical cloud-cavern.

After the cavern settled back into full silence, the equally resonant voice of Gerasen replied, "And who would disturb my slumber?" The voice carried a noticeably playful quality, just underneath the surface.

"Your visits are many of late, Bevriedak," Gerasen continued in a trice, with a stronger hint of amusement sounding within the dragon's words.

"Aye, that they are," Bevriedak replied, in a light-hearted fashion, as he proceeded forward into the chamber.

Towards the center of the cavern, the grand form of Gerasen lay curled upon a raised oval surface. The sizeable platform appeared to sprout from the ground in a continuous outgrowth of the spongy, white matter that formed the plains, hills, surfaces, walls, ceilings, and just about everything else across the expanses of the Elders' great havens.

The surface of the dais was markedly uneven close to where Gerasen's body lay. It sloped down where it disappeared beneath the dragon's girth, the depression forming a distinct shape matching the contours of the Elder's massive body.

The rays of warm sunlight raining down through the floating particles were cast into a flurry of sparkles and reflections all along the shiny surfaces of Gerasen's multitudinous scales. The color of the titanic dragon was of the deepest ebony, like midnight in a starless sky. In his elemental features, he was very similar in form to Bevriedak, though noticeably greater in both height and wingspan.

His two front claws were crossed before him, one atop the other, while his rear legs were tucked underneath, at his sides. His wings were folded, resting snugly against his long body.

Gerasen slowly raised his huge head, as if he had just been awakened from the tranquility of a deep, uninterrupted slumber. The broad nostrils at the end of his rounded snout flared widely, as the dragon inhaled several deep breaths.

The dragon's vivid, sapphire eyes, flecked with gold, regarded his friend with more than idle curiosity. The rounded, piercing black irises constricted in the brightness of the surrounding light, as Gerasen peered intently at Bevriedak.

"I would not disturb you so soon, without good reason," Bevriedak stated.

"It was no small reason that brought you before, little more than one day ago," Gerasen replied firmly, as if to remind his friend of the recent meeting.

Gerasen uncrossed his claws and stretched them out in front of him, lifting his head higher and extending his massive neck. His sleepy eyes widened a little more, further exposing the bright, sparkling orbs that looked far more rare and precious than the most desired jewels found within Ave.

"Is the Saxan with you this time?" Gerasen asked, with a stern lilt.

Bevriedak was not surprised by the grave concern present within the dragon's voice. Gerasen knew Wulftsan had rested on the outer boundary of his refuge during Bevriedak's recent visit.

The ebon dragon did not share Bevridak's favor for the creatures dwelling upon Ave's surface. Gerasen had not been pleased that Bevriedak found it acceptable to lodge a living human within the Forbidden Dominions. He had let Bevriedak know clearly that he was not in alignment with the silver dragon's judgement.

"He is now resting in my own dwelling lands. I meant no offense to your wishes the last time I was here. It was only a matter of necessity that brought the human with me, and nothing more. I will be here only for a short time, as my task presses me to suffer the pain of the Ban again soon," Bevriedak informed Gerasen, in a placating tone. "I also bring you some new word from below."

"And I have some word for you as well," Gerasen replied, shifting his substantial weight around, such that he propped the bulk of his upper body up further, squaring it towards Bevriedak.

"I fear the word I bring now will not bring you joy," Bevriedak announced, the timbre of his voice changing, like a dark thundercloud passing over the face of the sun.

Gerasen paused, reacting to the intense look on the other's face. "Tell me what you will, and I shall tell you of what has happened since you were last here."

"You already know well the Unifier brings war and death to the kingdoms of the lower world," Bevriedak replied. "Some yet hold out, but two of these have been invaded, and Midragard will likely be attacked very soon."

"I have thought long upon this, though all that our kind can do is watch, as has been our great burden for these many ages," Gerasen reflected aloud, in a more subdued tone. His bright eyes seemed to dim and narrow, as if reflecting the weight of his inner thoughts. After a few moments, his gaze rose to meet that of Bevriedak. "And this burden grows, for I have come to believe that this Unifier, of Avanor, is the Chosen One of Jebaalos, maybe His very Son … sent into our world from the vile renegade's hellish realms. Is that what you would tell me?"

"Only a part. And it is not all I have to say, my friend," Bevriedak responded, his head bowing, as he looked downward with a melancholy countenance. He found his spirit was sagging under the ponderous weight of the apprehensions he felt, in light of what he was about to say.

"Not all that you have to say?" Gerasen replied, looking to Bevriedak solemnly.

"I have already broken the Oath. And I will break it again. Perhaps so many times it will be hard to count the transgressions," Bevriedak declared. "I would not leave the Five Realms, Saxany, and Midragard to face this Unifier alone, knowing what I know, and believing what I now believe.

"I am going to enter this war as often as I am able, and do what I can for the people of these desperate lands. May the Almighty forgive me, but my soul tells me I do not break the greater laws, those transcending the very foundations of the world"

A cumbersome tension mounted, swiftly filling the chamber, as Gerasen silently pondered the words of Bevriedak.

"You have broken the Oath, and you openly resolve to break it again and again?" Gerasen responded incredulously, with a wisp of exasperation. His voice continued slow and purposeful. "And what do you think to accomplish? None of us can hope to stand against the Ban's power. It cannot be undone, unless the Almighty willed it directly."

Bevriedak held Gerasen's hardened stare, refusing to let go of the Elder's steely gaze. He wanted Gerasen to know just how ardently committed he was to his newfound path.

"I know we believe that it is not our place to intervene," Bevriedak replied grimly. "But much intervention occurs already by the darker powers spreading across the lands below us. Forces of a very powerful nature intervene everywhere for the benefit of the Unifier, whether we choose to act or not. I fear that even some among our kind are being swayed towards darker purposes, if they have not been turned to a dark path already."

"Such would only mean the End of Days are upon us," Gerasen responded curtly, plainly vexed with Bevriedak's intentions.

Bevriedak did not answer Gerasen immediately. He kept staring at the other Elder, with a look conveying a silent confirmation of Gerasen's supposition.

"Always the End of Days. You sound like so many of the monks from below," Gerasen responded, with an irritated timbre showing he understood Bevriedak's meaning well enough. "Tidings of war, famines, droughts, earthquakes. Always signs of the End of Days.

"I do not condemn you for looking for an end to our ages of exile. Why would I not desire the ending of the Ban, when we can finally rejoin the world in its fullness? Do you not think my spirit would soar upon receiving such a hope, even if we had to endure a brief time of conflagration at the cusp of attaining it? No, Bevriedak, none of this talk is new. The End of Days has always been proclaimed."

"I do not seek to speak for you, but I could not stand by idly," Bevriedak responded steadfastly. "The human Wulfstan, who was willing to die just in trying to reach my dwelling lands, has helped me to see what should have been clear to me years and years ago. I do not think our kind should be idle, when those seeking to enslave all of creation place no limits upon their own actions. But it is for each of us to decide on our own."

The implication was direct and intended. It was also a momentous personal admission. With all the ages of knowledge and experience an Elder possessed, it was difficult to even conceive that a better way could be gleaned from a mortal human.

"You ask me to cast aside the Oath we have followed for very good reason, for numerous centuries? Are these truly such new times that we must seek to break the Oath?" Gerasen asked. His next words bordered on outright accusation, "Do you wish to deny the will of the All-Father?"

Bevriedak studied the face of the other dragon closely. He sensed Gerasen was deeply troubled, far more so than when Bevriedak had seen him during his last visit. A part of Bevriedak knew the manifest signs of discomfort in Gerasen were not only due to the new tidings. There was something else occuring, an element hidden, which laced Gerasen's last questions with a perceptible trace of guilt.

Bevriedak honed in on his cognition of that trace, seeking to bring more of the deeper truth to the surface. "What more has happened, Gerasen? What have you yet to tell me?" he asked, with an intense, pressing interest.

Gerasen looked highly pensive at the query. His voice was low and restrained, when he finally replied, "I did as you asked, Bevriedak."

The words carried the undertone of a reluctant confession. The Elder then added, after a few taciturn moments, as if needing to justify himself, "Though I did not do it myself, and I did not transgress the Ban in the lower world."

The silver dragon was greatly intrigued. "What did you do?" Bevriedak prodded aggressively.

He was caught by surprise at the answer that followed, having come to different conclusions following his last visit. As the answer was given, Bevriedak's thoughts turned to the prior encounter with Gerasen. The details played out vividly within his mind.

When he had visited with Gerasen during the return from Midragard, Bevriedak had been aflame with exuberance as he related his findings of otherworlders present within the southern land. To a great extent, it was that fact alone that prompted him to choose Gerasen's haven as the location where he would take a brief hiatus, to regain some strength.

He wanted Gerasen, more than any other Elder, to know about the incredible findings. Beyond his own affinity for Gerasen, he still would have felt a deep urge to bring the discovery to the attention of the black dragon.

Tidings of otherworlders within Ave were of paramount interest to all of their venerable kind. The momentous revelation corresponded to the most ancient of prophecies. It was a resplendent beacon of hope, shining amid the host of unsettling developments down on the lower surface.

On his previous visitation, Bevriedak felt certain Gerasen would have enthusiastically shared his elation regarding the discovery in Midragard. He had expected to fly from Gerasen's haven with a powerful ally, willing to risk the effects of the Ban at Bevriedak's side. Instead, it had been quite the opposite.

Bevriedak had been stunned and angry when he had departed the Elder's haven. He had found himself as alone as he had been before his arrival. It had taken an act of will to steady his turbulent mind in the aftermath of the visit.

During the visit, Gerasen had listened attentively all throughout Bevriedak's detailed account. Gerasen had displayed a stoic mien during the entire telling, not betraying even a sliver of his feelings on the tidings one way or another. The anticlimactic reaction suprised the silver dragon.

In fact, Gerasen had been so subdued that Bevriedak had left the Elder's cavern with the strong impression his friend doubted his veracity on the entire affair. Gerasen's quiet, noncommittal reaction, and maddening lack of a substantive reply, had made no sense to Bevriedak. He knew beyond any doubts that Gerasen held a great interest in the ancient prophecies, which fundamentally applied to the sundering of their race's lengthy, burdensome exile.

Now, hearing indications that Gerasen had seen the spirit of the Ban in a different light, if not having directly transgressed it, as Bevriedak had done, reflected a change completely unforeseen. Admittedly, it was a most welcome turn of events, from what Bevriedak anticipated in the light of Gerasen's previous, lukewarm response.

Yet the reply indicated that Gerasen was unsettled, and not entirely resolute about undertaking new, uncertain directions. There was no doubt he was greatly troubled over whether he had already committed a trespass against the Oath, even if his actions had not specifically brought the Ban's punishing grip onto his own body.

Bevriedak understood the other dragon's reservations. Contravention of a sacredly held paradigm, one adhered to faithfully for centuries upon centuries, implied a tremendous transformation of attitude and understanding, as well as harboring an element of great risk.

"Messages were sent forth upon small black wings, conveyed far distances, to the attention of our mortal cousins in their mountainous holds," Gerasen stated. "Our cousins are, after all, living within the very lands where you claim to have found these otherworlders. The messages asked our smaller cousins to watch closely over Midragard. I asked them for their help ... to do what I would desire to do myself, were it not for the Ban.

"If these humans you saw in Midragard are indeed the ones

spoken of in the great prophecies, then it is certain to me that the Unifier is searching for them with an insatiable hunger. The Sundering matters to Him, as much as it does to us. And you know well the reasons why.

"More tidings have since come to me, and it would seem my fears were well-founded. The Unifier is hunting, and His reach spreads far and wide across the world below.

"A demonic servant of the netherworld reached deep into Midragard. It sought to take an invidual alive, a foreigner who might well be one of the ones you spoke of. This troubling word reached me a short time before your arrival."

"Where are the otherworlders now? Do you have word of them?" queried an anxious Bevriedak, hoping against hope that his discovery had not already been rendered futile.

"The foreigners of unknown origin are safe enough … for the moment," Gerasen responded. "Our brave cousins have taken to flying in the highest skies over Midragard, in numbers. They accepted my requests without dispute. Their trust and diligence saved us from a terrible predicament.

"They were the ones who came across the Fire Realm's Arcamon. The Arcamon was mounted upon a hell-spawned steed, out in the open light of the sun. Several of our cousins followed them at a distance, observing and looking to discern the Arcamon's purpose."

Bevriedak's eyes widened at the mention of an Arcamon. Such a baleful, infernal creature required remarkable exertions of power to manifest within the mortal world. Not even the mightiest of Wizards aligned with Jebaalos could bring through such a being on their own power from the depths of the Fire Realms.

Bringing an Arcamon into the physical realm required a great exercise of power. The Arcamon, which had been identified as a servant of the Unifier, was a living testament to Bevriedak's position regarding the true nature of the enigmatic being dwelling in Avanor.

"An Arcamon. In the skies of Midragard. One from the unending fires of the nether realm, and a declared servant of the Unifier," Gerasen said, uttering the words with inflections of distaste and consternation, mixed with a strong dose of trepidation.

"The Arcamon attacked a trio of sky riders, mounted upon Fenraren, slaying the two who were Midragardans," Gerasen continued. "The third, a foreigner who I learned has been a guest of the Midragardan king, was regarded with great importance. Jebaalos' emissary did nothing to harm him, when it could have easily destroyed him. It called upon the human to submit. This was when it claimed its allegiance to the Unifier. The Arcamon was circling the human, awaiting a response, when the human tried to escape. The dragons watching this take place from a distance moved to attack the Arcamon, catching it completely unawares.

"It would be no surprise to me if this human was one of your otherworlders. Why else would the Arcamon spare him? Why would the Arcamon take such interest in him?"

Bevriedak felt a rising unease. There was much to be pondered regarding an Arcamon within Midragard, in light of what Bevriedak had discovered there. The implications were foreboding and far-reaching.

Arcamons were usually relegated to the confines of lore, even more so than the Elder. An incarnate Arcamon would only be utilized for the most vitally important tasks by its ultimate lord, Jebaalos.

"It is no inconsequential servant the Adversary sends forward to do His bidding," Gerasen proceeded, echoing Bevriedak's thoughts. "You and I both know that. Yet even this one is bound by the physical nature it embraced in this world. The fire of our cousins could harm it, and it was successfully driven from the skies of Midragard.

"It fled before their pursuit to the very ends of Midragard, with others of our smaller kin joining in the chase. By the time it reached the outer boundaries of Midragard, a horde of our kin were close upon the Arcamon's steed's tail.

"The creature the Arcamon rode upon was swift enough, and given to unnatural strength. The infernal mount was able to pass beyond the borders of Midragard without showing any signs of tiring, carrying its hell-spawned master far beyond the reach of our cousins."

"Then it is no mystery," Bevriedak stated resolutely. "We can see the Unifier suspects there are humans in Midragard who are very possibly related to the ancient prophecies."

"It would seem this is indeed so," Gerasen replied, a faraway, deeply thoughtful expression on his face.

"Can you not see now? This is a time like no other that has happened, in all the ages of the world, " Bevriedak declared, a sense of conviction emboldening him. "We cannot deny the cries of millions below us, those yet free, and enslaved in the Unifer's grip."

"If Elder break the Oath to defy the Unifier, and if some of our kind are being swayed towards Jebaalos's seductions, as you claim, then an unprecedented time may drive any renegade Elder further into breaking the Oath," Gerasen then exclaimed.

His tone was heavily laden with concern. Bevriedak perceived the severe dilemma Gerasen was describing. The breaking of the Oath could be undertaken for more than one justification.

"You may well find yourself driving Elder not of our mind or heart into the fight below," Gerasen said. "Would you see many Elder brought under the direct power of the Unifier? That is what may happen, even if it is not your intent."

Bevriedak understood Gerasen's fears, but he was not about to allow the worries to become too ingrained in his friend. Still, he had to proceed very delicately, as Gerasen was an Elder extremely strong of mind. Bevriedak could not afford to appear dismissive, or even slightly patronizing.

"Those who would be swayed by Jebaalos have already sealed their minds. I believe they would break the Oath, even were you and I to sleep through the next thousand years," Bevriedak replied carefully, in a level tone. "While we would willfully choose not to act, fearing we would encourage them to break the Oath, I believe they would still willfully break the Oath in their own time, a time of Jebaalos's choosing. They would bring great strength to the cause of the Enemy. Elder would then be in the lower world on the Adversary's side, with none to oppose them."

Gerasen grew very quiet at Bevriedak's words. The black dragon remained subdued long after the other finished, appearing to be lost deep in thought.

"You ask me to break the Oath," Gerasen said at last, the look in his eyes suddenly lancing into Bevriedak. "You believe strongly that any Elder with allegiance to Jebaalos will eventually break the Oath. Whether sooner or later. What does that truly say about all of this?"

Tension coalesced thickly in the air between the two Elder, as Gerasen's searing gaze held Bevriedak in place. Bevriedak remained steadfast in his resolve, although he did not yet know what Gerasen was ultimately implying. He patiently waited for his friend to resume.

Gerasen's voice was all but a hiss, as he tersely proceeded, "What does that possibly say about you? What does it say about me? Regarding our own transgressions of the Oath? Intent is not always equal to the action taken. It can lead to something quite opposite. In the end, we may well find ourselves doing the Adversary's work, as might all Elder who break the Oath … for any reason."

The last three words bit deeply into Bevriedak. "Have no illusions that we are anything like those who hearken to Jebaalos. Not for a single moment."

He felt indignant, feeling the sharp sting from Gerasen's implication that all who broke the Oath would most likely end up doing Jebaalos' will.

"And what if you are right, Bevriedak? What if we are not doing the Adversary's will? The Lord of the Deep Abyss will certainly pour forth even darker creatures and powers, if Elder come forth in strength against the Unifier. I have no doubt of this, if the Unifier is truly the Chosen One," Gerasen countered.

To Bevriedak, it was as if the other Elder was grasping for any shred of reasoning that would prevent him from taking an unprecedented course. For the moment, Bevriedak was stymied. He paused to collect his thoughts, as he considered his own response.

"Would you be the cause of loosing even more of the Adverary's dark powers upon those living in this world? Powers greater than Elder?" Gerasen prodded. "What is this, but a choice between doing the Adversary's Will, or provoking a much more terrible doom upon Ave?

Feeling ever more sensitive to the verbal barbs, Bevriedak forced himself to maintain his composure. He was barely able to restrain himself from delivering the snapping response welling up within him. The moment was very precarious, and everything rested upon his reasoning through his position carefully, in response to Gerasen's stated fears.

He spoke with a calm timbre. "The Unifier will do what He will do, and Jebaalos will do what He will, with or without our interference. Do you think they will hold anything back when the enslavement of all Ave is within their grasp? The Five Realms, the Midragardans, and the Saxans are in a desperate fight for survival. The flames of war now blaze inside the borders of the Five Realms and Saxany. I fear it will not be long before this conflagration is brought into the very heart of Midragard."

Bevriedak paused. He delivered his next words more slowly, knowing what was hanging in the balance. "This war will then be carried to our smaller cousins, as it will surely be taken to all upon Ave who will not bow their heads to the Unifier. The Unifier, and Jebaalos, will accept only submission or destruction. They will not spare even a single human realm, and they will not spare the mountain realm of our cousins. There is no time to delay. I have no choice. I cannot leave those who remain loyal to the All-Father to their fate … not without being willing to share it myself."

"It is not for us to change the Oath. The Ban holds against us still, does it not?" Gerasen asked, after a few moments, his gaze remaining steady upon the silver dragon. Bevriedak returned the steely look, with unwavering confidence in his heart. "We cannot dispel the Ban by an act of mere will. You did not seem to be able to do so. The signs were written all over your body when you came to see me in this very haven, during your last foray."

There was no denying Gerasen had witnessed Bevriedak's extreme state of weakness, just after the silver dragon had come from Midragard. It was irrefutable that whatever justification Bevriedak saw for his own breaking of the Oath, the Ban still exacted a heavy tool for descending into the lower world.

In Bevriedak's eyes, there was another way of looking at the entire matter. The Ban did not necessarily judge whether or not Bevriedak's purpose in violating it was rightly guided. It was merely an impartial power, falling upon any Elder who left the Forbidden Dominions.

Bevriedak simply could not pierce the enigmatic shroud draped around the tantalizing scenarios. The Ban might well render some manner of evaluation upon a transgressor, or it might be a power blind to purpose, applied to all, regardless of their necessity or motive.

Regardless of the truth, Bevriedak's heart and mind were in full harmony with his decision to cross the longstanding barrier to the lower world. He felt entirely at ease, within the deepest region of his conscience.

After seeing and learning more about what was happening in the world, he believed that Wulfstan had saved him from a great folly. The thought of remaining uninvolved was now abhorrent to his core, merely continuing his immortal life in a state of inactive exile, while the world below was engulfed in a conflagration of wickedness.

Bevriedak had also learned a few more things regarding the nature of the Ban. Before Wulfstan had come, Bevriedak had only known that the Ban was not something affecting an instant death. It was known to be cumulative, applying its degredations gradually, designed to provide an increasingly onerous warning for any wayward Elder who became too impatient over the long ages.

The Ban's very essence was, therefore, not to immediately destroy. Rather, it was to offset the potential specter of recalcitrant Elder, in the ages following the Ban's establishment.

Bevriedak had gone into the lower world without knowing exactly how long it took before the penalties of the Ban became insurmountable. It was the kind of knowledge that singularly determined how long he could spend on the surface of Ave, without passing a point of no return. In some ways, he had taken a great risk in leaving the Havens behind.

Now, the great Elder had tested the boundaries of the Ban. He had learned so much more about how it took effect, at least under fairly normal circumstances. Admittedly, the powers of the Ban acted upon him much quicker than he had ever imagined, but not so fast that it prevented him from enduring periodic forays in the lower world.

Nevertheless, the advancement of the Ban's effects under calm circumstances caused him great concern regarding other types of encounters. Bevriedak feared what would happen if a sorcerer or Wizard invoked the Ban's powers upon him. Further acceleration of the Ban's force was nothing he ever wanted to experience.

"Tell me, Bevriedak, did you dismiss the Ban's effects by your strength of will," Gerasen pressed, breaking another long, pensive silence.

"You know the answer. As you said, it was written plainly enough upon my body when I returned from Midragard. The Ban did not spare me, and I know it would not have spared me from death had I challenged it far enough," Bevriedak acknowledged. His voice took on an adamant, almost challenging tone. "Yet it changes nothing for me. Even if my choice causes the Ban's power to slay me one day.

"I know what question you would soon raise, and I will answer now, for my part. I believe that it is not certain my sufferings show my action was wrong. It just shows that the Ban's effects held me in their power. The rains fall on the good and the evil in the world below. The Ban may simply be impartial, even regarding the most noble of intentions.

"I do not deny there is no sign or proof I can give that I am right in my choice. May the All-Father forgive me if I have chosen wrong, but I will fight, and I will act, in this darkening age."

LOGAN

Erika, Antonio, and Janus were slow in arriving for the midday meal. Logan was not about to reward their tardiness, already indulging in the ample repast by himself.

He had spent enough hours in the relative confinement of his bedchamber. Logan still felt like a glorified prisoner, as he and the others were still in the dark about what was going to be done with them.

Reason stated there was little sense in worrying too much about their current situation, as they had no control or choice in the matter. They were escorted everywhere by armed guards, such as the two now standing just outside the hall entrance.

A couple of servants scurried in and out of the high vaulted chamber, set in the forefront of the lengthy structure nestled at the base of the terrace's outer wall. The chamber was close to the tower where the four prisoners were quartered. Within, the servants had assembled a trestle table at one end, with benches for the prisoners' use.

The servants were primarily occupied with the two sideboards in the large room, set against one wall. One was a dresser, an open table upon which food was assembled before it was served. The other was an aumbry, provided with an open top surface, with shelves filled with platters and drinking vessels underneath.

A young girl, no more than fifteen, brought in a platter of freshly-made bread. She laid it down momentarily on the dresser, while a middle-aged man with a beakish nose mixed wine at the aumbry.

The mild weather outside demanded no fires in the recessed nich just to Logan's right. The weather had been one of the few comforting aspects surrounding his current plight, having remained mostly clear and radiant since they had arrived.

Daylight streamed through a number of small, arched windows, set in paired intervals down the length of both sides of the hall. A mild level of ambience was provided by the series of paired openings, the alternating pools of darkness and light breaking up the continuity of the hall's interior.

Logan had chosen to sit towards the end of a bench, within one of the dark swathes, as it was much easier on the eyes. The pocket of shadow also had a gentler, cooler touch upon his skin than unbroken streams of sunlight.

His spirits dusky, Logan had never felt more out of control over his own affairs, being completely at the mercy of their captors. Yet he could not deny having a little pleasure at the constant presence of servants. From those assigned to their quarters, to those providing them with refreshment and meals, all of his needs were diligently attended to.

He smiled and nodded to the old man, who had finished mixing the wine. Logan held out his drinking vessel of fine silver, and the old man approached with a ewer in hand. After filling Logan's cup, the old man nodded dutifully, and backed away.

His other three companions finally entered the chamber, as Logan took a long sip of the wine. There was little mystery about where they had come from. Like Logan, they had made their way up or down the spiral stairs, from their respective chambers, to a doorway on the fifth story of the tower.

From there, it was a straightforward path down the short series of stairs to the curtain wall. The path continued alongside the battlements, to the top of the stairs heading down from the wall-walk to the ground of the bailey. At the base of the stairs, it was a brief jaunt to the complex of domestic buildings set along the wall, which included the hall and a small stone chapel.

The dilatory trio's footsteps crunched on the fresh rushes, tied together in small sections effectively carpeting the stone floor underneath. Logan regarded his companions calmly, while finishing off his chalice of red wine. He found he was having trouble limiting his sips, as the rich wine from the northeast region of Gallea had turned out to be a very welcome discovery. Along with the cider native to Avanor, the Gallean wine took its place without delay as a favorite of Logan's in his new environs.

Without a word of greeting, he took a full bite out of a leg of roasted fowl. The meat was most succulent, and utterly gratifying to his tastes. After he had first sampled it, he had called the young servant girl over to make sure his platter was provided with a considerable helping of the savory meat.

He was already very grateful he was not a practitioner of the principle religion found in Avanor. Those following the Western Church observed a regular, midweek fast, a fact Logan heard from one of the attending servants back in the tower chamber. He had also gleaned that the Western Church demanded fasts on other days, forbidding the consumption of meat on the designated periods.

The servant had inquired gently whether Logan observed the dietary practices of the Western Church. From the way the servant asked, Logan sensed he had a choice in the matter. The servant did not seem entirely suprised when Logan requested that their meals not be governed by the dietery strictures. For his own part, Logan indicated that he had no intention of causing offense. The servant reassured Logan that the nobles of Avanor rarely worried about fasting days, their meals regularly including meat, poultry, and eggs. As he swallowed the chunk of garlic-seasoned fowl, and took another prodigious bite, he was thankful he had been assertive in the matter.

A pensive-looking, middle-aged man serving as a ewerer came forth at their approach. With a pitcher in one hand, and a basin in the other, he attended them as they took their places at the trestle table. Antonio sat down directly across from Logan, with Erika at his right, while Janus took his place at Logan's left.

Following the etiquette of the place, Erika put her hands forward, as the ewerer saw to her first. Setting the basin underneath her hands, he poured flower-scented water over them.

Logan shot her a momentary glance of appraisal, as her attention was distracted with the hand rinsing. He had to admit that her new attire was very flattering to her form, even if it covered most of her body.

Her head was ensconsed in a white linen wimple, and a veil of similar fabric was secured about her head by a narrow, green headband. The combination allowed only her face to be seen, covering her head and neck, and wrapping under her chin.

Her upper body was laced into a full-length, snug-fitting tunic of fine green linen. From her waist downward, the tunic flared out a little as it descended towards the bottom, where it lightly brushed the ground. A long, dark green belt was secured loosely about her waist, the extended ends dangling down freely in the front.

Her face betrayed her discomfort in the attire. As if in reflex, he shifted in his seat at the thought, as he was still getting used to wearing braies and hose, under his long tunic of fine, blue-dyed linen.

"Looks like you didn't bother to wait for us," Erika remarked, catching his eyes.

"Maybe it's the fact you're late, and I am very hungry. Only two major meals a day around here, you know," Logan retorted. "Lunch is dinner in this place, unless you haven't caught on to that yet."

"That's about all we've learned here, so far," Erika responded somberly, as the ewerer moved on to Antonio.

When Antonio was finished cleaning his hands, other servants moved in with platters and vessels, placing them before him and Erika. The custom in Avalos was to serve meals to pairs of individuals, providing each with a trencher of old, hard bread, which served as a disposable plate absorbing excess sauces and juices.

After his hand rinse, Janus was given his trencher. He reached across to take a few portions of food from the platters already set down for Logan. Though Logan had partaken copiously, there was more than enough remaining to fill Janus' trencher.

For their part, Erika and Janus opted for a standard kind of ale, which Logan had tried before, one that was weaker in potency than others he had sampled. Antonio took Logan's suggestion, and had his chalice filled with the rich, red Gallean wine, whose aromatic favors permeated the nose, and whose flavors burst generously within the mouth.

"Well, I'm happy to say some have learned not to eat their plates," Logan remarked with a slight grin, looking across at Antonio.

During their first meal in Avalos, Logan had been unable to stifle his amusement when Antonio tried taking a bite out of his trencher, after finishing the food on it. An attending servant had looked absolutely horrified, remarking quickly that the trenchers were good for nothing other than throwing to the beggars gathered beyond the walls on the fortresses' lowest level. Antonio had looked shocked as well, his expression souring instantly with a mouthful of the stale, old bread.

"That's not what I meant," Erika replied curtly. "We've been here long enough that we should know a little more about things other than food and drink."

"I know what you meant," Logan responded. "And I agree."

Amusements aside, Logan understood what Erika was saying. They had been held in tacit incarceration for a few days, and still knew little more about life in Avalos than when they had first arrived.

Other than the provision of new clothing, their chambers in the tower, and routines of food and drink, they had largely been left to themselves. Their interactions had been confined to a small circle of servants and guardsmen, along with a rather energetic scribe by the name of Euvroin.

"The trencher might not taste too good … but this is wonderful, Logan, without a doubt," Antonio commented, through a robust mouthful of the roast pork, flavored richly with garlic and onions.

Having indulged in an ample serving of the roast pork, Logan could not dispute Antonio's assessment in the slightest. "I'll concede you that," he replied, before settling back into silence.

Based upon earlier comments from the servants, Logan gleaned that they found the meal to be a fairly modest one, but to Logan it was a sumptuous feast. The roasted fowl and pork were accompanied by a number of other excellent suitors courting their various palates.

There was a very tasty pottage, made thick with herbs, vegetables, and salt beef. Also among the bounty were finely sifted white flour bread, rich butter, cheese tarts, apples, peppered eggs, and a few different kinds of fresh cheeses. Salt cellars were set on the tables for the access of those dining, who would need to use a knife for serving themselves an individual portion to season their food.

The meal continued in relative silence, with no significant impetus for conversation amongst the four companions. Aside from a few pleasantries about the food and drink, the quartet remained subdued.

They would have finished the meal in such a state, were it not for the sounds of footsteps surging towards the entrance of the hall. A metallic rustling, growing steadily in volume, augmented the chorus of heavy steps tramping in rhythmic unison. The marching sounds came to an abrupt end at the entrance of the chamber, as a tall guard clad in helm and mail entered the hall.

He looked towards Logan and the others with the impassive demeanor of a soldier dutifully executing orders. Wasting no time in his purpose, he announced in a firm voice, "The Unifier requests an audience with you. You will all come with us now."

The guard's timbre left no room for making any other choice. Though they had not finished their meal entirely, Logan was not about to argue. If anything, the interruption was a welcome boon. They were finally going to break the dreary monotony, and hopefully obtain a few answers regarding their circumstances and confinement.

The four slowly got up from the table. With Erika in the front, they filed in behind the guard as he led them out of the chamber. Standing outside was a group of about twenty other warriors, all equipped with spear and shield.

The warriors enveloped them as they marched along the grounds of the outer bailey. They headed towards one of the towers with a spanning bridgeway, connecting to the base of the terrace above them.

A timber staircase ran up to a doorway on the second level of the tower. Once inside, they began a long climb up the interior steps. His stomach full, Logan breathed much heavier by the time they reached the level with the connecting bridgeway. Without pause, they marched across the fortified bridgeway, to the bottom of the next terrace.

To Logan's mounting chagrin, the burden of climbing staircases with a full stomach did not end with the terrace. The guards continued escorting the group through towers and across bridge-like pathways as they surmounted two more levels, progressing on up to the sixth terrace of the lofty mountain-fortress.

Though they maintained a steady pace, Logan managed to gain more than a few unobstructed glimpses of the two terraces above the one they were quartered on. Both were sights to behold.

The fourth level was filled with lush, green foliage, flowers, and water, within which a broad stone building was nestled. The pools of water glistened brightly in the daylight, reflecting the rays showering down upon their rippling surfaces. Gently swaying trees, branches filtering the breezes caressing the mountainside, beckoned invitingly.

Logan espied a few other buildings of stone within the verdant level, the structures shrouded thickly by the abundant growths. A few men and women labored among the host of plants and trees. Some carried buckets of water, and others were on their hands and knees, attending to various specimens amongst the bounteous flora.

It was as if the richness of an opulent spring was contained within the confines of the terrace. Bursts of color flowed from the beds of flowers, as well as the flowers ornamenting a number of trees and shrubs. Bright yellows, deep blues, regal purples, and lush reds saluted the sun in the fullness of health and vigor.

Logan regretted having to take his eyes away from the jubilant vision when they crossed the bridgeway to the small postern gate set in the walls of the fifth level. It took an act of conscious will to keep from pausing for one more look.

The nature of the layout within the walls of the fifth level was not made clear until they had already stepped onto the crosswalk, starting across towards the lower edge of the sixth terrace. Looking down over the sides of the crosswalk, Logan could see the reason why. The fifth terrace contained a dense series of buildings, the arrangement of which was obstructed from the ground level.

Some were smaller outbuildings, while several prominent stone structures were arranged into a square layout. The latter buildings harbored a cloister garth. The edifices around the garth were at least two stories in height. To Logan's eyes, the tallest, and largest, of the buildings was likely some kind of church.

The revelation of a cloister garth was not the only unveiling at the height of the bridgeway. Looking to his left, just before they stepped onto the walkway, Logan regretted that they could not linger to take in the phenomenal view spread before his eyes.

The walkway was situated close to the far end of the semicircular curtain wall, at the southernmost edge of the mountain itself. The close proximity to the body of the mountain offered Logan an intimate view of the peculiar black rock comprising it. It looked to be volcanic, and was fascinating enough to look at, but it was not the cause of his momentary hestitation.

Rather, the spot offered a tremendous view of Avalos, and the adjacent ocean stretching far and wide, reaching into the vast horizons. The effect of the panoramic sight was breathtaking, the resplendant vision seemingly having no boundaries. Sparkling expanses of water, and a teeming city, both illuminated brilliantly by the sun's radiance, formed a picturesque image that Logan would not soon forget.

Logan's group bunched up momentarily, as they funneled into pairs, and started across the narrow bridgeway. Standing towards the rear, he was afforded a few extra, precious moments, as he stared off into the distance.

There was so much to take in. Logan took notice of a few elements that he had not taken account of when they had first passed into Avalos.

The hazy outline of an island could be seen off in the distance, set just off the shoreline running down beyond the southern edge of the bay's expansive mouth. Out of all the possible things to focus upon, there was something about the mysterous island that kept pulling at his attention.

"Looking towards that island?" Janus suddenly remarked, from behind him.

Logan glanced back, to where Janus was gazing upon the splendid panorama. "I was," he confirmed.

"I was, too. I can't help wondering what is on that island," Janus said in a low voice. "There is something about it that immediately drew my eye."

Logan agreed with Janus as he looked again, this time with a little more conscious scrutiny. He could see that the island was covered with buildings. The structures rose up the steep slopes towards its summit, the highest edifice sending a great spire soaring towards the bright sky above.

"I suppose we can ask," Logan said, before turning towards one of the guards standing alongside them. He gestured towards the island. "What's on that island? Off beyond the end of the bay there, with the spired building on top of it."

The guard's eyes followed Logan's pointing hand, and he nodded curtly. He then replied, in a nonchalant manner, "That is the Mount of the High Archon."

Another guard within hearing snickered derisively. "High Archon indeed. The Unifier's mount is the truer mount, in tribute to an even higher Archon. It's why this mount is beholden to One, and One alone, while that little mount needs two patrons … and even had to drop one of its older ones. Just be glad you are on a mount that only needs one patron… and, you are about to meet Him in person."

"Patrons?" Logan asked, intrigued to learn more. "Of that island?"

"Religious patrons … that island is dedicated to the High Archon who leads the legions of the All-Father, or so they say. It is also dedicated to the celestial Queen," the first guard informed him.

"Who was the first patron, who got replaced?" Logan asked.

"Used to be the monk that founded the place … and all he got was a hard knock on the head by the High Archon himself, so they say, when he wouldn't get underway on building the place," the guard commented, with a light guffaw. "Must've knocked the dirt out of his ear. The monk listened then, I suppose, 'cause there's the mount today."

"Just a legend," the second guard added, with a sneer.

"I only know what I hear," the first guard said, with a dispassionate shrug.

"So you see? The High Archon and Queen of all Palladium have that little, miserable island dedicated to them, while the Unifier has this great mountain honoring Him. Over there, you may see a few statues, and a handful of weak, harmless monks. Here, you are about to meet the

Unifier, alive and manifest right before you. You're in the right place," the second guard remarked haughtily.

Logan heard the tones of a man who was much more than a mere admirer of the Unifier. The guard spoke with the reverence of a devout believer in a faith. It was a very interesting, intriguing distinction, though the guard's stoic face betrayed little else.

There was also a clear hostility present in the man, directed towards those to whom the island had been dedicated; as if the small island's otherworldly patrons were considered outright enemies, to be loathed.

In a city where the vestiges of faith were everywhere, not the least represented in the numerous churches dotting the city, Logan found it highly interesting that not one of the guards within earshot challenged the mocking statements. The lack of reaction only made sense if all of the guards inwardly shared similar sentiments.

All fell into silence, as the rest of the group finally funneled onto the bridge, crossed the high pathway, and went through yet another narrow postern, into a passageway through the wall of the sixth level. Logan felt queasy as they walked through the dark passage, and the muscles in his leg carried a smoldering burn within them, after the long climb. Yet his mind was on other things than physical discomforts.

As they drew near to the end of their extensive hike, the notion that they were about to meet the Unifier, in person, began to mount steadily. The full magnitude had not quite hit Logan yet, but he felt a considerable anxiety swelling within.

Logan could see the great authority and power of the Unifier reflected all around him. It was manifest in the majestic city and soaring fortress, both of which testified to tremendous degrees of wealth and might.

He had sensed the presence of great, underlying fears in the words of servants and guards regarding the Unifier, including the normally ebullient Euvroin. The coif-wearing scribe had shed a little light on the scope of the Unifier's power, and the state of affairs in Ave. He had described the Unifier as unrivaled, a regal being whom even the greatest of kings feared, and to whom affluent emperors and mighty sultans sent dutiful, placating embassies.

It seemed like utter madness that the tribal people of the Five Realms had chosen to set themselves in opposition to such a massive power. As Logan saw it, if the tribal people had just cooperated with the desires of the Unifier, their village would not have been reduced to shards.

Logan could not dismiss the ferocity and merciless nature of the attack on the village. Yet neither could he understand the obstinance of the simple villagers, now that he had a keener appreciation of the might wielded by the Unifier. Submission to the Unifier might have seemed distasteful to the tribal people, but opposition loomed as a pursuit of great, reckless folly.

At the moment, he and his three companions were completely at the mercy of the Unifier. Stubbornness would profit them little, and perhaps much more could be gained by cooperation, a sobering lesson Logan had not missed in witnessing the ordeal befalling the Five Realms.

Logan took a deep breath, and exhaled slowly, steeling his resolve as they came to the end of the passageway. They walked out into a large, open bailey, within which was a massive, square keep.

The keep ascended a few stories to a crenellated roof. Square turrets rose above the main roof, extending upward from each of the blocky structure's corners. The individual turrets were each provided with a crown of alternating square merlons and open crenels.

Logan tilted his head up farther, sending his gaze past the keep towards the enceinte of the seventh level above. From his current vantage, he could see only the walls and, rising high above them, the lofty, circular tower set on the uppermost height of the mountain. The tower, effectively acting as a finial for the mountain itself, soared towards the underbelly of the sky.

He brought his eyes down to the huge keep immediately before him. The difference between seeing the edifice from high and afar on their flight into Avalos, and standing right before it, was vast. Logan remembered the general shape of the keep well enough, but it had not looked nearly as immense when looking upon it from the back of a Harrak steed.

As with the rest of their long ascent, they were given no time to stop and regard the wondrous architecture. Logan and the others were led by the guards towards the bottom of a short flight of stairs, which climbed up to a small, square landing.

An iron-banded timber door stood directly in front of them at the top of the stairs. Another staircase led upwards to their immediate right. Without hesitation, the accompanying guards conducted them up the stairs, which culminated in a broad landing.

A stout outer wall shielded the staircase, forming a type of forebuilding. The stairs had been left unroofed, completely open to the skies above.

Glancing up, and pausing briefly, Logan quickly saw the reason. Any attackers assaulting the keep would be mercilessly exposed to missiles pouring down from defenders positioned overhead. Small windows and loopholes were placed in the wall of the keep on each level, all the way up to the crenellated battlements.

A couple of cloaked, spear-bearing warriors, clad like the ones accompanying Logan's group, met them at the top of the stairs. Upon recognizing the guards escorting Logan and the others, the soldiers quickly stepped aside to make way for the group.

Logan surmounted the last few stairs, following Antonio from bright sunlight into the cool shade pooling under the roof of the enclosed landing. Set into the wall on their immediate right were two small, narrow windows. The aperatures looked beyond the wall of the forebuilding, and allowed some light into the dimmer environs.

Set just to the right, in back of where Logan now stood, was a timber doorway. It led into a small room or chamber formed within the thick wall of the forebuilding.

While he was looking, another soldier emerged from the doorway to watch them pass. The Avanoran gazed upon them with an expression of heightened curiosity.

Not knowing precisely how he was expected to react, upon catching the soldier's eye, and not wanting to inadvertently cause offense, Logan nodded his head in a slight bow. The guard gave a curt nod in return, though his expression remained stern.

Directly ahead, across the landing, was a much wider door fashioned of stout oak. The door was an entrance into yet another chamber, formed into the corner of the forebuilding where it wrapped around the main body of the keep to the immediate left. To the left of the door itself, running between the walls of the keep and the chamber, was a much narrower set of stairs rising up the keep's other side.

The confined passageway forced any traffic to condense into a tight, single file. The staircase pressed on up to the second major level of the keep's outer forebuilding. The roof covering the landing and two chambers gave way once again to the open sky, as Logan was jostled forward by the guard behind him. Cooperating fully, he moved out from the shade into the encompassing warmth of the sun.

After several steps in the congested boundaries, the staircase abruptly broadened to a width more than double its initial size. The increase allowed those ascending it to walk comfortably in pairs.

The steps within the wider segment stretched to a noticeably greater breadth than did those in the set leading up to the first guarded landing. The wall to their left remained largely constant, broken only by a doorway with iron studding and banding, leading directly into the keep. The doorway was fronted by an especially deep stair, which formed a kind of mini-platform before it. The guards paid the entrance no heed, continuing straight past it.

Having already passed a couple of doorways into the keep, and two entrances to chambers in the forebuilding, Logan's curiosity grew regarding their ultimate destination within the great edifice. About halfway up the wider section of the staircase, another defensive feature had been added to the elaborate structure. The group's ascent was slowed, as they carefully crossed a lowered wooden drawbridge, spanning a broad gap.

The drawbridge could be pulled up on the farther side of the gap, to rest within the frame of what looked to be a small gatehouse. The section housing the drawbridge was topped with a roof of its own, provided with crennclated battlements.

After passing through the tower-like gatehouse, the climb resumed. A narrower set of steps emerged into the open air once again. It was only a short climb to the final landing, a long, enclosed platform roofed with battlements.

Five guards were standing attentively on the elongated surface, as the party surmounted the final steps. Behind the Avanorans was a wooden door.

To the immediate right, spaced a few paces apart just beyond the forefront of the landing, were a couple of narrow breaks in the wall. Visible through the openings were a few stairs ascending to what appeared to be a long stone vessel, looking to Logan's eyes like a great trough.

Towards the end of the landing, the escorting contingent of guards led the prisoners into an opening on the left. At last, they entered the main body of the keep.

The soldiers standing near the landing's end stood rigidly still as the prisoners and accompanying guards walked by them. Right hands firmly gripping the ash shafts of their spears, impassive expressions were etched upon their faces.

Nevertheless, Logan felt the weight of their eyes, their gazes emitting much more than a passive interest. He had little doubt that he and his companions would soon be the main topic of conversation at the dining tables of the keep's garrison.

Once inside the walls of the main keep, a small vaulted chamber opened up on their immediate left. Logan peered into the room as they slowly filed by it.

Even in the dimness, he saw what looked to be some kind of well, in the form of a raised, cylindrical construct. It was equipped with a pulley assembly and wooden bucket, the latter resting idly over the dark, circular opening gaping just beneath.

Just past the well was another rectangular stone vessel, possibly a small cistern for water storage. A couple of lead pipes ran a short distance from the object, descending downward and away from the stone vessel, and disappearing into the rest of the keep.

A few wide steps rose just ahead of the party. They came to an end before an ornate door crafted from solid bronze. An image of a muscular winged figure had been artfully worked into the door. The entity looked to be in the act of ascending, with arms outstretched above it, following the contours of its upward-pointing wings. Its human-like head looked to be gazing in the path of its ascension, eyes raised towards the heavens.

The image on the bronze door was graceful and noble, but Logan's gaze did not linger for long upon it. He was soon staring in disbelief at what he had first thought to be huge statues.

It quickly dawned on Logan that the massive shapes were not inanimate objects. Flanking the steps, rising up from each side at their lower base, were the looming shapes of two hulking, living beasts.

Each of the massive sentries carried extraordinarily large lances. The thick shafts of wood were fitted into the sockets of long, broad spear-blades of dark iron. The sharp blades were large enough to serve as daggers, or even short swords, for a human. The extensive weapons were far too unwieldy to be used by anything other than creatures like them.

The four prisoners stood stil, gazing upon the two creatures with looks of sheer awe spread upon their faces. Logan's own face went partially slack at his initial comprehension of the heavily-muscled, inhuman sentinels.

Both of the monstrosities rose up to well over nine feet in height, the tops of their heads resting not far from the ceiling above. With their girth, they gave off a presence that filled the space before the short flight of steps leading to the bronze door.

The two beasts were clad in little more than roughspun, black woolen tunics, which reached down to the top of their stout knees. A narrow, hempen cord bound the dark tunics about their ample waists.

Simple hide shoes covered their feet. The shoes were fitted with a short slit at the top and center along their front, and bound around the circumferences of their ankles by rugged leather thongs. Between the shoes and the hem of the tunic, the leathery, grayish skin of their lower legs was left bared to view.

A short-cropped, bristly mane crested their great heads. The wide, spiky strip ran straight down the center of their elongated, capacious skulls. Beginning from a high point on their foreheads, the crest extended all the way back to the nape of their broad necks.

The creatures possessed extended snouts, out of the end of which two great tusks emerged from their lower jaws. The sharp tusks conferred a feral aspect to the guardians.

Each of the creatures wore small pendants of silver and iron, dangling at the end of leather thongs strung around their bullish necks. The circular-shaped pendants held the form of a radiant star within, the lustrous image inlaid upon the darker surface. The gleaming silver of the stars showed brightly in contrast to the duller, dark iron of the background.

The two beasts stared down silently upon the approaching party, with dark eyes recessed deeply on each side of their faces. The look within was anything but welcoming. The gaze was hardened and dangerous, hinting at something threatening, as if duty was a cage that kept a raging beast contained.

In addition to the two beasts, there were three men in view, standing in between the towering creatures. The three humans looked diminutive next to the massive sentinels.

Two appeared to be regular guards, similar in all outward respects to the ones escorting Logan and the others. They stood to either side of a very stately-looking man, whose refined outer appearance announced that he was possessed of a much higher status.

He carefully regarded the approach of the prisoners, and Logan found himself a little unsettled under the pressing weight of the emotionless stare. There was a noticeably sharp, perceptive look about the man, one that Logan was not about to underestimate.

He had a long, narrow face with a high forehead. His brown hair was cut into a bobbed style just below his ears, with his bangs evenly trimmed above thin, high-arched eyebrows.

His tall, lean body was dressed in a white, sleeveless surcoat hanging down to his knees. Underneath the surcoat was a blue, long-sleeved tunic that extended farther, to where the lower hem ended just short of his ankles. Both garments were fashioned of finely softened linen.

The surcoat and tunic underneath were both slit at the front, the cuts running from the lower hem up to just under his waist level. The hem and neckline of the outer surcoat held intertwining patterns embroidered from golden threads. The triangular neck opening of the surcoat featured a short slit descending down in the front, held together by an ovular brooch of lustrous gold.

Though he could not tell its precise form, Logan could see that the brooch's surface was inlaid with some kind of star-shaped design. It looked very much like the shapes rendered on the pendants of the two massive, inhuman guards.

Brocaded green panels, interlaced with more of the abstract, curling golden designs, embellished the cuffs culminating the long sleeves of the blue, underlying tunic. The décor was continued in the edges of the tunic's round neckline, poking into sight just within the opening in the surcoat atop it.

The man's leather shoes had been dyed a deep black. Gold foil was embossed into swirling patterns, the latter carved into the upper part of the shoes.

"Lord Rogier, here are the four guests, as you requested," the guard in the lead of Logan's group announced, giving a slight bow as he addressed the exquisitely attired man. The guard's tone held polite deference, rendered in the presence of a greater authority.

Rogier gave a slight nod in acknowledgement, his eyes continuing to fix upon the new arrivals. "Wait here for a moment. I shall inform our Great Lord they have arrived, as well as our good Steward Sir Richard," he replied, in a smooth, elegant voice.

Turning his back to them, Rogier left the party standing near the edge of the steps. The guards attending Rogier moved up the stairs before him, one opening the bronze door. They waited patiently for Rogier to pass through the ornate door, before going through behind him.

The small party waited in an uneasy silence, but it was not long before Rogier and the two guards returned. Standing at the top of the steps, Rogier beckoned to them.

"If the four guests of our Great Lord will now follow me," he announced.

The two guards with Rogier gestured for Logan and his companions to continue forward. The guards who had escorted them cleared aside, lingering behind as the prisoners walked slowly up the steps.

Logan could not help looking towards the bestial sentinels as they ascended. The creatures' heads remained fixed forward, but he flinched as his eyes met those of one whose gaze had swiveled to watch his group pass. The look within its eye was foreboding, sending an icy wave ripping down his spine.

As they passed through the entrance, they turned to the left and halted. The bronze doorway was set into the side of a great hall at its far end.

A grand stone archway with large doors inset stood about midway down the length of the rectangular chamber's wall, to Logan's right. The doors were currently open, revealing a chamber of similar size lying beyond. The wall to the right provided further support for a network of stout timber beams, forming the structure for a sharply slanted roof high overhead.

Positioned at regular intervals, window alcoves harborning pairs of rectangular openings could be seen on a second level running around three sides of the chamber. The openings allowed ample amounts of light to flood into the immense hall, and timber railings on the inner side of the gallery overlooked the floor below.

A few additional arched openings led off the hall. A couple of them were behind where Logan now stood, and another was just to the right of the bronze door as one entered the chamber. Each contained a small closed wooden door.

A couple of open doors were set within the wall at the hall's far end, one to the far right, and one to the far left. More light streamed into the hall through window alcoves in the outer walls of small chambers lying beyond the two doorways.

The stone blocks of the walls were covered over with a thorough coating of plaster. The surfacing was extensively painted with bright murals, depicting extravagant scenes featuring numerous figures, animals, and landscapes, colored in vibrant shades of blues, greens, reds, and yellows.

Logan eyed a rendition of a great hunt, complete with a host of dogs racing alongside a number of armed horseriders with flowing cloaks. He felt a little pang of sympathy for the majestic hart bounding desperately amid the trees, just ahead of the pursuing mass of dogs and men. It was not that long ago that he had felt hunted himself, in the wooded lands of the Five Realms.

Sizeable woven tapestries were hung intermittently down the sides of the walls, some covering portions of the mural images. Like the murals, the tapestries contained images of nature, battle, and a few things of a fantastical nature.

A very conspicuous tapestry was positioned centrally, at a point between two of the upper level alcove windows at the far end. The bottom of the prominent tapestry rested just above the arched opening of a large fireplace set between the two exits leading out of the chamber.

The images in the tapestry were spectacular. An exquisite figure similar to the one worked into the bronze door at the chamber entrance was portrayed in vibrant threads. The winged entity was in the act of ascending towards the skies, with wings, arms, and burning red eyes angled upwards. The majestic, angelic-looking figure exuded a proud, graceful bearing, and displayed a particularly fierce countenance upon its winsome face.

Unlike the image on the door, the being on the tapestry was set against an expansive backdrop. The peak of a lofty, dark mountain could be seen, rising from the land far below the regal entity.

An uncountable host of other winged beings could also be seen within the background, soaring up in the wake of the main figure. They looked to be funneling outward from the direction of the mountain itself.

The foreground being was clearly the preeminent focus, the greatest of a vast host. Logan even perceived the connotation that the being held precedence over the world itself, with the largely featureless rendition of the land and the lone mountain.

Little of the fireplace underneath the elaborate tapestry was visible. Only the upper curvature of the top arch could be seen from where Logan stood. A raised platform spanning most of the chamber's width had been erected several paces in front of it.

The timber platform supported a long table, set close to its front edge and continuing down much of its length. The table itself was covered in snowy, white cloth.

Two other cloth-draped tables were set on the lower floor, oriented perpendicular to the raised platform. Several individuals lined the outer sides of the lower tables, seated upon long settles placed end to end.

The scribe Euvroin was one of those seated on the side tables. Ever the image of a scribe, he was seated a short distance down the table to Logan's left.

A studious expression resting on his face, and wearing his white linen coif, he was holding a stylus and wax tablet in his hands. He was the only individual at the floor tables with whom Logan had some familiarity.

Other than a slight nod of recognition to Euvroin, Logan gave the others no more than a passing glance. His gaze was irresistably drawn to the platform at the hall's far end.

At the raised table were eight prominent figures seated upon high-backed chairs. Three were set off to the right, and four to the left, of a distinctive chair elevated a little higher than the rest. The seats were occupied by a very diverse array of individuals, who collectively exuded a presence that filled the hall.

Though he found his gaze increasingly funneled towards the direct center, Logan took account of all the individuals on the platform.

On the right side of the occupant of the higher chair were two women and a shrouded individual, whose nature or gender could not be ascertained. Logan felt a chill course through his entire body as his eyes met those of the two women. The feeling grew icier as his gaze drifted across the dark, featureless opening of the hood covering the head of the shadowy figure at the table's far end. The trio's collective gazes seemed to clench him like the talons of a hawk, pulling away from an attacking swoop with its prey tightly secured, and rendered helpless.

Logan did not know why he suddenly had such intense and apprehensive feelings. While the hooded figure was undeniably foreboding, the two women were strikingly attractive.

The woman closest to the central seat had a bountiful, curling mass of red hair that fell gracefully about her shoulders. She had an angular, narrow face with a straight nose. Her eyes could have been fashioned from jade, for such were the jewel-like hues they held.

She was dressed in a bright red, silken tunic cut to fit snugly along the course of her upper body and down her long arms. The hem of the well-fitted sleeves culminated at the cusp of elegant hands, which rested lightly on the table's surface.

Several of her slender fingers were embellished with beautiful rings. A couple were solid circlets fashioned of precious metals, one of gold and the other silver, while the others held glittering gemstones.

Golden earrings dangled from each ear, both finely set with round emeralds. Another precious stone encased in gold rested upon the center of her chest, in the form of a ruby pendent hanging from an exquisite gold chain.

Logan found that the resplendent jewelry adorning her could do nothing to enhance her exceptional comeliness. She was simply stunning.

The woman to her immediate left was a raven-haired beauty with sparkling blue eyes. Ebony locks fell in gentle waves to wash over her shoulders, framing a face and neck whose unblemished skin was a smooth, creamy white. She had short, full lips that were set straight, accenting an expression hinting at either detached amusement or ardent austerity.

Her clothes were formed of the finest linen. A pure white tunic covered the outside of her body, fashioned with wide, flaring sleeves exhibiting an equally opalescent chemise underneath. The tunic was decorated at the cuff lines and rounded neck opening with brocaded blue patterns, which looked to be a continuum of intertwined serpents. The serpents coiled about each other, linked in a repetitive manner where each serpent's outstretched mouth was engulfing the tail end of the next.

A sizeable, circular sapphire was set into an amulet hanging down in front, standing out prominently from the white linen underneath. Elegant fingers graced with several ornate rings led up to wrists displaying several alternating silver and golden bracelets.

The hooded figure to the right of the women deeply unsettled Logan. The dark folds of the figure's outer cloak covered a lean body that was slightly hunched over, as if bent by age, frailty, or some concealed deformity.

Nothing could be seen of its features, as even the figure's hands were hidden underneath the table's surface. Logan could sense a powerful scrutiny coming from the hood's interior, and found that he was not eager to see the face within the dark opening.

The cloak was fastened in front by a lone silver, penannular brooch. A golden amulet suspended from a narrow, silver chain emerged from the shadows of the hood to rest below the brooch. The shape of the shiny amulet was indiscernable, obscured by the folds of the cloak.

Arrayed to the left of the central chair sat four men. Two had the strong, rougher appearance of warriors. The other pair gave off a decidedly more sagely, high-cultured impression.

One of the two stalwart-looking men sat closest to the highest seat. His outer appearance had a very chiseled, rigid ambience about it. Wide of chest and shoulder, his long, thick arms rested with hands clasped loosely together on the table in front of him. He had a long face with a prominent, aquiline nose.

A dense, short-cropped beard and moustache covered his squared jaw. His short, broad eyebrows angled downward, towards his nose, evoking a trace of anger even though his expression was nominally placid. Wavy, thick black locks, parted in the middle, swirled about the sides of his face and came to rest on the top of his capacious shoulders.

He was clad in a black supertunic with extended, loose sleeves. Silver-threaded embroidery formed a continuing series of small, interlocking rings around the circumference of his wrists and hemline. The man had a calm, poised look about him, and studied Logan carefully with his dark, alert eyes. While Logan knew nothing about the man, there was no mistaking he was a warrior.

To the immediate left of the warrior was a man with a far less militant character to his appearance. His clean-shaven face was a work of balanced symmetry. His narrow, straight nose, mildly protruding eyes, and relaxed mouth were in excellent proportion to each other, lending him a fairly handsome appearance. His hair was combed straight, falling to just below his ears and parted in the middle of his modest forehead.

Like the warrior to the right, he wore a long-sleeved supertunic, though his was dyed a deep scarlet. Intertwining blue and green rings were woven into the various edges of the supertunic, the latter covering a solid black tunic underneath.

A round, snug-fitting cap crafted of black felt sat atop his head. His long fingers displayed a few silver rings, situated on smooth hands whose even complexion gave no evidence of usage in significant physical labors. Leaning slightly forward, his posture betrayed his keen interest in the newcomers.

To the left of the scarlet clad fellow was a man who Logan took immediately to be another warrior. He had a burly, barrel-chested build, with a broad, rounded face. His large nose was uneven along the bridge, where it had obviously been broken more than once.

Curly, brown hair covered his head, and shadowy, rough stubble surrounded his wide mouth. His eyes were a light hazel in hue, and were currently narrowed in a state of rapt examination, as he scrupulously looked over the four outlanders.

His attire was a little more simplistic than the others at the raised table. A sleeveless, black surcoat rested over a dark green tunic, devoid entirely of ornamental designs. A singular ring of silver sat upon his right hand, with a red garnet set into it.

At the far end of the table was a diminutive, elderly man, draped in a blue tunic of fine silk that featured a narrow collar. Thinning gray hair fell down in scraggly tendrils to the top of his shoulders, while the ends of a voluminous, elongated beard rested upon the top of his chest.

A long, sharp-ended nose cradled the top of his moustache and upper lip. His eyes were small and recessed, the dark pupils darting sequentially between the newcomers, and giving evidence to a spry alertness underneath his aged exterior.

All sitting upon the platform had their own unique, powerful carriage about their persons. Yet Logan's attention finally centered upon the one whose presence surpassed all the others. The other seven were little more than fanciful accoutrements to the majestic figure, for such was the commanding, noble presence the being radiated.

The great chair that the figure sat upon was fashioned of a dark-hued, intricately carved wood. The high backing had been meticulously crafted to form the image of high, arched wings, evenly framing the one who sat upon the ornate chair. The ends of the chair's stout arms would have otherwise seemed as nothing more than palm-sized orbs, were it not for the fact that their globular surfaces were etched with several raised, amorphous shapes.

To Logan, the designs looked uncannily like the outlines of continents, islands, and oceans, like those portrayed upon a globe representing his own world. Yet if it was such a display, the orbs did not feature renderings of his former world, but rather depictions of his strange new one.

The smooth hands of the one seated upon the chair rested comfortably upon the globes. Long fingers curled down along the curving surfaces, exhibiting no tension as they held a light, relaxed grip upon the orbs.

The one seated upon the high-backed chair was a most radiant, elegant figure. The regal man looked to be in his early to mid thirties, in the bloom of his physical prime with no hint of advancing age.

His lustrous black hair was close cropped, perfectly laying upon his scalp and framing his beautiful face. There was only the slightest undulation along the length of the short, ebony strands.

He was clad in a silken robe of the most immaculate white sheen. The splendid garment served to bring out the olive complexion of his flawless skin.

A prominent, equine nose edified his long, angular face. With full lips and a slightly upturned slant to his eyes, it was hard for Logan to even begin to guess at the man's ethnic background. If anything, the man was an almagamation of all ethnicities, bringing a host of diverse attributes into well-balanced harmony.

His dark eyebrows harbored his most remarkable feature underneath them; a set of striking blue eyes, whose great brilliance was evident even from the considerable distance at which Logan stood. He could not recall having ever looked into eyes that held such fathomless depths within. Logan stood as if mesmerized, as the man's gaze came to rest upon him.

The slightest hint of amusement came to the man's face. A spark glinting within the deep pools of his eyes, the slightest trace of a grin played upon his well-formed lips.

Another unexpected feeling passed through and over Logan. He tried to fight back the irrational impression that the man's eyes could, and indeed were, looking right through him.

It was as if Logan suddenly realized he had failed to don clothes prior to his coming into the chamber, and was abruptly exposed in his most bare elements before the princely figure's transfixing gaze. A cold sweat broke out upon Logan's forehead, bringing a clammy feeling to his hands. It was all he could do to maintain his composure, though his breath shortened, as rising anxiety drove it to catch in his throat.

There was a swirling sense of danger and a suggestion of invitation beckoning in the air. It was diffcult to pinpoint the subtleties, but some things were abundantly clear. Logan knew without a doubt in his heart that the prominent figure was far greater than any king or emperor.

section iv

BEVRIEDAK

The black dragon's stare bored into Bevriedak, as a brooding tension again gripped the stillness surrounding the two winged juggernauts. Yet Bevriedak did not feel any threats from having spoken so openly about his intentions for the future. The strain in the air was fueled by another source entirely.

Bevriedak knew Gerasen's struggle within himself. The black dragorn was trying to come to terms with, or reject, the conclusions Bevriedak voiced.

Bevriedak's position was not easy to embrace. To many other Elder, even the mere consideration of what Bevriedak had done was akin to abetting a great heresy. Some would have regarded Bevriedak as little more than a renegade, worthy of nothing but contempt.

Yet if any of the Elder could understand Bevriedak's heart, and might consider joining with him, it would be Gerasen. There were a few others who exhibited continued concern for Ave, such as the exalted red dragon Maraghen, but such Elder had become an outright rarity. Over the ages, most had gradually become detatched in their thoughts and interests, increasingly giving themselves over to lengthy periods of unconsciousness.

Gerasen had proven to be one of the enduring exceptions. Like Bevriedak, he had maintained a regular stream of tidings, with the assistance of ravens. The diminutive, dark-feathered messengers the two Elder utilized carried word gathered from all corners of Ave. Over the long centuries, the pair had become as diligent as the most assiduous human scholars in all the world, from any age.

Now that Bevriedak had made his full intentions known, he would see whether or not he had made a good calculation in his justifications to Gerasen. The Oath had stood without transgression for a few thousand years, still as potent as ever in the midst of the eighth marked age of the world. The All-Father had allowed the Wizards to enact the great sundering of Natural Law in forming the skyward sanctuaries that served for millennia as the abodes of the Elder.

The Natural Law, brought into being by the All-Father to govern the elements of the physical world, was not something suspended for minor reasons. The All-Father had allowed the breaking of Natural Law to such a great extent for only one other major endeavor in all of Ave's long history.

One dispensation had been granted for the uppermost reaches of the sky. Another had been granted for the deep fathoms of the sea.

Two miraculous havens had been created during that distant age, both of which defied many aspects of the Natural Law. Both were destined from the beginning to serve as isolated, comfortable refuges for two particular races needing separation from the rest of Ave.

Gerasen was indisputably correct about the matter facing all the Elder, including Bevriedak. The Ban could not simply be willed away, even with the pure force of righteous conviction.

The azure hues of Gerasen's eyes were highlighted prominently by the cascading light from the aperture in the cavern's ceiling. Yet the dragon's mien remained entirely impassive, as he stared rigidly into Bevriedak's face.

The light glinted off the golden flecks within the blue orbs, as if echoing the myriad activities that Bevriedak knew were occurring within Gerasen's mind. Bevriedak knew there was a great inner tumult transpiring behind the stoic posture of his friend.

"Bevreidak flies in the lower world once again … Arcamons are let loose in the world, called forth from the Nether Realms," Gerasen stated heavily, with an undeniably lugubrious intonation that did nothing to abate the unease pervading the air. "Renegade Elder may soon appear once more, forgetting the dire fates the last rebel Elder met with. And if all of that is not enough, the last refuge left to our little brothers and sisters is likely to be a battleground.

"It may well be the time when our long years of exile draw to an end, and we can return to the world again. But what kind of world will this be? Is it one that any of us who remain true would even wish to be a part of?"

Gerasen's nostrils distended widely, as his chest swelled and ebbed with an extensive, slow breath. His voice had the presence of calm resignation when he continued. "It brings me no joy to agree with you, Bevriedak, that this may truly be the final age, the End of Days. The time of the Ragnarok, as it was once called in Midragard."

As much as every Elder desired the end of their exile, there could be no joy taken in the onset of such a storm of horror, as the End of Days represented. The events implicit in the last age of the world would see a reign of unprecedented terror and upheaval. Tremendous numbers of innocents would endure a frightful age, of unprecedented darkness. A much greater number would not survive the period to begin with.

"Not another rumor of war, or common earthquake?" Bevriedak remarked casually, his provoking query drawing a sharpened look from the black dragon. Bevriedak studied his comrade carefully, wanting to determine the mindset Gerasen was embracing.

"Must I caution you that only the All-Father knows when the End of Days will take hold in Ave? There are signs, but do not presume you know the hour, Bevriedak," Gerasan stated.

"Then would you endure the Ban, if you felt in your spirit that the cause for doing so was just?" Bevriedak asked, finally letting his distant hope out.

Gerasen's expression was unreadable, as Bevriedak anxiously awaited the black dragon's response.

Finally, Gerasen responded, "I am tempted to endure the Ban for our little brothers and sisters. But I must speak what is on my mind, as I stand on this precipice you have beckoned me to. I ask you now, why the humans? Most show little or no will to resist this Unifier. Most stand by, and do nothing, as their kings and emperors bend their knees in submission to this walking abomination. Are they not to receive what they rightfully deserve, and have chosen?"

The black dragon's nostrils flared, as he breathed in deeply. Bevriedak would not have been surprised if a little burst of flame escaped when Gerasen finally exhaled. Bevriedak knew his friend did not hold outright hatred for humans, but rather was filled with a tremendous amount of disgust towards the majority of the race.

Bevriedak could not deny Gerasen's sentiments. The history of humankind substantiated the black dragon's outlook. It was of little surprise that Gerasen harbored an abiding reticence to help humans.

"They will flock to any banner, if it feeds their bellies, provides them with trivial amusements, or whispers to their ravenous vanities," Gerasen snarled derisively. His head extended towards Bevriedak, as he hissed his next words, "And you know this is so, Bevriedak."

"It is so, Gerasen," Bevriedak acknowledged firmly, without even a moment's hesitation. In his heart, he hoped he could somehow temper the ire rising within the black dragon. He then stated, "But it is not that way with all of them, and you know that is also so."

"Yet as a race, it is their way," Gerasen retorted curtly.

Seeing Gerasen's acerbic reaction, Bevriedak's hopes began to sag once again. He knew Gerasen all too well, and could make a reasonable forecast of where Gerasen's thoughts were taking him.

Gerasen's stubbornness would soon rise to the fore, following the bout of anger, all prompted by the contemplation of human history. Before too much longer, Gerasen would become implacable.

"I do not feel we should allow the slaughter of those humans still willing to fight," Bevriedak stated, steadfastly. "Were it just a hundred gathered in a final stand, arrayed against an army of thousands upon thousands, we should still commit to the fight below. I tell you solemnly, I would fight for one Wulfstan, even if there were ten thousand upon ten thousand unworthy for every rare one like him. He alone is worth fighting for.

"I feel that if we do not act, then we are little better than those who openly assault the faithful of the All-Father. Failure to act is failure in itself, as much as wrongful action is. That failure is widespread in this world, among those allowing their kings and emperors to bend their knee to the Unifier, and among those of our own kind, whom I fear will do nothing in the darkest age below.

"Such inaction is likely the greatest of failures. It is complicity in wickedness. Surely you understand what I mean by this. Do you, Gerasen?" Bevriedak silently awaited his friend's reply, and the ensuing moments seemed like years in the passing.

"You bring far too much to mind, my old friend, when you speak of the failure to act, though you are merciful for not giving open voice to it," Gerasen responded at last, speaking in a weary-sounding voice.

The massive black dragon slowly turned his head away from Bevriedak. The air of stalwart defiance evaporated swiftly, leaving a sense of emptiness in its wake. An unsettling disquiet emanated from Gerasen, as he stared silently ahead, with a gaze looking far beyond the physical space of the cavern.

At first, the reaction caught Bevriedak by surprise. A keen understanding then came over him, as time itself seemed to freeze. He realized what caused the abrupt downturn in Gerasen's attitude.

The other Elder was recalling one of the most painful memories for their immortal kind. The retrospection centered on a momentous failure to act, and a part of Bevriedak was sorrowful for invoking the dark remembrance.

Though faded in the deep mists of time itself, the course of events during a faraway age was not dimmed in Bevriedak's mind either. It called to mind an extraordinary age that saw many Elder crowned as gods, an abominable season when creatures were deified by other creatures.

It was a dark and frightful age, wrought with titanic wars unleashing enormous fires and bloodshed across the surface of Ave. The full danger of the Elder's power had been revealed, in all of its terrible might. The stygian age of violence and terror set in motion the events leading directly to the creation of the Oath.

The wielding of such immense power as the Elder possessed had hurled storms of disruption into the affairs of all living things within Ave. Great maelstroms had fallen without discrimination upon evil and innocent alike, and, as such, the Oath had been fairly easy to accept and endure during its earliest years. It was not difficult to look upon the Ban as a saving grace, halting the Elder from stumbling over the precipice of disaster.

The Elder in the Forbidden Dominions had been in unity then, resolved to wait until the End of Days set them free once again. That time of cohesion was when most of their kind began to take to the long sleep. The few like Gerasen and Bevriedak, who had elected to remain conscious and watch over the affairs of the world, soon arrived at stark, troubling realizations.

Their loyal, black-winged emissaries had not been the only creatures the Elder such as Bevriedak and Gerasen interacted with during the first ages following the Ban. Through the ravens, Gerasen maintained a sustained, if distant, contact with the Elder's lesser kindred; the race of mortal dragons.

Bevriedak could not dispute Gerasen's passion for the well-being of the mortal dragons in Ave. The smaller dragons were all that was left in the world serving as a visible reminder of the primal, immortal Elder. The Elder might have chosen to remove themselves from the affairs of the world, but they did not wish for dragon-kind to vanish from the spectrum of life dwelling upon Ave's surface. Nor did the Elder wish to be entirely forgotten.

Gerasen and the great red Elder Maraghen, nearly alone of all their kind, had felt a burning obligation to sustain some manner of connection with their lesser kindred. The pair's interests came to rest with the western breed of the mortal dragons, the ones the two Elder most closely resembled. There were also two other Elder, similar in disposition to Maraghen and Gerasen, who tended to the Eastern Ones in a like manner.

Maraghen was a very solitary, reclusive individual, and Bevriedak could not say what transpired over the ages between the huge red and the various generations of mortal dragons. With Gerasen, Bevriedak knew that his friend often extended valuable wisdom and guidance to the mortal dragons. The contact between Elder and mortal dragons never involved significant interference in the latter's worldly affairs. As such, Gerasen had never seen the interaction being a threat to violating the essence of the Oath.

Over the long course of time, the ongoing interaction brought terrible revelations, and a particularly horrid dilemma. The price of knowledge and the limitations of the Ban eventually collided in a major, devastating fashion.

As Bevriedak watched Gerasen now, he took a quick sojourn into the halls of his own memory. He hastened back to the age when the great hunts had been launched in western lands, not long after the Second Age of the world was underway.

At first, the reports trickling in seemed to be little more than dark rumors, of such a bizarre nature that they begged disbelief. Yet not much more time transpired before the veracity of the disturbing accounts could no longer be denied.

Tragic stories rose in ever increasing abundance up to Gerasen's abode, carried by dark-feathered witnesses. The ravens arrived at the Elder's haven from many wide and diverse lands, all speaking of similar, dismaying tales, full of blood, fear, pursuits, entrapment, and death.

The smaller, mortal race of dragons dwelling in the westernmost lands of Ave were being slain one by one, or rooted out, violently driven from their wilderness refuges. Not long after, the incidents spread like a creeping plague, pushing eastward, and wending deeper into the southern lands.

The Eastern Ones, with their more open connections with humankind, were spared the ordeal of the western kind. They were embraced, and even revered, within the human cultures where they existed, while the Western Ones became creatures that were feared, and viewed as outright pariahs.

The humans pressed the widening slaughter with ferocity. They were unceasing in their efforts to rid the kingdoms within the western and southern regions of Ave of all dragons.

Dragons, like humans, were each possessed of the capacity for good or evil. Bevriedak knew that some cruel, malignant dragons brought their own doom upon themselves, by their own actions, but a majority of the persecuted dragons had never once harmed humankind.

If anything, a few had sought, or enjoyed, open friendship with humans, desiring to be benefactors. Most, though, had simply wanted to live their lives without undue disturbance, embedded deep in wilderness regions where they had no interactions whatsoever with humankind.

The onslaught made no distinctions amongst the dragons. Malefic, benevolent, and indifferent alike were hunted down with great fervor, condemned to the same bloody fate. It was a genocidal hunt, pursued with the singular, vile purpose of extinction.

As the bloodletting unfurled, the western dragons reached out desperately for the help of the Elder. Yet none of the former's more powerful, sky-dwelling brethren heeded the urgent pleas. In every instance, the Ban was invoked as the sole reason for the Elder's refusal to come to the direct aid of the western dragons.

Without intervention, the mortal dragons looked doomed. Intervention was to come, as the western dragons survived that dark epoch of time, but it came from a source other than the Elder; a source that did not involve any manner of dragon-kind.

As Bevriedak now watched his friend, he knew Gerasen was dredging up, and squarely facing, the harsh truth of his abject failure to act in those grievous times. Bevriedak's firm decision to act, and his powerful remarks about failures to act, had done much to evoke the unpleasant history and dark memories abiding within the black dragon. Gerasen was now recognizing a bitter, searing truth that had existed all along; the verity that he could have acted to help the dragon-kind that he so loved.

Under the wings of the Elder, the ravenous, wicked hunger seeking to consume the western dragons to the last could have been held at bay. In the icy, merciless light of reality, Gerasen saw that he alone was responsible for making the choice not to defy the Oath during that troubling age.

A remote haven had eventually been located for the western dragons, in the far southern, highly mountainous regions of Midragard. The dragon-haven within the lofty Drakkar Mountains had safeguarded the bulk of the survivors.

After the exodus of the dragons to southern Midragard, the great Wizard Wodan sent word of the refuge to Gerasen through his two great ravens, Huginn and Muninn. It was then that Gerasen discovered Wodan and other Wizards of substantial power had acted during the dragon's greatest time of peril. Even a few humans had taken significant part in the salvation of the western dragon's race.

The Midragardans, for their part, reverenced dragons enough that they were willing to enter into a compact with them, overseen by Wodan himself. The resulting covenant allowed the mortal dragons the freedom to inhabit and roam the Drakkar Mountains, the range sprawling across the deep southern region of Midragard. They would no longer be hunted or purposely slain, as long as none of them claimed human life.

The great range of mountains was then given fully over to the dragons to live, hunt, and breed in. It was a place where they recovered in security, and, in the course of time, thrived once again.

Gerasen knew the people of Midragard and the efforts of Wizards made all the difference in helping the dragons to survive the horrid ordeal. At the same time, Gerasen had also known he had done nothing.

His friend then expressed the deep affliction he had been enduring for ages. Rearing back, he loosed a deafening roar that would have shaken a mountain if they had been down on Ave's surface. It was a mournful symphony woven of guilt, regret, and sorrow, rending the air all about the two Elder. Torrents built up and restrained for numerous centuries were finally given unrestrained vent.

The great dragon's chest swelled up again, as he inhaled deeply. He let free another sonorous roar, mixed with a withering jet of fire that shot across the cavern. The column of flame slammed against the far wall, spreading rapidly as it covered the opalescent surface, before burning itself out. It was quite fortunate the white substance constituting the structures of the formations within the Forbidden Dominions was not flammable.

Gerasen's head tilted downward, and a saddened look came to his eyes. Head bowed, he exhibited a posture that looked like one of surrender, though Bevriedak knew his friend was simply sagging under the weighty pressure of his consuming, inner torments.

Bevriedak had to look away from his crestfallen friend, knowing the pain gnawing within Gerasen was little different than the nature of the unending flames searing condemned souls in Jebaalos's nether-realm. It was a fire Bevriedak could not hope to quench by his own efforts, but he could always try to do his part.

"I know this is very difficult, Gerasen. It would seem we were given an impossible choice when we took the Oath, now that we have seen how the events of this world have unfolded," Bevriedak said. He spoke carefully, in a softened voice, delicately venturing his thoughts forward. "We can see all of that plainly now. But you must know we could not see so clearly in those days. We could not know the future. It was shrouded deep in gray mists that our best efforts could not hope to pierce. We should not condemn ourselves for that."

Gerasen made no effort to respond, and there was not even a flicker in his stony expression. After a moment, Bevriedak decided to proceed a little further.

"You know I believe that we must now break the Oath, and suffer the Ban as long as we can endure it below," he continued, carefully watching Gerasen. "We must help those who fight against the Unifier.

"You will be helping our own kindred by doing so. They now face a threat far greater than that of the past ages. Our smaller kindred are opposed to the Unifier, and you know the Unifier seeks to vanquish all who oppose the coming order, wherever they are in the world. We are at the dawn of a great darkness seeking to shroud Ave in its wickedness.

"There will be no refuge, not even the Drakkar Mountains. No dwelling place will be left untouched if the Unifier's hand grasps the entire world. This time it will be all dragons that are hunted, even those in the east. All who refuse to submit will be brought to destruction. All Elder, all dragons, whether immortal or mortal, whether western or eastern."

The last words hung thickly in the air. Bevriedak hoped with all of his heart that Gerasen saw the looming implications, and the comprehensive scope of the threats facing them.

Gerasen brooded in melancholy silence, his head remaining downward, and showing no signs of reaction. The black dragon's voice was heavily tinged with regret when he finally raised his head up, and answered his friend.

His eyes had a strange, tortured look as he stared deep into Bevriedak's eyes. Bevriedak sensed that the words coming out of Gerasen were some of the hardest utterances the great Elder had ever spoken.

"I cannot give you an answer that is to your liking. Maybe some of the others will come to join your path, even if I do not. I would not condemn them for making such a choice, as I do not condemn you.

"I cannot yet break the Oath, no matter what has happened, and is happening, in the world. It means that I may have to live with inner suffering that will never subside, at least until the End of Days. Maybe there is more suffering yet to come.

"Perhaps we would have done better by ourselves had we gone into the embrace of the deep sleep. Maybe this is our punishment for keeping an interest in a world that we are not allowed to act within.

"We must remember what brought us to the Oath in the beginning, and what was in the balance then, when we flew free in the skies over Ave. I remember all too clearly the great destruction and bloodshed that imperiled our immortal souls, in the age before the Oath and the Ban. It is all burned into my mind, as if it was yesterday. Were it not for the Oath, we may well have ended our life's journey in the unquenchable fires of the nether realm. Many of us likely were headed towards such a perilous end, even if we thought our loyalty was to the All-Father. Such is the great power of deception Jebaalos wields.

"The world is meant to run its course without us, and we only harm ourselves by meddling in Ave's affairs. That is the bitter lesson I learned in the age before the Oath, and I cannot disregard it now."

Bevriedak felt empty and forlorn as he listened to Gerasen's momentous words. He finally gave a slight nod, trying not to let his face show the deep sadness, and sharp disappointment, he felt at Gerasen's choice.

He kept his voice steady, trying to mask his own despondent emotions. His words came out slowly. "As you wish, Gerasen. We must all choose our path. For my part, I do not believe the world was meant to run its course without us. We are creatures of Ave, and we have our purpose too.

"There is no feeling of anger towards you for this decision, for I know you respect the serious nature of the Oath, as much as any of the others. And you have incurred great loss and suffering over the ages to honor it."

His response lingered in the air for a few extended moments, as he took account of Gerasen. There was a glistening to the other dragon's eyes that had not been there moments before.

"Know that there is no anger held towards you, for taking a different path than I, Bevriedak," Gerasen replied, in a heavy tone. "We are of the same mind and heart, in so many ways. Do not forget that. And I do hope that you show me to be wrong, and that you are able to do whatever you are setting forth to do in the world below."

Bevriedak knew Gerasen's soul was bleeding, from wounds accumulated over long ages. He did not know how he could help to heal his friend's raw, inner wounds, but if he was right about the imminent arrival of the End of Days, a day of true healing was not all too far away. At the very least, that sliver of hope gave Bevriedak's troubled spirit a little comfort.

MIDRAGARD

Mounted upon the fleetest among the race of Fenraren, messengers had gone forth at King Hakon's bidding to all ends of Midragard. Visiting jarls and chieftains of all the coastal regions and waterways, they hearkened wherever any kind of sea service was owed to King Hakon in times of war.

Some of the chieftains they visited controlled little more than an off-shooting finger of a fjord. Other greater jarls controlled entire regions, including some that were strategically critical for Midragard. Yet whether greater or lesser, they controlled the storied longships representing the greatest center of power in all Midragard.

Over the long ages, one absolute truth always stood forth; whoever controlled the seas and waterways, controlled Midragard.

The lesson was one well-heeded by King Hakon, who had long maintained several of the land's greatest longships. From the heralded Southern Storm, commanded by Svein, to others of great renown such as the Sea Wolf, Warrior's Soul, Water Dragon, and Spirit of Thunder, King Hakon held dominion of a wondrous, formidable array of vessels.

The famed ships had not come into being easily. During the midst of past winters, diligent searches had been made throughout the forests for the most exceptional oaks. Remarkable specimens had been found and lugged back with tremendous effort. Then, they were turned into the keels of King Hakon's vaunted longships. Where most Midragardian ships were of a size allowing for twenty to twenty-five pairs of oars, and celebrated ships around thirty-five pairs, none of the King Hakon's elite warships had less than forty.

Southern Storm had a previously unheard of fifty oars per side. It was an exquisite longship, with its ornately carved prow and stern. The uppermost strakes arced elegantly upward, to where they were crowned with a carving fashioned in a pronounced, swirling shape evocative of an oceanic maelstrom.

The curling figurehead was not simply a representation of the power of weather. Along the course of its outer surface, etched by expert hands, was a multitude of images. Great wolves, hulking bears, streaking dragons, proud ravens, and several armed Midragardan warriors were rendered in detail within the timber. Interspersed among the living figures, at regular intervals representations of axes, swords, and shields.

Southern Storm's outer line of shield-battens allowed for an impressive display of warriors' shields. The thin battens alongside the top strakes were provided with wooden cleats allowing for the array of round shields without impeding the use of the ship's oar holes.

When its high mast was raised, and the great square sail unfurled, its gilded bronze weather vane flew proudly in the winds from the oaken mast's lofty summit. Containing intricate, swirling scroll-work reminiscent of the carved prow and stern heads, the weather vane was both aesthetic and highly functional.

While pine was quite acceptable material for the fashioning of masts and many other elements of well-crafted ships, Southern Storm and the other prime vessels of King Hakon used pine only for deck planking. The thorough use of oak not only made for very strong, exceptionally seaworthy vessels, but also served as a clear testament to King Hakon's high status and wealth.

All the jarls and chieftains of the coastal districts had long been encouraged to indulge in shipbuilding. Ships could not be built overnight. King Hakon knew from his earliest days as a recognized king that Midragard could not afford to be taken by surprise, in the eventuality that a grave threat beyond its borders manifested.

He was well aware of the powers growing far to the north. The longstanding appeal to the jarls and chieftains to engage in shipbuilding turned out to be one of the wisest, most foresighted undertakings the king had ever embraced.

The leidang was invoked in full, as the hints of coming storms appeared on Midragard's horizons. The timing of the leidang was very fortuitous.

Many newly-fashioned ships could be seen across Midragard that spring, with most of the size requiring twenty to twenty-five pairs of oars. Shipwrights made skillful use of whatever was available in their particular region. Where oak and pine was scarcer, they made use of lime, willow, birch, and ash for upper strakes and other elements.

The coasts and rivers of Midragard witnessed the common sight of new ships being set into the water for the first time. Outer strakes covered with many coats of pine tar, the vessels were evaluated by the shipwrights in regards to how they sat in the water, and whether they had any leaks. If the results of the trials were satisfactory, the masts were stepped, oars fashioned, and other finishing touches added.

A bountiful crop of longships followed a carefully tended winter of shipbuilding. The ensuing yield of many magnificent craft had recently entered the seas, fjords, and rivers alongside their other brethren. From the fast, sleek longships, to the sturdy, broader knarrs that had been an exceptional achievement of Midragard's fabled shipwrights, the potential of a combined Midragardan fleet was as beautiful as it was deadly.

While King Hakon and the greatest jarls appreciated the artistic accomplishments of the shipwrights, it was the pragmatic nature of the ships that would be of the most regard to Midragard's leaders in the coming days of trial. The longships, low and narrow in profile, were graced with excellent speed. They also held the ability to navigate shallow waters, and beach easily upon shorelines, enabling a rapid, dexterous maneuvering of Midragardan warriors along coast, fjord, or river.

The broader and shorter knarrs were very seaworthy vessels, whose elegant frontal profiles had earned them the description of being 'swan-breasted' in the sagas of the land. Their midship holds could contain solid quantities of goods and livestock.

Collectively, up and down the coastlines, up wide rivers, and down the great fjords and their narrow offshoots, the final preparations were made. The components of a great and unprecedented war fleet were being assembled with alacrity.

Any longships still sheltered in special, quartering buildings, or naust, were brought out from where they had lain during their winter slumber. Rope made of hide, hemp, or bast fibers was assiduously collected for use in rigging. Casks, chests, and more durable foodstuffs were gathered for provisioning and storage aboard the longships and knarrs. Caulking and repairs of existing ships was executed with diligence, often making use of elements gleaned from older, discarded vessels.

A king in Midragard's power was never greater than in a time of war, and no greater threat of war had ever loomed over Midragard than the one spoken of by the Elder Dragon. King Hakon had acted decisively, taking little time to issue the official dictates and summons involved with the comprehensive leidang. The already impressive influx would not take much longer to coalesce into a seaborne juggernaut.

JANUS

Everything in Janus wanted to cry out. His hackles rose under the weight of penetrating stares directed his way from the high platform. A part of him wondered if it was how the mouse felt in an open field when the shadow of the descending hawk finally closed over it. Perhaps the sensation was similar to that of an old deer, tiring and running out its last burst of desperate energy before a relentless pack of slavering wolves.

He could not explain why he was gripped with such a paralyzing fear, but it was rife within him nonetheless. He averted his eyes from the platform for a moment, instead looking down at the floor.

Coated in a coarse plaster, the floor was covered with a layer of rushes woven into a series of small mats. Janus kept his eyes fixed upon the mat immediately beneath his feet, concentrating on the weaving pattern. He took in a few slow, calming breaths, seeking to stabilize himself.

"Please forgive the seeming detention, my honored guests."

The voice conveying the words was even and articulate, belonging to the prominent-looking man seated in the most elevated chair on the far platform. Janus slowly brought his eyes back up, partially recovered from the wave of fear that had just come over him. The disquiet still lingered within, but it had ebbed.

Though nothing had physically changed about the man in the few seconds Janus had looked away, he felt as if a profound transformation had taken place. The intimidating, scrutinizing atmosphere in the chamber was no longer palpable.

Janus found himself drawn to the face of the preeminent man, instantly taking notice of the figure's striking blue eyes. The azure depths held a gentle, even kindly look to them. The feeling was highly surreal, if not a little disconcerting. At the distance Janus stood from the platform, it was remarkable that he could have gained such a strong and encompassing impression.

The white-attired man looked to each of the foursome slowly, with a concerned-looking mien. In some indescribable way, the look transmitted an acute awareness that Janus comprehended clearly within his own mind. An understanding forged of pure thought, it seemed as if the man somehow shared their discomforts and anxieties, and was sorrowing empathetically over their confusion, troubles, and fears. The enigmatic gaze practically compelled Janus to trust the man's spoken words.

The remaining vestiges of fear Janus had been fighting seemed to instantly evaporate as he continued to look straight into the man's mesmerizing eyes. The becalming dissipation of fear served to encourage Janus further towards holding on to the words of the mysterious figure. It was a strange, hypnotic experience, one that completely overcame him, like nothing he had ever encountered before.

"It is an unfortunate necessity, in these times of war and uncertainty," the man continued in his remarkably soothing tone, following a brief pause.

His voice was reassuring and amiable, reaching out to wrap around Janus with a comforting sense of security. Yet all was not in perfect harmony. Janus began to find himself gradually becoming attuned to some underlying subtleties in the enveloping feeling of solace; hinting of an almost imperceptible discordance.

The distant sensation tugged ever so slightly at the far edges of his consciousness. Even though the feeling was diminutive, it starkly contrasted with the ostensible intentions of the man's words and demeanor. The man's unified message to the four companions, rendered in spoken words, visible countenance, and perhaps something intangible, urged trust and offered refuge. The words had all the appearances of being spoken with true sincerity.

Though his mind could not rationalize the incongruent elements present within the appearances and perceptions, the words and other conveyances from the man seemed to lack something intrinsic. Janus scarcely noticed the subtle anomalies at first, yet the more he focused his mind upon the newfound aspects, the clearer they became.

It was like there was no underlying warmth within the tones of the highly persuasive voice; even if the prior sense of riveting fear had seemed to so abruptly scatter in the wake of the man's direct attentions.

There was simply a rising, discernible matter of something being askew, though Janus could not hone in on the exact nature of the cognition. The emerging perception troubled Janus greatly.

Even worse, it was as if the deeper observation was being constantly obfuscated in his mind, elusively becoming ephemeral at the very brink of realization. As such, Janus' mind hovered right at the very edge of defining the troubling feeling, while being somehow prevented from taking the minute step that would help him grasp full understanding.

As frustrating as it was, Janus was left with little choice but to either trust the faint instinct or accept the powerful impressions flowing from the eminent man. He was not left with much time to ruminate further, as the man proceeded to gracefully rise to his feet.

He walked slowly down the length of the platform, in back of the table and the others sitting at it. He then took a few steps down at the right end of the platform. Passing around the end, He walked out to stand directly in front of Janus and his three companions.

Janus could now appreciate His considerable height, rising to at least three or four inches above six feet. The close-fitting, full-length white tunic He wore revealed a very solid, well-proportioned build underneath, replete with broad shoulders.

The man was doubtlessly in a state of perfect health, with absolutely no softness about his body, posture, or alertness. Janus judged that the man was not likely given over to the kinds of indulgences continuously available to those of extreme wealth and authority. There were absolutely no signs of extravagances or telltale indications of intemperance. As such, the man's mere appearance bespoke an individual who resisted temptations and valued discipline, scrupulously maintaining the qualities himself.

He emanated a radiating aura that seemed to saturate the entirety of the hall chamber. Whether a figment of his mind or not, Janus felt the sensation coalescing stronger with the man's close proximity.

The sense was so pervasive that it caused Janus to momentarily forget there was anyone else within the great hall. He even ceased to think of the three with him who were from his own world. Janus blinked his eyes a couple of times, adamantly willing himself to hold onto a leveled focus, and at least a remote semblance of awareness.

The man took a couple more purposeful steps towards the four otherworlders, quietly regarding them with an amiable expression displayed upon His face.

"I know just a little about each of you, Erika ... Antonio ... Janus ... and Logan...." He said, looking to each one of them as He spoke their name aloud. "Euvroin described you well enough, and told me what little he has learned of you. There is so much more I want to know. It is not often that we are privileged with such guests."

He paused for a moment, letting the final word sink in before continuing. Whatever murk surrounded the intentions of the man, it seemed very important to Him that the four otherworlders viewed their confinement as being some kind of visitation. Janus innately knew there were further clues to the greater truth he was seeking reflected within such a desire.

The man proceeded to formally introduce Himself. He was exactly who Janus thought He would be when the four otherworlders were escorted into the hall, and got their first look at those upon the high platform.

"Perhaps you wish to learn a little more about Me first. I am known as the Unifier, for I desire nothing more than to bring a harmonious, prosperous order to the world of Ave, an order this world has never seen before.

"I seek first and foremost to end all wars, to bring the divided lands of Ave together under one unity transcending all the petty struggles of humankind. To bring to an end the senseless conflicts for wealth, power, or religion, which have so dominated and blighted the history of this world.

"As my honored guests, you will see that this is true in time, and I invite you each to discover this awareness for yourself."

The actual words sounded reasonable on the surface. There was nothing undesirable within the man's stated aims. The same sources of conflict that the Unifier identified in Ave's history were the very same besetting Janus' former world.

Additionally, Janus could not deny that he was increasingly relieved by the fact that no less than the Unifier Himself was referring to the otherworlders as guests. The open clarification on the otherworlders' status by Avanor's exalted ruler informed Janus of another imminent reality. It was perhaps the lone, precious gemstone within the dark rock of their ongoing struggles.

Janus and his companions held some kind of special, intrinsic value at the present moment. Most importantly, that value was being acknowledged in the eyes of the highest person of authority in the land they were in.

It was not likely to be a minimal value either. It had apparently restrained a much more forceful approach by their captors, preventing Janus and his companions from being treated more overtly as the unwilling, incarcerated prisoners that they perceived themselves to be.

Yet Janus was not so far outside himself that he failed to continue discerning that faint trace of dire warning. He reached vigorously for that small shred of intimation, grasping it as if it were a solidly anchored object that could prevent a fall into a gaping abyss. It was an instinctive reaction, a reflex coming from the most primal element of his spirit.

Janus deliberately adjusted his eyes from directly meeting those of the Unifier, while continuing to look in a general sense at the man's face. He had no desire to commit any affront to the regal individual who now held their ultimate fates in His hands. Janus focused in upon the tall man's forehead, at the boundary where the Unifier's neatly cropped ebony hair ended just above smooth skin that showed no telltale furrows of worry or hardship.

Janus tried to maintain an ambiguous expression on his own face. At the very least, it was the mien of one who was politely attentive.

The Unifier seemed not to notice anything untoward in Janus' slight shift. He turned and gestured towards the diverse figures seated in the high-backed chairs on the platform behind him.

"Those you see seated at my side are the members of my Great Council. To each, much is given … and from each much is demanded. All have served me loyally and capably. It is my hope that you will come to know them very well in the days ahead," the Unifier stated in His eloquent manner.

The Unifier gestured towards the far, left end of the long table, where the old, gray-bearded man was sitting. "Niketas Palaeologos, formerly of the Empire of Theonia, and from one of the most storied families there," the Unifier said, as the old man gave the otherworlders a slight nod. "One of the greatest scribes and historians of our age, and, I would suggest, any age.

"Long did he capably serve the Theonian emperor. He now serves me with his academic counsel, to remind all of us of the lessons in history that are there for the taking. He also oversees my library, and the creation of new histories and biographies to record the developments and successes of our new world effort."

The Unifier then moved on to indicate the man to Niketas' left side. "Baron Dragone, My loyal castellan of the great castle at Gesoras."

The burly man gave Janus and the others little more than a glowering look, and a curt inclination of his head. Baron Dragone's stony countenance was filled with a sense of intimidation, and Janus suspected the conveyance was quite intentional.

As if taking note of the man's callous disposition, or perceiving Janus' thoughts, the Unifier continued after a moment's pause. "You must understand that he has a hard demeanor, well-suited to the task of war. He holds the status of a Lord General, and is first among them. His castle is in the Querellen. Long has he held it capably for Avanor."

The Unifier moved His attention onward to the next man in the line, seated at Baron Dragone's left hand. "Lothario Dandolo, of Venezia."

The refined-looking man named extended Janus and the others a charming smile. The expression contrasted very sharply with that of the Lord General. Even so, the amiable countenance did nothing to mask the piercing look held within Lothario Dandolo's keen eyes.

The Unifier continued forward with the introduction. "Venezia is now the greatest sea-power of the north, the strongest, most prolific, and perhaps most advanced of shipbuilders. They are the most proficient traders of the northern waters, first and foremost among the Lombar city-states that have taken to the seas of Ave so remarkably.

"Lothario has an exceptional gift for strategy, whether in war, government, or in matters of trade. In this way, he serves the interests of Avanor, as well as keeping strengthened relations for Avanor with Venezia's esteemed Doge, Mastino Fausto."

"Earl Reginald FitzOsbern of Norengal," the Unifier proceeded, looking towards the final man of the quartet seated to the left of the Unifier's empty seat. "His prodigious lands reside both in Norengal and Gallea, a legacy of the time Avanor conquered Norengal. The earl represents my interests in both lands, spending time at the courts of both kings, those of Norengal and Gallea. Like Baron Dragone, the earl is also a Lord General, and is ingenious in matters of war."

With His back largely turned to Janus and his companions, the Unifier took a couple of slow steps to the right. He drew to a halt, standing with His body in relative alignment with the first of the trio of individuals seated to the other side of His vacated chair.

He rotated his body a little more to His left, so that He could better see the four otherworlders. The Unifier then gestured gracefully towards the individual who had been seated at His left hand up on the platform, an astoundingly beautiful woman.

She was graced with long black hair that tumbled down in a midnight cascade over her elegant shoulders and about her enchanting face. The youthful luster of her skin was not enough to mask the intriguing depths within her enveloping gaze. It was the kind of look whose blade was sharpened with a richness of experience and knowledge. She gave a slow, smooth nod to the guests, never once taking her bright blue eyes off of them.

"Gyriel," The Unifier stated.

Gyriel's lips remained closed, but spread wider in the semblance of a smile. The expression was as frigid as was the penetrating gaze cast by her icy, cerulean eyes. Her attention lingered upon Janus for a few extra moments, heightening a tumultuous mix of fear and attraction within him, feelings that both pulled and pushed, repelled and beckoned.

"She is my greatest Sorceress, of the highest rank of the practitioners of the Mysteries in Avalos," the Unifier said. "She dutifully serves me in my relations with the lords, kings, and emperors of the lands of Ave, as well as interacting with the great merchants and communes. Gyriel is an emissary like no other."

Janus could not disagree with the Unifier's last statement, doubting that any common emissary could rival the beauty of Gyriel. He found he had a little trouble taking his eyes off of her, as the Unifier progressed to the female to Gyriel's right.

The next woman was no less enrapturing to look upon, and Janus would have found it hard to say which of the two women were the more resplendent. The two women were simply mesmerizing, each spellbinding in their beauty.

"Morrigan," the Unifier intoned, as the second woman arose slowly from her sitting position.

Her fiery red tresses coursed down in abundance, with effulgent green eyes that beheld Janus and his comrades with much more than a passing interest. To Janus' eyes, she was an image of perfection in symmetry and grace.

"One of the greatest of the Wizards of Ave," the Unifier announced. "Always a true friend to Me, and to our greater struggle in this world, all throughout the long ages."

Janus sensed something of great significance in the Unifier's words, but his immediate thoughts focused in on a subtle, but quite perceptible, change in the Unifier's delivery. He silently reflected on that noticeable difference, regarding the way that the Unifier addressed Morrigan.

With all of the others, the Unifier had spoken in a polite, formal tone. Yet He had not addressed them with the kind of inflection that carried genuine affection, like that woven into his words concerning Morrigan. Janus could sense the Unifier held some kind of sincere affinity for the carmine-tressed, beautiful woman.

It seemed then as if a cold chill suddenly gripped the chamber, as Morrigan dragged her intense gaze across the faces of each of the otherworlders. As with the Unifier, Janus averted his eyes from directly connecting with those of Morrigan, willfully maintaining careful discretion. He settled his vision on the unblemished skin of her high cheeks. Morrigan emanated a coiled, dangerous vibe, which felt to Janus as if it were at the very cusp of lashing out.

Janus did not want to make any wrong assumptions, or take any risks, by letting her emerald gaze delve into his own. There was something quite extraordinary about the fiery-headed woman. Janus decided to trust to his instincts, even if he did not have an explanation for his pressing trepidation.

Displaying a dazzling, opal smile towards them, an amiable expression that was not reflected in her cool green eyes, she nodded to the otherworlders, and smoothly sat back down into her chair. The Unifier then looked towards the final member of the Great Council.

The figure, for Janus could not tell if it was a man or woman, remained hidden within the dark shadows of its concealing hood. If the temperature in the great hall had seemed to cool rapidly when Morrigan was introduced, it now plunged further, becoming icy.

"Not least among my Great Council is Ahriman," the Unifier stated resonantly.

The hooded figure made no outward motion, and could well have been carved out of stone. Despite the stillness, Janus knew a keen intelligence was regarding Janus and his companions from within the impenetrable blackness of the hood. A prickly sensation came over his skin, and his heartbeat began to escalate.

"Ahriman is one of the most powerful Wizards that has ever walked upon the surface of Ave, made incarnate once again," the Unifier said. "His great stronghold is far to the east, crowning the vast ShadowLands. I am most grateful for the service he has given Me, even before My arrival in Avanor."

As with Morrigan, the Unifier's tone contained an undisguised trace of affection towards Ahriman. Likewise, it hinted at something far greater in the relationships involving the two Wizards and the Unifier.

As both of them were introduced as Wizards, Janus could only postulate there was something intrinsic to Wizards that raised their esteem in the Unifier's eyes. Janus wished he knew more about what a Wizard in Ave truly was, or meant.

Both Wizards, from their positions at the table, and their manner of introduction, were clearly under the Unifier's authority. Yet there was something extant that made them quite distinct in comparison to the other members of the Great Council.

The Unifier then spread His arms wide, swiveling such that the grand gesture encompassed the lines of people seated behind each of the side tables running along the floor level. Briefly, the Unifier introduced each of the remaining attendees.

Predominantly men, they represented a wide array of interests. A few were leaders from the great guilds in the city of Avalos, while others were high-ranking clergy from the Western Church. Some, like Euvroin, were scribes and clerks, while still others were proud warriors, knights of high renown. Religious, economic, or martial, they were powerful individuals in their own right, though far lesser in status than were the exalted seven seated on the raised platform. None gave off even a flicker of the kind of presence the other seven had, and certainly nothing reminiscent of that exuding from Morrigan and Ahriman.

When finally finished, the Unifier turned to squarely face the four outlanders. "I know you have come from another time, and another world. I can only imagine the uncertainty, the worry, and the fear that must come with arriving in a new world, and being suddenly taken out of one you had always called home."

He paused, and smiled warmly at each of them. The look carried a congeniality that otherwise would have been unquestionable, were it not for the faint fringe of disharmony Janus clutched onto within the recesses of his mind.

"You have probably heard many things about Me. I doubt that anything you might have heard was pleasant regarding Myself, as you have been living among My enemies for a time," The Unifier continued in a relaxed and friendly manner. "But you will soon see there is another side to the stories you have been told. I am sure you have many questions to ask of Me, and there is much I desire to ask of you as well."

He looked towards the members of the Great Council, and cast a few sideways glances to the extended gathering. His next words were addressed to all of them, "You have held council with me for a long time today, and have been held from your duties, but I desired that you could meet these refugees from a faraway land. There is much I wish to do to help them, not the least of which is discovering a way to help them get back safely to their own world."

The unexpected words nearly took the breath away from Janus. It was the first statement by anyone within Ave regarding the possibility of an actual return back to his own home world.

Out of the corners of Janus' eyes, he could see that the other three with him had visible reactions to the statement. Nervous anxiety played all about Antonio's face, while sheer disbelief was written into Erika's features. Logan's expression displayed signs of anger, as if sorely reacting to the perception of a false promise.

Janus had felt his own heart skip a beat or two, and knew that his face betrayed his attempts towards maintaining a placid expression. Yet as eager as he was to know of the tantalizing possibility of a return to his own world, a part of him did not wish to confront the drab grayness saturating his former place of existence.

The new world of Ave had bestowed him with a constant stream of new stimuli. Even including the great perils he and the others had faced, the swirl of events had effectively served to keep the numbing, encompassing sorrows inside held farther at bay; even if they were buried just underneath the surface of his soul.

Janus quickly stifled the swell of tormenting memories and thoughts threatening to surge once again into the fore of his consciousness, but not before a gaping hollowness manifested deeper inside. A terrible dilemma existed, pulling at him from opposite ends.

Without a doubt, the notion of returning to a world where the deep sorrows within him would likely be restored to full dominion was greatly dismaying. Yet Janus also knew that he would willingly confront such a trying existence, in order to be reunited with his family and the other friends he had left behind.

Thoughts of his mother struggling with her own sorrows, in the midst of chronic physical ailments, were becoming sharper pangs upon his conscience. His only comfort regarding the matter was in knowing that his sister would be looking out for her, and that she would not be alone.

As if He were allowing a few moments to permit the concept of returning to their own worlds time to settle further into the minds of the otherworlders, the Unifier fell into an extended silence. He quietly looked to each of them in turn, as if studying their reactions one by one. His scrutinizing look fixed upon Logan longer than the rest.

The Unifier's placid expression was unreadable, even if His interest in Logan was quite obvious. Janus wondered as to the particular reason for the Unifier's conspicuous regard, seeing that Logan appeared to have the only negative reaction to the Unifier's assertion.

The Unifier finally broke the weighty silence. His former, serene manner returned, and the pervading heaviness dissipated quickly from the air. A pleasant expression emerged on the Unifier's face, one that conveyed understanding and benevolence.

"The Great Council for this day is finished," the Unifier announced in a smooth tone that carried throughout the chamber. "I now dismiss all attending this day's Council. Go forth with strength and diligence to your tasks, for it is indeed a great Work that we labor towards."

At the conclusion of His words, the various members of the Great Council, as well as those seated at the side tables, rose without uttering a single word. Those arranged at the sides of the hall bowed low to the Unifier before exiting the chamber. The hushed assemblage filed slowly down to the farther end of the hall from the raised platform, departing through the same bronze door that Janus and his companions had entered through.

The seven members of the Great Council were the last ones from the convocation to go. Like the others, they also rendered the Unifier a bow, only they lowered themselves even further than had the others. They also held the more deferential posture for a few additional seconds, before finally rising back up.

Five of the Council's members left by the way that the ones seated along the sides had used. Janus felt more than a few furtive glances as the prominent quintet passed by his group.

The remaining two members of the Great Council took a different exit. They departed the hall through the large arched doorway set midway down the wall to the right.

Janus made a mental note of the fact that the two heading into the adjoining hall-chamber were both Wizards; the rapturously beautiful Morrigan, and the shrouded, enigmatic Ahriman. As if to secure the Unifier's privacy, Morrigan turned to shut the chamber's door behind her.

Janus caught the radiance of her bright jade eyes one final time, as she paused to look upon his group for a brief moment. In the instant their eyes connected, Janus felt his breath catch in his lungs, as an icy shiver gripped him tightly. The reaction was inexplicable to Janus, as her stunning beauty was something that he otherwise would have desired to gaze upon. Yet he found himself extremely relieved when the iron-bound, oaken door closed shut, blocking his view of the mysterious Wizard.

The Unifier waited until every last one of the Council attendees exited the chamber before returning His full attention to the foreigners standing before Him. There were no guards to be seen anywhere, not even the ones who had escorted Janus's group.

The development caught Janus by surprise. He could not imagine any powerful rulers choosing to allow themselves to be left alone with four complete strangers. It was especially inconceivable when the strangers in the current instance were from another entire world.

Having been forcibly abducted and brought to Avalos, snatched away from their former hosts, it could be reasonably assumed that the four otherworlders might well harbor a deep grievance. They had not yet been made privy to the other side of the story that the Unifier had made reference to before the Council.

Under any circumstance, it seemed to Janus as if the Unifier was taking a great, and unnecessary, risk. Yet he also surmised that the Unifier's action was a calculated chance, one meant to make a very particular statement. Janus' first guess was that the Unifier was endeavoring to establish some trust with his group, making such a gesture to begin eroding misgivings and resentments.

There was also the strong possibility that the Unifier simply felt no threat in being left alone and outnumbered with four beings from another world. That prospect was a sobering warning to Janus in and of itself, one that resonated harmoniously with the subtle discord he had been sensing at the edges of his consciousness.

The Unifier's head swept towards Erika, as if suddenly reacting to her, even though she had not moved or spoken. "You all have questions on the tip of your tongues, and perhaps you most of all, Erika. Please, do not be afraid. Go ahead, and ask what you will, freely and without fear."

Erika's eyes widened at the Unifier's invitation, and her mouth opened ever so slightly. Janus could sense that she was highly surprised about something, and he fixed his mind to ask her about the matter later in private.

"I have a question that I must ask, then," Erika said, looking a little rattled. She paused hesitantly for another few seconds. Visibly regaining her composure, she finally queried, "If we are called guests, then why do You keep us held in this place like prisoners? We were taken against our will. While we haven't been abused or harmed, we certainly don't have freedom here inside your walls."

It was the very question that any one of the four could have asked. Janus appreciated Erika's boldness in voicing his own prime question for Avanor's ruler, and waited with great interest to hear the Unifier's response.

BEVRIEDAK

Dipping out of the upper stratosphere, Bevriedak bolted forward with a torrential speed through the skies over Saxany. The ground below, with its rivers, towns, villages, hills, forests, mountains, and plains grew to be ever more of an amorphous blur. It was not long before the immense dragon angled into an even sharper path of descent.

After a great many leagues fled by, the dragon slowed considerably. A tumultuous, violent scene, of the vast battle on the Plains of Athelney, was arrayed before him.

The skies farther ahead were dotted with clusters of the enemy's sky forces. The sudden, swift movements on their part reflected their recognition of the dragon's approach. Their skittish response was not warranted, at least for the moment.

The cacophonous sounds of battle filled the air, pervading Bevriedak's exceptional sense of hearing with an infernal chorus. The shattering of wooden shields, the harsh impacts of steel on iron, flesh, and bone, the pulsing rumble of war drums, the blasts of horns, and the frenzied cries of men and beasts, attacked or attacking, all coalesced into a hellish, discordant song of war.

The plain before the Saxan ranks was filled with an immense, surging mass of enemy warriors. It was a shifting, undulating vision of martial power. Extensive and continuous, the ranks of the invaders formed one gargantuan beast, a menace far beyond the stature of a horde of Elder.

Bevriedak was amazed at the sight. The enemy hosts had mustered in enormous strength. Even a cursory glance at the two sides revealed that the Saxans would be unable to hold back the seething tide forever.

An extensive shield wall was still in place on the Saxan side of the field of battle. While it was clear the shield wall still held, the size of the reserve kept in back of the line, at the center, was small. There was little to patch any cracks or fissures created by the enemy. As soon as the shield wall eroded further, the Saxan line would be highly vulnerable to collapse.

All of Saxany would then be left wide open to the seemingly unending horde massed out on the plains. Bevriedak did not want to think of the bounty of evils that would inevitably be visited upon a subjugated population.

As a great commotion rose from the Saxan ranks at the sight of his return, Bevriedak glided down and landed within an expanse of ground situated far back from main battle lines. He saw he was not all that far from where he had set down the previous time.

Stretching his huge right claw forth, he turned it over slowly and opened it, allowing Wulfstan and the sky steed access to the ground. Bevriedak's heart was heavily laden with disappointment regarding Gerasen, but he was no less determined. The Ban would continue its relentless assault, and it was likely there were sorcerers, or even Wizards, among the enemy ranks, but his mind was fixed upon one thing.

"Tell the others what you have seen, and what is in motion within the Five Realms," the Elder boomed, his eyes staring towards the western horizon. "If the brave warriors of Saxany need to fall back, to regroup, and continue to resist this vile invasion, I may yet be able to gain time for your people. The Elder are still held in the Ban's grip, but there are some things we can still do in this world."

The Saxan warrior gazed upward, into Bevriedak's face, with a narrow smile that held an equal degree of sadness and joy. "I will," Wulfstan replied. "I hope to see you again. You are a friend … to me and all of Saxany."

"As are you, Wulfstan of Saxany. What will come, will come, but we must walk our chosen path," Bevriedak replied.

He eyed the small form of the Saxan warrior below him, sharing Wulfstan's hope that they would see each other again. While he wished to conserve every last shred of strength for the undertaking he was about to embrace, Bevriedak decided to delay for just a few moments more. Some things needed to be said, as the future was never certain.

The great dragon continued in a softer tone, lowering his head closer to the Saxan. "Whether or not some may say that you embraced folly, you showed what one man can do, where many, many thousands failed to even try to act. Take that strength with you, wherever you go, and take pride in it, come whatever may. You held faith in the midst of a faithless world. You are to be congratulated, and you may yet move mountains, Wulfstan of Saxany."

He quietly regarded the Saxan for little longer, before lifting his head back up. A number of camp attendants, injured warriors, and a few others had begun to gather around, but Bevriedak could not turn his attention to them. There was no more time to waste, as the state of the ongoing battle was precarious, and he had only so much time that he could withstand the Ban.

Looking about, the silver dragon oriented his body towards an empty stretch of ground. He peered carefully along the surface, striving to make certain he did not overlook any humans within the space. Once he was satisfied that it was clear, he stretched his wings, and let loose a deafening roar that froze the nascent gathering in place. As he had intended, the Saxans beginning to cluster around remained rooted in place, and did not blunder into his path.

Flapping his vast wings, and trundling forward upon all four of his legs, Bevriedak threw up chunks of debris as he built up speed. He launched himself upward, dipping a little as his wings clutched the air.

His wings snapped down with explosive power, urgency coursing through him as he climbed. The Elder wanted to make use of each and every moment he could sustain within the immutable, suffocating embrace of the Ban.

Higher and higher the Elder ascended, his silhouette growing steadily smaller against the sprawling mass of white clouds blanketing the sky. Thousands upon thousands of eyes, on both sides of the battlefield, strained to catch the last glimpse of him, as the dragon's huge body finally disappeared into the dense vapors.

Soaring upward, on a steep incline, Beviredak carried himself to heights that no common Harrak or Himmeros could hope to reach. It was the outlying edge of the boundary regions, at the cusp of the lofty places where the Elder havens existed.

The silver dragon had no interest in seeking sanctuary. He had spent far too many centuries there already. Leveling out, and adjusting his bearings, he streaked forward at a blistering rate of speed. In a couple of moments, he surmised that he was flying over the invader's massed ranks.

Any sorcerers or Wizards serving the Unifier were likely to be situated close to the actual lines of combat. Even if they were not, Bevriedak still hoped to take the enemy so suddenly that any practitioner of magical arts would need more than a few moments to simply gain their senses, and react.

Nonetheless, he knew that what he was about to do carried tremendous risk. If any sorcerers were somehow prepared for him, the swift invoking of the Ban could well kill him before he could make any difference in the terrible conflict raging below.

Despite the daunting possibility, he was fully prepared to take the peril-ridden chance. Angling downward, bringing his wings in close to his sides, he plunged at a dizzying speed through the lower cloud layers. The terrain was revealed very suddenly when he plummeted through the underside of the lowest clouds.

Even with the great speed, Bevriedak was disciplined enough to take swift account of his position. The contested area of the battlefield was behind him, just to the east, but the encampments of Ehrengard,

Avanor, and Andamoor were sprawled out beneath him. Masses of carts, tents, merchants, and other camp followers were gathered beyond the principle encampments, a little distance to the west.

Aggregated foodstuffs and supplies, painstakingly gathered and amassed over months and months, were foremost on the dragon's mind. The food and materials were stored within the main camps, as well as within the smaller encampments formed by the merchants and camp followers.

The innumerable carts, casks, hempen sacks, chests, and other containers, filled with ale, wine, grain, cheese, weapons, horse harness, and all kinds of other supplies, was the vital lifeblood of any army. The masses of food and material were especially indispensable to an army the size of the one besetting the Saxan lands. The precious supplies were also quite vulnerable to an attack of the sort Bevriedak had devised.

A few small squads of Trogen riders on Harraks were patrolling the lower skies as the massive dragon abruptly burst into view. He hurtled down so fast that he was already past the highest of the patrols before they even knew he was in their midst.

The Trogen warriors would not have been surprised to see Saxans upon Himmerosen, but they were definitely not expecting one of the legendary Elder to manifest from above. No army or individual since the First Era of the world had been made to face such a gargantuan juggernaut.

The Elder were titans among dragons, and Bevriedak's presence threw the Trogens' minds into states of temporal oblivion. Stunned with fear, it took a few moments for the Trogen riders to break free of their mental paralysis.

A frenzied outcry arose, both in the skies and upon the ground. Those on the ground beheld the spectacle above with unfettered anxiety and terror. Their eyes stared in disbelief at the monstrous shape racing towards them out of the formerly calm skies.

In moments, pandemonium was rippling across all of the invaders' encampments. Pack and draft animals, from the brawny horses and stout oxen quartered among the Avanorans and Ehrengardians, to the camels and mules among the Andamoorans, stampeded in desperate fear. Herds of animals brought along to victual the various armies' needs broke into a chaotic rampage, as goats, sheep, and cattle bounded anywhere and everywhere they could.

SPIRIT OF FIRE

The maelstrom of reckless animals levied a growing host of injuries, and more than a few deaths, upon the scrambling warriors and camp attendants caught within the spreading mayhem. Many dived for cover wherever they could, hunkering down by barrels, or taking shelter under wagons and carts.

The sky patrols, faced with a suicidal stand against the dragon, fled the vicinity of the encampments. Most set out in the direction of the main battlefront, where they could regroup at a distance.

Even the staunch reserve forces behind the main Avanoran contingent quailed, their commanders working desperately to maintain a cohesive order. Frightened warhorses kicked, bucked, and reared, tossing heavily armored knights out of their saddles. A fair number of infantry broke away in the grips of sudden madness, scattering in many directions.

None of the Avanorans had any way of knowing that they were the least of Bevriedak's interests. Neither were most aware that the encampment was not entirely vulnerable. They had no inkling that a monstrosity such as an Elder could have anything to fear.

With the combined intensity of hundreds of blazing furnaces, Bevriedak blasted forth a murderous torrent of flame. He swung his head from left to right, sweeping the bathing stream of fire across the encampment. The inferno was spread in a wide swathe engulfing innumerable tents, masses of carts, piles of sacks, and large concentrations of barrels.

The dragonfire hungrily built into a furious tempest, consuming both grain and livestock, while voraciously swallowing countless barrels and casks. Vitally precious stocks of ale, wine, oil, and even water seeped into the ground, set free from the destroyed containers. Making matters worse, some of the casks' contents were flammable, adding to the potency and reach of the fire.

After turning about in a tight arc, Bevriedak spurred forward, exerting himself with all of his will. He lowered for the second of what would be several more passes over the territory of the three sprawling encampments.

Though Bevriedak's focus was entirely upon the stores of foodstuffs and supplies, the raging fires were not selective. The darkening air was soon filled with the cries of dying men and animals.

The skies were also filling with swiftly expanding pools of smoke, buoyed from a forest of columns rising from the stricken encampments.

Eyeing the swirling black testaments to his withering attack, Bevriedak sped onward, continuing past the farthest edge of the encampments, shadowing the course of the main roadway approaching Saxany from the west.

The invaders had traveled along that very road on their eastward route. The road itself was little more than a wide pathway of dirt, packed hard by the tramping of tens of thousands of feet, both human and animal, and cut through with striations from cart and wagon wheels.

At the moment, the road was largely devoid of traffic, with the exception of a few merchant caravans trundling east with goods and foodstuffs. Their wagons, carts, and saddlebags were heavily laden, and the merchants orchestrating the caravans were drawing closer to collecting the great profits that such a massive invasion bestowed. The first of the incoming caravans, an operation of modest size, was less than a league from reaching the outskirts of the encampments.

Mercifully for the merchants, their servants, and their guards, the Elder's approach could easily be seen, coming from afar. Most abandoned the carts and wagons as fast as they could, running and tumbling towards either side of the roadway. Tripping, scrambling, and crawling, those who could not keep to their feet used every method they could to get as far away from the doomed caravan as possible.

With terrified shouts and cries, they threw themselves down upon the ground as the dragon closed the distance. Scraping, shuffling, and scooting on hands and knees, they strove to gain every last inch that they could from the vicinity of the hapless wagon train. The previously meticulous order of the merchant caravan was rendered anarchic, as abandoned draft animals, still affixed to the carts and wagons, desperately tried to escape.

The giant dragon strafed the stalled mass of carts and wagons with a searing river of fire that cloaked everything in its path. He continued onward for several leagues, levying withering destruction along the roadway as he struck a couple of other caravans farther down.

He was determined to ensure that there would be no immediate succor for the invaders, in the wake of their own losses. The dragon did not pull away from the road until there were no wagons or carts within several hard days' travel of reaching the invasion forces.

A voracious army was now denied its most essential needs for a sustained invasion. Even if the huge Darroks were put to emergency use, there were not enough of the creatures to ferry the proper amounts of food and materials needed by the armies of Ehrengard, Andamoor, and Avanor. The invaders could not hope to address the enormous deficiencies caused by Bevriedak's strikes.

The great size of the invasion force, once a daunting strength, had been rendered into a weakness. The supply stocks of the armies had been crippled. The silver dragon had struck powerfully at the greatest vulnerability of a massive army, as he had fully intended. Bevriedak's objectives had been achieved far more comprehensively than even he had anticipated.

When his farseeing gaze could espy no more caravans coming along the road, he lifted back upward, heading into the higher skies. He did not have much more left within himself to create the blistering torrents of flame, possibly another two or three blasts, at the most. His body would need extended time at rest to regenerate the inner fluids so essential in the creation of the flames, the fluids having been nearly exhausted in his fierce attacks.

His body was rapidly weakening, as the Ban's pain continued to expand all throughout him. His breathing had tightened considerably, a condition he had not noticed during the adrenalized fury of his assault. There was little doubt he did not have very long to live, unless he could soon reach the sky refuges of the Elder.

Out of the corner of his eye, Bevriedak beheld the first sign of the only thing he had feared. It was the very reason why he had not attacked the battlefield directly, and had chosen to pass far above it.

The enemy had finally recovered its senses and was responding. Coming towards Bevriedak in a resolute manner was a tight formation of sky riders upon Harraks. They were much higher in altitutde than he was, flying far above, near the uppermost boundaries of their steeds' reach. Driven harshly, the winged beasts were being pushed to the limits of their speed. The riders intended to gain the sky over the dragon, or intersect with his path as he ascended.

Bevriedak was left with little to no choice, as there was not even a moment to lose. The first feelings of panic stabbed into him. He had to reach the Forbidden Dominions immediately. He laboriously flapped his wings, severely alarmed at the weakness of his body, as he tried to lift himself towards the upper heavens.

The Harraks rapidly closed the distance, with every passing heartbeat. Bevriedak was drawing close to the level they flew on, and was not altogether sure he could reach it before they arrived and crossed his path. The Elder was too far away to hurl his last plume or two of fire at them, but it mattered little. Bevriedak knew his enemies would call upon their ancient arts, well before he came within range.

He could see two distinctive figures, robed in scarlet, positioned within the center of the approaching formation. Their hoods were thrown back, exposing grim, determined visages, with brows furrowed in reflections of intense concentration. They were decidedly human, but Bevriedak knew they called upon powers far transcendeding the things of the mortal world.

Bevriedak could see their lips moving rapidly, and their gazes had all the subtlety of a murderous lance thrust. Each of the pair extended a free hand in a grasping motion towards him, with the other holding firmly to the reins of their steeds. Their hands widened and closed, the muscles of their exposed forearms flexing rigidly. An invocation, calling upon powers that sealed an ages-old compact, was being performed, with skillfull precision and discipline.

The next feeling the Elder experienced was unbearable. It seemed that the air surrounding his body suddenly became an enormous set of claws, clutching him tightly. He still had freedom of movement, but the torments plaguing him from the inside out rose sharply, throughout every last bit of his body. At the same time, it felt as if his very sides were being squeezed with tremendous, unrelenting force.

He began choking, gagging and gurgling as he realized the sorcerers' invocations of the Ban were taking away his capacity to generate dragon-flame. Their arts drained the strength needed to enact the combustible bodily fluid stored within his body. Bevriedak now had nothing to hurl towards the oncoming attackers.

The great dragon strained with every shred of will he could muster to gain altitude, clenching his immense jaws in throes of spiking pain. His anguish-ridden eyes remained locked on the sky above, holding desperately to the only chance he now had. His mind began flickering between blinding, white flashes, and brief instances of coherence.

The oncoming riders crossed the remaining distance with alacrity, as the invocations of the two Sorcerers of Avalos grew ever greater in strength upon Bevriedak. Their hold upon him was comprehensive, fully summoning the powers of the Ban. Over long centuries, Bevriedak had often wondered how Wizards or sorcerers able to invoke the Ban would affect an Elder. He had never witnessed an Invocation of Binding with his own eyes, or spoken with any Elder that had suffered one.

Now, he knew the answer intimately, and it reflected the worst of his fears. The Oath had been taken with the evocation of immense concentrations of power. The Ban drew upon the original might of the Oath-born power as strongly in the present day, as on the day the Oath was taken. An invocation by a sorcerer enacted the Binding with rapid effect upon a severe transgressor such as himself.

It did not matter in the least what justification Bevriedak had for breaking the Oath. The purity of the sacred pact was assiduously enforced by the Ban, the latter overwhelming and pitiless in exercising its great might.

In a state of incredible agony, Bevriedak forced his wings to move, keeping them flapping with his last vestiges of willpower. In his terrible pain, the Elder loosed an undulating cry, an eerie fusion between a roar and a high-pitched screech.

He knew he had only a few precious moments left before he would cease to be able to control his faculties. The white flashes extended longer, and the instances of coherence lessened considerably. His great mind, honed and advanced throughout the passage of thousands of years, had been reduced to one simple, singular fixation; keeping his wings in motion.

His focus clung desperately onto that lone task as he crossed the level of the oncoming Harraks, just ahead of their arrival. It now felt as if a swarm of thin, razor-sharp bindings were constricting all over his body, cutting through his armor of scales and tearing into his very flesh.

The massive dragon gasped and gulped as his wings pumped laboriously, dragging him into the vaporous mass of the lowest cloud layer. He felt the cool mist envelop him as he passed through the clouds, though the damp chill provided him no measure of relief.

The Elder were immortal, but they were not eternal, in a physical sense. Sickness and age could not claim them, but the great dragons could be slain.

Never before had Bevriedak felt so completely helpless. The Elder's eyes misted, his vision blurring in the pitiless grip of the Ban, as he emerged from the cloud layer. He could barely make out the pure, white shape higher above. In his degenerating mind, he could not recognize whether it was the haven he sought, or simply another mass of clouds.

His grip on reality was slipping fast, as his mind began turning to other last thoughts.

As a race, the Elder knew very little of what death was like. A number of tales streaming up from below spoke of individuals experiencing light at the edge of death, and Bevriedak's fading mind wondered if the hazy brightness filling his vision was that foreboding boundary.

Behind him, the pursuing riders burst through the lower clouds. He caught traces of their forms at the edge of his peripheral vision; shadowy, featureless shades, racing after him with malefic intent.

He knew he was not going to reach the safety of the high sanctuary. The refuge was still too far away, and his time had run out at last.

Bevriedak had risked everything, gained everything, and was now at the cusp of losing everything. Yet there were no regrets whatsoever residing within, as the pain began to ebb at last, gradually being replaced with a seeping, encompassing darkness. His eyes fluttered for a few moments, and finally closed.

Thousands of years, reaching back to the dawn of Ave's First Era, were about to dissipate in his mind and spirit. Yet the great dragon felt no sense of loss. Bevriedak found only that he was content with the very thing draining the last shreds of life from him; the breaking of the Oath, in order to help the remaining faithful.

He could only hope that was taken into account when his lifespan was weighed and balanced before the Golden Throne, in the celestial court of Palladium. The thought of the heavenly realms brought a last drop of joy to his consciousness, enough to counter the oceans of pain wracking his body beyond endurance.

Like a final spasm, he felt a wrenching, violent pain impact thunderously upon his body, in several places. The sensation was like powerful claws digging far into him, the piercing ends of lengthy talons penetrating well past his toughened hide. An instant later, it was as if the invisible bindings on him jerked rigidly taut, for one brief moment, snapping his body abruptly upward.

Then all was peaceful, as the terminal threshold of pain was crossed, and a peaceful calm descended swiftly over his numb body. He experienced a weightless, lifting sensation, as if he were floating upon the currents of the wind. His mind sank beneath the waves of consciousness, gently letting go, comforted by the notion that he was drifting off into the depths of a new, everlasting sea.

THE UNIFIER

The Unifier's gaze lingered upon the young woman as He recalled her given name; Erika. She was so very shapely and attractive, but He knew that He could not charm her with anything superficial.

He sensed the presence of a markedly defiant instinct within her. Defiance itself was of a neutral substance. As such, it could be made to serve any interest, but it could also become a powerful adversary.

With a woman as vitally important as Erika was, the Unifier needed to proceed carefully, lest that defiance harden against Him. Each and every man and woman from another world was of tremendous significance. He could not take even one such individual for granted. In the end, just one single person could make the difference in tipping the balance in the great struggle.

Of the four now present before Him, the Unifier could see that Erika had the fewest weaknesses in the areas that were of greatest interest to Him. "I know that you were probably very well treated by my enemies. And you now find yourselves with guards, behind walls, and your movements restricted," the Unifier answered Erika gently, infusing the words with the hint of apology. "It is true this makes Me and Mine look like the enemy, but My enemies only wanted to use you for their own purposes. You will soon know of these purposes which they desired of you, because you are from another world. You will see that I have saved you great trouble. For now, I must continue to keep you safe, however regrettable it is to place any restraints upon your freedom. I do so for your own protection, and your own well being. In time, this need for heightened protection will change, once the dangers to you have passed and been eliminated."

His words were suffused with sentiments of reason and genuine regret, using an approach that He believed would appeal to the young woman on many levels at once. His eyes remained riveted upon her. She had an edge in her eyes that told Him at once that she did not entirely believe His words.

He then looked to the others, to sense what kind of reaction they had to His answer. It provided another moment for His deeper senses to reach forth and take a better assessment of them.

There was confusion in the one named Janus, though the Unifier could sense that the inner turmoil was born out of a desire to find the real truths underneath His words. This was a soul who was a natural seeker, whose vision sought after the depths underneath the outer surface of things. The human was not one easily convinced by mere appearances.

In some ways, such a disposition presented many challenges for one such as the Unifier. Yet the inclination to delve into past appearances did not entail everything about the otherworlder.

A cloud of desolation hung thickly around the young male, the distinctive mark of a badly wounded soul. The Unifier could sense that an onslaught of sorrows had effectively crippled the young man's spirit.

A numb, wearied soul was a vulnerable one, though it was also a potentially volatile one. Coupled with Janus' predilection to see things from a broader perspective, the Unifier knew He would have to proceed cautiously in His approach with the young man.

The stocky young male who stood next to Logan, the one who was named Antonio, was fairly straightforward in his inner response. He even appeared to be somewhat disposed towards accepting the Unifier's words, in the context of their literal meaning.

Antonio was the sort of soul not easily given to questioning, a spirit harboring a tendency to trust others. His unquestioning, trusting nature was due to the fact that Antonio was inherently honest himself. He could not easily conceive that others would be much different in nature than him. It was a combination that boded well for the Unifier's purpose.

On his own, a soul such as Antonio would not be inclined to even begin to suspect the far deeper, and much more complex, nature of the Unifier. Antonio possessed a very weak guard mechanism in the face of a transcendent being such as the Unifier, a Power who wielded the subtlest of arts rooted in untold ages of wisdom and experience. Among the foursome, the young male might well require the least effort on the Unifier's part.

The last one, named Logan, now exhibited a placid demeanor where there had been undeniable hints of simmering ire just a few scant moments before. Apart from the other foreigners, the Unifier knew Logan was carefully weighing His explanation, balancing it against everything he had experienced in the new world.

There was a great amount of skepticism residing within Logan, bolstered by an elemental distrust of others. Yet there was also openness to change within the young man, as well as a deep hunger for growth and insight. All of the attributes could be strengths, and similarly all of them could be weaknesses, in terms of their value to the Unifier's intentions.

At the moment, the Unifier honed in upon the strong angers and resentments percolating within the man. Like peeling off a concealing surface layer, the recognition of the angers within Logan revealed deeper, more exploitable parts of his soul's nature. The anger was generously fed by a number of other aspects residing in the shadows of Logan's heart, such as a feeling of powerlessness in the world, a burning hatred of false hopes, and an insatiable need for tangible realities.

It was not that Logan had been angry at merely the voiced idea of finding a path back to his own world. Rather, he had been incensed about the prospect that a known impossibility, or willful deception, had been given serious, deliberate utterance. The perception of intended guile on the part of the Unifier had triggered a sharp rise in acrimony within Logan, almost like a reflex. It had taken several moments for the brooding ire swirling within Logan to ebb.

In a mildly amusing way, it was the very kind of anger that many of the people who rejected the Western Church directed towards its clergy. Such people saw the priests, friars, monks, and others as individuals engaged in the propagation of false hopes, rendering promises that the proponents themselves did not really believe. In viewing the priests and other clergy as speaking about covenants that were nonexistent, and devoid of any sanctioning by a Higher Deity, the substance of a simmering, deeply resentful anger was nurtured in them.

The Unifier's attention was then disturbed momentarily. A brief, unfamiliar sensation rippled through Him as He continued to look upon Logan. He had no thoughts as to the specific reason for the unsettling feeling. It was simply an instinctive sensation, one that seemed to encourage the Unifier to take a particular interest in the dark-haired foreigner.

The feeling was no mere whim that He would soon dismiss. The Unifier most certainly would heed the interior inspiration, and give special attention to Logan in the future.

The Unifier's own Lord did not always commune in a direct manner with the highest servants of the Fire Realms. Sometimes guidance from the dark depths of the abyss manifested in the form of intuition, or an abrupt perception. The Unifier had learned to take such feelings very seriously, long ages before the restraints had fallen that finally allowed Him to take an incarnate place in Ave.

It was definitely one of the more difficult parts of His path, living as a distinct Person, as opposed to the more perfect union He had shared with Jebaalos in the Fire Realms. Still, with every passing moment, the Unifier was becoming better accustomed to His current state of existence.

The Unifier took a couple of steps forward, right into the midst of the otherworlders. Two of them stood to His immediate right, and two were on His left. He felt the four humans instantly tense as He bluntly invaded their space.

"While you are under My care, I will do everything to make your stay here a pleasant one. I will do everything to make sure that no harm comes to you," the Unifier announced.

"So why do you want us? Why such concern for our safety? We do not have wealth…or power. What could you possibly need from us?" Erika asked Him insistently, as if she could no longer restrain some nagging frustrations. She had nonetheless echoed the questions that He knew were on all of their minds.

"Even though you may not have been in this world for long, I must ask you to see through my eyes, at least for just a moment," the Unifier replied patiently. He showed no sign of taking affront at her bold tone, though He tolerated far less from emperors and kings. "When you are alone, take some time to think upon My situation. I suddenly became aware that My sworn enemies were concealing persons from another time and age amongst them. This news came to my attention during a time of war and struggle, when I have come within reach of finally being able to bring the whole world to a level of peace and cooperation, of a kind that it has never known in any age.

"I represent the hopes and ambitions of many lands and kingdoms, encompassing the lives of many millions. Of course, as you surely understand, I must strive to be aware of all threats to these hopes. I must know what My enemies plot against me. I could not know whether you were a weapon to be used against Me, brought forth by their arts. Neither could I know whether you were innocent of this ongoing struggle, and brought into this world to choose your own pathway within a much grander design.

"The only way to know the answer was to bring you before Me, as I have. I can only ask you to think about this further. There are always two sides to every tale. I ask that you hear that other side, before you come to your final conclusions."

He noted that three of the four around Him outwardly nodded in response, apparently finding His request reasonable enough. The lone exception amongst them was the stubborn woman. He conceded that it would take a very focused approach to gain the full cooperation and trust of Erika.

"Now, tell me something of yourselves," He inquired of them, a pleasant smile spreading on his face.

With occasional input from Antonio and Erika, Logan proceeded to relate the bulk of the otherworlders' incredible story. Janus remained silent, and a little aloof, during the telling, sometimes looking as if his thoughts had drifted far away from the chamber.

Logan spoke thoroughly of their unexpected arrival in Ave through the encompassing mists. With the periodic contributions from Erika and Antonio, he continued the account right up to his group's capture among the Midragardans on the small island off the shores of the tribal lands.

The Unifier sensed an affinity within the otherworlders towards the tribal people and Midragardans. Further, the otherworlders did not hesitate to inform the Unifier of the gruff treatment they had received at the hands of Bohemond's men on the sea vessel, as well as from the Trogens who had escorted them to Avalos. Nor did they forget to mention the much greater freedom they had enjoyed while living with the tribal people.

All of it was in sharp contrast to their very restricted manner of living in Avalos. Given their very different experiences with those serving the Unifier and His enemies, it was no wonder that the otherworlders would not have a propensity to easily accept the Unifier's overtures.

The parts of their story concerning the woodland stranger encountered in the Five Realms both fascinated and worried the Unifier. It had been that woodland traveler who had bestowed the enchanted amulets upon the four; the pendants enabling the otherworlders to understand all languages, and speak fluently in them.

The Unifier knew He would be consulting with Ahriman and Morrigan later that very day. The Unifier needed to see what they could infer from the story, and from the type of amulet bestowed on the otherworlders.

It was extremely possible that the pendants came from an enemy Wizard, and a very powerful one at that. The Unifier would not be surprised if such was the true nature of the woodland stranger. If the mysterious wanderer in the forest was indeed a Wizard, the Unifier already had some deep suspicions regarding his identity.

The Unifier needed to ascertain the identity of the woodland benefactor. At the very least, the knowledge would provide a strong clue as to why the amulets had been given.

Other than the concern regarding the amulets, the tale seemed straightforward enough. He had no doubts that they had little idea as to the truth of why they had been taken to Avalos, and were important to the Enemy.

He sensed that their fears concerning their ability to get back to their own world were growing. The Unifier wholeheartedly intended that kind of blossoming. It was precisely why He had addressed the Great Council outwardly of the possibility of finding a way for the four to return back to their own world.

Festering, growing desires created fertile grounds for influence. After they had finished relating the main aspects of their story, He gave them a warm smile. He decided to reinforce their desires further, leaving matters of influence for a more propitious time.

"Thank you for sharing your story with me. I will consult with my Great Council about your plight, in the hopes of finding answers, and maybe a way for you to get back to your own world. I do not say that idly…" the Unifier stated, looking to Logan, in order to gauge his response. The young man's countenance clouded briefly, but the irritated look did not linger quite as long as it had before. "As for now, I must attend to other matters concerning My realm, but orders have been given to provide you with a special feast tonight."

He then dismissed them politely, in a cheerful manner, before calling for His guards. Two Avanoran warriors entered the chamber, to escort the four prisoners back to their own quarters.

The Unifier quietly watched the otherworlders depart the chamber through the bronze door, knowing they were of immense importance. They represented a full third of the number of individuals that could affect the Sundering. They were four of the eleven outlanders that could possibly exist in all of Ave. They also comprised exactly half of the number needed for the Unifier's invocations to bring about the Sundering.

The four otherworlders were a vibrant, indelible mark of the momentous Age in which the Unifier had manifested within the world. They could never have appeared during the long ages the Unifier had been restrained from incarnating in Ave. The two events were closely intertwined, distinct harbingers of the approach of the End of Days.

Circumstances had placed a great boon right in the Unifier's hands. With the four otherworlders in His firm grasp, the Enemy's Prophecy and designs were now much closer to being denied the necessary conditions of being brought into fruition.

Even so, the Unifier sorely wished that He could simply eliminate the otherworlders. As long as they drew breath in Ave, they could still be of use to the Enemy.

Yet He was not so reckless that He failed to acknowledge that the same laws holding dominion in Ave did not fully govern the four. Their origin and nature was from another entire world. Something transcendent had superseded all natural law to bring them into Ave.

The Prophecies simply indicated that there would be twelve that would be involved with the Sundering in the Final Age, with all but one coming from another world. If He killed those now in His grip, He had no idea as to whether or not others might simply manifest elsewhere on the planet. He was not about to take any risks of having otherworlders fall into the Enemy's hands again. Four were now under His firm control in the heart of the immense fortress where His worldly throne had been set.

Even so, the matter was complicated. Locking the otherworlders deep within the fortress was not an advisable option either.

The four otherworlders represented an unsurpassed opportunity. The same paradigm by which the Enemy sought to defeat the Unfier could be turned to the Unifier's own purposes and advantage. Only eight of the prophesied twelve were needed by the Unifier to open the Gates between worlds, and bring about the Sundering on behalf of the Fire Realms.

Achieving the opening of those Gates would require a conscious, willing acquiescence on the part of the otherworlders. Everything of significance in the great Conflict was contingent upon acts of freewill. The greatest powers lay in the exercise of the will. Creation itself had come about by the Will of the Enemy, just as the great Rebellion, and the Fire Realm, found their origins in the Will of Jebaalos.

The Unifier would have to be very careful in His approaches to the four otherworlders, but there were always useful elements that could be cultivated in all manner of humans. Jebaalos had long ago revealed those truths regarding humanity to the Unifier, during the more perfect state of union they shared before the Unifier's incarnation.

The genuine art lay in discovering what such elements were within a particular individual. The Unifier was already well underway in that regard.

He would next seek a private talk with the one named Logan. The brief sensation He had felt while studying Logan had a purpose and a reason, and the Unifier was determined to uncover it as soon as possible.

In the very place where Jebaalos had fallen following the Great Battle at the dawn of time, the Unifier would now begin the final labors to prepare the way for His Lord's coming ascension. There was so much to be done, and much more that needed to take place, but the Unifier would see to it that all was accomplished.

Jebaalos' return would irrevocably shake the heavens, and the Unifier would find a throne at His Lord's right hand as a new age dawned. The union He once had with Jebaalos would be restored.

AELFRIC

The main herepaths and other roads leading towards the east were packed with wagons, carts, pack-horses, soldiers, merchants, camp followers, and any others the Elder Dragon's unexpected actions had spared.

Aelfric was among the last to leave the cluttered, bloody field of battle. The Saxan commander lingered on the Plains of Athelney as long as possible, gazing upon the widespread carnage.

Light cavalry contingents remaining behind to screen the vast retreat were readying to depart. Aelfric sat astride Midnight and silently watched the movements of the numerous horsemen, including considerable forces from Rouenum and Poitaine.

Streams of resolute faces flowed by Aelfric underneath their protective iron. Moving with well-practiced, tight cohesion, the throngs of horsemen kept a deterring presence on the Saxan side of the hellish clash.

Far across the battlefield, Aelfric saw the distant forms of several huge Gigans. The creatures roared out challenges underneath the Trogen sky patrols drifting over them in the skies above.

A number of Avanorans had begun to gather a short distance beyond the Gigans, but they were far too few in number to elicit worries from Aelfric. Dismounting their steeds, they were gathering in a loose circle. Few spared anything more than an occasional glance towards the withdrawing Saxans.

Aelfric's temper was still cooling down after a few tense moments in which he had firmly insisted that Prince Aidan depart with the King's Guard. The young Prince had wanted to be among the very last to leave the great field of battle, but Aelfric was not about to underestimate the guile of the enemy.

Prince Aidan had gained invaluable experience, and the Kingdom of Saxany would need the rapidly maturing leader desperately in the months to come. Aelfric was not about to let the enemy snatch one of the few small victories left to the Saxans in the form of the surviving Prince.

Not willing to brook dispute, he had effectively commanded the Prince to depart. The Prince's eyes had widened slightly in surprise at Aelfric's sheer forcefulness, but the young Prince finally deferred to the judgement of the Saxan Ealdorman.

The sight of the returning Prince in Aixen would cheer the old, venerable king's heart, especially since Alcuin was facing the realm's terrible darkness in a state of loneliness. Aelfric felt a great sympathy for the king. No matter how wise or strong of character King Alcuin was, he was still a man. He was not impervious to the strains and sorrows endured by all loving fathers.

Queen Baldhild was living out her final days in a nunnery, preparing herself for the journey into the next world. Her absence from Aixen had likely left the aged king with a heavy heart, made even more weary when he had watched his eldest son go forth in the company of the Royal Guard.

Aelfric took some joy in imagining the face of the king when he saw that Prince Aidan had lived through the immense battle. Yet it was not only kings that would soon be experiencing emotional reunions.

Great numbers of farmers and village artisans in the General Fyrd were now on the way back to their homes. Against all odds, thousands were returning alive to villages, hamlets, and homesteads strewn all throughout the Saxan region.

Many of the villagers, and even artisans from burhs, would be gathering up their families to press on farther, to flee ahead of the inevitable Avanoran thrust. Some would stay and take their chances, hoping they could somehow weather the coming Avanoran storm.

Staying in place was a grave risk, Aelfric knew, as conquering forces were rarely lenient on the populaces they subjugated. His only comfort was that the force of Halmlander mercenaries had been eliminated.

While Aelfric did not begrudge any villager's desire to return to home and hearth, there was an underlying strategic component to the returns that worried the commander within him. The peasants' great numbers included an overwhelming majority of the available archers for the Saxan forces.

As most all of the peasant archers traveled by foot, they would not be easy to summon in the precarious times to come. Beacon fires set along a succession of hilltops could bring the household guards of thanes and burh garrisons at haste upon their horses. Foot-bound peasants were a different matter, and a troubling delay would have to be accounted for when the need came again to bring up the mass levies.

Still, there was little practical choice in the overall matter. The Saxans could not feed so many mouths for any extended period of time.

Even so, there were more than a few unsullied rays of light that gladdened Aelfric's increasingly clouded heart. Soon there would be numerous outbursts of joy and great relief, as a host of tearful reunions took place throughout the rural heartland of Saxany.

Fear-ridden and deeply anxious young sons, daughters, and wives would find prayers answered. Dimming hopes would be filled beyond all expectation as they set their eyes upon beloved husbands and fathers striding along dirt pathways into sight of their fields and homes.

Yet a dreadful, gloomy pall would still hang heavily over the many thousand survivors; peasant, ceorl, and thane alike. Nearly to a man, all had lost one or more individuals who had been a close part of their lives. Such bonds were the norm in a kingdom where generation succeeded generation within villages and market towns.

After the jubilance of reunions took place, the fortunate survivors and their families would soon be taking notice of numerous others living among them whose fathers and husbands would not be returning home. Scenes of euphoria and sorrowful tragedy would commence side by side, wherever there were Saxan communities.

An overarching melancholy would soon begin to settle over those who returned, as well as those who greeted them. There were few illusions regarding the recent conflict among the survivors of the battle. Almost to a man, they knew in their hearts that the great battle at the Plains of Athelney had largely been lost at the point of the sudden, miraculous intervention by the titanic dragon.

The invaders had not been turned back or destroyed, but merely wounded and stymied. An abiding, dark sense of inevitability traveled back with most of the returnees. Aelfric knew it would be like a spreading disease to the spirit of resistance within Saxan hearts, eroding resolve and morale.

MAGNUS

With an increasingly comforted state of mind, moments after he had taken the first bites of freshly cooked elk meat, Magnus realized just how ravenous his appetite was. Brynhild laughed more than once in great amusement as he proceeded to voraciously devour a sizeable haunch of the spit-roasted meat.

All around them, the wolves of their respective packs were spread out amongst the surrounding trees. Several were lounging, a few resting and nursing wounds incurred during the recent hunt. Fortunately, as it was not always the case, none of the wolves had died or endured severe injuries in taking down the massive Midragardan Elk.

Others were playing and bounding about the trees, crouching, leaping, and colliding into each other with a series of impish bites and spirited bouts of wrestling.

A few of the lowest ranking members of the packs were just now finishing their own meals, situated around one of the remaining elk carcasses with meat still on it. They had been forced to patience as their fellow pack members of higher rank gorged themselves.

There was little worry for the wolves of lowest rank. There had been more than enough meat to go around, even for the least of the two packs. It had been a veritable feast for all involved in the successful hunt.

Magnus sat cross-legged near the stone-ringed fire he and

Brynhild had fashioned among a stand of elm trees, where they had decided to make camp for the evening. The chill of night was partially offset by the warmth emanating from the flames, though Magnus still pulled a woolen cloak he had borrowed from Brynhild more tightly about himself as he ate.

If he listened carefully, he could hear the softly flowing waters of a stream close by. Cool waters licked and tumbled energetically about the stones resting within the bed of the narrow channel.

The stream's steady, easeful movement created gentle night music. The soothing waters had already been a wonderful grace in a physical sense. Magnus had taken full advantage of the waters to refresh his face and skin, thoroughly cleansing his body of the build-up of dirt and sweat incurred since leaving his home village behind.

He still wore his new leather belt around his waist. Fastened with a bronze buckle, and pulled snug against his woolen tunic, it was provided with a new seax. The blade's leather and wood sheath, lined with oiled wool, was affixed to the belt by copper fittings.

The single-edged seax was not only broader and longer than his previous one, but it was also provided with some skillfully worked inlay of copper alloy. The fine lines of inlay were visible running in a strip along the top of the weapon, opposite the blade's lone, sharp edge.

Runic inscriptions ran in an unbroken line underneath three small panels visible in the strip of inlay. Ironically, the center panel held the snarling visage of a wolf's head. The flanking two panels displayed artistic renditions of ravens with outspread wings. The blade itself was fitted into a wooden hilt, and had no pommel.

Magnus had never had such an ornate weapon in his possession, but then again he had never before been given any access to the equipment of a Midragardan jarl. The exquisite craftsmanship of the blade almost made him regret that Brynhild made him stay back with the groups of wolves when they reached the outskirts of the jarl's estate. At her insistence, she had proceeded onward alone to procure the new items for him.

Nearby was his new long bow, now unstrung. Fashioned from the stave of a yew tree, it rested next to the cylindrical quiver of arrows holding a couple less shafts than it did when the day had started.

Swallowing another morsel of juicy elk meat, Magnus looked across the fire towards Brynhild and smiled contentedly. Her presence continued to pour into his eyes and mind, the pleasant sensation continuing ever since the previous day, when he set his gaze upon her for the very first time.

Her toned, chiseled body was an image of strength, though it was still complimented by graceful, feminine curves. It was accented well by her piercing blue eyes, and the flowing locks of raven-black hair that framed her comely face. She had a wild kind of beauty that reflected the life she had chosen. Within all of it was something intensely attractive to Magnus.

Brynhild already had his deepest respect. It took a rare individual to become one of the Wolf Kin; the kind of person willing to wager their very lives. As it was uncommon among the Midragardans for a female to seek the path of the Wolf Kin, there was already much to admire about her dedication and courage.

There was no doubting her sense of communion among the wolves, both as an authority and as an accepted friend. The wolves with Brynhild responded to her with a keen sensitivity, as well as a fierce loyalty that was stirring to behold. She moved among them with a melodious harmony that Magnus slightly envied. He inwardly knew that he had not arrived at such a level of association within his own pack.

"How long has it been since you were accepted among them?" he ventured quietly, watching her idly scratch the ears of one of the large, younger males from her pack who had wandered up to sit on its haunches beside her.

"About three years ... maybe a little longer," Brynhild replied with a thoughtful expression. The light from the fire sparkled in her eyes as she looked back towards him. "I never have had much interest for villages or market towns, or the All-Moots, or for seafaring. I have always felt alive when I have been out here, free under the open sky, and not beholden to the trivial things occupying the minds of most people. I stop to visit my father a few times a year, though each time I find that I understand other people even less."

"Or maybe the truth is that you understand them even more," Magnus interjected, with a partial grin.

A wistful smile crossed her face. "There is that way of looking at things. Though I think if I stated how I could care less about silver, and have no desire to ever own any gold, in front of a sea-going party of warriors, they would look at me as if I was gripped in throes of sheer madness."

She raised up the amulet hanging from her neck, the surface flickering in the dynamic light cast by the fire. "I could have cared less if this was wooden, bronze, pewter, or silver. I just care about what it represents. That is the only thing that gives this object any meaning."

"Are you a believer?" Magnus asked her, curious as to her attitudes on the faith that had not long taken root in Midragard.

"The more I live," she replied, smiling across at him, as she gently let the amulet rest back in place below her neck.

"I have struggled with much ... and the ways of the new Church seem so strange. In some ways, I wish the old ways were true. They were much easier to understand," Magnus replied, echoes of frustration in his voice as he thought of his frequent mental wrestling over the strange teachings of the new Church.

"If you understand it fully, then it is not of the All-Father," she responded, with a light-hearted gleam in her eyes. "That much I do know."

Magnus shook his head, hearing at once the depth in her esoteric words. "Yes, it all seems to be a swirl of seeming opposites, riddles, and mysteries."

"If you are going to live forever, you've got to have something left to think about. Would you want otherwise?" Brynhild asked. After a momentary pause, she continued, "So I'm glad we always have something new to realize and grow in, and that we do not know everything. It would be a tragedy to find out we are stagnant with nothing to dream of, or aspire to."

Magnus grinned back. "Yes, there is that way of looking at things too."

She looked across with a more serious countenance. "In a way, it does help on the path we are both on. I think we are moving towards answers that align fully with the truth the new Church shows us."

"Then this new Church is no easy road to walk," Magnus said.

"It is a narrow road, true, but even if it was not wide enough for two people to walk upon side by side, an endless multitude could still walk in a single column ..., one following the one in front, and leading the one following behind," Brynhild commented.

Magnus chuckled. "You have put a lot of thought into this."

The broad smile returned to her face. "Those of us on this path have a lot of time to contemplate. Do we not?"

"Yes, time is one thing we do have in abundance," Magnus

agreed. "There is not much to distract us in the wilderness, as there is in the villages."

"Other than herds of elk moving through our pack's hunting territory," Brynhild responded with a wry smirk.

"I don't think I could be distracted by another herd if it were to come through here right now," Magnus said, patting his full belly and laughing softly.

"Many more herds like that one, and we will soon have to seek larger tunics to wear," Brynhild jested, a low laugh escaping her.

Magnus could not even begin to imagine a soft edge to her form. "I still cannot believe I had not at least heard of you before. Jarl Guttorm's hand stretches out over Glittering River," he remarked, shaking his head in mild disbelief. "I would have thought some trader or traveling poet might have given a hint of such a fascinating tale. The daughter of our very Jarl ... taking the path of the Wolf Kin. Such is the heart of great sagas. I thought I was aware of most of the others nearby who walk our path, at least those who have not yet taken the Passage."

Brynhild smiled. "It does not surprise me that you have not heard of me, and that our paths have not crossed before. These wolves keep steadfastly to a modest range of territory. A small river to the east forms a natural boundary, and within this area are several streams and some rich open meadows. There is ample game here for the wolves ... herds move through here often enough. There is not much human settlement, and I do not have to go too far from my father's lands."

"Almost perfect," Magnus observed.

"I would not want to be in a larger territory. I have come to know every detail of this land, and I know my friends well," she said, giving the wolf at her side a vigorous rub on the top of its head, and smiling affectionately at the creature. Brynhild then added after a brief pause, "It is sometimes better to know a small land well, than a large land sparsely."

"There is truth in what you say, but I'm afraid I don't even know my own small land well," Magnus confessed.

"Do you return to your village often?" Brynhild asked.

"I did, and at one time I thought I had a good reason," Magnus replied, his voice lowering. His eyes suddenly broke away from her and looked downward, as he grew deeply silent.

"The woman of the village?" Brynhild asked gently, after a few moments passed.

"Men are simple creatures, are they not?" Magnus replied with a bittersweet grin.

Brynhild did not answer, simply waiting patiently for him to continue. He had not spoken much to her of his troubles at the village. In light of the friendship she had offered him, and the help she had given him, he knew that he owed her a little more in the way of explanation.

"I once had a taste of the happiness of love, only the woman was not the woman my mind had made of her. It took me until a couple of days ago to finally realize that," Magnus admitted ruefully. "It was not an easy lesson."

"Who was the other man?" Brynhild asked delicately.

"The reason I cannot return to the village. He is the man of highest stature in our village, and he is to be one of your father's warriors. A man named Njal, son of a man named Thorgils, who raised me as a son," Magnus related to her.

A dark look crossed her face, and her next words were laced with disgust. "And even Midragardans decide things such as status over simply how many metal rings or sheep a man has."

"It is the way of things," Magnus responded with a regretful tinge. "But Njal turned his hate against me just because Thorgils treated me as a son."

"Jealousy and envy," Brynhild remarked. "More poisons to the spirit. And this Njal took interest in this woman because you had an interest in her ... and she was showing an interest in you."

Magnus raised his head up a little in surprise at her keen insight. "Yes, that is the way I see it."

"You said men are such simple creatures," Brynhild remarked. "But I would rather say that men such as Njal are simple creatures. I know a little of him as well, and what drives him is what drives all men who seek my father's favor."

"But even the simple can cause great harm," Magnus replied.

"Yes, that is unfortunately true," Brynhild agreed. "I am sorry to hear of this, as I can sense the pain and loss you continue to feel deep inside. I have not walked in your path, so I cannot say I can relate to you in this. When I decided to walk on my path, there were no men who I had any interest in."

Magnus smiled, and shook his head. "Now that comes as a surprise. A woman like you could choose any man of her liking. I can already sense that no man could ever tame you to do, or be, anything against your liking."

A bright smile filled Brynhild's face. She seemed to be both amused and complimented by Magnus' words, and laughed lightly. "You are very kind, Magnus … and you are probably right in that it would indeed be hard to tame me. I have always been stubborn, as my father would agree."

"Well, for my part, I am glad you have not had to go through anything like I did," Magnus said.

"Do not be too sure of that," Brynhild said. "There are things you have learned, even if terribly painful, which may help you grow far beyond me. Times of pain offer us two paths … one to take us toward destruction, and another, harder path that through each agonizing step can make us greater in many ways. Which one you choose is up to you, but I sense you are taking the more difficult path. I see no hardness of heart in you, or consuming anger."

Magnus held her eyes for several heartbeats, finding that he wished he could look into such a fathomless gaze all night long. In Brynhild's eyes a refuge beckoned. Finally, he lowered his eyes toward the flames of the fire.

"I am not ready to give up hope just yet," Magnus said, "Even if that hope seems like a sliver."

Brynhild smiled again. "Hope is what we have, or this is just a world of rusted metal, rotted timber, and dry bones. It would be a total waste. Is that all the All-Father desires? An entire world that means absolutely nothing in the end? I think not. And I must say that I choose hope too."

Her radiant confidence filled him with an immediate sense of reassurance. "Then hope it is," Magnus replied firmly, smiling.

"If I had some mead here, we would take a deep draught together to that thought," Brynhild declared, while raising her hand up as if she had a drinking horn grasped in it.

Magnus set down the remains of his meal and leaned back, bracing himself on his hands. He looked up at the stars twinkling through the swaying boughs, feeling the cool night air upon his face. There was virtually no cloud cover, and the sky sent its invitation with white jewels set into an ebony cloak.

He basked in the moment, fully content. His heart was at peace, and his mind finally at rest from its ceaseless running in recent days. Closing his eyes, he took a long, slow inhalation of the night air, feeling the crispness as it filled his lungs. It was almost as good as a horn of mead.

"It is a good night to take a jaunt," Brynhild said in a low voice. "We can still share stories. I can show you around this territory."

Magnus brought his head back down and slowly opened his eyes. Having a vision of Brynhild's radiant face meeting his eyes was yet another reason for feeling gratitude.

"We should enjoy the peace we still have left to us," Magnus said, leaning forward, and slowly easing himself up. "A hike would be good."

"I was hoping you would say that," Brynhild replied, also standing up.

She took a couple of moments to put out the small fire. As she did so, Nightheart, the great black wolf that was the leading male of her pack, trotted up. As the wolf came to stand next to her, the other wolves of Nightheart's group rallied themselves and converged toward Brynhild.

Brynhild looked over to Magnus and laughed. "I hope your wolves are up for a walk … or are they too full of belly as their human friend might be."

She laughed and rubbed the head of the great black wolf exuberantly, leaning over and taking both sides of its broad head in her hands. The hulking creature whined playfully, extending its long snout up to lick her face enthusiastically.

Magnus grinned, "I know you already have his agreement. You have a way with them… And no, I am not too full, and neither are my wolf friends."

"Well, the night is not going to last forever," she quipped, with a teasing look upon her face.

Magnus grinned, closing his eyes as he reached out to Sky Star, inwardly summoning his pack and its venerable leader. He slowly reached out with his consciousness, a deep mystical art that was part of both the Wolf Kin and those who had undergone the Passage to become Ulfhednar. It was a most special gift, one passionately cherished by those few who could truly convene with the great wolves of the Midragardan lands.

Words were inadequate to describe how the interior process was done. It was not something that was taught, or truly could ever be taught in a traditional sense. Rather, it was something revealed and discovered. Though Magnus sometimes spoke out loud to his wolves, the real communion was done through the conveyance of the purest forms of thought and image.

As he reached forth, he felt Sky Star immediately, and Magnus' wishes were made known in a flash of an instant. Almost at once, he understood the enthusiasm that Sky Star held towards an evening jaunt through the star and moonlight dappled woodlands.

He also perceived a clear sense that Sky Star was well pleased, both with Nightheart as well as Brynhild. The disposition of the silver wolf was akin to a saturating warmth, emanating affection and harmony, a feeling that alone brought a buoyant smile to Magnus' face.

The big, silver-furred wolf loped up briskly to Magnus, nearly barreling its great head into his side. Sky Star's large ears flattened, spreading out to each side of its head as Magnus petted and scratched the huge wolf for a few moments.

Within that time, the rest of the wolves who looked to the authority of Sky Star traipsed up and collected themselves around Magnus and the stalwart pack leader. The whole brood of both packs was now fully gathered, the combined groups numbering thirty-three wolves.

The two humans faced their silent lupine brothers and sisters, and shared a gentle look between themselves. In the chasm of the sorrows, frustrations, dashed hopes, and broken dreams within Magnus' spirit, a bright, tiny spark was lit.

With a radiant smile of his own, he took in another extended inhalation, breathing out slowly and contentedly. "Shall we?" Magnus intoned softly, smiling brightly.

Smiling with an equivalent radiance, Brynhild started forward. The two of them walked side by side as they moved out into the woods with their numerous companions padding along in their wake. It was most certainly a favorable night for a hike, more so than any night had been as long as Magnus could remember.

AELFRIC

Aelfric was lost within a morass of heavy thoughts as Midnight walked forward. The herepath they now trod had entered woodlands a short while prior. He was now fully encompassed by a scene of restful serenity, one that contrasted starkly with the blood-soaked plains he had left behind.

The gently swaying branches of the trees filtered the sun's light, sending cascades of soft, flickering shadows across the forest floor and the column of men moving slowly through the woods. The air itself was fresh and clean to the lungs, entirely devoid of the bitter stench permeating the battlefield.

Birds twittered and flew freely about the high branches. The winged denizens of the forest joined their melodious voices with the sounds of the undulating breezes coursing placidly through the leaves. Looking carefree and full of life, the birds were wholly liberated from the poisons that the experience of battle left within a warrior.

The effect brought on by the surrounding ambience was timeless, as if Aelfric had entered some kind of place still unscathed by the taints of war and tragedy. At the moment, it would not have entirely surprised him if he had. A part of Aelfric was still in disbelief regarding the turn of events enabling the Saxans to retreat.

The rustles, clinks, shuffles, clopping hooves, and tramping steps of the long, bedraggled column of warriors sounded behind him. Most were men of the Select Fyrd, or the household guards of thanes, the latter including his own. They were all exhausted. Many endured the pain of wounds, some very debilitating, but those in the column were nonetheless alive and marching upon their own two feet.

The healthier warriors were heavily laden down with weapons and armor gleaned from the fallen on the battlefield. Some had long axes looped behind their leather belts, with their hands entirely occupied in the carrying of multiple swords.

The small number of ox-pulled carts travelling along with the column was filled with bundles of spears, helms resting atop cart posts, stacks of shields in usable condition, and many other war implements. Even the sides of the carts were being used for the hanging of excess mail shirts. The dutiful oxen plodded along with a treasure that was, at the moment, far more valuable than chests filled with newly minted silver coins.

Everything that could be salvaged in the short time available to the Saxans as the retreat was sounded had been hastily gathered up. The high quality weapons and armor would be of great use in the arming of other Saxans, and it provided immediate replacements for the many sorely damaged implements among the warriors. The access to replacement items was fortuitous, as any available blacksmiths across the land would soon be overwhelmed in tasks of repair.

The simple reality that there was a sizeable column of household guards, ceorls, thanes, warriors from burh garrisons, and others coming back from the battle was something to take heart from. Each and every man in Aelfric's wake was a living reminder that even in the darkest of hours a hope yet remained.

For his own part, the Saxan Ealdorman of the Wesvald was resolved to never forget the greatest lesson from the Battle at the Plains of Athelney; the one regarding hope. The hard-earned scouting reports continuing to trickle in certainly did nothing to dispute that lesson. A tremendous intervention had occurred, in what was possibly the last hour the Saxan line could have held up from collapse.

Saxan scouts had pushed as far as they could, some by horseback and others by sky steed. They had braved enormous dangers to gain an accurate perspective regarding the aftermath of the Elder Dragon's attack. Several had even died in the reconnaissance effort, having been intercepted by Trogen patrols in the air, or Avanorans on the ground.

Yet enough survived to form a clear evaluation of the status of the enemy. Their various accounts strongly corroborated each other as a concise image steadily formed.

The Elder Dragon had spread catastrophe all throughout the enemy encampments, including the principle roadway leading in from Erengard to the west. There had been no sightings of any merchant caravans drawing closer to the stricken enemy camps. There had been ample evidence of many destroyed caravans along that road, marked by the charred remains of numerous draft animals, wagons, and carts littering the stretch of hard-packed earth.

The encampments themselves had been left in shambles. The dragon's fires had spread quickly enough, and the herds of animals brought along with the invaders had been frightened into frenzied stampedes. The signs of that chaos were everywhere, not the least of which was the greatly reduced number of animals that the scouts witnessed under orderly, enemy control.

A tremendous number of wagons, carts, tents, tuns, barrels, and other storage and transport elements had been reduced to useless wreckage. Adequate supplies and foodstuffs necessary for the basic needs of an army the size of the invader's forces would take many weeks to arrive from the west at the earliest, if not several months. Even the great flying monstrosities controlled by the Avanorans would be unable to ferry enough food in to sustain a full drive of the invading forces into the east. The awesome force, on the verge of a decisive blow on the battlefield, had been soundly crippled in the one area that could not be easily, or swiftly, adjusted to.

The Avanorans and a significant part of the contingent from Erengard remained in place following the battle. They now held the fortress and lands formerly belonging to the traitorous, allodial Lord Godric. Aelfric did not doubt that the enemy would anchor themselves there for the time being.

While the overall invasion force was much reduced, with the reported departure of the Andamoorans and several of the princes and bishops from Erengard, it was still a force more than capable of subduing Saxany. Avanor had gained a foothold, one the Saxans were ill-prepared to confront.

Yet there would be a respite. With the crisis in food and supply, the enemy would not likely be making any broadly aggressive moves within Saxany in the near future. Aelfric hoped to get an idea as to Avanor's next areas of interest, but, in the meantime, the Saxan counts and ealdormen would be afforded some time to replenish and repair.

Stramangel was not too far away from the region Aelfric's column was now traveling through. Situated on the Langstenam River, Stramangel was a stout double-burh. The sizeable fortifications consisted of high earthen ramparts and thick palisades on both sides of the river, connected to each other by a wide timber bridge. A royal mint was located there, as well as a sizeable market, and a well-respected Reeve. But Stramangel was far greater in importance to the kingdom than any typical burh.

The Langstenam River had once served as a boundary line between the northern and southern kingdoms. Fed by a multitude of tributaries, it was a deep waterway for most of its considerable span to the sea. It offered no truly effective places to ford it along its western reach.

The place where Stramengal stood had been a carefully guarded crossing point held by the northern kingdom. If Stramengal were to be taken by the enemy, it could lead to the division of the entire Saxan kingdom. The taking of the double-burh would allow for unfettered movement between the northern and southern regions of the kingdom. If Aelfric was the enemy commander, it was precisely where he would strike.

He knew many of the warriors were aching to see their own families and friends again, but he would have to keep the bulk of the Select Fyrd together. They would have to be kept within close range of Stramangel, at least until Aelfric had a better idea of the enemy's intentions.

There was no room for error in judgement, a consummate, weighty truth Aelfric was unceasingly aware of. It was a great burden to bear for any leader, but he was not about to shy away from the onerous task.

Aelfric cast another glance back along the meandering line of forlorn faces, feeling the sorrows and worries emanating off the weary men. "Emmanu be with us," he whispered quietly to himself, as if in reflex to the melancholic sight of his heavy-hearted men.

The words of invocation had come quickly to his lips. Yet as he thought of it further, there was a lesson of hope within that particular story as well; a man subjected to extreme humiliation and beatings, executed gruesomely with five spears driven through him in front of jeering, mocking crowds had become a living, timeless beacon of hope.

Aelfric mused that nothing could have seemed more despairing for the followers of Emmanu than seeing Him stripped, bloodied, and naked, impaled through his pummeled body with the five lances where he was bound spread-eagled to two rough planks of wood crossing diagonally. Yet all of them had emerged in the years after that sorrowful time to face torture and death without hesitation, passionately spreading the fires of their testament among the poor, the outcast, and those whose hearts had grown.

Nothing would have seemed more improbable on the day Emmanu was executed than the widespread promulgation of His teachings regarding the All-Father. Nothing could explain the enormous shift in the morale of his dismayed followers than Him returning from the bonds of death to walk victoriously in the flesh once again.

Aelfric could not help but suffer a momentary smile to himself as he looked down the narrow pathway through the woods ahead. Though hemmed in by the wilderness of Saxany, it still marked a clear way forward.

Without thinking of what he was doing, Aelfric's right hand strayed upwards, and idly fingered the spear-shaped silver amulet hanging from his neck. Hope did indeed remain, no matter how despairing things might appear to be.

AETHELHERE

Aethelhere's vessel was in the midst of a host of ships plying the waters along the northern coast of Saxany when the startling commands of Aelfric arrived by way of a few riders upon Himmerosen. The hard-driven steeds were frothing when they arrived on the deck of his great war galley, Honor Bound.

Aethelhere implicitly understood the urgency of the situation before he even looked at the seal on the parchment handed to him by the sky riders. Before the first rider opened his mouth in introduction, Aethelhere knew time was of the greatest essence.

He had commanded men long enough to read their mannerisms, expressions, and postures capably. The sky riders' dispositions were abundantly clear from the moment they alighted.

Not long before the arrival of the sky riders, Aethelhere had espied the great dragon flying along the coastline. The incredible sight brought a jolt of fear to him, but when the dragon did no harm to the ships, passing swiftly down the coast to the west, Aethelhere recalled some of the older, more fascinating legends he knew.

The Himmerosen-mounted messengers had come shortly thereafter, after being sighted at a lower altitude than the dragon. They had been traveling along the same route, and Aethelhere suspected a correlation between the close appearances.

He had been stunned to hear the tale of what had transpired on the Plains of Athelney. The riders themselves appeared amazed that they were rendering the fantastical account to Aethelhere, of something they had been eyewitnesses to.

He had been even more astonished to meet the one called Wulfstan, who had arrived on a lone Himmeros shortly after the other sky riders. Wulfstan, Aelfric noticed immediately, had flown in from the direction the dragon had gone.

Wulfstan had turned out to be a simple ceorl from Sussachia, the lands under Ealdorman Byrtnoth's governance. Wulfstan was the one from the rider's tale who had braved the farthest heights reachable by man and beast. He had come upon the Elder dragon and somehow brought its formidable aid behind Saxany's terrible struggle.

The dark-haired, blue-eyed warrior described how he had been carried, along with his steed, in the Elder Dragon's immense claws. Evidently, he had developed a unique friendship with the huge dragon. As much as it all mystified him, Aethelhere was immensely grateful for everything.

Aethelhere's worries drifted constantly to the fates of his wife Emma, his sons Wystan and Wynoth, his brother Aethelstan, and a great number of kin and friends back in Wessachia. The forested hills and mountains there would not prove easy territory for an invader, but Aethelhere knew that Ealdorman Morcar and all his thanes, including Aethelstan, would be heavily engaged in the defense of Saxany.

That fact alone created grave worry for Aethelhere, as one of his sons, Wynoth, was fostering with Aethelstan. His only relief came in the knowledge that his brother was married to a woman of great judgement and wisdom. In addition, Aethelstan's first thoughts before leaving Bergton would have been put to providing as well as possible for the security of his family, including his nephew Wynoth.

Aethelhere loathed being so far away from those he loved, kept in a fog of uncertainty as the entire kingdom faced a massive invasion. As always, he had to trust that ultimately everything was in the hands of the All-Father.

The bulk of the Saxan war fleet had been assigned to watching the waters off the north and northeastern coastlines of Saxany. No immediate threats were suspected. The ocean waters to the immediate west, narrowing into a strait running between Gallean lands and the farthest western reach of Saxany's northern coastline, were treacherous, impassable for even the best of ships.

It was not likely that enemy fleets would come down from the direct north either. Any vessels would have a long distance to navigate, far from any friendly lands and ports.

Word would long precede any movements of large numbers of

ships. Sleek Midragardan vessels, among others, regularly plied the waters to the north and east of Saxany. The presence of an Avanoran fleet would have stirred up some warnings.

Therefore, it was largely a precaution that the main Saxan fleet was out at sea warding the northern coastlines, but Ealdorman Aelfric and King Alcuin were not the types to make reckless assumptions. As the majordomo, or army commander, for King Alcuin, Aelfric insisted that the fleet assemble and put to sea while the land forces moved to defend Saxany's western borders.

Aethelhere had no misgivings that the Saxan fleet was put out to sea in the early stages of the response to the tidings of Avanor's approaching invasion force. Mustered and already at sea, the Saxan vessels were in a favorable position to respond swiftly to any urgent request sent by Aelfric or the king himself. Such a need had now indeed manifested, born as Aethelhere conferred with Wulfstan and the sky riders sent by Aelfric.

Aethelhere had a considerable number of vessels at his disposal, as the Saxans had assembled a sizeable war fleet. It consisted primarily of galleys, of a couple of main types.

One type of galley was similar in appearance to Midragardan longships, only the Saxan versions were a little larger and wider of beam. Like the Midragardan ships, they were single-masted, clinker-built, and featured one large square sail.

The other principle style of galley present within the Saxan fleet showed the influence of Theonian dromonds, based upon warships first constructed by the legendary southern king Carloman the Great. The larger monoreme galleys were equipped with one bank of oars. In essence, they were cataphracts, with the entire array of rowers protected underneath a full upper deck.

With both single and double-masted vessels, the dromond-style war galleys used the triangular lateen sail. They also displayed robust spurs projecting above-water from their bows. The spurs were designed for the effective breaking of oars down the sides of enemy ships, or for ramming enemy vessels, such that they were tilted over and took on water.

The fleet had grown larger since the first batch of ships had responded to Aelfric's directive. Aethelhere had already put in to shore a few times to gather up more supplies. Additional ships were hastily collected during the interludes, requisitioned under the royal authority conferred on Aethelhere wherever they were found.

While a few of the additional vessels were galleys, there were some single-masted trading cogs and hulks. The flatter bottomed cogs were designed with steep stems at bow and stern. Using the spade-shaped firrer steering oar, with its T-shaped handle, the ships made use of a lugsail for maneuvering. Their flat bottoms allowed for the coastal traders to beach when the tide was out.

The hulks were not entirely dissimilar to the cogs, except they had a decidedly more curved profile that did not feature the prominent stems used in the cogs. Their rounded bottoms allowed for steadier performance at sea, as well as creating more effective bilges within.

The capacity of the hulks and cogs for cargo would come in very valuable in the endeavor Aethelhere had just been charged with; albeit the cargo they sought to attain was a human one. He could only hope fortune was with the Saxans, as the trading cogs and hulks would largely be at the mercy of the winds. The cogs normally were not taken out of the sight of land, but the persistent use of sky steeds would help to make sure the cogs stayed on course, if there ever was any separation from the other vessels.

The tops of the masts of the cogs and hulks were crowned with the spear-shaped symbol of Emmanu. The conspicuous style of mast-tops hailed all the way back in time to Carloman the Great's reign, reflecting the peaceable tradition of trading the ships enabled.

A few of the requisitioned trading ships were currently away from the main fleet. They were in the process of stocking their holds for departure, giving an added boon to the Saxan fleet in the form of an additional influx of supplies and foodstuffs. Aethelhere delegated some of his men to detail everything taken on board, so that fair compensation could eventually be rendered to those who owned the cargo.

Aethelhere even deliberated seriously over thoughts of using some of the larger river ships, such as a very particular, single-masted type with a curved profile. Almost sixty feet in length, their masts were set about a third of the way back from the bow. In some ways, the river ships were evocative of the rounded trading hulks. With no stem posts or main keel, operated with the use of a lugsail, and with only two oars for maneuver, the sleek river ships were also exceedingly dependent on wind for propulsion.

After weighing the risks, Aethelhere finally opted against the use of them. The river ships, whose few side strakes meant that they sat very close to the waterline, would incur far too many risks in the unpredictable stretch of open sea the Saxan fleet would have to cross.

Even without pressing the river ships into duty, Aethelhere had more ships than he ever expected to have as the journey to the north began. Collectively, the assemblage of capable vessels represented a formidable fleet upon the water. It was one that could aptly transport a great number of people.

Aethelhere had also been able to summon a small contingent of Himmerosen kept in reserve specifically for the assistance of the war fleet. The group joined up with the fleet just as it began its movement towards the north. Aethelhere had watched them landing on the open decks of the larger vessels until their principal officer, a stoic thane from Essachia named Felgild, sought Aethelhere's counsel.

A small number of Felgild's Himmerosen could now be seen in the air above. Their winged forms appeared diminutive off in the distance. A few were visible in each principle direction away from the core body of the fleet.

The riders in the sky were part of a disciplined group of patrol rotations implemented by Aethelhere and Felgild. They sustained a constant lookout for the naval force during daylight, and would be invaluable in helping the hulks and cogs keep to their course if the vessels lagged behind due to a downturn in the winds. As the fleet crossed the unavoidable stretch of open sea for the precarious jaunt required to reach the coastline of the Five Realms, the sky riders' consistent presence above was of inestimable value.

A robust, steady wind was currently in the Saxans' favor. All of the ships, galleys, hulks and cogs alike were able to take advantage of their prominent sails, whether square, lateen, or lug in style.

Aethelhere stood at the bow of Honor Bound, feeling the misty spray of the sea on his face, and its salty taste on his lips, as the vessel smoothly traversed the ocean's rolling surface. His thoughts were fixated on the horizons, both the one ahead and the one behind.

The men were in fairly even spirits, perhaps as good a mood as he could hope for, as they moved about the ship and attended to the rigging and other various tasks. Underneath their relatively calm, and sometimes jocular, demeanors, he knew full well that the men harbored a considerable amount of apprehension.

With the favorable winds negating the need for using oars, many of the men on Honor Bound would be able to get some rest or engage in amusements, such as stories, song, or games of chance. If Aethelhere could have his way, the men would be able to experience a relatively uneventful passage to the coast of the Five Realms.

He had little doubt that things would be much different when they drew near to the Water-Head Cradle if the tribal people and Midragardans had been able to reach it.

The Saxans would almost certainly need all of their strength and focus when that momentous time arrived, no matter who it was they encountered on the foreign shore. For his part, first and foremost, Aethelhere intended to return to his homeland with the Saxan fleet intact; along with a large number of new passengers lifted out of harm's way.

section v

LOGAN

Logan found himself restless, despite the comforts of a sizeable, four-posted bed. Sheltered within a full canopy, it was provided with ample pillows stuffed with the softest feathers.

Having pulled the canopy back, he found himself peering into the shadows hovering and pooling around the small chamber. Most were cast from the sylvan moonlight pouring through the lone tower window he had left fully open. A few came from the flames yet dancing in the recessed fireplace, which a servant had recently attended to at Logan's request.

The murky ambience echoed his ambiguous mood. Logan was so lost in the depths of thought that it took him a moment to react to the firm knock upon the door to the chamber. With an annoyed groan, he lifted himself upward, peeled the covers off, and swung his legs over the side of the bed. Gaining his feet, he ambled sluggishly towards the door.

Pulling the door open, he stood back and beheld three warriors in conical helms standing just outside. Their expressions were humorless. Each carried a spear and was equipped with kite-shield and a sword resting in a scabbard at his waist.

"The Unifier wishes to meet with you," the foremost warrior announced, with the slightest of nods towards Logan.

Logan knew the words were no invitation. They were a politely worded command. "Give me just a moment, to dress myself," Logan replied, his curiosity piqued.

The Unifier held the fates of Logan and his companions within His hands. The invitation beckoned towards an opportunity to gain a little more awareness regarding the situation facing the four otherworlders.

He took a few moments to don a pair of leather boots, trousers, and loose-fitting woolen tunic, buckling a hide belt into place before leaving the chamber. As they started up the winding stairway of the tower, he fumbled with his belt until the outer tunic was pulled more snugly about his waist.

They did not disturb any of the other occupants of the tower, exiting at the wall-walk. The group continued to the stairway down to the ground, and descended.

The night was cooled with swirling breezes, buffeting the men as they reached the bottom and crossed the open ground. The guards led

Logan towards another of the high towers set into the outer wall of the terrace.

Logan's eyes gravitated towards the bridging extensions running from the upper level of three towers, crossing on their huge arches to the edge of the next terrace on the lofty mountainside. The stout span of masonry was broken only by the exposed wooden platform set near the midpoint.

"They say those are the work of Andamoorans, or at least mimic it," one guard commented, having taken notice of Logan's intent gaze.

"Andamoorans?" Logan replied quizzically, glancing sideways to the guard walking at his side. "And why are they designed that way?"

"Never been in their lands. Those are far to the north of here. But they say the Andamoorans have such towers, set beyond the outer walls of their fortifications. That kind of tower doesn't rise above the walls, but is built with walkways leading from their tops, bridging from main walls to the exterior tower.

"As you can see, this type of tower can be used to defend, and to connect the rising levels of this fortress. It is said the design of many things within this great fortress hearken from a number of faraway lands."

"Fascinating," Logan commented, with no trace of the sarcasm so often lacing his words.

Dark forms moved high above him, as several guards strolled slowly along the circuitous wall-walk looming ahead. A couple of others met Logan's party as they climbed a short wooden staircase, and entered the tower with the spanning walkway.

When they reached the open, crenellated top of the square mural tower, the winds greeted the party, coursing steadily over them and carrying salty hints from the glittering ocean. A couple of merlons were currently being used to support the weight of two sentries leaning idly against them. The crossbow-bearing men straightened up quickly, putting on alert expressions as Logan and the others emerged.

The vibrant, misty breezes frolicking through the air livened Logan's senses, as the escorting guards guided him towards the bridging span. They started across, and after several paces the crenellated sides of the bridge came to an abrupt end. Logan felt a slight weightlessness in the pit of his stomach as they stepped out onto the wooden span. With the wind whistling in his ears, Logan felt his heart speeding up, hearing the creaking of the timber under his feet.

Having so recently beheld the dizzying drop just inches beneath the soles of his leather boots, and feeling increasingly light-headed, he looked upwards, trying to keep his mind off the long fall. A couple more terrace-levels rose above, culminating in the great, singular tower soaring skyward from the pinnacle of the mountain. The tower was limned with light from the larger of the bright moons, the edifice appearing to bisect the gleaming orb. The sheer heights the tower commanded, looming over the deep levels of the terraces below it, drove Logan's eyes back down mercifully, moments before he was hit with a disorienting sensation. He gave his head a shake, forcing his legs to keep moving onward.

He breathed deeply in with relief as his feet met the solidity of stone once again. The reappearance of the raised, crenellated sides gave him needed reassurance. He followed the lead guard with a little more haste in his step, as they headed towards the postern gate set into the wall ahead.

The gate was opened a moment later by a guard from within, and the party entered the narrow passageway single file. Logan looked up and saw small patches of deeper blackness breaking the continuity of the ceiling. Having read much on castle defenses growing up, he knew what the holes represented. It almost made him shudder to think of the death that could be rained down upon an unfortunate attacker trapped within the cramped space of the passage.

Passing through the thickness of the outer wall, they found themselves on the edge of an open expanse of ground. It led towards a glistening pool of water, backed by a palatial, exquisitely-fashioned edifice. The open ground, pool, and edifice, in turn, were surrounded by a host of lush foliage and trees, swaying and rustling gently in the night breezes flowing throughout them.

A small stone building, rectangular in shape, stood within the broad pool of water. The visible side of the structure was decorated with a series of tall, ornamental, arch-like recesses, arranged in a concentric pattern. There were two such adornments, each enveloping a double-arched window whose lancets were separated by narrow, coupled columns shaped into twisting forms.

A narrow stone bridge, supported by a low, singular arch, proceeded from the grounds out to the structure rising up from the water. The bridge entered the building through an arched opening that rested within a broadening series of archivolts skillfully molded around it.

From within the opening, Logan could hear the distinctive sound of water cascading down, undoubtedly from some kind of fountain housed inside. Beyond the enclosed fountain was the façade of a similarly embellished palace building, rising upwards for three demarcated levels.

The ground level contained two narrow openings, as well as one much wider and of a notably greater height. All three openings were constructed of pointed arches, graced by more of the concentric archivolts.

The second and third levels contained a multitude of double-arched windows. Similar to the fountain building in construct, they were surrounded by concentric moldings, and supported on coupled sets of small, twisting columns.

Skirting around the edge of the pool, the guards led Logan towards the higher, broader archway set in the middle of the larger structure. Drawing closer, Logan espied the tops of arched openings down at the water's surface, where the pool met the larger structure, channeling the water into the interior of the greater palace-building.

Two spear-bearing guards attended the central ground-level archway. They made no move to hinder Logan's entrance, nor did they make any demands of the warriors with him.

Once he was through the entrance, Logan looked about with a feeling of wonderment. The interior was lit by a number of flaming torches set into wall brackets, as well as several substantial, gleaming braziers placed throughout the area. The firelight gave the interior a warm ambience, one seemingly alive with its steadily undulating flickers and shadows.

A part of him wanted to explore the spaces beyond the adorned arches leading off to the left and right, as well as the magnificent tapestries lining the walls. He drifted behind the guards, slowing his pace as he gazed around.

The guards quickly made it known they were not about to dally for aesthetic reasons. They caught his wandering attention, gesturing firmly for him to follow them towards a more brightly-lit area just ahead.

The short passage opened into an opulent chamber rising all the way up through the center of the structure, culminating in a honeycomb-like ceiling far above. The presence of galleries ringing the central chamber on both the second and third levels gave evidence to a number of other chambers and rooms shooting off the central area.

The grand chamber itself was lit by a number of ornate, and sizeable, oil-filled lamps. Fashioned of various colors of glass, the lamps were placed all about the room on stands crafted of gleaming bronze. The floating wicks of the lamps gave off enough light to provide a soft, dynamic illumination. The elaborate, swirling shapes of the lamps themselves, and their wide variety of colors, boasted of exceptional artistry in their making.

A marble table fashioned into a semicircular shape dominated the center of the main chamber. Amply cushioned benches were placed all along the larger of its curving edges, suggesting a manner of reclined attendance, rather than upright sitting.

With the serene ambience, and the reality that the central table could only accommodate a small number of individuals, the chamber held the appearance of an intimate dining area. It was a vision simultaneously impressive and inviting, beckoning guests towards comfort even as it showered them with images of splendor.

A lone figure of tall stature stood towards the farther side of the table, at approximately its midpoint. Though the back of the individual was turned to Logan, he implicitly knew the figure was the Unifier. The guards held back, one of them nudging Logan forward, as he slowly took a few steps deeper into the chamber.

The hackles on his neck rose as a tingle ran over his skin. He had the distinct impression that eyes were watching him from the innumerable shadows off to the sides, and within the gallery levels farther above. A couple of times, he thought he saw larger shadows shift out of the corners of his eyes, firm movements contrasting sharply with the characteristics of flame-cast shadows. He quickly admonished himself to stop letting his mind play tricks, willing his lungs to breathe in deeper.

As Logan neared the semi-circular table, he found himself relieved when the voice of the Unifier finally broke the oppressive stillness. "I trust the walk here was not too tiring. I have not spent much time lately in this part of my palace. I thought this might be a suitable place for us to visit," the tall man said, turning and regarding Logan with His mysterious, luminous eyes. His face exhibited a charming smile, as He walked around the edge of the table. Drawing to a halt just a couple of paces away from Logan, the Unifier seemed even taller than the roughly six and a half feet Logan estimated Him to be.

"Thank you ... your Majesty ... It felt good to take a walk, and get to see more of your … palace," Logan replied awkwardly, giving a slight bow. He found himself hesitant, stymied with uncertainties about the proper way to address the Unifier.

The Unifier smiled, and there seemed to be a sparkling glitter within His eyes, as if He was highly amused by Logan's choice of address to Him. "I am not a king, Logan. And I would like to speak openly with you, so you do not have to use any lofty titles. Be welcome here, and speak plainly, and comfortably. This is no gathering of court officials and nobles that would beg pageantry or formalities."

The Unifier cast a momentary glance towards the semi-circular benches and table. "You will have to join Me for a meal here, sometime very soon. This level of the palace complex is one of My favorites because of this very building.

"This chamber is arranged in an older, more Theonian style. Some in these western lands might find it to be unusual, but it is one I find to be quite relaxing, and very conducive to conversation. But you have likely eaten already, am I correct?"

"Yes, and I would like to say that we have been fed very well during our stay. Thank you very much," Logan replied politely, with sincere gratitude.

"That is good to hear. Anything less I would find to be very unacceptable. I will have to see that those attending you are commended. Come with Me now, and let us talk together for a time," the Unifier invited amiably.

Logan could do little more than nod in response. He turned to follow in the wake of the Unifier, as the graceful man strode past Logan and headed back out the way Logan and his guard escorts had just arrived.

Once outside the building, the Unifier led him off to the right of the central archway. No guards followed them, and none were in the area they headed into.

The cool breezes caressing the surrounding foliage and the shimmering pool to their left complemented the tranquility reigning in the night air. The Unifier came to a stop where the covered fountain in the midst of the pool was just across the water from them. The sounds of flowing water provided an unbroken rhythm to the spectacular vision of the fathomless, richly-adorned night sky above.

The Unifier silently gazed upwards, a contemplative expression on His face. Logan felt the stress leaving him as he peered up at the sky, enraptured by the purity of the vista.

"The beauty of the world. An ebony curtain of jewels," the Unifier remarked in a low voice, as He continued staring upward at the dark canopy generously decorated with bright stars. Assertive tendrils of wind ruffled His dark, thick hair, and rippled through His flowing, loose-fitting robes of white silk.

Without waiting for an answer, He started forward slowly. Logan, who was still taking in the view of the sky, had to take quickened strides just to catch up. His curiosity rose as he walked behind the Unifier, heading towards the outer curtain wall lining the terrace.

The Unifier proceeded towards a stone staircase ascending the inside of the wall, up to the wall walk. With fluid steps, He surmounted the stairs with ease, coming to a halt on the allure near the edge of the battlements. Keeping pace with the Unifier, Logan found he was a little winded after the quick climb.

"An even broader vision of the night sky from the edge of this wall. A sky above, and a sky below," the Unifier commented.

His words drifted off, as a faraway look came into His eyes. The Unifier's gaze descended slowly from the sky towards the great city spreading outward far below.

The starry firmament did seem much vaster in scope than before from Logan's new vantage. Even so, the expansive view of the sky was not the sight ultimately taking his breath away in captivated awe. The perspective of Avalos, reaching out far and wide before the massive, mountain fortress, fully engaged his sense of wonder.

He looked out over the countless buildings, roads, walls, and incalculable other structures within Avalos. The city's features looked so small from the substantial height as to seem surreal in nature. Logan's own proximity to the lower terraces of the palace-fortress helped produce a dizzying sense of the towering loftiness from which he beheld the incredible view.

With each lower level, the terraces jutted out farther from the mountainside. They lost detail with the increasing distance, from the more distinctive form of the high tower where Logan presently resided, to the faint triple walls and moat running along the base of the mountain palace.

As if it were the surface of a great lake reflecting the starry firmament spread so far above, a vast host of firelights below formed an enchanting sight. Comprised of the torches set on street posts, lights in the windows of primarily larger buildings, torches or braziers at various watch points, and a wide assortment of other locations, the host of firelights broke apart the wider stretches and pools of shrouding darkness. Though the land fell to near total black farther out beyond the walls of the city, the entirety of the area within the city walls contributed to a powerful scene conveying immensity and timelessness.

"The whole world seemingly right before your eyes. So small, and yet so vast. Am I correct?" the Unifier remarked, bringing Logan out of his near trance. Logan had not noticed that the Unifer had turned to face him. "I have often felt the same sensation, looking out during nights such as this."

"It does feel that way," Logan said, keeping a step away from the edge of the crenellated wall. He felt a light dizziness continuing to run throughout him, and had to close his eyes for a second, to regain a little more equilibrium. A strong gust of wind washed over him, bringing with it a taste of the night's chill.

He opened his eyes again, and saw that the Unifier was still patiently regarding him. Strangely, he was not unsettled by the undivided attention.

The face of the Unifier was warm and pacifying. It was not the visage of a baleful creature like that painted by those in the Five Realms. The tall figure before Logan was a vision of reassurance and confidence.

Despite the placid impression, Logan still could not deny the horror of the Darrok raid on the Five Realms village. The vivid remembrance prevented him from feeling entirely at ease in the powerful man's presence, though he kept his sense of revulsion at that tragedy buried deep within. He found it difficult to focus upon such terrible things while in the company of the Unifier, and surrounded by such magnificence.

"It is a vision filled with wonder. Of a world that is not always so wonderful," the Unifier stated. His sharp, bright smile faded a little, as if He had caught an echo of Logan's latter thoughts. "It is a world most difficult to bear, with difficult choices to make. It is not so easy, for anyone. The village farmer laboring in the countryside, beholden to unpredictable elements, and the threat of pestilence. The merchant in his guild hall, navigating politics, personalities, and all manner of unforeseen developments, to keep his business in order. The warrior in the castle guardroom, or the leader of thousands, both needing to be vigilant, ready to respond to a threat at a moment's notice. The choices do not always go as we wish, or as we have intended. Within even the most noble of pursuits, there are often things that happen which are far from noble in nature, would you agree?"

"I would have to agree … with everything you've said," Logan answered a few moments later, in a subdued voice, seeing that the Unifier was waiting for his response. He had spoken in truth, as there was little argument to be had with the Unifier's assertion.

"Much has been said of Me, Logan. Some things you may have already heard, perhaps some things that are far, far from pleasant. Just remember that what you may have heard comes from the mouths of my enemies. I would ask you to consider whether such comments may have a bias. I trust that you have some questions for Me," the Unifier said in a congenial tone. "Please, do not hesitate to ask."

Logan cleared his throat, trying to keep his nerves and outward composure in order. Once begun, his questions poured out in his eagerness to acquire some answers.

"I don't know where I should begin. I do have many questions. Why have we been brought here? Why are we under such confinement? Why did we have to be captured by force? And maybe some things nobody can answer, such as why are we here in this world, and how can we get back to where we came from?"

The Unifier nodded, and fell silent for an extended moment, as if reflecting upon each of Logan's queries. His tone was calm when he responded, "These are very troubled times. A comprehensive order is being brought to fruition, once and for all time to come, to mitigate the long ages of humankind's unstable existence within this world. Humanity, and indeed all races of Ave, have endured a state of being that balances itself on the edge of chaos. I work to bring everything back to the sure footing of a complete, enduring order.

"One cannot look at such times from the usual perspective, as it is entirely unprecedented. I regret that great precautions have had to be taken on your behalf, and that those who were sent out to retrieve you did not understand all ends, or reasons, for themselves.

"It is no mystery why My enemies sought to have you think of them as genuine friends, and of myself as some kind of villainous adversary, perhaps even a monster. They merely desired to use you and your friends against me, as a weapon of war. They wished to use you as a means of helping them to preserve a flawed world in the face of the bold, new one I am bringing into existence. They wish to remain in error, while the rest of us progress.

"I can assure you they would not have been so welcoming otherwise. Once you are more settled, a visit to My library, or the one housed and maintained by the Cathedral, would show you much more about them that they have not shared with you. Things they do not want you to know. The Five Realms have been less than gentle with their neighbors. You should read the accounts of what they have done to their captives, even eating their flesh. And Midragard? Midragard's longships have visited terrors in abundance upon lands not their own. Burned defenseless monasteries to the ground, pillaged helpless villages … Keep all of this in mind when considering what you have heard regarding Me, from Midragardans and tribal people that have hid their own shameful actions from you "

The Unifier paused, as if wanting Logan to digest the words before He resumed. "And there are also those who would seek to harm you, among those that would use you. I understand that I risk being seen by you and your companions as having imprisoned your group. Your security is for your own protection and interests. I only hope that in time reason shall speak clearly to you.

"There is not yet an answer as to how you can return to your world, but I may know something as to why you are here. Prophecy in our world speaks of a time when those from another age, time, and place would enter our world … otherworlders, just such as you are. It is said that this will take place during the time of the Last War, a time when mighty gods would fight their final battle. Do you know of things such as this?"

"It sounds like a battle talked about in our world's own religions," Logan replied. "And what gods do you worship here?"

"Many have been said to exist, and many who are creations themselves have been worshiped," the Unifier replied. "But there are only two paths, as I see the world. The true god, the one I serve, and the hidden, tyrant god that my enemies truly serve."

A cloud passed over one of the moons, or the perception might have been his own invention, but to Logan's eyes the Unifier's gaze darkened and hardened considerably, as He spoke of the gods of their world. The change proved ephemeral, as when He finished speaking, the Unifier's features returned back to a relaxed, amiable state.

The Unifier cupped His hands together before Him, and a small flame burst from within His palms. The flames quickly grew, reaching outward, wrapping and curling around His body while not singeing so much as one strand of hair on His head.

Logan watched in stunned amazement, feeling the heat wafting from the expanding flames. He remained firmly in place, somehow knowing the flames less than an arm's length away would not harm him.

"Fire can be so many things. A source of warmth to save a traveler from death by cold. A weapon to drive back an enemy set to kill you. A means to prepare food to safely nourish an empty stomach. A power to consume a diseased corpse, and protect those yet healthy from the touch of death itself," the Unifier commented, His voice gradually becoming more commanding in tone. "I am bringing this world a peace it has never known, and a freedom to its people that has never been experienced. How could anyone believe there are those who would willingly choose to fight against this? Sadly, there are far more than you might think, whether misguided, or of ill-intent."

Logan listened closely to the words, even as he continued watching in astonishment as the flames extended farther above, curling and coalescing in the air just a few feet over the Unifier's head. The fire strands formed themselves into the shape of a great bird of prey, an eagle to Logan's eyes. The firebird flapped its wings, and soared up into the night air, before dissipating into smoke.

Logan's heart gave a start as he looked back down, and saw that the Unifier was staring directly into his eyes. A gentle smile returned to the Unifier's face, but His eyes continued to hold a serious edge.

"Just an illusion. Nothing more. Born of magic," the Unifier stated solemnly. "Yes, magic is a reality in this world, capable of much more than mere illusion. I can see from your face it is not something common in your own."

Logan slowly shook his head in disbelief, trying to gain some understanding of the extraordinary act he had just witnessed. "No, and the magic we have in our world is only simple illusion, nothing more. And even the illusions there are nothing like what I have just witnessed here."

"And only the beginning of what you will witness in time," the

Unifier said, with a lighthearted laugh. As if a sprite youth, He suddenly leapt to the edge of the crenellated wall, his soft leather shoes landing squarely between two stout merlons with perfect balance.

Logan's heart dropped into his gut watching the effortless motion. The Unifier folded His arms across His chest, looking outward. Logan thought of the last strong blast of wind that had come through only moments before, and became even more queasy inside.

"Forgive me if I frighten you, but there is so much to behold. So much for you to learn of the new world you are now in. Come, follow me," the Unifier invited with a broadening smile, gesturing with His outstretched left hand.

Logan suddenly felt himself being picked up off the ground, as if clutched by an unseen force. He was carried slowly towards the Unifier. Helpless to stop it, he blanched as he continued past the wall. His feet dangled in the air, with nothing to break his fall to the terrace below them.

His heart raced in his chest, pounding furiously. Logan's mind was a blur of panic. He feared he would lose control of his bladder in another moment or two. His attention was mercifully distracted, seeing the Unifier float out from the wall. The Unifier came to a hovering rest before Logan, sharing the open sky with him.

"Nothing to fear," the Unifier said calmly, his demeanor completely at ease. His unalarmed words filled Logan with both reassurance and strength, in and of themselves. "Remember, there is real magic in this world, and so many new things for you and yours to learn and experience."

Logan kept his eyes rigidly focused upon the Unifier, not wanting to let his gaze drift downward for even a second. The weightlessness beneath the soles of his shoes was more than enough of a warning. His heart rate slowed down only a couple of beats, his gripping fear unable to dissipate significantly.

Mustering his will, he spoke with a little unsteadiness. "It certainly seems there is real magic in your world. Nothing at all like our world."

"Maybe it is in your world, but remains hidden to you and those of your world. You are afraid now, but magic can be something you come to know very well. I can sense great abilities within you. Otherwise, you would not have been brought into this world," the Unifier replied, as another warm, friendly grin spread across His face. "I believe that you have the ability to do what you call magic. In time, I may even teach you to unlock such gifts, so you can wield a great force for the good of this world.

"Would my enemies do the same for you? Did they tell you of such a hidden skill? Did they offer to let you access its powers and wonders for yourself? Learn this power within my friendship, and who can say where the limits are? All you see below and beyond may be yours in time. I ask only for your loyalty. I can bestow the things of this world on those I wish, as they have been given to My authority ... by the One Who holds authority over all the world."

Logan saw a peculiar gleam creep into the Unifier's eyes as He spoke the enigmatic words. Yet just as he started to take notice of the odd manifestation, the Unifier's manner eased abruptly, and He suddenly changed the subject.

"But enough of that for now. I do not wish to overwhelm you, or frighten you, but I had to leave you with something significant to ponder as you consider the slander directed at Me by My declared enemies."

The Unifier then made another gesture, and the two of them drifted smoothly back towards the battlements. They passed over the top of the merlons, setting down lightly upon the stone of the wall-walk. Logan took a deep breath, wiping away some sweat that had beaded upon his forehead. A flood of relief entered him with the reassuring feeling of solid ground beneath his feet.

Once safely on the wall-walk, Logan finally let himself savor a taste of the electrifying thrill his fears had tamped down during the incredible experience. Now that he felt secure, the lingering sensation was allowed to emerge to the forefront.

"Magic has its thrills, yes?" the Unifier inquired, once again seeming to read Logan's mind.

"Yes, it does, most certainly," Logan replied, permitting himself a nervous smile.

"There is so much more to come, if you choose," the Unifier replied. His tone softened as He continued. "But you have beheld a vision of Avalos, in a way very few have before."

"It was absolutely incredible, thank you," Logan said, before querying, "And if you don't mind my asking, when might I be able to see Avalos down below? I would love to walk the streets of Your city."

"I will see that you are able to go into the city tomorrow, but not without an escort, for your own safety," the Unifier answered. His features darkened, in the manner Logan had witnessed a few times before. "I spoke of it before, but hear My words, Logan. Understand them, and what they mean.

"There are those among My enemies who will want you dead. There are those who would only seek to use you, like the ones whom My forces took you from. Even behind the city walls, it is not safe for you, or your friends. I do not wish to see harm come to you, and must keep you protected."

The thought that anyone wanted him dead placed things far beyond any anxieties Logan had wrestled with in his own world. He still did not know what to think of the Unifier, for the man before him contrasted greatly with the things he had previously been told. He would need some time to think everything through before coming to any conclusions, but the Unifier had given him much to think about.

It was inarguable that he was within the power of the Unifier, and he was not foolish enough to think he was in any position to try and test the boundaries of that power. Furthermore, he wanted to explore, and learn more about the city of Avalos. The Unifier held the authority to grant him that privilege, and Logan was not about to abuse the first steps of progress since his initial arrival in Avalos.

"I would definitely enjoy a trip down into the city, and I do understand the need for guards," Logan replied. "I promise I will not cause any troubles for You, or the guards You provide."

"Then it shall be arranged so," the Unifier said, another smile coming to His face. "You will learn more in time. For now, go and rest. Tomorrow I will have guards sent to escort you into Avalos."

The Unifier nodded towards the staircase. Logan walked over and began the descent. When he reached the ground, he saw the three guards who had escorted him from his chamber. They were gathered close to the postern gate by which they had first entered the terrace level.

"Rannulf, see My guest back to his quarters," the Unifier commanded, from where He stood a couple of paces behind Logan.

The guard bowed his head. "As you wish, my Lord."

Not sure how to gesture himself, Logan turned and gave the Unifier a similar, low bow, before departing with the three guards. In moments, he found himself back through the postern gate, and on his way to the tower with his private chamber.

It would be a long while before he succumbed to the serenity of sleep. His mind raced with numerous thoughts and visions. The Unifier's mere suggestion that Logan could work magic himself nearly staggered him. The incredible sensations he had experienced during his visitation with the Unifier were wonders to be savored, over and over again, within his head.

His spirits were lifted greatly from the deep brooding he had found himself mired in before Rannulf had knocked upon the chamber's thick wooden door, and summoned him to the unexpected audience with the Unifier. Unexpected and momentous possibilities now beckoned, and Logan was more than intrigued.

SAXAN FLEET

The Saxan fleet was well on its way towards the coastline of the Five Realms. The weather had bequeathed the fleet with remarkably good fortune, manifest in the form of a steady wind flowing from behind. The waters were not overly turbulent, allowing for progress without undue hardship on the part of the crews manning the vessels.

All of the Saxan vessels remained under sail, though the galleys were prepared at a moment's notice to switch over to oar power. It was not yet necessary, but the Saxans would not hesitate to use brawn to keep the ships moving at a swift pace. Aethelhere and the other Saxan ship commanders knew that every moment was precious. Even one moment lost was one that could not be afforded.

Never in the history of Saxany had such a mass of ships moved as quickly as the fleet now did. Tight rotations were maintained, allowing short, periodic rests for the crews. All who were aboard the ships did their part in executing the wide assortment of onboard tasks.

The shared urgency aided in the overall progress, as every adjustment that could possibly be made was assiduously attended to. The ships of the fleet, both large and small, moved in solid order.

A few particularly robust winds provided some welcome bursts. The winds filled main sails to capacity, propelling the vessels faster across the sea.

Yet despite the favorable conditions, there were problematic realities left to consider. The area of coastline the Saxans now sought would normally have been four, perhaps even five, days away, moving at a pace consistent with the one maintained prior to the emergence of propitious winds. By any measure, it was a great distance to cross, fraught with risk. The paucity of time facing the Saxans made even the favorable pace the fleet now enjoyed something that might ultimately prove to be a false hope. It was still more than possible for them to fall short of reaching the projected rendezvous.

Failure to reach the Water Head-Cradle in time was not acceptable at any level to Aethelhere. The fleeing mass of tribal people would be left stranded and vulnerable, backed up against the sea, with a merciless army bearing down upon them.

The invaders were bent on their subjugation at the very best, and destruction at the worst, with all manner of oppression and suffering in between. Neither extremes of fate were palatable to a people wishing to live by their own self-determination and sovereignty.

Aethelhere had a grave decision facing him. The fleet might well have to be partially split up, with galleys given over to a relentless effort with oar power, and sailing vessels left behind. Aethelhere had not yet settled upon a new projection, working to assimilate the increased pace into his previous estimates. Only time would tell if the swifter rate of travel would continue to be a factor. The decision would be made for the fleet by outside forces if the wind ebbed to any significant degree.

The various ship commanders kept a constant, studious eye on the skies overhead, taking regular account of any shifts in the air's temperature or direction. So far, the weather had held rather consistently, with largely clear skies, but all of them knew how quickly everything could change on the open seas.

A very treacherous state could be imminent. Every hour they were crossing the open swathe of water, to reach the southern coast of the tribal lands, the fleet was taking a very dangerous risk.

MAGNUS

Another beautiful night spread its soft touch across a tranquil land, having donned its sparkling, jeweled robe just a short time before.

SPIRIT OF FIRE

The temperature was mildly cool, with silken breezes streaming through the foliage. The leaves spoke in low whispers from their perches on the branches of trees, perhaps conversing in hushed tones about the living beings moving by just underneath.

Magnus and Brynhild walked side by side, strolling casually across a low saddle stretching between two hills covered in oak and elm. Their footfalls, fashioned by long practice, made almost no perceptible sounds, mimicking the silence of the wolves padding forward around them.

Magnus felt a pang of guilt and regret. The dragons' last words echoed once again in the back of his mind. He found himself recalling the words with greater frequency.

A very serious duty was going to be asked of him soon, if the dragon was correct. Of that he held little doubt. Yet there was so precious little that was ever certain, and he was not about to try and predict what loomed just ahead. Magnus had definitely not expected the swift turn of events after the dragons had taken back to the skies. He had plunged into abyssal depths, only to soon rise up to unimaginable heights.

His world had become enchanted ever since his unexpected encounter with Brynhild, filled with a sustaining hope. Having walked in dark shadows for so very long, traversing a world draped in an ashen pall, a glimpse of warm, living light evoked a famished hunger within him.

He was starved for such feelings, wanting more than anything to immerse himself in that beckoning light, like a single drop of water falling into a vast sea. Yet he knew he had to gird his resolve, for the dragons spoke of a solemn duty to seek others, and to protect Midragard.

The dragons told him that much would be asked of him, and had implored him not to be afraid of what was to come. Such words from the mouth of a dragon were not to be taken lightly.

Most cryptic of all were the references to an Elder having spoken, and the suggestion that healing would soon come to completion in the Age of Fenris. Magnus knew very well that such an Age was to be the culmination of everything in his ancient Order, the pinnacle of long eons encompassing a cascade of generations.

In the light of such an approaching age, he could not indulge personal dreams, no matter how heartfelt. Even if the tiny spark of hope within could have become a genuine flame of realization in due time, a powerful river of events would soon enough carry him along in an irresistible current.

Therein was the cause for an underlying melancholy, sobering the tinges of giddiness buoying his spirits in the company of Brynhild. Even if the coming era were to be one of unprecedented spectacle and finality, the course of his life would not be much different than before. He had known little other than disappointment, hardship, and heartache. The trio of bitter companions had only been temporarily evaded in the solitude of the deep forests.

The drinking horn of life offered was often filled with the liquid of suffering. There would be no other path if he were to remain true to the inner lights he embraced in his heart. The path of righteousness and honor was precariously narrow, the reason why so few in the world trod upon it. Magnus knew deep inside he would do nothing less than put his lips to the vessel offered to him, and drink deeply of its bitter contents.

"So there is talk of war abroad?" Brynhild asked, bringing a welcome interruption to his grim pondering. "My father heard of some such tidings from traders who had traveled recently to the far north."

"Yes, wars and rumors of wars. I learned much regarding this from Mershad, the outlander," Magnus replied. "The wars are commanded by the man called the Unifier, and visited upon more than one land. It is even thought this Unifier may gather a great invasion force to send against Midragard itself."

"You do not speak with much confidence, Magnus," Brynhild said. "The three great territories of Midragard, of Axe, Sword, and Shield, will not be easy for the taking. Not at sea. Not in the air. Not upon the land."

"This Unifier gathers forces from many lands. I fear He can gather a strength far greater than you and I could even envision," Magnus said.

Brynhild looked to Magnus, and spoke with a confident tone. "Do not speak with such despair, Magnus. The land is wide. Where a large force may fail, small, faster ones may succeed. I listened carefully when my father related tales to us from past ages, when great raids from Midragard were sent against the lands to the north and west.

"Even if I do not agree with the motivations of those raiders, there are some truths present in those accounts. The sudden appearance of Midragardan warriors on longships created advantages. Landing at unexpected places, the raiders often found their quarry vulnerable and unprepared. More often than not, Midragard's raiders overwhelmed their targets by sheer surprise. Why could not those lessons be applied to this age, to wreak havoc on any who come to do us harm?"

Magnus quietly took her words in, knowing she spoke much truth. He had also heard the stories of the sleek longships slicing up the rivers of foreign lands in ages past. Landing without any warning, they returned to the seas more often than not laden with a variety of treasures, while incurring very few casualties.

The great wolf packs of Midragard could move with incredible speed and stealth. Those aligned with members of Magnus' and Brynhild's Order could put such movements to effective purpose.

Furthermore, members of the Order who had undergone the Passage comprised a potent force. Even the appearance of an Ulfhednar or Berzerk was more than enough to put all but the hardiest, most disciplined of warriors to flight. It was highly doubtful that a vast invading army would be composed solely of such unwavering fighters. They would be warriors far from their own homes and hearths, in a strange, unfamiliar land. Such individuals would be fertile ground for sowing the seeds of anxiety and fear.

"It would be possible for our Order to cause great damage to an invader," Magnus finally replied, seeing the possibilities unveiling before him. "But do we even know how numerous our Order is? We have no jarls or kings among our kind. Each undergoes revelation and the Passage alone, and we have no greater convocations that could give us an idea of our collective strength."

"No, we do not," Brynhild admitted. "But should that deter us? Perhaps we should seek to find an answer." A sparkle flickered in her eyes, as if a broader idea had begun to take root.

Magnus grinned. "You are thinking of something already?"

"To the north of my territory is Kvedulf. He has already undergone the Passage. He is a very powerful Ulfhednar. I could not begin to imagine many being greater than him. His time as one of the Kin was very short," Brynhild said, with a hint of admiration in her tone.

"A good name for such a man," Magnus remarked, already impressed, as only the most exceptional in the Order could quickly attain the Passage. A man whose name meant 'evening wolf' was probably destined from the moment of birth to become a great Ulfhednar.

"Towards the east is Leif. Still one of the Kin, though I do not think for much longer. The Passage will beckon to him soon. You can sense his depth and strength when you are with him." Brynhild continued.

"Both have packs even larger than those with us here. It is a start."

Magnus nodded. "And at least it is an action."

Brynhild suddenly became distant, as if distracted by something. She slowly closed her eyes, and brought herself to a stop, her brows furrowing in a look of concentration. Magnus knew what she was doing, sensing easily enough that she was slipping into a deep communion with one of her wolves.

"Several large elk. Bulls. Cows. A herd night foraging most likely," she said quietly, her eyes remaining shut. "Not far from here. They are just now coming out of the trees into a clearing I know well enough."

She opened her eyes slowly, blinking for a second as she reoriented her focus. "Follow me," she said, lurching into motion.

At a run, her loping strides fell lightly upon the ground. Her body was a fluid harmony of form and balance. Magnus hurried to catch up with her, inwardly wincing as he perceived his own steps making much more of a commotion than hers. Compared to any of the men from the village, his own movements were exceptionally smooth, but when put in comparison with her gracefulness, he felt ponderous and clumsy.

They continued swiftly towards the crest of the next hill, slowing down as they arrived closer to the summit. The spot afforded them an advantageous view over a low meadow spread out on the other side.

Magnus reached out to Sky Star. He quickly sensed that the wolf had already moved off with the others of his pack. They had joined their number with Nightheart's group, and the two packs were fanning out along the high ground looming over the meadow.

Even as Magnus laid his eyes on the objects of their interest, he was well aware that a deadly ring was forming around the unsuspecting elk. The moonlight was unobstructed, bathing the open meadow in a soft, silvered light that revealed a number of dark shapes. As Brynhild had indicated, the large creatures had moved out from the tree cover, and were now scattered across the open ground as they grazed. Night had bestowed the prime opportunity upon the hunters, as the elk herds normally kept to the trees during daylight.

Broad, palmated antlers adorned with tines identified several bulls, including a couple of particularly massive specimens. But the cows were far from helpless, as even without antlers they could put explosive strength behind lashing hooves.

For the more widespread variety of wolves found in Midragard, neither bull nor cow would have been easy prey. One bull alone could square off against a full pack of common wolves, and a successful hunt could be dragged out for days with a hardy adult elk. In those instances, the smaller kin of the wolves with Magnus and Brynhild would typically strike at the haunches, seeking to cause significant blood loss, or perhaps bite at the elk's sensitive noses, a manner of attack that could cause them to freeze in place.

The rarer, larger breed of wolves that the members of the Order bonded with could attack more aggressively, and chance strikes that would get one of their lesser kin easily killed. Yet even for the larger kind of wolves, great danger from hooves and antlers yet remained.

A quick survey of the herd revealed more than a couple of individuals that would be favorable options for the pending hunt. There was more than one younger elk within the group who did not have the size, savvy, and maturity that a fully-grown elk possessed. More often than not, a young bull or cow's inexperience would prove to be their greatest vulnerability, even more so than their unfulfilled physical development.

Opposite the younger ones were the eldest among their group. Though imbued with size and years of experience thwarting hunts, their physical decline, including various ailments and slowing speed, created optimal weaknesses for a wolf pack to exploit.

Yet despite the aged elks' advancing burdens, they would not be taken down easily. The older ones were still powerful fighters to be reckoned with, and the bulls were adept at using their great antlers to deadly result.

Magnus and Brynhild slowly crept forward, descending the slope shrouded in silence as they moved towards the clearing. Ahead of them, and all around, the circle of wolves was gradually tightening. Numerous lupine hunters edged ever closer on their broad paws towards the outskirts of the meadow.

Briefly, Magnus mentally connected with Sky Star. He could feel the energy and anticipation rising within the noble pack leader. Sky Star was already at the cusp of the meadow's outer edge, looking out of the darkness, safely downwind, towards the striding herd. He had already set his eyes upon a particular old bull, moving with a noticeable hitch caused by ailment or injury.

The breeze shifted, and several large elk abruptly started, becoming aware of the wolves moving in behind them. Now downwind, the elk sensed the wolves' presence right as the majestic hunters broke from cover. A multitude of wolves bursting out of the shadows and trees set the elk herd into panicked flight, a flurry of heavy thumps erupting from their hoofbeats.

Magnus always marveled at how wolf packs aligned with one of the Kin hunted with far more diverse methods than did a pack of unaligned wolves. The present hunt was no exception, as the wolves of both packs moved with an astounding degree of coordination.

As the elk bolted for the refuge of the forest, the rest of the wolves sprang out from their cover. The sudden emergence of many more wolves, directly in the path of the elk, induced absolute chaos in the formerly placid meadow.

The great wolves bounded in from all sides, several besetting the old bull Sky Star had chosen. With a powerful kick, the elk reared up and sent one wolf reeling off to the side with a curt yelp.

A couple of other wolves leapt onto the elk, inflicting deep wounds with their crushing jaws. A few of the attackers suffered wounds as the old bull snapped its antlers about, thrashing in a desperate effort to defend itself.

More than one set of powerful jaws clamped down upon the legs, neck, and even the broad mouth of the creature. Weighed down by the swarming onslaught, the old bull finally succumbed to the inevitable. Its legs buckled as it fell to the ground, as more wolves raced in to assist their pack mates.

As the wolves had moved in on the old bull, Magnus set an arrow to his bow. He lined up his aim with another older bull who had not been singled out by the wolves. With a deft pull and release, he sent the shaft flying through the air to bury itself into the side of the bull just behind the shoulder.

Standing at his side, Brynhild had focused upon the same target, drawing back and releasing her own arrow. Her shot also embedded deeply within the side of the hapless bull. With two arrows landing true, puncturing both its lungs, the elk was already dead when its bulk crumpled to the ground.

The feverish hoof beats of the fleeing elk faded, as the meadow gradually ebbed into silence. The struggles were over, as the surviving elk bounded into the depths of the woods. A few snarls and growls from the wolves lingered in the air, during the aftermath of the tumult.

In addition to the old bulls, other wolves had downed one of the young ones on the far side of the meadow. It had fallen within just a few strides of reaching the woodlands.

As they always did, Brynhild and Magnus moved quickly to see to the status of the wolves. In the battle for the first old bull, the wolf that had been kicked was struggling with a bad limp. The wolf was straining laboriously in its breaths, likely suffering some cracked ribs from the thunderous blow.

The wolves incurring wounds from the antlers had largely avoided serious injury, though one exhibited a sizeable patch of matted fur at its left side. That wolf had taken a ripping slash from a pointed antler tine, soaking the fur around the open wound with blood. Another wolf had taken a similar kind of wound on its other side, in bringing down the younger bull.

Magnus knelt by the side of the wolf who had received the kick. A few moments later, he sensed Brynhild kneeling down next to him. The wolf was one from his pack, a younger male whose recklessness had resulted in the vicious strike of the bull's sharp hoof.

The wolf whimpered and whined in pain, in between short, agonized breaths coming from its muzzle. Magnus was trying to think of how he could address the creature's injuries, when Brynhild set a hand upon his shoulder.

"Will you allow me?" she asked.

Magnus looked into her eyes, and saw resolve and concern present there. He nodded in response, hoping she might have some ideas on how to treat the significant injury. He was not thinking of anything further than that, even if his instincts told him Brynhild's meaning was greater.

Brynhild turned her eyes to the injured wolf, laying both of her hands gently upon the area of impact. She closed her eyes, as a low sound started to emerge from her throat. Her body began to lightly sway, as the sound grew more distinctive.

Not human, and not of wolf, the sound was like a hybrid between the two. As it reached a harmonic unison, deep, rumbling, and resonant, Magnus' eyes widened, as he realized what was happening.

He had never witnessed a faith healing in person, knowing only that it was a superior ability attained by those who were nearing the Passage. A slight glow outlined Brynhild's hands, and Magnus knew it was no trick of the silvered moonlight from above. The light was being generated from within her, strong enough to be visible to the eye.

The wolf's whining lessened, and its breathing began to grow steadier. Its side seemed to pulse with some strange activity just underneath its fur and skin. In a few moments, the light faded, as Brynhild withdrew her hands. Her own breathing had become heavier, and she had a look of great fatigue as she opened her eyes.

"A ... faith healing," Magnus said in a low voice, with undisguised wonder.

A tired smile arose on her face. "It takes much of one's vitality to do."

"Thank you. Shadow is not one of yours," Magnus said with gratitude, looking down at the wolf.

The creature had already rolled over onto its belly, and had nuzzled its nose under Brynhild's hand. "They are all one of ours," Brynhild replied gently, stroking Shadow's head. "And you are welcome."

She looked down at Shadow. "And you, my friend, need to be more careful in your hunting."

"The others will be able to heal on their own," Magnus said, concerned that Brynhild would drain herself further with the other injured wolves. He could see the obvious debilitating effects that the healing had bestowed. "I will clean and attend their wounds, as I can."

"I will go with you, just in case there is anything we may have overlooked which is more serious," Brynhild said. The look in her eye would not allow for any objection.

They took some time to carefully inspect the wounds of the other wolves. Magnus looked to the injured as best he could. Brynhild expended a little more of her waning energies on the wolf that had received the large gash. Magnus, knowing what was to come, watched the process with fascination as the healing light emerged from her again, accompanied by the rumbling intonations in her throat.

Fortunately, there were no others needing any kind of special attention. The remaining wounded would heal well enough by themselves, with only a few more nicks and scars added to their bodies.

The higher-ranking wolves had already begun to feast upon the carcasses of the first old elk and the younger male. They kept away from the elk with the two arrows embedded in it, allowing Magnus and Brynhild first access to the carcass. Using their single-edged knives, the two humans cut off chunks of meat to take back to their campsite. Unlike the wolves, Magnus preferred meat to be fire-cooked.

Once they moved away, some lower-ranking members of the two packs, who had not yet been able to gain a place at the sides of the other elk carcasses, trotted quickly in. They wasted no time in delving into the waiting meal.

"A very good hunt, Magnus," Brynhild remarked, as they walked off, "I am glad we both got to share in this hunt".

"Yes, it was a good hunt. And not one of our good wolves were injured beyond hope," Magnus replied. "Thanks to you."

"I hope to hunt with you many more times," Brynhild said gently, with a serious undertone.

Even though she looked fatigued, her eyes flashed a lively spark within. The look she gave him caused Magnus to tremble with a wave of warmth and kindled hope.

"And I ... with you," was all he could offer in reply, past the sudden dryness gripping his throat.

THE UNIFIER

As Logan exited through the postern gate, the Unifier turned and walked back along the way they had come. After a few strides, He was amid the lush garden ringing the pavilion and pool before the opulent palace hall.

As if summoned implicitly, two of the diabolical creatures sent from the depths of the Infernal Regions by the Lord of Fire emerged from the deep shadows to His left. Their white-hot eyes gazed down at the Unifier, as their towering, brawny forms entered the argentine light of the moons.

The mere presence of the creatures greatly pleased Him. Though very rarely present within the world of Ave, they were a harbinger of the world to come, having come from a realm where they were countless in number.

"The battle for the mind and for the will begins," He intoned. The demonic beings with him were by nature brutish and violent, and there was little use in addressing them other than for the Unifier's own personal whims. Nonetheless, the creatures stood in rapt silence, as if they listened intently to each and every word coming from His lips. "More is known of these otherworlders, and I am finding that there are few differences between what they are, and what those of this world are. I am certain they are of the Twelve, spoken of by Prophecy. This is no small matter, as it relates to our ends."

Others upon His Great Council shared His deep concerns regarding the otherworlders, in regards to the Prophecy and its interpretation. It was a Prophecy that especially consumed Ahriman and Morrigan, though for very different reasons.

Morrigan advocated slaying any member of the Twelve they could get their hands on. The Unifier had spoken truly enough to Logan when He had said there were those who wished him dead. He had simply chosen not to mention that such individuals were within His own Great Council.

According to Morrigan, killing the otherworlders would disrupt the Prophecy completely, and bring all of their own paths into a future with no prophecies lurking about to ever confound or defeat them. Without the Twelve, the Final Battle could never be fought in the manner their hated enemies prophesied. By her rationale, the peril would be eliminated in a simple, easy stroke.

The logic seemed simple enough, notwithstanding a deeply held desire of the Unifier to see the Final Battle waged at last. He lusted after that titanic, conclusive battle, in which the course of creation itself could be brought under the full dominion of Jebaalos, Lord and Master of the Infernal Powers. Morrigan's position was admittedly based in a logic of ultimate caution, one that might gain them domination of the mortal realm, but would deny them power they would need to bridge to the heavens, to strike into the heart of Palladium itself. The Unifier knew He could never rest until the heavens burned.

The Unifier also could not ignore the nagging thought that where several otherworlders had been drawn into Ave, others could follow. If Morrigan had her way, and the otherworlders already in their hands were struck down, there was nothing to ensure that new otherworlders would not manifest elsewhere in Ave.

Ahriman was just as vehement regarding his own perspective. It was true that there were two visions of the Prophecy. The one espoused by the followers of the tyrant god stated that their god would inevitably win the Final Battle over the Lord of Fire. A different version had long existed among the more clandestine followers of the Lord of Fire.

Ahriman was at the summit of that particular group, fiercely holding to its prediction. This version stated that if the Unifier, who was the true Son of the Lord of Fire, was able to gain the will of eight of the Twelve otherworlders, then the defeat of the tyrant god would be inevitable. With the balance of will and power tilted towards Jebaalos, the way to Palladium itself could then be laid bare for the ravenous hordes of the underworld. Palladium would burn, and the First War would be fully avenged.

Ahriman had salivated describing the imprisonment of the tyrant god, and His followers of all kinds, confined for all eternity within a new hell the Lord of Fire would create for them. The Unifier shared Ahriman's enthusiasm, though He conceded it was very dangerous to assume interpretations of prophecies.

Between Morrigan and Ahriman, the latter's position held a stronger appeal, even if it carried greater risk. Following council, mediation, and supplication to the Lord of Fire, the Unifier had finally decided in favor of winning over the will of at least eight otherworlders.

Success in that endeavor held the promise of overwhelming power to be harnessed for His god and Father. It was the path to ultimate vengeance, without which neither the Unifier nor Jabaalos could ever quell the burning in their own spirits.

"A greater burden than that of the Enemy ... but still, only eight," the Unifier said aloud to the two towering entities.

He mused about the astounding thought that the wills of just eight frail humans could be decisive in bringing down the seemingly unassailable gates of Palladium. A step in that direction had just been taken with Logan, bringing the Unifier a morsel of satisfaction. Gaining Logan's confidence was an important start towards gaining the cooperative will of eight otherworlders.

The Unifier's final moves to subjugate the entire world, and open the pathway for the ascension of Jebaalos, did not look so far off anymore. Looking into the macabre countenances of the two creatures with Him, the Unifier smiled broadly.

"This world will soon be yours to roam, and its inhabitants to do with as you will," He told them, a feral, hungry spark glinting in His own eyes.

DEGANAWIDA

Deganawida trudged onward through the incessant aches and strain, keeping near to the back of the sprawling mass of refugees. He watched as a couple of horses, heavily laden with leather pouches and other containers, were coaxed forward by a couple of exhausted-looking warriors.

The horses were likely overburdened, but everyone was being pushed to their limits on the journey to the Water Head-Cradle. Only a few dogs from the wrecked villages trotting along with the refugees were handling the arduous journey somewhat well.

It was still a little more than a couple of days from the Water Head-Cradle, at the speed the refugees were currently traveling. If they slowed down at all, the estimate would quickly rise.

The Water Head-Cradle was now the single most important place in all of the tribal lands. Everything depended upon reaching it, assuming the Saxan fleet would be able to reach it in time as well. With no other options left to them, Deganawida had to trust that the giant Dragon was not guiding them towards a hopeless last stand.

Deganawida found himself calling to mind a very particular element within the sacred stories of his people. It was said that a dragon had once helped the Great Mother of the tribal peoples, far back at the genesis of the world itself. If that cherished tale was indeed true, then a dragon could help the tribal peoples once again.

Deganawida felt a fiercely burning pride regarding the contingent of warriors accompanying the main body of refugees. From all five of the tribes, representing all of the various clans, they were aptly demonstrating that the blood running in the veins of their people was still strong and resilient.

Despite throbbing, sore muscles, and long-empty stomachs, the fatigued warriors at the heart of the great exodus pushed themselves to the extreme. They took hold of supply pouches, helped with makeshift stretchers for the sick, elderly, young, and wounded, and acted as perimeter scouts for the hundreds upon hundreds coursing through the trees.

They did so with little thought for their own welfare, and Deganawida knew that each and every one of them was ready to fling himself at any attacker without hesitation. He also knew the warriors would press onward until they collapsed or reached the Water Head-Cradle, whichever came first.

Deganawida sorely wished they had the help of some of the great Wizards affiliated with their people, such as the Light Brother, and the legendary Deganawida. The continued absence of the benevolent Wizards during the midst of such dark times was a tremendous mystery. Deganawida could not fathom that they would abandon the tribes within such a perilous hour.

The Wizard named Deganawida had been the one to establish the Great Council. He had led the very first instance of the revered convocation at the legendary white pine tree, called the Tree of Peace, so many years ago. That sacred site had been hidden by some art or design during the long ages that followed, but Deganawida did not think that the Wizard would willingly allow so great and terrible a darkness to swallow the sacred lands of the Five Tribes; at least, not without resistance.

The wanton bloodshed now occurring was not of the tribal people's making. There had been no provocation on their part, and there were no riches of precious metals or jewels to be gained by the invaders. It was simply naked aggression of the vilest sort, seeking absolute power over the land and people of the Five Realms.

Deganawida felt that his people were alone in the terrible struggle. The tribes were reduced to relying upon their own means as they fled towards the coast. There were no Wizards to be seen anywhere, and even the Little Ones, blessed with incredible healing arts, and often of assistance to tribal hunters, had seemingly vanished from the forest.

Yet Deganawida had to be grateful that the refugees had not been forced to openly contend with the Dark Brother, who would relish a baleful doom like the one imminently facing the tribal peoples. The uprooting and destruction of the tribes would be a welcome feast to the Dark Brother, perhaps the only thing that could placate the voracious hunger the malevolent Wizard had harbored throughout the ages.

The disturbing thoughts gave Deganawida sudden pause, as he wondered whether the terrible plight encompassing the tribes could possibly be a wicked harvest sown by the Dark Brother. Even more troubling, the Dark Brother might well have had something to do with the absence of the Light Brother, Deganawida, and other Wizards of benevolence.

Making such matters worse, the Dark Brother would be far from alone in any onslaught against the tribes. There were many powerful witches and shamans in league with the Dark Brother, given wholly to the pursuit of dark mysteries. These fearful beings could well be serving as spies or lookouts for the enemy, augmenting the enemy's efforts through the use of dark arts.

As spies, witches would be formidable adversaries. In the forms of natural, commonly encountered creatures, such as snakes and owls, witches would be especially unnoticeable to the retreating, beleaguered refugees.

As he thought about the powers of witches, Deganawida quietly fingered the small hide pouch he carried at all times, holding a large, quartz crystal inside. He would have to remind the other sachems and tribal warriors to remember to use the crystals often, just in case witches were about, or had filtered amongst them in the ongoing chaos. At least the quartz crystals would betray the presence of those who had committed their hearts to darkness.

Shrill cries from warriors in the rearguard a short distance behind ceased his ruminations, and compelled the venerable sachem to stop and turn around. He could not yet see the warriors through the trees, but knew cries heralded the approach of newcomers.

Scouts and smaller war parties had become a regular sight, venturing in and out of the main body of refugees. Bringing information, they acquired a few supplies, saw to repairs, or procured new weapons for use in the desperate effort to slow the pursuing Gallean forces. Deganawida sensed Ayenwatha was among the incoming group, the inspiration confirmed a few moments later as a band of warriors emerged into view, led by Ayenwatha.

Deganawida watched Ayenwatha's approach with rising interest. The war sachem was accompanied by a most unusual sight. Towering over Ayenwatha, and walking right alongside him, was a heavily muscled Trogen warrior with a fearsome demeanor.

Deganawida was fascinated by the physical appearance of the enemy warrior. The brawny figure's upper and lower jaws protruded forward, like a short, broad muzzle, lending the Trogen a feral appearance. The Trogen was unarmed, and Deganawida readily noticed the warrior was also without any sort of restraint to arms or legs.

Deganawida met Ayenwatha with a greeting embrace. The younger war sachem looked both buoyed and relieved to see Deganawida.

"Deganawida, I am very glad I have found you," Ayenwatha said wearily.

Signs of fatigue were exhibited everywhere. The look deep in his eye, the tone of his voice, the slight slouch to his posture, and much more spoke loudly to Deganawida of Ayenwatha's debilitated condition. The older sachem could see the younger man resisting his weakened physical state with sheer willpower, projecting the full aura of a war sachem to the men he led.

A few warriors with Ayenwatha paused, the Onan warrior Sky Arrow standing at the forefront of them. Ayenwatha turned aside.

"Go onward, and see to your own needs now. You will not have much time to do so before we have to go back," Ayenwatha urged them.

With Sky Arrow leading, the war party continued towards the mass of refugees ahead, with the particular exception of the huge Trogen, who lingered at Ayenwatha's side. Deganawida found himself in growing wonderment at the exceptional physical presence of the foreign warrior. He could easily see why their race had gained such a fearsome reputation, and could also sense a measure of trust between Ayenwatha and the enemy warrior.

"You are making progress," Ayenwatha commented, turning back to Deganawida. "We had to cover much more ground than we thought to catch back up with our people."

"I am pressing forward as fast as these old legs will carry me," Deganawida replied, with a tight grin announcing his own state of weariness.

"It may be that your legs are worth more than these younger ones," Ayenwatha responded, letting out a long exhalation. With no other warriors near, Ayenwatha did not bother to feign a more hale appearance.

"It is a terrible burden that all are shouldering," Deganawida observed. "But I know you endure more than most, both within your heart and your body."

Deganawida lay his hand upon Ayenwatha's shoulder, gently patting the younger warrior in reassurance. He smiled with deep empathy, looking upon Ayenwatha, and then glanced purposefully towards the silent Trogen.

Ayenwatha nodded, understanding the cue. "This is Dragol, a Trogen warrior encountered in the woods. He lost his sky steed. He has proven that he embraces honor. I owe him my own life. Without his actions, I would not be speaking with you now. Of course, he must be taken with us. I desire to have him remain with you, and the rest of the people," Ayenwatha said, glancing over at his massive companion. "I must return to help slow our pursuers."

"He has a means of understanding and speaking with us," Ayenwatha continued. "The Wanderer traveled with him, and he has an amulet like those from the other world."

"Dragol, welcome," Deganawida greeted the Trogen politely, giving the tall creature an amiable smile. "I am Deganawida, sachem of the Onan, and First Sachem of the Grand Council."

The Trogen responded with a brief nod. Deganawida did not take the silence and curt gesture as an affront, suspecting the Trogen simply did not want to respond in an improper way.

Deganawida looked into the Trogen's hard, deep-set eyes, his curiosity greatly piqued. The Wanderer did not often appear within the woodlands, and the fact that the venerable Wizard had bequeathed one of the strange, powerful amulets to a Trogen warrior, of the very kind worn by the otherworlders, was not a small matter.

"It would seem that the Wanderer finds a purpose in you," Deganawida said.

"If he did, he did not share it with me," the Trogen responded gruffly. The words sounded to Deganawida's ears in perfect Quoian, flowing as if the Trogen had always spoken the language of the Five tribes. The Trogen then shook his head, displaying a sense of frustration. "That man was a living mystery, one I could not understand."

Deganawida smiled. "You truly walked with the Wanderer. A mystery he is, Dragol of the Trogens."

While the Wizard whose name he carried and the Light Brother were absent, perhaps the Wanderer was actively helping the Five Realms. The notion gave Deganawida a little comfort, something for his flagging hopes to clutch onto.

A couple of warriors from the rearguard then strode into sight. Their presence signaled that the end of the refugee formation was about to pass by them.

"Come, let us walk together, so we do not fall too far behind the others," Deganawida stated, though internally he was highly grateful for the few moments of respite.

Ayenwatha nodded, and they all turned together and headed in the wake of the refugees. Ayenwatha filled Deganawida in on the full story involving Dragol, giving the Great Sachem much detail as the trio wended their way through the trees.

"Astounding," Deganawida commented upon the story's completion, casting a glance back toward the huge Trogen warrior following a few paces behind.

"There are few surprises left in these strange times," Ayenwatha replied with a slight grin, the good humor reflected within the expression stained with a little sadness.

"No, most definitely not many surprises left," Deganawida replied, thinking of how one of the legendary Elder had intervened at the right moment, to bring the light of new hope to his forlorn people.

"Needless to say, we must reach the Water Head-Cradle in time, hopefully with no other surprises," Ayenwatha exclaimed, concern thick in his voice.

"We will have to survive a few days before the Saxan fleet can even reach the Water Head-Cradle," Deganawida replied.

"And I must return, so that you and all of our people have that chance," Ayenwatha said. His countenance hardened as he looked behind them, staring for a moment towards the deep woodlands now being filled with hostile invaders.

Deganawida then drew to a halt, bringing Ayenwatha and the Trogen warrior to a stop a moment later. "Then take some supplies with you, Ayenwatha... and heed me ... keep up what strength you can. Eat and replenish your body. It does those you lead no good to deprive yourself too much. You cannot fight well and lead others if you collapse. Our warriors would much more prefer that you continue to wield a war club, and let arrows fly from your bow, than how much you are willing to sacrifice. They already know your heart."

Ayenwatha nodded.

Deganawida's expression then softened, "And do not worry yourself regarding the Trogen. I will vouch for Dragol, as you have done. Go with a free conscience on that matter."

Ayenwatha inclined his head towards Dragol, a grim smile emerging upon his face, before giving the elder sachem another embrace. The tired war sachem then broke into a jog, heading in the direction taken by the other warriors of his band.

Deganawida hoped Ayenwatha took his counsel, and saw to his physical needs for sustenance, and possibly later a little rest. The younger war sachem was not overly stubborn or headstrong, and Deganawida decided not to worry himself too much.

He waited for a few moments, and then beckoned for the Trogen to draw closer. With a couple of quickened strides, the massive Trogen was standing beside the Onan sachem.

"The people of the tribes speak their minds, and speak them plainly, Trogen. Do not take offense at what I have to say to you now," Deganawida said in an even tone.

The Trogen nodded quietly, and said nothing, waiting for Deganawida to continue.

"War is a part of all people, perhaps the greatest scourge of this world," Deganawida said. "The Wizard who has the same name as I sought to eliminate the spirit of war from among our tribes, when he called together the first fifty at the Tree of Peace. While we have grown in many ways since, war has never left our lives."

Deganawida paused for a moment, and searched the Trogen's face closely. There did not seem to be any anger or deception within the Trogen's gaze. Deganawida relied more heavily upon the look within another's eyes, as it often betrayed what a stoic face could otherwise hide. Deganawida could only hope his current judgement was still sound, despite his considerable exhaustion.

"It was Trogens who took part in the attack that destroyed our villages, and drove us from our homes into the depths of these woodlands. You were among those forces, and you fought in those attacks, Dragol. Those who have lost many from their families, and who have seen their home villages shattered, will despise the sight of you. In truth, many hearts will wish you dead."

The words were severe, but undeniably true. The Trogen might have some purpose in the eyes of the Wanderer, but the tribal people would still see the Trogen as nothing more than an enemy, stained with the condemning blood of innocents.

As Deganawida brought the matter out into the open, he felt the stirrings of sharp revulsion in his own heart towards those who had brought death and suffering to the tribes. The Trogen warrior before him had been a part of the merciless attacks, and as such embodied the crimes committed against the Five Realms.

Given a burst of impetus, the seed of antipathy grew and spread within Deganawida's heart, as he looked upon the enemy warrior. He kept his face inscrutable, but knew his eyes were growing hardened by the moment. The images of broken, torn bodies of men, women, and children flashed through his mind, a ghastly carnage strewn amid the wreckage of a destroyed village.

Each one of those innocents was a precious, irreplaceable being. Deganawida's eyes narrowed further, as he fought to tamp down the fast-rising ire.

"This is not our fight," the Trogen finally responded in a low, deep-toned voice, one devoid of any trace of confrontation. "We fought in this war for the promise of aid long sought. We desired assistance in lifting a terrible oppression from our own kind, one that has lasted for many, many generations. "We have seen Trogen villages destroyed in blood and fire, and our kind slain without mercy for endless generations. This is why our clan chieftains agreed to fight for the Unifier … so that the evil inflicted upon my kind for centuries could be finally brought to an end."

Deganawida reflected deeply upon the Trogen's words. He found it disquieting that one race subjected to the horrors of violent oppression would be so driven by desperation that they would acquiesce to visiting the very same terrors upon another people.

The explanation did not excuse the actions of the Trogens, in assaulting a people with whom they had no quarrel. Still, it did offer a reason behind the Trogen participation in the bloodshed that was something other than a lust for power and conquest.

Despite the righteous anger now boiling within Deganawida towards the Trogens for what they had done to his people, desperation could not be entirely discounted as a powerful factor. Born out of desperate circumstances, more than a few atrocities had been committed by individuals within the five tribes, transgressions very far removed in nature from the offender's previously demonstrated character.

Whether or not the Trogen warrior before Deganawida could someday find redemption, the elder sachem could not say. As Deganawida wrestled with his deep resentment about the indiscriminate violence the Trogens had levied from the skies, a gentle, soft-toned voice emerged within the midst of the raucous chorus of stirred emotions. Though like a calm whisper emitted among raging shouts, it was what the old sachem heard most clearly inside his conscience. He trusted that particular inner voice the most, when rasher impulses threatened to supersede his better judgment.

Deganawida nodded slowly, after several moments of heavy silence transpired. The look in his eye became more blunted, if not entirely losing its sharp edge. "And who knows what our people might have done, if we had a similar story to tell? Would we also have participated in a war in a foreign land to remove a storm over our own? Perhaps ... perhaps not."

The Trogen's eyes widened in surprise at Deganawida's words. The enemy fighter likely found the sachem's response to be an extraordinary concession in the stark light of the current situation.

"I cannot judge your kind's reasons, or what lies in your own heart, but it is certain that our people did no harm to the Trogens," Deganawida continued. "It is also without dispute that the Trogens participated in the brutal attacks destroying our villages. Trogens continue to fight in the assault driving our people like prey through these woodlands. As your kind endured destroyed villages and being slain without mercy, so your kind has done exactly the same to us, as a willing part of the Unifier's army."

His last words were thick with accusation, and the heated ire that had threatened to overflow moments before flared once again.

"Nothing you have said can be denied," the Trogen admitted somberly. The conciliatory tone underlying the Trogen's words was instantly disarming.

There was a great tension present in the Trogen, but Deganawida could see without a doubt that it derived out of a sense of inner conflict, rather than any measure of defensiveness or hostile anger.

The macabre, corruptive genius of the Unifier had orchestrated the use of one oppressed race to plague another in a similar fashion. Deganawida had little doubt that recognition of a deep state of hypocrisy was at the root of Dragol's increasingly pensive demeanor.

"Then know it would be best for you to keep a constant distance between yourself and my people. I will remain with you, and I will vouch for you, but it would not be wise to try and move freely among the people. They are tired, hungry, desperate, and hard-pressed ... and they are well-aware that your kind bears a great accountability for their current condition. The resentment harbored among them is not without good reason, and nor would their resistance to your presence be without just cause. I cannot assure you of the safety of your person if you choose to disregard my advice.

"There is a purpose for the path you have now taken, Trogen, even if it cannot yet be seen by my eyes, or yours. That is something my heart tells me, and while I do not absolve your kind of what they have done to my people, I do not wish to see any harm come to you."

"Then I will do as you have asked," the Trogen responded, accompanied by a slight inclination of the head.

One thing was for certain. The Trogen was very courageous. Deganawida could only imagine the kind of fortitude it took for the Trogen warrior to willingly approach thousands of his former enemies, right in the midst of ongoing conflict.

War was such a strange, corrupting entity, Deganawida mused as he quietly looked upon the Trogen. It transformed an individual into becoming the very thing that the individual once vigorously opposed.

His own people were not immune to that pungent type of conversion. The inter-tribal wars that had taken place in the woodlands for centuries were an ebb and flow of such a discordant reality.

The very warriors who had endured great, bitter losses, losing friends and loved ones in the violence of another tribe's raid, responded by violently taking the lives of friends and loved ones of the warriors in the other tribe. The other tribe's warriors, gripped in the wrath of renewed outrage, returned to do the same; and so it continued ever on.

The insanity of those wars had been considerably dampened by the Wizard Deganawida's Grand Council, and the ensuing confederation of the tribes, but only amongst themselves. Wars and retribution had continued without respite, with the tribes outside of the confederation such as the Wendaton. The somber fact prompted Deganawida to wonder why the lessons and wisdom learned from the Wizard's wondrous gift had not been applied universally.

Perhaps the Trogen standing with him was coming to a broader perspective of the follies of war. Defending oneself and one's lands against an attacker was never a wrong, and a warrior had a very definite place among a sovereign people, but unnecessary cycles turning oppressed into oppressor, and then back again, had to be broken asunder at some juncture. Otherwise, the lands and populaces of the world would remain trapped within an endless cycle of blood, sorrow, and death.

Deganawida eyed the Trogen carefully, again noting the powerful muscularity in the being's great body. The real question at hand was whether the Trogen was strong enough on the inside. Breaking ages-old cycles took a far greater strength than any matter of muscle, speed, and reflex.

Deganawida thought back to what Ayenwatha had told him about Dragol's actions after being captured. The mere fact that Dragol had adhered to his given word, ardently resisting the Galleans to uphold it, and willingly putting himself into the hands of his former enemies, indicated that he just might have a rare and special kind of strength. What that might mean in the greater tapestry of life, woven with diverse lands, peoples, and beings of all kinds, could not be predicted. Only time would tell.

"Stay with me now, Dragol. Let us continue to walk through these woods for awhile. It will not be long before a halt is called, and I will have food and drink brought to you," Deganawida bid the Trogen, with a kindly smile. "As for now, we shall talk more. You will quickly find that I am not as mysterious a traveling companion as the Wanderer."

The flicker of an amused grin played about the Trogen's face at the mention of the Wanderer. "That is a relief," Dragol acknowledged.

"Shall we proceed?" Deganawida asked the Trogen, taking the first steps. His moccasins brushed against a little of the trillium spread across the forest floor before them.

With another nod, Dragol set into motion, keeping close to the side of the Onan sachem as they strode together after the masses of tribal refugees.

MAGNUS

As the light of a fresh day unfurled, spreading throughout the Midragardan skies, Brynhild and Magnus walked side by side, as their wolves paced nimbly along. The two large packs were spread out in a wide perimeter, crossing through the high grasses of an open meadow.

Magnus had managed to get a solid rest the night before, dreaming wonderful dreams, despite the looming presence of war and continuing uncertainties facing him. He had found his mind constantly wandering back to thoughts of Brynhild, hearkening towards a young man's panacea for the troubles of the world.

Magnus felt a slight quickening of his heartbeat every time he caught her piercing gaze, bringing a smile to his face that he could not hope to mask. A feeling of child-like giddiness rifled through him in such moments, stirring the blood to run faster in his veins.

Fortunately, he could perceive a corresponding reaction in Brynhild as well. It was reflected in the way her eyes sparkled, and in the manner she smiled whenever they spoke or shared glances.

A few times, he wondered whether he had already crossed the legendary Bridge of Rainbows, or stepped into the afterworld of the churchmen. He felt weightless enough during such moments to wonder if he were still a creature of flesh and blood, or had perhaps become a spirit.

Magnus and Brynhild were both examples of a unique type of individual, of a kind capable of living on their own in the wilderness. They had both attained one of the highest callings of the Midragardan world; becoming part of an elite brotherhood and sisterhood, a mythic order that had endured for ages.

Remarkably, Magnus was afraid to openly express the feelings now percolating within him, and it seemed to be the same way with Brynhild. Potent feelings were being held back, restrained right at the brink of flowing freely between the two.

Magnus wished he knew a way to lower whatever barriers remained inside of him. As good as he felt with Brynhild, he also found himself caught within an undeniably awkward state.

"I feel fantastic today," Magnus exclaimed brightly, as they neared the midpoint of the sun-bathed meadow.

He took in a deep, cleansing breath of the cool morning air. The tops of the high grasses moved like little waves, as a breeze swept through them. Looking over, he smiled broadly at Brynhild, feeling a return of the light-headedness as he took in the sight of her.

"And I likewise," she replied softly, a smile gracing her own face.

A part of him felt that they had just drawn a little closer to openly admitting their sentiments. Magnus suspected that both of them had just been talking about how they felt in each other's presence.

Brynhild's radiant smile was accented with her ebony tresses of hair, tossed gracefully about her face by the sinuous breezes. Her appearance was at once wholly untamed, and irresistibly alluring. With a little effort of will, Magnus turned his head and looked forward, the resplendent image of Brynhild resonating in the eyes of his mind.

He then came to an abrupt stop, as the wolves around him halted and momentarily flattened their ears. Their hackles raised, and their muscles tightened with readiness to react.

Their ears perked back up a moment later, and their tensed bodies relaxed, as Magnus's eyes settled upon the forms of two strong-looking figures who had just emerged from the trees on the opposite side of the meadow. The two beings moved with a light step, and both wore telltale pelts fashioned from the skins of wolves.

The pelts had not been garnered from the efforts of any hunter. Rather, they were free gifts from the ones they had cloaked in life, to the ones who wore them now. Magnus knew at once that both of the men were Ulfhednar.

Before the two had gotten any farther across the meadow, both Brynhild and Magnus lowered their heads and eyes reverently towards the ground. Full-fledged Ulfhednar were of the highest rank in their shared mystical order, and as such Magnus felt compelled to accord all proper respects to the two men.

"A brother and a sister to the wolf, Kin traveling together. This is indeed an unexpected surprise," the man on the left commented, his pelt black-furred.

"We were coming to summon you, Brynhild. There is a duty we come to ask of you, involving a matter that our kind has been asked to help with. A charge has been asked of us, by no less of a man than King Hakon himself," the other man stated, garbed in a silvery pelt. He looked towards Magnus, eyeing him closely. "I am afraid I do not yet know of your friend, though I see and recognize that he is indeed a Master."

"Magnus, formerly of the village at Glittering River. His pack's territory is adjacent to mine own," Brynhild answered in a subdued voice, openly deferential to the two Ulfhednar.

The pair of Ulfhednar gave Magnus a slight nod of acceptance, as the one with the silver cloak proceeded, "Well met, Magnus. Then it may be beneficial that I have found the two of you together. We have need of you and your pack, Brynhild, and you may assist us with yours, Magnus. It would bring us even greater help in the task we have been given… assistance that would be very welcome."

"It would be an honor," Magnus replied immediately, in a low voice, bowing his head slightly again.

Inside, he was extremely pleased to have been invited so quickly to assist. Ulfhednar did not come in person to summon another of their order for trifling purposes. Whatever had been asked of them was undoubtedly of considerable significance to Midragard.

"Then come with us now, both of you. We will move with haste. There is a very special individual, of great importance to King Hakon, who must be conveyed safely to the Drakkar Mountains," the black-cloaked Ulfhednar stated.

"It is an individual whose origins may be difficult to understand," added the other. "It is said he comes from another world, though such a thing is hard for me to even conceive."

Magnus eyes widened a little. "Do you know the name of this individual?"

"A man named Mershad. One said to look like those from the Sunlands," the second Ulfhednar, with the silver pelt, responded.

"I know him. He spent some time at Glittering River. And I came upon him when he was driven from the skies by an Arcamon," Magnus replied.

A brief, unmistakable flicker of surprise crossed the faces of the other men. "Indeed, it is one named Mershad that we have been tasked with conveying to the Drakkar Mountains" the second Ulfhednar replied after a moment's pause.

"Your familiarity may bring Mershad more comfort in the journey," observed the first Ulfhednar.

"Familiarity or not, we must not tarry here further. Magnus, you can tell us this tale of yours, as we travel together. I know that both of us would like to hear of it," the second Ulfhednar said.

Without further comment, both of the Ulfhednar then turned and set a swifter pace with their long strides. Like Brynhild, Magnus did not have to ask what was expected of him, and he followed suit, heading in the wake of the Ulfhednar. The wolves of both packs picked up their pace, and bounded along with them, easily able to keep stride with the humans.

The two Ulfhednar did not wait long before asking Magnus to relate his tale of how he had come to know of Mershad. Still not believing his incredible turns of fortune, first meeting Brynhild, and now being included in fulfilling a King's request to the Ulfhednar, Magnus began the telling. His rested body coursed with an enthusiasm that infused his gait with a light, energetic step. Striding briskly alongside Brynhild, with no less than two Ulfhednar, he knew he would not easily tire.

THOMAS

Thomas paused to catch his breath. He leaned heavily against the plastered outer wall of a two level residence, astride the corner of one of Avalos's innumerable streets. The cool air lingering within the merciful pool of shade was a panacea for the fatigue clenching onto him, both of a mental and physical nature. As a stream of people passed by, heading in each direction, he inhaled slowly through his nose. He felt a rivulet of sweat streaking down the side of his face.

Breathing in through his nose was not perhaps the best of choices. He wrinkled his nose, and shook his head in disbelief at his luck, moving a few feet down from where he had halted. The inhalation instantly revealed that he had stopped far too close to an ample pile of recently deposited horse droppings. Such an aroma was far from uncommon on Avalos's streets, but it was one he preferred to keep a little more distance from.

Whether he imagined it or not, he felt as if his entire head was sore from the midday lessons with Father Anselm. Thomas definitely had taken his fill for the day with wax tablets and rhetoric. A part of him felt guilty for harboring the dour thoughts. He knew his father had gone through some considerable trouble and effort to get him the opportunity for an education, the latter most often being the sole realm of those with greater means.

'You never know what the world may bring, and a sharper mind will have you better prepared for all things. I want you to climb the ladder even higher than me, just like your brother Hugh is doing.' The words of his father echoed within his head.

His family had done really well for weavers, reaching an impressive level. Good numbers of journeymen had to gather at the beginning of each week within Avalos just to seek employment for one more week. The promise of anything more than that was uncommon, and such individuals lived with constant uncertainty. Even many master weavers lived with their families crammed tightly into crowded tenements, scratching out as much gainful work as they possibly could.

It was always considered a natural progression to take the trade of one's father, Thomas suspected his own father did not want him to miss any opportunity for greater things; if the very uncertain, rare possibility ever arose.

The station of a person in Avanor, or anywhere in Gallea for that matter, was largely fixed at birth. Any changes in fortune were usually for the worse. The ability to advance in life was slim, but Thomas was aware that his father held tightly onto a miniscule shred of hope on his son's behalf.

He was now a good way from Father Anselm's parish church, and the Street of the Weavers. He had already passed by the formidable-looking, square building of stone serving as the local commandery for the Order of the High Altar. He had finally reached the district where some of the more elite merchants kept their sizeable homes and capacious warehouses.

"Hello young Thomas," a kindly voice said, calling for his attention.

Thomas turned his eyes towards a figure shuffling slowly along the outer edge of the street, carefully avoiding the quicker traffic, and occasional carts and wagons rumbling along the center. Thomas nimbly worked his way over towards the same side of the street as the figure, striving to avoid becoming an unwanted obstacle as he crossed.

"Good day to you, Hubert," Thomas cheerfully greeted Old Man Hubert, whose crooked posture had been the price of many, many years spent laboring as a fuller.

Thomas had a great liking for the elderly man, and the beaming smile on his face was entirely genuine. To Thomas, Old Man Hubert seemed eternal, as old as the mountain looming over Avanor.

Old Man Hubert was retired now, succeeded by his sons. They still had hale, youthful bodies, but worked no less hard at the strenuous occupation. Hubert's family was one of many who still did the arduous work of a fuller by themselves, in the traditional way, stamping about endlessly in troughs.

Thomas was cognizant that more of the work nowadays was being taken on by huge hammers, driven by water mills, but a part of him held on to a desperate hope for the sake of those such as Hubert and his sons. It was the incessant hope that the more efficient, mill-driven hammers would not take the paying work away from the fullers, destroying their occupation and driving them into becoming beggars.

As Thomas saw it, new inventions did not come without exacting painful costs. Hubert's sons had a right to continue in an honest, time-proven trade, just as their father had been afforded one in his lifetime. He wondered what good new devices really were if they ended up reducing large numbers of people into lives of suffering penury. Thomas was also wise enough to know that where one invention threatened fullers everywhere, another could be developed that would threaten weavers.

"Heading towards Hervee's storehouse?" asked the old man, in a raspy tone.

Thomas nodded, answering respectfully. "Yes, Hubert. On an errand from my father."

The old man held up a large, folded piece of woolen cloth that he had been carrying, which Thomas recognized as being of high quality. "Hervee is still good to this old man, even if this rickety body cannot handle the troughs any more."

"With all the work you have done for him, and that your sons do for him now, I imagine he will always appreciate you, Hubert," Thomas replied politely.

"Hervee is an uncommon man among merchants," Hubert remarked. "Many dyers, weavers, fullers, and tenters in Avanor are very fortunate."

"They are," agreed Thomas, knowing his own father felt much the same way about the beneficent merchant.

"And you are certainly growing up fast, young man. Not long before you sit at your own loom," Hubert commented.

Thomas grinned, not quite sure how to reply. Hubert would not likely share Thomas's father's zeal for having his sons educated, which seemed to imply that his father did not want either Thomas or Hugh to end up as weavers like him. In a world where sons took up the trades of fathers, Thomas, even at his young age, recognized that his was an unusual situation.

"I will do my best," Thomas finally replied, hoping the answer was good enough.

"And how is your brother? Have you heard any word since he

went to the Island City?" Hubert asked.

"Not recently. They keep him very busy in his studies, and he does not get much time to travel," Thomas replied.

The old man smiled. "Well then, now that I have tidings of the both of you, I will continue on my way ... these old legs are getting tired fast. It was good to see you again, young Thomas."

"And you, Hubert. I will be sure to tell my father that I saw you as well," Thomas said.

"Give him my blessing and best wishes," Hubert replied congenially, as he took a step forward.

Thomas parted from the old man, and resumed his trek into the harbor-side merchant's district. He gazed up at the large houses built of stone, perched close to where the main business of their wealthy occupants was transacted.

He looked upon the opulent constructs with a sense of wonder and curiosity. Seeing how wide the buildings were, Thomas could only imagine how sizeable the rooms and chambers inside were. He had heard the descriptions of large stone fireplaces in main chambers, rooms lit by whale-oil lamps, and other amenities enjoyed by the upper classes, told from the lips of household servants employed in the district.

Even the interior walls were said to be anything but bland. They were described as covered with epic scenes, of feasts, battles, and tales of the Western Church, rendered on painted cloth, embroidered panels, tapestries, or even painted directly on the walls.

Thomas could only begin to imagine what kinds of meals were served in such places. It was hard for him to envision much of anything inside the large residences, coming as he did from an environment of narrow rooms, with undecorated, plastered walls, and lit by smoky, tallow candles.

Thomas continued onward, striding down towards the water's edge. The long, vaulted warehouses of the great merchants were lined up in rows close to the quays and jetties of the harbor. Thomas could see the harbor spread out beyond, dotted with vessels of all sizes. The waters were in perfect view, as he descended the street to the particular row where Hervee's warehouse was located.

The ocean breezes washed over him, an invigorating feeling that always sparked his spirits. To Thomas, the breezes hinted at adventures, beckoning from the open sea and the magnificent lands far beyond. The harbor was living evidence of those lands, as ships from all over the south and west were gathered there, even a few vessels from the north, and the Sunlands.

Thomas turned and walked down the facings of a couple of warehouses, waiting patiently as a team of oxen pulled a heavy wagon laden with wine casks from one of the storehouses. Reaching the third warehouse in the row, he turned and walked through the wide, arched opening.

The extensive interior was dim. What light there was came through sun beams reaching through the entrance itself, and a series of small, upper windows set at even placements into the side walls. Few lamps were utilized in such a place, where a single fire could devastate huge stores of cloth and textiles in moments.

Jehan, the son of Hervee of Delshire, smiled amiably as Thomas passed through the front entrance. Jehan did not pause to talk, as he was concluding business with a man standing next to a horse-drawn cart piled full of various types of cloth.

Thomas halted for few moments, as he was always in awe of the mass of contents within the capacious warehouse. Knowing how much cloth his father produced in his workroom gave him a finer appreciation for the tremendous quantities and varieties present within the lengthy chamber.

The barrel-vaulted ceiling rested on walls lined with shelves filled with stockpiles of finished cloth and other textile items. There were expensive cloths of all varieties, including linen, wool, cotton, and even silks. Several of the more expensive types were of thicker material, provided with teasel-groomed finishes. Much of it would be shipped to markets in distant lands, or taken to the great yearly fairs now approaching. All would bring Hervee sizeable profits.

There were also bales of coarser linens and woolen cloth, including prodigious stores of broad cloths in an array of different colors. These were largely set aside for the city's needs, such as those of Avalos' tailors and cappers.

"Hervee is one of the best merchants in this area, if not all of Ave itself! If anyone has some high quality, scarlet cloth for tunics, Hervee will," boasted a raised voice, as a small party of men entered the warehouse.

The voice belonged to a man that Thomas instantly perceived to be some kind of city official. He wore a haughty expression, and partly aloof demeanor, seeming to regard Thomas as invisible even though the boy was standing almost right before him. He was a tall, slender man, with narrow features such as a sharp, long nose, and a thin, tightly set mouth.

With a décor including several jeweled rings, an ornate necklace of beautifully crafted silver links with a jeweled pendant, and a silver belt buckle, the man exhibited all the trappings of luxury. A brimless, low-sitting cap of felt topped his head.

He wore an overtunic dyed with a carefully executed combination of weld and madder that produced a distinctly golden hue. His purple undertunic was no less rich in appearance, and both garments displayed exquisite embroidery along their edges.

A single leather pouch attached by two short straps hung from his narrow belt of fine leather. The ivory hilt of a small knife protruded from the exquisite scabbard fitted into one of the short straps.

Respecting the power of the official-looking man, Thomas stood cautiously to the side. He observed the entrance of the prominent party with great interest.

A half-dozen guards of the city garrison, with conical helms, cloaks, and mail-shirts, armed with lances and carrying round-topped, triangular shields, accompanied the pompous speaker and a pair of other individuals. Thomas wanted to deliver the message his father had given him for Hervee, concerning the status of some finished cloth, but his piqued curiosity temporarily put aside his charge as he studied the incoming group.

"A visit from the citadel, yes? I am truly honored," Hervee exclaimed, displaying genuine pleasure as he walked into sight to greet the men.

Thomas' interest was kindled further as he focused upon two of the men escorted by the six guards. From the complexions of their skin, he could tell one was probably from the north, most likely one of the kingdoms in Eberias. The second could have been from Gallea, or any one of the southern or western lands.

The lighter-skinned man had thick, shoulder length hair. raven black in color. Above average in height, he had a solid build, though not as robust as the imposing guards escorting him. His eyes were of a deep blue shade, and he had a strong jaw line, lending him a naturally serious expression.

He was clothed in a fine array of colors, from his green supertunic, to the light blue tunic underneath. The blue tunic's close-fitting sleeves were long enough to poke several inches past the end of the overlying supertunic.

Both sets of cuffs, on the supertunic and tunic, were exquisitely embroidered, as was the hem and collar of the supertunic. The lower half of a pair of high, black leather boots was visible below the hem of the supertunic.

The expensive attire all attested that this was also a man of importance and stature, as did the garb upon his companion. The man with the darker skin tone was a little shorter, dark-eyed and full-lipped. His oval face looked friendly enough, if somewhat apprehensive at the moment. He exhibited a full shadow of growth on his face, and had short-cropped black hair.

He wore a sleeveless yellow surcoat, over a green tunic, with matching green trousers and crème-hued, soft leather shoes. Like his companion, the hints of a necklace could be seen just inside the embroidered collar of the inner green tunic, tucked underneath.

"So, Hervee, what have you in the way of bright reds, to fashion a special tunic from?" inquired the arrogant Avanoran official, in the polite, articulate tone of a man given to few other modes of speech.

"It would not be so difficult, if the bugs would not be so stubborn about which oak trees they preferred... They are so maddeningly particular," quipped Hervee with a good-natured timbre. Thomas almost chuckled, knowing the pretentious city official just wanted a succinct answer, but would instead receive an abundant response from the loquacious Hervee of Delshire. "But you are in some good fortune, for one of the dyers I work with did receive a shipment of some of the valuable paste, and managed to work up a rather good quality dye. Came all the way from the lands of the Fahtamid Khalif ... even despite the situation there. Word has it a new upstart named Ibn Amal has annexed a fair portion of the Khalif's territory. Just be glad that while rulers may change, trade continues, my good friends."

"Ah yes, Ibn Amal ... Baron Osbern recently set out with a strong force to confront him," remarked the Avanoran official, courteous, but clearly having no interest in the banter. "But I am glad that you have some good scarlet cloth in."

"Finely finished too, I might add. Soft linen, or fine wool. I might even have some stock from wheel-spun cotton from southern Lomilas too," Hervee responded. "I make use of every bit of Kermes dye that I can."

"Do you have some of my father's weave dyed with that?" piped in Thomas. As soon as he spoke aloud, he blanched, not intending to be so brazen. His fascination with the talk of the Kermes dye had gotten the better of his focus.

He felt the eyes of the guards snap upon him. With Thomas being a commoner, and a youth at that, they made little effort in response other than looks of annoyance at the sudden interruption. Their duty was to offset genuine threats, and Thomas was obviously anything but that.

"Hello Thomas," Hervee said congenially, noticing him for the first time. He looked to the others and smiled, showing no sign of displeasure at the interruption. "His father is truly one of my best weavers here in Avanor. A family I could not do as well without."

Hervee's response instantly defused the flare of tension, and eased Thomas' nerves. He wanted to thank Hervee for not admonishing him, and also felt pride at the open commendation given his father by the elite merchant.

The Avanoran official nodded politely in response, though Thomas could tell the man held absolutely no interest in learning tales of mere weaver's sons. Thomas had encountered the type often enough, and recognized the detached, albeit civil, expression written upon the official's slender face.

The official's disinterest did not deter Thomas, as some impetus arose now that he had drawn some attention. An opportunity lay before him, and though he was nervous, he surmised he could rely on the bravado of youth.

He knew he could not turn back now that he had made his presence known. He did not shrink away, looking directly to the two strangers just behind the official.

"Do you know much about cloth?" asked the dark-haired, lighter-skinned stranger. He had a very unusual accent, from no land Thomas could identify.

Thomas nodded. "I do a lot of work with my father. I do not work the loom myself yet, but I know many things about cloth. He has taught me much."

"My name is Logan, what is yours?" the man asked.

"Thomas, son of William the Weaver," Thomas responded politely.

"Nice to meet you. This is my friend Antonio," he said, indicating the darker-hued man at his side.

"Very nice to meet you Thomas," Antonio said, his accent matching that of Logan.

"And you as well," Thomas returned cordially.

Logan looked towards the Avanoran official, who was now displaying signs of impatience. "Let us give some support to this boy's father. His confidence tells me his father is skilled."

Hervee motioned for a thin, modestly-dressed man standing nearby to come over. The man must have manifested shortly after the others had entered, as Thomas had not taken any notice of him. Yet Thomas was not surprised to see Hervee's dutiful hireling. The man hustled over without delay, his face attentive.

"Alan, would you see if any of William's cloth was dyed with the Kermes dyes?" he asked. He looked back to Logan, Antonio, and the city official, as Alan headed into the depths of the warehouse. "William does produce an excellent quality of woolen cloth for me, though I fear I might not have had any dyed with the scarlet hues."

Alan returned a few moments later, and shook his head. "Some in Indigo, but none in the Kermes dye," Alan replied.

"I would like an Indigo tunic," Antonio interjected.

Hervee looked outwardly pleased with the response, and sent Alan off to procure some of the Indigo-dyed woolen fabric that Thomas's father had woven.

Logan smiled. "I would like some scarlet linen."

"Exquisitely soft, and finely finished," the Avanoran official added, with a pretentious lilt to his words.

"Of course," Hervee stated evenly. The subtle narrowing of his eyes, and the slight tensing of his face, hinted at being affronted at the very idea he would proffer anything less for such distinguished customers.

Logan turned to look at Thomas. "As my friend here is giving your father some support, and as I am fixed on having scarlet, I still don't want to leave here without making a contribution to a good weaver's son."

Logan took up a pouch from where it was tied to his outer belt. He retrieved a couple of shiny golden coins from within, and handed them over to Thomas. At first Thomas hesitated, and it took Logan to reach down and brush the coins against Thomas' right hand before he opened his palm to receive them.

He felt the cool metal of the gleaming coins as they settled against the flesh of his hand. Thomas' eyes widened as he gazed upon two gold besants from Eberias, each one worth fully twenty-four silver deniers. It was hard for him to believe what had just transpired. He had seen gold besants before, when loitering around market areas, or during his periodic visits to Hervee's warehouse, but he had never in his life actually held one in his hands.

"For your good advocacy, as I admire loyalty," Logan stated, with the trace of a grin.

"He is a very good boy, and I assure you he is indeed worthy of such a good boon," Hervee added, as if in endorsement of the stranger's incredible beneficence.

"Thank you," Thomas retorted in a low voice, a little uncomfortable regarding how he should properly respond. He was anxious and thrilled at the sudden good fortune he would be able to bring his parents that very day. Such a spontaneous display of generosity was extremely rare within Avalos.

"I would like to stay and talk more, Thomas, but we need to be getting back to the fortress. I am just a guest, and I don't want to keep my generous hosts waiting too long," Logan commented politely. He ended his address in a more formal air. "It was very nice to meet you, Thomas, son of William."

"And you ... thank you," Thomas replied in the low tone, bowing his head, and falling into silent attendance.

"Then shall we settle our business?" Hervee queried, casting a sideways smile at Thomas, obviously amused and pleased at the incident. Not all merchants would have acted so favorably, yet another distinction between Hervee and his peers.

Murmurs of assent came from the others, especially the Avanoran official, who did not exhibit the same enthusiasm as Hervee towards the interlude. Thomas waited quietly while Hervee concluded the remaining business with Logan, Antonio, and the Avanoran official. It was ultimately a small sale, especially in comparison to the cart-loads regularly exiting the long, vaulted warehouse, but Hervee was plainly in great spirits as an exchange of substantial value was made.

When the men finally resolved their transactions and departed, Thomas quickly delivered the messages from his father to Hervee. The merchant seemed pleased with the updates, and did not have anything particular for Thomas to convey back to his father. He congratulated Thomas again on the good fortune involving the stranger.

Taking his leave, Thomas left the warehouse. As soon as he was outside the building, he quickened his stride. He hurried to catch up to the group from the citadel, guessing their route as being the most direct one back to the mountain-palace. Before long, he had caught sight of them, and began shadowing them at a distance.

For a short while, Thomas watched the entourage moving through the crowded streets. The teeming masses in the streets parted quickly at the sight of the three well-dressed men, accompanied by six heavily-armed garrison escorts.

Thomas wondered what kind of story was behind the two strangers, who had behaved so differently from the usual nobility he had seen and encountered around the city. They had spoken very clearly in his language, and they were dressed in the manner of wealthy Galleans, but they were most certainly not from anywhere near Gallea.

He knew he could not follow them forever, and would have to accept that his curiosities would have to be sorely frustrated for the present. Nonetheless, he was ecstatic for the unexpected, exciting rendezvous, feeling the pair of gold coins held securely within his tightly clenched fist.

When the escorting party finally proceeded beyond his sight, turning onto another main thoroughfare leading towards the towering citadel of the Unifier, Thomas turned away with reluctance. With a long exhale, akin to a sigh, he started back home.

The trip was a near blur, as all sorts of thoughts raced through his inspired mind. It was as if his mind was somewhere else entirely, his body simply traversing the route out of sheer memory. If asked later, he could not have recalled much of anything about his journey back to the Street of Weavers that day.

Thomas paused a step inside the front doorway to his house. Seeing that his father was not present in the main workroom, he resumed his pace, and bounded up the timber stairs to his left, heading up to the second level.

His mother was sitting on a stool in the main solar, attending to the familiar task of hand-spinning wool. His sister Emma sat upon another stool nearby, with her own spindle and distaff. Both looked up abruptly at Thomas' sudden appearance.

"Worth forty-eight silver deniers!" Thomas exclaimed jubilantly, striding briskly over to his mother. He finally opened his right hand, and extended the two gold coins to her. "This is a little good fortune for you, mother, and for father!"

His mother set down the spindle and distaff, with a surprised look on her face, as she eyed the resplendent gold coins. Slowly, she accepted the coins from Thomas, cupping her palm as he dropped them gently into her hand.

Emma stopped what she was doing and waited expectantly, as if for some kind of explanation. Her eyes roved to the gold coins in their mother's hands, and a look of wonder was reflected in them.

His mother then abruptly shot Thomas a firmer look, her eyebrows narrowing. Though somber, the mien held no trace of anger, as of yet. He knew she was suspicious, but not yet ready to make an accusation.

"Now where did you come by two gold coins?" she asked slowly, her tone compelling Thomas to hide nothing from her.

He knew he could not, even if he had wanted to. She had a Wizard's ability to see past any attempt at deception, by either himself or Emma. They had learned the hard way that obfuscation was not an advisable path to take with her. In detail, Thomas related the story of his trip to Hervee's warehouse, and the unanticipated interaction with the generous strangers.

"Then it is indeed a legitimate gift, and you have done no wrong in obtaining it. A gift freely yours," his mother stated at the culmination of Thomas's tale, her face softening. "And I thank you for bringing it home, when you had a right to keep it to yourself."

Though she seemed genuinely grateful, and a little relieved at Thomas' explanation, he could still sense something was troubling her.

"You and Father can make better use of it for the family than I could. I know any good it does for the family will be good for me and Emma," Thomas said quickly. He then gave a shrug, as he conceded, "I'd probably waste it on a whole lot of cloves and ginger. That would be a waste of two gold coins."

"And I might have to buy you a few cloves and ginger out of this, at the very least," his mother replied, her expression brightening, as the radiant smile he liked so much dawned.

"The man named Logan, who gave me the coins, was really nice and generous, mother," Thomas explained, finally sensing the source of the subtle trepidation.

"Yes, Thomas, very generous. But those men had to be very important. It is not unimportant folk who can throw gold coins at a weaver's son. You have to be very careful about who you talk to in these days," she replied in a more even tone, the words clearly intended as a gentle admonishment.

"Yes, Mother. I saw the guards all around him, but he seemed friendly enough. So did his friend. I just wanted to see what they were like. I want to find out who they really are. Probably rulers of another land, great warriors, or even generals of some kind," Thomas exclaimed, growing more excited as he spoke openly of each fascinating possibility. He then burst out, "Maybe even Wizards, Mother!"

"Or maybe just wealthy merchants of another type, or administrators for another king," his mother replied with noticeably less ebullience than Thomas.

"Maybe so, but I think not," Thomas lightly protested.

"Do not let your wild imagination get the best of you, my boy," she responded. His mother then looked down at the shining gold pieces in her hand, bold symbols of sorely needed relief for a struggling family. "But your father will indeed be very happy at this unexpected boon. It should help greatly with some of our debts, perhaps putting some to rest for good."

Thomas' giddy excitement faded as he was starkly reminded of their incessant financial plights. They lived better than most weavers, and his father had gained good favor with a most kind merchant in the person of Hervee, not the most common of situations among those in the weavers' trade. Yet day to day life was still very difficult, with an assortment of burdens and challenges that never allowed much room for comfort.

"Do not be troubled, I do not mean to discourage imagination. Just do not lose hold of reason, my boy," his mother said, apparently misinterpreting the fretful expression on his face.

"I just wish Father could get ahead, enough so that he did not have to ever worry," Thomas said forlornly.

She shook her head and smiled. "Even Hervee of Delshire, with all of his wealth, has sleepless nights, my boy. I do not think there is anyone who goes through this life and does not encounter worry at some time. It may even be that those who have much have more to worry themselves over. Do not trouble yourself unnecessarily, my boy. We all know there are enough times of worry in this world. We should not miss enjoying the carefree moments. Now go, and be carefree, before your chores for Father Anselm."

Thomas stepped forward and threw his arms around his mother, giving her a tight hug that was returned with even greater intensity. She tousled his hair, kissing him lightly on the forehead as she released her embrace.

"Now be off with you, I have much to do around here, and you do not have all day until you have to go provide some worthy recompense to Father Anselm for your lessons," she pronounced, with a boisterous surge. "Waste not another moment!"

Thomas needed little further encouragement. In a few seconds, he was off down the stairs and out the front door. His mind was firmly set on finding some of his friends, before it was time to report to Father Anselm for an afternoon of sundry labors around the parish church.

Hidden within his heart, he carried a burning urge to find out if anyone knew anything about Logan, or his friend Antonio. The two strangers were undoubtedly direct guests of the Unifier, and were so very different in their mannerisms from anyone Thomas had ever seen or met before.

He was well aware that it was no minor encounter he had experienced that day. It was without a doubt one that was quite exceptional for the son of a weaver in Avanor. The event ignited a thrill within a life all too often mundane, where imagination normally had to suffice to provide such stimulation.

DEGANAWIDA

Having left the big Trogen in the company of a few very trusted Onan warriors, men who he knew could control their passions under the mounting strains of the ongoing hardship, Deganawida had spent the better part of the morning walking amongst the people as they moved eastward. The sight of a Trogen warrior would only inflame the raw emotions of the people, and while Deganawida did not wish to leave the Trogen out of sight for too long, his first priority was seeing to the care of his people.

Lending encouragement wherever he could to lift sagging hopes and spirits, Deganawida endured the pain of watching the exhausted masses of refugees continuing their perilous flight through the forest. There had already been several casualties from the arduous travel, mostly involving the oldest and frailest.

It wrenched Deganawida's heart to watch families hurrying to fashion makeshift, unmarked graves for venerable, respected elders who had finally succumbed to the bitter tolls exacted from their weary bodies. The people had no choice in the manner of burial, sorely pressed to avoid leaving the beloved elders' remains out in the open. There was no time for the proper, traditional ceremonies.

The situation struck mercilessly at the heart of long-held practices, depriving the people of some of their most sacred observances at a time they needed them the most. They could not delay to construct the timber platforms used to hold bodies high off of the ground, away from scavengers. Even if they had the time, such platforms would not be able to serve the intended, proper function, of storing bodies until the Festival of the Dead, which so many tribal people adhered to.

Those sacred days, when family members tenderly carried the bodies of loved ones to a great pit of internment, helped bring some closure to the pain suffered by the living, as well as eliciting hope of worlds beyond. The medicine given by the Festival of the Dead could not be realized in any way when the tribes were being forcefully driven out of their homelands.

Others within the tribes who preferred the use of grave mounds to honor those who had passed to the higher realms were not given the consolation of their traditions either, prevented from forming proper earthen tombs within the deceased individuals' homeland areas.

The tragic situation did not involve just elderly victims. There were also several vulnerable young ones who had fallen to debilitating sicknesses, unable to recuperate in the pressing haste of the exodus. Deganawida had witnessed a few heartbreaking scenes involving infants, innocents who even the most gifted members of the great Healing

Societies could not begin to help.

Deganawida could not even honor the wishes of a few who petitioned to have funeral pyres for either elder or youth, as the rising smoke would send a clear signal across a vast distance to their relentless enemies. As much as it tore him up inside, he and the other sachems had to deny the pleas of grieving mothers and other despondent survivors.

War scouts had labored earnestly to bring up the latest tidings of the enemy pursuit. The enemy forces were advancing along a broad front, in incredible numbers, and there now seemed to be little that could be done to stop them.

The enemy's front line kept stretching farther and deeper as they swept through the forest, driving Deganawida's people onward. Judging from the reports, the enemy ranks were swelling by the day, and he did not doubt that more levies were arriving from Gallea.

Troubling word had also come that more support from the eastern Anishin tribes, especially the Wendaton, was pouring into the fray on the Unifier's side. Unable to threaten the Five Realms on their own, the Wendaton and others saw a tantalizing opportunity to revenge themselves for ages-old conflicts, whose fires still burned fiercely within their hearts.

The brave warriors of the Five Realms, and their remaining Midragardan allies, were doing everything they could possibly do to divert, stall, and throw back every forward push of the invaders. It was all to little avail, and no sachem could deny that there was simply not enough strength to stem the Gallean advance.

The war of attrition was exacting a cost that could not be recouped. For every warrior of the Five Realms felled, there was none to replace. For every Gallean warrior slain there were two, if not three, fresh warriors being brought in from the west.

Deganawida's mood darkened as he faced the stark inevitability of the situation facing them. It was increasingly possible the refugees would be overtaken before they reached the sands of the shoreline at the Water Head-Cradle.

Steeped in dour ruminations, Deganawida did not immediately take notice when Ayenwatha and a large war party emerged from the trees off to his left. Ayenwatha did not break stride as he approached the venerable tribal leader, whose saddened eyes rose to meet those of the younger war sachem.

Ayenwatha looked about Deganawida as he drew nearer, as if expecting to see someone else, and a concerned expression formed quickly on his face.

"The Trogen is well-cared for. I had to move among the people, and could not bring him into their midst," Deganawida said, in response to the unvoiced question.

Ayenwatha nodded, with a look of relief. "No, you could not. He should be kept out of their sight, as much as possible."

Deganawida looked into the younger sachem's eyes, and saw a fierce determination burning within the warrior's gaze. After witnessing so many with breaking spirits, here was one Onan man who was yet unbowed.

"What dangers have you evaded on your latest foray with the war band?" the older sachem inquired.

"Firakens, this time," Ayenwatha said. "My answer may have surprised you, and I do have a story to tell."

"You need to be wary of them," Deganawida replied, knowing well of the forest-dwelling carnivores who served as the symbol for Ayenwatha's clan.

Ayenwatha chuckled in a rare moment of levity, though Deganawida saw the other's expression was still tinged by a little bitterness. "Gallean patrols have not learned that lesson yet. It is a tale you must have me relate to you later. You may find some amusement within it, though at the time my heart was racing fast. It is only the Creator's grace that allowed me to get away from there. I was very close to becoming a Firaken's meal."

"I am glad that did not happen, and it sounds as if you have a good tale to share," Deganawida replied. "Though I wish it were otherwise, I know the Firakens are not going to stop all the invaders. What is your next task?"

Ayenwatha then took a deep breath, as the smile faded from his face. "A new war party is to be gathered, to meet with Gunnar's warriors," he iterated. "I will be going forth with them, and not much time remains before we will be moving back out. Tired warriors replacing other tired warriors. How is the retreat proceeding?"

Deganawida stifled an emotional burst that welled up as the vivid image of a mother's forlorn, agony-riddled face, cradling her still-warm, yet lifeless, infant in her hands, loomed within his mind's eye. For some reason, that singular, powerful image was evoked by Ayenwatha's question.

In so many ways, the haunting image answered the query thoroughly. Deganawida's eyes glistened reflexively, as the strains of the retreat caught up to his consciousness.

"It seems ever harder and harder," he answered Ayenwatha, in a subdued voice echoing his inner burdens. "The old ones cannot endure much more. Our people cannot go any faster than they have. It is ever harder for me to watch five proud tribes fade, and maybe vanish before my eyes. There is little to hold onto, as we will be nothing but an exile race, if any of us survives this terrible trial."

Ayenwatha gently shook his head, as he listened to Deganawida's melancholy words. He looked away, as a pained, sorrowful expression broke through, replacing the stoic, determined demeanor the younger war sachem usually presented.

"Deganawida, no. It is not that way," Ayenwatha finally replied, in a low voice. He clenched his right fist, brought it up to the middle of his chest, and pounded against it emphatically, as a spark came to his eyes.

"Here. The Five Realms is always right here," Ayenwatha continued more adamantly, indicating his heart. "As long as it exists here, we will continue to be a people, and the tribes will continue to be tribes, and the clans will remain as clans ... wherever our paths may take us in this big world. Even if we never come to these shores again, even if the days ahead are very dark, we can survive as a people, as long as we hold onto what is carried inside all of us.

"It has never been the trees, rocks, and creeks that have made us a people since the beginning. It is us, and us alone, who have made this land our land. It is what has always kept us together. If we never surrender that, they can never take it from us. Not with the largest army in all of the world."

A poignant silence hung in the air between the two dedicated tribal men. A lone tear escaped Deganawida's right eye at last, as he internalized the sharp, pure wisdom radiating from the emphatic young warrior. Ayenwatha held his gaze for a moment longer, before giving Deganawida a gentle clasp upon his arm.

Extending Deganawida a slight bow, Ayenwatha turned and signaled to a number of warriors from the war party he had arrived with.

They had respectfully lingered in wait for him, several paces away, during his interaction with Deganawida. Though looking outwardly exhausted, the warriors sprinted away. Deganawida presumed they had been sent to gather the others who would soon be heading out with Ayenwatha, to see to the overwhelming task of holding the approaching enemy storm at bay.

In just a few moments, the last warriors of Ayenwatha's war party dissipated into the depths of the foliage. With a look that was both weary and resolute, Ayenwatha stated to Deganawida, "It is not much farther to the Water Head-Cradle. May the Creator shield us in these final, decisive hours."

Deganawida gave Ayenwatha another embrace, before the younger warrior headed off, to rejoin his war party. After Ayenwatha could no longer be seen, Deganawida reverted his attention back to the masses of people streaming through the trees to the right.

He watched a mother clasping her very young son and daughter by the hands, virtually pulling the tired children along with her. Deganawida read the substantial fear and worry within her countenance, even as she spoke soothing words, rendered in soft, light tones, to her haggard children.

An older man using a stout walking staff to help navigate his path stumbled suddenly, in the grip of his own deep fatigue. A beautiful, unwed female, hair fashioned into two long braids, moved swiftly to help stabilize the old man before he fell to the forest floor.

A few younger males, in the height of adolescence, then came into view, dragging a couple of infirm people upon leather-spanned stretchers. The expressions of the young males were drawn tight as they concentrated upon their labor, taking great care with their living burdens.

All of them, from the elderly dragged upon the stretchers, to the young mother with her children, to the warriors diving back among the trees to defend the rear, were indeed the essence and vital substance of the Five Realms.

Ayenwatha was right, and Deganawida was not one who was headstrong, refusing to glean insight over a petty difference in age and experience. Sometimes it took the young to remind the old of what should never have been forgotten to begin with.

If the tribal people held fast to the things that had brought them together, the qualities that had fashioned the wonderful, strong confederation of tribes they had become, he knew they could remain so; no matter what faraway land their journey might take them to.

Still, the specter of harsh, imminent reality remained. For the present, they would simply have to survive, an aim far from certain as the tribes were pushed ever closer towards the Great Waters.

section vi

SVEIN

Far to the south of Saxany, a second large fleet of ships plied ocean waters on a northward passage.

The elder gods appeared to be with the Midragardan fleet, as well as the new God, Svein reflected. He steadied himself on the bow of the great longship Southern Storm, with its meticulously carved, colorfully painted prow. Rising well above Svein's head was the swirling figurehead containing so many iconic, Midragardian images, so skillfully etched into its surface. It was a fitting symbol to serve as the vanguard for the teeming mass of vessels sailing in Southern Storm's wake.

The ship flowed up and over another rolling wave, sending up a salty spray of the kind that always seemed to invigorate Svein. He felt the bow lifting upward again, as the ship glided up the slope of another wave.

The wind was blowing his hair from behind with sustained force, such that he could only see directly ahead for the mass of hair framing each side of his forward vision. Yet the same generous wind billowing his hair about was vigorously thrusting Southern Storm and the other longships onward by means of their great square sails. The favorable air currents sent the elegant ships slicing across the sea's undulating surface.

The day was bright and clear, and no storm beckoned. The conditions were about as ideal as they could possibly get for sailing.

At the current rate of travel, Svein knew the fleet was well ahead of schedule, but he could presume nothing. The often harsh lessons learned during his past experiences had taught him that it was best not to assume that optimal conditions such as this would be sustained perpetually.

The spirits of the men on the ship were excellent, and for that Svein was eminently grateful. They were all on a harrowing journey to save two faraway lands. It was a voyage that would likely earn them places in the Great Hall of the elder gods, if such a place existed.

It was a thought that Svein did not want to linger upon for too long, even if he was renowned for his iron-solid courage. His presence alone had bolstered the men, who were surprised enough that King Hakon had sent so many of his greatest household retainers and vessels to lead them to Saxany's distant shores.

Shading his eyes with his hand, warding against the beaming, unfettered light of the sun, he watched the progress of a skyward patrol mounted on Fenraren, gliding upon the air currents on the distant horizon.

The sky warriors had reported nothing troubling so far. Excellent scouts, each possessed of sharp-sighted vision, their range had been extended far outward. Svein wanted as much advance notice of anything deemed to be of even a remote concern. The relaxed and methodical patterns of the distant sky patrol were a reassuring sight.

"How far do you think we will get before nightfall?" a deep, gritty voice inquired. It belonged to a stout warrior who had just come up to join him at the bow. Svein felt the plunging sensation in his stomach, as the bow dipped down again.

"Likely the second or third of the Stepping Stones, that is, if we continue as we are," Svein replied confidently to Herigar.

His back still turned to Herigar, Svein smiled, knowing the robust warrior already knew the answer. If there was ever a veteran of the seas who Svein wanted by his side at a difficult moment, Herigar would be his undisputed first choice.

Herigar grunted his agreement, not the kind of man given to excessive verbiage.

"The first Stepping Stone is not far off now," Svein added. He nodded off to the right, where a small number of seabirds were drifting lazily through the air.

The ability to use Fenraren in the skies had certainly made navigation easier on the open seas, but the Midragardans manning the vessels never became lax regarding their traditional scrutiny of wave forms, clouds, birds, and even whales. The sun was also a capable enough guide, and there were some useful tools that had been discovered or developed over time.

The Sun Stones from the Ice Island, which were truthfully crystals, were one such discovery, with their remarkable sun-seeking properties. Though they had been found in the natural world, and had not been given to the Midragardans by any Wizard, the Sun Stones seemed like a thing of magic. Even fog and overcast skies could not hinder their ability to indicate the direction of the sun.

The invention of an eight-pointed bearing dial was another wonderful instrument, with markings arranged for northeast, northwest, southeast, and southwest, to go along with the principle four directions.

Svein believed strongly that it did not hurt to check and recheck all available signs, especially when out of sight of land. Being out of sight of land was by far the most precarious time for any longship, the dangers expanded to a manifold level for a fleet of the great size that Svein now led.

The journey to Saxany would not involve tremendous stretches of open sea. The wondrous Stepping Stones helped greatly in that regard. They were a series of islands beginning a full day's sailing from the highest point of the northern coast of Midragard. The islands held a wide range of sizes, but were all fortuitous landmarks. A good number served as suitable sites for landfall.

The Stepping Stones were immensely useful for reaching Kiruva and Gael. They had also marked the way for ships seeking Saxany, and the lands to the north or northwest.

The route Svein was now taking followed along the same ancient route legendary Midragardan war fleets once took. It was the first part of the path taken for the storied raids and conquests driving as far to the north and west as Gallea, and what was now the kingdom of Norengal. It was also the initial path leading to colonization in Gael and Kiruva, the latter leading to the establishment of an entire realm. Oddly, it had been those very excursions that had led to the famous settlement that had given birth to Avanor so long ago.

The relation of their current path to those past, storied ages was never lost on Svein, always conscious of Midragard's great sagas and history.

Svein turned his head and glanced past Herigar, taking in the spectacular vision of the massive fleet following Southern Storm. No matter how often he looked back, he could not help being astonished. Svein found himself wondering whether the immense array of vessels behind him was one of the greatest that had ever been assembled and sent forth from Midragard.

The magnificent fleet was an effusion of luminance and color. The prows of many of the sleek ships were adorned with gold and silver, displaying fabulous embossments of geometric patterns or figures from the natural world. The gilded prows positively sparkled with radiance in the sunlight. Bulls charged forward thunderously, dolphins crested in elegant leaps out of the water, dragons unleashed mighty blasts of fire, and warriors stood proud with swords and axes raised high, among the host of vivid forms rendered in precious metals.

The sails, whether displaying a checkered pattern, or alternating vertical stripes, exhibited a broad array of paired, contrasting colors.

Yellow and black, blue and white, red and white, were just a few of the vibrant combinations in evidence.

Snarling wolves, fanged serpents, roaring bears, fire-breathing dragons, sleek ravens, and many more iconic visages graced the carved figureheads surmounting the prows of many vessels. Some longships had gilded bronze weather vanes mounted at the prows, instead of figureheads, inset with elaborate scrollwork. The weather vanes were themselves often mounted with small figures of birds or other creatures.

All of the ship elements, whether practical or for adornment, contributed to an incomparably majestic vision filling Svein's eyes. The fleet embodied the pride of Midragard, a people who had mastered the seas, and proven their mettle and character time and again, over so many long ages.

Yet the sprawling fleet was also a vision of vulnerability, and Svein was wise enough to realize that as well. He knew that he had to be very careful, no matter how hard they all wished to press onward. One lone storm could scuttle all of the might arrayed behind him within a speck of time, a terrible lesson meted out more than once in the long history of Midragard. Svein was not about to see the wondrous fleet become a terrible tragedy.

"We will put in to shore for the night, Old Sea Wolf. Probably will have to divide the fleet between the second and third islands of the Stones. Coordinate communication using the Fenraren. Have the tents assembled on the ships, we want a quick breakdown and departure tomorrow," Svein instructed. "Men can go onshore for cookfires, but I want little holding us back when dawn's light breaks."

With frames assembled out of long, narrow boards of ash wood, the flexibility of the gable-ended tents to be used on ship or land was something Svein now appreciated to the fullest. The men would have the comfort of shelter, but they could remain on the ships.

There would be enough preparatory duties that needed attending. Everything involved with stepping the mast, getting the furled sail in place, setting stays, and other preparatory tasks would occupy the earliest part of their day.

Svein hoped that they would be able to head forth on the morrow under sail from morning onward. They would put out to sea and maneuver themselves by oar power first, before giving the vessels over to the power of the wind. Once the sails were unfurled, and having dealt with the necessary issues of bowlines, halyards and other necessary adjusting elements, the fleet would hopefully be traveling as efficiently they were today.

Herigar nodded at Svein's words and gave another assenting grunt, before heading back towards the main mast. He stepped down from the raised platform at the bow, to the loose deck planking of the vessel. Svein could rest assured that his related instructions would be communicated and carried out to the last detail. Herigar was as meticulous as he was coarse.

Aside from the steering oar at the starboard side of the stern, and a few attending to the many lines involved in the sail rigging, most of the men aboard Southern Storm were currently indulging in some welcome leisure.

Some strolled along the shield-battens and talked amongst themselves, while a few stood and quietly watched the passing sea. A couple were curled up and napping, while others were occupied with one of the popular Midragardan games, versions of 'tables' based around timber boards, bone dice, and either pegs or pieces fashioned of glass, amber, stone, or bone.

The sight of the relaxed crew members was of no worry to Svein, as a state of readiness could be summoned in a hurry. The mast of Southern Storm could be lowered fairly quickly, making use of the exceptional Midragardan design involving the keelson and sizeable, overlying timber mast-fish that gained its name from its visual profile.

Its mast lock, the piece curved in the fore and flat-edged at the rear, could be easily withdrawn from its seating in the mast-fish, the latter set immediately behind the upright mast itself. The mast could then be lowered into an aft groove, without the need to lift the towering mast out vertically in its entirety. While newer Midragardan ships increasingly made use of a crossbeam rather than a mast-fish, Svein preferred the time-tested method of the latter.

The oars were now resting on the upright racks rising well above the decking down the center of the ship. They could be fitted to the now-shuttered oar holes quickly enough. It would take only moments to synchronize two long lines of men seated upon timber sea chests. Oars would then dip in a powerful, rhythmic unison, as the ship was propelled forward swiftly.

Yet at the moment, there was no need to interrupt the crew's relative leisure. The voyage was going very smoothly, and Svein uttered a silent prayer of thanks to both his elder gods and the new God. As he had never really heard a response from any of them, he hoped his gratitude got through to at least one deity.

Taking an extended inhalation of the salt-tinged breezes, he rested his hands on the top strakes of the prow and looked resolutely forward, as the ship rose and fell over another wave. With each wave crested, the shores of Saxany were drawing ever closer.

THOMAS

The morning had not yet showered her light over mighty Avalos. The massive city was still held within the embrace of shadows, and the mild luminance provided by a vast array of torches placed nightly throughout it. The rising sun was just starting to break the crest of the horizon, when the door to Thomas' dwelling resounded with strong, insistent knocks.

His heart racing as he awoke abruptly. Thomas silently got off his straw-filled mattress. Glancing back, he saw that Emma was also fully awake, sitting up on the mattress with her eyes wide in apprehension.

A second series of intrusive, forceful knocks came to his ears, sounding noticeably louder, and more demanding. After firmly bidding Emma to stay right where she was, Thomas padded over to the stairs leading down to the second level, from the garret where he and his sister had their sleeping quarters.

He heard his father slowly making his way down the wooden staircase from the second level to the first floor, calling out irritably to the one knocking to hold their patience. Thomas moved slowly, stepping carefully down to the landing just beyond the end of the stairs. He paused, recognizing the outline of his mother as she descended the wider set of steps to the first level.

Wary of every step, Thomas crept to the top of the staircase and peered down to the workshop level. Though he could not yet see anything, the deep voice of the one pounding upon the door reached up to him, arrogant and authoritative. "We have reason to believe you were among those who slew several students last night!"

"Say what you have to say!" Thomas heard his father growl in response. There was a sharp edge to his father's voice that Thomas had not heard before, confrontational, and laced with defiance.

Thomas had little idea what the specific incident being talked about was. He knew his father had returned home early the previous evening, greatly agitated, as a loud uproar developed outside in the streets. He had firmly ordered Thomas and Emma to stay inside with their mother, before retrieving a crossbow he had kept carefully hidden.

His mother had told Thomas that things were very dangerous outside, and that the students of the University in Avalos were rioting violently throughout the streets. His father did not know the cause of the riot, but it was evidently causing injury to people, and damaging the property of those who had no part in whatever grievance had aroused the students' wrath.

It was not the first time that the University students had rioted in Avalos, nor would anyone in their right mind think it would be the last. From Thomas's own observations, and from what others said, it seemed to Thomas as if fighting and rioting was a prerequisite for those seeking to master the seven main arts taught at the University.

The students constantly appeared to be in a state of agitation, at odds with the local populace. Even so, Thomas could not begin to imagine his brother Hugh engaging in such barbarous activities within the Island City.

From what Thomas gathered from his mother, the unrest was a direct result of the students' provisions for lodging and learning in houses and tenements. There were no demarcated facilities for University students, who conducted their pursuits side by side with the regular citizens of Avanor. Just as the first floor of most houses were used as shops or workshops, the first floor of a master's home was where University students sat upon straw-strewn ground to attempt to enrich their minds.

One such master, the respected John of Monepelle, lived right around the corner from the Street of Weavers. Likewise, a number of tenements near to John of Monepelle lodged a substantial number of students.

Every once in a while, the students living under these conditions grew belligerent due to perceived affronts, whether real or imagined. In some of these circumstances, they grew in anger until finally exploding into violence.

The previous night, Thomas had only been able to gather that his father and other tradesmen had decided to fight back against the unruly mobs of students. They did not wish to see their families and friends beaten and assaulted, and had chosen to protect their own streets.

The choice to resist had put them on an immediate collision course with the stratification of society within Avalos. Many of those that the tradesmen set out to fight were the sons of nobles. Additionally, all of the students of the University were considered clerics, tonsured and under the jurisdiction of the Western Church. Those were the two factors where Thomas' father and others had gone very wrong, even if it was inherently right to resist the destructive, reckless behavior of the students.

"You will face royal justice, weaver, for these killings take this beyond the justice of guild or clergy," the deep-voiced speaker replied, in a cadence indicating the declaration was absolute.

"We have also been ordered to search your home," the voice continued. "And to take you to the Tomb Hall."

Thomas' heart sank precipitously, for the notorious Tomb Hall was where people were imprisoned while awaiting a hearing before a royal representative. Underneath the Seneschal's castle, the Tomb Hall was named as such as it held the remains of many people from much older times; from long before the ancient catacombs had been adapted for the holding of individuals awaiting justice.

"Find what you will," his father replied firmly. There was no sense of apology, or any attempt to evade the speaker. "A man has every right to defend his family and property against lawlessness."

The hackles rose on Thomas' neck. He knew that this was no mere guild violation, demanding the payment of a small fine. His mind turned to the crossbow he knew was clandestinely owned by his father.

It was readily known throughout the city that certain weapons were not to be carried by its dwellers, unless it was expressly a time of war. The weapons restrictions were not lightly regarded, especially in the case of crossbows.

The crossbow was a weapon that had even been banned at one of the Great Vicar's formal Councils, for it had the power to enable a mere peasant to slay a knight with the greatest of ease. The ban had stopped short of discouraging its use against infidels in the Sunlands, as a matter of course, for nobody could argue against its martial effectiveness.

Even with the ban, the weapons were regularly employed in warfare among kingdoms of the southern and western lands. Yet the possession of them was strictly regulated within the cities. A person such as Thomas' father, a simple weaver, was strictly forbidden to have a crossbow in his keeping.

The other voice took on a crueler, haughty edge. "You foolish weaver. Slaying the son of a baron. Should have been happy to have a home of your own, and work to keep bread in your stomach. You have learned before that collusion with your fellow weavers will do you little profit."

The barb was stinging, referring to the many struggles faced by weavers, as well as a major protest the weavers had undertaken in Avalos that had assumed the form of a work stoppage. The storied outburst had resulted in a ruthless, armed suppression of the weavers, a bloody lesson all within the trade had taken to heart.

"Would you have done anything to them, had they killed me?" his father challenged the speaker, his voice rising in volume.

"You have carried weapons that are not permitted. You have slain a baron's son," the firm voice responded, as if the statement summoned everything up irrefutably.

"Would you have arrested them?" his father angrily retorted. "Or will you not give voice to truth?"

Thomas then heard the sounds of a vigorous scuffle, and many raised voices, as the front door was forced inward. He heard his mother cry out in alarm, which almost caused him to dash down the steps. From the sounds below, Thomas knew there were now several more individuals in the room beyond his father, mother, and the speaker. After a few moments, all fell quiet once again.

Anxiety froze Thomas in place, his heart beating faster as his eyes watched the top of the staircase to the first level. Slowly, he backed up a few more steps, ascending halfway to the garret, where he could be better hidden in shadow.

The stairs creaked as the cold metal of an iron-brimmed kettle-helm came into view. The hard eyes of one of the city's militia watch bored into Thomas.

The look was unforgiving, dispassionate, and altogether immovable. Thomas wondered what kind of guild could provide such a hard-looking man for the city's watch.

Thomas had barely noticed his mother coming up the stairs just behind the watchman. An intractable, defiant look was reflected within her own eyes.

She moved deftly around the watchman, blocking his path towards the narrow stairs to the garret, as well as the short passage running back to Thomas' parents' bedchamber.

"Move out of the way, woman," the guard stated curtly.

"This is my home. You have no right to do this," Alice Weaver replied in a tight, challenging voice.

The militia man continued forward until he stood directly in front of her, glaring down into her eyes. He stood a full head taller, was clad in a padded gambeson, and was half again as wide. He took another step forward and reached out with his right hand, shoved her violently backward towards the solar.

Thomas scrambled down the stairs to go to his mother's side, his ire overwhelming his fear. The man whirled upon him, and gave him a backhanded blow sending Thomas spinning into the arms of his mother. Pain lanced through him, and tears came to his eyes.

His mother stormed towards the watchman, glowering at him as she raised an arm to strike the man. Striding forward, he met her advance, and pushed her unceremoniously back towards Thomas.

Thomas hoped with all his heart that Emma was wise enough to remain concealed. He knew she was listening to every word from her place up in the garret.

"Do not think to resist, you or the boy," he warned her, shooting a baleful glance in Thomas' direction. With a darker, more threatening tone, he continued, "We can make this much harder for every last one of you."

Two others of the city watch came up behind, clad in a similar manner to the first man. One proceeded back to the bedchamber, while another entered the solar.

Entering the rooms, they began a search, looking through chests, prodding the walls, and tapping the floor as they probed for secret compartments. One of the watchmen used the haft-end of a lance to tap forcefully upon the walls, and the wood of the floor.

"Say, what have we here?" he inquired abruptly, stopping his tapping in a spot located approximately in the middle of the solar's wall, opposite the stairs. The tapping had taken on a noticeably different timbre.

Setting the lance aside, he took out a short axe hanging at his hide belt. With a sudden, forceful stroke, he cleaved into the plastered wall. The powerful stroke shattered the section into a burst of wood and plaster fragments, revealing a hollow in the wall that had been obscured by a panel.

Reaching in, and grinning widely, he brought out a sword in its scabbard. "Well, would you look at this," he said, beaming triumphantly, as he stood up straighter. He looked to Thomas' mother, with a cold, unfeeling expression. "We came looking for a crossbow, and now I find a sword."

"No, please give us mercy," Alice pleaded, her expression abruptly changing from defiance to that of a supplicant beggar at the sudden discovery. "He meant no harm. He is just a simple weaver."

"A simple weaver? Bearing a crossbow? Harboring a sword?" the guard riposted.

"Mercy, please, in the name of the All-Father," Alice entreated him.

Thomas' eyes widened. He knew his father had once possessed a sword, but had been led to believe it had been gotten rid of long ago. His father said that he had disposed of it when many types of military weapons within the city's confines fell under new laws of the Unifier.

"Mercy? Your husband has clearly broken the Laws of Avanor. A weaver cannot carry a sword, much less use a crossbow. Know that he will pay a great price," the man said icily.

"No, please. You don't understand. My husband is needed badly here. We will be on the streets if he is taken away. As it is, we struggle to pay for this dwelling," she stammered, fear strangling her words. "For our sakes, not his, spare him."

Thomas knew enough of his mother's past to know she had not been a stranger to hard times, even having lived through the dark time when the weavers rebelled together with their refusal to work. Her own uncle had been one of the weavers' number during that arduous, painful time.

The plea had no effect upon the militia man. His steely, unforgiving eyes regarded her quietly for a few tense moments. He then spoke in a low, purposeful tone. "He is going to be given a proper place in the Tomb Hall. He will likely have his own Tomb soon enough, foolish woman. You should have counseled him better."

Thomas ran up to the man, breaking out of his silence as he was overcome with emotion. He did not even hear his mother cry out for him to stop what he was doing, as he fell at the man's feet, clutching at his leg. "He does not need to be in the Tomb Hall! Take the sword, good sir, but do not take my father. Show us mercy, please!"

"Your father broke the law," the watchman growled, his hand flashing out to grab Thomas by his tunic at the shoulder. With a forceful yank, he wrenched Thomas up to his feet, and held him in place. It was clear there would be no chance of parley with the watchman.

Even so, Thomas still pleaded further with the watchman in his desperation, but his words were like a clay vessel dropped against a stone floor, fracturing into uselessness. The anguish he felt was too much to hold back, as he started to sob.

The watchman gruffly pushed by him, continuing the investigation of the rest of their dwelling. He muttered to his comrades, "Let us see what else can be found under this roof."

They resumed the search of the abode, soon finding the crossbow, and a few remaining bolts. "Do you own twenty livres of property? I do not think so," sneered another watchman to Alice, as he held up the crossbow.

The reference was to recent laws that had firmly restricted ownership of crossbows and bolts to the more wealthy classes. Weavers were definitely not to be found in those classes.

No corner was left unexamined, and Emma was discovered as well, up in the garret. Fortunately, the guards had already found what they were searching for and paid her little heed. She slipped quickly down from the garret and moved to Alice's side, where Thomas had also taken his place.

Though his sister said nothing, there was as much anger as there was fear in her expression, and Thomas did not miss the faint quivering of her lips. He could only hope that she did not lash out, as the telltale sign indicated a level of indignation and defiance that was on the verge of exploding.

The militia guards finally stopped when they deemed that the residence had been thoroughly scoured. The watchmen produced a small cache of silver coins, deniers stowed away by either Thomas' mother or father. With a mocking smile, the watchman who had first climbed the steps placed the coins in a pouch strung on his waist.

"Did not find any coins, though," he said, with an air of derision. "These were in my pouch from the moment I entered this place, yes?"

Thomas hated the man, wishing he could wield a sword, or lay his hands on the crossbow to defend his mother, sister, and father. The man was displaying lawlessness, even as he claimed to be upholding the laws of Avalos. The recognition of the hypocrisy grated bitterly within Thomas, but he felt his mother's hands firmly holding him at the shoulders, from behind.

He clenched his teeth, shaking with rage, though he stifled a vocal response. He knew such an act would profit nothing, and would likely bring more harm to his family.

Emma displayed as much restraint and discipline as Thomas, and did nothing to provoke the armed men, but the emotions churning within her finally boiled over as several tears began trickling down her cheeks.

A few moments later, the men from the city watch left with Thomas' father in their custody. His hands bound tightly, William was prodded along through a crowd of onlookers and gawkers, who had begun to gather in front of their home.

Thomas had watched the spectacle after breaking free from his mother and stumbling down the stairs, after his father, hardly believing what was happening. He heard Emma following close behind. Everything was surreal, like the contents of a nightmare he wished he could wake up from.

His attention was so hemmed in by the ongoing nightmare that he could not even sense the throbbing ache on his face where the watchman had landed the backhanded blow. He strode through the front door and into the street, drawing a few eyes in his direction.

Thomas felt antipathy welling up towards the crowd of spectators. Not one moved the smallest muscle to defend his father, who had done nothing less than what they would have done, if their own streets were threatened by a violent mob of students. Not a peep of protest emerged from the crowd. To Thomas' eyes they all looked to be little more than sheep.

Though Thomas had no way of knowing, several of the faces in the crowd had taken part in the fighting with the rioting students. They now kept quiet, avoiding attention as none wanted to share the fate of Thomas' father.

Thomas looked around as he felt his life spinning rapidly out of control. Town houses and shops, as long as Thomas remembered, had always leaned towards each other on the narrow city streets. It had never distracted him before, or seemed odd in any way. Now, those same constricted avenues and tilting structures seemed to be pressing in upon his very self. It was like his entire world was closing in upon him.

The same sensation applied to the plethora of bad smells permeating most any urban street, buoyed by the refuse and animals contributing daily to the pungent aromas. To Thomas, the stench was now more noticeable than ever before. He had the impression it was driven not just by physical waste or animals, but by the nature of the people crowding the street.

Things of his normal, daily existence were quickly taking on immensely personal, hostile meanings. He had never felt such a torrid anger in his entire life. His resentful thoughts turned to which one of the onlookers had betrayed his father to the watchmen, as he knew with certainty that someone had done so.

The rising humiliation and anger was cut short, as he fixed his eyes upon the erect posture of his father. Head held high, his father cooperated with the militia watchmen, giving them no cause to abuse him further.

The scene was deeply embedded in Thomas' mind. Even in that dark moment he found shreds of pride in witnessing the dignified disposition of his father. His father did not cower or grovel, carrying himself with honor in the face of the terrible pageant playing out.

"Come, Thomas, Emma … come with me," a soft voice said, as his mother gently hugged Thomas and his sister to her, from behind.

He could hear her fighting back the sobs thickening in her voice, trying to be strong as she walked back with them into the street level door. Emma halted in the doorway, her face tear-stained as she looked back and watched their father being led away like a common criminal. Thomas put his arm around her shoulders, gently pulling her away from the terrible sight and into their home.

Thomas was glad they did not delay in moving his father onward. Enough of a display had been presented to the surrounding rabble.

A sense of hollowness gripped Thomas, as his mother shut the door behind. He stood silent for a long time, and neither he, nor Emma, or his mother moved from the dark, heavy stillness inside the closed door. The sounds of the street resuming early morning activity reached their ears through the wooden planks

A gentle knock came at the door after a few more moments passed, quite unlike the one that had come earlier that morning. Wordlessly, his mother turned, and slowly opened the door.

She stepped back to let an elderly man in. Almost shuffling more than walking, wearing an old, brown tunic descending well below the knees, Thomas' grandfather, his mother's father, entered the workroom.

His thin, gray hair had receded greatly, and his creased skin displayed the kinds of spots not uncommon to one so advanced in years. His eyes, though, were anything but dull, the blue color still sparking with the vitality of the sharp mind resting just behind them.

Thomas watched as his mother moved to embrace the older man, exclaiming, "Father! We are destroyed!"

From the embrace, the old man reached over and placed his hand gently on Thomas' head first, and then on Emma's, in gestures of compassion and empathy.

"Tell me. Tell me what has happened," he implored Alice in low tones. "I was kept outside, as I was on my morning walk. I cannot abide long in the hospital, even if the monks and Sisters mean well enough."

"Let me get you a seat, Father," she replied through reddened eyes, walking across the workroom to retrieve a stool for the old man to sit upon.

A stark thought struck Thomas as he eyed the simple wooden stool. There would be no use for it by the loom that day, or perhaps any other. A terrible pang hit him in the gut at the recognition, and his eyes welled with tears of sorrow and helplessness.

His mother related what had just transpired, including the events of the night before. She paused several times to regain her breath, in the midst of a cavalcade of words and tears.

The old man's thin, haggard face could still evince an ample display of anger. His eyes narrowed, and his mouth tensed, as the story was told. Thomas noticed his grandfather's hands, clasped together in his lap, were gripped tightly such that his gnarled knuckles grew whiter as the telling proceeded.

His cracking voice spurted his furor, "When a man can no longer protect his own homestead, he cannot hope to ever be free … for a free man has the means and right to defend his family and home from harm.

This is indeed a dark, dark day … in a very dark age, my daughter."

He looked over to Thomas and Emma, and his look softened. He beckoned to them. "Come here … the both of you … come here."

Thomas stepped forth with Emma, and they wrapped their arms around their grandfather, tears of his own breaking free and streaming down his face. His father and mother were the backbone of everything he had known. He had just seen the foundations of his life shaken to the core. In the aftermath of the shock, emotions were surging within.

The old man slowly raised his hands, and lightly patted Thomas and his sister upon their heads. "I wish I had the money to make things different. Alas, my life has been one of strife and poverty. I have never apologized for my station in life, but I regret now that I was not born to a higher station."

"But you are a rich man, even now," his daughter, now looking up at him, returned with a suddenly fiery countenance. A measure of Alice's spirited nature had come back in the wake of her father's lament. "They can never take that from you, or my husband."

The old man smiled. "Aye, I am rich in the things that can be taken from this world. You are wise to remind me of that, though I have not forgotten it. And I am not poor in other ways, some of which may yet be of use."

"What will happen to Father?" Thomas asked, fearing the answer even as he voiced the question.

"I have no good answer. They will take him to the tombs under the castle, and hold him there until he goes before royal justice. I will not lie to you, Thomas. There is little hope that things will go well for your father, though I wish I could say otherwise," his grandfather stated heavily, his eyes filled with sadness.

"I cannot believe that. Surely there is a way to plead to the Unifier," his mother said, her eyes showing that a desperate hope was yet clinging to her.

"To hell with the Unifier," Thomas shot back defiantly. "Father is no danger to anyone. He was only defending our homes and the people being hurt in the riots. He was not the attacker. The watchmen were doing nothing to defend us. Why can they not see that? Why must they lock him up?"

"Justice is not something achieved by the rulers of men," his grandfather replied. "Your father was not wise to keep the sword or the crossbow … though in a truly just world he would never have feared to possess them. I worried that the weapons would be discovered some day, and told him it was ill-advised to keep them, though I confess I shared his reasons for harboring them.

"I heard the talk already on the street. Students rioting once again for lower rents, for yet more rights. They become a crazed, uncontrollable mob. For claiming to be dedicated to things of the mind, it is indeed amazing how bestial and brutal they become. They should simply be grateful they can learn and not be made to plough a field," the old man finished, with a tone of disgust.

He turned to fix Thomas with a piercing stare. The young grandson saw the sharp look within the eye of his grandfather, an admonition in itself.

"Say nothing about the Unifier where ears can hear. You may think whatever you may in the privacy of your mind, but you must learn to control what comes out of your mouth. You will only invite trouble that you cannot hope to overcome. You must choose the time to speak, and the place to speak, Thomas, with great care," his grandfather admonished.

Thomas felt an overpowering sense of helplessness engulf him. As he saw things, there was no one who could stand up to the Unifier. There was no one that could oppose His vast armies, culled from all across the known world. Worst of all, there was no one who could help his father. Thomas had never felt so utterly small, as he did not know how he could ever hope to save his father.

Overwhelmed with a debilitating feeling of loss, he lowered his head, feeling a little ashamed as he continued to cry. A few tears fell downward, striking the tiny mark that had recently been made on his left wrist. The blemish on his skin was part of the unprecedented requirement of the citizens of Avalos, one evidently being demanded all over Avanor.

Normally, he thought little of the mark. Now, he absolutely hated the sight of the mark. It represented the powers who had taken away his father. If he had a blade, he knew he would have sliced it right off in that moment.

He felt the gentle hand of his grandfather rest again upon his shoulder. "Even the greatest of empires and kingdoms eventually fall. That is a lesson any student of history knows. It is what each of us do in our lives that we must account for," he said, benevolently. "Live your life to the utmost, and you will surprise yourself at the force one man can become. Just one man can affect history by his actions."

The words halted the despair sprawling uncontrollably within Thomas, as they rang with the force of undeniable truth. Slowly, Thomas brought his eyes back up to meet those of his grandfather.

"One man can really affect history?" Thomas asked.

His grandfather nodded resolutely, and replied with confidence, "Yes, just one man, Thomas. That is all it takes sometimes to change the course of the world."

Thomas' gaze then hardened, as a feeling of resolution took hold within his heart. His voice held no trace of the choking sobs of a few moments before, as he replied with a defiant timbre, "Then, grandfather, I promise you that the Unifier will know one day that I am one such man."

AETHELHERE

Athelhere once again found himself musing upon home and hearth. His weathered, thickly-callused hands rested on the top edge of the warship's side, where he stood near to the bow of the stout, monoreme war galley Honor Bound. The memories both soothed and tormented him, as he had no way of knowing whether his young wife and sons were secure, or were under threat.

His wife Healfwina, and one of his sons, the youngest, a boy named Wyfrith, were now in Landahn. The strong port-city, perched on the eastern edge of Saxany, was still far beyond the main battle lines. But Aethelhere knew that ominous shadows were spreading all across their world, and the city could not avoid their baleful reach forever.

Though he tried not to think of it, the tilts and shifts of the war might already have pushed those battle lines much closer to Landahn, without him even knowing about it. Yet despite the icy fears, he knew Healfwina and Wyfrith were likely in much better stead than they would have been if Aethelhere had followed his emotions, and brought them along on the voyage.

His other son, Wynoth, who had been fostering with his brother Aethelstan, was another matter entirely. Wessachia was inescapably near the front lines of the conflict. Aethelhere could not help but think that Wynoth was facing imminent danger, or, even worse, had already been swept up in the traumatic events of the war.

He struggled to keep the paralyzing fears out of his mind, mental torments buoyed by the Avanoran-led invasion that had so swiftly turned his world into an unpredictable maelstrom. He wrenched his mind from the deep troubles, as dwelling upon the worries would improve nothing.

The immediate world before him came back to the fore of his thinking, with a little further concentration. At last, his surroundings came into focus, as the anxieties were tamped back down.

The sun gleamed on the gentle waters, the weather continuing to remain favorably calm. A rolling, undulating field of shimmering sparkles extended far and wide.

Fortune had indeed blessed the Saxan fleet, as they had encountered no enemy fleets, sudden tempests, or the threats inherent in some rarer kinds of sea creatures. Even more promising, the winds had been generous, allowing the vessels to continuously make use of the power of sails.

The ship crews had been able to handle the routines required without undue strain. The position of sails were altered from time to time, and a multitude of chores focusing on feeding, cleaning, and general ship readiness were attended to without distraction. Muscle was put to oar only occasionally, when the winds slacked. The favorable situation far exceeded Aethelhere's wildest hopes.

Aethelhere wanted the crews well-rested and in good spirits, taking full advantage of the propitious conditions. It was a great boon to his overall plan that he was able to keep the crews in such a good state of morale and readiness. They were in excellent shape to meet whatever trials might suddenly befall them.

Other than keeping a close eye out for the anticipated moment that the contours of a shoreline broke the distant horizon, there was relatively little to occupy himself with during the travel. He knew it would not be much longer before that moment arrived, as scouts on far-ranging Himmerosen had indicated land was approaching fast to the north.

There was only one minor incident that day, with the sighting of a huge sea serpent. Winding its way harmlessly along the surface, it had glided through the center of the fleet.

Over one hundred feet long, and four times as wide as a man, the serpent's scaly form had broken the water's surface just off the port side of Honor Bound. The serpent was certainly large enough to create mischief, or worse, for various ships in the fleet, had it been so inclined. Fortunately, the serpentine leviathan paid the Saxan ships little heed, as it traveled peaceably onward.

Other creatures provided far less trepidation, such as a large group of dolphins that had traveled alongside the starboard side of the fleet for many leagues. Gracefully bounding in and out of the water, the dolphins evoked much joy and laughter from the ships' crews and warriors. Aethelhere felt a little melancholic when the dolphins finally parted ways with the fleet.

The dampened feeling did not last long, as the fleet was visited shortly after by another oceanic throng. Even more laughter was elicited from the ship crews by a boisterous pack of sea bears. The spirited creatures swam in from the east, seeking to fill their curiosity at the presence of such a vast fleet of humans traversing the territory they were now hunting in.

Though much larger than seals, the burly sea bears were obviously related to the more commonly seen ocean denizens. The sea bears had longer, broader heads, and substantial girth, which all brought to mind thoughts of the land-dwelling bears who had given rise to their name. The sea bears were reputed to possess great intelligence, and could be found ranging far from any known land source, even within the middle waters of the great Dranian Sea.

Bolstering the overall sense of excitement was the fact that sea bears were an uncommon sight for Saxan ship crews. Even among those who often traveled upon the seas, few could tell of seeing the brawny sea creatures more than once. The only rarer creature of their oceanic ilk was a wolf-resembling breed, which was said to exist in the waters off the coast of Midragard.

For such great size, the creatures moved with exceptional speed, which came as a surprise to many observing them. They kept pace easily enough with the ships, and a few of their number even began to dip and dart among the ships in the midst of the fleet. Their large eyes carried a keen edge, as they carefully scrutinized the humans watching them from the ships.

While cautious, the sea bears did not seem to greatly fear the ships. It was as if they could somehow discern the lack of threat, or knew by experience what ships were. What little timidity they initially exhibited eroded gradually, as they became more familiar with the Saxan fleet. The sea bears increased their boldness, several coming close alongside the dromonds, galleys, and other vessels in the sprawling formation.

Aethelhere had laughed aloud as a particularly large sea bear kept up with the bow of Honor Bound, looking almost quizzical as it stared towards the Saxan commander. To Aethelhere's eyes, the creature had the pleading look of a dog, as if it were begging for food in a manner not unlike the canines populating Saxan settlements, villages, and the long halls of thanes.

"Sorry lad, I can't spare any food for you! We're going to need all we have for this journey!" Aethelhere had called out to the creature. "Maybe find me when all this is over!"

The creature stared at him for another couple of moments, not showing any sign of whether it registered Aethelhere's response or not. Aethelhere laughed heartily at the playful fellow.

The sea bear's head then abruptly jerked back, as if startled. It descended quickly under the surface, as a sudden commotion broke out among the other sea bears. With a chorus of throaty barks and yelps, and a flurry of violent splashes of water, the pack scurried from the fleet in great haste.

A pang of anxiety touched him, as Aethelhere wondered what could possibly have startled the creatures so much. Moments later, his answer manifested as the huge dorsal fin of a shraka broke the water just off the starboard bow. The gargantuan, shark-like hunter was no threat to the ships, but was a tremendous danger to the sea bears.

Though the rapid departure of the sea bears was a great disappointment to those on the ships, it was probably better for the fleet that they left the vicinity. The plump, friendly sea bears would have become a lingering distraction to ship chores and tasks during the extended monotony of an uneventful day.

Even so, Aethelhere whispered a silent prayer of encouragement for the sea bears to prove their mettle as evasive prey to the massive shrakas lurking in the oceanic depths. The shraka near the vessel was likely trolling casually through the waters, as the predators tended to strike up at their prey, rising from beneath. Most likely, the pack of sea bears would all remain intact, a comforting proposition to Aethelhere's mind.

The Saxan fleet commander always savored the positive experiences during a sea voyage. He had been on many seafaring excursions, on single ships and as part of fleets, during the course of his passage to becoming the highest naval commander in all of Saxany. While his older brother Aethelstan had remained landward, awaiting his installation as a prestigious thane over the market town and royal mint at Bergton, Aethelhere had gained as much experience as he could on the decks of ships plying the waters off Saxany's coast.

He had come to know many types of ships intimately. He knew the various rowing and sail craft used on rivers, as well as the larger galleys built in the northern part of Saxany, vessels not altogether unlike those of Midragardan design. The ship he knew best and enjoyed most was Honor Bound, of the particular type long constructed in the south.

From crews to ships, he knew what his range of expectations should realistically be, for many different scenarios. The current voyage, despite the desperate circumstances looming over them, continued to go smoother than almost any other in his recollection. It was fast becoming far more than a welcome surprise, as the whole mission had been a hastily arranged effort, of unprecedented proportions.

Every ship deemed capable of making the journey and able to be be scraped up had been brought along. While most of their best warships and galleys formed the core of the fleet, there were a few ships that might not have been used had there been less daunting challenges facing them. As it was, they needed every last bit of capacity they could muster, forcing some risks should inclement weather arise, or enemy threats emerge.

He did not regret taking on the risks. To Aethelhere's memory, Saxans had never before tried to provide rescue to the people of an entire land. There simply was no precedent to consider, and he had to do everything he could to carry out his onerous charge.

"Lord Athelhere! Lord Athelhere!" cried the lookout, a young lad named Eosterwine, from where he gazed out over the ocean from the single basket mounted high on the main mast.

The air filled swiftly with a bevy of excited cries, coming from both near and far, originating from the other warships in the vicinity. Numerous trained eyes had focused upon a most welcome new sighting.

The grizzled Saxan fleet commander moved quickly down the length of the deck, striding from the bow to the base of the main mast.

He was followed by two of his most senior crew members, who joined him below the elated lookout.

Shielding his eyes from the bright sun, Aethelhere turned his head upwards and squinted at the lookout. He could not see the joy etched in the young man's face, as the light striking directly from behind rendered the lookout into a small shadow-figure leaning over the basket's edge.

"What is it now, lad?" Aethelhere called up, his voice eager, as he had a good idea as to the nature of the cries echoing all around. He then jested, unable to stifle a grin, "Better not be any more worries of large Shrakas! They don't much like sinking their teeth into wood."

"No, my lord, no Shraka at all!" the young man responded, in obvious delight. "It is a long line of land ahead. A rising and falling line. I would say it is a land that is hilly, and thick with trees."

"And I would say it is a land we have been expecting to see!" Aethelhere shouted back to Eosterwine, thrilled at the news.

A radiant smile broke out over Aethelhere's face, bursting from the midst of his dense beard. He turned to the men standing attentive at his side. "It seems we have finally reached the lands of the Five Realms. I would hope they have reached the beaches at the Water Head-Cradle, so that we may pluck them out of their danger, and make our way back swiftly to Landahn."

"What would you have us do now?" inquired one of the senior crewmen, a burly, pock-marked man named Sigfrid.

"Let us not relax and depend upon the sail now. Let us begin our final approach with oar. Furl sails, and let us make double haste on the power of oars. Strength need not be conserved in full now," Aethelhere stated. "Send forth sky scouts to find out what has happened with our friends that we seek to meet. We need to confirm if they have indeed made it to the beach. Ready the men for the possibility of battle as well. We do not know what we may soon be confronting."

"I shall see it done," Sigfrid replied somberly, before striding down the ship and calling others to him.

Aethelhere waited calmly, knowing Sigfrid would carry out his charges well. Sigfrid commanded a high level of respect from the men of Honor Bound, as well as the captains of the other vessels.

In just a few moments, the loud, swelling blares of horn signals filled the air, conveying the message to the other ships of the fleet.

Following the horn signals to the others, Sigfrid's booming voice could be heard disseminating Aethelhere's orders to furl the sails and ready the oars, as the fleet commander turned his eyes toward the forward horizon.

It would not be much longer before they reached their intended destination. Aethelhere hoped with all of his might that they would not be arriving too late. Taking a deep breath, he began to whisper some prayers to the All-Father.

THE UNIFIER

Tongues of fire licked the darkness from the huge torches set into wall brackets. The firelight flickered off the smooth black walls, as the Unifier prostrated Himself within the center of the unholy chapel.

The chapel had been built deep within the mountainside palace, accessible only to the Unifier and any He chose to bring with Him. It was a place diligently warded, by diabolical guardians that bore a ravenous hunger to swallow anything of purity and innocence.

Directly underneath, and fully surrounding Him, a broad image had been carved deep into the stone surface. It took the form of a circle with six even shards radiating out from its center. It was a representation of the Dawn Star, the Unifier's personal sign, and a symbol of His own Infernal Lord.

Before Him was another Dawn Star, forged of black iron, and hanging from thick chains descending far down from the rib-vaulted ceiling. It was suspended directly over a simple altar of ebony stone, no more than a rectangular slab set atop two short, robust columnar supports upon the summit of a low dais reached by six steps.

Murmuring ancient chants, in a language whose origins were not rooted in Ave, the Unifier locked his mind out of the awareness of His immediate surroundings. He focused His inner being on His encompassing servitude to the Lord of Fire, Jebaalos, giving all His thoughts and will over to His transcendent overlord. Only within the absolute semblance of servitude and submission could He ever see fit to make a request of the Lord of Fire.

Outside His body, as if smoke sifting from the stone flooring and walls, black, foggy tendrils emerged slowly and began to swirl about the chamber. The deeply-etched Dawn Star beneath began to glow all along its edges, as did the Dawn Star hanging above the black altar. New tongues of flame were given birth, expanding in magnitude until the Unifier was ensconced within an inferno of blistering heat.

No harm came to His body or silken clothing, though the dense, ebon smoke filling and obscuring the small chamber would have choked any mere mortal to death quickly. Similarly, the searing heat being generated would have rapidly consumed any mortal flesh.

Once the chamber was saturated, the Presence finally arrived. Enveloping the chamber and its lone occupant, The Presence filled every last speck of space within the enclosed chamber.

An aura of unfathomable sentience and power rippled throughout the chamber. The inferno still blazed, and black smoke wafted in abundance, but an unimaginably icy chill, issuing from the purest essence of death and oblivion, replaced the scorching heat. The chamber was soon freezing, and no living being in Ave would have been able to last even a heartbeat within its embrace.

The feeling of the Presence deeply soothed the Unifier, as He drew into full harmony with Its essence. In His mind and spirit, the Unifier prostrated Himself in unconditional humility and obeisance to the Lord of Fire.

He cast forth only the single desire to locate more of the otherworlders, as a part of His committed service to His Father and Lord. His mind's eye saw only an impenetrable blackness, the darkness of pure oblivion, as He intoned His supplication again and again.

As if the Dawn Star was unveiling from within Him, progressing in a manner not unlike the symbols in the chamber, a circular pool of cold light emerged from a central point in the absolute blackness. Six large rays emanated and spread outward, to reach the edges of his mind's eye. The spaces in between the rays were gradually filled by an increasing number of light shards radiating from the center.

As it became ever more solidified, forming into an enormous pool of light taking up the Unifier's entire vision, other images began manifesting within it. Taking on recognizable forms, murky shapes clarified into vivid renderings of great rocks and a waterfall, before twisting, and coalescing, into a spectacular view of towering, snow-capped mountains.

The alternating visions repeated, growing in detail. Figures began to take form within each of the animated pictures.

Broad shouldered, thick bearded warriors wrestled in the open air, as crowds of gleeful onlookers surrounded them. Standards were planted in the ground, displaying a distinctive image flowing in the breezes; the head of a white wolf, upon a black background. The Unifier instantly recognized the image, and who it represented.

As if from the heights of a flying bird's view, the scene changed, altering to take in visions of horse races, merchant stalls, dancing, eating, and other activities. The view ascended, taking in an expansive field filled with tents and semi-permanent structures. As the vision grew, it revealed that the tents and shelters were situated not far from a large cluster of permanent buildings. A majestic, gable-ended hall in the midst of the edifices marked the heart of a powerful homestead.

Another standard was visible among the buildings of the homestead. It displayed black streaks of lightning across a white backdrop. A stark moment of recognition came to the Unifier, in regards to the identity of the individual represented by the sigil.

Another series of visions emerged. New images of mountains formed into clarity, though the rises were not nearly the size of the gigantic ones within the earlier revelations. Noticeably smaller peaks, they were draped in trees, and no deposits of snow crowned their summits.

A modest village with a number of figures moving around was then revealed, nestled within a small valley. The figures unveiled were humans, a mixture of people going about a number of menial daily tasks. Some bore wooden buckets of water, others were leading ox-drawn carts along a narrow path, while still others were attending to woodwork and carpentry.

Their clothes were those of peasants, including dull leather shoes, earthen-colored trousers and tunics on males, and long tunics of similar hues on females. Many of the men wore distinctive puttees, narrow strips of cloth wrapped around the lower length of their trousers up to their knees. Some of the men also wore a unique kind of woolen hat, which had forward-tilting apexes.

In a general sense, it could have been a scene derived from a large number of mountain villages within the western lands. At last, a figure wearing a shirt of chain mail, with an iron half-helm of a spangenhelm design atop his head, came into view. The man's sharp eyes looked about, as he scratched the emerging whiskers of a newer beard growing to catch up with the matured moustache resting above his mouth.

Gazing upon the attire, The Unifier was swiftly able to narrow the possible location of the mountain village now being revealed to Him. Outside of His body, the fire and smoke eventually receded, as the chamber returned to its former state. The permeating energy of the Presence occupying it just moments before swiftly vanished, taking a cumbrous weight from the air.

Only when the Presence fully departed the chamber did the Unifier begin to emerge from the trance-like state. To the Unifier, a feeling of great absence and separation came in the wake of His severance from full communion with the Presence. It was not the release from an oppressive, overwhelming force, as any bystander able to endure the conditions of the chamber would have felt, but rather the deprivation of the innermost part of His being.

An agonizing emptiness pervaded Him, and His spirit cried forlornly for a return back to complete union with the Presence. Every moment was torturous, as The Unifier endured the worst portion of His deep meditation during the moments the Presence withdrew.

It was quite some time before the Unifier was able to return to a full mode of consciousness, with awareness of His surroundings. Very slowly, He lifted His face from the umber floor, straightening His back as He rested for a few moments on His knees. He looked towards the Dawn Star hanging above the altar, feeling a deep longing that resounded throughout every element of His being. After a brief pause, He stood up in one graceful, smooth motion.

A renewed energy flowed into Him, and proceeded throughout Him, enriching His physical form, as it always did when He visited His Father's mystical sanctuary. To the Unifier, it was a true refuge, an oasis of spirit within the great palace complex.

His times in the chamber wove the aspects of a healthy life into the physical vessel of a being whose truest nature was aligned with an absence of life. At the same time, He knew His own powers had been sorely taxed. While He could tirelessly conduct affairs in a physical sense, it would be a little while before He could exert himself to the level it took to bridge realms of existence.

For a time, He would be vulnerable to the most powerful of His enemies, if they were aware of the reduction in strength accompanying His audiences with His Father. It was a reasonable risk, though, as He had become confounded by the lack of knowledge concerning the whereabouts of otherworlders not yet within His grasp. His enemies would have a limited amount of time to exploit His temporal weakness, as He would soon rejuvenate His supernatural energies.

There were things He could do to speed the recovery process, as blood and sacrifice were potent tools. Yet even those personally beneficial practices would have to be deferred until a later time. There was so much to be done, and not a moment to lose.

He knew where the first visions guided His attentions, with no doubts at all. The second group of visions was much less clear. The lands shown in the second group of visions was understood easily enough, but there would yet be many variables needing to be discerned.

Even as His Father's power helped to identify His targets, the Power of the Enemy would be working to obstruct His efforts. The Enemy would cast a dense mist over His special sight, even as His Father strove to bring things into clarity. It was a constant struggle, within a relentless war that had not let up for even an instant since the dawn of time itself.

His calf skin boots striking firmly upon the stone, the Unifier strode rapidly across the chamber. He paused only to unlatch a thick, iron-banded wooden door in the wall opposite the black altar.

Once He was across the threshold, and into the unlit passageway beyond the chamber, The Unifier turned and locked the door. He then walked many paces to the base of a winding stairwell, paying no attention to the ethereal gazes falling upon Him from the chamber's fearsome guardians. Without breaking his stride, He took the first step, and began the long climb upward.

THOMAS

"Here … just down this way he is, the old, surly bird," the Sister remarked cheerfully, her reference to Thomas' grandfather given in obvious jest.

With a warm smile, the nun led Thomas down the wide, vaulted chamber, lined on both sides by a fair number of large mattresses set upon the floor. The Sister had a light step and deceptively rapid stride.

Thomas found himself needing to quicken his own pace just to keep up with her. Her long tunic swished gracefully with her movements, as she continued down the center of the chamber.

An interior wall pierced by a couple of wide arches separated Thomas and the Sister from another section of the sprawling ward. The opposite wall contained a few windows looking out upon the outside world, which seemed so far away in the midst of the special environment surrounding Thomas.

He had not often visited the Hospital for the Aged, a charitable establishment once donated by the beloved Gallean King Louis the Faithful. Then again he had not often felt compelled to.

His grandfather had visited Thomas's own home often enough, and had ardently discouraged visits by the family to the hospital. Times had now changed, though, and Thomas found himself with a great need to visit the old man in the tumultuous wake of his father's arrest.

The dim chamber was filled with elderly men, often more than one to a mattress, as well as an assortment of Sisters and monks moving amongst them. The dutiful religious figures were bearing everything from cups of weak ale to strips of cloth, as well as herb poultices for dressing open sores, wounds, or other types of ailments.

Thomas could see at once why his grandfather loathed spending much time there. It was not the kind of scenery that tended to lift one's spirits. Yet for the aged poor, it was a wonderful boon, as it provided shelter, food, and medical care for a great many who otherwise would have had nothing.

His grandfather certainly did not begrudge the place, speaking well of the Sisters, monks, and Louis the Faithful's generous foresight. But neither did he try to claim the place was anything other than it was; a hospital for the aged and infirm.

Thomas' grandfather was seated on a little stool, set by one of the mattresses abutting the interior wall. His head was angled downward, his face a mask of concentration, and prayer beads were gripped lightly in one hand, as Thomas and the Sister approached. As if conferring a mystical grace upon his praying grandfather, warm rays of the sun bathed him, entering the chamber through one of the tall, narrow windows spaced evenly along the opposite wall.

There was a small wooden bowl with a spoon resting inside it on the floor, smeared with the vestiges of some type of pottage, as well as an empty wooden cup. A small, square wooden chest rested against the wall, nestled by the mattress on the side his grandfather was seated on. A couple of woolen blankets lay in a disheveled state upon the hemp-filled mattress. The items represented almost the entirety of his grandfather's worldly possessions.

"Here he is, the irascible fellow," the Sister indicated with a chuckle, as they drew near to the old man.

His grandfather slowly looked up as the Sister spoke. He said, in a subdued voice, "Just paying my respects to the Sacred Lady, Sister." He raised the prayer beads in his right hand, as if to offer proof,

"Always a good thing, Wace," the Sister commented brightly. "Helps one to see the better things in this world, and even sometimes a hint of what is ahead and beyond."

"As I get older, I have come to see that you are right," his grandfather replied, with a gentle smile. "And it is never a bad thing to wish for the healing of this corrupt world. Though sometimes I grow impatient with what I see out there."

"As do I, Wace, but the fact that you see the corruption for what it is shows you are indeed a soul whose world is not this one. Take some heart in that," the Sister replied with a hint of sagacity. She then smiled, turning to include Thomas in her gaze as she continued to face his grandfather. Her voice returned to its merrier tone. "And now that you two are together, I must beg leave, as there is never enough time to do what needs to be done around here."

"I'll not take up much more of your time, but I do appreciate you bringing me my grandson," Wace said.

"It is a light task that I wish I had much more often than others," she replied merrily.

"And I will try to be less … irascible, as you say," Wace added with a chuckle of his own.

"I always like seeing you a little irascible, as it reminds me you've got some fight left in you," the Sister riposted.

"Then I will continue being so," Wace said, laughing.

As if an afterthought, she bent downward to retrieve the small bowl and cup.

"Thank you, Sister, for helping me," Thomas said.

"You are very welcome, and may the All-Father's Light go before you, young man" she said warmly, before walking away to tend to other beckoning duties.

One look around the chamber told Thomas that her statement regarding her work was no exaggeration. He watched as an older monk holding a small bowl gently spoon fed a very ancient, frail-looking man on the opposite side from his grandfather. The various chores and needs in such a place were quite possibly endless.

When they were alone, his grandfather said to Thomas, "Sister Eleanor is indeed a good spirit, journeying on the right path. And no, I do not give her much trouble. So, young Thomas, what brings you here today? This is not the kind of place for a young boy with the grand adventure of a full life ahead of him."

"Everything is getting worse, grandfather. Faster than I can handle," Thomas said bluntly, his voice low, and burdened with the weight of everything he was feeling. His posture sagged as if the restraints within finally gave way.

"Here, sit on the floor, you can do so while you are young," his grandfather directed, eyes brimming with concern.

Thomas crossed his legs as he slowly sat down on the floor, before his grandfather.

"Go on," his grandfather gently urged.

"Hervee of Delshire has said nothing, but I know that he will not let us keep the house forever. We will not be able to keep up with the rents. Nicholas will have to seek work elsewhere, and you already know the watchmen stole the deniers saved by my parents," Thomas said. His heart felt increasingly heavier as he pointed out each of the considerable pressures affecting his family. His greatest concern was the last one he gave voice to. "And Mother does not speak much at all these days. Some days it is like Emma and I are invisible to her. She grows distant, and there seems to be nothing we can do to help her."

"Maybe the guild will see to her difficulties, at least through the Brotherhood of Saint Onofrius," Wace responded.

"But she is not a widow," Thomas said.

He left the brooding, dreadful worry that constantly plagued his thoughts of the future unspoken. Thomas was not naïve in regards to matters of royal justice, even as young as he was. It was a very real possibility that his mother would become a widow very soon, and that he and Emma would find themselves fatherless. The mere thought of that likely reality clenched at his gut, with a merciless, unrelenting vigor.

"Perhaps they will still find a way to help her, even if she is not a widow" his grandfather stated reassuringly.

"But she cannot care for Emma and myself, and I have no true trade, as of yet," Thomas said ruefully. "I can work all day, and still not provide well for them. I have been trying to think of a way I can help, but nothing comes to me."

"It is good of you to think of these things, for it shows you have the heart of a man," Wace said, his face slowly becoming pensive.

His voice was soft, and filled with compassion. Even his wrinkles seemed deeper, as if his face was streaked with new, additional lines of worry. "It is a hard matter to be faced with, so suddenly, at your age," Wace said, after a long pause.

"But it must be faced. I cannot live with mother and Emma being in any kind of trouble or hardship," Thomas replied, somberly.

"I would not expect you to accept anything other than their well-being," Wace stated.

"Hugh is not a tradesman either, and I do not wish to see him pulled from the University at the Island City," Thomas continued. "Father wanted so much for him to be there, and I wish for him to be able to stay there."

"Your brother is on a good path. The Church sponsors him in his studies, so he is of no additional burden to the matters now facing your family," Wace replied calmly. "And you are right, in that it means much to your father that Hugh is studying at the University."

"So what do I do?" Thomas asked, looking up slowly.

His words sounded a little of desperation. The stoic manner he was struggling to project was blurred with the fears and uncertainties of a normal twelve-year old boy; caught up within an unexpected maelstrom.

The gentle continuum he had known, allowing him to grow into full adulthood in a smooth, determined fashion, had been ripped right from under him. He had to accelerate everything about life in an impossibly short time.

With his father being held within the Tomb Hall, he fathomed that only his grandfather might have some sort of direction for him to take. His eyes fixed upon his grandfather with a slim hope, the latter straining valiantly against the growing despair clouding his heart.

Wace's eyes bore down on Thomas, and his voice was imbued with the sort of conviction that could only come from a perspective gleaned through a lifetime of struggles and experiences. "You must be open to the possibility of opportunity. You must not give in to hopelessness, no matter how hard it presses upon you now. You are not destroyed, and neither is your family. A chance is a chance, no matter how dark the skies."

"What opportunity? What chances?" Thomas responded dourly. "There is little such for the son of a weaver. How do you know there will ever be an opportunity? How can one wish for something that will likely never be?"

His grandfather laughed, and there was a spark of bright gaiety in his eyes. "I imagine that is hard to believe, hearing it from one who must now live in a charitable house for old men and women of no means. What wisdom can possibly be taken from a poor old man in the Hospital for the Aged, yes?"

"Mother and father always wanted you to stay with us," Thomas replied firmly, feeling a little defensive, as he had suggested nothing disdainful about his grandfather's condition.

In truth, he had always felt the same way as his parents had, harboring an abiding affection for his grandfather. At the very least, he had thought that by coming to see his grandfather within the hospital, he would have plainly conveyed how much he valued his grandfather, and how much he needed him.

"The humor is my own, no offense intended to you, young Thomas," his grandfather replied, evidently perceiving the youth's raw sensitivity. "Yes, your mother and father insisted for me to stay in your home. And I know that you and Emma would have welcomed me happily. It was I who refused. It was all my choice, one made for much the same reasons that you worry yourself about right now.

"I did not wish to be any sort of burden, and I knew this place would let me lay my head down with a roof over it. It would also keep some food in my stomach," Wace stated, slowly and succinctly. "I do not have much longer before I journey to the realms of the All-Father, for greater adventures yet to come. So I do not worry about enduring some discomforts here, for the short time left to me. You could say I am waiting my time out, until I am called to be my true self."

"True self?" Thomas asked, inquisitively. His curiosity was a kind of mercy, enabling him a moment's escape from the worries plaguing him.

STEPHEN ZIMMER

Wace rolled up his loose-fitting tunic sleeve and pinched a fold of leathery skin along the lower part of his arm. With an amused expression, he asked, "Do you think for a moment that this is your true self? Truly I tell you, Thomas, it is simply a shell, one taken on and then cast off like a tunic, as one is born and dies. This truth I am fortunate in telling you, in that I can say it with great certainty."

"It is what the Church says, what we are to believe," Thomas said, matter-of-factly. His voice took on a tilt of curiosity, as he continued, "but how do you know with great certainty?"

Wace smiled. "That, my young friend, and dear grandson, is a long story, coming from years ago. But I have been in my spirit before. I know that everything that we are can truly exist … aye, indeed thrive … apart from this bag of bones."

Thomas' eyes widened, as the curiosity within him was stoked further. He knew little of what his grandfather had done in his life, other than that he had been on many far travels as a pilgrim to holy sites. Out of the relatives he was aware of, his grandfather was regarded as the most devout with regards to the Western Church.

Thomas listened closely, as his grandfather began to speak. His anticipation was rampant towards the revelation that appeared to be forthcoming.

THE UNIFIER

Chilling winds blowing across the aging night caressed the unblemished face of the Unifier. The ground passed by in a blur far beneath Him.

His own sky steed, a particularly regal, powerful Harrak, was one that had been ceremoniously presented to Him by the great Trogen chieftain Framorg, on behalf of all the Trogen clans. The elegant creature passed gracefully forward on the steady winds, soaring ever farther beyond the lofty palace-mount of Avalos.

Given the name of Pyrinos, the wondrous steed would have been deeply envied by any veteran sky warrior, its powerful frame gliding seemingly effortlessly upon the flowing air currents. A prince of its kind, the creature behaved as if it was fully conscious of the vast authority of

622

its Master.

Other massive, prideful Harraks required a determined, disciplined rider to control them. In contrast, the Unifier's Harrak complied with His desires, to such an incredible degree that it appeared as if the creature could somehow anticipate the Unifier's every whim.

The Unifier guided Pyrinos with a relaxed ease, as they flew over the huge city spread out below them. Rider and steed continued onward, flying towards the open, rolling lands lying beyond the outermost suburbs of Avalos. They soon passed directly over those suburbs, a teeming mass of buildings and market spaces stretching far beyond the city's main walls.

The suburban mass outside the walls contained many open workspaces for the various trades requiring such ground, like the fullers, dyers, and tenters. The outer areas also provided for the necessary crafts not quite as welcome within the more congested spaces inside the city's walls, such as tanners, butchers, and larger livestock merchants.

During the day, the suburbs were awash with activity, but at the moment, the entire area seemed deep in slumber. Occasional sounds of animals broke the stillness. A few dogs barked excitedly at the overhead fliers. Other sounds included the eerie shrieks of a pair of cats scuffling in the darkness, as well as the whinnies of a few horses, sounding from where they were quartered on the grounds of the horse market.

The Unifier sensed the eyes of many gazing skyward from below. There was little doubt guards of the city watch were taking full note of the contingent flying overhead. Whether coming upon craftsmen breaking guild rules by working at night, or discovering homeless individuals who had not taken refuge at one of the ubiquitous churches throughout the city, the men fulfilling militia duty were quickly aware of any aberrations within their often dull routine.

Fanned out a short distance beneath the Unifier was a group of orderly, highly-disciplined warriors from the elite palace garrison. Culled from the best of His palace warriors, the large cluster of Avanorans were hardened, dedicated souls, fighters not easily unnerved.

All were revered knights of Avanor, carrying themselves with proud bearing. Each was covered in links of mail, effectively wrapped in iron from head to foot. The upper portion consisted of a knee-length chain mail shirt, with full-length arms ending in cloth-palmed, mail mittens. The lower part included full chain mail leggings, which the mail shirts overlapped, protecting the knights from their upper thighs down to their encased feet.

They sat tall in their saddles, their sleeveless white supertunics reflected the bathing moonlight streaming down from above. Their visor-affixed, flat-topped helms, pierced with numerous ventilating holes, glinted and shimmered in the silvery luminescence. They turned their determined gazes from side to side, and up and down, assiduously scanning the area for any unexpected disturbances.

They had long since become accustomed to unusual sights, the latter increasing in frequency. Serving as messengers, escorts, and as the center-most element of the palace guard, there were no others who would have been appropriate for the unique task now at hand.

To the Unifier's immediate right and left, riding upon steeds far different in nature than his own, were the shrouded forms of two powerful Arcamons. Only the ends of their hideous, elongated faces pushed out from the depths of the hoods encompassing their heads. Eyes like searing flames burned deep inside the black sockets set within their taut, leathery visages.

The location of the evening's rendezvous had been prearranged well in advance. The cloaking cover of darkness, and the remoteness of the meeting site, would largely shelter the participants from any widespread observation. The only risks involved a few scant rumors and ale-imbued mutterings derived from the mouths of peasants, all of which could be easily dismissed, or even suppressed, if ever the need arose.

The Unifier set his eyes upon a wide, cleared meadow, situated close to an outlying, and secluded, small village. He took his steed into a gradual descent, before landing in the center of the open expanse.

Virtually no sound was made as the Arcamons landed their own reptilian steeds to each side of the Unifier. The escorting band of Avanoran warriors remained above, breaking their cohesive formation apart. They divided into a host of pairs, undertaking an assortment of low, wide-ranging patrols covering the entire vicinity.

All eyes, even those of the Unifier, were soon focused upwards. In unison, they all looked expectantly towards the night skies.

They did not have long to remain in a state of anticipation. The last arrivals expected at the moonlit gathering finally arrived.

No crier would be required to herald their presence, though their authority and potency were far beyond that of any mortal kings. The mere sight of them could make a fierce army shudder to its core, but they caused no anxiety to the Unifier, or to the Arcamons waiting patiently on the ground below.

The colossal forms lowered, descending from the uppermost heights. They cast expansive, rapidly growing shadows, fueled by the light of the two moons. The lunar orbs and the immense, dark forms were largely unobstructed in the clear sky, which was only sporadically crossed with thin tendrils of clouds.

A puissant turbulence was generated by the approach of four Elder dragons. The force whipped up caused the branches of nearby trees to bend to such an extreme degree that many snapped loudly, submitting to the pressing, unyielding strain placed upon them.

The escorting Avanoran warriors had already given the meadow a wider berth. The riders had hastily spurred their steeds at the initial approach of the massive dragons, seeking to gain a far distance from the enormous creatures' landing area. They were desperate to avoid being cast about helplessly within the increasing force of the winds, forcefully generated by the beating wings of great dragons.

A few riders and steeds were momentarily tossed about about like wayward leaves, caught in the outermost fringes of the turbulence. The riders held on tightly as the Harraks struggled against the overpowering force. Much to the relief of the riders, the Harraks finally regained their equilibrium, and passed safely beyond the outer grip of the dragon-generated tempest.

The flying monstrosities were not wholly unexpected by the Avanorans. The Unifier made sure the knights knew what to expect. Yet the Elders' close presence, and their sheer size, caused more than a few Avanorans and their steeds to quaver in fright.

Though the nearby village slumbered quietly in the unconscious depths of night, a few Avanoran knights landed in its midst. After alighting, the warriors positioned themselves carefully, setting up a close watch on the thatch-covered, timber buildings housing the village's humble occupants.

They looked assiduously for any peasant foolhardy enough to think the sounds of turbulence outside were anything other than the offspring of a passing storm. Any emerging to catch a glimpse of the sky-born gathering would meet death quickly.

No word of the gathering with the Elder would be allowed to spread. The Unifier made that abundantly clear to the Avanorans delegated with enforcing His will. Unsheathed, steel-edged blades would be used to accomplish the grave charge.

The immense size of the oncoming dragons did not unsettle the Unifier in the least. Their great power was resolutely committed to His own Father, a factor giving Him power and authority over the winged titans.

They had already received the Hallowed Flames in the ceremonial ritual of Claimancy. With the Lord of Fire's Grace upon them, the four Elder would be safe from being swiftly immolated once across the veil between worlds, but the same power could also be used to consume them utterly, if they were to relent on their newly-rendered oaths.

When they alighted, the land underneath the huge, clawed feet of the four giant dragons gave a shudder and rumble upon their collective impact. The colossal beasts had landed where the Unifier desired, with the Unifier and two Arcamons centered in the midst of the winged juggernauts.

The gargantuan shadows cast by the beasts almost completely blotted out the meadow, even after they had folded their leathery wings into their elongated bodies. The eyes of the dragons smoldered, as they reacted to the first tinges of the Oath's baleful price. Despite the anger and resentment they felt at the onset of the draining sensation, they remained stoic, and fully attentive towards their new Master.

The Unifier knew the great dragons were filled with an insatiable hunger, whose relief could only be granted by the final victory of Jebaalos. The debilitation caused by the Ban was a small cost for them to endure, in contrast to the rewards they now stood to receive.

There were many immortals, great warriors, and exceptionally learned beings from across the history of Ave who would have understood the gravity of the moment. They would have found themselves beset with great dismay at the sight transpiring within the shadow-laced meadow.

The lofty dragons were four of the greatest among the ancient, mythical race of the Elder. Their race's presence had been virtually unknown to the world for countless centuries, ever since the Oath had been taken towards the end of the world's First Age.

In a trace measure of thought and glance, the Unifier could recognize the implications inherent in the Elders' presence. More than a few involved remembrances that condensed centuries of diligent, purposeful efforts, involving the courting of Elder possessed of dispositions susceptible to the seductive influence of Jebaalos.

His vision had observed the history of the Elder unfold from the moment of their race's inception. Each of the towering creatures now standing before the Unifier were ancients among the ancients of Ave, being one of the few races of living beings that time itself could not slay or weaken. The fiery eyes gazing down upon the Unifier in obeisance and deference had witnessed every Age of Ave's history, ever since their origin at the dawn of the world's Creation.

The Elder were so primeval in nature they had even beheld the genesis of the race of Elves. Among the creatures of Ave, only the venerable Wizards had known existence in the world for a longer period of time. In truth, the Elder had even existed since the Battle of the Great Schism, when the Lord of Fire had led the rebellion against the Order of the Creator.

The Unifier stifled an outbreak of rage threatening to surge from within at the bitterly hateful memory of the monumental Battle. He reminded Himself that the Elder in the meadow represented the immeasurable recovery, hope, and strength that had ascended from the ashes of that terrible defeat.

In the aftermath of that gargantuan battle, Jebaalos and the insurrectionist hosts of Archons had remained unbowed, and unrepentant. A new Kingdom arose to defy the Creator, founded in the depths of a fiery abyss. The reach of the infernal realm had quickly stretched from its stygian core to all corners of Ave. It had been nurtured, built upon, and advanced to incredible heights of power, of a magnitude whose full realization was now beginning to unfold.

Despite the great promise inherent within the current age, the turbulent periods of the past still had a claim on both the present and the future. The Unifier's thoughts regarding the four Elder broadened to contemplate others of their kind; the First Ones, Elder who had not taken the Oath, and gone into Exile.

Undeniably, the First Ones would always be foremost among the Elder in the mind of the Unifier. They had stood boldly with Jebaalos, at the dawn of the Great Rebellion. Their sacrifice and arduous state of existence since that fateful age could never be overlooked.

The four Elder in the meadow were not from that legendary group of Elder. Rather, the quartet represented an emerging vanguard of a newer force; one that would vastly increase the Unifier's power within

Ave.

The new Elder's mere appearance in the meadow heralded a potent new development within the Great War. The Unifier welcomed the commencement of the new phase in the War, embodied by the ancient creatures surrounding Him. Yet even in the midst of the triumphant moment, there was still an unmistakable taint of bitterness as thoughts of the First Ones returned to Him.

They had fought ferociously for the Lord of Fire at the beginning of the world, hurling their considerable might at the Heavens right after the creation of the first humans. The First Ones, despite being few in number, had shaken the heavens during the Battle of the Great Schism. In the aftermath of the galling defeat, the First Ones had been rendered outcasts. They had been numbered with the Lord of Fire and His battered legions of fell spirits.

The First Ones had tumbled down with all the others in the long, fiery descent that had followed. The echo of fury and pain from that horrible time still reverberated within the Unifier's consciousness. First Ones and Archons alike had plummeted far down, into a horrific realm comprised of shapeless, molten seas and unbound horizons of impenetrable darkness.

The Unifier stilled His roused emotions, as He felt Himself momentarily immersed within a feeling of blackest despair. He had to remind himself of the realities that ensued from the moment the netherworld had first begun to be molded by Jebaalos. Such realities entailed both the First Ones, and the faction of Elder represented by the four standing before Him.

A semblance of time and focus of Will were the sources of the clay with which all things already created could be reshaped into newer, mightier forms. They were also the means by which a pathway that led towards ultimate renewal and revenge could be traveled. It was a radiant course filled with promise. Tributaries involving the shifting of loyalties and the severing of oaths merged irrevocably into an immense river of power.

A tremendous reality beckoned, as a reunion spanning deep ages loomed. The Elder who had been steadfast from ancient times, the First Ones, would soon be joined with many others of their kind.

Not long ago, Jebaalos had allowed for a very special word to seep from the shadows, and spread among the Elder remaining in the havens in Ave. Whispers from the unseen world spoke of the unrepentant First Ones, swiftly catching the attentions of Elder whose hearts had gradually been filling with darkness.

Long since cast down and banished to suffer the horrors of the netherworld, memories of the First Ones had faded in the thoughts of those in Exile. Yet the Elder in the havens knew well that their renegade brethren had not been permanently destroyed.

The words sent from the abyss spread the tidings that the First Ones were soon to be guided back to the mortal world. It was said they would soon reunite with any brethren of theirs who would stand forth, and serve Jebaalos.

The Elder now serving the Unifier had since come to know that the return of the First Ones was more than just a rumor on the wind. Rather, it was a truth defiantly roaring at the heavens, buoying the commitment of the newer contingent of Elder to even greater heights. From seeming destruction within seas of fire, the fabled First Ones would rise anew, and take their place once again in the world.

To witness signs of that truth, the four Elder in the meadow had been chosen for the journey on the night at hand. Astarol, Iklan, Shogaul, and Gargartian were the strongest of the Elder in the Havens who had freely given their allegiances over to the Lord of Fire. They had also been the first to initiate the breaking of their loyalties to the old Oath, and consciously seek the favor of the Lord of Fire. As such, the Unifier was bestowing them with special favor, to be the first Elder since the beginning of the world to lay their eyes on their brethren who had been separated from them.

"A New Age dawns soon, and not a moment too soon," the Unifier stated, serenely.

Despite his diminutive physical form in proportion to the Elder, His voice carried amply to the massive dragons. He looked upward, gazing quietly at the behemoths gathered around Him.

Without exertion, He held their undivided attention as His commanding, powerful voice rang out boldly. "The New Kingdom shall rise in Ave, and you shall all be rewarded ten-fold for your service to our Lord, my Father".

He paused to read the minds of the beasts, the gateway made possible by their submission to the Lord of Fire. Their intelligence and cunning had always been as great as their physical size, but their motivations were elemental. The Elder sought to learn ancient mysteries and powers, and return to the world in full, with the bonds of the Oath and the Ban broken asunder. They desired prominence in the world once again, and to have other races accede to their rule.

The Unifier mused that the dragons were not so different from humans, at the basest level. He found irony in that reality, as the fate of the human race had once been a prime reason behind the justification for the Oath's creation.

The Unifier was not disturbed in the least that selfish motivations took precedence over any pure passion for serving Jebaalos. It was that way with most living beings comprised of spirit and flesh, even with most of those serving His Father's eternal enemy, the All-Father, the Lord of Light.

Over time, if the four Elder desired to learn the hidden arts, their motivations would have to transform into a more unsullied loyalty. Nonetheless, no matter what manner of reasons now spurred them towards dedicated service, they would all be needed in the volatile days to come. Elder were enduring the effects of the Ban to aid the Unifier's enemies, such as the one named Bevriedak, and there were few better counterparts for an Elder than another Elder.

The Unifier spread his arms wide above Him, slowly closing His eyes, as a light breeze gusted over His body. The sole intended purpose for the gathering was now at hand.

"Brothers in the eternal faith, bearers of the Light of the Morning Star, now bear witness unto Me. You have beheld the power given to me by the One who sent me, the ancient power by which I command in this world. You remember the former ages. Do not let yourselves be deceived any longer. Now, behold a vision of the New Kingdom, and the vast might awaiting the opening of the Gates for the Final Battle of the Great War."

The Unifier slowly clenched His fists. Veins slowly emerged, pushing up to the surface of the smooth skin along His exposed arms and across His forehead. Visibly shaking, His face was locked in a tense contortion, born of the deepest exertion and concentration.

He invoked tremendous powers through the use of arts buried deeply within the most arcane of mysteries. No sorcerer or Wizard that had ever lived could have commanded a force such as the one He accessed now.

After just a few moments, the space within the meadow began to shimmer and distort. It was as if the light of the moon was being bent, curved, and twisted by some inexplicable force. The empty air itself was a refracting prism, transforming reality into something malleable and alterable.

The prior, crisp reality of the world, encompassing all gathered within the meadow, was now pulsing and jittering within the controlling grasp of the Unifier's summoned power. Starting as a mere sliver of a breeze, a hot wind surged into a powerful current that began to circle in an unbroken continuum around the four Elder, the two Arcamons, and the Unifier.

The Avanoran escorts still gliding high above looked downward in total astonishment. Fear and uncertainty gripped them, as the forms of the dragons, the Arcamons, and the Unifier slowly faded from their sight.

Only their unwavering loyalty and solid discipline kept the riders and sky-steeds in their flight pattern. The Unifier had expressly ordered them to maintain the course of their patrol, no matter what they might see transpiring beneath them. They now adhered rigidly to His command, as they always had, keeping their nervous steeds under control as they continued their watch.

For the Elder Dragons, the Arcamons, and the Unifier, a new sight displaced the view of the world surrounding them scant moments before. The bending light was gradually straightened, and the flickering sensation ebbed, until a nightmarish realm manifested all around the group.

Garish skies of dark crimson and ash spread infinitely onward, leaving a blood-red sky draped in violently churning, undulating cloud masses. It was as if the sky itself was on fire, flames surging and coursing throughout endless masses of black, billowing smoke.

The unusual cloud layers were lit up sharply, time and time again, with a vicious, unrelenting lightning. The streaking bursts raced furiously along the expansive formation's rolling underbelly. Fierce columns of the surreal lightning were hurled with terrible force at the depths far beneath them. Like the cloud masses, the violent lightning could be seen in all directions, reaching beyond the farthest edges of sight.

The air was filled with the roaring of hot winds now rushing over the bodies of those who had just appeared on the rocky surface. The relentless air currents carried a searing, brutal heat, one that would have engulfed and consumed the flesh of any living being from Ave.

Mercifully for the four Elder, the torridity of the scorching gales ebbed just as they graced the skins of the Unifier, the Arcamons, and the dragons. It was like a special aura had been conferred upon the newcomers, shielding their corporeal bodies from physical harm while within the environs of the infernal realms.

The small group, standing in a quiet, tree-bounded meadow just a few heartbeats before, now found themselves at the upper culmination of a towering rock structure. It was not unlike a great stalagmite in form, reaching to a staggering height.

As far as the eye could see, in any direction, there were innumerable structures of the type, some taller, and some shorter. Many, such as their own, had flattened upper surfaces, while a number came to a jagged or rounded end. All appeared to be formed out of a rough, obsidian rock, and most flared wider as they descended to where a molten sea engulfed their bases.

The surface of the violently raging sea was far too distant to observe in any detail, even for the far-seeing Elder. A couple of the dragons, Shogaul and Gargartian, allowed their attention to linger, straining to make out what appeared to be dark, flying forms gliding just above the thrashing, surging, liquid tempest.

Molten waves crashed thunderously against the bases of the tower-rocks, sending great plumes of fiery spray soaring upward. The flying forms espied by Shogaul and Gargartian kept above the uppermost reaches of the temporal, blazing fountains.

The Arcamons and the Unifier were figures of absolute calm within the surrounding maelstrom, solemn and expectant. The scaly steeds of the Arcamons, returning back to the world of their origin, rested placidly as they awaited the command of their masters.

Even Pyrinos remained composed. A little hint of nervousness flickered within the depths of its eyes, but the beast seemed to draw confidence from the exalted rider mounted upon its back. The Unifier's own expression grew into a mien of something like serenity, similar to that of a wearied traveler returning home, after enduring a long odyssey.

The Elder, despite possessing long centuries of experience, observance, and knowledge, were clutched with fear, as well as a debilitating unease they had never known before. The massive dragons' heads turned slowly about, as they struggled to gain some manner of grasp upon the encompassing, supernatural environs they found themselves within. Their eyes were pools of chagrin and confusion, finding themselves in the midst of something far greater, and more ghastly, than any calamity unleashed by nature in Ave.

"My Father's Kingdom," the Unifier stated, in a firm, and indisputably prideful, voice. The Unifier's once blue eyes shifted, as black and grey hues pulsed and ebbed at their surface. As He spoke, His voice swelled with a boastful strength. "Once a world covered in nothing but a sea of flames, molten rock, and burning sulphur. A despairing Pit, created by the Enemy, into which my Father was once cast ... intended to be a prison. It is now a testament to His power and might ... reshaped by the unshakeable willpower of my Father."

The Unifier's voice reached a crescendo, taking on a fierce, defiant edge. "It was He alone Who stood up to the Order of Creation. It was He alone Who challenged what we did not choose. It was He Who bent no knee before the lesser things of the world. It was He Who sought to exalt the strong. It was He Who refused to elevate the weak.

"You now stand on the edge of worlds vast and diverse, filled with all manner of wonders and visions ... more than you could explore in a thousand upon a thousand years. Even then, not all is as it seems to your eyes. Look closer ... as I guide you forward. Follow Me, without fear."

The Unifier spurred Pyrinos forward. The Harrak took a couple of steps towards the edge of the rock-tower's summit, stretching its wings outward. It then leaped forward in a burst of motion, dipping into a glide that carried it swiftly away from the rock-tower. The two Arcamons followed close behind, their reptilian steeds also settling into a glide.

The Unifier's mind expanded in awareness, taking in the feelings of the dragons still standing on the rock surface behind them. He sensed their sharp fears, and took some amusement at their plight.

At first, the four dragons hesitated, seeming to find it incomprehensible that they could take to flight in the face of the powerful winds rushing by all around them. Tentatively, seeing the smooth ease by which the Harrak and the two steeds of the Arcamons navigated the seemingly turbulent air, they moved carefully towards the jagged lip of the rock-tower.

First of the four, Shogaul tensed his powerful muscles, and sprang from the edge of the rock, snapping his giant wings outward. The Unifier could feel the swirling rush of terror and anxiety saturating the great dragon as it braced for what it feared would be the inevitable embrace of the mighty, infernal winds. As powerful as the creature was, it was not so foolish as to deem the force of those winds as anything less than irresistible.

A spirit of pure helplessness reigned within the huge Elder, as its body left the solidity of the rock-tower. The Unifier deeply relished the vulnerable sensation, awakening black hungers that could only be sated within His Father's realms. Indeed, He had already spent far too long out of His own elements, and the remaking of Ave could not come a moment too soon.

A feeling of amazement and relief washed away the torturous dread within the dragon a moment later. The dragon's form went into a graceful, downward-curving path, and then up again, lifted as if on favorable currents of air.

Taking heart from the sight of their companion's flight, the other dragons then bounded off the rock, one after the other. Like Shogaul, Gargartian, Iklan, and finally Astarol found themselves flying with ease, heading away from the rock-tower.

The winds that the dragon feared would batter them mercilessly did not hinder their flight at all. It was as if the winds somehow altered their course at the last possible instant, so that they flowed over the contours of the Elder's immense bodies.

A slight grin came to the Unifier's face, as He sensed the four dragons struggling to rationalize the seeming contradiction they found themselves within. They could sense that the strong winds were still swirling all around them, a veritable maelstrom, yet the forceful currents had absolutely no effect upon them, as they flew in the wake of the Unifier.

The dragons had still not yet accepted that they were within an entirely different realm of existence, one that was not governed by the laws of the physical world from which they had come. The Unifier knew they would come to appreciate such differences in time, now that they had irreversibly taken the path of His Father.

Once all were airborne, the group settled into a loose formation. The Unifier flew a short distance in the lead, with the Arcamons just in back of Him. The Elder flew a little farther behind, trying to keep pace as close as possible. On Ave, there was no difficulty keeping up with any Harrak, but in this unfamiliar world, the titanic Elder had to exert themselves to keep from falling far behind.

The Unifier guided them slowly upward, until they were comfortably over the reaches of the tallest rock-towers rising from the tossing, volcanic seas. They continued at great speed, covering a tremendous distance as all sense of time evaporated.

The Unifier felt anxious streams of thoughts racing through the bewildered minds of the four dragons. The dragons had long since realized that the effects of the Ban had ceased, ever since the moment they entered the nether realm. They were now absorbing the dawning fact that no fatigue was accumulating within them. It was as if they possessed a boundless energy within the new realm, able to sustain the pace of a flying sprint over incredibly vast distances.

The Unifier could have revealed other modes of reality within the nether realm to them. He could have shown the Elder senses far surpassing the limited ones that they had known in their lives. Yet for their first visit to the nether realm, He had chosen to take them on a course that would at least have a close resemblance to the reality that they had known.

Far ahead, on the edge of the horizon, a sharply-pointed structure came into sight. It was accompanied by a vertical, slender object, which also culminated in a focused point. The pair of edifices rose far above the stalagmite-like forms the flying group had been passing over. The rock-towers looked miniscule, a host of diminutive spikes dwarfed by the two mountainous forms.

It was self-evident that the ordered appearances of the two objects had been constructed with a purposeful design, as opposed to the ubiquitous stalagmite-like structures scattered in the molten seas around them. By contrast, the teeming, rocky projections seemed to have been formed at random, the result of atmospheric, geological mechanisms mirroring those found in Ave.

Crossing through the air at a blurring swiftness, the Unifier surged forward on His steed, leading the group directly towards the two great objects. As they drew ever closer, the two structures loomed steadily larger, revealing more of their nature with every passing moment.

The more massive structure of the pair was an immense pyramid. The outer perimeter at the lowest visible level of the structure, where the walls immersed into the fiery, raging sea, was colossal scope.

It was impossible to ascertain how deep the flaming seas were from the high vantage. Yet the Unifier knew only a modest fraction of the gigantic structure was visible above the burning ocean's surface.

The other edifice, situated in close proximity to the pyramid, was a soaring obelisk. Its pointed summit was not unlike a pyramid itself, set atop a smooth-sided, square shaft of dizzying height.

While the pyramid was of a staggering scale, the measure of the even-sided obelisk's periphery was very extensive in and of itself. The monolith descended with no aberrations visible upon its immaculately smooth, unmarred surface, before finally plunging into the raging seas and the hidden depths they contained.

A broad, arched bridge, with unobstructed edges ending in a sheer drop-off to either side, connected the two imposing structures. One end of the bridge was aligned centrally against the base of a sloping side at the uppermost, pyramidal area of the obelisk. From that juncture, the bridge arched up and over an extensive distance to culminate in a corresponding location in the facing of the huge pyramid. The substantial width of the bridge was such that all four of the Elder could stand side by side upon its surface, with room to spare.

The fiery cloud masses high above were reflected dynamically within the metallic-gold surfaces of the giant edifices. The saturation of moving images served to lend a peculiar appearance to the objects, lending the gigantic pyramid, the connecting bridge, and the obelisk the uncanny sensation that they were living organisms.

The Unifier landed His Harrak at the center of the bridge, towards the end where the obelisk loomed. He set the steed down in a graceful landing, emulated moments later by the Arcamons following on their scaly mounts.

The Elder took a little more time to alight. At first, they circled in the air, right above the bridge, slowly spreading apart from each other.

Shogaul touched down on the bridge's surface first, followed by Gargartian, then Iklan, and finally Astarol. Once on the bridge, the four Elder tucked their wings tightly against their bodies, and moved closer together. They came to stand in two orderly pairs, just behind the Unifier and Arcamons. Shogaul and Gargartian formed the front rank, within Iklan and Astarol behind.

The Unifier glanced back, to make certain the dragons were well-situated before turning to face the obelisk. "Behold, the seat of the great throne of Hauras, one of the great Dukes of my Father!" the Unifier called out, in a powerful voice that shook the air. The sonorous declaration was only a prelude, as the Unifier then spoke with an unnatural voice containing the strength of tens of thousands. "Hauras, the Son of Jebaalos stands before your exalted throne. My Father's authority has been given in full to me. Come forth now, to attend to Me!"

As the Unifier's words concluded, far behind the Elder, at the opposite end of the bridge, a huge opening formed within the facing of the pyramid. The four dragons sensed the movement immediately, swiveling their heads to see what was transpiring.

An impenetrable blackness gaped in the side of the pyramid, though something stirred within its light-less depths. Issuing from the dark, rectangular opening, pouring forth in a massive swarm, were many thousands of macabre, winged entities. Their frenzied cries and wails filled the air with a hellish chorus. Moving swiftly, thickly massed ranks ascended in broad columns towards the churning skies above.

None of the creatures rode upon any manner of steed, as all of them possessed pairs of outstretched, leathery wings. The black, membranous appendages flapped vigorously, rapidly bearing the demonic beings aloft.

Lean, highly-protracted arms were connected into elongated, narrow, and noticeably gaunt torsos. The torsos continued into a proportionate set of hips, out of which a short, stubbier pair of legs emerged, the latter ending in wickedly sharp-looking sets of reptilian, clawed feet.

The creatures were roughly one and a half times the size of an average human man. Though emaciated in appearance, the quick, purposeful movements of the flying entities gave outward indication of the great vitality and strength contained within them.

The Unifier soaked in the stunned reactions of the Elder, as the dragons witnessed the emerging storm of diabolic entities. He could sense their rattled nerves and fear, sensations rarely felt by an Elder.

The dark horde gazed upon those gathered on the bridge with eyes virtually incapable of expression. Small, white orbs, set deeply within recessed, black hollows, their eyes echoed the lonely emptiness ceaselessly tormenting every last one of the creatures.

Only a small sliver remained of whatever kind of being they had once been. Their former existences were now distant, far-faded memories, now that they dwelt within a malefic world forged out of the blackest nightmares imaginable. Their icy, stony gazes, and sneering, slavering visages reflected the pitiless creatures of rancor they had all become.

Perhaps the most unusual aspect of their outward appearances, one that the Elder had quickly taken notice of, was that the creatures were not fully opaque. It was an observation readily ascertained when the first among the creatures reached the upper skies.

Watched closely enough, the incessant movements of the churning cloud masses, and the sharp reverberations of lightning rifling throughout the vaporous masses, could actively be seen through the slightly translucent bodies of the multitudes. The fell spirits were of an incorporeal nature, a type of existence entirely mysterious to the ages-old Elder.

While many of their bodily features carried close similarities in structure, their heads demonstrated a much more extensive variety of forms from creature to creature. Several were possessed of small, rounded craniums, which were connected to prominent, forward-extended sets of lower and upper jaws. The elongated sets of jaws were rounded at their extremity, like those seen on many varieties of apes existing within Ave.

Others had faces more resembling feral canines, extended snouts lined along both upper and lower portions with ferocious arrays of sharp, brightly glistening teeth. Still others exhibited very pronounced, beak-like visages. Spiked, downward-curving extensions were displayed at the end of the beak-like portions, like those found on birds of prey.

An abundance of other facial variations existed among the swirling host, blending the forms of humans and animals. While diverse, all held in common a fearsome, predatory aspect to their appearances.

Humanoid and bestial.

Sentient and rabid.

They were a teeming, deadly mass, imbued with a furious, ravenous intent. All were bound and condemned to serve as lowly thralls to the great lords of the Hallowed Kingdom, driven by madness and anger. There was little doubt that only a single word from any one of their dark Masters would set every one of them feverishly upon a rampaging, murderous course of action.

The Unifier knew the Elder could keenly sense the violent urges and insatiable hungers permeating the swirling masses. Unlike the Elder, the Unifier held the certitude that any attempt by the creatures to harass or attack them would be entirely unthinkable. Harboring no such assurances, the Elder continued to struggle with fear and anxiety, watching thousands upon thousands gathering right above them.

The ranks of entities reaching the upper heights rapidly swelled into an incredible multitude. Their formations deepened to many layers thick, stratified one above the other. It was not long before the expansive masses of creatures effectively blotted out the view of much of the sky immediately overhead. The impenetrable procession continued ascending for a considerable length of time, unbroken from the opening within the pyramid up to the aggregate in the sky.

When the torrent finally ebbed, the Elder stared upward in unison, rife with wonder and trepidation. Countless thousands now flew, darted, and soared in monstrous, living, and sentient cloud banks of their own making.

The Unifier had little doubt the Elder would have been incredulous to learn that the forces above represented only a few mere legions of spirits. The dense ranks were just a small portion of the vast hordes of fell spirits in thrall to Haurus, whose throne the Elder now stood before. The dragons had not even begun to realize that the greater hordes serving Haurus, far exceeding the force they were now witnessing, were likewise a fraction of the innumerable ranks serving Jebaalos. Since the terrible Fall, the power of Jebaalos had expanded exponentially, founding numerous realms populated by the bounteous harvests of spirits culled from the living world.

The rising cacophony generated by the raging maelstrom of beings above sharply subsided, as the many thousands of fell spirits sensed the approach of far greater powers. A wave of fear rippled through their sprawling ranks, demanding instantaneous obedience.

Another opening manifested at the opposite end of the bridge, the new portal opening and expanding within the sloping face of the obelisk. A stream of dark entities came forth, moving so smoothly that it looked as if they glided just over the surface of the bridge. They headed straight in the direction of the Unifier and those standing behind Him.

The column split apart, flowing gracefully into two equal, orderly formations. One group oriented to one side of the bridge, with the second aligning with the other.

Drawing to a halt, lining the edges of the bridge, their ranks extended continuously from the Unifier to the opening in the obelisk. A clear, unobstructed channel passed down their midst.

The new host of creatures emanated a power significantly greater than the far more numerous ranks of malicious creatures swarming overhead. Ancient, and regal of stature, each of the entities on the bridge was significantly taller and brawnier than the lesser kin above. They had broad, muscular chests, provided with bulging shoulders that flowed into powerfully-built arms. The latter ended in huge hands, each exhibiting long fingers culminating in razor-sharp talons.

Their right hands firmly gripped the hilts of long, wicked-looking sabers, which appeared to be composed entirely of vigorously-burning flames. The fiery blades were laced with both red and white-hot flames, rippling up and down the length of the supernatural weapons. The darkly majestic creatures held the unique swords out silently before them, the upper tips of the fire-blades pointed straight upward.

Their heads were not wholly unlike humans, in that they each possessed two eyes, two ears, a nose, and a mouth. Also like humans, there was a noticeable variety in their faces, from individual to individual.

Yet there were many sharp differences. Hairless on both face and head, the creatures were covered in a tightly-drawn layer of skin that had a dark, leathery appearance. Prominent, pointed ears, set higher on the sides of their heads than those on humans, could swivel and move independently of each other.

They possessed long, thin noses, which descended from pronounced, bony-looking ridges running across their heads above the cavities holding their deep-set eyes. Their eyes burned a solid red, matching the color of flames burning along the surfaces of the fiery blades they held so resolutely.

Their broad mouths, now closed, sat above jutting, elongated chins. Out of proportion to the rest of their face, their sizeable mouths and chins gave their appearances a distorted quality.

Upon closer scrutiny, the disturbing sense was conveyed further by the rough, scarred texture of their outer skin. The marred skin testified to the sufferance of burns terrifying in scope, endured many long ages before. Exposed clearly, with no effort made to subdue the terrible scars, it was obvious the ranks of infernal warriors wore their blemished, maimed forms as an outward symbol of their loyalty, and defiant origins.

A robust set of wings extended from their wide, upper backs, the top joints of which rested high above their heads. It took little imagination to see that their tightly-folded wings, once spread, would easily unfurl into a great span.

There was a faint translucent quality to their dark forms, shrouded somewhat by the deep, ebony hue of their astral bodies. While not fully corporeal, they had much more density than did the flood of smaller winged-entities above them.

A sudden stillness then fell upon the newly-assembled ranks. Their fiery eyes turned in unison to gaze towards the towering opening from which they had just emerged. A palpable anticipation filled the air, as something moved within the deep blackness of the opening set within the crowning element of the monolith.

The first figure to come forth from the darkness, passing between the assembled ranks of attendant demons, was a large, solitary figure nearly human in most outward respects. The figure walked with long, purposeful strides along the platform.

Two broad wings protruded from the back of the stately entity. Powerful in appearance, and abundantly feathered, the appendages were similar to those of eagles.

The being was half-again as tall as the Unifier. A strange, full-length robe, fashioned of what appeared to be thick, churning smoke, covered much of the figure's body. The bottom of a pair of heavy black boots protruded from the lower edge of the long, swirling robe. The boots struck the bridge's surface with authoritative, booming beats, as their regal wearer approached the Unifier. The hilt of a sheathed sword, topped with a bright golden pommel in the shape of a perfect orb, could be seen at the being's left side.

The entity's face was very angular, with a sharp chin point, a set of large, pointed ears carried erect, and a highly-pronounced lower jaw-line. An aquiline nose rested between two eyes glowing fiercely, an unnatural fire blazing within their depths.

The being's head exhibited a receded hairline, situated high above its broad forehead. Thick locks of hair sprouted from that line backward, flowing into long, dark tresses framing each side of its face. The effect of its locks and hairline created a passing resemblance to a lion's mane.

Elegantly, the tall entity lowered its eyes to the ground, and made a low, reverend bow before the Unifier. It was a gesture infused with deference and obeisance. The figure then took one step to the right, and stood quietly.

Gliding from the depths of the towering fortress a moment later was a crow of exceedingly large form, larger than any eagle that had ever dwelled within Ave. In silence, the creature drifted forward and alighted on the ground before the Unifier. The creature lowered its head in an unmistakable bow, before stepping to the side opposite the entity who had preceded it. Its sentient eyes were alert and inquiring, as the huge crow flicked its curious gaze briefly towards the hulking Elder looming nearby.

An even stranger sight followed the enormous crow, in the form of a powerfully-built man sitting astride a regal griffin, whose wings and fur were of the deepest ebon hue. The griffin stepped with feline grace, carrying itself with a proud bearing.

The image of the man on the griffin's back was one of a great warrior, rippling with muscle, and clothed in a simple tunic and trousers, both of pure white. A silver belt of great radiance was bound about his midsection.

Thick, curly black locks tumbled around his wide face to where they ended just above his broad shoulders. A shining circlet of gold surmounted his bearded head. His eyes blazed with a cold, fell light, beneath bushy eyebrows.

When they reached the Unifier, the griffin lowered its forequarters, while the man leaned forward, rendering a harmonious gesture of deference to the Unifier. The griffin then backed up next to the winged humanoid, as the man kept his eyes lowered.

Behind the griffin-riding entity, a gigantic leopard padded slowly forward. Its baleful, glaring eyes, and mouth filled with glistening, extensive fangs, created a strong presence; one radiating the raw, unabated danger of a dominant predator.

Nearly the size of a war horse, the creature walked with a sanguine, measured gait, until it neared the other prominent figures who had just emerged from the fortress. Like the others, the great leopard prostrated itself before the Unifier.

The Unifier paused in His thoughts to take account of the impressions now taking place within the Elder behind Him. Their states of mind were just as He had expected them to be.

The Elder Dragons watched the proceedings nearly as still as statues, entirely mesmerized by the unprecedented sights they were witnessing. The reaction was no small matter for such venerable, powerful creatures. Living long ages in Ave, almost since the beginning of life upon that world, they had never experienced anything like the events transpiring before them.

Their heightened amazement increased further as the forms of the winged entity, the man upon the griffin, the great crow, and the huge leopard started to blur and coalesce upon themselves, at the initiation of a sweeping transformation into entirely new forms. Their features melted and faded into black mist, before slowly regaining a semblance of solidity.

Where the several distinctly different entities had been standing were now four congruous types of beings. With a few notable distinctions, they were similar in appearance to the ranks massed to each side of the bridge.

Unlike the two lines of guardians, the four had smooth, unblemished skin, displaying an appearance of complete substantiality. They were also noticeably larger than the beings within the guardian ranks.

They were unable to fully mask the horrific corruption brought upon them in their legendary Fall, of ages past, having been hurled into a fiery sea that had seared and charred their truest forms. Yet they had still managed to retain a distinctive sense of the elegant, dignified aura they had maintained before the Fall.

A crown of fire rested upon each of their great heads, construed of flames born of the infernal realms, as refashioned by the will of Jebaalos. The flames rose and fell around the circumference of the burning crowns, forming a continuously changing cascade of lofty tines.

The four noble entities, each in their own turn, prostrated themselves again, in a display of total humility. The gestures were much more pronounced and dramatic than the ones each of them had rendered to the Unifier following their emergence.

Likewise, the ranks lining each side of the bridge also laid themselves low, in an outward gesture of complete reverence and submission towards the Unifier. They set their fiery swords down flat upon the bridge's surface, at their right sides, where the weapons continued to burn.

The four prominent beings, and the ranks of elite warriors, made no move to get up, keeping their faces close to the bridge. When the Unifier finally broke the lingering impasse, He spoke in a language entirely unexpected by the Elder.

The massive dragons could not hide their awe, as it was written plainly upon their visages when the Unifier spoke words in a tongue they had not heard since the titanic struggles of the First Era. The language had faded from Ave soon after the great celestial battle that had cleaved several of the Elders' own number in the teeming Fall of Jebaalos' forces.

Hearing the words of the ancient, otherworldly language, the huge dragons were held in a spellbound state. Nearly alone among all the creatures of Ave, the immortal dragons understood the meaning of the words.

"Arise, Haurus," the Unifier thundered. He extended His right arm forward, palm up, towards the fourth of the crowned entities, the one who had just recently been in the guise of the great leopard.

The Unifier then turned purposefully towards the third figure, the one holding the form of the stout man upon the large griffin. "Murmas, arise."

To the second, who had emerged in the image of a giant crow, the Unifier stated, "Raum, arise."

Finally, focusing upon the final entity of the august quartet, the first to come forth from the obelisk, in the appearance of a winged humanoid, the Unifier enjoined, "Focalor, arise."

Four noble powers of the netherworld, exalted commanders of over one hundred legions of condemned spirits, stood up slowly before the Anointed Son of their Lord and Master. Their eyes remained lowered in a continued sign of their obedience.

"Faithful of my Father, Warrior Archons of the First Legions, arise!" boomed the Unifier, calling to the ranks prostrated to the left and right sides of the bridge.

"All hail the Son of Jebaalos, He Who Will Open the Gates! He who goes to prepare the way!" the assembled warriors cried out in deafening unison, once they had risen to a standing position. They raised their flaming swords high, the blades now burning almost entirely white-hot, in a zealous salute. As the clamor died down, they resumed their initial postures, standing in place with the burning swords held point-upward in front of them.

The Unifier looked again to the four prominent entities from the obelisk. "Focalor, step forward," the Unifier stated.

"In Your service," Focalor rumbled in a deep voice, as he stepped forth, still speaking in the arcane language used by the denizens of the

SPIRIT OF FIRE

Hallowed Kingdom.

"From your throne, turn your gaze to the seas of Ave, to the south, and the coming assault upon Midragard," the Unifier said. "With the powers that My Father has bestowed upon you, I desire to see the vessels of our enemies sinking below the waves, as I desire to see ours reach Midragard's shores. We have already suffered enough blows upon the waters of Ave."

Focalor gave a slight bow. "It shall be done, my Lord."

"I do not have to tell you that in doing so, you will enjoy a feast of human death," the Unifier added, a smile crossing His face.

Focalor returned the expression, his lips pulling back into a broad smile. His countenance was laced with anticipation.

"Go forth, see to the Will of My Father, and the sooner you shall gain the reward," the Unifier declared.

With another bow, Focalor spread his great leathery wings, and departed from the bridge. As the powerful Archon ascended, a small contingent of the demonic warriors lining the bridge took off and followed in his wake. In just a moment, they vanished from sight.

The Unifier then turned his eyes back to the remaining three Powers.

"Raum, come forward," the Unifier said.

The powerful Archon who had previously assumed the form of a great crow stepped towards the center of the bridge, coming to stand just in front of the Unifier. Bending at the waist, the Archon bowed low, and replied. "In Your service."

"Examples must be made of those who resist. Turn your eyes to the conflicts raging upon Ave, most especially the precious Power we are cultivating to the East. Know that this Power is of great importance to Me, and to My Father.

"Instill a hunger within the mortals serving My Father's Will, that they will not hesitate to level an entire city if it will subdue the desire to resist those who conquer by My Father's Will. If an example is made, see to it that such an example will shake the surface of Ave, and spread terror across all the kingdoms. I can think of no other Archon more suited for this task ... perhaps this work can be done through the Power in the East, when the time comes to reveal him."

"All shall be done," Raum replied firmly.

"You will find great reward, as the pride of countless humans will

645

be brought into humiliation and death," the Unifier said. "Go now, and do My Father's Will."

Raum, like Focalor, gave a bow, and departed the bridge, taking along with him another mass of escorting demon-warriors.

When Raum and the contingent of warrior Archons were gone from sight, the Unifier turned towards the Archon who had first appeared as a warrior upon a griffin.

"Murmas, come forward," the Unifier ordered.

Murmas walked forth and bowed, replying in a deferential tone, "In Your service."

"All knowledge must be gained and discovered, to help us find the otherworlders, to know them better, and to learn of those seeking to use the otherworlders for the purposes of our Enemy," the Unifier said, in a particularly grave tone of voice.

"Many souls who have recently descended into the Hallowed Kingdom following their death in Ave may possess useful knowledge," the Unifier continued. "Your task is to conduct an inquisition all across the Hallowed Realms, to glean what you may from the souls who have fallen into My Father's Dominion.

"Any knowledge you gain must be conveyed to those serving My Father in Ave. Make your abilities available to the Wizards serving the Hallowed Kingdom. This is a time of great war in Ave, and there has been an abundant harvest of souls recently within these realms… You have a mind with a grasp for the subtle, Murmas … apply it well."

"I shall, as always for the Will of Jebaalos," Murmas replied, before being dismissed. Like the other two High Archons, he departed with a small throng of demonic warriors.

Unlike the other two, Murmas left with a steely expression fixed upon his face. There had been no mention of a reward. Success in his task would help to bring about the greatest of rewards; Jebaalos's ascension, and coronation over all of Creation.

The philosophical, intellectual creature needed no intricate interpretations to understand the enormity of his undertaking, or the extreme priority it held in the Unifier's eyes. The otherworlders could either seal victory for the Hallowed Kingdom, or undermine everything to a most disastrous end.

It was one area in which there could be no recovery from failure. The mission of Murmas was perched on the precarious balance between everything and nothing.

The Unifier paused for a moment, staring after Murmas for several moments after he flew off. Finally, He turned towards the last Archon yet remaining, of the four who had emerged from the opening in the obelisk.

"Come forward, Haurus," the Unifier said.

Haurus obeyed, bowed, and replied, "In Your service."

"It is long since I have visited with you. Let us speak plainly now, as we often have before," the Unifier exclaimed, in a more casual voice.

The other slowly looked up in response to the Unifier's bidding. The Unifier's own voice proceeded to soften from its commanding edge, as He continued speaking with a greater air of familiarity.

"Since My Incarnation, I have not had the luxury of your company as before, Haurus," The Unifier said.

Hauras was one of the Unifier's favorite entities among the High Archons serving His Father. As a being who concerned itself with matters of time, both future and past, Hauras was also most useful to consult.

"I trust your service to My Father proceeds well," the Unifier said. "Indeed, you have a form that is as solid as a physical one. It cannot be other than good favor from my Father."

The Unifier's transcendent vision easily delineated the subtle differences between the forms of Raum, Murmas, Focalor, and Haurus, though all appeared identical to the physical eyes of the Elder. There was a slight insubstantiality to the other three, which the Unifier knew was his Father's way of reminding them that they now drew all of their substance from the Hallowed Kingdom.

Haurus evidently enjoyed a special confidence from Jebaalos, one that had not escaped the keen, otherworldly vision of the Unifier. The Unifier could not deny that the recognition pleased Him greatly, as He personally held Haurus in high esteem.

Haurus nodded slowly, with an air of sincere humility. "That I cannot deny. Your Father, my Lord, has all of our powers in full trial to His Will. Know that I do not rest when favor has been given. We prepare ceaselessly for the coming age."

"As do I, now that I am no longer held back ... at last able to take incarnate form within Ave," the Unifier said, with an edge of triumphant vindication.

He then stifled a sliver of anger that threatened to surge, a reflex

He had not managed to yet suppress. It reflected the hostility He always felt towards the exceedingly long, painstaking efforts that had been required to surmount the Enemy's barriers to His physical manifestation within Ave. At least that time was now well behind Him. The Enemy could no longer hold back the Son of Perdition.

"This is a time and age we have long awaited, my Lord," Haurus replied.

"Yes … a time we have both long awaited, indeed," the Unifier agreed. After a wistful pause, His voice took on a different timbre, as He queried, "Is all well from your throne, Great Duke of the Hallowed Kingdom?"

"Through great arts, many spirits from my dominion have transcended the increasingly sundered barriers to the mortal world. Ever more power is available to them, to work, and to appear when need be. This is a welcome sign as the new age dawns," Haurus answered. "Much word has been brought to me that the spirits of the Enemy are also moving abroad in the mortal world, also in greater number. I can assure you we are eager to take to the skies against them. My legions thirst and hunger for open battle."

"And soon you shall assail the Enemy, in such open battle," the Unifier pronounced, a broad grin emerging.

A sharp glint flickered in His eye, akin to the gleam of a starved individual at the sight of an imminent feast. A sense of great pride in His Father, the Lord of Fire, welled up powerfully. The Final Age had arrived, and the grievous wrongs done to Jebaalos were going to be undone, at last. Everything would be set to rights, as Ave, and even Palladium, would become mere continuations of the Hallowed Kingdom.

"We are even now conquering the last vestiges of resistance upon the mortal world," the Unifier continued. "Soon, we will have brought the world's entire focus and power to the service of My Father, our Lord."

"We have heard it said there are relatively few lands that must yet be brought to their knees, before our Lord," Haurus stated.

"Two of these last, recalcitrant realms, who would yet defy, are indeed being conquered, even as we speak together here," the Unifier responded.

A brief, anger-spurred haze crossed the surface of His blood-red eyes, as He recalled the many frustrations incurred in both instances. Neither Saxany nor the Five Realms were falling as easily as He had hoped, though victory over both loomed nonetheless.

"You have brought Elder of the living world here with you, a surprise that I must confess I did not anticipate," Haurus commented, turning the subject back to the present. He looked past the Unifier, and up at the huge dragons, all of whom were looking back at them attentively.

"It is time to give them a vision of true strength, of the vast power of the transcendent Lord they now serve," the Unifier responded. "This is one reason why I have come Myself to the seat of your throne, and commanded you and the other three great Archons to attend to Me here. The Elder must witness you, and you must witness them, as new strength comes to our great war effort in Ave."

"They say that Elder are involved on the part of our enemies. It would seem that the Oath has already been broken asunder by our Enemy," Haurus then said, with a hint of concern.

"What you have heard is true, in that Elder are now directly involved on the part of our Enemy. This is why I am readying our own force of Elder for the coming days," the Unifier answered.

"But of the Oath?" questioned Haurus.

"The Oath still holds power over all the race of Elder within Ave, but sides are being chosen. The Enemy's Elder must be countered, lest we suffer any disadvantages or unwanted delays to our purposes. Do not worry yourself in this matter, Haurus, we may soon even have the advantage of numbers among the Elder."

The news seemed to please Haurus greatly. His sharp teeth showed in a mockery of a smile, while his eyes blazed all the brighter. His voice resonated strongly, when he responded, "Then all is truly going well."

Shadows flickered around The Unifier's face, as He became lost in thought for the moment. His face clouded darkly from the surging worries he contemplated within.

"No, not everything," the Unifier responded, in a solemn tone, the grin fading from His face. "There was an unexpected rebellion among the Kiruvans, near the port of Thessalas. This rebellion undermined our main sea fleet, obstructing their coming task to invade and conquer Midragard. It was the very reason why I commanded Focalor to turn undivided attention to the southern seas. This rebellion has given those resisting us time to organize their strength.

"The Enemy Elder you have heard word of was just one creature, by whose actions the total destruction of Saxany's forces was denied to us. The interference greatly delays my conquest of Saxany, and the humbling of their king, who foolishly fails to bend his knee to Me."

"Even so, it is still just a matter of time, My Lord," Haurus said, clearly seeking to reassure the Unifier. "This is a war they cannot win. The armies I see coming under Your power are bringing You strength far greater than any remnant loyal to our Enemy could hope to oppose."

"Truly spoken, Haurus," the Unifier replied, nodding His head slowly. "It is simply a matter of My impatience. I wish to be in full control of Ave, to prepare the glorious coming of My Father into the world, and the launching of the Great Assault against our Enemy. I seek only a chance to bring down the barriers setting this world apart from the mortal one.

"I vow that it will not be long before the passages between the worlds are lain wide open. You will soon be able to bring the full might of your armies and powers from here … all your legions … to loose them in full strength upon the mortal world and beyond. You will at last gain vengeance for that which was denied us ages ago."

A glow filled with elation and anticipation rose across Haurus' countenance, as the bothersome doubts in the Unifier finally retreated. A master of history and augury, Haurus' farseeing gaze dwelled almost ceaselessly upon the matters of past and future. Haurus' genuine excitement was a cause for encouragement to the Unifier.

Even without Haurus's reaction, the Unifier had reason on His side. It was undeniable that the combined forces under the Unifier were virtually incalculable in scale. Those of the Enemy were well-accounted for, decidedly far lesser in strength, and steadily dwindling.

If it were not for the presence of otherworlders within Ave, the Unifier would not have suffered the need to hold any concerns about the situation. As it was, with otherworlders physically manifested in Ave, He could not afford to take the slightest of chances. He had to draw as many of them as He could under his control, and seduce them to His willing service.

"Do you wish me to call forth the First One?" Haurus asked, as the Unifier realized He had become quiet for several moments. "He has been summoned, as You have desired, and awaits Your call."

The Unifier looked towards the four Elder. As before, they were watching the proceedings with great scrutiny. Turning back to Haurus,

He nodded, "Yes, you may call the First One forth. It is time these four bear witness."

Haurus's fiery eyes shut for a moment. The Unifier's awareness perceived the summons issuing from the mighty Archon.

Not long after, a gigantic form burst from the underbelly of the cloud masses, exploding into view in an eruption of fire and smoke. The great form rapidly disengaged from the clouds, hurtling downward, as the swirling denizens occupying the upper skies made great haste to scatter out of the winged titan's way.

The Elder standing behind the Unifier looked upwards, beholding the spectacular entrance of one of their own brethren; one they had not seen since the very origins of the world.

The creature was much larger than any one of the observing Elder on the span. It swooped lower, and began to circle around the pyramid and obelisk.

The behemoth's form possessed an abundance of unnatural elements, heralding that the monstrosity was no longer a creature of Ave. Its massive head swiveled around to fix the four Elder with a deadly, penetrating stare.

Pools of madness and rage churned within its baleful gaze. Its enormous jaws were far disproportionate to the rest of its head, a chasm lined with wicked-looking, ebony teeth resembling a host of swords.

The ghastly creature was riddled with advanced signs of decay, baring raw bone in many places. Openly exposed muscle, where skin and scale had been torn away, dappled the surface of its gigantic body.

Once a lustrous green, the rest of the creature's exterior was mottled black and dark green, with charred, ebon swathes scattered amid patches yet holding a faded hint of their original hue. The horrific aggregation of lacerations and defacements were ages old, vividly calling to mind the torturous suffering the First Ones endured in the Great Fall, and its hellish aftermath.

The creature's vast wings, extensively frayed and tattered along their outer edges, flapped steadily as the spectral dragon came to hover to one side of the bridge. The ancient First One, having existed within Jebaalos' diabolic realms since the onset of Ave's history, continued glaring towards its smaller brethren.

The Unifier felt the tremors of ire racing through the creature. After so many ages dwelling in a world of darkness and fire, after entering

its netherworld existence while still in a physical form, the First One had evolved into a living, titanic nightmare.

The Unifier knew it was a deeply unpleasant reunion for the First One. Waves of resentment and antipathy wafted from the creature, as it regarded the four Elder.

The Unifier let a slight smile grace His lips, savoring the unprecedented levels of fear pervading the four Elder with Him. All of them stared in near disbelief at the sight of one of their own kind within the Hallowed Kingdom. Once just like them, the First One had been transformed into something far mightier, and far greater.

"Behold, Regarthoth! Loyal since the dawn of the Hallowed Kingdom, one of the sacred First Ones," the Unifier announced proudly. He then turned and commanded the First One, "Come, Regarthoth. Stand before your brethren!"

With several beats of its sweeping wings, the enormous dragon lifted higher into the air, and made its way slowly to the bridge. Angling downward, it touched its huge claws upon the broad span, behind the four Elder. Its colossal mass filled the width of the span.

The gaze within Regarthoth's eyes remained venomous as it peered down, towards the four Elder. The Unifier knew the creature derived some pleasure from their obvious discomfort.

Unknown to Regarthoth, the Unifier sensed that the four Elder had almost cowered before the infernal dragon, the moment it had landed close to them. Brimming with menace, the First One had intimidated the four Elder.

Regarthoth reared back, tilting its massive head upward, and blasted a searing column of fire towards the sky. The lengthy eruption soared rapidly, hurtling towards the bristling clouds. The intense column of flames smashed into the cloud masses with thunderous impact. The dragon-flame spread outward, in expanding, concentric rings, like those from a stone dropped into a lake.

The First One followed the torrent with a sonorous roar, throwing its head back again in a flare of exultant pride. The creature opened its enormous jaws wide as the deafening clamor emitted, its extraordinary, gigantic arsenal of teeth displayed in striking fashion.

The four Elder watching the scene unfold looked stunned, witnessing the astounding reach of the fiery blast. The stormy inferno far outdistanced the strongest eruption any of the four had ever loosed during their entire existence. The destruction the First One was capable of was bewildering to even contemplate.

The Unifier calmly looked towards the four Elder. "Shogaul, Gargartian, Iklan, and Astarol, you have taken your first steps upon a new path, one that will take you, and many of your kind, to heights none of you ever knew before. Serve well, and you will also gain supremacy among the rest of your kind."

Potent desires were taking root within the creatures. Desire had always been one of the most useful tools, one the Unifier and Jebaalos were well-acquainted with; and proficient in utilizing.

THOMAS

"The true self is all that really matters, Thomas," Wace stated. "You think of physical things because we live in a material world, the only place you have known, so I know it is not easy to grasp what I am telling you."

Thomas eagerly waited for his grandfather to expound upon what one's 'true self' was, but Wace paused. His eyes appeared to sparkle from within as he looked up into his grandson's eyes, or perhaps it was simply a trick of the mid-morning light. With a little effort, Wace got up to his feet, and shuffled forward.

"Thomas, come with me, and let us continue this conversation elsewhere. A little walk will do me some good right now," Wace said.

Thomas accompanied his grandfather out of the hospital, situated next to a large monastery compound in one of the older sections of Avalos. The day was mild and sunny, with scattered cloud-cover, the latter providing the city with periodic, cool respites between warmer sequences of direct sunlight.

The streets outside the compound were filled with activity, spanning the gamut from running children to itinerant peddlers. It was much the average day in Avalos, but still presented considerable challenges to an elderly man with an unstable step.

"Glad you are with me, to help shield me in this throng," remarked Wace with a chuckle, as they started out together, into the street. "I will brave this rabble as long as I can command my muscles to move this husk

I'm now stuck in, but it is nice to have some company today."

Thomas and his grandfather were benefited by a slow-moving wagon, whose wheels rolled through the deep ruts countless wagons and carts had carved into the ground over the years. Keeping in its wake, they were able to navigate the wide thoroughfare as if it were a steadily parting sea.

"The effort it takes to reach some open space," his grandfather muttered tersely. "Here, we can take this alleyway."

Turning to the right, they continued down the backside of several densely packed houses, of a type quite common within that district. Wending his way to its end, his grandfather looked to Thomas and smiled. "Real treasure is on this street."

Wace gestured in both directions of the street now crossing their path. Thomas looked up and down the thoroughfare, taking appraisal of the wealthy attire on those strolling the length of it. He peered at the images carved and painted into the small wooden signs perched over the entrances to the various shops, recognizing what they indicated easily enough; a street of booksellers.

"You keep up with your lessons from that priest, and you'll be able to take in wealth far greater than gold with what is contained in those shops," his grandfather commented, as they waited for an opening in the foot traffic. He then added, with a rueful grin, "Though it would admittedly take much gold to own what is in these shops."

Thomas had no argument. He could not even imagine possessing a single book, or keeping one within his own home. The possibility of owning one of the expensive, hand-copied tomes, as the son of a weaver, had never entered his mind. Wax tablets and some sheaves of parchment at Father Anselm's church were his mode of encounter with the world of letters.

Merging into the foot traffic, and walking past the booksellers, they eventually came upon a large bridge. Traversing the great river coursing through the midst of Avalos, the bridge's narrow middle passage ran between shops and residences packed next to each other, on either side of the stone-built span.

"Hold for a moment. When you get older, endurance is not as it was before," Wace stated, before turning aside, into a small public structure provided for calls of nature.

Thomas waited patiently until Wace emerged, and they proceeded across the bridge. Walking a pace or two in front of his grandfather, Thomas bore the brunt of the nudges and bumps from the crowd, as he shouldered his way through them.

After reaching the opposite side, they turned onto a cobbled roadway traveling down the length of the riverbank. They soon came upon a gently sloping embankment extending down to the water's edge.

A number of women were engaged in the washing of clothes by the flowing waters. Some chattered amiably amongst themselves, and others were wholly engrossed in their labors. They barely spared more than a glance towards the newcomers, as Wace led Thomas down the slope and to the right, guiding him into a section of trees that offered cool, soothing shade.

Within the trees, there was a good measure of privacy. Wace sat down, and settled onto a large root, resting his back against a trunk of fair girth. He sighed, gazing over the passing waters for a few moments, as Thomas found a place to sit down close to him.

"This is a spot I stumbled across on one of my sojourns around this city," Wace commented. "A good place, when you simply need a few moments to breathe and think. It will suffice well for our current purposes."

The place was indeed secluded, affording a beautiful backdrop for any type of conversation Wace had in mind. Thomas watched a couple of small, single-masted sailing vessels, and a river barge, as they glided along the river's shimmering surface.

"What I have to tell you is hard to believe. But you must listen to me," Wace said, in a somber tone that drew Thomas' attention. His grandfather's countenance matched his voice, fixed into a serious mien.

Thomas nodded, not quite sure what his grandfather was talking about. Nevertheless, he wanted the old man to know he was dutifully listening. He could do no less than accord his grandfather a respectful demeanor, no matter how outlandish the upcoming tale might be.

"Before we go any further in this discussion, there is the matter of your mother's needs," Wace stated. "I have been to see the good monks who run the Saint Therese Hospital for Widows. I even had the privilege of speaking briefly with the Abbess of the Sisters who serve there. I have also been to speak with some of your father's fellow tradesmen, who belong in the Brotherhood of St. Onofrius. I am certain we will be able to get substantial help for your mother. That is very important for you to know, for what I have to tell you now."

Wace paused, as the solemn conclusions sank in. Thomas felt a heavy sadness draping over him, as he realized what his grandfather was talking about. He had been trying to stave off the tormenting thoughts as best he could, but he did not always have the strength. His mattress up in the garret had been wetted with an abundance of tears, in the depths of the last few nights.

His father was locked away in dark confinement, awaiting a trial that would quite possibly demand his life. Even worse, Thomas was utterly powerless to oppose the horrible situation, or even influence it. His family did not have the kind of wealth necessary to help his father avoid the gallows, if the provost of the city rendered such a dreadful judgement.

The only word Thomas had received of his father came from a single message, conveyed by one of the Gray Friars tending to the men and women held within the catacomb prison. His father had sent a message of encouragement and love to his family, though it did little to assuage the dire feelings weighing upon Thomas, his mother, and his sister.

The message told them nothing more, which did not come as a surprise. They all knew William well enough to know that no matter how much he was suffering, he would endeavor to lift their spirits.

"I will try now to explain what I mean when I say I have been in spirit," his grandfather asked. "Are you ready to listen to me with an open mind?"

"Yes, I am, grandfather," Thomas replied, a little hesitantly.

He caught the shift in tenor within his grandfather's voice. He sensed that his grandfather had returned to the verge of making some type of revelation, or discussing a matter of great importance.

His grandfather nodded, slowly. "Well, then, know that I have done so more than a few times. In truth, I do so very often. It is a special gift I stumbled onto when I was much younger. For whatever reason, the All-Father granted me a great boon with this gift. It has helped me to look upon this aging body, and my dwindling future in this world, as things to have no undue concern with."

"Why is that?" Thomas asked, his curiosity rising, though he did not have an inkling of what his grandfather was speaking about.

"I do not look upon death as an ending, not in the least bit," his grandfather replied, smiling towards Thomas with a lively glint in his eyes.

Thomas' brow furrowed. "But does not the Church say that we will live onward? We will live past when we die here?"

"Yes, and what they say is quite true, Thomas, though relatively few live their lives as if they truly believe it. If every person only knew the certainty of this, I believe the world would be a much different place," Wace said, wisps of regrets laced in the tone of his words. "Your perspective on life itself is more clear when you have actually experienced something like the state I speak of, the full state of your spirit … knowing who, and what, you really are."

"Can this be learned?" Thomas asked, excitedly, suddenly enamored with the possibilities.

"I do not know," his grandfather replied. "For obvious reasons, I have spoken little of this to anyone, so there is little for me to compare this to. My loyalty to the Church is without question. My heart and life are pledged to Emmanu, the All-Father, and the Life Spirit, but there are many who would not understand a gift such as this, and would instantly liken it to some dark, nefarious art. Do you understand that danger?"

"Yes," Thomas replied sincerely, wondering what Father Anselm would think of his grandfather's strange gift. For some reason, he was not so sure Father Anselm would condemn it outright.

Admonishments against darker arts, and the wiles and seductions of the Lord of Fire, Jebaalos, were reinforced at every turn in the life of the faithful. Public performances of stories from the Sacred Writings, held during feast days and other civic occasions, were often bolstered with fearsome images of demons. Lurid portrayals complete with fire, smoke, and cacophonous noise were staged, as hapless transgressors of moral law were indelibly held to account.

Such themes were echoed during the course of innumerable Church services, with detailed descriptions of what lay in wait for those given over to the authority of Jebaalos. Realms filled with grotesque monstrosities, searing heat, torn flesh, and, worst of all, the absence of all hope, were said to be under the Lord of Fire's domininion.

Several particularly gruesome depictions of Jebaalos's infernal kingdom had given Thomas and Emma great nightmares; which they had woken up from drenched in cold sweats, with eyes wide and hearts racing. Better that a soul had perished from existence, than to find itself claimed by Jebaalos after the End of Days.

Father Anselm's words during Church services took a markedly different path. Tending to have much more focus on the mystery, beauty, and merciful nature of the All-Father, they did not emphasize the fears and macabre descriptions of hellish realms that so many other priests stressed so heavily. Thomas mused as to whether Father Anselm would find his grandfather's gift part of that mysterious, seemingly unknowable element of the nature of the All-Father; or whether he would attribute it to some guile or deception of the demonic.

Yet even if Father Anselm did not condemn the gift, Thomas was certain there were many others who would not be willing to even consider the matter. The fate of an espouser of heresy was little better than that faced by his own father.

Thomas knew the stories regarding the efforts to root out a large heretic movement in eastern Gallea, involving a massive military campaign in the time of his grandfather. A great many unfortunates adhering to the heretical sect were said to have been burned alive, in horrific pyres whose fires and acrid stench served as daunting warnings to any others tempted to embrace false teachings.

Father Anselm attributed that war to being one of the greater mistakes in the Church's history, in which Jebaalos had deftly maneuvered the faithful into doing wicked actions, justified as necessities in smothering a heresy. Father Anselm said the war had left terrible scars on the Church and on their own souls, of the kind that did not fade away quickly.

Yet Father Anselm's insights rarely reflected the general consensus within Avalos, and Thomas always had to keep that in mind. The present time was no exception, and Thomas resolved to keep his wits about himself.

"You understand I am taking a terrible risk, by even talking to you of this?" his grandfather asked.

Thomas nodded again, and spoke firmly, "Yes, grandfather. I know, and I would do nothing to get you in trouble."

A trace of bemusement came to his grandfather's face, and he seemed pleased by Thomas's answer. "Then, young Thomas, answer me another question … do you believe in Archons? And I mean, really believe," his grandfather asked, voicing the latter words with a careful, purposeful emphasis, which seemed to urge Thomas to think the question through before rendering an answer.

Thomas thought of the fantastical, legendary servants of the All-

Father, whose celestial choirs were said to shake a listener's soul down to the innermost foundations. He had learned the various stories of Archons as told in the Western Church. They ranged from the spectacular tales of the towering, flame-sword bearing Archon warding the entrance to the primeval sanctuary of Eden, to the immensely powerful High Archon Mika'il, who led heaven's hosts in throwing down Jebaalos and the vast army of rebel Archons at the dawn of creation. He also knew of Gavri'el, who had heralded the birth of Emmanu Himself.

The tales always stoked the higher levels of Thomas' imagination, filling him with hope and a sense of wonder. It was a great comfort to believe the All-Father had delegated such powerful champions to come into the world on behalf of humanity. In a world filled with darkness and death, even said to be under the authority of Jebaalos, the ethereal warriors and messengers from Palladium were, at the very least, comforting symbols to inspire and gird the heart.

Yet whether Thomas truly believed the stories was another question entirely, as he had never set his own eyes upon an Archon. While Archons were said to be actively warding those serving the All-Father, terrible things continued to happen to good, faithful people. No Archons Thomas was aware of ever showed up to defend those he had witnessed suffering and enduring injustices.

None of the winged powers had been forthcoming in the matter of his father. Thomas was certain his father was pitiably alone in the damp, cold darkness of the gaol known as the Tomb Hall. As Thomas bitterly saw it, the reality of life did not harmonize with the accounts contained within the Sacred Writings.

Thomas shrugged noncommittally, giving a conceding sigh. He chose to answer the question honestly, even though he did not want to answer in a way that disappointed his grandfather. When he spoke, his tone was apologetic. "I'm not sure. I cannot say they don't exist, but I cannot say they do. I've never seen one, Grandfather, though I know we're supposed to believe what we are told."

"An honest answer … very much so," Wace replied, with a gentle smile. "Much more so than those who say they are certain Archons do not truly exist. They are the ones who amuse me the most, the ones who cannot possibly possess all existing knowledge, but then claim to have it on one matter or another."

"So do you believe in Archons?" Thomas asked pointedly,

perceiving something intriguing in the things left unspoken within Wace's reply.

"Had I your experience in life at this point, I would probably answer as you have," Wace said. "But I have had some very good fortune in life, most especially in the matter of this gift the All-Father has allowed me to possess ... such that I can speak with certainty. No, I do not believe Archons exist."

His grandfather paused, and Thomas felt the shock rippling through him, feeling a sharp pang of dismay. While he harbored doubts, he had always hoped one day to learn that Archons were real beings. While Thomas was gripped in the throes of despair, his grandfather's smile broadened, as he added a few more words to complete his statement.

"...because I know Archons do indeed exist."

Thomas' heart leaped at the concluding words. A thrilling sense of hope raced through him at the conviction contained within his grandfather's answer.

"Really? Truly, Grandfather?" Thomas queried, nearly stammering in a mixture of incredulity and excitement. "You have seen a real Archon?"

"Yes, and they tend to be a little different than you have seen depicted, when painted or sculpted," Wace commented. His eyes had a distant look to them, as he raised them towards the midday sky. "Beautiful creatures, not dense in substance at all, like you and me. They are filled with sparkling grains of light. That is the best way I can describe them, though words are limiting in the matter of their beauty. Indeed, they have a form consisting of light in its purest essence. Radiant and wondrous beings, far beyond anything you have ever seen in this world. No art in any church, or image painted on any noble's wall, can do them justice. You will know what I mean, when you see one for yourself. Everyone will, some day."

Wace appeared lost within his thoughts for several long moments. A tranquil, dreamy expression took form upon the old man's face, and Thomas wished he could see whatever image or experience his grandfather was envisioning.

Watching the sun's rays sparkling on the river surface, Thomas tried to imagine what a creature composed from elements of light would look like. It was a difficult notion to get his mind around, but the effort was like adding fresh wood to a fire, stoking flames of excitement and curiosity.

"I have told you that your mother is cared for, for a good reason," his grandfather said, bringing his gaze back upon Thomas. "You have wondered what you will do, for your mother, your sister, and even for your father. You may have an opportunity, to take a new path, one that may well help you in all these matters. Though I know little of what form it may be."

Thomas felt an upsurge of confusion as he listened to his grandfather. It was an unwelcome discordance, and he wondered how a discussion of being in one's spirit, the reality of the existence of Archons, and the terrible situation facing his family could all relate together. On the surface, they seemed completely unrelated matters.

"What are they like?" Thomas asked quickly, working to tamp down the nascent bewilderment forming in his mind. At the least, he wanted to know a little more about the celestial beings before Wace pursued another tangent.

"You are intrigued, young Thomas, aren't you? I was about to bring all of this together, believe it or not. But I will pause to give you an answer. Visiting with an Archon is as real as you and I talking right now … every bit as real. My experiences are definitely not dreams, young Thomas. How do you think I knew to be near your street, on the day your father was arrested? I was told I would be needed, though I did not know why, at the time," his grandfather said. He then took a deep breath, and his voice became more solemn in timbre. "And it is such a visit I am here to speak with you about … a visit relating to your situation. It took place just two days ago, during the calm of night. I was given to know something that seems of great importance. I was in my spirit, and I encountered an Archon, something I have done often enough."

His grandfather paused again, and his hazel-colored eyes searched Thomas' face carefully. Whatever Wace was looking for, he seemed satisfied with what he saw reflected in Thomas' face, as he continued with his account.

"I looked upon the encounter as a special opportunity, given what has been happening in this world to our family. I asked the Archon about you, and if anything could be done to spare your dear father. I received a most unusual answer … I had expected just simple counsel, but I do not yet know what to make of the response given me by the Archon."

His grandfather's story was getting ever stranger, and Thomas did his best to keep a perplexed expression from displaying too openly on his face. He did not want his grandfather misinterpreting anything, perhaps mistakenly coming to think Thomas was taking his words with anything less than the utmost seriousness.

"The Archon told me you can choose to leave Avalos by the wings of a great dragon ... and that this would stay your father's life," Wace stated slowly. He then added, more quickly, shaking his head, "I know, it sounds impossibly strange. I do not have the first idea what to make of it, but that is what the Archon said. I asked the Archon to explain more about this message, but was given no further response."

"What?" Thomas replied, in absolute bewilderment at the Archon's bizarre message.

A part of him wondered whether his grandfather's mind was indeed taking a turn for the worse, though the old man appeared very lucid. There was not the slightest hint of jest, and his eyes reflected sincerity.

"I know, I know, it sounds like I am entering senility," Wace stated, as if he had picked up Thomas' wavering thoughts. "But I heard the words as plain as the water in that river ... and even more clearly than words. You see, when you communicate with an Archon, it is like images and thoughts form within your own mind; things that are more clear, and better understood, than anything spoken words could ever convey. You have to experience it, to know what I am struggling to describe.

"It is not as if the Archon is incapable of human methods. The Archon could easily choose to speak with me aloud using the words of our Gallean tongue. The Archon did, in fact, place words for me to remember within my own mind, even as it transferred a purity of meaning and intent. This is why I can speak to you with certainty regarding the message, even if I do not understand it."

"Grandfather ... it all sounds so strange," Thomas replied, incredulous. "Leaving Avalos by the wings of a dragon to save my father? I would go if I knew I could save my father's life. But I've never even seen a dragon, like I've never seen an Archon. And a dragon, here in Avalos?" Thomas looked down and shook his head in exasperation, his thoughts increasingly muddled.

"So, if you saw a dragon in Avalos, you might believe in Archons as well?" queried his grandfather, with a lighthearted grin.

The question brought to light an intriguing notion, at the very least. "If I saw a dragon in the middle of Avalos ... and I could leave with the dragon … I would believe in Archons," Thomas said matter-of-factly, though believing the extraordinary scenario to be far too absurd to take seriously.

"Be careful of what you declare, young Thomas. You may someday be required to adhere to it," Wace replied, with an even broader grin.

"Grandfather, I don't think I'm going to see a dragon in the middle of Avalos. Definitely not one that offers a chance for me to fly away with it," Thomas replied, rife with disbelief.

Like Archons, dragons were brought to life within the imagination by the voice of a skilled storyteller. They were the subject of artistic representations. There were many, many accounts of the creatures, some even set near to the current age, but never had Thomas seen one of the legendary winged beasts in the flesh.

It would not likely be otherwise. Dragons were believed to have been hunted down or driven out of Gallea and the western lands long ago. Shards of rumors, and a few rarer tales, alleged that a few survivors had found refuge deep in Midragard, near the southern edge of the world itself. It was held that the creatures survived within a great range of mountains, unhindered by the affairs of humankind.

Very few took such claims seriously, most of sound mind finding them to be preposterous. The populaces of those faraway lands were well-known for having imaginative, mythical tendencies. It was not a stretch to believe that the Midragardans had fomented tales a dragon haven.

Midragard was, after all, the source of the barbarous raiders who had descended like a plague in Gallea and other western lands not all that long ago. The raids had eventually ceased, and it was known that large groups of Midragardans had settled in Norengal and Gallea, but their blood-stained legacy of fear had not dissipated. It was more than appropriate that a fearsome creature like a dragon would be reputed to survive, even flourish, in such a myth-rich land.

Thomas doubted there were any dragons in Midragard, just many fertile imaginations. Yet like the matter of Archons, the tales of dragons were prevalent enough that Thomas believed there had to be some root of truth to them. While he was skeptical of Wace's fantastical tale, within the depths of his heart he hoped fervently that his grandfather's words could somehow be true.

Thomas turned his attention towards another aspect of his

grandfather's strange experiences. "So how do you really know you are… in spirit? How does it happen?" Thomas ventured cautiously, hoping his grandfather did not find the pointed question entirely distrustful.

"When I am in spirit, I am as conscious as I am right now," Wace answered. "I am as clear of mind and focused as I am when fully awake, perhaps even more so. I can even perceive my own body lying on that old, hemp-stuffed mattress in the long chamber, as if it were something completely separate from me. Leaving my body is quite different from dreams. The process of your spirit lifting out of your physical body is often very loud, and you go through a lot of strange, jarring sensations. Sometimes you even feel like you cannot move for a few moments, like you are trapped in your own body."

As if an amusing afterthought struck him, he added with a laugh, "Of course, you would imagine that stepping out of your body, in your spirit, would be a little more exciting than finding yourself looking down upon long rows of snoring old men. Even worse, you can see them snoring much clearer, as you don't need much light to see by when you are experiencing that state of existence."

The words stopped Thomas' thoughts in their tracks. Even his breath stalled in his throat, and he felt a light chill draping over him. The further illumination from his grandfather was not the answer he had expected, but it certainly elicited some very pertinent recollections.

Thomas had experienced several dreams of a very unusual nature before; or at least dreams were what he thought they were. The incidents left vivid impressions, and bore striking parallels to what his grandfather had just illustrated.

The events started with similar perceptions of loud noises, accompanied by the distressing sensation of being in an entirely immobile condition. During those moments, he nonetheless found himself with a clear-headed state of mind, in full command of his thoughts and focus.

He would have thought he was wide-awake, were it not for some things impossible to reconcile with the physical world. In each of the various instances, he had perceived himself as floating above his body. Looking downward, he had gazed upon the gentle rising and falling of his chest, as breath moved steadily in and out. A couple of times, it was so surreal he had not realized at first that it was his own body he was looking upon, thinking for a few moments it belonged to somebody else.

During a few of the bizarre experiences, he had floated out from the garret, moving right through the timber frame and clay tiles of the roof as if they had no material substance. Outside, he had gazed upon an ethereal nighttime scene, able to see more clearly than the available light from moons, stars, and watch fires should have allowed. Many things seemed to give off their own glow, limned by some mysterious, inner source of light.

Following initial reactions based in sheer wonderment, anxieties and fears always began welling up. Inevitably, he started thinking of his body back in the garret; afraid of whether or not he would be able to get back inside his physical form. The experiences ended almost instantly at those moments, snapping him back to reality as he woke up on the mattress. The times where he had concentrated for too long on the sight of his breathing body had also ended in such an abrupt, jarring manner.

Opening his eyes within the dark of the garret, he had always deemed the odd experiences to be some manner of special dreams. A few times, He had briefly spoken of them to his mother, but she had told him they were nothing more than dreams. The one or two times he had mentioned them to Emma, she had chided him for having an overactive imagination. He had never ventured to tell his father about the incidents at all.

No matter how real the experiences seemed, Thomas had come to accept his mother's explanation. Dreams formed the only plausible scenario, as he could think of no other satisfactory possibility.

Since then, he had kept the incredible memories to himself, the last such experience having transpired well over a year ago. His grandfather's words brought great upheaval to his settled mind, forcing him to revisit the exotic experiences once again.

"Thomas?" his grandfather queried, looking at the youth with a furrowed brow.

Thomas blinked his eyes, realizing how distracted he had become. He smiled at his grandfather, trying not to look shaken. For the moment, he wanted to keep his troubling insights and recollections to himself. "I'm okay, grandfather. It's just a lot to take in."

"It is a lot to take in ... but a lot has been thrown upon you, young Thomas," his grandfather replied sympathetically, his face easing into a gentle grin.

"Grandfather, I've always wanted to have a great adventure, like the tales of the knights who go off to the Holy Wars, or the Saints traveling in far off lands," Thomas said. "I always wanted to know about your travels as a pilgrim. Now, you speak of something that is amazing to me, something I can hardly believe. It sounds just as wonderful as those other things I have wished for."

"I wish I could do something right now, right here, to prove the truth of it all to you, beyond doubt," his grandfather said softly. "But it is not the way of things. What happens, happens. Some see with their own eyes, while others do not, and these have to choose whether to believe or not. I am no sorcerer. I cannot compel something to happen, though I wish it were otherwise.

"I only know what I know, and I can only say I am completely convinced that this message was of tremendous importance. As crazy as it may sound to you now, look out in the future for a dragon that can take you from Avalos. Know that will be an opportunity that can give you a chance to save your father. A chance, mind you, but a chance nonetheless, and that is certainly better than having no chance at all.

"If such an occasion rises in your future, do not hesitate to act on it due to worries over your mother. As I have said, she will be well provided for. "

"And Emma?" Thomas asked.

"She will also be well taken care of, right alongside your mother," his grandfather replied.

The likelihood of a dragon appearing in the midst of Avalos, when none had been seen in all of Gallea during Thomas' lifetime, was staggeringly infinitesimal enough. The chance of a dragon manifesting in Avalos that would be accessible to Thomas was even more miniscule.

It sounded so ridiculously absurd, and Thomas wished he had a way of obtaining some sort of validation without unduly offending his grandfather. The whole scenario was so entirely bizarre that Thomas could not help but think his grandfather had, at the least, misunderstood the Archon.

"I will remember what you have told me, grandfather. And don't worry, I won't talk about this to anyone else," Thomas stated after a few uneasy moments, mustering as much surety in his voice that he could.

"I thank you for that, young Thomas. I cannot expect you to do any more with these strange words from the dry lips of a poverty-ridden old man, other than keep them to heart," his grandfather responded.

With a little groan, his grandfather slowly began getting up from where he was sitting on the large tree root. Wincing, he stretched his back for a moment, the movements accompanied by a few perceptible cracks and pops.

"Ah, to be your age again, at least in the physical world," his grandfather remarked, chuckling, as another considerable pop sounded.

Thomas got up, and found he was not entirely unscathed, having acquired some stiffness and soreness within his own muscles. He took a few moments to stretch out his limbs, and arch his back, managing to limber up much quicker than his grandfather had.

"Let us be on our way, so that the good Sisters do not think I have gone ahead to the All-Father just yet," his grandfather said, shuffling away from the tree and working his way back towards the long slope leading up to the roadway.

Thomas followed at his side, keeping close, so he could provide assistance where necessary. The women laboring at the riverside washing clothes remained engrossed in their activities as they departed.

Lost in a swirl of thoughts, Thomas barely took account of the city's sights as they returned over the bridge and proceeded to the Hospital for the Aged. For the most part, they traveled in silence, an atmosphere broken only when his grandfather grumbled aloud about the travails of poverty, when they passed a crier standing in front of an undercroft tavern.

The crier was heralding the recent arrival of some type of Gallean red wine, of a certain kind that Wace expressed having a great fondness for. The crier's pronouncement caused his grandfather to bitterly lament the thin ale he would be drinking instead that evening.

Thomas wished for a moment that he still had one of the gold coins given him by the stranger from the Unifier's mountain-palace, so he could buy his grandfather some of the wine. The desire sharply reminded him that he did not have even one denier in his pocket. He knew he would be hard-pressed to scrounge up anything in the coming days, weeks and months, in light of the grave poverty he and his family were now facing. The dire thoughts left him with a heavy heart, as he continued in silence with his grandfather.

They managed to reach the hospital without incident. After greeting one of the Sisters, Thomas bid his grandfather a good evening, and started off for home. The sun was far advanced in its travel across the skies, and the shadows were shifting and lengthening by the time

Thomas entered the oppressive silence of his home.

He paused inside the front doorway, taking account of the vacant horizontal loom within. The unattended loom was now a visual source of distress, an inanimate, unrelenting witness to the travails besetting his family.

Thomas wondered how Nicholas was faring, hoping that Hervee of Delshire had been able to find the man some good work with another weaver. Thomas had not yet learned whether or not this was so, but he greatly missed the buoyant journeyman's presence. Nicolas had been such a day to day fixture in Thomas's little world, to the point he was regarded as a kind of family member, in some ways.

Thomas never thought he would see the loom sitting still for days on end, without being worked for even a moment. Weaving had been done in his home ever since the day he was born. In truth, his own birth had occurred within the home he was now standing in; the only home he had ever known.

Any notion of permanence within the physical world was an illusory deception. Though the revelation was greatly discomfiting, Thomas could see through the facades of the world clearly enough now. Though undeniably true, the transitory nature of life still brought a great sadness to Thomas' heart, as he trudged past the silent, dust-gathering loom.

He knew that no matter how kind Hervee of Delshire was, the loom would not remain silent for much longer. When it resumed the tasks for which it was intended, Thomas had no doubts his family would find itself cast into a whirlwind of change.

A new weaver, with other apprentices or journeymen, would soon be working the treadles previously tended by Nicholas and his father. Thomas, Emma, and his mother would find themselves in a place other than the house they had known for year after year, ever since his very first memories.

Thinking about the depressing realities, he hoped with all his heart that his grandfather had indeed received a message from a genuine Archon. It would be so reassuring to know there was a chance, no matter how slim, for Thomas to do something that might somehow save his father from an unjust fate.

Though it seemed so mundane, and unlike the fantastical aspirations Thomas usually fancied, seeing his father back working at the loom would truly excite him more than any promise of adventurous journeys into exotic, faraway lands. He knew without a doubt that he would give up such a chance in an instant, in order to see new cloth being fashioned by his father in the little room once again. As he ascended the steps to the second level, he could not prevent his eyes from misting over, as the frustration of it all overwhelmed his suffering heart and mind.

MERSHAD

The tendrils of a bitter chill whipped around the timbers holding up the roof, coursing through the open space of the house interior. The icy shards of air entered through the smallest of crevices, piercing between the rough wooden planks of the hall-house's sides.

The probing winds fanned the low flames of a fire slumbering in the central, stone-lined hearth, stirring them up momentarily. The creaking of timbers, enduring the onslaught of unyielding winds outside, woke Mershad from his troubled sleep with a start.

Reflexively, he pulled the thick sheepskin covering tightly about him, as a flash of lightning splashed evanescent slivers of brilliant light into the dimness. After another roll of resonant thunder, he sat up in the darkened room. Tapestries hung strategically on the side walls to help block the cold were not fully effective. Looking around, he saw he was alone.

With nobody awake to tend the fire, Mershad knew it should have been put out. Yet none of the three quartered in the hall-house had gotten used to the absence of warmth and light that came with extinguishing the hearth fire at night.

Mershad wondered how long it would be before his friends sought to settle down for the night. He surmised that most of those yet awake were probably gathered inside the king's great hall.

They were likely waiting out the storm through some rounds of a game resembling tables, or perhaps listening to incredible tales, making bawdy jests, or listening to the music of lyre or flute. What was for certain was that they would be drinking copious amounts of ale and mead.

Kent would undoubtedly be striving to make better acquaintance with one of the highly attractive women living on the king's estate. At least

Derek would be there to make sure Kent did not blunder into anything that would result in him being on the receiving end of a Midragardan warrior's ire. The thought brought a grin to Mershad's face.

He was about to get up from the mattress when he heard a firm rapping on the door. It was more of a notice than a request. A moment later, a lone human figure opened the door and entered, along with a formidable, four-legged companion padding a couple of paces behind. Mershad instantly recognized the outline of the figure, as well as the lupine companion.

King Hakon paused a moment to secure the door behind him, as the winds pressured its iron hinges. The great wolf strode slowly towards the center of the room, its eyes glowing in the firelight, as it silently regarded Mershad.

"Humor an old king," King Hakon gently greeted, as Mershad awkwardly rose to his feet and bowed his head respectfully.

"King Hakon," Mershad stammered in reply, surprised to see the king entirely unattended within one of the guest houses of the settlement.

Clad in little more than a tunic, trousers, and a long cloak, worn so that it formed a hood to protect his head from the outer elements, King Hakon ambled over to a wooden stool just beyond the farther end of the hearth. Behind him, treading noiselessly, the black wolf Heder followed closely.

The huge beast circled for a moment before curling up at the King's feet, resting its great head upon its broad paws. The wolf's golden eyes remained alert, trained upon Mershad, but its posture was relaxed.

"Please, be at ease," King Hakon implored in a calm tone of voice. "We are just two men here, along with a particularly large wolf."

Mershad walked closer towards King Hakon, and sat down upon one of the two raised, wood-faced earthen surfaces running along the length of the chamber's sides. The front facing of the low earthen platform began just to the king's immediate left.

"You might find it the folly of an old man, but I do not mind a walk in the midst of thunder and lightning," King Hakon remarked, with a soft chuckle. "It speaks to my soul sometimes, and I am afraid I am in no state of mind for idle games or mead this evening. I hope I am not disturbing you much."

Mershad shook his head, "No, not at all. Kind of hard to sleep, with the commotion of the storm out there. I probably should have taken a walk myself."

The old king of Midragard smiled. "Our ways are calling to you already."

"So does Heder enjoy these nights as well?" Mershad asked, glancing at the ebony shape sprawled out on the ground. He knew he had nothing to fear, but the close presence and glowing stare of the huge wolf nonetheless cultivated a little nervousness within him.

The king leaned over and scratched the great wolf between the creature's triangular ears. "He has certainly seen a few storms in his time. This is not one that could rattle him much."

The king then grew silent, and seemed to be pondering something that troubled him. After a few pensive moments passed, Mersad decided to be a little forthcoming.

"What troubles you, King Hakon?" he asked gently, before adding, hesitantly, "If I may ask you … of course."

The old king lifted his head slowly and looked to Mershad. "Svein has left these lands with a great war fleet. Midragard girds for a war like no other. I, for one, cannot find any peace of mind. Even my dreams haunt me. They no longer provide a refuge where I can evade the troubles of the world."

Mershad could see that the king's face was heavily laden with worries. In that moment, he also realized that the king needed a place and a time where he did not have to appear strong and inviolable, a façade Hakon would always need before such a valorous and hardy people as the Midragardans.

Mershad recognized that he was one of the very few individuals the king could talk to during such a time. As a widower, the king likely had nobody to fully confide in. Even in the company of his most trusted retainers, he could not necessarily allow himself to be entirely candid.

Mershad felt honored that the king had chosen to place a deeper trust in him. Hakon could let his guard down and become just a man with Mershad, for a few precious moments, and not worry about being an embodiment of Midragard.

"It must be difficult for you, as you are far from your lands, and even your world," the king said, as if in further reflection.

"I try not to think about that too much, even if I can never forget about it completely," Mershad replied quietly, with a slight shrug. "I have found that if I think of my circumstances too much, I can only damage myself for living in the present. Reality is reality."

"There is much wisdom in what you say," the king replied. He clasped his hands in his lap, and looked down for a moment, before continuing. "Even so, my dreams are a premonition at times. The ones I have suffered recently offer nothing but dire portent.

"I keep dreaming that the Unifier seizes you and your companions, and we are utterly powerless to stop Him. In my dreams He is beyond resistance, you are under His full control, and all of Midragard falls under His shadow."

"I hope that dream never happens," Mershad said, keeping his fears about the matter at bay. He worked to keep his face as serene as he could for the benefit of the king.

"There is more that burdens my mind, though these worries existed long before you came to our shores," King Hakon said. "I believe it is only right to tell you, so that you, and those with you, know of it too."

The king then explained how his dreams seemed to relate to the matter of an old prophecy passed along by the Midgragardan people for many generations. It was a prophecy concerning the appearance of people from another world, who would hold the balance of the world within them.

Mershad listened with fascination and interest, especially in light of the fact that he began to realize King Hakon truly regarded Mershad and his companions as being three of the prophesied people he was speaking of. In that context, the tale Hakon revealed was all the more incredible to Mershad's ears.

Crossing barriers between worlds, the presence of the prophesied otherworlders would herald the approaching time when the boundaries between the realms of gods and mortal beings were fully breached. It would bring about a climactic age, when a final doom fell upon the entire world.

As King Hakon explained, the Western Church of the new religion spoke of such a final cataclysm, as did the old religion once followed in Midgard. Both described a titanic clash involving all of the world, and all the powers of the spirit world, out of which a new world would emerge.

King Hakon made mention of how he had found it highly intriguing when he had first learned that the Western Church spoke of the emergence of new heavens and a new world following the final battle. As the old religion followed for ages by Hakon's people had also predicted a new world to rise from the ashes of the old, there was a congruent prophetic element within the heart of both religions. The strange similarity had been something that greatly amazed the king, as he came to embrace the ways of the new religion.

The gateway to the All-Father's spiritual realm, according to the prophecies relating to the Western Church, would be found in the mythical First Gardens. Death held no presence in the First Gardens, which had been hidden from the view of mortals and immortals alike in Ave since the beginning age of creation. Once the incorruptible Gardens were found, the individuals from another world would somehow invoke the gateway, and help breach the barriers between the realms of existence.

The sundering would then enable celestial powers serving the All-Father to come in full numbers into Ave, unrestrained and without hindrance. The Archons would then be able to aid those still resisting evil during the last days.

Another version, perhaps a broader telling of the prophetic revelations, was much more foreboding. It was derived from the prophetic traditions of the Western Church's enemies, those who followed the Adversary, Jebaalos.

The more diabolical prophetic traditions said that the prophesied ones from other worlds could also be gathered for the purpose of opening a dark gateway. The other gateway was said to be located at the very place where the self-crowned dark god once fell from heaven and struck Ave, following the Celestial War of the Schism.

The ancient, unholy place, mythical in nature as its location in Ave had never been identified, was called the Place of Lightning. The impact of the malevolent Adversary's fall was reputed to be incomprehensible in its sheer force, and blinding radiance. It was said to have left a great scar upon Ave, marking where the Adversary's passage had burned straight through existence itself; piercing the world of matter and descending into the fiery, molten realms of hell.

Hakon had then remarked that he found it difficult to believe that the location of such an important and monumental place had been forgotten, if the Fall of Jabaalos had been remembered in such powerful detail. Nevertheless, the alternatives to the Western Church's prophecy were clear within the words of the dark prophecy. A gateway between the material and spiritual realms could likewise be opened by an assemblage of otherworlders at the Place of Lightning.

Demonic powers would then be able to pour into Ave, in all of their infernal might and fury, to seek the conquest of Ave and assail Heaven itself. A nightmare of blood and fire would be unleashed upon the world, before the ravenous hordes turned their attentions to higher realms.

Banished Archons would rise with Jebaalos at their lead, accompanied by a vast, innumerable force formed in the depths of the abyss since the beginning of creation. They would wage war upon Palladium itself, the assailants burning inside with insatiable hatred.

Creation would then be remade, in Jebaalos's baleful image. Death, hell, and oblivion would then be brought to reign over all worlds. The mere thought that such a horrific travesty could even be considered as possible chilled Mershad.

Yet as prophecy tended to be, there were many aspects of the prophetic verses of both kinds that were very nebulous. There were also some things that were resoundingly clear.

It was certain that the issue of free will was involved in the fabric of both main prophecies. The balances of force could be shifted one way or another, either for heaven or hell, before the Final Battle was commenced.

It was also manifest that there would be twelve individuals, understood to be otherworlders, whose freely-made choices would be crucial during the course of the momentous events. Only four out of this special group of twelve would be necessary to bring about the sundering between dimensions with respect to the opening of the Celestial Gateway, in the First Gardens. In a similar way, eight individuals from the appointed twelve would be needed to open Hell's Gates, at the Place of Lightning.

The greater burden fell upon the darker forces serving the Adversary. Mershad began to wonder as to the reasons behind the disparity in individuals necessary to open the two gates, when Hakon indicated there was a specific reason for the difference. The explanation reached back to the beginning of the great conflict, at the dawn of time.

It was said the proportions needed to open the gates somehow reflected the balance of the original forces arrayed at the first battle. Discordance gripped creation at the moment of the Great Rebellion, cleaving an existence of pure harmony asunder. For the first moment in all of existence, the Will of the Creator had been rejected. The cataclysmic, transcendent moment left an indelible legacy, one that reverberated all the way to the present age.

As the dark god was said to have swept a third of the stars from the heavens at the beginning of time, the original division affected events at the end of time. Mershad saw that the proportions involving the two prophecies were the inverse of the ratio existing at the first battle.

As two out of three had sided with the All-Father in the First Battle, only one out of three was needed to enact the Sundering. Likewise, as one of three had sided with the Adversary at the onset of time, two of three were needed to unlock the gateway to the Infernal Realms.

The proportions fulfilled a certain type of unity, or completeness, from the beginning of the world to its end. Mershad could not begin to fathom a deeper explanation. As to why the full number of possible candidates for enacting Sunderings was twelve, King Hakon could not say.

Forebodingly, a group of twelve potential candidates allowed for the possibility that both of the gateways could be opened during the same time. It would take a very precise alignment of wills, where exactly eight chose to enact the Sundering at the Place of Lightning, and exactly four chose to enact the Sundering at the First Gardens.

It all looked to be an overwhelming quandary, fraught with all kinds of dilemmas for those who hoped for the triumph of justice and hope. Even if four otherworlders could be gathered together, willing to commit to the All-Father, the First Gardens would still have to be located. As it had been hidden from humankind since the beginning age of creation, even finding it seemed like a near impossibility. Without the location of the First Gardens, all efforts could easily be for naught.

It was a relief that the opposing prophecy was similarly burdened, with the location of the Place of Lightning lost within the murky depths of myth and legend. In actuality, the enemy's encumbrances were significantly worse, with the need for a much greater proportion of willing otherworlders to open their dark realms.

Mershad nonetheless felt little better about the overall situation. The implications of the prophecies, especially with respect to the presence of Mershad and his companions in Ave, were enormous to consider. The slim prospects of achieving success in the end were daunting, any way he looked at it.

"You should gather nine of us together. Keep us out of the hands of the Unifier, and this Sundering can never happen, at least with respect to the second version of the prophecy," Mershad commented, shortly after King Hakon finished his oration. "And you would have more than enough of us available to fulfil the first version of that prophecy, if anyone could ever discover where these First Gardens are located."

The king shook his head regretfully, his countenance rueful, "Had I known more of this, at a much earlier time, we could have worked towards such an end. Even so, as it is, there is still hope … in many ways.

"There may not even be twelve from your world in all of Ave. It is also possible the Unifier may not be able to acquire eight, whether there are twelve in Ave or not. Even if the Unifier does capture eight, they would have to be willing. I find it hard to believe anyone would choose to help open the gateways of hell itself.

"Perhaps, too, the prophecy speaks of yet something more, a veiled aspect none of us have thought of." Hakon's expression looked weary, belying the hopes he had just mentioned.

"Whether there are more from my world existing in this world or not, beyond those I know of already, none of us can afford to fall into the hands of the Unifier," Mershad rationalized. "That I can say for certain."

"And such is my great burden. I am still just a man, but now I am afraid I am involved in events involving unimaginable, immortal powers. How can a mere man, here breathing upon Ave for a mere flicker of years, measure up to such an impossible task?" the king lamented, closing his eyes, and taking a deep breath.

Hakon let out his breath slowly, sat up a little straighter, and opened his eyes again. The flicker Mershad then perceived was not one of years, but of resolve.

"Yet I must do what I can," the king continued in a firmer tone. "The voice of my heart says to have you taken to the great Drakkar Mountains, to the south, where the dragons abide within their longstanding refuge. Perhaps some dragons would agree to harbor you in safety, in a place that no effort of humankind can assail. They have protected Midragardans in the past. We have fought and bled for them, even as they have been driven out from other lands, or been hunted down and slain."

Mershad thought back to the towering, fierce monstrosities that visited Bergthora's village. He also recalled the behemoth that had made its presence known when the Arcamon beset Mershad. Like the one that had visited King Hakon's estate, the larger dragon was a living legend to the Midragardans.

The vivid memories of the gigantic Elder dragons brought a chill to him, one not born from any effects of the weather. If dragons such as those winged titans, or even their formidable smaller relatives, chose to take Mershad under their protection, he did not see how the Unifier could hope to reach or capture him.

"It would be for a time of safe keeping," the king went on, "until a better grasp of this war can be attained. Until we can find out more of what comes against us in the world. I cannot deceive myself in regard to this war. It is likely to come very soon to our lands."

A heavy silence fell upon them, as Mershad thought of the massive burdens carried within the old king. Mershad had intimately known the kinds of feelings evoked within his own heart, not so long ago, by a war launched by his adopted country against his ancestral homeland.

A powerful, seemingly unstoppable force had commenced that war. The circumstances of the two wars, in two different worlds, were indeed different, but in terms of the scale of power being wielded it was a situation not entirely unlike the threat Midragard was now facing.

He remembered how he had endured the terrible war in a surreal environment. The strangest part of the experience was the stark contrast of daily living between the two nations at war. His day to day existence had been spent amid a populace effectively unobstructed in their daily lives. Life proceeded unscathed for nearly everyone, save for the families and friends of the comparatively few casualties incurred during the overwhelming onslaught.

For every soldier of Mershad's country that died, a hundred or more soldiers and civilians died within his ancestral land. The signs of war in his own land consisted of reports on the news, the occasional, miniscule protests around campuses, and displays of flags and banners. The signs of war in his ancestral land were the constant rumbling of deadly thunder, and staccato rains of lead, which reduced cities to rubble and soaked the dry, desert land in crimson showers.

With each passing day, with every fleeting moment, he had lived in a terrorized state of mind where he knew he might well lose his extended family, and some very dear friends, in the explosive flash of an instant.

The black columns of smoke from massive explosions within the major cities shown on television were not just images to Mershad. They represented a horrible fear. It was that enormous, constant tension, of knowing that the lives of his family and friends were truly under a cloud of unceasing threat, that pounded mercilessly upon Mershad's emotions.

This king of Midragard, Mershad recognized, viewed his entire realm as an extension of family. The king also saw the same kind of dark cloud spreading menacingly over all of Midragard, poised to burst with a downpour of horror and death over his own lands.

Mershad knew the essence of the worries, fears, and anxieties the king must have been facing for quite some time. He had not missed the furrowed brow and glint of sadness within the king's eyes when Svein and several other retainers had left for the coast, to coordinate the final assemblage and departure of the Midragardan fleet. It was a look genuinely reminiscent of a father looking upon departing children, not knowing whether or not it was for the last time.

The expression occurred in an ephemeral moment, when the king had not thought any others would be studying his face. Most had not been, their eyes fixed upon the men about to lead an impressive armada of sleek war vessels forth from Midragard's shores.

Mershad was the exception, and his witness of the brief, unguarded moment made a heartfelt impression. The look had struck him to the core, emblazoned on his mind such that he could recall it distinctly even now.

Yet beyond the aspects Mershad could personally relate to, the burden held by the old king held a second component that Mershad could not. In addition to the signs of Hakon's tremendous affinity for his people, Mershad could see that the king also cast an incredible strength forth, one that appeared to radiate across the lands of Midragard. He was a king who truly bonded the realm together, in his wisdom, leadership, and his very person.

Mershad had seen the inspiration and influence of the king reflected in the faces of merchants, warriors, craftsmen, mothers, and many others, whenever the name of King Hakon was brought up. He had seen it in the gazes and postures of all the people, whenever the king passed by; reflections of sincere respect, and genuine reverence.

The people of Midragard had enjoyed great prosperity and fair justice under the king. An unassailable bond between the noble monarch and his people had been forged, woven through blood and traditions strengthened over the course of a great many centuries.

As Mershad saw it, after learning more about his generous hosts, their most heartfelt traditions and values were rooted primarily in all forms of strength and loyalty; to friend, kin, and leader alike. Such characteristics were reflected and celebrated within their great Sagas, and undeniably held in the quiet deep of their souls. Midragard was a living expression of a rich heritage, culture, and its greatest treasure, the people themselves.

The thought of the king's inherent goodness, strength, and resolute bond with his people brought a sudden gladness to Mershad, causing him to smile broadly. The feeling engendering the smile instantly lightened the heaviness in his heart.

"There is reason to smile at this?" the king queried. Eyes widened, and eyebrows raised, Hakon looked to be a little surprised, if not mildly baffled by the unanticipated reaction.

"Maybe there are always reasons to smile," Mershad replied, as the smile lingered upon his face. "Even in the midst of a great darkness."

The King must have found something pleasing in Mershad's visage or statement, as a slight smile was elicited from Hakon's overwrought face. The heavy gaze in his eyes shimmered with a little levity.

"Maybe there are," the King intoned, a few moments later, as his smile grew wider. "Maybe it takes an honored young guest from another land, in a different world, to remind an old King of what Midragard is, come what may on the field of battle."

"I carry my own heritage with me, whether in a foreign land in my former world, or now, in entirely new lands, of an entirely new world," Mershad stated. "I will go on any path you deem to be wise to travel. Midragard has been a great, kind, and generous friend to me, and I hope only that I can repay this kindness in some way, someday."

The words were not idly spoken, nor were they simply polite utterances meant to soothe the old king. They were deeply heartfelt, thought Mershad did not know how he could ever possibly contribute something of significance to the lands that had gone to such great lengths to assist him and his companions.

The king smiled again, as he slowly got back up to his feet. At the king's upward movement, the great wolf at the king's feet roused itself from the ground, and stood at the king's side. Its head remained squarely oriented upon Mershad, eyes still aglow from the light of the low fire.

"Thank you, Mershad. Truly, thank you. I cannot begin to understand what you must be going through, in a land that is not yours, in the midst of a great war that you and your friends had no part of," the king said, with an unmistakable air of compassion. "The fact that you can find some light reminds me that I can too. That is no small thing, with what I have been enduring in my weary heart. Have a good rest, as I may just have a good rest tonight myself, something I have not had for a very long time."

The king looked over to where the front door rattled on its hinges, battered from outside by the storm gripping the building. A rumble of thunder ensued, encompassing and reverberating.

Hakon's smile gleamed as he looked back towards Mershad, giving him a merry wink that stripped many years away from his countenance. When he spoke again, his voice even carried a more youthful lilt. "Looks like a good time for a stroll outside, one fit for a king of Midragard."

The king and Mershad shared a final moment of warm laughter together, as Hakon turned and walked to the door. With a little effort he opened it against the winds drubbing against it. Heder dutifully followed the king outside, into the tempestuous night. When the door was closed shut at last, Mershad was left alone once again.

He had not consciously sought to achieve anything, but he had somehow brought an honorable old man some sorely needed relief. It did not matter whether the old man happened to be a great king, as Hakon definitely was. It would have been just as satisfying to Mershad if Hakon had merely been an elderly thrall on the estate.

When Mershad lay back down upon the mattress, slipping underneath the sheepskin covering once again, he was not nearly so restless as before King Hakon visited. Likewise, the power of the storm did not disturb him quite so much as it did before.

He settled down easily, with a more contented heart, knowing he would have a good night's sleep. Perhaps Midragard was calling out to him now, and perhaps a part of him had answered.

THOMAS

After putting away the trestle board, and setting the solar back in order, Thomas assisted Emma down on the first level of the house with tidying up the kitchen. Once finished, he quietly climbed the two flights of stairs to the bed that would not be his for very much longer. As usual, his mother had said little during the evening meal, barely making a dent in the simple pottage, or the small chunk of bread set before her.

By the time Thomas was feeling his way up the dark staircases to the upper garret, she was already sequestered in the sleeping chamber at the rear of the second level. He kept his step light as he ascended, not wanting to disturb her. The thought of her sleeping alone night after night saddened his heart greatly. He was carrying a double burden nowadays, struggling over her sufferings as well as his own great sense of loss.

Emma lingered below in the kitchen, and Thomas knew she would likely spend awhile there by herself. Her own sorrows had manifested in the form of restlessness and tense disquiet, interrupted by periodic breakdowns of crying under the cumbersome emotional weight. He suspected she was enduring one such moment right then, as her eyes were already glistening when he had wished her a good night, and left her behind in the kitchen.

Thomas slowly got undressed, down to his breeches, tossing his shoes and tunic into a near corner of the garret. He settled onto the wide mattress, pulling one woolen blanket up over his body, as he lay flat upon his back. He stared silently at the underside of the roof, the timbers of which were just a few arm spans above him.

There was little to see, as the room was cast in deep shadow. Just a little moonlight filtered in through a small window at the far end of the garret space, the shutters of which Thomas and Emma usually kept open on warmer evenings. They needed all the air circulation they could get, as there were times the garret reached the verge of stifling during hotter mid-summer nights.

Thomas wished he could have one strong confirmation to tell him his grandfather's message was genuine. Gradually, with that sole, specific desire resting thickly on his mind, he began drifting off into the depths of sleep; at last letting his heavy eyelids settle shut.

A deafening roar came to Thomas' ears moments later. The clamorous sounds startled him at first from his deepening slumber. As the sensations continued, he decided to relax, and see what might transpire. Having thought so much about the special dreams that afternoon, he quickly recognized the noise as being one of the distinctive attributes of those strange experiences of his; of the kind that correlated with the descriptions of those experienced by his grandfather.

He felt a little surge of joy as well, as the experience was not something he had ever consciously willed. To have such an experience, so soon after talking with his grandfather, appeared to be a stroke of good fortune. At the very least, it enabled him to approach the onset of a new experience with a little less fear, and much more enthusiasm.

As he relaxed, he felt a powerful, shaking sensation throughout his entire body. Though it was a turbulent, discomfiting feeling, he was able to still his thoughts, and take in the potent feelings without undue alarm.

If the current encounter was to be anything like the others, he knew he could float and move through simple matter like the timber and clay composing the roof above him. As such, his thoughts turned towards the open air above the garret in expectation, envisioning the lofty view in his head.

In a flash of time, he found himself fully there, hovering gently over a wide spectrum of clay, lead, and slate-tiled rooftops, filling up his vision as he looked out over the adjacent streets.

Thomas found he was lucid, and entirely cognizant of himself, with a conscious awareness as focused as it ever was. He knew he was immersed in one of the strange experiences, feeling further elation at the notion while he looked out in amazement over the slumbering city.

The shadowy streets and buildings were dotted with the firelights of torches and braziers, most of which indicated contingents of the city watch. Almost every building was steeped in darkness, and devoid of any signs of activity. It was no surprise to Thomas, as it was long past the hour when strict guild and city rules required fires to be put out within residences, demarcating the time when most forms of work were expected to cease in accordance with the guild rules.

As he continued hovering in the air over his house, he recalled his grandfather's talk of Archons. He remembered how his grandfather had spoken of meeting the Archons when he was in spirit. If Thomas was now in spirit, like his grandfather, then it followed logically he was in a state where he might be able to find an Archon.

If there was any place in the city to begin searching out Archons, and perhaps encounter one, Thomas believed Father Anselm's church would be as good a place as any. He thought of the stone parish church, calling to mind the image of it within his mind.

He found himself rushing through the air in a blur. In a scant moment, he came to an abrupt halt. Looking directly downward, Thomas eyed the familiar, spear-shaped finial ornamenting the pinnacle perched above the lead-tiled, pyramidal roof of a bell-tower.

The four-sided bell-tower, at the western end of the church, held the arch-enclosed entryway at the ground level. The tower abutted the main body of the church, which continued down the spine of its high-pitched roof to its eastern gable end. The limestone used to construct the small edifice appeared to have a light glow along its surface, emitting from the stone itself.

Thomas quickly took account of the fact that his vision was much stronger than it should have been naturally, with the minimal light available from the two moons, faint stars, and scattered watch-fires. Circling around briskly on the ground below, and looking upward from the open yard before the church entrance, was a familiar, four-legged shape.

Father Anselm's stout, imposing dog, Pierre, moved briskly about, his body giving off a glow of its own. Pierre looked to be full of energy, more animated than Thomas had ever observed before.

Pierre trotted out from the yard and into the street, wagging his tail excitedly. The dog continued peering up towards Thomas, as three men of the city's night watch drew into sight, walking slowly along the street in front of the churchyard. The three patrolling watchmen paid no heed to the dog, nor did they take any notice of Thomas. The men strode forward without hesitation, and, astonishing to Thomas, they passed right through the body of the dog.

The incorporeal dog was not the only incredible part of the scene. Thomas's enhanced vision focused in upon a very thin, barely perceptible strand running from the dog, and continuing into the small house sitting adjacent to the parish church.

A significantly larger, brighter glow, one he had not noticed before, attracted Thomas's attention. He looked away from the watchmen and the dog, peering down towards the doorway at the base of the church's bell-tower.

Filling the entrance, a spectacular being stood at a height exceeding the lintel. The stone arch over the wooden doorway was like a framing aura for the entity's radiant head.

White-robed, the wondrous figure had eyes of pure white light, which were oriented towards Thomas. Long, flowing tresses of silver hair undulated from the being's head, as if buffeted steadily by a light wind.

Like a human, the being exhibited two arms, two legs, and other analogous features, but its outer surface was far unlike anything Thomas had ever seen. He could not bring himself to describe it as skin, as it formed the substance of the robe-like garment too.

Deep blue, and partially translucent, the surface gave off a smooth, luminous glow. It contained a myriad of tiny specks of light within it, like a miniature reflection of the immense spectrum of stars shining high above in the night sky. The miniscule lights were dynamic in nature, gliding slowly throughout the being's form in such a way that the creature's body had a constant, shimmering quality to accompany the soft glow.

Unlike a human, the ethereal being had a pair of broad wings spread wide behind its back. The tips of the great appendages reached all the way to the edge on each side of the bell-tower.

Thomas cast a quick glance back towards the street, thinking there could be no possible way the watchmen could miss the incredible manifestation. To his astonishment, the watchmen were still casually proceeding down the thoroughfare. Save for some momentary glances at their surroundings, their focus was on each other, as they talked amongst themselves. The men showed absolutely no awareness of the stunning figure within the church entryway.

Pierre, however, had padded directly up to the winged figure in the interim. The winged-being slowly laid its right hand upon the head of the dog, gently stroking the docile canine between its ears. The being smiled warmly, at it gazed upon Pierre.

Thomas watched in amazement, as Pierre was normally very boisterous in his approach to those he liked, and highly wary of those he did not know. His behavior at the moment fit neither category. The dog was showing a unique response for the ethereal figure.

"Will you remain up there long, young spirit?" a soft, amiable, feminine voice reached to Thomas. The enchanting voice contained a musical quality, which he would have described as choral in nature.

Thomas flinched, experiencing the speech simultaneously with a clear image appearing inside his head. He could see himself hovering in the sky, and the winged-being beckoning him downward, juxtaposed with another vision of him standing before the being in the churchyard.

The intertwined understanding born of images and words, and especially the interior visions, were a type of communication that he felt as much as interpreted. Thomas understood at once what his grandfather had been trying to describe.

Not really knowing exactly how movement worked in the light, floating body he now found himself in, he imagined drifting down into the churchyard. As if his body echoed his thoughts, he started descending slowly, easing down towards the ground in front of the churchyard.

He imagined having the ability to stand on the ground in a more natural manner, just like the celestial figure was doing. Again, as if some governing power acquiesced to his conscious intent, he felt a familiar sense of form, as he came to stand upright upon the grass.

Pierre nearly tackled him when his feet alighted upon the ground, but Thomas managed to remain standing. He brought his arms up and around the dog, giving the canine a big hug, even as Pierre's tongue flicked out to lick his right cheek. Thomas felt the rough tongue on his skin as vibrantly as if it were entirely physical.

The dog then disengaged, as if called back from Thomas. The melodious, kindly voice, and accompanying mental images, returned once again to Thomas.

"So, will you keep in mind what your grandfather has told you?"

Images involving his recent visit with his grandfather, and the strange message his grandfather had given him, flooded his mind in an instant. The feeling was not overwhelming, but rather one of absolute clarity, in which he had the sense he was recalling every single word his grandfather had spoken, in one singular moment.

Thomas knew that if the bright figure asked a question about anything his grandfather had said, then he would have been able to recall it with ease. He was surprised he felt no extreme fear in the presence of the extraordinary, unquestionably non-human creature. He knew, at the worst, that the being before him filled his own conception of an Archon.

The recognition of the being as possibly being an Archon brought with it a powerful inner confirmation that the being was indeed such a creature. Thomas felt a saturating warmth flood through him, bringing a sense of peace like being held in his mother's loving embrace.

He brought his eyes up slowly, uncertain of how to respond or show respect to the magnificent being that was at the very heart of his own spiritual beliefs. A kind smile spread across the being's face, a welcoming mien involving a harmony of its narrow chin, elegant cheeklines, full lips, and sharp nose, which all gave the creature a decidedly feminine appearance. Thomas looked awestruck into the being's face, gazing upon incredible beauty, imbued with celestial grace.

Thomas started to kneel, then straightened up, fumbling for words and hesitant on how to proceed. At last, he fell down clumsily to his knees before the hallowed Archon. The being moved towards him immediately, though whether it stepped lightly across the ground, or drifted just above its surface, Thomas could not tell. His eyes were fixed upon the Archon's tranquil, exquisite face.

An even brighter smile, filled with gaiety, was on the Archon's face as it laid its hand down gently upon Thomas' shoulder. He could feel, even more than hear, hints of merry laughter coming from within the being. It was a soothing laughter, of the kind derived from a sense of amusement and affection.

"Do not be afraid young spirit, and do not kneel before me, for I am a fellow servant of the All-Father," the Archon stated calmly, as Thomas felt a strong, compelling impulse to arise.

Keeping his eyes riveted upon the Archon's serene face, Thomas cooperated, getting slowly to his feet. "Sorry ... I don't know ... what I'm supposed to do," he mumbled, his thoughts trailing off, as he looked straight into the fathomless depths of the Archon's eyes.

The hint of mirth resonated strongly in the Archon's gaze, accompanied by another bright smile. "You have not often met with my kind?"

Thomas had no doubts the Archon knew the answer, before it had even asked the question. "No ... this is the first time," Thomas finally mustered.

"Now you have, so you may know that what your grandfather speaks of is true," the Archon replied.

A trace of amusement lingered, though a distinctly serious undertone was conveyed within the Archon's meaning. There was no need for discernment, or interpretation, as Thomas perceived the shift within the core of his being.

"And … my father. What is going to happen to him?" Thomas asked, realizing his opportunity to petition the Archon for help, in a more direct fashion than any prayer he had ever uttered in his life. "Can you save him?"

The Archon grew silent for a few moments, the look on the creature's face becoming much more somber. The serious demeanor of the Archon was intertwined with an unmistakable sensation of true compassion, as well as sadness, all of which poured strongly into Thomas' mind. He felt a slight dread towards the impending answer.

"The world you live in now is a world where great evil or great good can happen. Time takes its course, the forces of nature act, and creatures of will make their choices," the Archon stated slowly. "It is a realm where rain falls upon both the innocent and the corrupt. For those of the All-Father, it is a passage through a valley of shadow, the movement of flocks of little lambs through forests teeming with ravenous wolves."

A deep, ponderous sadness descended upon Thomas as he listened to the Archon's words. He inwardly perceived a host of vibrant images, and within his mind he understood for the very first time just how dangerous, and fundamentally unstable, the physical world was. A world in which a person had full latitude to choose actions ranging between the purest good and the purest evil allowed for all manner of things along the vast spectrum in between.

Beyond some basic laws governing the structure and function of physical things, it meant that such a world was rife with all possibilities. It meant that injustice had just as much potential as justice to manifest, and transpire. It meant that evil intent had the ability to be realized, and brought to fruition, in the very same manner that good intent could be confounded and stymied.

It also meant that there was just as much of a place within this kind of world for the things born of purely random chance. Even at a young age, Thomas understood that the forces of chance were dispassionate, and entirely indiscriminate regarding who or what they affected.

The storms at sea shattered apart the vessel of the rapacious marauder, just as easily as it did a sailing ship filled with pious pilgrims. It made no distinction at all between one group bent on murder and pillage, and another en route to honor and revere the All-Father and Emmanu in the Holy Lands. Both could be unceremoniously cast into frothing waters, condemned to a drowning fate. Even worse, the vessel of the sea raiders could well find itself under sunny skies, with favorable winds, while the occupants of a pilgrims' vessel could find themselves staring up at dark, menacing thunderheads in the skies above.

The life one experienced in such an uncertain, vulnerable world was no performance upon a stage, of the kind Thomas often watched during holy feast days on the streets of Avalos. Those staged events involved actors executing predetermined roles, within the context of a familiar story that the audience watching already knew well by heart.

If the world was to be compared to a stage, then it was one in which the actors determined the course of the performance, improvising with each and every moment. Something entirely original was created in the process, a vast, growing story that no audience observing would be able to predict.

There were many very uncomfortable, and undeniable, truths as far as such a world was concerned. A brutal, self-centered lord could find himself enjoying the resounding success of his intended aims, no matter how corrupt, oppressive, or blood-soaked. To all looking, it could seem as if the avaricious noble's life was constantly blessed with bounty and good fortune by the All-Father. At the very same moment in time, a kind weaver with a loving family could find no hope of pardon or mercy, for having done a most reasonable thing born out of loyalty to friend and family.

The particular noble whose son had died in the melee between the townspeople and the violently rioting students, and would likely ensure the execution of Thomas' father, was more like the former man. So was the city's provost, who would soon render the final decision, a man carrying a heavily stained reputation amongst the lower classes, but nonetheless led a life of comfort and authority. Neither man, the noble nor the provost, were known to be given to mercy, as much as they were given to matters of silver, gold, power, and land.

The whole judgement affair was not to be a matter of grievance over a heartfelt injury, or sincere loss, as much as it was merely a reaction against a slight; an infraction against a rich man by one who had the misfortune of being born within a lower class. The relation between the noble and his son was nothing like that between Thomas and his own father. Thomas understood that now, clearer than ever before.

In truth, the noble had an eldest, favored son who was standing in succession to his father's Avanoran lands. The youngest son, the one who had been killed as Thomas had learned since his father's arrest, had been a tonsured student for a very clear reason having nothing to do with familial benevolence.

He was being pushed towards a career in the church precisely to get him off his father's hands, and away from entertaining any notions that would interfere with the noble's intentions regarding succession and patronage of his three other sons. It was probably just such an environment that influenced the young son to turn into the angry, violent man Thomas' father had confronted, and who would have hurt or killed innocent townspeople had William not intervened.

Such was the way of things in the distant world of the nobles. It was a world where children were largely detached from their parent's presence at a young age, and set on predetermined paths, set in place by their mere order of birth.

For that reason alone, Thomas was grateful he had not been born into a noble family. He was thankful he had come to have a good, close relationship with his father, even if the loving relationship now was the source of the great, gaping pain deep within him. It was, Thomas fully realized in the presence of the Archon, an area of true wealth where the nobles were the ones suffering poverty; even if they never consciously understood that kind of poverty during the entire course of their lives.

Even so, the knowledge was of little consolation at the present moment. The implacable truths burned within Thomas, as he was bluntly confronted with the world's sheer unfairness and its real effect in his own life. He thought of his father, and what his father would be denied in life as a consequence of the world's fundamental nature.

He then thought of what his mother would be denied, and what he and Emma would be denied, as the terrible loss reverberated outward, affecting every single life that his father significantly touched. All of the things taken from William, and all those he loved, converged in a torrent of vivid, unrestrained perception.

The onerous feelings manifested in a bevy of hot tears, ones somehow reflecting more intensely in Thomas's current, non-physical state. The tears streaked down his face, dripping towards the ground, in a grieving rain as his body started shaking with the overwhelming emotions seizing him.

The Archon moved closer, gracefully reaching its arms around Thomas. The Archon took him into a full embrace, delicately drawing

Thomas' trembling body inward, pressing him against the celestial being. The movement strangely seemed natural, as if Thomas had experienced such a thing many times before.

The wings of the creature tilted forward, curving around Thomas' back, as if sheltering him and expanding the scope of the encompassing embrace. Thomas slowly felt an ebbing sensation occurring within, even as he felt a tremor in the body of the Archon. Thomas felt something liquid dripping upon his own head, and slowly brought his eyes upward, to look into the Archon's face.

The Archon now exhibited a visage of mournful sadness. Tears flowed copiously from the measureless depths of its eyes. Thomas realized the creature had truly embraced, and fully willed itself to share, the thundering pain wracking him to his core.

It did not fully eradicate the sting that the understanding regarding the world's nature had brought to Thomas, but it undeniably brought it down to a level he could endure. In that moment, he understood something very fundamental about Archons, at least the ones who were in service to the All-Father.

"Through ... all the years that people have lived ... you have taken these kinds of burdens on yourself?" Thomas asked, carefully voicing the question.

The response was a faint nod, and a resounding sense of confirmation within his mind. Thomas had always envisioned the Archons as simply messengers, or awe-inspiring wards against evil spiritual powers, like they were portrayed in all of the Church's accounts. He had envisioned them wielding fiery swords against demonic powers, driving monstrous evils back under storm-rived skies.

Now he saw they were wards in another, much deeper, sense. They were guardians in a way likely imperceptible to the persons the Archons suffered to aid in such an intimate, profound way. Unseen and unheralded, the Archons absorbed the pain of the living. Thomas realized that the Archons of the All-Father willingly embraced tremendous levels of suffering, on behalf of people everywhere.

The world, for reasons that Thomas did not yet understand, had to take its full course. The Archons could not openly intervene to eradicate struggles, injustice, and random tragedy, as if they were ethereal sorcerers employing great powers to make changes in the physical world. They were bound to a certain degree, just as much as evil, otherworldly powers were not entirely free to wreak havoc in the world.

Thomas had the distinct sense that the Archons of the heavenly realms did indeed combat evil spiritual powers, and acted as messengers in very special instances. Yet now he saw that the Archons had a very prevalent duty in the lives of humankind. It was an unseen, arduous task, of a guiding, empathic nature.

"Please … do not cry … I will be fine," Thomas said, gently pulling back from the Archon's embrace.

He found himself deeply troubled by the vision of the being's profound suffering, feeling a great sympathy for the Archon. Perhaps it was a good thing such actions could not be viewed under normal circumstances by humans, as Thomas doubted he could ever tolerate allowing such a beautiful, pure being to take on, and endure, such sadness and pain.

Thomas felt a vigorous pulse from the Archon, right before he took a short step backward. The pulse seemed to move in both directions, flowing from him into the Archon, and from the Archon into him.

"You will withstand the world's trials, young spirit," the Archon stated. "One day you will find your way home."

Thomas was then given a keen sense of a time and place lying far beyond the moment he was living in, if time and place could even be appropriately used to describe the indescribably beautiful environment he inwardly perceived. The spark of understanding brought a momentary levity within him, all cares in the world vanished for that instant.

Yet the flashing hint of a wondrous future was only a consolation, and it did not remove the needs of the present. Thomas waited expectantly, knowing the Archon had not yet finished with matters of important concern.

The Archon gazed down upon Thomas for a moment, as the tumult within him continued to subside. "Return to Father Anselm tomorrow. When he speaks to you of the Great Archon Mika'il, and of the dragons who stood with Mika'il when the Enemy was thrown down, remember this moment. When he speaks of the dragons who stood with the Enemy, and of a battle where true good stood against true evil, then know this was no dream, and that the words of your grandfather are spoken true," the Archon related to Thomas.

The words, and their insistent nature, were emblazoned within Thomas' head, and he could have quoted the Archon without a single error. "I will go to see him, tomorrow," Thomas assured the Archon, nodding.

"Have you forgotten your body, back upon your mattress at home?" the Archon then asked him, with a jovial, slightly mischievous timbre.

The Archon's words prompted Thomas to think of his body lying back within the garret. As soon as the thoughts crossed his mind, he was hit with an instant sensation, of a kind he had felt before. It happened even as he recognized how subtle and clever the Archon had been in ending Thomas' audience with it.

In choosing the suggestive method that it had, Thomas found that the Archon possessed a sense of humor. He felt himself pulled back to his body in an instant of time, his journey ending with him wide awake on his mattress under the timbers of the roof.

He found that he could not move his limbs for a few moments, but at last his inability to control his physical body faded. Thomas sat up slowly on the mattress, and ran his hands through his hair, taking several deep breaths. He had returned to consciousness, and sat up just in time to see his sister surmounting the last few steps to the level of the garret.

As if a lingering remnant of the kind of perception he had possessed just moments before, he knew at once that Emma had indeed been weeping down in the darkness of the kitchen. "Hi Emma," he called out gently.

"Thomas," she acknowledged, stepping quietly towards the bed.

"We are going to find a way to make all of this okay," he stated resolutely, trying to sound as confident as he could. Tomorrow, he would find out whether the message from the Archon had validity or not, as he set his mind on visiting Father Anselm.

"I hope … that we can," Emma replied, a brief sob choking her words.

"Come over here, Emma," Thomas said, a notion hitting him. He tossed the wool blanket aside, swung his legs out, and stood up at the side of the mattress.

"What is it?" she replied, stepping towards him with a curious expression on her face.

He wrapped his arms around her, and imagined having broad wings that he could curl about his sister's form. "Sometimes, you just need to have a hug, Emma," Thomas said, drawing her in tightly against him, hoping that he could somehow absorb her sorrow and pain as well.

DEGANAWIDA

The rocky eastern shores gave rise to lofty outcroppings that jutted out of the sea, towards the southeastern tip of the Five Realms. Just to the south of the continuum of high, imposing cliffs, there was a thin beach edging the ocean waters. The sandy strip of land arced into a crescent forming the confines of a small bay.

Seen from the heights, the bay held the general shape of a small child's shoulders and head. Long ago, the bay had been given its name, the Water Head-Cradle, as a result, taken from tribal people flying over the area on the backs of their winged Brega mounts.

The old and infirm, as well as a multitude of women and children, were now huddled together along the curving, sandy, waterfront, having emerged from the deep forests only a short time past. They gathered closer to the water than they did to the tree line, almost touching the lapping waves of the rising tide, as it began caressing the higher areas of the narrow beach.

The disposition of the refugees reflected a desire to be as far away from the forest as possible. It was a melancholy sight to behold, taking place mere paces from the sheltering branches and abundant growths garbing their cherished homeland.

The same elm trees used to build long-houses were now just another part of a forest swirling with deadly hostility. Their former haven and homeland now harbored terrifying dangers, ones tirelessly pursuing them with lethal intent.

Great peril and encompassing fear had shattered everything they had known. It was all that many of them could do to keep from letting the horrid experience fracture their deepest-held beliefs.

A shaken, broken people, they had endured an exhausting journey, driven forward by a relentless enemy. Worse, they had surmounted all the obstacles only to find themselves facing the thick, gray mists of the unknown looming before them.

Near the northern side of the bay, a fair distance beyond the edge of the massed refugees, a few tribal men attended a throng of nerve-rattled Bregas. Most were females, who had been pressed along in the retreat with their young. Only a few adult males were left in the small herd that had been salvaged. The remnants were securely tethered and roped to obstruct them from flying off in the panic of their fears.

SPIRIT OF FIRE

Countless hide packs, woven baskets, stretchers, bark barrels, and a multitude of other items cluttered a large swathe of area encroaching on the water's edge. A small cluster of horses was also being tended by a few tribesmen. Anyone could see the horses were worn out, having been heavily encumbered and pressed to their limits in the desperate exodus. In their depleted condition, most would not have lasted even one more day.

A number of dogs, tails wagging, trotted amongst the gathered masses. Of the non-humans participating in the exodus, they were the only ones not exhibiting considerable fatigue or agitation.

The lively canines had given many children welcome distractions during the arduous trek, and had even brought a few smiles to the faces of sorely beleaguered adults. In many ways, the dogs were a tremendous blessing, about the only occupants on the beach exhibiting even a remote semblance of normalcy; content as long as they were with the humans familiar to them.

Deganawida silently regarded the faces of his people, as they stared out across the shallow bay waters. He was used to the sight of fear in their eyes by now, but the nascent signs of hope within their exhausted gazes buoyed his spirit.

A wondrous sight had greeted them when they had emerged onto the beach, but the same vision evoked a sense of trepidation; Finality and unfamiliarity were at the forefront of the pervading anxiety.

The Saxan fleet had arrived, in time.

The Saxans wasted no time in sending a number of vessels towards the beach as the refugees came into sight. Many rowing craft, and a few smaller, single-masted galleys were approaching the shoreline. The waters teemed with the smaller ships drawing steadily closer to the beach, a glorious sight to Deganawida's eyes.

A host of galleys and other sizeable vessels remained a little farther out in the water, gathered towards the mouth of the bay. Deganawida could see numerous Saxans standing along their decks, carefully watching the progress of the evacuation.

For a majority of the tribal people, the sight was both incredible and unprecedented. Most had never seen such large ships before, or such a great number of foreigners.

The shock of their dire circumstances and the unusual vision spread before them was more than enough to unnerve a good many of the refugees. A number of mothers strove diligently to calm crying, scared children, as well as agitated babies perceiving the discomfort in the atmosphere. Most often, the efforts of the tired mothers were futile, as they fully shared the fears of their children.

To Deganawida, the vision of the Saxan fleet was anything but frightening. It was a miraculous sight, which gave him renewed assurance and hope. The Saxans had made the journey successfully, were not a moment late in their arrival.

Deganawida strode onto the beach, moving among his people as the flotilla of vessels drew ever closer. Though exhausted, and filled with turbulent emotions at the mere thought of being forced from his homelands, the old sachem kept darkened or saddened expressions at bay. He knew that a good leader had to forego personal travails and burdens during the hours when the people of the Five Realms badly needed to witness an air of inviolable strength. It was one of those times where the external expression he displayed was far more important than any internal reality.

From group to group, the venerable sachem went, giving embraces, words of encouragement, and clasping many upon their arms or shoulders. There was no artificial façade to his actions, and the genuine concern he displayed for each individual was recognized by all. It took great concentration to avoid reflecting on the sight of their collective pain, as he looked upon frightened children, mournful wives, broken husbands, and forlorn elders.

The latter were probably the most distressing sight of all to Deganawida; old men and women utterly bereft of hope, as they prepared to depart the lands they had always known during the ebbing twilight of their lives.

It was a wickedly cruel reward for lives that, in most cases, had been lived with honor, and had entailed long labor and sacrifices for the betterment of families, clans, and tribes. The elders had given everything of themselves, only to have what little rest or enjoyment remaining in their final years ripped right out from under them.

Deganawida managed to keep his face taut, his voice strong and steady, and his posture erect. It took a very great effort, but the resolute presence he exhibited worked wonders among the populace.

In pocket after pocket amid the teeming masses, he could feel the lightening of the heavy air as he visited with his people. The emotional burdens weighing them down noticeably ebbed by the time he moved from one group to the next.

All of his life, Deganawida envisioned the land and the people as one. From the genesis of the sacred alliance of the tribes until the present moment, it had been that way for a long line of wise and noble sachems.

Now, as he watched his people preparing to leave the shores of their homeland, he experienced a curious sensation; that the land itself was somehow leaving with them. It was a strange, confusing perception, which initially made little sense to Deganawida.

Looking back towards the forest, there was a corresponding emptiness. As if the very spirit of his homeland was now dissipating, he was stunned by the cold, desolate sentiment washing over him as he eyed the treeline. He wondered whether what he saw before him was merely a great illusion.

It was as if the forested lands of their ancient, beloved homeland were not what he saw spread before his eyes. Rather, it felt as if his eyes gazed upon a foreign place.

None of the feelings made any sense to him, and he wondered whether the stress, sorrow, and perhaps even his age, were finally catching up with his sanity. The Dark Brother, in Deganawida's view, must have gained considerable dominion over the day at hand, for no other reason explained the irrational notions pulling and tugging strenuously from within his mind.

He carefully worked his way over to the beach area where the first Saxan craft were now arriving. A tall, burly, thick-bearded man stepped out of the closest boat, a moment before it came to a full halt. His beard and hair was divided disproportionately between strands of black and gray, with many more of the former than the latter. The Saxan's face and hands had the leathered, cracked texture evidencing long years spent in the sun's rays upon open seas. His gray eyes were steady, alert, and warm, those of an honest man, a perception Deganawida took notice of immediately.

"Good fortune has brought you here, in a great hour of need," Deganawida stated, using the pendant he had borrowed from the Trogen Dragol, "I am Deganawida, a sachem of the Onan, and the First Sachem of the Grand Council. We humbly thank you, for heeding our call."

He gave the man a slight bow, in a manner he knew would show respect towards the Saxan. In some ways, he found that the look of the

Saxans was reminiscent of the Midragardans his people had come to know so well.

The Saxan's eyes flared wider for a moment, obviously taken unawares at hearing the tribal sachem speak the Saxan tongue with perfect fluency. He recovered quickly enough from his surprise, his features settling back down into their prior, earnest state.

"I am Athelhere, thane of Ealdorman Morcar of Wessachia, and loyal servant of King Alcuin of Saxany. Were that we met under different circumstances," the Saxan warrior replied to Deganawida in a gritty voice, his tone laden with regret. He gave a low, respectful bow towards Deganawida. "I fear time is no ally to either of us. Haste may be our only ally. We must begin moving your people to the ships with no delays."

Deganawida sensed grave concern and anxieties present within the Saxan noble. He quickly called out to some nearby tribal warriors, who rushed over right away. The sachem delegated the task of assisting with the mustering of the refugees.

When Deganawida looked back to the Saxan thane, the Saxan's face wore a look of puzzlement. "You speak in Saxan to your own?" the man asked, incredulously.

Deganawida smiled, lifting up the borrowed pendant. "No, though you understand me as such. I am using a very useful gift, given to one with us from one called the Wanderer who has long been a friend of our people."

The Saxan's eyes widened in surprise again, and Deganawida heard the hope in his voice. "The Wanderer is with you?"

Deganawida shook his head, but was not entirely surprised the Wanderer was known to the Saxans as well. The Wanderer was an enigma, as well as a benefactor. "Not with us, but I believe he is helping us. This is no mere token I wear."

"I had wondered how we would speak together," the thane stated. "There was no time for much planning. Our fleet was already in the northern waters off our coast, keeping watch, when word was sent to me of the great dragon's message."

"And you arrived here in time, and I hope safely enough, " Deganawida said, casting a glance towards the armada deeper in the bay.

"We did not lose one ship during the passage. How many from Midragard are here?" the thane asked, with a hint of impatience.

"A small force. They are with the warriors holding the enemy tide back even now, not far to the west of here," Deganawida said.

"Do they have their longships?" the thane asked.

"No," Deganawida replied, somberly. "The enemy has either captured or destroyed their ships, unless a few were able to escape. The Midragardans here on the land have no other way out, and will be coming with us."

"They will be of great help on the journey back, excellent masters of the sea that they are," Aethelhere remarked, in a tone of sincere respect. "And I have brought some men to be of help to you and your people, as we get your people onto the ships. These Saxan warriors are excellent fighters, who will give any of your enemies who try interfering with our departure a full taste of Saxan steel."

Deganawida could tell the Saxan's last statement was not delivered as a boast, but as a reassurance during a troubled hour. Any additional fighters would come as a welcome boon, and looking upon the strong-looking, well-armed men with Aethelhere, Deganawida had no doubts they were quite capable at arms.

The Saxan thane turned and waved towards a few small rowing vessels idle on the shore. They were about to be joined by several similar craft just now pulling up onto the beach. Men jumped out of the incoming craft to help pull the vessels up further, lodging them onto the shore.

A few of the vessels were filled with Saxan warriors, many carrying bows, and most others armed with sword or spear, and great round shields. Sunlight gleamed brightly off helms, mail shirts, and iron shield bosses. As the boats emptied out, the warriors disembarking moved swiftly up the beach towards Aethelhere

A couple of very robust-looking men strode a few paces ahead of the rest. They carried themselves with the conspicuous air of men of authority, looking expectantly towards Aethelhere. Further distinguishing them were the long-hafted war axes they bore with them.

"Lads, we will need you to gain us some time, and bolster our friends from the tribes and Midragard," Aethelhere said to the two. He looked back over to Deganawida. "Show them where they can be of help."

Deganawida saw the confusion on the Saxans' faces, as they witnessed the tribal sachem reacting with perfect understanding to instructions voiced in the Saxan tongue.

"He has an understanding of our tongue, through an art I will explain to you later, when we are back at sea," Aethelhere explained quickly, evidently perceiving their shock.

Deganawida summoned a couple more tribal warriors, and turned aside to speak briefly with them. The tribal warriors looked up when he was finished, and one gestured for the Saxan warriors to follow them.

"Go with these warriors, and they will show you where we seek to hold a line of defense, while the refugees depart this beach," Deganawida addressed the Saxans.

As the two axe-carrying men nodded, they stepped towards the tribal warriors. The other Saxan warriors streamed behind them, as they all headed up the beach towards the trees.

Seeing well-armed foreign warriors storming towards the forest's edge, a few refugees cried out, while others shuffled and scurried aside to give them a wide berth. The nervous reactions had no basis in reality, as it was readily apparent the Saxans, escorted as they were by tribal warriors, represented no threat.

"Thank you, for allowing your warriors to stand with ours here," Deganawida said to Aethelhere, as he watched the cluster of stout Saxan fighters disappear into the tree line. He knew the Saxans were there to help the tribal people escape, but they were under no obligations to risk their own fighters in battle.

Aethelhere gave a shrug that was accompanied by a rueful grin. "We stand against the same enemy. The Unifier has invaded both of our lands."

"A very dark time it is, Aethelhere, though it heartens me greatly to see us standing together, strangers though we might yet be to each other," Deganawida replied.

Aethelhere nodded quietly in reply, as the two leaders looked back towards the water's edge. Several other rowed vessels were gliding in towards the beach. The beginnings of several groupings of tribal refugees, guided by the warriors Deganawida had delegated, were now gathering where the waves broke and tumbled against the sands.

The process of loading people onto the smaller watercraft was quickly underway. Many Saxans joined with the Five Realms' warriors in assisting the first of the children, women, and elderly aboard the boats. There was no need for translation between the Saxans and tribal people, as all understood the urgent task. Gestures and tones served well enough for communication, as the intentions were simple.

A quantity of baskets, leather pouches, and some pottery containers, loaded with foodstuffs and items salvaged from the villages, were then carried forward and placed among the people that had boarded the vessels. Deganawida and Aethelhere engaged in a short discussion regarding the logistics of the departure, and the number of people and other items Aethelhere judged the Saxan fleet to be capable of taking onward. Deganawida had to make a few quick judgements, and soon dispatched his conclusions through some message-bearing runners.

Responses from other sachems were brought back quickly, and Deganawida relayed the decisions to Aethelhere and the runners. He was relieved to find thorough consensus.

A good portion of the tribal possessions brought along would have to be discarded. What little space was available beyond that allocated for the people and bare essentials would be set aside for the animals who had shared in the great sacrifices made.

The remnant of the Brega herd, the exhausted small band of horses, and the dogs would be taken along. It would be very difficult bringing the Brega, in particular, but Deganawida was not about to leave the precious creatures to the mercy of the invaders.

Deganawida noticed a few members from the various tribal Societies tenderly bearing the sacred masks they had managed to salvage onto the watercrafts. The masks were covered up, hidden from view, but Deganawida could not fail to see the reverent, delicate way in which the items were handled.

The Healing Societies, with their masks of carved wood, and the Bounty Societies, with their masks of braided corn husks, were carrying much more than physical objects with them. In truth, they were carrying forth the sacred traditions of the Five Tribes. With the Societies still present among the refugees, invaluable bonds would be preserved for the murky times ahead, which would be of tremendous importance during the daunting trials that all would face in the forthcoming exile.

Not everything would be taken, though. Some of the innermost secretive Societies, themselves ensconced deep within the Healing Societies, were facing a worse fate. They were about to be removed from the very elements they were dedicated to. This included the Society whose focus lay with the Little Ones of the forest, as well as others associated with certain mystical creatures.

The debacle facing the special Societies would create new challenges. There was no way of knowing whether there would be any elements relating to those particular Societies within the new lands they were going to.

Nevertheless, the most important tribal essences would be preserved; the lore and the traditions of the Five Realms. Those intangibles were perhaps the most valuable of the salvaged treasures, symbolized by things like the sacred masks, that were being loaded onto the Saxan vessels.

Within a very short time, the first wave of boats was filled to capacity. The Saxans and Five Realms' warriors then pushed the heavily laden vessels back off the beach, sliding them into the bay waters. A few Saxans boarded the boats, to row them towards the larger galleys and sailing ships waiting for them.

Athelhere and Deganawida walked down to the shoreline together. They continued talking and sharing what information they each possessed, all the while observing the diligent evacuation labors from close proximity.

Deganawida listened as Aethelhere described the coming of the great dragon, and the urgent message delivered from Aelfric. The Saxan thane spoke of pressing his men hard in response, assembling the rescue fleet and departing for the Water Head-Cradle.

Those who had brought Aethelhere the message from Aelfric had also related a few tidings of a great battle taking place in the western region of Saxany. Aethelhere did not yet know the outcome of the battle, but Deganawida marveled at the account of how the Saxans were resisting the combined forces of three armies.

There was a tremendous undercurrent of concern in Aethelhere's voice. Deganawida could not imagine how difficult it was for the Saxan thane to undertake the sea journey, while his own homeland was under such a vicious assault.

Aethelhere then listened to Deganawida, as the Onan sachem described the ferocious rearguard battles fought to stave off the onslaught of forces invading the tribal lands. Deganawida could read Aethelhere's expressions clearly, and sensed that the Saxan was increasingly relieved he had arrived when he had. The Saxan could comprehend quickly enough that there had not been much time left.

The Saxan expressed his sympathy to Deganawida regarding the struggle of the exiles, as they had been made to hasten just ahead of the voracious enemy pursuit. While Deganawida was relating the last stages of the non-combatants' harrowing plight, he looked up to see a number of warriors upon sky steeds flying in from the west.

At first, he tensed, but relaxed a little as he noticed the unique nature of the steeds, and the brightening countenance upon Aethelhere's face. The profile of the winged creatures became clearer with each moment, stripping away the anxieties that had just erupted. Without a doubt, they were not the Harraks that the enemies of the tribes rode upon.

A rider and steed broke away from the small force, descending until they landed near Deganawida and Aethelhere. The rider guided his steed across the beach towards the Saxan leader, responding to the thane's broad gestures.

Deganawida was familiar with three kinds of Skiantha; the Bregas of their own lands, the Fenraren of the Midragardans, and the formidable Harraks flown by the enemy. He could not remember ever encountering a Skiantha like the one now standing just a few paces before him. The creature had a very robust form, provided with expansive wings. It looked in many ways like a powerfully-built canine, with a broad head, short muzzle, and a lustrous black and tan coat of short fur.

Seeing Deganawida's curious expression, Aethelhere remarked, "Himmerosen. The winged Skiantha steeds that come from our homeland."

"A very beautiful creature, and very strong in appearance," Deganawida observed, appreciatively.

"Hardy indeed, and their kind has been of excellent help to the Saxan people for many, many years. And of great use on this very journey," Aethelhere responded. "They helped to orient the fleet perfectly towards the Water Head-Cradle, so we didn't lose a moment."

The rider dismounted quickly, and trotted over, giving respects to both Deganawida and Athelhere in the form of bows. The Saxan proceeded to announce that he and a small scouting force had surveyed the land and skies just a little to the west of the shore.

He indicated that substantial enemy forces were closing in fast, now less than a league away and pressing aggressively forward. There were signs of intense battles taking place among the trees, though much was obscured by the dense foliage. The scout also related that a small number of enemy sky warriors, upon Harraks, had sped off at the sight of the Saxan sky contingent.

The two leaders listened with solemn expressions, and Deganawida was greatly troubled at the disturbingly close proximity of the invader's vanguard. The enemy forces were likely salivating at the prospects of falling upon the surviving populace of the Five Realms, with the tribal people's backs against the sea. The enemy would need little motivation to press their attack as swiftly as they could. If the enemy became aware of the Saxan fleet, Deganawida knew they would respond with a ferocious surge, to ensure that their herded quarry did not escape the seaside trap they had been methodically driven into.

Athelhere turned towards Deganawida at the conclusion of the scout's report. His face was a visage of sheer determination. "It seems time is indeed our enemy, as I knew it would be. Let us work to set up a firm shield for your people. I have many capable warriors here with me, to help form the planks, rivets, rim, boss, straps, and grip of such a shield."

He then dismissed the scout, sending him to the Saxan galleys to summon more warriors to the beach. Gruffly, he called out several orders to a number of Saxans who had come on another wave of small boats that had reached the shore moments before. A fair number of warriors were rapidly gathered together, soon forming into a concentrated group.

Aethelhere then bid Deganawida's leave. The Saxan thane personally led the contingent towards the rear of the mass of refugees, where the armed warriors from the first wave had gone.

Deganawida wasted no time in assembling a moderate force of Five Realms' warriors, soon leading them up the beach in the wake of Athelhere's force. They came upon the Saxans amongst the trees, and quickly combined their strength, as Aethelhere explained the Saxan methods of war to Deganawida, and what he had in mind.

Deganawida cooperated fully with the thane's plan, which he deemed very sound, and not all that much different from the Midragardan ways of war. The Saxan warriors were rested and unscathed, and it would be best for them to fight in the manner they were most comfortable with.

The two leaders worked to arrange a motley type of shield wall, made of Saxan warriors and Deganawida's own people. A thin, forward line of Saxan spearmen was backed by a slender number of archers, the latter derived from both Saxans and tribal warriors.

An even smaller number of Saxan swordsmen, mixed with a few club and hatchet bearing Five Realms' warriors, were sprinkled amongst the archers. They would act as a kind of reserve, addressing any sudden breach in the shield wall that might arise.

The force of Saxans and tribal warriors had just finished arraying when a large outcry of terror erupted from behind the two leaders, coming from the masses back on the beach. The sound was mixed with the bold, fierce war cries of Trogens, coming down from overhead.

Deganawida's head snapped upward at the sound of the deep, throaty war cries, just as a significant number of Harraks swept through the air just over the tree tops. To his horror, they were angling down towards the hapless, exposed occupants of the beach.

THOMAS

Short of stature, burly, and with a full, dense beard, Father Anselm was an image of stalwartness. Yet despite his robust appearance, and his deep voice, he was far from being a somber or dour clergyman as some Thomas had encountered tended to be.

Father Anselm's eyes sparkled with merry laughter, and his smile gleamed as he looked up to see Thomas strolling into the front yard of the church. He was wearing his full-length, white woolen tunic, with a pair of simple leather shoes. His tonsured head was open to the elements, little of a risk on a clear, breezy day.

Thomas glanced towards the spear-shaped finial atop the bell-tower, and then down towards the arch-enclosed entryway of the church. He saw in his mind the incredible, ethereal vision of the Archon he had witnessed during the previous night.

Out of the corner of his eyes, he beheld a large form bounding swiftly towards him. He turned to the right, and braced his legs at the last instant. It was just in time to avoid being toppled, as he managed to keep upright despite the significant force of the impact.

"Pierre! Your enthusiasm is a credit to you, but your zeal may end up sending my young student here to the All-Father well before his time," Father Anselm boomed. The robust priest laughed heartily at the sight of the boy and the dog, clearly in a state of great amusement.

Thomas struggled to keep his feet, as the dog reared up fully, placing his broad paws down firmly upon the youth's shoulders. The dog's positioning held his long body in place, while the canine relentlessly licked Thomas' face. Thomas felt the considerable weight of the dog pressing down on him, and had the dog been able to stand entirely upright, Thomas would have been looking up to the sizeable creature.

"I sure didn't choose him, and I sure can't get rid of him," Father Anselm quipped, as the dog finally dropped down to stand on all four of his legs, mercifully freeing Thomas.

The truth was that the dog was like a devoted personal guardian of Father Anselm, accompanying him faithfully whenever he left the church grounds, night or day. As if trained specifically for the task, the dog would patiently wait wherever Father Anselm visited, until he was ready to return home. Then, the dog would trot along at the priest's side, or keep a few steps before him, all the way back to the church.

The dog had originally shown up out of nowhere, fully grown. Pierre had never been claimed by anyone, despite obviously good breeding that had lent it the size of a forest wolf. To Thomas' eyes, Pierre looked like a wolf indeed, with gray fur, a long muzzle fronted by a set of fearsome, intimidating fangs, a barrel-chest, and a pair of high, triangular ears. Yet no feral wolf Thomas had ever imagined could possibly have been as well-behaved, and quintessentially tame, as Pierre was.

Then again, there were precedents for amiable relationships between clergymen and wolves. In fact, the saint-founder of the Gray Friars was commonly said to have befriended a wolf during his worldly life.

Father Anselm liked to blame his mentor, a certain Father Jean de Bosquier, for the dog's surprising, timely appearance. Father Jean had been the one to suggest that Father Anselm petition the All-Father for special help, after Father Anselm had endured a few traumatic experiences. Rogues and petty thieves in the alleyways of Avalos had waylaid Father Anselm more than once, when the priest had been about the city seeing to the various needs of the members of the parish.

As the needs surrounding such instances often involved urgent summons regarding dying men or women, desperately desiring the administration of the Transition Rites, Father Anselm could not even consider ceasing to make the dangerous journeys within the city at night. Therefore, Father Anselm had prayed fervently for help, at Father Jean de

Bosquier's insistence.

Pierre might well have been an answer, as no rogues had threatened Father Anselm ever since the dog's unexpected arrival, soon after. Father Anselm's ministry to the people of Avalos had proceeded unhindered, and he had been far less bloodied and bruised during the course of his religious tasks.

Thomas could not help but stare at the huge dog for a few moments, shaking his head as he took note of the fact that there was no thin fiber running from the dog's body. The dog moved with noticeable grace for its great size, but now resembled more of a juggernaut than the light-footed, highly-energized version Thomas had witnessed with the Archon.

"Hi Father Anselm... sorry for the delay in greeting you. I had to recover from Pierre's welcome," Thomas finally said, now a little disheveled, looking back to the priest after recovering from the canine ambush.

"Pierre is demanding, and you certainly can't ignore him. I can't blame you for delayed courtesies at all. So, are you ready for today's lessons?" Father Anselm asked enthusiastically, patting Thomas upon the shoulder.

Thomas nodded, feeling much more resolute about adhering to his education with his father held in prison. At the very least, honoring his father's wishes on the matter of erudition was a small, but genuine, way that Thomas believed he could demonstrate his respect and love for his father.

He had not even made one solitary complaint to his mother about the lessons with Father Anselm when she had insisted Thomas continue with them. Even when Father Anselm had firmly abrogated the need for chores around the parish, due to the difficult circumstances facing Thomas and his family, the boy had continued in his tasks.

Father Anselm led him on towards the entrance of the church, opening the thick wooden door, and holding it back for Thomas to proceed inside. The dim interior of the small church was rather plain in form, certainly in comparison to the huge, elaborate new cathedral rising up further by the day in the midst of Avalos.

A simple barrel vault surmounted the open nave, with a short arcade resting on thick piers designating two narrow side aisles. Above the aisles, a few pairs of round-headed clerestory windows, each filled with glass and set into a larger rectangular framing, let in modest amounts of daylight.

The walls themselves were covered in painted murals of various church figures and references to stories from the Sacred Writings. The portrayals utilized a wide array of colors, which had faded a little over the long years the church had existed.

A wooden partition erected towards the farther eastern section of the church served as the principle boundary before the main sanctuary. The wooden partition stood as a clear line of demarcation for all those entering the church; whether for the celebration of an Offering or any other function.

The open space leading to that wooden screen was very public, often used by members of the parish for various types of meetings. A few small craft guilds, who had no special hall or building of their own, periodically utilized the area for assemblies.

Beyond the screen was an area strictly off limits to the public, a section including the main altar. It was accessible only to Father Anselm, or those involved directly with the functions of the Western Church's services, such as the main, ritualistic service known as the Offering.

Thomas had stood with his family in the nave before that screen countless times, on Seventh Days and holy days alike, as Father Anselm, his back to the parish members, faced the far end's apse with its prominent Spear of Emmanu. Some on cushions, some on stools, and others directly on the floor, the congregation sat, stood, and kneeled during the Offering at the designated moments, in a manner of worship that had existed for centuries.

The words of the ancient language of Liantan, hearkening from the grand, legendary city where the Great Vicar now held his seat, had echoed off the walls countless times, in chants and as part of the ritual. Liantan was the language of the rites of the Western Church, even though the Sacred Writings themselves were rendered in the letters of two other tongues, as Father Anselm had instructed Thomas.

Even though the space was used for common meetings of a purely secular nature, Thomas could not help but keep his voice low, out of a sense of reverence. In his mind, he could see Father Anselm, colorful mantle-like chasuble placed over his long white tunic, lifting up the silver chalice containing the Waters of Life. The plain water initially placed in that chalice was believed to become the very essence of Emmanu Himself, transforming once consecrated by the priest.

Thomas had taken the notion of that real presence to heart, even if it was a doctrine that had always been difficult for Thomas to get his mind around. The liquid in the chalice following the consecration still seemed no different in appearance or nature than the water he pulled from the public fountains for his household.

Yet the notion that the water did undergo a transformation nonetheless contained a bold sense of the deep mystery within the Western Church; beckoning to something transcending the rules of matter and the mundane world. That unique sense, though hard to define exactly, had imprinted an abiding respect within Thomas, whenever he was within the building.

"Today, young Thomas, I thought you might enjoy a story of great battle," Father Anselm announced, with a broad grin, his voice resounding within the confines of the church space. "As you always love tales of adventure, I thought I would share it with you, though this one has great relevance to our Church."

Thomas felt his breath quicken at the mention of a great battle, already recalling the words of the Archon. He also felt a sharp pang of embarrassment, knowing full well how he had often urged Father Anselm to procure accounts of the Holy Wars to use in Thomas' study of letters.

"You might have noticed this strong fellow before," Father Anselm said, gesturing towards one of the figures meticulously rendered in paint within the wall murals.

Wings stretched out, wearing a flowing white robe, and holding high the hilt of a sword, whose long blade was comprised of red flames, was the broad-chested, square-jawed, powerful figure of the Great Archon, Mika'il. Mika'il's regal head was wreathed with a golden halo, and his large, blazing eyes seemed to be looking directly down at Thomas.

Thomas felt a tingle at the nape of his neck, a strange sensation that coursed over the rest of his body as he gazed upon the tall, powerful-looking image. Everything seemed to be aligning with the Archon's words.

"This story involves dragons too, something else I thought you might enjoy," Father Anselm continued, casually.

The words froze Thomas completely in place, and for a moment he forgot to exhale.

"Now don't tell me that you are reticent about tales of battles and dragons, after all the grief you've given your poor teacher," Father Anselm stated, with a slight chuckle.

"What story?" Thomas asked, finally remembering to breathe.

"I figured we would talk about the Great Archon, Mika'il, commander of the All-Father's celestial armies," Father Anselm replied. "And the great battle against Jabaalos. There are legends of a race of great, massive dragons taking part in that ancient battle. Many were loyal to the All-Father, and had to fight some among their own brethren, who had declared openly for Jebaalos.

"Archon against Archon, dragon against dragon, probably the greatest battle that has ever taken place in the history of the world. Much larger than any that has taken place in the Holy Wars. Even more intriguing, it was a battle with one side dedicated to a pure good, against another dedicated to pure evil.

"You will not find such a stark division in all of the wars of mankind, where souls leaning towards good or evil fill the armies of both sides of warring kingdoms or empires."

Thomas was rendered speechless, as each of Father Anselm's words entered his ears. It was as if he were hearing the Archon's words repeated from the previous evening, spoken simultaneously within his mind. He accepted immediately what it implied, or, more accurately, confirmed.

The experience of the previous night, and the words of his grandfather, were affirmed without a shadow of a doubt in his mind. As insane and improbable as it sounded, if a dragon did indeed appear in Avalos, with an opportunity for Thomas to fly away with it, he would do so with the knowledge he was grasping onto a fighting chance to help his father. The means of doing so might not yet be clear, but he resolved to trust himself to such a path, in the instance it somehow occurred.

Thomas had to smile, realizing he would be incessantly searching the sky for dragons, with every step he took outside in Avalos. At the very least, it would make the coming days a little more interesting, and inject a small spark of hope into the desolate atmosphere he had been enduring.

"Thank you Father Anselm, very much, I think this will be very interesting," Thomas stated, grinning brightly.

Thomas' eyes drifted back towards the painting of Mika'il. He looked at the figure in an altogether new way, knowing with certitude that there was a very real being, one who truly existed, represented by that painting; one of whose celestial kind Thomas had personally met, just hours before.

The resulting feeling bordered on giddiness, as if Thomas had just discovered he had a whole new outlook on life. In many ways, he did.

"You look excited," Father Anselm commented. "I should have chosen this topic much earlier. You would probably already be a master of the Seven Arts!"

Father Anselm directed Thomas towards a pool of light by one of the windows where he had already positioned a stool for himself, as well as materials for the day's lessons. Thomas took a seat upon the rush-strewn floor, gripping the now-familiar bone stylus and accompanying tablet, filled with its smooth, green wax surface. The latter would be etched upon and scraped bare many times before the next few hours were through, and for once Thomas looked forward to the process.

"Father Anselm, wherever did you get the idea to use this story for today's lessons?" Thomas finally asked, unable to stifle his rising curiosity.

Father Anselm grinned and shrugged. "Who can say? Maybe an Archon whispered the idea into my ears while I slept last night!"

DEGANAWIDA

Deganawida reacted quickly, running through the trees towards the beach. He broke free from the treeline with Aethelhere close by his side, scanning the skies immediately to assess the threat.

Several Trogen sky warriors completed a full pass along the edge of the beach, before curling around for another, brandishing weapons and roaring out challenges to the Saxans and Five Realms' warriors. A portion of the Trogen war party came to a relative halt, drawing their steeds into a hovering position high in the air. The warriors in this group were armed with great bows, and they shortly began loosing arrows at the boats and those endeavoring to board them.

Though the archers aimed for warriors, the non-combatants densely gathered around and on the boats were not immune to the lethal rain. Anguished cries riddled the air, as several arrows found fleshy, living targets, bringing down warriors, elderly, women and children alike.

It was not much longer before a responding formation of sky warriors from the Saxan vessels had been grouped together and put into the air. Once concentrated into a single mass in the skies over the main body of the fleet, they moved swiftly to press a counterattack.

The Saxan formation greatly outnumbered the Trogens. A few of the Trogens shouted orders, bringing all of the enemy warriors to cut off their attack. Taking up the reigns of their steeds, the throng of Trogen warriors sped back towards the west.

Despite the outbreak of panic from the surprise attack, the firm, disciplined leadership of Saxans, clan matrons, male elders, and a few tribal warriors around the shoreline quickly regained order. Before long, the evacuation activity was resumed in full, which was an immense relief to Deganawida.

More boats were heading in to shore, while others, fully loaded, passed them on their way towards the larger Saxan vessels just within the bay's mouth. Many hundreds of refugees had already been removed from the beach, but a few thousand more still crowded the shore.

Even though the boats shuttling back and forth across the bay took no respite, it seemed as if progress was at a crawl. Deganawida knew it would take many, many more boats, and a much longer time, before the beach would be completely cleared of its desperate inhabitants.

After a little while, the first waves of defenders from the primary rearguard finally began to reach the bay area. Several injured warriors, many very badly, were assisted without delay down to the water's edge. Strain and weariness were heavy upon the faces of those escorting the wounded, while pure agony splayed across the faces of the stricken warriors.

The hurried reports emerging as the warriors stumbled onto the beach spoke of strong enemy forces drawing closer to the bay with every heartbeat. The air thickened with foreboding, spurred by the initial hints of looming conflict.

Faint cries could be heard through the trees, heralding the main battle lines as the enemy advanced. The rearguard, it was said, was vigilantly resisting the final push of the enemy forces. The sight of several blood-spattered, maimed warriors gave testament to the tremendous cost incurred to achieve a few extra moments of time.

Despite the best of their efforts, the defenders could only slow the invaders. The enemy pressed forward with every moment, bolstered by the knowledge that their quarry had nowhere else to run.

The pace of the exodus was pressed as fast as it could be, as a sense of desperation rippled throughout those involved in the departure. Death salivated at the brink of the shoreline, and everyone was aware of its iniquitous presence.

Many tiring Saxan oarsmen, assiduously rowing undermanned boats to maximize capacity, kept the cycle going without complaint, returning to the shoreline after offloading tribal refugees at the larger ships. The Saxan rowers drew upon all extra reserves of strength left in their bodies, diligently ferrying terrified refugees away from the beach, draped in a deepening shadow of danger.

All eyes, those of refugee and rescuer alike, kept up a nervous vigil watching the edge of the forest and the skies above. Many of the airborne Saxans had returned after driving off the Trogen force, and a few now hovered in the upper skies, keeping an unwavering eye upon the horizons.

The sounds of war drew closer and closer, the cries and shouts growing louder and more distinctive. The crack of shields being shattered, and the sharp clang of iron rang through the tense atmosphere.

Soon afterwards, the Saxans in the sky became the harbingers of imminent new threats. With excited cries and alarmed blasts upon horns, the Saxans alerted their comrades below on the decks of the galleys.

In moments, Saxan sky warriors were ascending from the galleys and coalescing into a loose formation. The sentinels who had just sounded the warnings streaked to join them, just as another formation thundered towards them from farther inland.

By then, the sounds of war were engulfing the beach area. The clashes of steel and the hiss of missile fire filled the air at the edge of the forest, spilling onto the shore area. Loud, defiant cries, oaths, curses, and screams spurred a renewed panic, and many refugees charged haphazardly into the waters in the grip of spiraling terror.

A second wave of tribal warriors from the rearguard came lurching or running out from the forest's edge and onto the sands. Many hauled injured comrades, in some cases carrying unconscious warriors across their backs. Their haggard expressions and sagging postures evidenced terrible levels of fatigue.

A few surviving Midragardan warriors, their formerly bright helms dulled, and colored tunics stained with grime and blood, began emerging in the midst of the retreating rearguard. After handing off their wounded comrades to those laboring on the beach to load the vessels, the exhausted warriors cast their weary gazes about the beach and out into the bay. A few were so worn out they swayed in place, entirely sapped of strength and unsteady on their feet.

Deganawida watched with an aching sorrow. With a stoic resolve, nearly all of the able-bodied tribal warriors and Midragardans began turning around. They raised their weapons and started back towards the forest with steely eyes.

The tumult of battle increased rapidly, as the emboldened attackers began to reach the outskirts of the defensive lines. Through the trees the enemy could see the beach and water beyond, as well as the throngs of vulnerable refugees massed there. The vision ignited a swell of fury, as the invaders hurled themselves at the narrow line of rested defenders formed by Aethelhere and Deganawida.

As the first violent exchanges erupted between the final defensive line and the first arrivals among the enemy forces, the source of the Saxans' worries in the skies finally reached the bay. A much stronger, far more numerous Trogen formation, accompanied with a chorus of bellowing war cries, raced towards the Saxans.

The Saxans held their lofty positions, letting the Trogens advance. As the Trogens drew close, horns sounded and the Saxans spurred their steeds forward to meet the attack. While the Saxans still enjoyed the advantage of numbers, the ferocious onslaught splintered their formation, scattering both sides into a frothing chaos of individual melees.

In that precise moment, the wiles and purposes of the Trogen leaders manifested, in a most deadly manner. Moving as a tight, cohesive body, the lead formation had cleverly masked a second group following a short distance behind. The condensed secondary mass remained in complete unison as the screening front line broke up the enemy formation, furiously besetting the numerically superior foe.

Deganawida could see the ruse unfolding from the ground below, though he did not immediately comprehend the purpose of the veiled force. The secondary group was mounted upon Harraks that were distinctly larger than the ones ridden in the vanguard, and each bore the burden of four large rocks tethered in pairs, suspended just underneath their bodies.

Deganawida's heart raced as he looked upon the powerful sky steeds dragging heavy stones through the air, perceiving their purpose with growing dismay. The stones held considerable bulk, which showed in the tight pull the rocks had upon the leather lines descending from the backs of the sky steeds, to where the cordage was tied about the stones. Such weight would transform them into exceedingly formidable missiles when dropped from a high altitude, which was clearly the intent of the attackers.

The steeds bearing the stones had been fitted with additional broad leather pieces secured about their shoulders and chests, which prevented the cordage from digging into their fur. The Trogen riders held short, single-edged blades positioned between the protective leather and engaged straps, readying to discharge the dreadful loads in an instant. Deganawida watched helplessly as the rock-bearing formation of Trogens angled farther upwards, proceeding to a much higher altitude, with the obvious intention of achieving greater impact for their heavy missiles.

Only a few Saxans moved to engage the smaller formation as it passed beyond the edge of the beach on its upward climb. The Trogens' path took them right over the flotilla of craft moving back and forth from the beach to the ships at the bay's mouth.

Just as they passed over the first Saxan boats, several Trogens cut their leather straps with a forceful, jerking motion, cleaving through the narrow leather. Each single strap, once cut, immediately sent two heavy rocks plummeting downward.

With closely-matched weight and positioning, the pairs of rocks dropped on roughly even trajectories, hurtling towards the targets below. A slight jostling occurred in the Trogens' saddles as the stones were cut free, as the Harraks reacted to the abrupt alleviation of weight. The Harraks readjusted quickly enough, keeping a steady pace as they flew onward.

Several of the plunging rocks splashed harmlessly into the sea, sending explosive sprays of salty water careening over the edges of nearby boats. A few found their targets squarely, eliciting cries mixed with the loud crash of splintering wood, as rocks smashed through the hulls of small rowing boats. Many individuals were cast from the boats by the thunderous impacts, thrown into the bay waters. Sickening thuds occurred on a couple of other vessels, where stone directly met flesh.

Among the boats hit, a few sustained the strikes well enough to remain afloat. Though crippled, the damage they had taken was in places that allowed the boats to continue along the surface without taking on enough water to sink.

Others began to sink immediately, with gaping rifts in the bottom of their hulls. Those on the doomed craft shouted and cried out as the boats sank, the vessels abandoning their horrified occupants to the mercies of the seawater.

There were a couple of boats hit by multiple stones, their forms brutally smashed and ripped asunder by the pulverizing strikes. Rowers and passengers alike were pitched violently into the bay, some flailing helplessly as they were cast far through the air.

Saxans and refugees were strewn along the waters of the bay after the first barrage from above. Several bodies floated lifelessly, as many had been slain by the devastating blows.

Boats that remained unscathed responded as swiftly as possible to the frantic cries of those thrashing and treading water. Every small boat in the vicinity altered course, regardless of whether the unharmed boats were heading towards the shoreline, or rowing back out with a full group of refugees aboard.

Despite the urgent responses, further tragedies were unavoidable, as several terrible scenes unfolded. The awful visions scalded Deganawida's eyes, as he watched helplessly from the shoreline.

Many elderly men and women, as well as a few smaller children, began succumbing to the waters, sinking below its surface before any boats could get near them. Deganawida could see the hopelessness on the faces of individuals weakened and overwhelmed, as their strength gave out at last. His heart sank again and again, as the chilly ocean waters swallowed up the bodies of many still alive.

The catastrophes compounded rapidly, as more than a few frantic mothers went under the waves to try and rescue their children. Their gallant, desperate efforts were for naught in many instances, and Deganawida's gut was wrenched as he saw more than one mother disappear after a child, never to return to the surface.

The Trogen formation bearing the stony missiles did not hesitate in their fearsome onslaught. The force continued further out over the bay, taking them over the larger war galleys and sailing vessels.

A number of arrows were loosed from Saxan archers upon the decks, though the missiles did not come close to reaching the altitude where the Trogens had guided their steeds. A few Trogens, their steeds having been unburdened of their complement of stones, disengaged from the others. They moved to confront the few Saxans pursuing the stone-bearers, as the distance between the combatants had closed significantly.

Spearheaded by leaders in the front emitting guttural cries, the stone-bearing formation then broke into two smaller groups. One continued on its path out over the galleys, discharging their remaining stones moments later.

Heavy rocks blasted into the timbers of a few larger vessels. A couple of galleys quickly began taking on substantial amounts of water. The crews of the stricken ships recovered swiftly enough, at least those who had not been thrown overboard from the jarring impacts. The Saxans did whatever they could to salvage as much as possible from the ill-fated vessels.

As a whole, the larger ships of the fleet came out relatively unscathed in the bombardment, and there were few casualties suffered. The Trogens discharged most of their rocks by the time they reached the greater ships, and only a small number of missiles succeeded in direct hits. Smaller craft moved with haste to help any who had fallen in the water, or needed transferring from a sinking vessel.

The rest of the stone-bearing Trogens curved around in a tight arc, flying at haste back towards the inner bay and curving shoreline. A number loosed their second pair of stones, once they were over a concentrated throng of smaller boats. Three more of the vessels were incapacitated beyond hope of utilization, with two additional boats broken apart.

Another flurry of calamities ensued in the waters around the newly-destroyed vessels. Few survived long enough to be rescued, as nearby boats reacted to the panicked cries of refugees battered about in the churning waves.

The stone-bearing Trogens were well-aware of the disadvantages faced by their larger, slower steeds, so they did not linger to bask in the success of their strikes. With no hesitation, and a chorus of loud outcries, they flew their steeds back out over the forest.

Though the group that had discharged stones over the galleys had a farther distance to go, most were able to reach the relative safety of the skies over the forest. Behind them, after a few brief skirmishes, the ones who had broken off to engage the counterattacking Saxans separated themselves from combat as soon as they could. On their lightened steeds, they rapidly fled the skies over the bay, following in the wake of their brethren. Though many had incurred injuries to themselves or their steeds, only a few in the secondary, stone-carrying formation had been lost in the fighting.

The deep braying of Trogen war horns reverberated powerfully in the sky. Those fighting in the much broader melee, unless immediately engaged with an opponent, soared away from the combat and raced inland after the other contingent.

The Saxan sky warriors out over the bay regrouped into a cluster. As a group they flew inland, and formed up just over the edge of the shoreline.

Both sides had sustained casualties in the larger melee, but the harshest impact had been delivered through the battle-guile of the Trogens. Their clever concealment of the small group of larger Harracks, bearing stony, formidable loads, had caught the Saxan defenders entirely unprepared.

Seeing an end to the attack upon the ships was a tremendous relief, though the overall threat to the refugees was far from diminished. Deganawida's heart ached sorely, and it was all he could do to bear the dreadful sights of refugees struggling desperately for their lives in the waters of the bay.

With the threats from the sky departed, he wrenched his gaze from the bay back to the engagement swarming behind him. On the ground, the fighting had surged to a furious level beneath the tree canopy.

Even the place Deganawida stood was an area of great risk. A couple of Saxan warriors with large round shields were positioned directly before the tribal sachem and Aethelhere, mitigating the most immediate of threats, deadly missiles now hissing through the trees.

Torrents of arrows passed each other, flying towards defenders or the oncoming enemy. The bellowing of Gigans could now be heard in the distance, though the huge creatures remained out of sight.

Cohesive formations of well-armed Gallean infantry were marching up behind the lines of the attackers, and the rhythmic thumps from their tread resounded through the trees. Led by knights with expressionless visages of iron, the formation would soon bring their strength to bear, though it would be a little time yet before they could engage the defenders.

A few Atagar then joined the fighting. The rat-like beings used their exceptional agility to climb the trunks of surrounding trees, moving nimbly along the branches.

Crossing lithely from tree to tree, they reached the limbs above the defenders in mere moments. Whether foolhardy or courageous, the diminutive warriors caused major disruptions along the defensive line. Several of the fierce rat-men dropped into the midst of the defenders, and attacked with inspired savagery.

Despite their crazed zeal, the Atagar were little more than suicidal in their assault. Though slain quickly, their presence still increased the burdens of the defending warriors, as eyes now had to keep watch on the heights of trees for potential enemy strikes.

The fresh Saxan fighters within the defensive line, in turn, caused some confusion amongst the enemy ranks. Gallean knights held back part of their forces as they recognized the Saxan presence.

Hail after hail of arrows was loosed at the enemy from Midragardan, Saxan, and Five Realms' bows. The missiles left a considerable number of casualties in their wake, punctuated by cries and screams.

That the enemy did not strike in full strength all along the line became a stroke of good fortune for the defenders. Sporadic enemy probes up and down the battle line were fended off, as the invaders took a new assessment in light of the Saxan warriors.

Aethelhere quickly proved his mettle as a formidable warrior, wading into the fray several times. The Saxan's sword was bloodied and his shield displayed many gouges by the time he returned back to Deganawida's side, after one particularly intense enemy sortie was beaten back.

Aethelhere's eyes carried the inflamed look of a man embraced by the passions of battle. The Saxan blinked his eyes, taking several deep breaths as he rested, as his calmer demeanor slowly returned.

Deganawida kept his wits about him while searching his mind for a course of action. The enemy's hesitation had not deluded him into a false sense of security. It would not be long before the enemy realized the true size of the Saxan reinforcements. The Saxan numbers were far too small to cause the enemy to reappraise their entire assault. A massive, overwhelming attack would be coming, soon enough.

Through the trees, Deganawida could see the continuous arrival of well-equipped enemy warriors, tromping up from the depths of the forest. It would not be much longer before the invaders reached a critical mass, one that could strike simultaneously at every point in the line. Like a great predator bunching its muscles and baring its fangs, the enemy was nearing the moment of springing upon its intended prey.

Deganawida watched Aethelhere lunge forward again, hustling to join his fellow Saxan warriors as another vicious clash broke out just paces away. Deganawida gripped the haft of the war club that had been brought to him when he had reached the treeline, a solid weapon crafted from heavy maple.

Though his combat years were long behind him, he still readied to fight if the breach in the defensive line was not sealed. He was resolved to face the same end as the tribal warriors, whether or not his slowed body allowed him to acquit himself well on the battleground.

Vigorously thrust spears and slashing swords sent wood fragments flying in bursts from shields. The hellish chorus of battle was darkly accented by the sickening sounds of tearing flesh, and crunching blows landing upon living bodies.

Deganawida was not cast into the throes of hand to hand combat, as the Saxans nearby drove the enemy fighters back, closing the break in the shield wall. The defenders fought with primal fury, knowing the last groups of children, women, and elderly were at their back, being loaded onto the rescue boats.

Deganawida chanced a short look towards the bay. A few medium-sized galleys had since drifted towards the shoreline, as the last of the smaller boats made their way out into the bay. Overhead, the Saxan sky formations had withdrawn from the shoreline, and were now covering the incoming galleys as they pulled in closer and closer on the rhythmic strength of coordinated banks of oars.

Having been around Bregas for years, Deganawida could see that the Saxans' steeds were showing telltale signs of great fatigue. The development was occurring at a very precarious time, eliciting new worries in the sachem's mind.

Deganawida looked back as Athelhere, with his sword and mail splattered in the blood of his foes, returned from the fighting. The Saxan glanced back towards the beach, before bringing up a horn from where it rested at his side. His chest expanded with a deep intake of breath, which he loosed through the horn a moment later.

The sonorous blast carried far outward, conveying the momentous signal across the waters of the bay. Deganawida glanced back for a few heartbeats, and then walked a few paces to the right, leaning over and picking up a thick wooden branch lying upon the ground. Using the branch as a makeshift walking staff, he braced his aged body.

Unexpectedly, the clear, distinct sensation he had felt earlier rushed back in that moment. He perceived the last essence of the tribal homeland leaving with the refugees on the boats. The land to the west held no substance, reduced to nothing more than an empty, foreign illusion.

Emptied of refugees, a flotilla of smaller boats started towards the shore in the wake of the incoming galleys. Deganawida knew there would be little time for the rescue of the warriors, as the enemy would not relent in its assault. The invaders would seek to drive them into the seas as they retreated, and the remaining Saxans, Midragardans, and tribal warriors would likely have to fight their way off the shore.

Deganawida saw that the Saxans had recognized the dilemma, as there were several archers on each vessel of the approaching flotilla, bows out and arrows notched. Yet beyond causing a brief hesitation, the bowmen could do little to prevent the enemy from falling upon the defenders as they tried to climb into the boats.

A braying chorus of enemy war horns then broke out among the trees. Deganawida whipped his head back around at the deafening blare, just in time to see a solid wall of Gallean warriors tromping forward. Shields raised, and lances lowered, they marched resolutely toward the defenders. The predator was now springing.

Near the center of the defensive lines, four massive Gigans, wielding huge maces and axes, formed a spearhead for the great surge. Well-armed ranks of Gallean warriors in helms and mail-shirts kept pace to either side of the brutish quartet.

Leaders amongst the defenders shouted out in frantic urgency in response to the Gigan-forged threat looming in the center. The Gigans threatened to punch right through the midst of the defensive lines, as nothing could hope to stand in the way of the lumbering juggernauts. A wide breach at the center would likely result in full collapse and rout. The attackers could then stream in to take the shoreline, and prevent any escape.

Saxan, Midragardan, and tribal archers alike concentrated their arrows upon the lumbering brutes, from wherever the bowmen were positioned. The concentrated flurries of arrows felled many Galleans around the Gigans, though not all of the arrows missed their intended targets.

Fletched shafts riddled the bodies of three of the Gigans. The bestial warriors slumped heavily to the ground, succumbing to the overwhelming barrage.

The fourth Gigan bellowed in pain as a couple of arrows lodged in its thick hide, but the injuries were negligible as it stomped forward, outraged, and eager to reach its tormentors.

The focus of the archers upon the central area of the enemy lines enabled many Gallean warriors to cross the remaining expanse of ground relatively unhindered. Clashes of steel and cries of men erupted everywhere, as the two sides locked in a deadly embrace.

Though arrows had culled many from their ranks, the Galleans in the center continued their advance without hesitation. They closed upon the defenders, as the last Gigan roared furiously. The towering creature raised its huge axe upward, trudging through the final strides remaining between it and the defensive line.

The last Midragardans gathered in the center suddenly pressed forward with spirited war cries, to meet the Gigan and spear-bearing infantry head on. Wading among them with slashing swords and maniacally-wielded axe blows, they fought with mythic ardor. Giving no thought for their own lives, striking and hacking in a frenzy, the last of them did not fall until a much greater number of Gallean warriors and the Gigan cluttered the blood-soaked ground.

The defensive line continued to hold, if barely. Deganawida knew the resistance could not be sustained for much longer, as the enemy possessed overwhelming numbers.

With a spike of alarm, he espied another large force of Galleans, accompanied by a sizeable contingent of warriors from enemy tribes, moving through the trees. Hearing the enemy tribal warriors' distinctive war cries, Deganawida knew them at once to be Wendaton. Their faces were contorted into masks of hatred, bent on settling ages-old enmities with the tribes of the Five Realms, once and for all.

A number of the last rescue boats were now gathered on the shore. Many Saxans glanced over their shoulders, at the sound of another extended horn signal from Athelhere.

Deganawida looked to the Saxan commander. Aethelhere quickly explained what was happening, and the sachem had runners relay the information on to the Midragardans and tribal fighters.

Up and down the defensive line, stalwart warriors readied for a hurried retreat. Far beyond the enmeshed lines of battle, past the advancing Wendaton and Gallean warriors, more contingents of fresh enemy warriors were mustering.

The tenuous balance was about to be tipped decisively in the attacker's favor. Wave after wave of the invaders' might was rolling to crash upon the fragile shield wall. The swelling might of the attackers would batter the weakening defense apart in no time.

Deganawida then took notice of a lone figure running at full speed towards the middle of the battle, heading towards the area where the sachem was standing. The man was a tribal warrior, and for a moment Deganawida eyed him as he raced down the backside of the defenders. The warrior was lost from view a few times as he hurried through the trees along the edge where foliage and earth made the transition into a sandy beach.

The venerable sachem could not allow himself to be distracted by any curiosities, though he had a very good idea as to who the figure was. At that moment, another breach occurred in the vicinity of the running man, who slowed to a halt and hurled himself into the fray.

The brittle line was finally breaking, and Deganawida knew there would be no time for the defenders to make it to the boats, much less load themselves onto the vessels. He thought quickly, wondering how he could possibly do something for his people.

He had learned special arts over the long years, which he had always employed for the benefit of the tribe. In other lands they were called powers of sorcery or magic, but Deganawida had never regarded them in an ill light. Countering the workings of witches and evil shaman sometimes required the kind of arts that were normally within the domain of Wizards.

Yet even the strongest of those powers would be useless against a force as strong as the invaders. Any magical working Deganawida employed would be nothing more than poking a great bear with a twig.

Deganawida did not have long to ponder the stark dilemma before him, as frenzied shouts broke out to the left in response to yet another break in the shield wall. The defense was crumbling fast, and there appeared to be no pathway out of the dilemma.

The brave warriors who had fought so vigilantly, and paid such a massive price, needed some kind of intercession. The refugees had to survive, and carry the Five Realms onward within their hearts and souls, or everything was lost.

There was no strategy to act upon, or forces to relieve the defenders. In desperation, and with every last vestige of willpower left to him, he poured his heart into one great supplication to the One Spirit.

Closing his eyes, he thought deeply of his people, and all the joy, sacrifice, and heartbreak accumulated across the years empowered his outreach, as his spirit cried out with soul-rending passion. Pure of intent and fervent, the prayer soared from within.

Gripped with waves of emotion, Deganawida's body shook. The sachem fell to his knees as if something had snapped deep within. Emptied of energy, he felt the hands of two individuals, faintly hearing their words, as they worked to get him back up to his feet.

The void he felt within did not last long. Clarity poured into his mind like a robust waterfall, filling him with long-obscured memories and experiences. The fog shrouding his mind and spirit for so many years was no more. Deganawida knew precisely who he was, and what he could do.

His supplication had not given him any kind of heightened powers, or brought down fire from the skies to destroy the enemy. The gift he had received was simply remembering who his true self was. A choice to act still remained in the aftermath of that knowledge.

The only path he saw before him would bring finality, but there was no other way. Deganawida knew the forest teemed with thousands of attackers, who would fall upon the defenders with overwhelming strength the moment the latter tried to reach the boats.

Deganawida realized he had lived an incredible life, and if he had to die, then he wanted to die with his feet set firmly upon the ground of his beloved homeland. In proclaiming the Peace Law and forging the Grand Council, Deganawida had shown the people a new way. Now, if the people were to survive, he would have to honor that way by making the greatest of sacrifices.

A momentous hour had arrived, a call to be at one with the lands that had cradled the tribes for countless generations. It was an hour to become one with the people who were the spirit and soul of the Five Realms.

Deganawida was also a sachem of the Onan, the Keepers of the Sacred Fire, and in that moment a deep understanding came to him. The carefully tended fire that had nearly been destroyed in the Place of Far

Seeing during the Darrok attack was not the true Sacred Fire.

Standing at the very edge of their lands, in the shadow of a great evil, Deganawida realized the genuine nature of the Sacred Fire. Burning with flames that no rain or attack of the enemy could ever hope to put out, the Sacred Fire was within.

As the inspirations unlocked further wisdom, Deganawida made yet another realization. In the truest sense of the word, Deganawida was a Keeper of the Sacred Fire.

A sensation of tremendous power thundered within him. With a loud outcry startling all the warriors around him, Deganawida used the thick branch to prop up his tired physical body. He let the maple-carved war club fall to the ground, raising his right hand with palm facing up towards the sky.

He began a chant filled with sorrow, longing, praise, strength, joy, and a host of other emotions, comprising the breadth of a long life spent in the care of his people. Reaching deep within, down to the most sacred, quiet core of his soul, Deganawida summoned the flame; the Sacred Fire burning inside.

The act recalled the image portrayed on the wampum shell-belt, the very one he had held so often when speaking before the Grand Council. The image on that belt was both symbol and reality.

Five images, four square shapes connected with a pine tree at their center, evoked a transcendent union now reflected in a much more radiant way; as five living tribes were embodied in one being, a Wizard choosing to lay down the grace of immortality on their behalf. The spirit in which the Five Realms had once come into harmonious fellowship was resurrected in full, in a way even Deganawida had not fully fathomed.

AYENWATHA

The mesmerizing sounds of the old sachem's resonant, rhythmic chants carried over to where Ayenwatha was standing. He was recovering his breath alongside several tribal warriors, who had all just barely managed to close another break in the shield wall.

His eyes, stinging from coursing rivulets of sweat carrying drops of blood within them, were drawn towards the old figure standing a short distance down the line. Engrossed with the spectacle of his wizened mentor and dearest friend, Ayenwatha did not think of the painful gash on his leg from the biting edge of an enemy spear.

Deganawida's arms were now outstretched, his left hand firmly gripping some kind of staff or branch. His gaze was oriented towards the skies, as he continued to powerfully chant.

While he did not know what was transpiring, Ayenwatha knew something of profound consequence was underway. While working his way to Deganawida, a sudden break occurred in the shield wall. He had already accepted the inevitable conclusion to the battle in his heart, as the shield wall broke apart and the defenders were swarmed by a horde of invaders. His last wish was to make a final stand by the side of Deganawida, and give his last breath defending the old sachem against the terrible fate engulfing them.

With grim resolve, Ayenwatha fought through the melee, making his way towards the old man. Of singular mind and purpose, it was as if nothing else existed in that moment.

Deganawida slowly looked towards him as he approached, and Ayenwatha was stunned by the sachem's look of peace and serenity. With the fires of battle raging all around them, his aura was an oasis, heralding another time and place.

"All this time, I should have known. " the old sachem said to Ayenwatha, in a calm, clear voice. "The Sacred Fire was never within the longhouse of the Grand Council. It could never be put out. It is within all of our people, and burns there still, in each and every one of them. I am a sachem of the Onan, the Keepers of the Sacred Fire, I hold the Grand Council position that I once established myself, so long ago"

The declaration astonished Ayenwatha, but Deganawida continued before he could respond. "Bear this staff of wood with you, and go with our people. I shall give you a sign, so that you and the others may understand. This sign will be an echo of a deeper truth I have come to know in this final hour ... one I believe you will be guided to in your heart."

Deganawida paused for a moment, and his gaze enveloped Ayenwatha, as he concluded his address in a low, purposeful voice. "Remember well the sign I give you on this very day. For most, it will be of great importance for the tribes, in the coming days. But for you, it will point to something much deeper. In future times, look for the One whose anointing is done with the Fire of the Living Spirit of the Creator, a Fire that burns within us all."

Ayenwatha took in each of the cryptic words, though they made little sense. Perplexed, amazed, and a little fearful, he looked to Deganawida, as he could feel something powerful coalescing in the air all around them. An expression of wonderment began emerging on the war sachem's face.

It was as if Deganawida's body was gaining in strength right before Ayenwatha's eyes. As he handed the branch-staff over to Ayenwatha, the sachem's posture straightened, and he showed no further need for any sort of assistance. If anything, the elder sachem displayed a youthful, hale ambience about his person. Years fell away swiftly from his countenance.

In one graceful movement, Deganawida removed the blue-gemstone pendant he had borrowed from the Trogen Dragol, and extended it towards Ayenwatha. The war sachem took the pendant from Deganawida, but found himself staring speechlessly at the old sachem.

Everything happening seemed so surreal, as if reality itself was spinning in place, with time itself suspended. Even the worrisome thoughts of the ongoing battle had fled from Ayenwatha's mind.

"Take this, and give this back to Dragol. He has a place in this struggle," Deganawida instructed gently. "He will show his true heart, and his kind will find their way after being led astray. Help him on that journey."

Ayenwatha silently nodded, feeling a strong sense of the huge, dog-faced warrior taking hold within his mind. The Trogen had been sent out among the first of the relief boats, to remove him from approaching combat, and the chance that the unavoidable clash transformed into a vengeful antipathy on the part of those around him.

Ironically, the Trogen had been one of the survivors of a sunken relief boat, when his kind had attacked from the skies above. He had shown the kind of heart he possessed, in the face of a threat to his own life. Ayenwatha had watched from the shoreline as the huge figure grasped no less than three small tribal children, saving them from a drowning fate. He staunchly tread water for all of them, keeping the chidlren from submerging, until the young ones were finally able to be passed onto a rescuing vessel. An old tribal sachem from the Onan had been sent with Dragol, to vouch for the Trogen and safeguard him, and Ayenwatha could only hope that he had survived as well.

As the resolve to protect Dragol took deeper root, his concern over the Trogen's fate receded in his mind. As if the intended message had been imparted, and it was time to move forward, Ayenwatha's attentions were once again consumed by the beloved, elderly figure before him.

"Go now, my dear friend. They need you. We will hunt together in a time to come," Deganawida continued, benevolently, his face emanating a confident reassurance as he turned back to face the treeline.

Time and the urgency of the moment snapped Ayenwatha back jarringly. No matter what abyss of sorrow was opening in his heart, he knew he had to act.

"To the boats! To the boats!" Ayenwatha cried out at the top of his lungs, forcing the words out with difficulty.

His eyes, reddened and stinging, were now being filled with tears, as deep, thunderous emotions surged up from within. Though he knew what he had to do, it still took a tremendous act of will to leave Deganawida behind.

In an afterthought, he slipped the Trogen's pendant over his head, for safekeeping. There would be no time for long farewells, or even to brace himself for what was now taking place.

With gut-wrenching fortitude, Ayenwatha implored haste among his comrades, calling out forcefully to them to fall back to the beach. His cry was taken up by others, and many of the tribal warriors began backing up, moving towards the shoreline while keeping their bodies squared to the forest.

From nearby, the bearded Saxan leader blew upon his horn, seeing Ayenwatha's warriors start to retreat. The Saxan leader had remained close, watching much of what was happening with Ayenwatha and Deganawida. He was now taking his cue from Ayenwatha's actions, and encouraging his men to pull back.

All along the beach, the line of defenders streamed towards the boats, as the last members of the defensive line moved out from the trees. They retreated slowly, still facing the forest with weapons poised. Those in the central area edged carefully by the shimmering Five Realms council elder, whose body was undergoing a spectacular transition, from mere flesh into a luminous, translucent form.

The enemy commanders must have perceived the sudden movements and horn signals to be some manner of planned ruse, and their suspicions worked to the favor of the defenders. The enemy did not press the attack, as horns blasted hurriedly from within their ranks.

Much of the defensive line was retreating orderly enough. Though much smaller, and thinned considerably, it was still no broken, routed force that the attackers faced.

The enemy archers and crossbowmen were not nearly as restrained as the commanders, as they continued discharging a showering barrage of arrows and bolts. The missiles dropped more tribesmen and allied warriors right in the path of their retreat, at the very cusp of reaching the waiting boats.

Strangely, not one of the arrows or bolts harmed Deganawida. Whether missing him, or passing harmlessly right through him, Deganawida was left entirely unscathed as he continued through the incredible transformation.

Emboldened after the storm of arrows and bolts, the enemy commanders finally signaled their ranks through sonorous horns. The reinforced mass of warriors, up and down the line, started marching forward, sending a rumbling sound rolling through the trees towards shore.

The first ranks of Gallean warriors stepped out of the forest, the sun's rays reflecting off their iron helms, weapons, and armor as they set foot upon the sands of the beach. The enemy line closed in rapidly upon the position Deganawida was warding. Those in the central ranks paused, their boldness stayed as they regarded the fully translucent, pulsating form of the tribal elder standing right in their path.

The advancing enemy was oriented towards the east, and it was as if a new sun was rising up before them. Deganawida's body emitted a blinding flash of fiery light. Sheets of flame erupted from his resplendent form, racing up and down the beach along an even line. Waves of heat washed over defender and attacker alike, and all who witnessed the phenomenon were held in place, awestruck.

The powerful emanation cleaved through the ground, scattering plumes of dirt and rock all through the area. Innumerable shards of the flaming light soared upwards, as if the lustrous rays streaked to pierce the sky above. Accompanying the visible elements, the ground itself began rumbling and shaking.

The enemy commanders were not foolish enough to have their forces recklessly continue into the sudden, expansive manifestation. Through the issuance of several curt horn blasts, they hastily brought all of their forces to a halt.

Scant moments later, a huge crevice opened in the ground. Rock, clay, soil, sand, and other debris from within the growing crevice piled up on the sides of the gaping opening, as if being pushed upward by a great power from deep within the ground.

Many terrified Gallean warriors cried out desperately, as they were caught around the edges of the forming crevice and the violence of the debris vomiting up from the depths. A number helplessly tumbled into the fissure, their screams fading into the darkness. Others were completely buried in the massive upsurge of rock and soil, knocked off their feet and embedded in the rampart forming at the lip of the chasm.

All across the line, the attack was brought to a complete halt. An eerie silence hovered over the ranks of the attackers, save for the scattered cries and shouts from survivors in the foremost ranks, who had the extreme fortune to be only partially buried in the upheaval.

Ayenwatha was no different from the other tribal warriors, Midragardans, and Saxans. Whether still getting into the boats, or rowing out towards the awaiting Saxan fleet, they all kept their eyes riveted on the wall of rubble that had seemed to sprout from the ground itself. Ayenwatha could not even see the enemy forces from where he was, shielded as they were by the substantial, earthen wall.

Saxans riding upon Himmerosen were still in the skies overhead. The bursts of fiery light into the skies had highly unnerved many steeds, causing some to bolt farther away from the shoreline in fright. After getting the steeds settled, the Saxan sky riders began pulling back further out over the bay. Regrouping, they shadowed the last waves of boats leaving the shore.

Ayenwatha was on the very last boat to be shoved off the sands and into the bay's waters. Gliding along the glistening surface of the Water Head-Cradle, Ayenwatha watched the aftermath in reverend silence.

Where offshoots of the skyward flame-shards had headed far into the skies, a strange, wonderful vision began taking place. As if a gentle, reddish snow, small tongues of fire drifted slowly down in great multitudes, angling towards the mass of boats clustered within the bay.

Something stirred deep within Ayenwatha, prompting him not to fear the tongues of fire as they cascaded downward. He felt a calming wave of solace flood throughout him, and he could not have forced himself to become alarmed if he had wanted to.

Each tongue of fire drifted down to settle lightly upon the head of a tribal refugee, from the greatest to the least, and from the youngest to the oldest. The unusual rain did not cease until every single individual from the five tribes was graced with a flame.

A second fiery rain, comprised of many more flames, followed. Lighter in hue, the second host of flames floated down in a great mass, and then separated. One flame was absorbed into each of the Saxans serving in the fleet that had come to the rescue of the tribal people. Likewise, tongues of fire from the second cascade anointed the few surviving Midragardans, the courageous, honorable warriors who had stood and fought alongside the tribal people throughout their terrible exodus.

The people on the crowded vessels were held nearly spellbound by the stunning visions, but the display was not finished. A mighty, white-hot column of flame streaked down from the sky, speeding towards the last of the small rowing vessels. It struck the wooden branch-staff that Ayenwatha still clenched tightly in his right hand, engulfing the wood in an instant.

Though caught by surprise, he somehow held his grip upon the staff. The staff burst into a pure white flame, one that did not harm his flesh. It cast a soothing warmth upon his face, and his body coursed with a vibrant, invigorating energy, drawing upon some mysterious power emanating from the essence of the flames.

Ayenwatha was emotionally shaken to his core, as he knew what the event represented, and what it would mean for his people. With wetted eyes, he looked up at the sky, and offered a prayer of thanksgiving to his friend, mentor, and most honorable elder, Deganawida.

"We will meet again … in a land of rich hunting. One that no dark power can ever drive us from, Deganawida. And I will strive to honor your sacrifice always, until that glorious day arrives," Ayenwatha stated, in a low, soft voice, laden with heartfelt emotion.

His eyes remained skyward, as the boat continued across the bay. None of the boat's occupants said a word to him, or otherwise interrupted him. Ayenwatha held the branch-staff reverently, the top flaming like a torch, though the fires did not consume the wood.

His boat eventually reached the edge of a galley, a large vessel with a lengthy bank of oars sprouting out from the side. Many hands helped Ayenwatha and the others up from the small boat, though all took great care not to come in contact with the burning staff in Ayenwatha's right hand.

A little smile of relief came to Ayenwatha's face, as he beheld the Trogen warrior, Dragol, looking back at him on the ship's decking. The brawny, tall warrior was standing with the haggard-looking Onan sachem who had been asked to accompany the Trogen. The sight of Dragol unharmed brought a spark of gladness to Ayenwatha's heavily laden heart.

Ayenwatha took notice of the stunned expressions lingering on the faces of the Saxans all around him. They looked to be trying to make some sense of the incredible, awe-inspiring visions.

A burly, thick-bearded man stood a pace ahead of the semi-circle of Saxans. He cradled a half helm in his right arm, his thinning gray and black hair stringy and matted. His face and coat of mail were amply spotted with blood, and the links of the chain mail were broken in a couple of places.

Ayenwatha recognized the man as being the first Saxan from the boats, the one who had stood with Deganawida. The Saxan gave a slight nod of acknowledgement, as he quietly regarded Ayenwatha.

The Saxan leader and his fellow warriors appeared somewhat entranced. It was also plain that they were very exhausted, having put all of their strength into the efforts to resist the attackers, and ferry the tribal refugees out to the fleet.

A number of tribal people, of all ages and gender, gradually began gathering around Ayenwatha. They stared in amazement at the flaming brand in his hand, seeing that it gave off no smoke, and did not burn flesh or wood.

With a voice choked by a juxtaposition of great sadness and joy, Ayenwatha spoke to the people of the five tribes, and all others who could hear him, "Deganawida knew ... he was the Keeper of the Sacred Fire. The Fire was within him. As it had always been. As it had been within those who served on the Grand Council that he once founded. Now it goes forth in all of us, as it always has been. In our people, wherever we are. He has shown us, in this great, final sign, what the nature of the Sacred Fire and the alliance of our five tribes truly was. No matter the hardship we may face, his revelation will ever give us strength."

His heart swelled with fiercely-burning pride as he thought of Deganawida. He suddenly had to look away from his fellow tribal people, as well as the Saxans. As powerful as his pride was, so was the thunderous emotion of grief, an abyss continuously gaping inside him.

SPIRIT OF FIRE

The wound to his spirit was raw and painful. He could acutely sense the saddened hearts within the tribal warriors, women, elderly, and children about him, as they also sorrowed over the tremendous loss of the well-loved sachem. Deganawida would be mourned for a long time to come, and he would never be forgotten.

Deganawida's one final act had done so much to save their people from destruction. It had spared the remaining warriors of the tribe, to go forth into an uncertain future with the women, children, and the elders. Though bought at a high, bitter price, all of the tribal people had been given an inviolate lesson in wisdom. It was one the five tribes would have great need of in the times to come.

A pall of sorrow hung over all the tribal people. The somber atmosphere was broken only by horn signals calling out from the surrounding ships.

After a short time spent to gather up the smaller boats and anchors, the galleys of the Saxan fleet lurched into motion with the power of a multitude of oars. Cadences were sounded, as rowers put their shoulders and backs into maintaining a unified rhythm.

His heart cumbrous, Ayenwatha stood quietly, watching the shoreline slowly disappear as the fleet left the bay's mouth, starting on its southward journey. There were few words spoken, and most exchanges were conducted between Saxans going about tasks on the galley.

The signal calls to the rowers, the lapping of the ocean's waves on the timber hull, and the splashes of oars in the water formed a sustained backdrop for the weary passengers. Like Ayenwatha, most of the tribal people stared forlornly towards the shoreline as they were carried farther and farther away from their homeland. Little could be said after enduring the great hardships, loss, and miraculous manifestations. There was so much to ponder and reflect upon.

Ayenwatha knew that healing would take quite some time, and each and every one of the tribal people must deal with their personal ordeals in their own way, even as they strove to aid each other. Even the children were not spared, having experienced horrific sights that no child should have been made to bear.

Yet there was a spark of hope within each of them, the war sachem could see, and the recognition of a flame burning deep within every last man, woman, and child. The nature of that flame was as individual as it was shared; an essence that transcended the world itself.

A wise, brave Wizard had helped them to see it for the first time, though it had always dwelt inside them. Still, the wisdom was a precious gift, which had been bestowed upon them in the form of an anointing.

It was now Ayenwatha's task to make certain that the Onan continued their charge in being the Keepers of the Sacred Fire. The sign of that Fire blazed brightly from the staff in his right hand, as the coast of his homeland passed into memory.

He turned away, and his eyes met those of a small child standing by her mother. As the child's eyes met his, her little face brightened and a smile bloomed upon her face. Ayenwatha's hope was rekindled.

appendix

AELFRIC: The designated majordomo, or top commander, of the forces of Saxany that are deployed at the Plains of Athelney. Aelfric is also the Ealdorman of the Wesvald.

AETHELSTAN: A powerful thane from Wessachia, Aethelstan leads a force to defend against an offshoot of the main invasion forces from the west.

AETHELHERE: Aethelhere is Aethelstan's brother, and is a thane who has been given command of the Saxan fleet.

AIDAN: The son of King Alcuin, Prince Aidan is heir to the throne.

ALCUIN: Current king of Saxany. His wife is Queen Baldhild, and his immediate successor one of his sons, Prince Aidan.

ANDAMOOR: Located in Eberias, the Andamoorans follow the Prophet, which puts them at odds with many of the western kingdoms. The Andamoorans have come under the sway of the Unifer, and have agreed to assist in the wars launched to unite all lands. Their cooperation with the Unifier has held threats to their own lands at bay.

ANISHIN TRIBES: A group of tribes occupying lands bordering those of the Five Realms, who have primarily been adversaries of the latter.

ARCAMON: Beings of hellish power, Arcamons come from the depths of the Hallowed Kingdom, the realms of the Lord of Fire, Jebaalos.

ATAGAR: The Atagar are from the lands of Yanith. Shorter of stature in comparison to humans, hey can walk upon two legs or four, and have a rat-like appearance.

AVALOS: Avalos is a great city that is the capital of the lands of Avanor.

AVANOR: Avanor is a duchy that is part of the Kingdom of Gallea, on its far western edge. Avanor is the home of the Unifier, who resides in the capital city of Avalos.

AYENWATHA: War sachem of the Onan, Ayenwatha is also a member of the Firaken clan. It is Ayenwatha who one of the major leaders of the resistance against the invasion forces from Gallea.

BERZERKS: The Beserks, or "bear-shirts", are part of a mystical order in Midragard that also includes the Ulfhednar. Just as the Ulfhednar form a special, close bond with wolves, the Berzerks are associated with the great bears of Midragard.

BEVRIEDAK: One of the Elder, it is Bevriedak that Wulfstan encounters when he seeks out the Havens.

BREGA: One of the types of Skiantha, the Brega are found in the lands of the Five Realms. The winged creatures echo the form of a bear in their appearance.

DARROKS: Huge flying, reptilian creatures that are kin to dragons. Many have been trained for the Unifier's forces, bringing new methods of warfare to Ave.

DEGANAWIDA: Deganawida is the First Sachem of the Grand Council, and is also a sachem of the Onan. He is named after a great Wizard who helped bring together the Five Realms long ago.

DRAUENIR: The father-jewel to the ones that the otherworlders and Dragol carry, given to them by the enigmatic Wanderer.

EASTERN ONES: Another type of Elder who have very different forms from Elder like Bevriedak and Gerasen. They reside in Havens far to the east of where Bevriedak's kind are.

EDEN: A sanctuary where death has no claim, now hidden from the eyes of the living in Ave.

EHRENGARD: Part of the Sacred Empire, Ehrengard is located just west of Saxany.

THE ELDER: An immortal race of gigantic dragons. The Elder were among the very first beings given life in Ave during its First Age, along with the Wizards and Elves.

FAHTAMIDS: A realm ruled by a powerful Khalif and populated by followers of the Prophet. Its capital is Caiandria.

FENRAREN: A type of Skiantha, these winged creatures have a wolf-like appearance and are found in the lands of Midragard.

FIRAKENS: Great hunting cats with six legs, the Firakens are fearsome predators. They can be found in the lands of the Five Realms.

FIRST ALLIANCE: The initial seven western kingdoms whose leaders gave their full allegiance to the Unifier privately.

THE FIRST ONES: Elder who sided with Jebaalos when the Great Schism occurred. They were cast into the Abyss along with Jebaalos and the Archons who sided with the Lord of Fire. They have a prominent place in the Hallowed Kingdom that rose up in the aftermath of that great battle.

THE FIVE REALMS: A confederacy of five tribes, two of which are referred to as the Younger Brothers, the Gayogohon and Onyota. The other three are known as the Older Brothers, the Kanienke, the Onan, and the Onondowa

FRAMORG: Supreme war chieftain of the Trogen Clans, Framorg is of the Mountain Bear Clan. It is he who commands the Trogen forces that are aiding the Unifier in the invasion of Saxany.

GALLEA: A large kingdom just west of the Five Realms.

GALLIDILS: Huge reptilian creatures that have a resemblance to large crocodiles, the Gallidils dwell in the subterranean world of the Unguhur.

GAVRI'EL: A powerful Archon

GIGANS: Huge creatures with boar-like countenances, the Gigans dwell in lands just east of Trogen lands. They have also been brought into the service of the Unifier, with Gigans fighting in the forces invading both Saxany and the Five Realms.

KIRUVA: A land that contains broad steppes and many rivers, just to the south of Trogen and Gigan lands. Kiruva is led by a Grand Prince, with other provinces ruled over by members of the Grand Prince's family in a hereditary system.

GUNTHER: Originally from Ehrengard, Gunther has had many journeys, including a time when he lived in the Empire of Theonia. Now, he is a reclusive woodsman dwelling in the wild forests of Saxany, along with a small pack of Jaghuns that he has raised and trained.

HAKON: The current king of Midragard. Hakon is often accompanied by his great black wolf, Heder.

HALLOWED FLAMES: Used in the ritual of Claimancy, binding a soul to the Lord of Fire, Jebaalos.

HALLOWED KINGDOM: One of the names for the realms of Jebaalos.

HALMLANDER: A legendary mercenary company, who come from Ehrengard. Formed of outlaws, oath-breaking knights, runaways, and others who have broken away from their former lives, the Halmlander are brutal and deadly. When wars break out, they are quickly employed by Kings of Ehrengard, not just because of their strong military value, but also to get them out of Ehrengard for a time.

HARRAKS: A type of Skiantha, the Harraks come from the lands where the Trogens dwell. Many now reside in Avanor, where a number of Avanorans have been trained to fly them and care for them. They have an appearance that echoes a brown hyena.

HIMMEROSEN: A type of Skiantha, the Himmerosen echo a dog-like form, and dwell in the lands of Saxany. Robust and thick-jawed, the Himmerosen are tough creatures well-suited to battle in the skies.

JAGHUNS: With powerful jaws, large, and fast, the Jaghuns are predators in the lands where they dwell in the wild, such as the Shadowlands. It is there that the woodsman Gunther found a young pair, who were brought back to Saxany where he bread a small number that he has trained and keeps as companions.

JEBAALOS: The Lord of Fire, which is just one of the many titles used for the Being also known as the Prince of the World. Jebaalos is the great Adversary who led a war against Palladium that involved a schism of the Archons themselves.

LICANTHERS: With lengthy upper canines that resemble curving sabers, the Licanthers are brawny, cat-like beasts that are found in the land of Yanith. The Atagar raise and train Licanthers for use as guards and for battle.

LNUK: One of the Anishin tribes. As of the events depicted in the Fires in Eden series, they are no longer in conflict with the Five Realms. They are known for their ocean-capable canoes, and regularly ply the coastal areas near the Five Realms and their lands.

MIDRAGARD: A great land far to the south, made of a people who excelled at seafaring. For many ages, the Midragardans traveled to many lands, raiding some, trading in others, and in some cases founding new lands, such as Kiruva.

MIKA'IL: High Archon and leader of the hosts of Palladium. The Mount of the High Archon, on an island near Avalos, is named after Mika'il.

ORANIM: A great underground city, carved out of the rock of a vast cavern beneath Saxan lands. Oranim is where a large population of Unguhur dwell.

ORDER OF THE HEALERS: An order of warrior-monks named for the numerous hospitals they established across the Sunlands. Their standards are red with a white spear of Emmanu depicted on them.

ORDER OF THE HIGH ALTAR: A powerful order of warrior-monks who also very involved in the handling of money. They have a presence that spans from the western lands into the Sunlands. Their standards are half-white and half-black.

ORDER OF THE SACRED LADY: An order of warrior-monks whose origin derives from Ehrengard. Their standards are black spears of Emmanu upon white backgrounds.

PLACE OF LIGHTNING: The place where Jebaalos struck the surface of Ave during the Fall from Palladium.

QUOIAN: The language of the tribes of the Five Realms.

SACRED FIRE: Bestowed by the Wizard Deganawida at the foundation of the Five Realms, the Sacred Fire has never been extinguished, carefully tended by the Onan, who are known as the Keepers of the Sacred Fire.

SAINA RIVER: A large river in Gallea that flows through Avalos to meet the sea.

SALJUKA: Ruled by a Sultan, Saljuka is a powerful land that borders the empire of Theonia. The majority of its people follow the teachings of the Prophet.

SELECT FYRD: Composed of thanes, household guards, and more skilled ceorls, the Select Fyrd is a special levy in Saxany that differs from the General Fyrd, which is a summons of all able-bodied men for the defense of the land. Under most circumstances, the Select Fyrd is all that is necessary to counter threats.

SHIMMERING RIVER: A great river that travels through the heart of the Five Realms.

SHRAKAS: With some resemblance to sharks, the Shrakas have some distinct differences, but they are massive ocean predators that ply the waters off the coasts of many lands.

SPIRIT WING: The Himmeros that Wulfstan took to find the Elder.

THE STEPPING STONES: A series of islands that break up the ocean stretches north of Midragard, helping seafarers on their way to lands such as Kiruva, Gael, and even Saxany.

THE SUNLANDS: To the far north are a number of realms that are collectively called the Sunlands. Many of these lands follow a religion founded by a great prophet, which has set them at odds with both the Eastern and Western Churches. Holy Wars have erupted pitting the followers of the Prophet against the followers of Emmanu.

SVEIN: A senior retainer of King Hakon of Midragard, Svein is perhaps the most trusted. He is often delegated the most important tasks by the king.

THEONIA: A powerful empire that has faded in strength at the time of the Fires in Eden series. Its capital is a majestic city called Theonium, which is the seat of the Grand Shepherd of the Eastern Church. It is constantly warring with the Fahtamids and the land of Saljuka.

TREE OF PEACE: a snow-white pine tree where the first convening of the Grand Council of the Five Realms was held

TROGENS: A muscular, tall race of beings that inhabit lands bordering the northeast of Kiruvan lands. The Trogens have a longstanding conflict with the Northern Elves, who have raided, pillaged, and enslaved Trogens over the ages. To get aid in their fight against the Elves, the Trogens have been persuaded to serve in the ranks of the Unifier's forces.

UKTENA: Great horned serpents that dwell in the depths, the Uktena possess incredibly lethal venom.

ULFHEDNAR: The Ulfhednar, or "wolf-cloaks", are part of a great, mystical order in Midragard that also includes the Berzerks. The Ulfhednar have reached the final stage of the order, and have been gifted with special powers that they use in the service of Midragard.

UNGUHUR: A race of beings that dwell in subterranean environments. They are strong creatures with grayish, rough-textured skin, which is the reason they are called Stone Hides by the tribal people of the Five Realms. A great population of them reside beneath the lands of Saxany, centered around a terraced city called Oranim.

WENDATON: One of the Anishin Tribes and principal enemy to the Five Realms.

WOLF KIN: The Wolf Kin include all who are a part of a mystical order in Midragard that have, or are forming, bonds with packs of great wolves in the land. The most fully-realized of them are the Ulfhednar, while the ones on the earliest stages of the sacred path are called Seekers.

WULFSTAN: A Saxan ceorl who acts upon dreams he has had for a long time, searching out the mythic Elder when it seems as if there is no hope to be found for the Saxans as a massive invasion comes at them from the west.

ABOUT THE AUTHOR

Stephen Zimmer is an award-winning author and filmmaker, whose literary works include the epic-scale urban fantasy series *The Rising Dawn Saga*, and the epic fantasy *Fires in Eden Series*. As of the first half of 2012, Stephen has six novels and several short stories published, including the Harvey and Solomon steampunk adventures.

As a filmmaker, Stephen's credits include the supernatural thriller feature *Shadows Light*, the horror short film *The Sirens*, and *Swordbearer*, a medieval fantasy short film based upon the H. David Blalock novel *Ascendant*.

Further information on Stephen Zimmer can be found at:

Website: www.stephenzimmer.com
Facebook : www.facebook.com/sgzimmer
Twitter: http://www.twitter.com/sgzimmer
Blog: http://stephenzimmer.blogspot.com
and he is also available on Google+

Check out the following pages to see more from

All Seventh Star Press titles available in print and an array of
specially priced eBook formats.

Visit www.seventhstarpress.com for further information.

Connect with Seventh Star Press at:
www.seventhstarpress.com
seventhstarpress.blogspot.com
www.facebook.com/seventhstarpress

Epic Urban Fantasy-The Rising Dawn Saga

A shadow falls across the world, and realms beyond, as a war that has raged since the dawn of time itself draws closer to a decisive clash. As groups aligned with a movement called The Convergence speed up their efforts to bring about a global economic and legal order, resistance mounts after the host of a syndicated radio show, Benedict Darwin, discovers the true nature of a virtual reality device that has come into his possession. The Rising Dawn Saga will take you into mythical, supernatural realms as it unfolds, as the most unlikely of individuals rise to confront powers that have existed since before the world began.

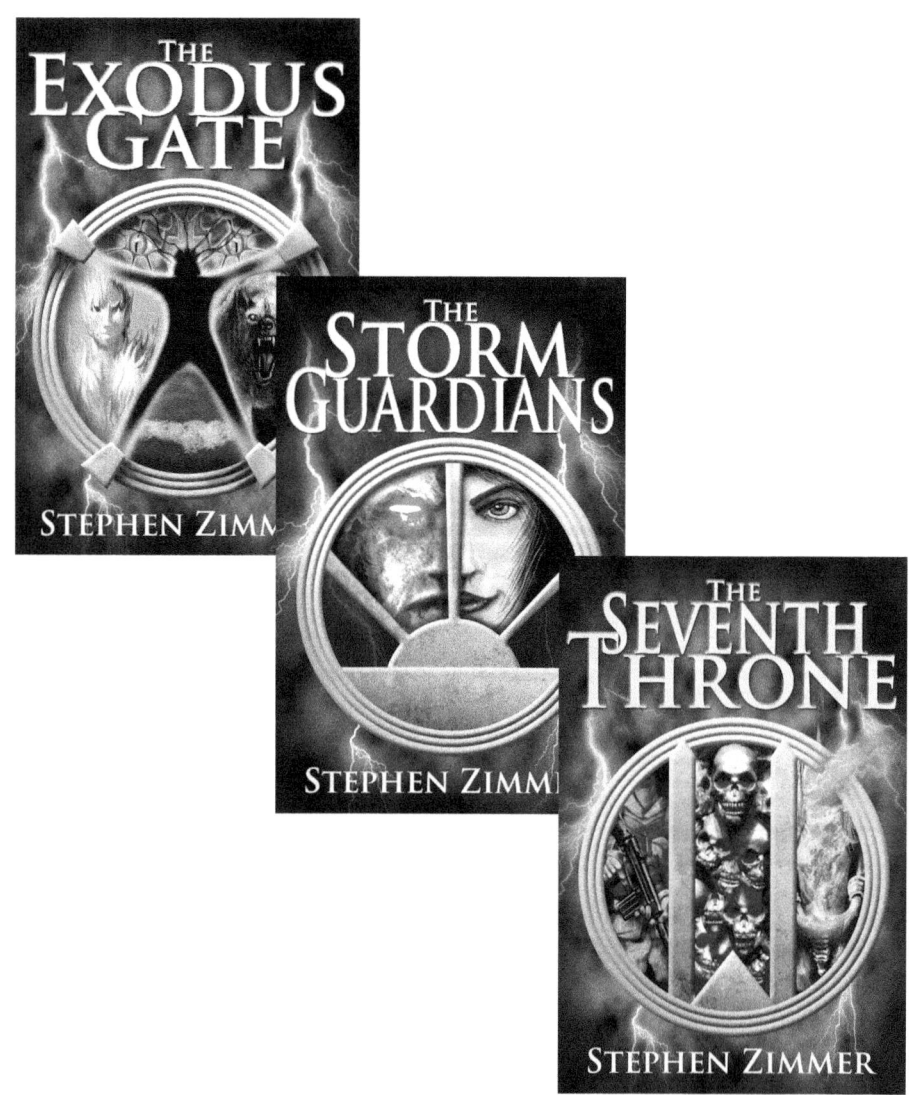

Book One: The Exodus Gate
ISBN: 978-0615267470

"With The Exodus Gate author Stephen Zimmer sets the stage for an adventurous new science fiction fantasy series that is sure to entertain the reader from beginning to end. Zimmer has weaved a tale of fantastic realms populated with exotic creatures. Keep a sharp eye out for this new series."
-Mark Randell, Yellow30 Sci-Fi

"…a book that Fantasy Book Review recommends for lovers of thoughtful-fantasy. It is also a book with an ending that is near-prophetic, written as it was before the world's economic meltdown."
-Fantasy Book Review

Book Two: The Storm Guardians
ISBN: 978-0982565636

"This novel transports me from my bedroom to the edge of an upcoming storm — a battle to be fought by incredible villains and noble heroes of all forms. I love Zimmer's imagination, as each of his creatures play a pivotal role in the bigger picture. Unfortunately, for every auspicious being there is an ominous beast lurking in the shadows. Zimmer's weave of fantasy and religious fables leaves the reader sated"
-Bitten By Books

"The scope of The Storm Guardians is massive, opening up and expanding on the conflict only hinted at in The Exodus Gate. The intrigue and action promised in the first book is fully developed and mercilessly exhibited. The Storm Guardians is a non-stop thriller that lives up to the promise of The Exodus Gate and points at an even more amazing denouement in the final book of the series. Once again, Zimmer has used his command of cinematic imagery to give us a spectacular vision of war both heavenly and hellish. Two thumbs up on this one."
-Pure Reason Book Review

Book Three: The Seventh Throne
ISBN: 978-0983740247

NOW AVAILABLE!

Now Available from Seventh Star Press, Steven Shrewsbury's hard-hitting, heroic fantasy novel THRALL, featuring illustrations and cover art by fantasy artist Matthew Perry!

Trade Paperback ISBN: 9780983108634
Hardcover ISBN: 9780982565650
eBook ISBN: 9780983108641

FOR GORIAS LA GAUL...
DELIVERANCE WILL COME

Set in the mists of ancient times, *Thrall* tells the story of Gorias La Gaul, an aging warrior who has lived for centuries battling the monstrosities of legend and lore. It is an age when the Nephilum walk the earth, demonic forces hunger to be unleashed, and dragons still soar through the skies … living and undead. On a journey to find one of his own blood, a young man who is caught in the shadow of necromancy, Gorias' path crosses with familiar enemies, some of whom not even death can hold bound.

Thrall is gritty, dark-edged heroic fantasy in the vein of Robert E. Howard and David Gemmell. It is a maelstrom of hard-hitting action and unpredictable imagery, taking place within an incredible antediluvian world. In Gorias La Gaul, *Thrall* introduces an iconic new character to the realms of fantasy literature. Thrall invites the reader to go on a perilous journey where it is not a matter of whether one has the courage to die, but whether one has the courage to live.

All Seventh Star Press titles available in print and an array of specially priced eBook formats. Visit www.seventhstarpress.com for further information.

**Now Available from Seventh Star Press, Steven Shrewsbury's continuing tale of Gorias La Gaul, OVERKILL.
Features illustrations and cover art by fantasy artist Matthew Perry!**

Trade Paperback ISBN: 9781937929800
eBook ISBN: 9781937929831

FOR GORIAS LA GAUL...
DELIVERANCE WILL COME

A great flood once wiped clean the earth, destroying everything upon it. Before the deluge, in a time now forgotten, the world was a place of warriors and witches, conflicts between kingdoms, and, until their extermination, dragons. In this world, men may live centuries, fallen angels have begotten terrifying spawn, and sometimes, the best hope can be found in a brothel.

In the land of Transalpina, a new religion spreads, and important men are dying mysteriously, slain by what can only be the fire of dragon breath. Summoned by the Queen Garnet, the legendary warrior Gorias La Gaul returns to the place where he once saved the queen's young granddaughter from treachery and enslavement. The Princess Nykia is gone, and soon others may try to claim the throne. The queen has little choice but to turn to the only man who ever told her no.

With the aid of one of the queen's elite guard, the battle maiden Alena, and the young palace servant Orsen, the old mercenary will face pirates and traitors, monsters and foul magic in the quest to find the missing heir and learn the truth behind the disconcerting murders.

Deliverance will come for Gorias La Gaul, but for now there are women to love, secrets to discover, and killing that needs doing.

Now Available from Seventh Star Press, D.A. Adams'
fantastic saga *The Brotherhod of Dwarves Series*, featuring
illustrations and cover art by fantasy artist Bonnie Wasson!

Book One: The Brotherhood of Dwarves

Trade: 978-1-937929-91-6
eBook: 978-1-937929-93-0

Roskin, heir to the throne of a remote, peaceful kingdom of dwarves, cravesexcitement and adventure. Outside his own kingdom, in search of fortune andglory, he finds a much different world, one divided by racial strife andoverrun by war. The orcs to the south want to conquer all dwarves and sellthem as slaves. The humans to the east want to control the world's resources. Caught in the middle, Roskin finds himself chased by slavetraders and soldiers alike as he discovers that friendship is the bestfortune of all. Just when he thinks he has triumphed, an act of betrayalsends him into bondage. His only hope of escape is the faltering courage ofa disgraced warrior whose best days are behind him...

Book Two: The Fall of Dorkhun

Trade: 978-0-983740-25-4
eBook: 978-1-937929-90-9

Crushaw, Molgheon, and Vishghu have liberated the Slithesythe Plantation. They must make their way to safe lands before being caught andreturned to certain bondage. Across the orc lands, they and Roskin recruitand train an army of freed slaves, for between them and freedom arethousands of well-armed, well-trained orc warriors. Near the Pass of HardHope, in the shadows of the eastern mountains, they make their desperatestand. But even if they succeed, Roskin's ordeal is far from finished, ashe is haunted by visions of something awful back in Dorkhun...

Book Three: Red Sky at Dawn

Trade: 978-1-937929-92-3
eBook: 978-0-983740-25-4

The Fall of Dorkuhn, the third installment in The Brotherhood of Dwarves series, continues the adventures of the dwarf Roskin. Having escaped slavery, and survived the Battle for Hard Hope, Roskin returns home to a kingdom divided by war with the ogres.

On one side, his father desires to restore peace. On the other, Master Sondious, hungry for revenge after having been crippled, seeks to escalate the aggression. Roskin and his friends hasten to the capital, to make a desperate attempt to resolve the growing rift, but unknown to the dwarves, new and powerful menaces threaten to destroy the entire kingdom...

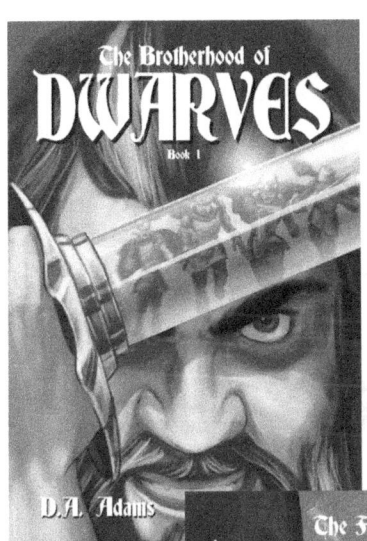

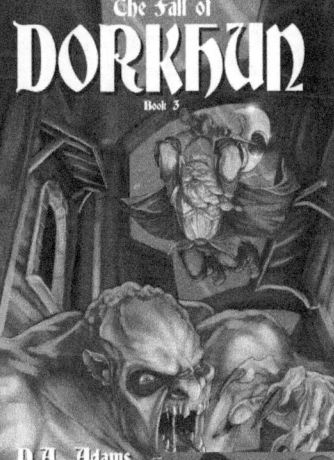

Now Available from Seventh Star Press, Jackie Gamber's fantasy novel REDHEART, featuring illustrations and cover art by fantasy artist Matthew Perry!

Trade Paperback ISBN: 9780983108672
eBook ISBN: 9780983108696

Enter the lands of Leland Province, where dragon and human societies have long dwelled side by side. Superstitions rise sharply, as a severe drought strips the land of its bounty, providing fertile ground for the darker ambitions of Fordon Blackclaw, Dragon Council Leader, who seeks to subdue humans or wipe them off the face of the land.

As the shadow of danger creeps across Leland Province, a young dragon named Kallon Redheart, who has turned his back on dragons and humans alike, comes into an unexpected friendship. Riza Diantus is a young woman whose dreams can no longer be contained by the narrow confines of her village, and when she finds herself in peril, Kallon is the only one with the power to save her. Yet to do so means he must confront his past, and embrace a future he stopped believing in.

A tale of friendship, courage, and ultimate destiny, *Redheart* invites readers to a wondrous journey through the *Leland Dragon Series*.

Now Available!
Jackie Gamber's Book 2 in the Leland Dragon Series: Sela

Trade Paperback ISBN: 9781937929893
eBook ISBN: 9781937929893

Peace is fleeting. Vorham Riddess, Venur of Esra Province, covets the crystal ore buried deep in Leland's mountains. His latest device to obtain it: land by marriage to a Leland maiden. But that's not all.

Among Dragonkind, old threats haunt Mount Gore, and shadows loom in the thoughts of the Red who restored life to land and love. A dragon hunter, scarred from countless battles, discovers he can yet suffer more wounds.

In the midst of it all, Sela Redheart is lost, driven from her home with only her old uncle to watch over her. As the dragon-born child of Kallon, the leader of Leland's Dragon Council, she is trapped in human form with no understanding of how she transformed, or how to turn back.

Wanderers seek a home, schemes begin to unfurl, and all is at risk as magic and murder, marriage and mystery strangle the heart of Esra. A struggle for power far older and deeper than anyone realizes will leave no human or dragon unaffected.

In a world where magic is born of feeling, where the love between a girl and a dragon was once transformative, what power dwells in the heart of young Sela?

www.ingramcontent.com/pod-product-compliance
Lightning Source LLC
Chambersburg PA
CBHW070532030726
47505CB00001B/18